The Knight and the Squire

"Don Quixote, a lanky scarecrow of a man with withered face and lantern jaw, dons his rusty armour and mounts his ramshackle steed Rozinante. With lance couched, he still rides through our lives, followed by his pot-bellied squire Sancho Panza."

With these words, Walter Starkie launches the new introduction to his highly esteemed translation and abridgement of Cervantes' great classic, a book that has enchanted generations of readers throughout the world.

Brimming with humor, rich in idealism and earthy common sense, vivid in its characterizations of men and women from every walk of life—nobles, priests, impassioned damsels, simple country girls, rogues and romantics—*Don Quixote,* in this zestful new translation, will win many new friends.

"Of the four translations I have had a shot at, Dr. Starkie's is the most inviting. The Knight and Sancho Panza are now applauded not as butts but as the supreme archetypes or symbols of two essential qualities, soaring idealism and earthbound common sense . . . Only a very great book could be admired in so many countries over so long a stretch of time and for such contrasted reasons. Cervantes has turned out to be a far more profound writer than he himself realized."—Raymond Mortimer, *Sunday Times,* England.

Walter Starkie, noted authority on Spanish history and culture, eminent lecturer, scholar and writer, was for over twenty years a professor at Dublin University. From 1940 to 1955 he was Director of the British Institute in Madrid. Among his many books are *Raggle-Taggle* and *The Road to Santiago.*

ST. MARTIN'S PRESS PUBLISHED THE HIGHER-PRICED HARDCOVER EDITION OF THIS BOOK

Don Quixote

OF LA MANCHA

by Miguel de Cervantes Saavedra

*An abridged version designed to relate
without digressions the principal adventures of
the Knight and his Squire*

Translated and Edited
with an Introduction

by WALTER STARKIE

A MENTOR BOOK

To my children
LANDI and ALMA
In Memory of our Readings
of *Don Quixote*

MENTOR
Published by the Penguin Group
Penguin Books USA Inc., 375 Hudson Street,
New York, New York 10014, U.S.A.
Penguin Books Ltd, 27 Wrights Lane,
London W8 5TZ, England
Penguin Books Australia Ltd, Ringwood,
Victoria, Australia
Penguin Books Canada Ltd, 10 Alcorn Avenue,
Toronto, Ontario, Canada M4V 3B2
Penguin Books (N.Z.) Ltd, 182–190 Wairau Road,
Auckland 10, New Zealand

Penguin Books Ltd, Registered Offices:
Harmondsworth, Middlesex, England

Published by Mentor, an imprint of Dutton Signet,
a division of Penguin Books USA Inc.

Published as a Mentor Book by arrangement with Macmillan & Company, Limited who
have authorized this softcover edition.

This book is sold throughout the British Commonwealth by arrangement with
Macmillan & Company, Limited.

This book is copyright in all countries which are signatories to the Berne Convention

First Mentor Printing, September, 1957

46   45   44   43   42   41   40

Introduction to the Mentor Edition © 1957 by Macmillan & Company, Limited, London

REGISTERED TRADEMARK—MARCA REGISTRADA

Printed in the United States of America

CONTENTS

INTRODUCTION

Don Quixote, a lanky scarecrow of a man with his withered face and lantern jaw, dons his rusty armour and mounts his ramshackle steed Rozinante. With lance couched he still rides through our lives followed by his pot-bellied squire Sancho Panza. The ill-sorted pair played a prominent part in the world of our grandparents and parents, and we transmit their message to our children and grandchildren.

The indissoluble pair rub shoulders with many other heroes—with the melancholy Ulysses "of the many wiles," meandering home to the faithful Penelope after the ten-year Trojan War, with Sinbad the Sailor and Ali Baba and his Forty Thieves, with Gulliver and Robinson Crusoe, with Mr. Pickwick and Sam Weller, with all the rest of the never-dead who linger in the hidden spaces of one's subconscious mind ready to be conjured up in moments of reverie.

Don Quixote has always been one of the world's best books for reading out to the family circle on Sunday evenings, according to a secular tradition observed in self-respecting families all over the world.

Don Quixote and Sancho refuse to grow old and musty, and they still amble on at the sweet whim of Rozinante and Dapple over the roads of Spain which, as Barbey d'Aurevilly said, *"ne sont nulle part décrites,"* and as we emerge from childhood we do not forget the *Knight of the Rueful Figure* and his squire, for now we begin to sympathize with the Don and we become

> piteous of his case.
> Yet smiling at his rueful length of face. (I)

We return to them both as if they were long-lost friends. In a sense they are more genuine than many friends we possess in real life, for they do not change from minute to minute, and we know that as soon as we open the book they will speak to us and take us into their counsels.

Their friendship is indeed inexhaustible, because, no matter how often we read certain chapters, we discover new qualities and sidelights in them, and they fill us with optimism, even in later life, when our mentor Montaigne keeps whispering in our ear that old age leaves more wrinkles on the mind than on the face.

Don Quixote has a message for man's seven ages: at school we roar with gusto at the spectacle of Sancho tossed in the blanket like dogs at Shrovetide: at college we freshmen seek out the story of the lovesick Cardenio and Luscinda of the emerald eyes, and when we write woeful ballads to our mistress' eyebrows we turn to the resourceful Dorothea. And in the recent world war, when we watched stray youths leaving their villages to respond to the call to arms, have we not recalled the stripling whom Don Quixote and Sancho met on the road, walking along, and carrying on his shoulder a sword with a bundle strung across it. And as he walked he sang:

> I'm off to the wars for want of pence,
> If I had any money I'd show more sense.

Who could go through University life without recalling again and again the bachelor Samson Carrasco, of Salamanca University, who though no giant in stature, was a very great wag? He was sallow-complexioned, sharp-witted, about four-and-twenty years of age, with a round face, a flat nose, and a large mouth—"all signs of a mischievous disposition," and of one fond of joking and making fun. And when we reach middle age and have passed the half-way period of wandering in the dark forest described by Dante, it is Part II of the immortal work that affects us more than Part I, for it not only opens up fresh vistas in the world of the Don and his squire, but conveys to us that sense of universality of outlook that we find in Shakespeare and Montaigne.

We think of Shakespeare in his later years when his writings had a relaxed quality and an artlessness in construction, for the field of romance was shifting back from the drama to the novel. The Bohemia of *The Winter's Tale*, the Britain of *Cymbeline* and the island of *The Tempest* fluctuate between Earth and a kind of fairyland. Prospero was preparing to break his wand and retire to his mansion in the country with its decoy partridges and ferrets and his library.

The aged hero of Lepanto, as he wrote his spiritual biography in *Don Quixote,* constantly dreamed of a life of moderate wealth in a spacious country house with the escutcheon of his family carved in rough stone over the hall door. In that house there would be a courtyard with a storeroom, and in the rear porch the entrance to the wine cellar with many *tobosan* jars. The joy of such a home would be its wonderful stillness which gave it the air of a Carthusian monastery, thus enabling him to bury himself from time to time in a healing solitude.

In this way our thoughts lead us away from Don Quixote and Sancho Panza towards the author of the immortal book. Too many critics have repeated that Cervantes was inferior to his own work. He was, they say, a typical Spaniard, like all the rest. He was a Catholic, he hated the Moors and he bowed to the Inquisition, owing to his loyalty to his religion. Then one day, with the help of his imagination and a certain number of romances of chivalry, he created Don Quixote and pitched him into the world to do battle with human society. In

x

consequence the world has paid attention to Don Quixote but has not studied deeply the personality and life of Cervantes.

Unless we become closely acquainted with the figure of Cervantes we shall find it impossible to understand the deeper meaning of *Don Quixote*. We have always been told that the book is a satire on the old romances of chivalry, and this is true to a certain extent, for Cervantes did satirize the extravagances of chivalry in its decadence, but he was as unqualified an admirer of *Amadis of Gaul* as Charles V, Saint Ignatius, Saint Teresa and all the finer minds of the sixteenth century. It is, indeed, true to say that Cervantes lived the whole of his life in the spirit of the Knight-errant, and *Don Quixote* swept away the romances of chivalry only because it was itself a romance of chivalry and the greatest of them all, since its action was placed in the real world.

Cervantes was a soldier by profession and would never have become a writer had it not been for his misfortunes which compelled him to write for money. "The lance has never blunted the pen, nor the pen the lance," was a saying of Don Quixote which admirably sums up Spanish history, for in no other country do we find the soldier supreme in literature from the earliest times.

Cervantes was a great personality and a brave soldier long before he became famed as the author of *Don Quixote*. Before he wrote of life he had spent his best years in learning the lesson of life.

He entered the world under the same handicap as so many great literary figures, such as Shakespeare, Dickens and Bernard Shaw, for his parents were poor. His father, Rodrigo Cervantes, a poor hidalgo, was a physician without a diploma, who suffered from acute deafness. The privations of early life and the necessity of keeping the wolf from the door acted as a spur to his ambition, and from the poverty of his early years Miguel learnt to be charitable and human towards his neighbour, and he also learnt to appreciate the value of family co-operation. In fact, through all his life we are continually struck by the self-sacrifice and generosity of his mother and sisters in moments of crisis. Poverty, nevertheless, is an ever-present tragic theme throughout all his works. Even in *Don Quixote*, when the Don after his lonely first sally determines to set out again in search of adventure, he made overtures to a certain labouring man, a neighbour of his called Sancho Panza, and the author adds—"an honest fellow (if such a title can be given to one who is poor)." Cervantes did not go as far as Bernard Shaw, who stigmatized poverty as a crime, but from childhood onwards he was as obsessed by it as Dickens, and he, like the author of *The Pickwick Papers,* had to endure the humiliation of seeing his father carried off to gaol for debt.

When he reached manhood Cervantes did not think of poverty, for he was of adventurous disposition, and he set out for the port of Cartagena to join the war as gaily as the stripling whom Don Quixote met on the road towards Saragossa. He was proud to have fought at Lepanto in 1571, when the fleet of Don John of Austria annihilated the power of the Turk in the Mediterranean. He fought heroically like a good soldier on that victorious afternoon and received wounds: his left hand was shattered and he received two gunshot wounds in the chest. These wounds he refers to on several occasions in *Don Quixote,* and he calls wounds received in action "the stars that lead men on to honour."

Misfortune, however, dogged his footsteps, and in 1575 when he was on his way back to Spain to receive preferment, the galley *Sol* in which he travelled was attacked by the Corsairs off Les Saintes Maries and he and his brother Rodrigo were taken prisoners and carried off to Algiers to be sold as slaves or held for ransom.

During his five-year captivity Cervantes made four attempts to escape, and on one occasion he and his companions managed to elude the vigilance of their gaolers for five months in a cave. On each of the four occasions, when they were rounded up by the armed forces, Cervantes assumed the entire responsibility for the escape. Indeed, such was his valour in the face of his accusers and the threats of torture that the Dey, who secretly admired him, bought him from his former master, and as he sent him back to his chains he murmured: "So long as I have the maimed Spaniard in my power, my Christians, my ships and the city itself are safe."

When Cervantes was ransomed in 1580 by the Trinitarian friars and returned to Spain, he found his family still more impoverished than before. His father's affairs had gone from bad to worse and his deafness had become a heavy burden. His mother and sisters had beggared themselves trying to raise the money for his ransom and that of his brother Rodrigo, and they were making desperate attempts to borrow money from all and sundry in order to pay off pressing debts.

Alas, no fixed employment came his way and all accounts agree that he was poor and down at heel. His pastoral romance, the *Galatea,* appeared in 1584 but did not bring in much money: his dreams of becoming a successful playwright faded into thin air; for just then the youthful Lope de Vega, "the Portent of Nature," entered triumphantly to transform the theatre by his genius, and the public flocked in their thousands to see his vivid plays based on the traditional *Romancero.* In later years Cervantes would write sadly in the Postscript of his *Journey to Parnassus* (1613): "When a poet is poor, half of his divine fruits and fancies miscarry by reason of his anxious cares to win his daily bread."

He married in 1584 a girl of nineteen, Catalina Palacios y Salazar from the village of Esquivias near Toledo, but he was unable to afford even a simple home for his bride, and he was forced to become a roving Commissary in Andalusia and La Mancha, raising supplies for the Armada before it set out for England in 1588, while his forlorn wife lived at home with her brothers at Esquivias. In 1587, and for the next fifteen years, Cervantes made Seville his centre and roved from village to village, requisitioning supplies of bread, wheat, barley and oil for the government and at times facing hostile demonstrations from the peasants and excommunication from the Church dignitaries whose wheat he commandeered. His pay was often in arrears, for in those days government offices moved even more slowly than they do today, so slowly in fact that King Philip II's ministers were called "ministers of eternity."

With characteristic humour Cervantes tells us in the prologue to *Don Quixote*, Part I, that his hero, "a dry, shrivelled, whimsical offspring" was begotten in prison "where every misery is lodged and every doleful sound makes its dwelling." This refers to the two occasions, in 1597 and 1602, when he was an inmate of Seville gaol.

Part I of the novel appeared in 1605, and within six months Don Quixote and his squire were celebrated all over the country and their names even used as nicknames at Court. Even across the ocean in the Indies the Don and his squire were already famous, and readers wrote saying that the title of the book should be changed to *Don Quixote and Sancho Panza*, "for Sancho," they said, "is worth as much as his master and amuses even more."

In spite of the national and international success of the book, ten years were to elapse before Cervantes wrote Part II, and when on October 31, 1615 he wrote the dedication of the sequel to his Maecenas, the Conde de Lemos, he added wryly: "In addition to being unwell I am also confoundedly short of money." The dedication was not merely an appeal for charity to his Maecenas, but also a signal of distress intended for his spiritual patron, the Cardinal Archbishop of Toledo. More than ever did he need help and consolation, for it was when he was writing the last part of his novel that he learnt that an apocryphal *Don Quixote*, claiming to be the continuation of his work, had been published at Tarragona by a certain Alonso de Avellaneda.

Our last vision of Cervantes comes from the prologue he wrote to his posthumous work, *Persiles y Sigismunda* (1617), when he describes his last ride from Esquivias to Madrid in the company of a student who was thrilled to meet "the hero of the maimed hand, the famous author, pride and joy of the Muses." When taking leave of the youth, the aged author says gently: "My life is slipping away, and by the diary my pulse is keeping, which at the latest will end its reckoning next Sunday, I must close my life's account. You, sir, have met me in an uncouth moment, since there is not enough time left for me to thank you for the good will you have shown me."

Four days before his death he wrote the last words of the dedication of his swan song to the Conde de Lemos: "Adieu, sweet grace of life; adieu most pleasing fancy; adieu my happy friends, for I perceive I am dying, and the one wish in my heart is that I shall see you all soon in another life." Then he added as a final refrain the words of the ancient ballad, adapting them to his own case:

> *Puesto ya el pié en el estribo,*
> *Con las ansias de la muerte,*
> *Gran Señor, esta te escribo . . .*

> (With one foot in the stirrup,
> And in the anguish of death,
> My lord, I write to thee.)

"Yesterday they gave me Extreme Unction, and today I am writing. The time is short; my agonies increase; my hopes diminish."

Four days later he died, on Saturday, April 23, 1616. Ten days later in England, where the calendar was still unreformed, Shakespeare died also (nominally) on April 23. In their death they were undivided.

WALTER STARKIE

University of Texas, Austin
May, 1957

PART ONE

I. The quality and manner of life of that famous gentleman Don Quixote of La Mancha

AT A VILLAGE OF LA MANCHA, WHOSE NAME I DO NOT WISH
to remember,[1] there lived a little while ago one of those gentlemen who are wont to keep a lance in the rack, an old buckler, a lean horse and a swift greyhound. His stew had more
beef than mutton in it and most nights he ate the remains
salted and cold. Lentil soup on Fridays, "tripe and trouble"[2]
on Saturdays and an occasional pigeon as an extra delicacy on
Sundays, consumed three-quarters of his income. The remain-
der was spent on a jerkin of fine puce, velvet breeches, and
slippers of the same stuff for holidays, and a suit of good,
honest homespun for week-days. His family consisted of a
housekeeper about forty, a niece not yet twenty, and a lad
who served him both in the field and at home and could saddle
the horse or use the pruning-knife. Our gentleman was about
fifty years of age, of a sturdy constitution, but wizened and
gaunt-featured, an early riser and a devotee of the chase. They
say that his surname was Quixada or Quesada (for on this
point the authors who have written on this subject differ), but
we may reasonably conjecture that his name was Quixana.
This, however, has very little to do with our story: enough
that in its telling we swerve not a jot from the truth. You must
know that the above-mentioned gentleman in his leisure moments (which was most of the year) gave himself up with so
much delight and gusto to reading books of chivalry that he
almost entirely neglected the exercise of the chase and even
the management of his domestic affairs: indeed his craze for
this kind of literature became so extravagant that he sold
many acres of arable land to purchase books of knight-errantry, and he carried off to his house as many as he could
possibly find. Above all he preferred those written by the
famous Feliciano de Silva on account of the clarity of his writ-

1 Cervantes was purposely vague in describing the birthplace of Don
Quixote. "En un lugar de la Mancha" is the beginning of the ballad "El
Amante Apaleado," which was familiar to our author.
2 Semi-abstinence fare because Saturday was kept as a fast-day in
memory of the defeat of the Moors in 1212 in the battle of Navas de
Tolosa. Others say the phrase "duelos y quebrantos" means "rashers and
eggs"—pot-luck fare in La Mancha. See note on p. 375.

ing and his intricate style, which made him value those books more than pearls; especially when he read of those courtships and letters of challenge that knights sent to ladies, often containing expressions such as "the reason for your unreasonable treatment of my reason, so enfeebles my reason that I have reason to complain of your beauty". And again: "the high heavens which, with your divinity, divinely fortify you with the stars and make you the deserver of the desert that is deserved by your greatness". These and similar rhapsodies bewildered the poor gentleman's understanding, for he racked his brains day and night to unbowel their meaning, which not even Aristotle himself could have done, if he had been raised from the dead for that purpose. He was not quite convinced by the number of wounds which Don Belianis gave and received in battle, for he considered that however skilful the surgeons that cured him may have been, the worthy knight's face and body must have been bedizened with scars and scabs. Nevertheless he praised that author for concluding his book with the promise of that endless adventure, and many times he felt inclined to take up his pen and finish it off himself as it is there promised. He doubtless would have done so, and successfully too, had he not been diverted by other plans and purposes of greater moment. He often debated with the curate of the village—a man of learning, who had graduated in Sigüenza—on the relative merits of Palmerin of England and Amadis of Gaul. But Master Nicholas, the village barber, affirmed that no one could be compared to the Knight of the Sun: and that if, indeed, any could be matched with him, it was Don Galaor, the brother of Amadis of Gaul, for he had a nature adapted to every whim of fortune: he was not so namby-pamby and whimpering a knight as his brother, and as for valour, he was in every respect his equal.

In short, he so immersed himself in those romances that he spent whole days and nights over his books; and thus with little sleeping and much reading his brains dried up to such a degree that he lost the use of his reason. His imagination became filled with a host of fancies he had read in his books —enchantments, quarrels, battles, challenges, wounds, courtships, loves, tortures and many other absurdities. So true did all this phantasmagoria from books appear to him that in his mind he accounted no history in the world more authentic. He would say that the Cid Ruy Diaz was a very gallant knight, but not to be compared with the Knight of the Burning Sword, who with a single thwart blow cleft asunder a brace of hulking blustering giants. He was better pleased with Bernardo del Carpio, because at Roncesvalles he had slain Roland the Enchanted by availing himself of the stratagem Hercules had employed on Antaeus, the son of the Earth, whom he squeezed to death in his arms. He praised the giant Morgante, for he alone was courteous and well-bred among that monstrous brood puffed up with arrogance and insolence. Above all, he admired Rinaldo of Montalvan, especially when he saw him sallying out of his castle to plunder everyone that came his way; and, moreover, when, beyond the seas, he made off with the idol of Mahomet, which, as history says, was of solid gold. But he would have parted with his housekeeper and his niece into the bargain for the pleasure of rib-roasting the traitor Galalon.

At last, having lost his wits completely, he stumbled upon the oddest fancy that ever entered a madman's brain. He believed that it was necessary, both for his own honour and for the service of the state, that he should become knight-errant and roam through the world with his horse and armour in quest of adventures, and practise all that had been performed by the knights-errant of whom he had read. He would follow their life, redressing all manner of wrongs and exposing himself to continual dangers, and at last, after concluding his enterprises, he would win everlasting honour and renown. The poor gentleman saw himself in imagination already crowned Emperor of Trebizond by the valour of his arm. And thus, excited by these agreeable delusions, he hastened to put his plans into operation.

The first thing he did was to furbish some rusty armour which had belonged to his great-grandfather and had lain mouldering in a corner. He cleaned it and repaired it as best he could, but he found one great defect: instead of a complete helmet there was just the simple morion. This want he ingeniously remedied by making a kind of vizor out of pasteboard, and when it was fitted to the morion it looked like an entire helmet. It is true that, in order to test its strength and see if it was sword-proof, he drew his sword and gave it two strokes, the first of which instantly destroyed the result of a week's labour. It troubled him to see with what ease he had broken the helmet in pieces, so to protect it from such an accident he remade it and fenced the inside with a few bars of iron in such a manner that he felt assured of its strength, and without making a second trial he held it to be a most excellent vizor. Then he went to see his steed, and although it had more cracks than a Spanish real and more faults than Gonela's jade which was all skin and bone, he thought that neither the Bucephalus of Alexander nor the Cid's Babieca could be compared with it. He spent four days deliberating over what name he would give the horse; for (as he said to himself) it was not right that the horse of so famous a knight should remain without a name, and so he endeavoured to find one which would express what the animal had been before he had been the mount of a knight-

17

errant, and what he now was. It was indeed reasonable that when the master changed his state, the horse should change his name too, and assume one pompous and high-sounding as suited the new order he was about to profess. So, after having devised, erased and blotted out many other names, he finally determined to call the horse Rozinante—a name, in his opinion, lofty, sonorous and significant, for it explained that he had only been a "rocín" or hack before he had been raised to his present status of first of all the hacks in the world.

Now that he had given his horse a name so much to his satisfaction, he resolved to choose one for himself, and after seriously considering the matter for eight whole days he finally determined to call himself Don Quixote. Wherefore the authors of this most true story have deduced that his name must undoubtedly have been Quixano, and not Quesada, as others would have it. Then remembering that the valiant Amadis had not been content to call himself simply Amadis, but added thereto the name of his kingdom and native country to render it more illustrious, calling himself Amadis of Gaul, so he, like a good knight, also added the name of his province and called himself Don Quixote of La Mancha. In this way he openly proclaimed his lineage and country, and at the same time he honoured it by taking its name.

Now that his armour was scoured, his morion made into a helmet, his horse and himself new-named, he felt that nothing was wanting but a lady of whom to be enamoured; for a knight-errant who was loveless was a tree without leaves and fruit—a body without soul. "If," said he, "for my sins or through my good fortune I encounter some giant—a usual occurrence to knight-errants—and bowling him over at the first onset, or cleaving him in twain, I finally vanquish and force him to surrender, would it not be better to have some lady to whom I may send him as a trophy? so that when he enters into her presence he may throw himself on his knees before her and in accents contrite and humble say: 'Madam, I am the giant Caraculiambro, Lord of the Island of Malindrania, whom the never-adequately-praised Don Quixote of La Mancha has overcome in single combat. He has commanded me to present myself before you, so that your highness may dispose of me as you wish.'" How glad was our knight when he had made these discourses to himself, but chiefly when he had found one whom he might call his lady! It happened that in a neighbouring village there lived a good-looking country lass, with whom he had been in love, although it is understood that she never knew or cared a jot. She was called Aldonza Lorenzo, and it was to her that he thought fit to confide the sovereignty of his heart. He sought a name for her which would not vary too much from her own and yet would approach that of a princess or lady of quality: at last he resolved to call her Dulcinea del Toboso (she was a native of that town), a name in his opinion musical, uncommon and expressive, like the others which he had devised.

II. Our imaginative hero's first sally from his home

AFTER MAKING THESE PREPARATIONS HE WOULD NOT DELAY putting his designs into operation any longer, for he was spurred on by the conviction that the world needed his immediate presence: so many were the grievances he intended to rectify, the wrongs he resolved to set right, the harms he meant to redress, the abuses he would reform and the debts he would discharge. And so, without acquainting a living soul with his intentions, and wholly unobserved, one morning before daybreak (it was one of the hottest in the month of July), he armed himself cap-à-pie, mounted Rozinante, placed his ill-constructed helmet on his head, braced on his buckler, grasped his lance, and through the door of his back-yard sallied forth into the open country, mightily pleased to see with what ease he had begun his worthy enterprise. But scarcely had he issued forth when he was suddenly struck by so terrible a thought that he almost gave up his whole undertaking: for he just then remembered that he had not yet been dubbed a knight, and therefore, in accordance with the laws of chivalry, he neither could nor ought to enter the lists against any knight, and, moreover, even if he had been dubbed, he should, as a novice, have worn white armour without any device on his shield until he had won it by force of arms. These thoughts made him stagger in his purpose; but as his madness prevailed over every reason, he determined to have himself knighted by the first one he should meet, like many others of whom he had read in the books which distracted him. As to white armour, he intended at the first opportunity to scour his own so that it should be whiter than ermine. In this way he calmed himself and continued his journey, but he chose whatever road his horse pleased, believing that in this consisted the true spirit of adventure.

As our brand-new adventurer proceeded he kept conversing with himself in this manner: "Who doubts but that in future ages, when the true story of my famous deeds is brought to light, the wise man who writes it will describe my first sally in the morning as follows: 'Scarcely had the rubicund Apollo spread over the face of the vast and spacious earth the golden tresses of his beautiful hair, and scarcely had the little painted birds with their tuneful tongues saluted in sweet and melodious harmony the coming of rosy Aurora, who, leaving the soft couch of her jealous husband, reveals herself to mortals through the gates and balconies of the Manchegan horizon, when the famous knight Don Quixote of La Mancha, quitting his downy bed of ease, mounted his renowned steed Rozinante and began to ride over the ancient and memorable plain of Montiel' " (and indeed he was doing so). Continuing his discourse, he added: "O happy era, happy age wherein my famous deeds shall be revealed to the world, deeds worthy to be engraved in bronze, sculptured in marble and painted in pictures for future record. O thou wise enchanter, whosoever thou mayest be, whose duty it will be to chronicle this strange history, do not, I beseech thee, forget my good horse Rozinante, the everlasting companion of my wanderings." Then, as if really enamoured, he cried: "O Dulcinea, my princess! Sovereign of this captive heart! Grievous wrong hast thou done me by dismissing me and by cruelly forbidding me by decree to appear in thy beauteous presence. I pray thee, sweet lady, to remember this poor, enslaved heart, which for love of thee suffers so many pangs."

To such words he added a sequence of other foolish notions, imitating the style of his books as nearly as he could, and meanwhile he rode slowly on, while the sun rose with such intense heat that it was enough to dissolve his brains, if he had any left. He travelled almost the whole of that day without meeting any adventure worthy of note, wherefore he was much troubled, for he was eager to encounter someone upon whom he could try the strength of his doughty arm. Some authors say his first adventure was that of the Pass of Lápice; others hold it was that of the windmills; but according to my investigations and according to what is written in the annals of La Mancha he travelled all that day long, and at night both he and his horse were tired and nearly dead with hunger. Being in such a pass, he looked round him on every side to see whether he could discover any castle or shepherd's hut where he might rest himself and find nourishment. He then saw, not far from the road, an inn, which was as welcome to him as a star leading him to the portals, if not to the very palace itself, of his redemption. He made all haste he could and reached it at nightfall.

Now there chanced to be standing at the door two young wenches who belonged to the category of women of the town, and they were on their way towards Seville in the company of certain carriers who halted for the night in that inn. Our adventurer, since he moulded by his imagination all that he saw in accordance with what he had read in his books of chivalry, no sooner had seen the inn than it assumed in his eyes the semblance of a castle with four turrets, the pinnacles of which were of glittering silver, not forgetting the drawbridge, deep moat and all the appurtenances with which such castles are depicted. And so he drew near to the inn (which he thought was a castle), and at a short distance from it he halted Rozinante, expecting some dwarf would mount the battlements to announce by trumpet blast the arrival of a knight-errant at the castle. But when he saw that they tarried, and as Rozinante was pawing the ground impatiently in eagerness to reach his stable, he approached the inn door, and there saw the two young doxies, who appeared to him to be two beautiful damsels or graceful ladies enjoying the fresh air at the castle gate. It happened also at this very moment that a swine-herd, as he gathered his hogs (I ask no pardon, for so they are called)[1] from the stubble field, blew a horn which assembled them together, and instantly Don Quixote imagined it was what he expected, namely, that some dwarf was giving notice of his arrival. Therefore with extraordinary satisfaction he went up to the inn and the ladies. But when they saw a man armed in that manner draw near with lance and buckler, they started to take to their heels, full of fear. Don Quixote, perceiving their alarm, raised his pasteboard vizor and, displaying his withered and dusty countenance, accosted them gently and gravely: "I beseech your ladyships, do not flee, nor fear the least offence. The order of chivalry which I profess, doth not permit me to do injury to any one, and least of all to such noble maidens as your presences denote you to be." The wenches kept gazing earnestly, endeavouring to catch a glimpse of his face, which its ill-fashioned beaver concealed: but when they heard themselves called maidens, a thing so out of the way of their profession, they could not restrain their laughter, which was so boisterous that Don Quixote exclaimed in anger: "Remember that modesty is becoming in beautiful ladies, whereas laughter without cause denotes much folly. However," added he, "I do not say this to offend you or to incur your displeasure, for my one desire is to do you honour and service." The strange language of the knight was not understood by the ladies, and this, added to his uncouth appearance, increased their laughter and his annoyance, and he would have proceeded further, but for the timely appearance of the innkeeper, a man who, by reason of his extreme corpulence, was of very peaceable disposition. As soon as he saw that uncomely figure all armed, in accoutrements so ill-sorted as were the bridle, lance, buckler and corselet, he felt inclined to join the damsels in their mirth. But out of fear of such a medley of warlike gear he resolved to give him civil words, and so he said: "Sir Knight, if you are seeking for a lodging, you will find all in abundance here, with the exception of a

[1] Even today the peasantry beg one's pardon when mentioning swine. Proximity to the Moslems, who, like the Jews, abhor pork, originated this superstition.

21

bed, for there are none in this inn." Don Quixote observing the humility of the Governor of the Fortress (for such the landlord and the inn appeared to him), answered: "Anything, Sir Castellan, suffices me:

> My ornaments are arms,
> My pastime is in war."

The host thought he called him a Castellan because he took him to be one of the Simple Simon Castilians,[2] whereas he was an Andalusian, one of those from the Sanlúcar shore, no less a thief than Cacus and not less mischievous than a truant scholar or court page. And so he made him the following repiy: "If so, your worship's beds must be hard rocks and your sleep an everlasting watching:[3] wherefore you may boldly dismount and I can assure you that you can hardly miss being kept awake all the year long in this house, much less one single night." Saying this, he went and held Don Quixote's stirrup, who forthwith dismounted, though with much difficulty, for he had not broken his fast all that day. He then told the host to take great care of his horse, saying that he was one of the finest pieces of horseflesh that ever ate bread. The innkeeper looked him over but thought him not so good by half as his master had said. After stabling him, he returned to receive his guest's orders and found the damsels disarming him (they had now become reconciled to him), but though they were able to take off the back- and breast-plates they did not know how to undo his gorget or remove his counterfeit beaver, which he had tied on with green ribbons in such a way that they could not be untied. It was necessary to cut them, as the knots were so intricate, but he would not allow this to be done, and so he remained all that night with his helmet on, and was the strangest and pleasantest sight imaginable.

And while he was being disarmed by those lights o' love, whom he imagined to be ladies of quality of that castle, he said to them with great charm:

> "There never was on earth a knight
> So waited on by ladies fair
> As once was he, Don Quixote hight,
> When first he left his village dear:
> Damsels to serve him ran with speed
> And princesses to dress his steed,

or Rozinante—for that, ladies, is the name of my horse and Don Quixote of La Mancha my own. I never intended to discover myself until deeds performed in your service should have proclaimed me, but the need of adapting to my present

[2] A play upon words here. Castellano means (1) a Castellan and (2) a native of Castile. Also the term "sanos de Castilla" in thieves' jargon meant frank, gullible native of Old Castile.
[3] The innkeeper caps verses with our knight by continuing the ballad.

22

purpose the old ballad of Sir Launcelot has made my right name known to you before the season. But the day will come when your ladyships shall command and I obey, and the valour of my arm make plain my desire to serve you."

The girls, unaccustomed to such flourishes of rhetoric, made no reply, but asked whether he would eat anything. "Fain would I break my fast," answered Don Quixote, "for I think that a little food would be of great service to me." That day happened to be a Friday and there was nothing in the inn but some pieces of fish, called in Castile pollack, in Andalusia codfish, in some parts ling and in others troutlets or Poor Jack. They asked him if he would eat some troutlets, for they had no other fish to offer him. "Provided there are many little trout," answered Don Quixote, "they will supply the place of one salmon trout; for it is the same to me whether I receive eight single reals or one piece of eight. Moreover, those troutlets may turn out to be like unto veal which is better than beef, and kid which is superior to goat. Be that as it may, let it come quickly, for the toil and weight of arms cannot be sustained without the good government of the guts." As the air was cool they placed the table at the door of the inn, and the landlord brought a portion of ill-soaked and worse-cooked codfish and a piece of bread as black and mouldy as the knight's arms. It was a laughable sight to see him eat; for, as he had his helmet and his beaver up, he could not with his own hands feed himself, and so one of the ladies performed that service for him. But it would have been impossible for him to drink had not the innkeeper bored a cane and, placing one end in his mouth, poured in the wine at the other end. All this he endured in patience rather than cut the ribbons of his helmet.

While he was at his meal, a sow-gelder happened to sound his reed flageolet four or five times as he came near the inn. This was a still more convincing proof to Don Quixote that he was in a famous castle, where they were entertaining him with music, and that the Poor Jack was salmon trout, the bread of the purest white, the whores ladies, and the innkeeper the governor of the castle. All this made him applaud his own resolution and his enterprising sally. There was only one thing that vexed him; he regretted that he was not dubbed a knight; for he thought that he could not lawfully undertake any adventure until he had received the order of knighthood.

III. *The amusing way in which he is dubbed a Knight*

AS HE WAS TORMENTED BY THAT THOUGHT HE MADE SHORT work of his meagre pot-house supper. Then he called for his host, shut himself up with him in the stable and fell upon his knees, saying: "I will never rise from this place, valorous Knight, until your courtesy grants me the boon I seek, one that will redound to your glory and to the advantage of the human race." The innkeeper, seeing his guest at his feet and hearing such words, stared at him in bewilderment, without knowing what to do or say. He tried to make him get up, but in vain, for the latter would not consent to do so until the boon he demanded was given. "I expected no less from your magnificence," answered Don Quixote, "and so I say unto you that the boon I have demanded and which you out of your liberality have granted unto me, is that, tomorrow morning, you will dub me knight. This night I shall watch over my arms in the chapel of your castle and tomorrow, as I have said, you will fulfil my earnest desires, so that I may sally forth through the four parts of the world in quest of adventures on behalf of the distressed, as is the duty of knighthood and knights-errant who, like myself, are devoted to such achievements." The host, who was, as we said before, a bit of a wag and already had some doubts about his guest's sanity, now found all his suspicions confirmed, but he resolved to humour him so that he might have sport that night. He told the knight that his wishes were very reasonable, for such pursuits were natural to knights so illustrious as he seemed and as his gallant bearing showed him to be. He added that he himself in the days of his youth had devoted himself to the same honourable profession and had wandered over various parts of the world in search of adventures: and, moreover, he had not failed to visit the Curing-grounds of Málaga, the Isles of Riarán, the Precinct of Seville, the Aqueduct Square of Segovia, the Olive-field of Valencia, the Rondilla of Granada, the Shore of Sanlúcar, the Colt Fountain of Córdoba, the Taverns of Toledo and divers other haunts, where he had proved the nimbleness of his feet and the lightness of his fingers, committing wrongs in plenty, accosting many widows, deflowering certain maidens, tricking some minors and finally making himself known and famous to all the tribunals and courts over the length and breadth of Spain. At last he had retired to this castle, where he lived on his own and on other men's revenues, entertaining therein knights-errant of every quality, solely for the great affection he bore them, and that they might share their goods with him in return for his benevolence. He further told him that in his castle there was no chapel where he could watch over his arms, for he had knocked it down to build it anew. However, in case of necessity he might watch over the arms wherever he pleased, and, therefore, he might watch that night in the castle courtyard; then the following morning, with God's help, the required ceremonies would be carried out in such a way that he would be dubbed a knight so effectively that nowhere in the world could one more perfect be found. He asked if Don Quixote had brought any money. "Not a farthing," answered the knight, "for I have never read in the stories of knights-errant that they ever carried money with them."

"You are mistaken," answered the landlord; "for, admitting that the stories are silent on such a matter, seeing that the authors did not think it necessary to specify such obvious requirements as money and clean shirts, yet there is no reason to believe that the knights had none. On the contrary, it was an established fact that all knights-errant (whose deeds fill many a volume) carried their purses well lined against accidents, and, moreover, they carried in addition to shirts a small chest of ointments to heal their wounds; for in the plains and deserts where they fought and were wounded there was no one to cure them, unless they were lucky enough to have some wise enchanter for friend, who straightway would send through the air in a cloud some damsel or dwarf, with a phial of water possessed of such power that upon tasting a single drop of it, they would instantly find their wounds as perfectly cured as if they had never received any. But when in past ages the knights had no such friend, they always insisted that their squires should be provided with money and such necessities as lint and ointments; and when they had no squires (which was very seldom) they themselves carried those things on the crupper of their horse in saddle-bags so small that they were scarcely visible. For except in such a case, the custom of carrying saddle-bags was not allowed among knights-errant. I must, therefore, advise you," he continued, "nay, I might even command you, seeing that you are shortly to become my godson in chivalry, never from this day forward to travel without money or without the aforesaid necessaries, and you will see how serviceable you will find them when least you expect it."

Don Quixote promised to follow his injunctions carefully and an order was given for him to watch over his armour in a large yard adjoining the inn. When the knight had collected all his arms together, he laid them on a stone trough which was close by the side of a wall. Then embracing his buckler and grasping his lance, he began with stately air to pace up and down in front of the trough, and as he began his parade, night began to close in.

The landlord, meanwhile, told all who were in the inn of the madness of his guest, the arms-vigil and the knighthood-dubbing that was to come. They were astonished at such a strange kind of madness and they flocked to observe him at a distance. They saw that sometimes he paced to and fro and at other times he leant upon his lance and gazed fixedly at his arms for a considerable time. It was now night, but the moon shone so clearly that she might have almost vied with the luminary which lent her splendour, and thus every action of our new knight could be seen by the spectators.

Just at this moment one of the muleteers in the inn took it into his head to water his team of mules, to do which it was necessary to remove Don Quixote's arms from the trough. But the knight as he saw him approach cried out in a loud voice: "O thou, whosoever thou art, rash knight that dost prepare to lay hands upon the arms of the most valiant knight-errant who ever girded sword, take heed and touch them not, if thou wouldst not leave thy life in guerdon for thy temerity." The muleteer paid no heed to this warning (it would have been better for him if he had), but, seizing hold of the armour by the straps, he threw it a good way from him. No sooner did Don Quixote perceive this than, raising his eyes to heaven and fixing his thoughts (as it seemed) upon his lady Dulcinea, he said: "Assist me, O lady, in this first affront which is offered to thy vassal's heart. Let not thy favour and protection fail me in this first encounter." Uttering these and similar words, he let slip his buckler and raising the lance in both hands, he gave the muleteer such a hefty blow on the pate that he felled him to the ground in so grievous a plight that if he had followed it with a second there would have been no need of a surgeon to cure him. This done, he put back his arms and began to pace to and fro as peacefully as before.

Soon after, another muleteer, without knowing what had happened (for the first still lay unconscious), came out with the same intention of watering his mules, and began to take away the arms which were encumbering the trough, when Don Quixote, not saying a word or imploring assistance from a soul, once more dropped his buckler, lifted up his lance, and without breaking it to pieces, opened the second muleteer's head in four places. All the people in the inn rushed out when they heard the noise, and the landlord among the rest. As soon as Don Quixote saw them, he braced on his buckler and laid his hand upon his sword, saying: "O lady of beauty, strength and vigour of my enfeebled heart! Now is the time for thee to turn the eyes of thy greatness upon this thy captive knight, who stands awaiting so great an adventure." These words, as he believed, filled him with such courage that if all the muleteers in the world had attacked him he would not have retreated one step. The wounded men's companions, seeing them in such an evil plight, began from afar to rain a shower of stones upon Don Quixote, who defended himself as best he could with his buckler, but he did not dare to leave the trough for fear of leaving his arms unprotected. The landlord shouted to them to let him alone, for he had already told them the

26

man was mad and, as such, he would escape scot-free even if
he killed every one of them. Don Quixote shouted still louder,
called them caitiffs and traitors and the lord of the castle a
cowardly, base-born knight, for allowing knights-errant to be
treated in such a manner. "I would make thee understand,"
cried he, "what a traitorous scoundrel thou art had I but been
dubbed a knight. But as for you, ye vile and base rabble,
I care not a fig for you: fire on, advance, drew near and hurt
me as much as you dare: soon ye shall receive the reward for
your folly and presumption." Such was the undaunted boldness with which he uttered those words that his attackers were
struck with terror. And so, partly through fear and partly
through the persuasive words of the landlord, they ceased to
fling stones at him, and he, on his side, allowed them to carry
off their wounded. After which he returned to the guard of
his arms with as much calm gravity as before.

The landlord did not relish the mad pranks of his guest, so
he determined to make an end of them and give him his
accursed order of chivalry before any further misfortune occurred. And so, going up to him, he excused himself for the
insolent way those low fellows had treated him without his
knowledge or consent, but he added that they had been well
chastised for their rashness. He repeated what he had said
before, that there was no chapel in that castle, nor was one
necessary for what remained to be done; for the chief point
of the knighting ceremony consisted in the accolade and the
tap on the shoulders, according to the ceremonial of the order,
and that might be administered in the middle of a field; that
he had performed the duty of watching over his armour, for
he had watched more than four hours, whereas only two were
required. All this Don Quixote believed, and said that he was
then ready to obey him, but he begged him to conclude with
all the brevity possible, for if he should be attacked again
when he was armed a knight, he was determined not to leave
one person alive in the castle, except those whom, out of respect for the governor of the castle and at his request, he would
spare. The governor being warned and alarmed at possible
consequences, brought out forthwith a book in which he kept
his account of the straw and barley supplied to the muleteers,
and with a stump of candle, which a boy held lighted in his
hand, and accompanied by the two damsels above-mentioned,
he went over to Don Quixote and ordered him to kneel: he
then read in his manual, as if he had been repeating some
pious oration. In the midst of the prayer he raised his hand
and gave him a good blow on the neck, and after that gave a
royal thwack over the shoulders, all the time mumbling between his teeth as if he was praying. After this, he commanded
one of the ladies to gird on his sword, which she did with

singular self-possession and gravity—and plenty was needed to prevent them all from bursting with laughter at every stage of the ceremonies; but the prowess they had beheld in the new knight made them restrain their laughter. As she girded on his sword, the good lady said: "God make you a fortunate knight and give you success in your contests." Don Quixote demanded then how she was called, that he might henceforward know to whom he was beholden for the favour received, for he was resolved to give her a share in the honour which his valour should obtain. And she answered with great humility that she was called La Tolosa and was a cobbler's daughter of Toledo, who lived near the stalls of Sancho Bienaya Square, and that she would always serve him and consider him her lord wherever she happened to be. Don Quixote replied, requesting her for his sake to call herself henceforth Lady Tolosa, which she promised to do. Then the other lady buckled on his spur and he addressed her in very nearly the same terms as the lady of the sword. He asked her name and she said she was called La Molinera and was daughter of an honest miller of Antequera. Don Quixote told her also to take a title and call herself Lady Molinera and he offered her his services. Now that the strange and unique ceremonies had been thus speedily finished, Don Quixote could not rest until he found himself mounted on horseback and sallying forth in quest of adventures. Wherefore, after saddling Rozinante, he mounted, and embracing his host, he said so many extravagant words in thanking him for having dubbed him a knight, that it is impossible to tell them. The landlord, that he might speed the parting guest, answered him in no less rhetorical flourishes but in briefer words, and without asking him to pay for his lodging he let him go with a godspeed.

IV. *What happened to our Knight after leaving the inn*

IT WAS ABOUT DAYBREAK WHEN DON QUIXOTE SALLIED FORTH from the inn, so lively and brimful of gladness at finding himself knighted that his very horse-girths were ready to burst for joy. But calling to mind the advice of his host concerning the necessary accoutrement for his travels, especially the money and clean shirts, he resolved to return home to provide himself with them and with a squire. He had in view a certain labouring man of the neighbourhood, who was poor and had children, but was otherwise very well fitted for the office of squire to a knight. With this thought in mind he turned Rozinante towards his village, and the horse, knowing full well the way to his stable, began to trot so briskly that his hoofs seemed hardly to strike the ground. The knight had not travelled far when he thought he heard faint cries of someone in distress from a thicket on his right hand. No sooner had he heard them than he said: "I render thanks to heaven for such a favour. Already I have an opportunity of performing the duty of my profession and of reaping the harvest of my good ambition. Those cries must surely come from some distressed man or woman who needs my protection." Then turning his reins, he guided Rozinante towards the place whence he thought the cries came. A short distance within the wood he saw a mare tied to a holm-oak and to another a youth of about fifteen years of age naked from the waist upwards. It was he who was crying out, and not without reason, for a lusty countryman was flogging him wi·h a leather strap, and every blow he accompanied with a word of warning and advice, saying: "Keep your mouth shut and your eyes skinned." The boy answered: "I'll never do it again, master. By God's passion I promise in future to be more careful of your flock."

When Don Quixote saw what was happening, he said in an angry voice: "Discourteous knight, it is a caitiff's deed to attack one who cannot defend himself. Get up on your horse and take your lance (for the farmer, too, had a lance leaning against the oak tree to which the mare was tied). I will show you that you have been acting a coward's part." The countryman at the sight of the strange apparition in armour, brandishing a lance over him, gave himself up for lost and so replied submissively: "Sir Knight, this youth I am chastising is a servant of mine, whom I employ to look after a flock of sheep in the neighbourhood; but he is so careless that every day he loses one, and when I punish him for his negligence or rascality, he says I do it because I am a skinflint and will not pay him his wages. Upon my life and soul, he lies."

"Have you the impudence to lie in my presence, vile serf?" said Don Quixote; "by the sun that shines on us I will pierce you through and through with this lance of mine. Pay him instantly and none of your denials. If not, by almighty God who rules us all I will annihilate you this very moment; untie him at once."

The countryman hung down his head and without a word untied his servant. Don Quixote then asked the boy how much his master owed him. He replied, nine months' wages at seven reals a month. Don Quixote having calculated the sum found that it came to sixty-three reals, so he told the farmer to pay up the money unless he wished to die. The fellow, who was shaking with fear, then answered that on the word of one in a tight corner and also upon his oath (yet he had sworn nothing) he did not owe so much, for they must deduct three pairs

29

of shoes which he had given the boy, and a real for two blood-lettings which he had when he was sick.

"That is all very well," answered Don Quixote, "but let the shoes and the blood-letting stand for the blows which you have given him for no fault of his own; if he wore out the leather of the shoes you gave him, you wore out his skin, and if the barber drew blood from him when he was sick, you drew blood from him when he was in good health; so in this matter he owes you nothing."

"The trouble is, Sir Knight," said the countryman, "that I have no money on me. If Andrew comes home with me, I'll pay him ready money down."

"I go home with him?" said the boy; "not on your life, sir! I would not think of doing such a thing; the moment he gets me alone he'll flay me like a Saint Bartholomew."

"He will not do so," answered Don Quixote. "I have only to command and he will respect me and do my behest. So I shall let him go free and guarantee payment to you, provided he swears by the order of knighthood which he has received."

"Take heed, sir, of what you are saying," said the boy. "My master is no knight; he has not received any order of knighthood: he is Juan Haldudo the wealthy, a native of Quintanar."

"That matters little," answered Don Quixote: "there may be Haldudos who are knights, especially as every man is the son of his own works."

"That's true," said Andrew, "but what kind of works is my master the son of? Isn't he denying me the wages of my sweat and toil?"

"I'm not denying them, brother Andrew," answered the countryman. "Do, please, come with me and I swear by all the orders of knighthood there are in the world to pay you, as I said before, every real down, and even perfumed into the bargain."

"I let you off the perfuming," said Don Quixote: "give them to him in good, honest reals and I shall be satisfied; but see to it that you carry out your oath. If not, I swear by the same oath to return and chastise you, and I am sure to find you, even if you hide away from me more successfully than a lizard. And if you want to know who it is who gives you this command, learn that I am the valiant Don Quixote of La Mancha, the undoer of wrongs and injuries. So, God be with you and do not forget what you have promised and sworn, on pain of the penalty I have stated." With these words he spurred Rozinante and in a moment he was far away.

The countryman gazed after him, and when he saw that he had gone through the wood and was out of sight, he turned to his servant Andrew, saying: "Come here, my boy; I want to pay you what I owe you in accordance with the commands of that undoer of wrongs."

"So you shall, I swear," said Andrew, "and you will be well advised to obey the orders of that good knight—may he live a thousand years: he surely is a courageous and good judge. By Saint Roch, if you don't pay me, he'll be back and he'll do what he threatened."

"Faith and I'll swear too," answered the countryman, "and to show you my good will I'll increase the debt in order to increase the pay." Catching the boy by the arm, he tied him again to the oak and gave him such a drubbing he left him for dead. "Now, master Andrew," said he, "call out to that undoer of wrongs and you'll find that he won't undo this one. Indeed I don't think I'm finished with you yet, for I've a mind to flay you alive, as you feared a moment ago." At last he untied him and gave him leave to go off and fetch his judge to carry out the threatened sentence. As for Andrew, he went off dejected, swearing that he would seek out the valiant Don Quixote of La Mancha and tell him all that had happened, and he would make his tormentor pay sevenfold. However, he departed in tears, while his master stayed behind laughing.

Such was the manner in which the valiant Don Quixote undid that wrong.

Meanwhile the knight was full pleased with himself, for he believed that he had begun his feats of arms in a most successful and dignified manner, and he went on riding towards his village, saying to himself in a low voice: "Well mayest thou call thyself the happiest of all women on earth, O Dulcinea del Toboso, peerless among beauties, for it was thy fortune to have subject to thy will so valiant and celebrated a knight as is and shall be Don Quixote of La Mancha, who, as all the world knows, received only yesterday the order of knighthood and today has undone the greatest wrong that ever ignorance designed or cruelty committed. Today from the hand of that pitiless foe he seized the lash with which he so unjustly scourged that tender child." Just then he came to a road which branched into four directions, and forthwith he was reminded of the crossroads where knights-errant would halt to consider which road they should follow. To imitate their example he paused for a moment's meditation, and then he slackened the reins, leaving Rozinante to choose the way. The horse followed his original intention, which was to make straight in the direction of his stable.

When Don Quixote had ridden about two miles he saw a big company of people who, as it appeared later, were traders of Toledo on their way to buy silk in Murcia. There were six of them and they carried sun-shades. They were accompanied by four servants on horseback and three muleteers on foot. No sooner had Don Quixote perceived them than he fancied a new adventure was at hand. So, imitating as closely as possible the exploits he had read about in his books, he resolved now to perform one which was admirably moulded to the present circumstances. So with a lofty bearing he fixed himself firmly in his stirrups, grasped his lance, covered himself with his buckler and stood in the middle of the road waiting for those knights-errant (for such he supposed them to be). As soon as they came within earshot, Don Quixote, raising his voice, cried out in an arrogant tone: "Let all the world stand still if all the world does not confess that there is not in all the world a fairer damsel than the Empress of La Mancha, the peerless Dulcinea del Toboso."

At the sound of those words the traders pulled up and gazed in amazement at the grotesque being who uttered them. Both the tone and the appearance of the horseman gave clear proof of his insanity, but they wished to consider in more leisurely fashion what was the meaning of this confession which he insisted upon. So one of them, who was a trifle waggish in humour and had plenty of wit, addressed him as follows: "Sir Knight, we do not know this lady you speak of: show her to us, and if she is as beautiful as you say, we shall willingly and universally acknowledge the truth of your claim."

"If I were to show her to you," answered Don Quixote, "what merit would there be in acknowledging a truth so manifest to all? The important point is that you should believe, confess, affirm, swear and defend it without setting eyes on her: if ye do not, I challenge ye to try battle with me, ye presumptuous and overweening band. Come on now, one by one as the traditions of chivalry declare, or else all together according to the foul usage of your breed. Here I stand waiting for you, trusting in the justice of my cause."

"Sir Knight," answered the trader, "I beseech you in the name of all the princes here present not to force us to burden our consciences by confessing something we have never seen or heard, especially when it is so prejudicial to the empresses and queens of Alcarria and Extremadura. Please show us some picture of that lady, even if it is no bigger than a grain of wheat, for the thread will enable us to judge the skein and we shall be satisfied and you yourself happy and content. I believe that we already are so much on your side that even if your lady's picture shows that one eye squints and the other drips vermilion and sulphur, yet in spite of all, to gratify you, we shall say all that you please in her favour."

"Drip indeed, you infamous scoundrels!" cried Don Quixote in a towering rage. "Nothing of the kind drips

32

from her eyes, but only ambergris and civet in cotton wool: she is not squint-eyed nor hunch-backed but straighter than a Guadarrama spindle. But you shall pay the penalty for the great blasphemy you have uttered against so peerless a beauty as my lady." With those words he attacked the man who had spoken to him, so fiercely with couched lance that if good fortune had not caused Rozinante to stumble and fall midway the merchant would have paid dearly for his rashness. Rozinante fell and his master rolled a good distance over the ground. Although he tried to rise he could not, for he was so impeded by the lance, the buckler, the spurs, the helmet, and the weight of the ancient armour. However, as he was struggling to arise and could not, he kept on crying: "Flee not, cowardly rabble. Wait, slavish herd! It is not through my fault but the fault of my horse that I am stretched here."

One of the muleteers of the company, who indeed was not over good-natured, when he heard the poor fallen knight say such arrogant words, could not resist the temptation to give him his answer on his ribs. So he went up to him, took the lance, broke it into pieces, and with one of them he so belaboured our poor Don Quixote that in spite of his armour he ground him like a measure of wheat. His masters shouted to him not to beat him so much and to leave off; but the fellow's hand was now in and he would not leave off the game until he had spent what remained of his rage. Then running to get the rest of the pieces of the lance, he splintered them all on the wretched knight, who in the midst of all this tempest of blows that rained on him, did not for a moment close his mouth, but bellowed out threats to heaven and earth and those villainous cut-throats (for so they appeared to him). At last the muleteer became wearied and the traders pursued their journey, carrying with them plenty of matter for conversation at the expense of the poor drubbed knight. And when he was alone he tried to see if he could get up, but if he could not do so when he was hale and hearty, how could he do it when he was bruised and battered? And yet he counted himself lucky, for he thought that his misfortune was peculiar to knights-errant and he attributed the whole accident to the fault of his horse.

V. Wherein is continued the account of our Knight's mishap

DON QUIXOTE, SEEING THAT HE COULD NOT STIR, RESOLVED TO have recourse to his usual remedy, which was to think of some incident in his books, and his madness made him remember that of Baldwin and the Marquis of Mantua, when

Carloto left him wounded on the mountain side—a story familiar to children, not unknown to youths, celebrated and even believed by old men; yet for all that, no truer than the miracles of Mahomet. Now this story, as he thought, exactly fitted his present circumstances, so with a great display of affliction he began to roll about on the ground and to repeat in a faint voice the words that the wounded knight in the wood was supposed to say:

> "Where art thou, lady of my heart,
> That for my woe thou dost not grieve?
> Alas, thou know'st not my distress,
> Or thou art false and pitiless."

In this manner he repeated the ballad until he came to those verses which say: "O noble Marquis of Mantua, my uncle and liege lord." By chance there happened to pass by just at that moment a peasant of his own village, a near neighbour, who was returning from bringing a load of wheat to the mill. And he, seeing a man lying stretched out on the ground, came over and asked him who he was and what was the cause of his sorrowful lamentation. Don Quixote, firmly believing that the man was his uncle, the Marquis of Mantua, would not answer, but continued reciting his ballad and relating his misfortune and the amours of the Emperor's son with his wife, just as it is told there. The peasant was amazed to hear those extravagant words. Then taking off his vizor, which had been broken to pieces in the drubbing, he wiped the dust off his face. No sooner had he done so than he recognized him and said: "Señor Quixana (for that must have been how people called him when he had his wits and had not been transformed from a staid gentleman into a knight-errant), who left you in such a state?" But he kept on reciting his ballad and made no answer to what he was asked. The good man then, as best he could, took off his breast- and back-plate to see if he was wounded, but he saw no blood nor scar upon him. He managed to lift him up from the ground and with the greatest difficulty hoisted him on to his ass, thinking such a beast an easier mount. Then he gathered together all his arms, not omitting even the splinters of the lance, tied them into a bundle and laid them upon Rozinante's back. Then taking him by the bridle and the ass by the halter he set off towards his village, meditating all the while on the foolish words which Don Quixote kept saying. And Don Quixote on his side was no less pensive, for he was so beaten and bruised that he could hardly hold himself on to the ass, and from time to time he uttered such melancholy sighs that they seemed to pierce the skies, where-upon the peasant felt again moved to ask him what was the cause of his sorrow. But it must have been the devil himself who supplied his memory with stories tallying with his circumstances, for at that instant, forgetting Baldwin, he remembered the Moor Abindarráez, when the Governor of Antequera, Rodrigo de Narváez, took him prisoner to his castle. So, when the peasant asked him again how he was, he answered word for word as the captive Abencerrage answered Rodrigo de Narváez, just as he had read in the *Diana* of Montemayor where the story is told: and he applied it so artfully to his own case that the peasant was distracted at having to listen to such a hotchpotch of foolishness. This convinced him that his neighbour was mad, so he made haste to reach the village and thereby escape being further plagued by Don Quixote's long discourse. The latter ended saying: "I would have you know, Señor Don Rodrigo de Narváez, that the beauteous Jarifa I have mentioned is now the fair Dulcinea del Toboso, for whom I have done, I do and shall do the most famous deeds of chivalry that ever have been, are or ever shall be seen in the world." To this the peasant answered: "Take heed, sir, that I am neither Don Rodrigo de Narváez nor the Marquis of Mantua, but Pedro Alonso your neighbour: and you are neither Baldwin nor Abindarráez, but the honourable gentleman Señor Quixano."

"I know who I am," answered Don Quixote, "and I know that I can be not only those I have mentioned but also the Twelve Peers of France and even the Nine Worthies, for my exploits would surpass all they have ever jointly or separately achieved."

With these and sundry other topics of conversation they reached the village at sunset, but the peasant waited until it was dark so that no one might see the belaboured knight so sorrily mounted. When he thought the time had come he entered the village and went to Don Quixote's house, which he found in uproar. The curate and the village barber, great friends of Don Quixote, happened to be there, and the housekeeper was addressing them in a loud voice: "What do you think, Master Licentiate Pedro Pérez (that was the curate's name), of my master's misfortune? For the past six days neither he, nor his horse, nor his buckler, nor his lance, nor his armour has appeared. Woe is me! I'm now beginning to understand and I'm as sure as I am to die that those accursed books of chivalry, which he continually reads, have turned his brain topsy-turvy. Now that I think of it, I remember hearing him say to himself many a time that he wished to become a knight-errant and go through the world in search of adventures. The Devil and Barabbas take such books, for they have ruined the finest mind in all La Mancha." The niece said the same, and a little more: "You must know,

35

Master Nicholas (this was the name of the barber), that it was a frequent occurrence for my uncle to read continuously those soulless books of misadventure for two days and nights on end. At the end of that time he would cast the book from his hands, clutch his sword and begin to slash the walls. Then when he was grown very weary he would say that he had killed four giants as big as towers, and the sweat which dripped off him after his great exertions, he would say, was blood from the wounds he had received in battle. Then he would drink a great jugful of water and become calm and peaceable, saying that the water was a most precious liquor which his friend the great enchanter Esquife had given him. I, however, blame myself for all, for not having warned you of my uncle's extravagant behaviour: you might have cured him before things reached such a pass, and you would have burnt all those excommunicated volumes (he has many, mind you), for they all deserve to be burnt as heretics."

"I agree with that," said the curate, "and I hold that tomorrow must not pass without a public enquiry being made into them, and they should be condemned to the fire to prevent them from tempting those who read them to do what my poor master must have done."

All this Don Quixote and the peasant heard; whereupon the latter finally understood the infirmity of his neighbour, and he began to shout out: "Open your doors, all of you, to Sir Baldwin and the Marquis of Mantua, who is grievously wounded, and to the Moor Abindarráez who is led captive by the valiant Rodrigo de Narváez, Governor of Antequera."

Hearing these cries, all rushed out and straightway recognized their friend, and they ran to embrace him, but he had not yet dismounted from the ass, for he was not able to do so. He said: "Stand back, all of you. I have been sore wounded through the fault of my horse; carry me to my bed and, if possible, call the witch Urganda to examine and cure my wounds."

"Bad 'cess to it," said the housekeeper at this juncture; "my heart told me clearly on which foot my master limped. Come on upstairs, sir; we'll know how to look after you here without that Urganda woman. Curses, aye, a hundred curses on those books of chivalry which have driven you to this."

They carried him to his bed and searched his body for wounds, but could find none. He said he was all bruised after a great fall he had with his horse Rozinante when he was fighting ten giants, the fiercest and most overweening in the world.

"Aha!" said the curate, "so there are giants too in the

36

dance? By the Sign of the Cross I swear I'll burn the lot of them before tomorrow night."

They questioned Don Quixote a thousand times, but he would give no answer. He only asked them to give him food and allow him to sleep, for rest was what he needed most. This was done, and the curate cross-examined the peasant closely about the condition in which he had found Don Quixote. The man told him all, including the extravagant words he had said when found and on his way home. This made the curate still more eager to carry out a project which on the following day he actually did, namely, to call in his friend Master Nicholas, the barber. Taking him with him, he came to Don Quixote's house.

VI. *The high and mighty inquisition held by the curate and the barber on the library, and the second sally of our good Knight Don Quixote*

THE KNIGHT WAS STILL ASLEEP. MEANWHILE THE CURATE asked the niece for the keys of the room containing the books, those authors of the mischief, and she gave them to him willingly. They went into the room accompanied by the house-keeper, and they found above a hundred large volumes very well bound, besides many of small size. As soon as the house-keeper saw them she ran hastily out of the room and returned with a crock of holy water and a bunch of hyssop, saying: "Take this, your reverence, and sprinkle the room: we may thus avoid being bewitched by one of the many enchanters from those books, who would wish to punish us for our resolve to cast them out of the world."

The simplicity of the housekeeper made the curate laugh, and he told the barber to hand him the books, one by one, that he might see what they were about, for some might be found which did not deserve the fire penalty. "No," said the niece, "there is no reason why you should pardon any of them, for they have all been offenders. It is better to throw them out of the window into the courtyard and, after piling them in a heap, set fire to the lot; or else they can be carried into the back-yard and the bonfire can be lit there, and so the smoke will not trouble anyone."

The housekeeper agreed with her, so eager were the two women for the death of those innocents. But the curate would not agree without first reading at least the titles.

The first that Master Nicholas handed to him was *Amadis of Gaul*, in four parts. The curate then said: "There is a mystery about this, for I have heard it said that this was the first book of chivalry which was printed in Spain, and that all the rest owe their origin to it. I am therefore of the opinion that we ought to condemn it to the fire without mercy because it was the lawgiver of so sinister a sect."

"No, your reverence," said the barber, "for I have heard also that it is the best of all the books of this kind: since it is unrivalled in its style it should be pardoned."

"That is true," said the curate; "and for that reason we may grant its life for the present. Let us see the other one near by."

"It is," said the barber, *The Adventures of Esplandian*, the legitimate son of Amadis of Gaul."

"Well," said the curate, "the goodness of the father is not going to help the son. Take it, mistress housekeeper; open the window, throw it into the courtyard and start the pile for the bonfire."

The housekeeper did so with alacrity, so good Esplandian went flying into the courtyard to await patiently the fire with which he was threatened.

"Continue," said the curate.

"This one," said the barber, "is *Amadis of Greece*, and I believe all those on this side belong to the lineage of Amadis."

"Into the yard with the lot of them," said the curate. "Only let me burn *Queen Pintiquiniestra*, *The Shepherd Darinel*, his eclogues and the devilish subtleties of the author, and I should agree to burn with them the father who begat me if he disguised himself as a knight-errant."

"I agree," said the barber.

"So do I," added the niece.

"Well, since that is so," said the housekeeper, "away with them all into the courtyard."

They handed them to her, and, as there were many of them, she saved herself the toil of the stairs and threw them out of the window.

All of a sudden, while they were thus employed, Don Quixote began to shout out, saying: "Here, here, valiant knights! Here ye must show the force of your mighty arms, for the courtiers are winning the best of the tournament."

As they rushed out to investigate the hubbub, the scrutiny of the remaining books was not continued. When they reached Don Quixote's room they found that he had already risen from his bed. He continued to rave and rant, cutting and slashing about him, as fully awake as though he had never been asleep. They caught him in their arms and forced him to go back to bed. After he had calmed down a little he turned to the curate and said: "Surely, Lord Archbishop Turpin, it is a great dishonour to us, who call ourselves the Twelve Peers, to permit the knights-courtiers to carry off the glory of the tourney so easily, when we, the knights-adventurers, have won the prize on the three preceding days."

"Hold your peace, dear kinsman," said the curate; "with God's help, fortune may change and today's loss may be tomorrow's gain. Look to your health for the moment; you must be well nigh in the last stages of exhaustion, if you are not wounded into the bargain."

"Not wounded," said Don Quixote, "but there is no doubt that I am bruised and belaboured, for that bastard Don Roland drubbed me with the trunk of an oak tree, out of pure envy because he saw that I alone dared to oppose his valour. But I would not call myself Rinaldo of Montalvan if, as soon as I get up from this bed, I do not make him pay the penalty, in spite of all his enchantments. For the present, bring me food, for I know that it will do me most good; as for revenge, leave that to my care."

They gave him a meal, after which he fell asleep again, and they all were amazed at his madness. That night the housekeeper burnt all the books she could find in the court-yard and in the house. Some must have been burnt which deserved to be preserved for ever in the archives, but their destiny did not permit it. And so in their case the saying was fulfilled that "the righteous sometimes pay for the sinners." One of the remedies which the curate and the barber prescribed for their friend's infirmity was to wall up the room where the books had been stored, so that when he got up he would not find them (once the cause had been removed the effect might cease). They agreed to tell him that an enchanter had whisked books, room and all away. The plan was carried out with great speed. Two days later Don Quixote got up, and the first thing he did was to go and see his books, and, as he could not find the room where he had left them, he strode up and down looking for it. He came to the place where the door used to be and he felt the wall with his hands, staring around him on all sides without saying a word. At last he asked the housekeeper where was the room in which he kept his books. The housekeeper, who knew exactly what she had to answer, said: "What manner of room are you looking for? There is no longer room or books, for the Devil in person took all away."

"It was not the Devil," answered the niece, "but an en-chanter who arrived on a cloud one night after you went away. He got down off a serpent on which he was riding and went into the room. I do not know what he did in there, but soon after he flew out of there and up through the roof, leaving the house full of smoke. When we set about investi-gating what he had done, we could see no books or room, but the housekeeper and I both remember full well that when the wicked old man was about to depart, he said in a loud voice that owing to the secret enmity he bore against the owner of those books and of the room, he had done damage which would soon be clear. He said, furthermore, that he was called Muñaton the wizard."

"Freston was the name he wished to say," answered Don Quixote.

"I don't know," said the housekeeper, "whether he was called Freston or Friton: I only know that his name ended in -ton."

"That is true," said Don Quixote. "He is a wise enchanter —a great enemy of mine, and looks upon me with a sinister eye, for he knows by his skill and wisdom that in the course of time I shall fight in single battle with a knight whom he favours, and I shall win in spite of all his machinations: wherefore he tries to do me all the hurt he can. But I affirm that he will never prevail against what has been ordained by heaven."

"Who has any doubts on that score?" said the niece. "But, dear uncle, what have you to do with such quarrels? Is it not better to stay peacefully at home instead of roaming the world in search of trouble, not to mention that many who go for wool come home shorn?"

"My dear niece," answered Don Quixote, "how completely mistaken you are! Before they ever shear me, I shall have plucked and lopped off the beards of all those who think they can touch the tip of a single hair of mine."

The two women would not make any further reply, for they saw that his choler was rising. As a matter of fact he remained a fortnight at home in peace without showing any signs of wanting to repeat his earlier follies. During those days he had much agreeable conversation with his two friends the curate and the barber. He would say that what the world needed most of all was plenty of knights-errant and that he would revive knight-errantry. The curate sometimes would contradict him; at other times he would agree, for if he had not adopted this procedure he could never have dealt with him.

Meanwhile Don Quixote made overtures to a certain labouring man, a neighbour of his and an honest fellow (if such a title can be given to one who is poor), but of very shallow wit and understanding. In effect, he said so much to him and made so many promises that the poor wight resolved to set out with him and serve him as squire. Among other things, Don Quixote told him that he should be most willing to go with him, for perhaps he might meet with an adventure which would earn for him in the twinkling of an eye some island, and he would find himself governor of it. With these and other promises, Sancho Panza (for that was the labourer's name) left his wife and children and engaged himself as squire to his neighbour. Don Quixote then planned to raise money for his expedition, and by dint of selling one thing, pawning another and throwing away the lot for a mere song, he gathered a respectable sum. He fitted himself likewise with a buckler borrowed from a friend, repaired his broken helmet as best he could, and informed Sancho of the day and hour when he intended to sally forth, so that the latter might provide himself with what he thought needful: he charged him particularly to carry saddle-bags. Sancho said he would do so, and he added that he was in mind to bring an ass with him, for he had a good one and he was not used to travel afoot. Don Quixote was a little doubtful about the ass and he tried to recollect any case of a knight-errant who was attended by a squire mounted on ass-back, but he could not remember any such case. Nevertheless, he resolved to let him take his ass, for he intended to present him with a more dignified mount when he got the opportunity, by seizing the horse of the first discourteous knight he came across. He also provided himself with shirts and other necessities, thus following the advice the innkeeper had given him.

After all these preparations had been made, Don Quixote, without saying farewell to his housekeeper and niece, Panza to wife and children, set out one night from the village without a soul seeing them go. They travelled so far that night that at daybreak they were sure that no one would find them even if they were pursued. Sancho Panza rode along on his ass like a patriarch, with his saddle-bags and wineskin, full of a huge longing to see himself governor of the island his master had promised him. Don Quixote happened to take the same road as on his first journey, that is, across the plain of Montiel, which he now travelled with less discomfort than the last time; for as it was early in the morning the rays of the sun did not beat down directly upon them but slant-wise, and so did not trouble them. Sancho then said to his master: "Mind, Sir Knight-errant, you don't let slip from your memory the island you've promised me; I'll be well able to rule it, no matter how big it is."

Don Quixote answered, saying: "I would have you know, my friend Sancho, that knights-errant of long ago were wont to make their squires governors of the islands or kingdoms they won and I have resolved not to neglect so praiseworthy a custom: nay, I wish rather to surpass them in it. For they sometimes, perhaps even on the majority of occasions, waited for their squires to grow old, and then when they were cloyed with service, having endured bad days and worse nights, they conferred upon them some title, such as Count, or at

41

least Marquis, of some valley of more or less account. But if you live and I live, I may before six days are over, even conquer a kingdom with a string of dependencies, which would fall in exactly with my plan of crowning you king of one of them. Do not, however, think this strange; for knights-errant of my kind meet with such extraordinary and unexpected chances that I might easily give you still more than what I am promising."

"And so," answered Sancho Panza, "if I became king by one of those miracles you mention, at least my chuck Juana Gutiérrez would become queen, and my children princes."

"Who doubts it?" answered Don Quixote.

"I doubt it," answered Sancho Panza, "for I truly believe that even if God were to rain kingdoms down upon earth, none would sit well on the head of Marí Gutiérrez. Believe me, sir, she's not worth two farthings as queen; countess would suit her better and, even then, God be kind to her."

"Commend it all to God, Sancho," answered Don Quixote. "He will do what suits Him best, but do not humble yourself so far as to be satisfied with anything less than the title of lord-lieutenant."

"I'll not indeed, sir," answered Sancho; "for a famous master like yourself will know what is fit for me and what I can carry."

VII. The terrifying and unprecedented adventure of the Windmills, and the stupendous battle between the gallant Biscayan and the puissant Manchegan

JUST THEN THEY CAME IN SIGHT OF THIRTY OR FORTY WINDMILLS which rise from that plain, and as soon as Don Quixote saw them, he said to his squire: "Fortune is guiding our affairs better than we ourselves could have wished. Do you see over yonder, my friend Sancho Panza, thirty or more huge giants? I intend to do battle with them and slay them: with their spoils we shall begin to be rich, for this is a righteous war and the removal of so foul a brood from off the face of the earth is a service God will bless."

"What giants?" said Sancho, amazed.

"Those giants you see over there," replied his master, "with long arms: some of them have them well-nigh two leagues in length."

"Take care, sir," answered Sancho; "those over there are not giants but windmills, and those things which seem to be arms are their sails, which when they are whirled round by the wind turn the millstones."

"It is clear," answered Don Quixote, "that you are not experienced in adventures. Those are giants, and if you are afraid, turn aside and pray whilst I enter into fierce and unequal battle with them."

Uttering those words, he clapped spurs to Rozinante, without heeding the cries of his squire Sancho, who warned him that he was not going to attack giants but windmills. But so convinced was he that they were giants that he neither heard his squire's shouts nor did he notice what they were though he was very near them. Instead, he rushed on, shouting in a loud voice: "Fly not, cowards and vile caitiffs; one knight alone attacks you!" At that moment a slight breeze arose, and the great sails began to move. When Don Quixote saw this he shouted again: "Although ye flourish more arms than the giant Briareus, ye shall pay for your insolence!"

Saying this, and commending himself most devoutly to his Lady Dulcinea, whom he begged to help him in this peril, he covered himself with his buckler, couched his lance, charged at Rozinante's full gallop and rammed the first mill in his way. He ran his lance into the sail, but the wind twisted it with such violence that it shivered the spear to pieces, dragging him and his horse after it and rolling him over and over on the ground, sorely damaged.

Sancho Panza rushed up to his assistance as fast as his ass could gallop, and when he reached the knight he found that he was unable to move, such was the shock that Rozinante had given him in the fall.

"God help us!" said Sancho. "Did I not tell you, sir, to mind what you were doing, for those were only windmills! Nobody could have mistaken them unless he had windmills in his brains."

"Hold your peace, dear Sancho," answered Don Quixote; "for the things of war are, above all others, subject to continual change; especially as I am convinced that the magician Freston—the one who robbed me of my room and books—has changed those giants into windmills to deprive me of the glory of victory: such is the enmity he bears against me. But in the end his evil arts will be of little avail against my doughty sword."

"God settle it his own way," cried Sancho, as he helped his master to rise and remount Rozinante, who was well-nigh disjointed by his fall.

They conversed about the recent adventure as they journeyed along towards the Pass of Lápice, for there, Don Quixote said, they could not help finding many and various adventures, seeing that it was a much frequented spot. Nevertheless he was very downcast at the loss of his lance, and in mentioning it to his squire he said: "I remember having read of a Spanish knight called Diego Pérez de Vargas who, when he broke his sword in a battle, tore off a huge branch from a holm-oak and with it did such deeds of prowess that day and pounded so many Moors that he earned the surname of 'the Pounder'. I mention this because I intend to tear from the first oak tree we meet such a branch, with which I am resolved to perform such deeds as you will consider yourself very fortunate to witness; exploits that men will scarcely credit."

"God's will be done," said Sancho. "I'll believe all you say; but straighten yourself a bit in the saddle, for you seem to be all leaning over on one side: but that must be from the bruises you received in your fall."

"That is true," answered Don Quixote: "and if I do not complain, it is because knights-errant must never complain of any wound, even though their guts are protruding from them."

"If that be so, I've no more to say," answered Sancho; "but God knows, I'd be glad to hear you complain when anything hurts you. As for myself, I'll never fail to complain at the smallest twinge, unless this business of not complaining applies also to squires."

Don Quixote could not help laughing at the simplicity of his squire, and told him that he might complain whenever he pleased and to his heart's content, for he had never read to the contrary in the order of chivalry.

Sancho then asked his master to consider that it was now time to dine. The latter told him to eat whenever he fancied; for himself, he had no appetite at the moment. Sancho no sooner had obtained leave than he settled himself as comfortably as he could upon his ass, and, taking out of his saddle-bags some of the contents, he jogged behind his master, munching deliberately; and every now and then he would take a stiff pull at the wineskin, with such gusto that the ruddiest tapster in Málaga would have envied him. While he rode on, swilling away in that manner, he did not remember any promise his master might have made to him, and so far from thinking it a labour, he thought it a life of ease to go roaming in quest of adventures, no matter how perilous they might be.

They spent that night under some trees, and from one of them Don Quixote tore a withered branch which might, at a pinch, serve him as a lance, and he fixed to it the iron head of the one he had broken. All that night he did not sleep, for he kept thinking of his Lady Dulcinea. In this way he imitated what he had read in his books, where knights spent many sleepless nights in forests and wastes, revelling in memories of their fair ladies. Not so Sancho Panza, whose belly was full of something more substantial than chicory water.[1] He made one long sleep of it, and, if his master had not roused him, not even the rays of the sun beating on his face, nor the joyful warbling of the birds, would have awakened him. When he got up he tested the wineskin once more and found it somewhat flabbier than the night before. This saddened him, for he thought that they were not in the way to remedy that loss so soon as would satisfy him. Don Quixote would not break his fast, for, as we have said before, he was resolved to nurture himself on savoury remembrances. They now turned into the road leading to the Pass of Lápice and they discovered it about three o'clock in the afternoon. When Don Quixote saw it, he said: "Here, brother Sancho Panza, we may thrust our hands up to the elbows in what they call adventures. But I warn you not to draw your sword to defend me, even if you see me in the greatest danger, unless you find me attacked by base-born scoundrels. In that case you may help me; but if they are knights, you are forbidden expressly by the laws of chivalry to help me until you are dubbed a knight yourself."

"Master, I can promise you obedience in this," answered Sancho, "especially as I am by nature a quiet, peaceable man with ne'er a wish to thrust myself into noisy brawls. Nevertheless, when it comes to defending my own person, I'm not one to pay much attention to such laws, for those laid down by God and man allow everyone to defend himself against any who would do him wrong."

"I agree," answered Don Quixote; "but in the matter of helping me against knights, you must restrain your natural impulses."

"I promise to do so," answered Sancho, "and I'll observe that injunction as religiously as the Sabbath."

While they were thus talking, two friars of the Order of Saint Benedict appeared on the road mounted on large mules —big enough to be dromedaries. They wore dust-masks with spectacles and carried sun-shades. After them came a coach accompanied by four or five horsemen and two grooms on foot. In the coach, it was learnt afterwards, was a Biscayan lady on her way to meet her husband at Seville. He was about to sail for the Indies to take up an important post. The monks were not in her train, but were travelling the same road. As soon as Don Quixote saw them, he said to his squire: "Either I am deceived or this will be the most famous adventure ever seen, for those black, bulky objects over there must surely be enchanters, who are abducting in that coach some princess. I must redress this wrong."

[1] Chicory water was the popular cooling drink of that age.

"This will be worse than the windmills," said Sancho. "Take heed, sir, that those are monks and the coach must belong to some travellers. Take heed what you are doing: don't let the devil lead you astray."

"I have told you before, Sancho," answered Don Quixote, "that you know precious little about adventures: I am telling you the truth and you will now see for yourself." With these words he advanced and stood in the midst of the road by which the monks were to go. When they had come near enough for them to hear him, he cried out in a loud voice: "Monstrous spawn of Satan, release this instant the noble princesses you carry away in that coach under duress! If not, prepare to meet swift death as the just chastisement for your evil deeds."

The monks stopped their mules and stood bewildered both by the appearance of Don Quixote as well as by his words. They then answered: "Sir Knight, we are neither monstrous nor satanic, but two monks of the Order of Saint Benedict wending our own way. We do not know whether there are any princesses being carried in that coach by force or not."

"Soft words do not influence me: I know you well, accursed knaves," answered Don Quixote. Then without waiting for any further answer he spurred on Rozinante, couched his lance and attacked the first monk with such ferocity that if the latter had not let himself fall from the mule, he would have toppled him on to the ground against his will and wounded, nay, even killed him. The second monk, when he saw the way his companion fared, clapped spurs into his fine, towering mule and began to speed away over the plain faster than the wind itself. Sancho Panza no sooner saw the monk fall to the ground than he leapt swiftly off his ass, rushed at him and began to relieve him of his habit. But two of the monk's servants came up and asked him why he was disrobing their master. Sancho replied that it was his due by law, as spoils of the battle his master Don Quixote had won. The servants, who knew nothing of spoils or battles, seeing that Don Quixote was at a distance speaking to those in the coach, set upon Sancho, threw him down, plucked every hair out of his beard, and so mashed and mauled him that they left him stretched on the ground breathless and stunned.

As for the monk, he straightway got up again on his mule. He was trembling, terror-stricken and as pale as death, and no sooner was he mounted than he spurred after his companion, who stood a good distance away observing the issue of the encounter. Without waiting for the end of the whole

46

incident they continued their journey, crossing themselves oftener than if they had the devil himself at their heels.

Don Quixote, meanwhile, was talking to the lady in the coach, to whom he said: "Beauteous lady, you may dispose of your person as you will, for your proud ravishers now lie prostrate on the ground, overthrown by this mighty arm of mine. And that you may not pine to know the name of your protector, learn that I am called Don Quixote of La Mancha, knight-errant and captive of the peerless and beauteous Lady Dulcinea del Toboso. In return for the service you have received from me, I demand nought else save that you should go to El Toboso and present yourself in my name before my lady and tell what I have done to liberate you."

All that Don Quixote was saying was overheard by a squire in the retinue of the coach, a Biscayan; as soon as he heard that the coach was not to pass on but was to return to El Toboso, he went up to Don Quixote and, taking hold of his lance, he said to him in bad Castilian and worse Biscayan: "Go away, Sir Knight, and the Devil go with you: by God who me create, if you no leave coach me kill you as true as me be Biscayan."

Don Quixote understood him very well, and with great calmness answered him: "If you were a knight or a gentleman, which you are not, I would have punished your folly and insolence, vile caitiff."

"Me no gentleman?" cried the Biscayan. "As me be Christian, me swear to God you be liar. Throw away lance, draw sword, and me soon show you how soon you carry water to cat.[2] Me be Biscayan by land, nobleman by sea, nobleman by the devil and you lie if else you say."

"You will see presently, quoth Agrages," shouted Don Quixote.[3] Flinging his lance on the ground, he drew his sword, clasped his buckler and rushed at the Biscayan with the firm determination of taking his life. The Biscayan, seeing him coming, would have wished to alight from his mule, which was not to be trusted, seeing that it was a hired hack and a sorry one at that. But he had not time to do anything but draw his sword. Luckily for him he was near the coach, whence he could snatch a cushion to serve him as shield. Then they fell upon one another as though they were

[2] "Llevar el gato al agua" (to carry the cat to the water) means to do something that is difficult and perilous. It was a saying often applied to one who was victor in a contest. It was derived from a game in which two cats were tied together by the tail, then carried near a pool of water. They had the water between them and the cat which first pulled the other into the water was declared the winner. The Biscayan inverts the phrase.

[3] This phrase from *Amadis of Gaul* became a proverb ("ahora lo veredes, dijo Agrages").

mortal enemies. The bystanders tried in vain to prevent the fight, for the Biscayan shouted out in his garbled language that if they would not let him finish the battle, he would kill his lady and everyone else who hindered him. The lady in the coach, bewildered and terrified, told the coachman to draw aside a little, and from a distance she sat watching the fierce struggle.

The Biscayan in the course of the fight dealt Don Quixote a mighty blow on the shoulder over the buckler, which, if it had not been for his armour, would have cleft him to the girdle. Don Quixote, feeling the weight of that colossal blow, cried out in a loud voice: "O Dulcinea, lady of my soul, flower of all beauty! help thy knight, who, to repay thy great goodness, finds himself in this great peril!" To say this, to grasp his sword, to cover himself with his buckler, to rush upon the Biscayan was the work of one instant, for he was resolved to risk the fortune of the whole contest on a single blow. The Biscayan, as soon as he saw him coming, perceiving by his ferocious mien his set intention, resolved to do likewise. He stood his ground, covering himself with his cushion, but he could not manœuvre his mule either to right or to left, for the beast, being already jaded and unaccustomed to such childish pranks, could not move a step. Don Quixote, as we said before, advanced towards the wary Biscayan brandishing his sword on high and determined to cleave him in twain. The Biscayan, on his side, waited for him with his sword also raised, and protected by his cushion. All the bystanders stood trembling in fearful suspense, dreading the result of these prodigious blows: the lady in the coach and her women servants were making a thousand vows and offerings to all the statues and places of devotion in Spain, that God might deliver their squire and themselves from so great a peril.

The first to discharge his blow was the choleric Biscayan, and he delivered it with such force and fury that, if his sword had not turned in his hand, that blow alone would have sufficed to put an end to this cruel conflict and to all the adventures of our knight. But good fortune reserved him for greater enterprises and turned aside his rival's sword so that, though it struck him on the left shoulder, it did him no other harm than to disarm him on that side, carrying away with it a great part of his helmet and half his ear; all of which with hideous din clattered to the ground, leaving him in a pitiful plight. Heavens above! Who on earth could adequately describe the fury which then flushed the heart of our Manchegan hero when he saw himself thus treated? It is enough to say that it was such that, raising himself again in his stirrups and grasping his sword more tightly with both hands, he brought it down with such force upon the Biscayan, hitting him full on both his cushion and his head, that it was as if a mountain had crashed upon him: blood began to stream from his nose, mouth and ears, and he reeled as if he was going to fall backwards from his mule, as no doubt he would have done had he not clutched her neck. Then he lost his stirrups, then let go his arms, and the mule, frightened at the terrible blow, began to gallop across the fields, and after a few plunges, threw her master to the ground. Don Quixote, meanwhile, stood calmly looking on: as soon as he saw him fall, he leaped off his horse, ran swiftly towards him and, setting the point of his sword between his eyes, ordered him to yield, or else he would cut off his head. The Biscayan was so stunned he could not answer a word; and it would have gone hard with him, so blind with fury was Don Quixote, had the ladies of the coach, who up to now had been terrified spectators of the fight, not come up and begged the knight earnestly to grant them the grace of sparing their squire's life.

Don Quixote replied with stately gravity: "Truly, beauteous ladies, I am most willing to grant what you ask me; but it will only be on one condition, that this knight shall promise me to go to the town of El Toboso and to present himself before the peerless Lady Dulcinea, that she may do with him what she pleases."

The frightened and disconsolate ladies, without considering what Don Quixote demanded and without enquiring who Dulcinea was, promised that their squire would do whatever he commanded. "Then," said he, "on the faith of that pledge, I will do him no more harm."

While all this had been going on, Sancho Panza, who had been somewhat roughly handled by the grooms, had got upon his legs and had stood attentively gazing at Don Quixote's combat. He kept beseeching God in his heart to give his lord victory, that he might win some island of which he might be governor as he had promised. Seeing the contest was now over, and his master about to mount Rozinante, he ran to hold his stirrups, and before he mounted, he knelt before him, and, taking him by the hand, he kissed it, saying: "Be pleased, my good master Don Quixote, to grant me the government of that island which in this terrible battle you have won. However big it may be, I feel myself able enough to govern it as well as the best in the world who has ever governed islands."

To which Don Quixote replied: "Take heed, brother Sancho, that this adventure, and others of this kind, are not adventures of islands but of crossroads, in which nothing is gained but a broken pate or the loss of an ear: have patience awhile, for the adventures will come whereby I may make you not only governor, but something higher."

Sancho gave him hearty thanks, kissing his hand again and the skirt of his habergeon.[4]

After helping him to get up on Rozinante, he mounted his ass and followed his master, who without another word to the people of the coach rode on rapidly and entered into a wood near by. Sancho followed him as fast as his ass could trot, but Rozinante went so fast that, finding himself left behind, he had to shout to his master to wait for him. Don Quixote did so, bridling Rozinante until his wearied squire overtook him. As soon as Sancho came up he said: "I'm of the opinion, sir, that the wisest course for us would be to retreat to some church, for you've left yon man you fought with in a parlous state. I'll wager they'll tip the wink to the Holy Brotherhood[5] and we'll be nabbed: and, mark my words—before we get out of prison we'll have to sweat our tails out."

"Hold your tongue," said Don Quixote. "Where have you ever seen or heard that a knight-errant was brought before the judge, no matter how many homicides he might have committed?"

"I know nothing about 'omicils',"[6] answered Sancho; "nor did I ever commit one against anyone: all I do know is that the Holy Brotherhood does have something to say to those who fight in the country; I'll have nought to do with t'other."

"Set your mind at peace, friend," answered Don Quixote. "I will deliver you from the Chaldeans, not to mention the Holy Brotherhood. But tell me now, have you ever seen a more valiant knight than I am on the face of the earth? Have you read in history of any other that hath, or ever had, more courage in fighting, more spirit in resisting, more dexterity in wounding, or more agility in felling his foe?"

"To tell the honest truth, your worship, I've never read any history, for I can't read nor write; but I'll dare wager that I've never served a more daring master all the days of my life: only please God we don't have to pay for this boldness in the way I've mentioned. Now I'd like to beg your worship to let me dress that ear of yours, which is losing a power o' blood. Here I have some lint and a little white ointment in my saddle-bags."

"That," said Don Quixote, "would have been unnecessary

4 To kiss the skirt of the habergeon or mailed shirt, according to the code of chivalry, was a token of respectful affection.

5 An old institution revived by Ferdinand and Isabel in 1476, for the purpose of suppressing highway robbery and the lawlessness of the turbulent nobles. It spread all through Spain and made the road safe for travellers. It was a kind of constabulary.

6 Sancho thinks "omecillos" is equivalent to "homicidios."

if I had remembered to make a phial of the balsam of Fiera-brás, for with just one drop of it both time and medicines could be saved."

"What phial and what balsam is that?" asked Sancho.

"It is a balsam the recipe of which I have in my memory, and whoever possesses it need not fear death nor consider any wound mortal. Therefore when I have made and given it to you, you have nought else to do when in any battle you see me cleft in twain (as often happens) but deftly to take up the part of the body which has fallen to the ground, and with the greatest nicety, before the blood congeals, put it up again on the half which remains in the saddle, taking great care to fix it exactly in the right place. Then you must give me just two draughts of the balsam I have mentioned, and you will see me become as sound as an apple."

"If that is so," said Panza, "I renounce from now the government of the promised island, and all I want in payment for my many good services is for you, sir, to give me the recipe of that precious balsam: I'm certain that an ounce of it must anywhere fetch more than two reals, and I don't need any more to enable me to spend my life with credit and comfort. But tell me, does it cost much to make it?"

"For less than three reals you may make three gallons of it," answered Don Quixote.

"As I'm a sinner," answered Sancho, "what is your worship waiting for? Why don't you make it and show me how to do so?"

"Hush, friend," answered Don Quixote. "I intend to teach you greater secrets than this, and bestow greater benefits upon you also. For the present let me see about dressing my own wounds; this ear of mine pains me more than I would wish."

Sancho took out of his saddle-bags some lint and ointment, but when Don Quixote saw that his helmet was broken, he well-nigh lost his senses. Putting his hand to his sword and raising his eyes to heaven, he said: "I swear solemnly by the Creator of all things and by all that is written in the four holy gospels, to lead the same life as was led by the great Marquis of Mantua, when he swore to avenge the death of his nephew Baldwin; which was not to eat bread from a tablecloth,[7] nor sport with his wife, and other things which, though I cannot now remember, may be taken as included, until I have taken entire vengeance on him who hath done me such an outrage."

When Sancho heard this, he said: "Take heed, your worship. If the Biscayan knight has done what you ordered him to do, and presented himself before my Lady Dulcinea del

[7] This was the sign of mourning as described in the ballads of the Marquis of Mantua and the Cid, and in the romances of chivalry.

Toboso, then he has paid what he owed. He deserves no other penalty, unless he commits a new fault."

"You have spoken well and hit the mark truly," answered Don Quixote; "and, therefore, I annul the oath in so far as it concerns fresh vengeance, but I make it and confirm it again to lead the life I have said, until I capture by force another helmet as good as this from some other knight. Do not, Sancho, think that this is mere smoke of straw on my part. I have a precedent to guide me, for the very same thing happened in the case of Mambrino's helmet, which cost Sacripante so dear." [8]

"Throw those oaths to the devil, master, for they do a power of damage to a man's health and conscience. Tell me now: what shall we do if we don't butt into a man armed with a helmet? Must you keep the oath in spite of so many hardships, such as sleeping in our clothes, roughing it out on the heath, and a thousand other idle penances, which that crack-brained old Marquis of Mantua swore to observe and which you now want to revive? Remember, sir, that armed men don't go gallivanting over those roads but muleteers and carters, who don't wear helmets and have probably never heard tell of them all the days of their lives."

"You are mistaken in that," said Don Quixote, "for we shall not haunt these cross-roads two hours before we see more men-at-arms than rode against Albraca to win Angelica the fair."

"So be it," said Sancho. "God's will be done: may all turn out for the best and may the time come for winning that island, which is costing me so dear. Then let me die, for all I care."

"I have already told you, Sancho, not to worry on that score, for even if there is no island, there is always the King-dom of Denmark or of Sobradisa,[9] which will fit you like a ring on the finger, and you ought to be all the more pleased as they are both on terra firma. But let us leave this to its proper time, and now see if you have anything for us to eat in your saddle-bags. Then we must go in search of some castle, where we can lodge this night, and make the balsam I told you about, for I swear to God this ear of mine is hurting me greatly."

"Here is an onion, some cheese and a few crusts of bread," said Sancho, "but that's not dainty enough fare for so brave a knight."

"How little do you understand!" answered Don Quixote.

[8] The story is in Ariosto's poem *Orlando Furioso*, canto xviii. Don Quixote is wrong. It was not Sacripante but Dardinel de Almonte whom Mambrino's helmet cost so dear.

[9] An imaginary kingdom in the romance *Amadis of Gaul*.

"You must know, Sancho, that it is the pride of knights-errant to remain for a whole month without eating, and when they do, they eat only what is ready to hand: you would know this if you had read as many books as I have. In all the books I have delved into I have never found that knights-errant ever ate, unless by mere chance, or at some costly banquets prepared in their honour. The rest of the time they lived in clover, and although we know that they could not live without eating or without performing all the other functions of nature, because they were men like ourselves, yet it is clear that, roaming as they did most of their lives through forests and uninhabited wastes without anybody to cook for them, their daily fare must have been coarse country food such as you offer me. Therefore, friend Sancho, do not be troubled about what pleases me, and do not try to make a new world, or lift knight-errantry off its hinges."

"Pardon me, sir," said Sancho; "seeing that I can neither read nor write, as I've said before, I've not yet understood the laws of the knight's profession, but from this day onwards I'll provide my saddle-bags with every kind of dried fruit for you who are a knight, and for myself who am not one I'll lay in a store of more substantial things that can fly."

"I do not say, Sancho," replied Don Quixote, "that knights-errant are obliged to eat nothing but those dried fruits; I only say that their ordinary nourishment had to be of such a kind, together with certain herbs they found in the fields, which were as well known to them as to me."

"It is a good thing," replied Sancho, "to know those herbs, and I'm thinking we'll need to use that knowledge some day."

He now brought out what he had in his saddle-bags, and the two ate their meal in good peace and company. But wishing to look out for a lodging that night they soon finished their dry and scanty repast, mounted at once and hastened to reach a village before nightfall. But both the daylight and their hopes failed them near the huts of some goatherds, so they resolved to spend the night there.

Although Sancho was grieved at not being able to reach the village, Don Quixote was more joyful than ever to sleep in the open, for he thought every time this happened he was performing an act which confirmed his title to chivalry.

VIII. Don Quixote and the goatherds, and the calamity that overtook him in connection with certain heartless Yanguesan carriers

DON QUIXOTE WAS WELCOMED MOST CORDIALLY BY THE goatherds, and Sancho, having tethered Rozinante and his ass as best he could, followed the scent of certain pieces of goat's flesh which were sizzling in a pot on the fire. Though he longed that very instant to taste and see whether they were ready to be translated from the pot into his belly, he did not do so, for the goatherds themselves took the pot off the fire, spread some sheepskins on the ground and swiftly laid their rustic table, to which, with words of good cheer, they invited the two to share pot-luck. Six of them that belonged to the fold sat in a circle on the skins, having first with rough courtesy invited Don Quixote to seat himself on an upturned trough. Don Quixote took his seat, but Sancho remained standing to serve him with the cup which was made of horn. Seeing him standing, his master said to him: "That you may see, Sancho, the true worth of knight-errantry and how certain those who exercise it are to arrive swiftly to positions of honour and esteem in the world, I want you to sit by my side in the company of these good people, and become one with me, your master and natural lord. I want you to eat out of my plate and drink out of my cup, for the same may be said of knight-errantry as of love, that it makes all things equal."

"Many thanks for your favour," replied Sancho, "but I must tell your worship that, provided I have plenty to eat, I can eat as well and better on my feet and by my lonesome than if I was perched up on a level with an emperor. To tell you the honest truth, what I eat in my own corner without fuss and frills tastes far better, though it's nought but bread and onion, than turkey at tables where I have to chew slowly, drink but a sup, wipe my mouth often, neither sneeze nor cough even when I'm dying to do so, nor do other things which a man is free to do when he's alone. So, dear master, let these privileges which you wish to give me as a servant and follower of knight-errantry, seeing as how I'm your squire, be exchanged for something that'll be of more use and profit to me; for, though I'll put them to my account as paid in full, I hereby renounce them from today onwards to the end of the world."

"For all that," said Don Quixote, "here you will have to sit, for God exalteth the humble," and taking him by the arm he forced him to sit next him. The goatherds did not understand this gibberish about squires and knights-errant, so they just ate, held their peace and stared at their guests, who with great relish and good humour wolfed pieces as big as one's fist. After the meat course was finished, the goatherds spread on the skins a great quantity of parched acorns and half a cheese, which was harder than if it had been made of cement. The horn, meanwhile, was not idle, for it went the rounds so often, now full, now empty, like the bucket of a water-wheel, that one of the two big wineskins hanging in view of the company was rapidly emptying. When Don Quixote had satisfied his appetite, he took up a handful of acorns, and gazing at them earnestly, held forth in the following manner:

"Happy times and fortunate ages were those which our ancestors called Golden, not because gold, so prized in this our Iron Age, was gotten in that happy time without any labours, but because those who lived then knew not those two words *Thine* and *Mine*. In that holy age all things were in common: to provide his daily sustenance no man needed to do aught but lift up his hand and pluck his food from the lusty oaks, which generously invited him to gather their sweet, ripe fruit. The clear fountains and running brooks offered him bountifully their transparent waters. In the clefts of the rocks and in the hollow trees the busy, provident bees fashioned their commonwealth, offering to every hand without interest the fertile harvest of their fragrant toil. The robust cork trees, inspired by their own courtesy alone, divested themselves of their broad light barks, with which men began to cover their houses built on rough stakes, using them only as a defence against the inclemency of heaven. All then was peace, all friendship, all concord. The heavy share of the crooked plough had not yet dared to open and expose the compassionate bowels of our first mother; for she, without compulsion, offered up through all the parts of her fertile and spacious bosom whatever could nourish, sustain and delight the children who possessed her. Then did the innocent and beauteous young girls trip from dale to dale and hill to hill with braided locks or flowing tresses, wearing just enough clothing to conceal modestly what modesty seeks and has always sought to hide. Their adornments were not like those now in fashion among people, who value so highly Tyrian purple and silk fretted in countless patterns; but being decked in some green dock-leaves interwoven with ivy, who knows but they outshone our court ladies of today arrayed in the rare, outlandish inventions which idle luxury has taught them. In those days amorous conceits found simple and un-affected expression in the very form and manner in which they were conceived, without any artificial circumlocutions to enhance their value. Neither fraud, nor deceit, nor malice had yet interfered with truth and plain dealing. Justice was then contained within her proper bounds; she was untroubled and unbiased by favour or self-interest, which today so be-little, disturb and persecute her. Law was not yet left to the personal interpretation of the judge, for then there were neither judges nor causes to be judged. Modest maidens went about, as I have said, alone, wherever they pleased, without fear of danger from the unbridled freedom and lustful desires of others; and if they did lose their honour it was only because of their own natural inclination. But now, in this detestable age of ours, no damsel is safe, even though she were hidden and shut up in some new labyrinth like that of Crete; for even there the amorous pestilence would enter through some cranny, or through the air, owing to the zealous plotting of some rascal, and drive them to perdition despite their seclusion. Therefore, as times went on and wickedness increased, the order of knight-errantry was instituted to defend maidens, to protect widows, and to rescue orphans and distressed persons. I belong to this order, brother goatherds, and I thank you for the entertainment and good cheer you are giving me and my squire, for though it is a law of nature that every human being is obliged to favour knights-errant, yet since you have received me and feasted me without being aware of this obligation, it is only reasonable that I should return my warmest thanks to you."

Our knight uttered this long harangue (which might well have been spared) simply because the acorns which they gave him reminded him of the Golden Age, and put him in the humour of making that unprofitable discourse to the goatherds. They listened to him in wide-eyed astonishment, without answering a word. Sancho, too, was silent, munching acorns and frequently paying visits to the second large wineskin that was hanging from a tree to cool. As for Don Quixote, he took more time over his speech than he did over his supper. When he had done, one of the goatherds said: "That your worship, Sir Knight, may be sure that you are heartily welcome, we would ask one of our fellows to give us a song." No sooner were the words out of the goatherd's mouth than they heard the sound of a rebeck, and presently there appeared a handsome young man of about twenty-two years of age, who, sitting him down on the stump of an old oak, tuned his instrument and sang for the company. When he ended his song, Don Quixote entreated him to sing another, but Sancho Panza, who was more disposed to sleep than to listen to songs, would not allow it. "Sir," said he, "you had better consider where you are going to rest this night, for the labour which these good men perform all day does not allow them to spend the night listening to singing."

"You, Sancho," answered Don Quixote, "go and lie down where you please. As for me, it is better for a man of my profession to watch than to sleep; however, it would be a good thing, Sancho, if you could dress this ear of mine again, for it pains me more than it ought."

Sancho did as he was told; and one of the goatherds, seeing the wound, told the knight not to worry about it, for he would give a remedy which would cure it. Then bringing a few rosemary leaves, which grew in plenty in the neighbourhood, he mashed them, mixed a little salt with them, and having applied them to the ear, he bound it up, telling him that he needed no other medicine; which indeed proved to be true.

Next day when Don Quixote had taken leave of the goatherds, he and his squire rode on in search of fresh adventures. After passing through a wood they came at last to a meadow of fresh grass, by the side of a delightful and refreshing stream, which seemed to invite them to stop and spend there the sultry hours of the day that were already becoming oppressive. Don Quixote and Sancho dismounted, and leaving Rozinante and Dapple loose to crop the grass that was there in plenty, they ransacked the saddle-bags, and without any ceremony master and servant ate the contents in peace and good fellowship.

Sancho had neglected to hobble Rozinante, for he knew that he was so gentle and little wanton that all the mares in the stud at Córdoba could not provoke him to any indecorous act. But fate or the devil, who is not always asleep, so ordained that a troop of Galician mares, belonging to some Yanguesan carriers, happened to be grazing in the same valley. It is the custom of those carriers to spend the noon with their team in spots where grass and water abound, and that where Don Quixote happened to be was very well suited to their purpose. Now it happened that Rozinante was smitten with the desire to solace himself with their ladyships the mares, and therefore, as soon as he got their scent, he changed his natural accustomed pace into a brisk little trot, and without by your leave to his master, he went off to pay his respects to them. But they, as it seemed, were more eager to feed than to respond to his advances, and received him with their hoofs and their teeth in such a manner that in a moment his girths were broken and he remained naked minus his saddle. But the worst of all was that the carriers, perceiving the violence he was offering to their mares, rushed over with pack-staves and so belaboured him that they knocked him flat on the ground in a wretched plight.

Then Don Quixote and Sancho, who had seen the drubbing of Rozinante, rushed up puffing and blowing, and Don Quixote said to Sancho: "From what I see, Sancho, my friend, those are not knights but base scum of a vile race. I say it, because you may help me to take due revenge for the outrage which has been done to Rozinante before our eyes."

"What the devil kind of revenge are we to take," answered Sancho, "when they are more than twenty and we no more than two, perhaps indeed no more than one and a half?"

"I am equal to a hundred," answered Don Quixote, and

without another word, he clapped hand to his sword and flew at the Yanguesans. Sancho Panza, excited by the example of his master, did likewise. With his first blow Don Quixote slashed a leather jerkin one of the carriers wore and wounded him grievously in the shoulder. The Yanguesans, seeing themselves so rudely handled by two men only, when they were so many, seized their pack-staves, and hemming in the two of them, began to lay on with great fury. In fact the second thwack brought Sancho to the ground and the same fate befell Don Quixote; his dexterity and courage availed him nothing, and as fate would have it he fell at the feet of Rozinante, who had not yet been able to rise. Whence we may learn how unmercifully pack-staves can batter and bruise when they are wielded by wrathful rustics. Seeing the mischief they had done, the Yanguesans loaded their beasts as speedily as they could and departed on their journey, leaving the two adventurers in evil plight and worse humour.

The first to come to his senses was Sancho Panza, who, finding himself close to his master, said in a feeble, plaintive voice: "Master! Master!"

"What is it, brother Sancho?" answered Don Quixote, in the same feeble and doleful tone.

"I wish, if it were possible, that you would give me a couple of sups of that balsam of Vile Blas,[1] if you have it ready to hand; perhaps it will be as good for broken bones as for wounds."

"If I only had it here, woe is me, we should want nothing; but I swear to you, Sancho, on my word as a knight-errant, that before two days pass, unless fortune forbids, I will have it in my possession, or my hands will have lost their cunning."

"In how many days, sir," said Sancho, "do you think we shall be able to move our feet?"

"For my part," said the drubbed knight, Don Quixote, "I cannot say exactly, but I take on myself the blame for all, for I should not have drawn my sword against men that are not knights as I am. Therefore I believe the god of battles has allowed this chastisement to fall upon me as a punishment for having transgressed the laws of chivalry. Wherefore, brother Sancho, take heed of what I tell you, for it mightily concerns the welfare of us both; and it is this, that when you see such rascally rabble do us harm, do not wait for me to draw my sword upon them, for I will not do it on any account, but put your hand to your sword and chastise them at your own pleasure; and if knights come to their assistance, I shall know how to defend you and attack them with all my power, for you have already perceived by a thousand signs and experiences how far the strength of my invincible arm

[1] Sancho says Feoblas ("feo-Blas"—ugly Blas) for Fierabras.

extends": so arrogant had the poor gentleman become since his victory over the valiant Biscayan.

But Sancho Panza did not much relish his master's advice, and he replied: "Sir, I am a peaceable, sober, quiet man, and can let pass any injury whatsoever, for I have a wife and children to maintain and bring up. Therefore let me give you a bit of a hint, seeing that it's not for me to order, that I will on no account clap hand to my sword either against peasant or knight. And from this time forward, I do pardon, in the presence of God, whatever insults have been or shall be offered against me, whether by high or low, rich or poor, noble or commoner, without any exception whatsoever."

His master, hearing these words, answered: "Would that I had enough breath to be able to talk easily, and that the pain I feel in this rib were less, that I might make you understand, Sancho, the mistake you are making. What would become of you, if I, after conquering an island, were to make you lord of it? You would ruin all by not being a knight, nor wishing to be one, and by having neither valour nor will to avenge your injuries or defend your lands."

"In this trouble that's fallen on us," answered Sancho, "I wish, master, I was furnished with the brain and the courage you talk of; but I swear on the faith of a poor man that this moment I'm more fit for plasters than palaver. Try, sir, and see if you can rise: we'll help Rozinante, though he doesn't deserve it, for he was the chief cause of all this mauling. Faith and I'd never have believed the like of Rozinante— why, I thought he was as chaste and peaceful a fellow as I am myself."

"Fortune," said Don Quixote, "always leaves one door open in disasters, and that beast of yours, Dapple, will now be able to supply the want of Rozinante and carry me hence to some castle where I may be healed of my wounds. And I shall not consider such riding a dishonour, for I remember to have read that good old Silenus, the tutor and guide of the merry god of laughter, when he entered the city of the hundred gates rode very pleasantly upon a goodly ass."

"He probably did ride as you say," answered Sancho, "but there is a great difference between riding as a gentleman and going slung across like a sack of manure."

To which Don Quixote answered: "Wounds which are received in battle rather confer honour instead of depriving men of it; wherefore, Panza, my friend, do not reply any more, but get up as best you can and sit me on your ass, and let us depart before night comes and surprises us in this wilderness."

"Yet I have heard you say, sir," quoth Panza, "that it is very common for knights-errant to sleep on heaths and deserts for most of the year, and they consider themselves lucky in doing so."

"That," said Don Quixote, "is when they cannot do otherwise, or when they are in love; and so true is this, that there was once a knight who, unknown to his lady, stood for two years on a rock exposed to sun and shade and the inclemencies of heaven. Amadis was one of that kind, when after calling himself Beltenebros, he bivouacked on Peña Pobre. I do not remember whether he stayed there eight years or eight months, but I know that he did stay there doing penance for some pique, I know not what, shown against him by Lady Oriana. But let us leave this, Sancho, and hurry before some mishap befalls the ass similar to what happened to Rozinante."

"That would be the devil and no mistake," said Sancho, as with thirty groans, sixty sighs and a hundred and twenty curses and execrations against whomsoever it was that had brought him there, he got up, remaining bent half-way like a Turkish bow, and without being able to stand upright. In spite of this, he saddled his ass, who also had taken advantage of that day's liberty to go a little astray. He then lifted up Rozinante, who, if he had only possessed the power of speech, would have complained as loudly as Sancho and his master. At length Sancho, after setting Don Quixote upon the ass and tying Rozinante to his tail, led Dapple by the halter and proceeded as best he could to where the high-road seemed to lie. And since Fortune was guiding their affairs from good to better, he had not travelled a short league when he reached a road where he spied an inn, which, to his annoyance and to Don Quixote's pleasure, must be a castle. Sancho insisted that it was an inn, and his master that it was a castle, and their dispute lasted so long that they had time to arrive there before it was finished. Sancho, however, without arguing any further, entered with all his team.

IX. *What befell our imaginative gentleman in the inn he supposed to be a castle*

THE INNKEEPER, SEEING DON QUIXOTE SLUNG ACROSS THE ass, asked Sancho what ailed him. Sancho answered that 'twas nothing, only that his master had fallen from a rock and had bruised his ribs somewhat. The innkeeper's wife, unlike those that are usually engaged in that trade, was by nature kindhearted and would grieve at the misfortune of her neighbours, so she immediately began to minister to Don Quixote. She made her good-looking young daughter help her to heal her guest. There was also serving in the inn an Asturian wench, broad-cheeked, flat-pated, snub-nosed, asquint of one eye and not very sound of the other. It is true that the comeliness of her body made amends for other defects. She was not seven hands high from her feet to her head, and her shoulders, which burdened her somewhat, made her look down at the ground more than she would have wished. This bonny lass now assisted the daughter of the house to prepare for Don Quixote a makeshift bed in a loft that had in days gone by served for straw. Here, too, lodged a carrier, whose bed was a little distance away from that of our knight, and although it was only made up of the pack-saddles and coverings of his mules, was much better than that of Don Quixote, which only consisted of four rough planks on two uneven trestles, a mattress no thicker than a quilt, full of knots which from their hardness might be taken for pebbles had their rents not betrayed that they were made of wool; a pair of sheets like the leather of an old target; as for the coverlet, if anyone wished to count the threads of it, he could not have missed one in the reckoning.

In this wretched bed they laid Don Quixote, and then the landlady, with the help of her daughter, plastered him from top to toe, while Maritornes (for so the Asturian wench was called) held the candle for them. The landlady, as she was plastering Don Quixote, noticed how black and blue he was in places, and said that the weals seemed to be more the result of blows than of a fall.

"They weren't blows," said Sancho; "but the rock had many sharp ends and knobs on it, every one of which left behind a bruise." He also added: "Please, lady, leave over some of those pieces of tow—somebody will be sure to need them; and as for myself, I tell you my back, too, is hurting me a bit."

"In that case," answered the landlady, "you, too, must have fallen."

"I didn't fall," said Sancho Panza, "but with the sudden fright I took on seeing my master fall, my body aches as if they had given me a thousand thwacks."

"That might well happen," said the landlady's daughter. "I myself have often dreamt that I was falling from some high tower and without ever coming to the ground; and when I did awake I have found myself as bruised and shaken as if I had fallen in good earnest."

"That's the point, lady," answered Sancho Panza. "I didn't dream at all and I was more awake than I am this minute, yet I find myself with more weals than my master Don Quixote."

"What's this gentleman's name?" asked Maritornes the Asturian.

61

"Don Quixote of La Mancha," answered Sancho Panza; "he's a knight-errant and one of the finest and strongest that the world has seen these many years."

"What is a knight-errant?" asked the wench.

"Are you so fresh in the world that you don't know?" answered Sancho Panza. "Know then, sister, that a knight-errant is something that, in two words, is cudgelled and an emperor. Today he is the most wretched creature in the world, but tomorrow you'll find him handing out two or three crowns of kingdoms to his squire."

"How is it, then," said the landlady, "that you haven't got an earldom at least, seeing that you're the squire of this good gentleman?"

"It's early yet," answered Sancho, "for it's only about a month since we have been gallivanting in search of adventures. Up to the present we haven't bumped into any adventure worth the naming, but perhaps indeed we look for one thing and light on another. But, believe me, if my master Don Quixote recovers from this wound or fall, and I be not crippled by it. I wouldn't barter my hopes for the best title in Spain."

Then Don Quixote, who had been listening attentively to this conversation, sat up in his bed as best he could and, taking the landlady by the hand, said: "Believe me, beautiful lady, you may call yourself fortunate in having harboured my person in your castle. For I am such a person that if I say little about myself, it is because men hold that self-praise debases a man; but my squire will tell you who I am. Let me just say that I shall keep engraved for all time in my memory the service you have done me, and I shall be grateful to you as long as I live. Would to high heaven that Love had not enthralled me and subjected me to his laws and to the eyes of the beautiful, ungrateful Dulcinea, whose name I whisper to myself, else would the eyes of this beauteous damsel here bereave me of my freedom."

The landlady, her daughter and the good Maritornes stood bewildered by the words of our knight-errant, which they understood as well as if he had spoken in Greek, although they realized that they were compliments and offers of service. Not being accustomed to such language, they gazed at him wonderingly and thought he must be a far different kind of man from those now in fashion. And so, thanking him in their rough pot-house phrases for his offers, they left. The Asturian Maritornes rubbed down Sancho, for he needed her care no less than his master.

Now, the carrier and she had agreed to spend the night together, and she had given him her word that, as soon as the people in the inn were all quiet and her master and mistress were asleep, she would come to him and satisfy his desires as much as he pleased. And it is said of this good-natured wench that she never gave her word without keeping it, even though she had given it in the woods without any witness; for she prided herself on being of gentle birth, and thought it no disgrace to be in service in an inn. In fact she would maintain that misfortunes and unhappy accidents had brought her to that state.

Don Quixote's hard, narrow, niggardly and rickety bed stood first in order in the middle of the dilapidated star-lit cock-loft, and next to it Sancho had placed his own, consisting only of a rush mat and a coverlet that seemed to be rather of napless linen than wool. Beyond those two beds was that of the carrier, made, as we have said, of the pack-saddles and the trappings of his two best mules out of the twelve he owned; sleek, fat and goodly beasts they were, for he was one of the rich carriers of Arévalo, according to the author of this story, who makes special mention of him because he knew him well. Now this carrier, after he had visited his mules and given them their second feed, laid himself down on his pack-saddles and waited patiently for the coming of his most punctual Maritornes. Sancho was already plastered and in bed, but though he tried to sleep, he could not do so owing to the pain in his ribs. Don Quixote for the same reason had both his eyes wide open like a hare. All the inn was sunk in silence, and there was no other light but that of a lantern that hung in the middle of the gateway. This wonderful stillness and our knight's thoughts, which unceasingly reverted to the adventures described at every step in the books of chivalry (the true authors of his misfortune), brought to his imagination one of the strangest follies that can be conceived. He fancied that he was now in a famous castle (for, as we have said, all the inns where he lodged seemed to him to be castles) and that the landlord's daughter (daughter of the lord of the castle), captivated by his gallant presence, had fallen in love with him and had promised to lie with him that night for a good space of time without her parents being any the wiser. Then, taking as gospel truth all this fancy which he had created, he began to feel anxious as he reflected on the perils which his honour would suffer, but he resolved in his heart not to be guilty of the least infidelity to his Lady Dulcinea del Toboso, even though Queen Guinevere herself should appear before him.

While he lay thinking of these follies, the hour approached (that was unlucky for him) when the Asturian wench, faithful to her promise, entered the room. Clad in her shift, barefoot, with her hair trussed up in a fustian net, she stole in with soft and wary steps, feeling her way towards her carrier. But scarcely had she reached the door when Don Quixote heard her, and, sitting up in his bed, despite plasters and pain,

63

stretched out his arms to receive his fair damsel; but the Asturian, crouching and holding her breath, kept groping her way in search of her lover. Suddenly she encountered Don Quixote's arms, who seized her first tightly by one of her wrists and then, pulling her towards him (not a word did she dare to utter), made her sit down on the bed. Then he felt her shift, and though it was of sackcloth he thought it was made of the finest and most delicate lawn. She wore on her wrists bracelets of glass beads, but he fancied they were precious pearls from the Orient; her hair, which was almost as coarse as a horse's mane, he took to be threads of the most glittering gold of Arabia, whose brightness obscured that of the sun; her breath, reeking of last night's stale meat-salad, seemed to him to shed a sweet and aromatic fragrance: in short, he transformed her in his fantasy into the likeness of one of the princesses he had read about in his books, who came thus adorned to see the grievously wounded knight, being overcome with love of him. And such was the infatuation of the poor gentleman that neither touch, nor breath, nor other idiosyncrasies of the good damsel undeceived him, though they would have made anyone else save a carrier vomit. He thought he held in his arms the goddess of beauty herself, and clasping her fast he began to court her in a low, tender voice, saying: "I wish, fair and noble lady, I were in a state to repay so great a boon as thou hast given me by disclosing thy beauty; but Fortune, never weary of persecuting the virtuous, has seen fit to lay me in this bed, where I lie so bruised and battered that, even though were I ready to satisfy thy wish, 'twere impossible for me to do so, for there is a still more invincible obstacle, namely, the faith I have plighted to the peerless Dulcinea del Toboso, sole mistress of my most hidden thoughts. Had this obstacle not intervened, I should not be so doltish a knight as to let slip the happy opportunity thy great bounty has bestowed upon me."

Maritornes all this while sweated in mortal fear at finding herself locked in Don Quixote's arms, and without attending or even hearing what he said, wriggled silently to free herself.

The carrier, whose lustful desires had kept him awake, as soon as he heard his moll enter the door, listened attentively to all that Don Quixote said. Full of jealous suspicions lest the Asturian wench might play him false, he crept forward towards Don Quixote's bed and stood still, waiting to see the outcome of the knight's discourse, which, however, he could not fathom. When he saw the wench struggling to get free and Don Quixote trying to detain her, he no longer relished the jest. So he raised his fist and discharged such a terrific blow on the lantern jaws of the enamoured knight that he bathed his whole mouth in blood, and not content with this he mounted upon his ribs and, using his feet like a trotting horse, paced up and down from one end to the other. Now the bed was unsteady and its foundations were not of the strongest, so, being unable to endure the additional load of the carrier, it collapsed to the ground with such a crash that it woke up the innkeeper. He as once suspected that it was one of Maritornes' nightly skirmishes, seeing that she did not answer when he called her. Nursing this suspicion, he rose, and, lighting a lamp, went towards the place whence he had heard the scuffle. The wench, seeing her master coming, and knowing full well his ferocious temper, was scared out of her wits and rushed for safety to the bed of Sancho, who was now asleep, where she rolled herself up like a ball.

The innkeeper came in, shouting: "Where are you, you damned whore? I'll swear these are your doings."

Just then Sancho awoke, and feeling such a bulk on top of him, fancied he had got the nightmare, and began to lay about him on all sides with his fists. Not a few of those blows descended upon Maritornes, and, at last, stung by sheer pain, she cast aside all decorum and paid him back with such stiff interest that she soon roused him from sleep, whether he would or no. And he, finding himself pummelled in that manner by one whom he could not see, raised himself up as best he could, caught hold of Maritornes, and the two of them began the most obstinate and droll skirmish in the world. The carrier, perceiving by the light of the innkeeper's lamp the dismal condition of his lady, left Don Quixote and ran to her assistance. The landlord did likewise but with different intention, for his was to chastise the wench, thinking that she was certainly the sole cause of all this harmony. And so, just as the proverb says, "The cat began to bite the rat, the rat began to gnaw the rope, the rope began to bind the stick", so the carrier drubbed Sancho, Sancho Maritornes, Maritornes Sancho, and the innkeeper Maritornes: all of them minced it with such expedition that they gave themselves no rest: and the best of all was that the innkeeper's lamp went out, and as they were in the dark they flogged one another so unmercifully that wherever a blow fell it left its bruise.

There happened to be lodging that night at the inn one of the officers of the old Holy Brotherhood of Toledo. No sooner did he hear the strange noise of the conflict than he seized his short rod of office and the tin box containing his warrants and groped his way in the dark into the room, calling out: "Stop in the name of Justice; stop in the name of the Holy Brotherhood!"

The first object he encountered was the battered Don Quixote, who lay senseless face upward on his demolished bed. Catching hold of his beard as he groped about, he kept crying out incessantly: "I order you to assist the cause of Justice"; but, seeing that the person whom he held fast moved neither hand nor foot, he concluded that he was dead, and that the people there were his murderers. Wherefore he lifted his voice and shouted: "Shut the inn door and let nobody escape: they've killed a man here."

These words startled the whole company, and each combatant stopped the fight at the exact point at which the shout had caught him. The innkeeper retired to his chamber; the carrier to his pack-saddles; the wench to her straw bedding: and only the luckless Don Quixote and Sancho were unable to move from where they lay.

The officer now let go Don Quixote's beard, and wishing to search for the criminals and arrest them, he went out to get a light; but he could not find any, for the innkeeper had purposely extinguished the lantern when he retired to his chamber. And so the officer was obliged to make use of the hearth-ashes, where after much time and trouble he managed to light another lamp.

X. *An account of the countless troubles that came upon Don Quixote and his squire in the inn that, to his sorrow, the former took for a castle*

BY THIS TIME DON QUIXOTE HAD COME OUT OF HIS TRANCE, and, in the same sad tone in which the day before he had called to his squire, when he lay stretched in the valley of the pack-staves, he again called to him, saying: "Sancho, my friend, are you asleep? Are you asleep, friend Sancho?"

"How can I sleep, blast it?" quoth Sancho, groaning and grumbling. "I swear all the devils in hell have been after me this night."

"You may certainly think so," answered Don Quixote, "for either I know nothing or this castle is enchanted. Now take heed, Sancho, of what I am going to tell you—but you must swear to keep this secret until after my death."

"Yes, I swear," quoth Sancho.

"I ask you to swear," answered Don Quixote, "because I refuse to take away the good name of anyone."

"I tell you I'll swear," quoth Sancho again, "and I'll keep my mouth shut until after your death, and, please God, I may be able to let it out tomorrow."

"Have I done you such injury, Sancho," answered Don Quixote, "that you should wish to see me dead so soon?"

"It isn't for that," quoth Sancho, "but because I am all against holding things for long. I don't want them to rot in my keeping."

"Whatever the reason," said Don Quixote, "I put still greater trust in your love and courtesy. I must tell you that last night I had a most extraordinary adventure. Briefly it was as follows: a little while ago I was visited by the daughter of the lord of this castle, who is the most talented and most beautiful damsel to be found over a great part of the earth. Just as we were in most sweet and amorous conversation, an invisible hand, joined to the arm of some monstrous giant, gave me such a buffet on the jaws that my mouth was bathed in blood, and, not content with that, so bethumped me that I am now in a worse state than yesterday, when, owing to the indiscretions of Rozinante, the carriers did us the outrage you know about. Wherefore I conjecture that the treasure of this damsel's beauty is kept by some enchanted Moor and she is not reserved for me."

"Not for me, either," quoth Sancho, "for more than four hundred Moors have so whacked me that the drubbing with the pack-staves was nought but tarts and fancy cakes in comparison. But, sir, tell me something: would you call this a good and rare adventure, seeing that we're left in such a pickle? It wasn't quite so bad for you, sir, for you hugged in your arms that incomparable beauty—but what did I get except the ruddiest drubbing I'll ever have in all my mortal life? Bad 'cess to myself and to the mother who bore me! I'm no knight-errant and I never mean to be one; yet in all our mishaps the lion's share of trouble always falls to me."

"So you have been beaten, too?" said Don Quixote.

"Plague on my race, haven't I told you I was?" said Sancho.

"Do not grieve, my friend," said Don Quixote: "I will presently make the precious balsam which will cure us in the twinkling of an eye."

At this moment the officer of the Holy Brotherhood, having lit his lamp, entered to examine the person he imagined to have been murdered. And as soon as Sancho saw him approach in his shirt, with a nightcap on his head and a candle in his hand, having an ugly expression on his face into the bargain, he asked his master: "Is this by chance that Moorish enchanter who's out to punish us again in case something was left over?"

"He cannot be the Moor," answered Don Quixote, "for enchanters never let themselves be seen by anyone."

"If they don't let themselves be seen, they let themselves be felt," quoth Sancho. "If not, let my shoulders bear witness."

"Mine might also," answered Don Quixote; "but that is not sufficient evidence to make me believe that this man whom we see is the Moorish wizard."

The officer when he found them chatting so calmly together paused in amazement. Yet it is true that Don Quixote still lay flat on his back unable to stir from bruises and plasters. The

67

officer then approached them and said roughly: "Well, how goes it, you fellows?"

"I would speak more respectfully were I such as you are," answered Don Quixote. "Is it the custom in this country, blockhead, to address knights-errant in such a way?"

The officer, finding himself thus rudely used by one of so scurvy an aspect, flew into a rage, and lifting up his lamp he dashed it with all its contents at the head of Don Quixote, and broke his head in one or two places. Then, as all was dark again, he retired.

"Surely, sir," said Sancho Panza, "this is the wizard Moor; he must be keeping the swag for other folks, and for us nought but punching and lamp-smacks."

"It is ever so," answered Don Quixote, "and we must not take any notice of these devices of enchantment, nor must we be angry or vexed with them, for as they are invisible and fantastical, we shall not find anyone on whom to take vengeance. Rise, Sancho, if you can, and call the warden of this fortress, and try to get him to give me a little wine, oil, salt and rosemary to prepare the health-giving balsam, of which I have desperate need at this moment, for I am losing much blood from the wound which the phantom gave me."

Sancho arose, not without aching bones, and crept in the dark to where the innkeeeper was. On the way he met the officer, who was waiting to hear what had become of his enemy, and said to him: "Sir, whoever you are, do us the favour of giving us a little rosemary, oil, salt and wine; we're in sore need of some to cure one of the finest knights-errant in the wide world. He is lying in a bed over yonder sorely wounded by a Moorish wizard who is in the inn."

When the officer heard this, he took Sancho Panza for a man out of his wits, but, as the day was now beginning to dawn, he opened the gate of the inn and called the landlord, telling him what the fellow wanted. The landlord provided what was needed, and Sancho carried it back to Don Quixote. The latter was lying with his hands to his head, groaning with pain from the blows with the lamp, which, however, had only raised two fairly big lumps; what he had supposed to be blood was only the sweat running down his face as a result of his agony in his recent adventure.

Don Quixote took the ingredients, mixed them all together into a compound and then boiled them a good while until, as he thought, they had reached the exact temperature.

He then asked for a phial to hold the mixture, but as there was not one in the inn, he resolved to put it into a tin cruse or oil-pot which the landlord gave him as a present. He, furthermore, recited over the cruse more than eighty paternosters, and as many aves, salves and credos, accompanying every word with a cross by way of blessing. These ceremonies were witnessed by Sancho, the landlord and the officer. As for the carrier, he had gone off peaceably to the business of looking after his mules.

No sooner had Don Quixote made the mixture than he resolved to test on himself the power of his precious balsam (for so he really thought it to be), and so he swallowed a good quantity of what remained in the pot after the cruse had been filled. No sooner had he drunk the potion than he began to vomit so violently that his stomach was emptied of every particle of food. Owing to his retchings and rumblings, he fell into a plentiful sweat, and so he ordered them to cover him up well and leave him alone. They did so, and he remained asleep for more than three hours. When he awoke and found himself so much relieved in body and so much the better of his bruises, he took himself to be cured and believed he had really compounded the balsam of Fierabrás. With that remedy in his possession he would be able henceforth to encounter, without fear, all brawls, battles and quarrels, no matter how perilous they might be.

Sancho Panza, likewise, considered his master's cure a miracle and begged him for leave to swallow what remained in the pot, which was no small quantity. Don Quixote consented, so he took the pot in both hands and, with good faith and better will, he tossed down very little less than his master had done. It happened, however, that poor Sancho's stomach was not as nice as his master's, so before he could vomit he was racked by so many bouts of writhing, retching and kicking, with such cold sweats and swoonings that he truly thought his last hour had come, and in his agony he cursed the balsam and the rogue who had given it to him. Don Quixote, seeing him in that pitiful state, said: "I am sure, Sancho, that all this trouble has befallen you because you have not been dubbed a knight, for I am sure that this liquor can only do good to those who are professed."

"If you knew that, sir," replied Sancho, "may God blast me and all mine if I can understand why you let me drink it!"

By this time the beverage began to work to some purpose, and the poor squire discharged so swiftly and copiously at both ends that neither the rush mat on which he had thrown himself nor the coverlet were of the slightest use to him: he sweated and sweated in such a paroxysm of strains and stresses that not only himself but all present thought he was at the point of death. This dreadful hurricane lasted nearly two hours, at the end of which he found himself not cured like his master, but so shaken and shattered that he could hardly stand.

Don Quixote, on the contrary, found himself eased and

cured, and was eager to set off at once in quest of adventures. He thought that every moment he delayed there meant depriving the world, and especially those in need, of his strong arm. His confidence, too, was strengthened by his implicit faith in his balsam. So, full of this determination, he himself saddled Rozinante, put the pack-saddle on his squire's beast and helped Sancho to dress and mount his ass. Then, getting on horseback, he rode over to the corner of the inn and seized a pike which stood there, to make it serve him as a lance. All the people that were staying in the inn, over twenty in number, stood staring at him, and among the rest was the innkeeper's daughter. Don Quixote kept gazing at her fixedly, and from time to time he breathed forth so doleful a sigh as if he had plucked it from the bottom of his heart. All, however, or at least those who had seen him plastered the night before, thought that the sigh proceeded from the pain in his ribs.

When both were mounted and at the door of the inn, he called to the innkeeper and said in a grave and solemn tone: "Many and mighty are the favours, Sir Governor, I have received in this castle of yours and I shall remain deeply grateful for them all the days of my life. If I can repay you by avenging some affront you may have suffered from some proud miscreant, remember that my sole function is to help the weak, to revenge the wronged, and to punish traitors. Ransack your memory, and if you find anything of this sort for me to do, you have but to utter it, and I promise you by the order of Knighthood which I have received, to procure you satisfaction to your heart's content."

The innkeeper replied with equal gravity: "Sir Knight, I have no need that you should avenge any wrong of mine, for I know how to take what revenge I think fit when one is done to me. I only want you to pay me the score you have run up this night in the inn, both for the straw and barley of your two beasts and your suppers and your beds."

"So this is an inn, then," exclaimed Don Quixote.

"So it is, and a mighty respectable one too," replied the innkeeper.

"All this time I have been deceived," answered Don Quixote, "for I really thought it was a castle, and no mean one. But since it is indeed an inn and not a castle, all that can be done now is to ask you to excuse any payment, for I cannot break the rule of the Order of Knights-errant, of whom I know for certain that they never paid for lodging or anything else in the inns where they stayed. For the good entertainment that is given them is their fair reward in consequence of the sufferings they endure, seeking adventures both day and night, winter and summer, on foot and on horseback, in thirst and hunger, in heat and cold, exposed to all the tempests of heaven and the troubles of earth."

"All that has very little to do with me," answered the innkeeper. "Pay me what you owe me, and a truce to your fairy stories and chivalries; my only business is to get what I'm owed."

"You are a blockhead and a bad innkeeper," answered Don Quixote: then clapping spurs to Rozinante and brandishing his lance, he sallied out of the inn without opposition, and without turning to see whether his squire followed him or not, was soon a good way off.

The innkeeper, seeing him depart without paying, hastened to catch Sancho Panza, who said that, since his master would not neither would he pay, for being the squire of a knight-errant as he was, the same rule and reason held good for him as for his master in the matter of not paying anything in taverns and inns.

The innkeeper on hearing this became very irritated and threatened that if he did not pay him speedily he would get it from him in a way he would not like.

Sancho replied that by the law of Chivalry which his master had professed he would not pay a farthing even if it cost him his life; for he would not be responsible for the loss of the good old tradition of knight-errantry, nor would the squires of the future have cause to rebuke him for breaking so just an enactment.

But poor Sancho's ill luck so ordained that among the crowd there happened to be at the inn at this time four wool-combers of Segovia, three needlemakers from the Colt's Square in Córdoba, and two natives from the market-place of Seville—all of them merry fellows, full of mischief and fond of practical joking. As if they were all fired with the one impulse, they came up to Sancho, and pulling him down off his ass, one of them rushed in for the innkeeper's blanket and hurled him into it. But looking up and seeing that the ceiling was somewhat lower than they needed for their job, they resolved to go out into the yard, which had no roof but the sky. There they placed Sancho in the middle of the blanket and began to toss him up in the air and make sport with him as they would with a dog at Shrovetide.

The cries of the wretched blanketed squire were so loud that they reached the ears of his master, who, pausing for an instant to listen, believed that some new adventure was at hand, until he realized that the shrieks came from his squire. Straightway turning his horse he rode back at a painful gallop to the inn gate and, finding it closed, he rode round the wall to see if he could find any place at which he might enter. But he scarcely reached the wall of the inn-yard, which was not very

71

high, when he saw the wicked sport they were playing with his squire. He saw him go up and down in the air with such grace and agility that, if his anger had allowed him, I am sure he would have burst out laughing. He tried to climb the wall from his horse, but he was so bruised and broken that he could by no means alight from his saddle, and so from on top of his horse he began to utter such fearsome curses against those who were tossing Sancho that one could not set them in writing.

Nevertheless, in spite of his threats the others did not stop their laughter or their labour, nor did the flying Sancho cease his lamentations mixed now with threats, now with prayers. But all were of no avail, for they carried on their merry game, until at last they stopped from sheer fatigue and let him go. They then brought him his ass and, mounting him on it, wrapped him in his cloak. The kind-hearted Maritornes, seeing him so exhausted, thought it best to give him a pitcher of water, which, that it might be the cooler, she fetched from the well. Sancho took it, and as he was lifting it to his mouth he stopped on hearing his master's voice calling to him, saying: "Sancho, my son, drink no water; drink it not, my son, for it will kill you. Behold here I have the most holy balsam (he showed him the pot of liquor); two drops of this will certainly cure you."

At these words Sancho, giving his master a squint-eyed look, replied in a louder voice: "You must have forgotten that I am no knight, or else perhaps you want me to spew up what remains of my guts after last night's bit of work. Keep your liquor to yourself, in the devil's name, and let me alone."

As he said these words he began to drink, but at the first gulp, finding it was only water, he would not swallow any more, and he asked Maritornes to bring him some wine, which she did willingly, and likewise paid for it with her own money, for indeed it is said of her that, although she followed that trade, she had some faint glimmerings in her of a Christian.

As soon as Sancho had finished drinking he dug his heels into his ass, and as the inn gate was wide open he rode out, highly pleased at having paid for nothing, even at the expense of his usual creditors, namely, his shoulders. The innkeeper, it is true, remained with his saddle-bags in payment of what was due to him, but Sancho was so flurried when he departed that he did not miss them.

The innkeeper wanted to bar the door firmly as soon as he saw him out, but the blanketeers would not allow him, being the kind of people who would not have cared two farthings for Don Quixote even had he been one of the knights-errant of the Round Table.

XI. The conversation that took place between Sancho Panza and his master Don Quixote, together with some adventures worth recording

WHEN SANCHO REACHED HIS MASTER HE WAS ALMOST TOO jaded and faint to ride his ass. Don Quixote, seeing him in this state, said to him: "Now I do believe, my dear Sancho, that yon castle or inn is without doubt enchanted, for those who so cruelly made sport with you, what else could they be but spectres and beings of another world? I am sure of this because, when I was by the wall of the inn-yard watching the acts of your sad tragedy, I was unable to mount it, or to alight from Rozinante, so I must have been enchanted. For I swear to you, by my faith in my honour, that if I could have mounted or alighted, I would have avenged you in such a manner that those bragging rascals would remember the jest for ever, even though to do it I should have had to disobey the rules of chivalry. For, as I have often told you, they do not allow a knight to take up arms against one who is not one, unless in defence of his own life and in cases of urgent and extreme necessity."

"I, too, would have avenged myself," said Sancho, "whether I was dubbed a knight or no, but I could not. And yet I believe that those who amused themselves with me were no hobgoblins or enchanted beings, but men of flesh and bones as we are, for one was called Pedro Martínez, and another Tenorio Hernández, and the innkeeper's name, I heard, is Juan Palomeque the Left-handed. So, sir, when you said you couldn't leap over the thatched wall nor get off your horse, I'm sure the reason did not depend on enchantment but on something else. In fact, what I can gather clearly from all this is that those adventures which we are after will bring us in the end so many misadventures that we shan't know our right foot from our left. The best thing for us to do, in my humble opinion, is to go back again to our village, now that it's reaping time, and look after our own affairs, and not go, as the saying goes, 'jumping out of the frying-pan into the fire'."

"How little you know of knighthood, Sancho!" answered Don Quixote. "Peace and have patience, for a day will come when you will see with your own eyes how fine a thing it is to follow this profession. Now tell me: what greater contentment can the world offer? What pleasure can equal that of winning a battle and triumphing over one's enemy? Undoubtedly none."

73

"It must be so," answered Sancho; "but I don't know. I only know that since we have been knights-errant. anyhow since you have been one (no need to count me among so honourable a band). we have never won a battle. except that with a Biscavan. and even then vou came out minus half an ear and half a helmet. Ever after that it has been nothing but cudgels and more cudgels, blows and more blows; then, as an extra, the tossing in the blanket falls to me, which, as it was done by enchanters. I can't take revenge on them, so I'm blest if I know what is that pleasure of triumphing over an enemy which vou talk of."

"That is my trouble and it should be vours also, Sancho," answered Don Quixote. "But henceforth I shall trv to provide myself with a sword made with such art that no kind of enchantment can touch him that wears it. Perhaps Fortune may bring me a sword like that of Amadis. when he called himself Knight of the Burning Sword. which was one of the best weapons ever worn by a knight: for it not only cut like a razor. but there was no armour however strong or enchanted which could withstand it."

"It will be like my luck." said Sancho, "that even when you find such a sword it will. like the balsam only serve those who are knights. while poor squires will still cram themselves with troubles."

"Do not be afraid of that, Sancho." replied Don Quixote; "Heaven will yet deal more liberally with you."

Such was the conversation of master and squire as they rode on, when suddenly Don Quixote saw a large. dense cloud of dust rolling towards them Turning to Sancho. he said: "This is the day. Sancho, on which I shall show the might of mine arm and on which I intend to do deeds which shall be writ in the books of fame for succeeding ages Do you see yon dust-cloud. Sancho? Know then that it is churned up by a mighty army composed of sundry and innumerable peoples that are marching this way."

"If so there must be two armies." said Sancho, "for here on this side there is as great a cloud of dust."

Don Quixote turned round to look at it. and seeing it was so, he rejoiced. for he fancied that there were indeed two armies coming to fight each other in the midst of that spacious plain. For his imagination at all hours of the day and night was full of battles, enchantments, adventures, follies, loves and challenges which are told in the books of chivalry, and all his words, thoughts and actions were turned to such things.

As for the clouds of dust he had seen. they were raised by two large flocks of ewes and rams which were being driven along the same road from opposite directions, but owing

74

to the dust they could not be seen until they came near.

So earnest was Don Quixote in calling them armies that Sancho came to believe it, asking: "Well, what are we to do?"

"What?" said Don Quixote. "Why, favour and help the distressed and needy. You must know, Sancho, that this army marching towards us in front is led by the mighty emperor Alifanfaron, Lord of the great island of Trapobane: this other which is marching at our back is the army of his foe, the King of the Garamantans, Pentapolin of the Naked Arm, for he always goes into battle with his right arm bare."

"Why do these two gentlemen hate each other so much?" quoth Sancho.

"They are enemies," replied Don Quixote, "because Alifanfaron is a furious pagan, and is in love with the daughter of Pentapolin, a beautiful, graceful lady, and a Christian. Her father refuses to give her to the pagan king unless he abandons first the false religion of Mahomet and turns Christian."

"By my beard," said Sancho, "Pentapolin does right and I'll help as best I can."

"Then you will do your duty," said Don Quixote, "for it is not necessary to be dubbed a knight to engage in battles such as these."

"I understand," replied Sancho; "but where shall we stow this ass that we may be sure of finding him after the scuffle is over? I think it was never customary to go into battle mounted on such a beast."

"That is true," said Don Quixote. "What you must do is to leave the ass to his own devices: let him take his chance whether he is lost or not, for after winning this battle we shall have so many horses that even Rozinante runs the risk of being exchanged for another. Now listen to me carefully while I give you an account of the principal knights in the two approaching armies. Let us withdraw to that hillock yonder whence we may get a better view of the two armies."

They did so, and standing on the top of a hill, they could have discerned the two flocks which the fantasy of Don Quixote had converted into armies, had their eyes not been blinded by the clouds of dust. But seeing in his imagination what did not exist, he began to say in a loud voice: "The knight you see yonder with the yellow armour, who bears on his shield a lion crowned *couchant* at a damsel's feet, is the valiant Laurcalco, Lord of the Silver Bridge. The other with armour flowered with gold, who bears on his shield three crowns *argent* on an *azure* field, is the fearsome Micocolembo, Grand Duke of Quirotia. The other, with gigantic limbs, who marches on his right, is the undaunted Brandabaran of Boliche, Lord of the Three Arabias. He is wearing a serpent's skin, and bears instead of a shield a gate, which fame says was one of those belonging to the temple which Samson pulled down when by his death he took revenge on his enemies. Now turn your eyes to this other side, and there you will see, in front of this other army, the ever victorious and never vanquished Timonel de Carcajona, Prince of New Biscay, who comes clad in armour quartered *azure, vert, argent* and *or*. He bears on his shield a cat in *or* on a field of *gules* with a scroll inscribed *Miau,* which is the beginning of his mistress's name—according to report—the peerless Miaulina, daughter of Alfeñiquen, Duke of Algarve." In this way he went on naming many knights of each squadron, as his fancy dictated, and giving to each their arms, colours, devices and mottoes, extempore: for he was completely carried away by his mad fantasy. Ye gods! How many provinces did he name! How many nations did he enumerate! giving to each, with wonderful speed, its peculiar attributes, so absorbed and wrapped up was he in all that he had read in his lying books. Sancho Panza hung on his words without opening his lips. Now and then he turned his head to see whether he could perceive the knights and giants his master named. Seeing none, he said at last: "Master, I'll commend to the devil any man, giant or knight of all those you mentioned who appears here: at least I cannot see them. Perhaps all may be enchantment like last night's spectres."

"Why do you say that?" said Don Quixote. "Do you not hear the neighing of the horses, the blaring of the trumpets, and the rattle of the drums?"

"I hear nothing," answered Sancho, "but the bleating of sheep and lambs." And so it was, for now the two flocks were close at hand.

"The fear you are in," said Don Quixote, "allows you neither to see nor to hear correctly, for one of the effects of fear is to disturb the senses and make things seem different from what they are. If you are so afraid, stand to one side and leave me to myself, for I alone am sufficient to give the victory to the side which I shall assist." With these words he clapped spurs to Rozinante, and, with lance couched, rode down the hillside like a thunderbolt.

Sancho shouted to him: "Come back, master, come back! I swear to God that those you are going to charge are only sheep and muttons. Come back! Woe to the father who begat me! What madness is this? Look! There is neither giant nor knight, nor cats, nor arms, nor shield quartered or entire, nor true azures nor bedevilled. Sinner that I am, what are you doing?"

Don Quixote, however, did not turn back, but charged

on, shouting as he went: "Ho! You knights who fight beneath the banners of the valiant Emperor Pentapolin of the Naked Arm: follow me all of you and you will see how easily I will take vengeance for him on his enemy Alifanfaron of Trapobane."

With these words he dashed into the midst of the flock of sheep and began to spear them with as much courage and fury as if he were fighting his mortal enemies. The shepherds and herdsmen who came with the flock shouted to him to leave off, but seeing that words were of no avail, unloosed their slings and began to salute his ears with stones as big as one's fist. Don Quixote took no notice of their stones but galloped to and fro, crying out: "Where are you, proud Alifanfaron? Where are you? Come to me, for I am but one knight alone and wish to try my strength with you, man to man, and take away your life for the wrong you do to the valiant Pentapolin." At that instant a smooth pebble hit him in the side and dinged two of his ribs. Finding himself in such a bad way, he thought for certain that he was killed or sorely wounded, and remembering his balsam, he took out his pot and raised it to his mouth to drink. But before he could swallow what he wanted, another pebble struck him full on the hand, broke the pot to pieces, and carried away with it three or four teeth and grinders out of his mouth, and badly crushed two fingers of his hand. And such was the force of those two blows that the poor knight now fell off his horse on to the ground. The shepherds ran up, and believing that they had killed him, they collected their flocks in great haste, carried away their dead sheep which were above seven, and departed without further enquiry.

All this time Sancho stood on the hillock watching his master's mad escapade, and tearing his beard and cursing the unlucky hour and moment when he first met him. But seeing him lying on the ground, and the shepherds out of sight, he came down the hill and went up to his master, and found him in a very bad way, although not quite unconscious. So he said to him: "Did I not tell you, sir, to come back, for those you went to attack were not armies but flocks of sheep?"

To which Don Quixote answered: "That thief of an enchanter, my enemy, can counterfeit and make men vanish away. Know, Sancho, that it is a very easy matter for such men to make us seem what they please, and this malignant persecutor of mine, envious of the glory that I was to reap in this battle, has changed the squadrons of enemy into flocks of sheep. Now, for my sake, Sancho, do one thing to undeceive yourself and see the truth of what I am telling you.

Get up on your ass and follow them fair and softly, and you will see that, when they have gone a little distance away, they will return to their original shapes, and ceasing to be sheep, will become straight, upstanding men as when I described them to you at first. But do not go now, for I need your assistance. Come and see how many of my teeth are missing, for I do not think I have a single one left in my mouth." Sancho went so close that he almost thrust his eyes into his mouth, and it was precisely at the fatal moment when the balsam which had been fretting in Don Quixote's stomach came up to the surface; and with the same violence that a bullet is fired out of a gun, all that he had in his stomach discharged itself upon the beard and face of the compassionate squire.

"Holy Mary!" cried Sancho, "what has happened to me? The poor sinner must be at death's door, for he's puking blood at the mouth." But reflecting a little, he was soon convinced, by the colour, smell and taste, that it was not blood but the balsam which he had seen him drink; and so great was the loathing he felt that his own stomach turned, and he voided its full cargo upon his master, and both were in a precious pickle. Sancho rushed to his ass to take something out of his saddle-bags to clean himself and his master; but when he did not find them, he was ready to run out of his wits. He cursed himself again and he vowed in his heart to leave his master and return to his home, although he would lose his wages for service, and his hopes of becoming governor of the promised island.

Don Quixote had now risen, and keeping his left hand to his mouth that the rest of his teeth might not fall out, with the other he took hold of Rozinante's bridle (who had not stirred from his master's side, such was his well-bred loyalty) and went over to his squire, who stood leaning against his ass with his cheek reclining upon his hand, looking the picture of a man in sorrow.

The knight, seeing him in that mood, and so full of melancholy, said to him: "Learn, Sancho, that one man is not more than another unless he achieves more than another. All those storms that fall upon us are signs that soon the weather will be fair, and things will go smoothly, for it is not possible for evil or good to last for ever. Hence we may infer that, as our misfortunes have lasted so long, good fortune must be near. So you must not vex yourself about my mischances, for you have no share in them."

"How not?" replied Sancho. "I suppose him they tossed in a blanket yesterday was not my father's son? And the saddle-bags which are missing today with all my chattels is someone else's misfortune?"

"What, are the saddle-bags missing, Sancho?" asked Don Quixote.

"Yes, they are missing," answered Sancho.

"In that case we have nought to eat today," quoth Don Quixote.

"Too true," said Sancho, "if the herbs of the fields fail us, which your worship says you know all about, and with which knights-errant down in the dumps like yourself generally supply their wants."

"Nevertheless," answered Don Quixote, "at the present moment I would rather have a quarter-loaf of bread, or a cottage loaf and a couple of heads of salted pilchards, than all the herbs that Dioscorides has described. But, good Sancho, get up on your ass and follow me, for God, Who provides for all, will not desert us; especially, being engaged, as we are, in His service. He doth not abandon the gnats of the air, nor the worms of the earth, nor the tadpoles of the water, and He is so merciful that He maketh His sun shine on the good and the evil, and He causeth the rain to fall upon the just and unjust."

"Your worship," quoth Sancho, "were fitter to be a preacher than a knight-errant."

"Knights-errant, Sancho," said Don Quixote, "knew and ought to know somewhat of all things, for there have been knights-errant in past ages who were as ready to make a sermon or a speech on the king's highway as though they had taken their degrees at the University of Paris; whence it may be inferred that the lance never blunted the pen, nor the pen the lance."

"Well, may it turn out as you say," answered Sancho. "But let us be gone and endeavour to get a lodging tonight; and I pray to God we may find a place where there are no coverlets, blanketeers, spectres or enchanted Moors; and if there are, may the devil keep the lot of them."

"Ask that of God, my son," said Don Quixote, "and lead me where you please, for on this occasion I will leave the choice of lodging to you. But give me your hand and feel with your finger how many teeth and grinders I have lost on this right side of my upper jaw, for there I feel the pain."

Sancho put in his finger and, feeling about, asked: "How many grinders did your worship have before on this side?"

"Four," answered Don Quixote, "besides the wisdom tooth, all of them whole and sound."

"Mind well, master, what you say," answered Sancho.

"I say four, if not five," quoth Don Quixote, "for in all my life I have never had a tooth or grinder drawn from my mouth, nor has any fallen out or been destroyed by decay."

"Well, then, on this lower side," said Sancho, "you have

only two grinders and a half, but on the upper, not even half an one, for 'tis as smooth as the palm of my hand."

"Woe's me," cried Don Quixote, hearing these sad tidings from his squire. "I would rather they lopped off an arm, provided 'twere not my sword arm; for you must know, Sancho, that a mouth without grinders is like a mill without grindstone, and a tooth is far more to be prized than a diamond. But all this must be suffered by those who profess the stern order of chivalry. Mount, friend, and lead the way, for I will follow you at what pace you please."

Sancho did so, and proceeded whither he thought it possible they might find a lodging without leaving the high-road, which in that region was much frequented. As they slowly continued their journey Sancho, seeing that the pain of Don Quixote's jaws gave him no rest, tried to entertain him and divert his mind by anecdotes.

XII. *The adventure of the corpse, and the never-seen and unheard-of adventure that Don Quixote terminated with less danger to himself than ever did famous knight in the world*

NIGHT OVERTOOK THEM WHILE THEY WERE STILL ON THE high-road, without having found a place where they might rest until morning, and what was more serious, they were famished with hunger, for by losing their saddle-bags they were deprived both of larder and journey rations. And to complete their distress, they had an adventure, or something that was uncommonly like one.

The night grew darker but they still plodded dolefully on, for Sancho hoped that, as they were on the king's highway, they would be sure to discover an inn within a couple of leagues or so. All of a sudden the ravenous squire and his master, who had a good appetite, saw coming towards them along the same road a great number of lights resembling a multitude of moving stars. Sancho stood aghast at the sight of them and Don Quixote himself felt uneasy: the former pulled at the halter of his ass, the other at the reins of his horse, and both stood peering earnestly in front of them. They saw that the lights were advancing towards them, and as they approached nearer and nearer they became bigger and bigger. At the sight of them Sancho began to tremble like one with quicksilver poisoning, and Don Quixote's hair stood on end. However, recovering somewhat, he said: "Sancho, this doubtless must be a very great and perilous adventure, where I shall need to show all my might and valour."

"I'm unlucky!" answered Sancho. "If this turns out as it seems, to be another adventure of ghosts, where am I to find the ribs to last it out?"

"No matter how many ghosts, press on," said Don Quixote. "I will not allow them to touch a thread of your garments; for if they made game of you on the other occasion, it was because I was unable to jump over the wall of the yard, but now we are in open country, where I can parry with my sword at will."

"What will you do if they enchant and benumb you as they did the last time?" said Sancho. "What good will it do us to be in open country then?"

"In spite of all, Sancho," replied Don Quixote, "I beseech you to keep up your courage, for experience will prove to you how great mine is."

"I will, if it please God," answered Sancho.

Both then turned to the side of the road and began to gaze again earnestly at the moving lights, wondering what they could mean. After a short while they perceived many persons robed in white.[1] At the dread sight Sancho Panza's courage was completely annihilated, and his teeth began to chatter like one who is suffering from ague, and his quivering and teeth-chattering increased when they saw distinctly what it was; for they perceived about twenty persons in white habits, all on horseback, with lighted torches in their hands. After them came a litter covered over with black, which was followed in its turn by six persons in deep mourning, whose mules even were in black down to the ground. It was quite plain that they were mules and not horses owing to the slowness of their pace. The white-robed folk kept muttering to themselves in a low, plaintive tone.

This strange vision appearing at such an hour, and in such a desolate spot, was quite sufficient to strike terror into Sancho's heart and even into that of his master. As for Sancho, he had pitched away all notions of courage. Not so his master. His imagination on the contrary immediately suggested that this must be one of the chivalrous adventures he had read about. He imagined that the litter was a bier on which was carried some dead or sorely wounded knight,

[1] This adventure is based upon an incident that took place in 1593. On December 14th, 1591, the great saint and poet Saint John of the Cross died in his monastery at Ubeda from a pestilential fever. In 1593 his body was secretly conveyed by night to Segovia by way of Madrid. Before reaching the village of Martos on a hill near the road, a man suddenly appeared, who called out, "Where are you carrying the body of the saint? Leave it where it was!" This caused such fear in the bearers that their hair stood on end. They thought that it was the devil himself who appeared to them. St. John was born at Fontiveros in 1542, not Segovia, and died at Ubeda, not Baeza. Martos was one of the places where Cervantes collected stores in the years 1591-3.

whose revenge was reserved for him alone. So without delay he couched his spear, seated himself firmly in the saddle, and with great spirit and courage took up his position in the middle of the road by which the white-robed procession must pass. When he saw them draw near, he raised his voice, saying: "Halt, knights, whoever you are, halt, and give me account of yourselves, whence you come, and whither you are going, and what it is you carry on that bier. For, as it appears, either you have done some injury to others, or others to you: wherefore it is necessary that I should know the truth, that I may chastise you for the evil you have done, or avenge you for the wrongs you have sustained."

"We are in haste," answered one of the men in white. "The inn is far off and we have no time to answer your questions." Then spurring on his mule, he pressed forward. Don Quixote was greatly enraged at this answer, so he laid hold of his bridle and said: "Halt, and answer my questions with greater civility: if not, I challenge you one and all to battle."

Now the mule was nervous, and, so soon as he touched the bridle, she started so violently that, rising on her hind legs, she unhorsed her rider. One of the footmen, seeing the man in white fall to the ground, began to revile Don Quixote, and he, being now thoroughly enraged, without more ado couched his lance and ran full tilt at one of the mourners and threw him to the ground sorely wounded. Then, turning on the rest, it was amazing to see with what speed he attacked and laid them low. It seemed, in fact, as if wings had sprouted on Rozinante at that instant, so nimbly and arrogantly he moved.

All the men in white were timorous and unarmed, and they gave up the skirmish in an instant. They then began to run over the plain with their lighted torches, looking for all the world like the masqueraders who run up and down on a Carnival night. As for the mourners, they were so wrapped and muffled in their trailing skirts and trains that they could not stir, so that Don Quixote with entire safety drubbed them all and drove them off the field against their will, for they thought he was no man but a devil incarnate from hell, striving to snatch away the corpse they carried in the litter.

Sancho, meanwhile, had been watching the fight amazed at the boldness of his master, and he said to himself: "This master of mine is surely as strong and brave as he says himself."

A torch lay burning on the ground beside the first man whom the mule had overthrown, by the light of which Don Quixote perceived him, and going up to him, he placed the point of his lance to his throat, ordering him to surrender on pain of death. To which the prostrate man replied: "I am already surrendered more than enough, for I cannot stir. One of my legs is broken. I beseech you, sir, if you are a Christian gentleman, not to kill me, for that would be a great sacrilege, as I am a licentiate and have received minor orders."

"Well, then," said Don Quixote, "what devils brought you here, if you are a churchman?"

"What indeed," answered the fallen man, "but my own misfortune?"

"A worse one is in store for you," said Don Quixote, "if you do not satisfy all my demands."

"You shall be satisfied, sir," answered the licentiate. "You must know, sir, that, though I said first that I was a licentiate, I am in fact only a bachelor of arts, and my name is Alonso López. I am a native of Alcobendas, and I come from the city of Baeza with eleven other priests, who are those that ran away with the torches. We are travelling to the city of Segovia as escort to the corpse lying in that litter. It is that of a gentleman who died in Baeza and was buried there till now. And we are carrying his bones to his tomb in Segovia, his birthplace."

"Who killed him?" asked Don Quixote.

"God," replied the bachelor, "by means of a pestilential fever he caught."

"In that case," said Don Quixote, "Our Lord has delivered me from the task of avenging his death, if any other had slain him. Since he fell by the hand of God, there is no other remedy but silence and a shrug of the shoulders, for I should have done the same if He had been pleased to slay me. I would have your reverence know that I am a knight of La Mancha, by name Don Quixote, and my office and profession is to go through the world redressing injuries and making crooked things straight."

"I cannot understand what you mean by that," said the bachelor; "for from straight you have made me crooked, by breaking my leg, which can never be straightened as long as I live: and the injury you have redressed is to leave me so injured that I shall remain so for ever. It was indeed a very great misadventure of mine to meet you, who are looking for adventures."

"All things," answered Don Quixote, "do not happen the same way. The trouble, Sir Bachelor Alonso López, was caused by your coming as you did, by night, arrayed in those surplices, with burning torches, chanting and clad in mourning, so that you really seemed to be something sinister from the other world. I thus could not but perform mine

83

obligation to attack you, and, let me tell you, I would have attacked you even if you had been, as I truly thought from the start, the devils themselves from hell."

"Since my fate so ordained it," said the bachelor, "I beseech you, Sir Knight-errant, who have done me such an injury, to help me to get up from under this mule, for my leg is caught 'twixt stirrup and saddle."

"I might have gone on speaking till the morrow," said Don Quixote. "Why did you wait so long before telling me your trouble?"

He then shouted to Sancho Panza to come, but the latter turned a deaf ear, for he was busily employed ransacking a sumpter-mule well furnished with belly-ware. Sancho made a bag of his cloak, and having crammed it full to the brim, he loaded his ass. This done, he gave heed to the shouts of his master and helped to release the bachelor from under the mule. He mounted him on his mule and gave him his torch, and Don Quixote bade him follow in the wake of his companions and to beg their pardon, in his name, for the injury which he had done them; for it was not in his power to have done the contrary.

Sancho said to him also: "If those gentlemen wish to know who the champion is who routed them, you may say that he is the famous Don Quixote of La Mancha, otherwise called the *Knight of the Rueful Figure.*"

When the bachelor had gone, Don Quixote asked Sancho what had moved him to call him the Knight of the Rueful Figure, at that time more than at any other. "I'll tell you," answered Sancho. "It was because I stood observing you a pretty while by the torchlight which that unlucky man was carrying, and truly at the present moment you make about the ruefullest figure I've ever seen in my life: this must be due, I'm thinking, either to your weariness after the fight or to the loss of your teeth."

"That is not the reason," said Don Quixote. "But the wise man, who has been entrusted with the task of writing the history of my deeds, must have deemed it proper that I should take some appellation as the knights of old have done; for one called himself the *Knight of the Burning Sword*; another *Knight of the Unicorn*; this *Knight of the Damsels*; that *Knight of the Phoenix*; another *Knight of Death*: by those names and devices they were known over all the surface of the earth. And so I say that the wise man I have just mentioned must have inspired your mind and tongue to call me the *Knight of the Rueful Figure*, as I mean to call myself from this day forward. And to make this name fit me better I am resolved, when an opportunity occurs, to have a most rueful figure painted on my shield."

"You need not spend time and money, sir, in getting this figure painted," said Sancho: "all you have got to do is to show your own face to the onlookers. Without any other image or picture they'll be sure to call you the *Knight of the Rueful Figure*. And let me, sir, say by way of a jest, that hunger and the loss of your teeth give you such a dismal face that you may well spare us the rueful picture." Don Quixote laughed at Sancho's wit; nevertheless he resolved to call himself by that name as soon as he could get his shield or buckler painted accordingly.

Now that the bachelor had departed, Don Quixote wished to see whether the corpse in the litter consisted of bones or not, but Sancho would not permit him, saying: "Sir, you have finished this adventure with less injury to yourself than any others I have seen. These people, though overcome and scattered, may perhaps reflect that they have been routed by one person alone, and, growing ashamed of themselves, they may rally their ranks and return to give us plenty of trouble. The ass is as he should be; the mountains are at hand; hunger presses; we have nought to do but retire at a decent pace and, as the saying goes, 'To the grave with the dead, and them that live to the loaf of bread'." Then, driving on his ass, he begged his master to follow him, and Don Quixote, thinking that his squire was right, followed him without a word. After travelling a short distance between two small mountains they found themselves in a large and sheltered valley, where they alighted. After Sancho had unloaded his beast they both threw themselves down on the green grass and, with hunger for sauce, broke their fasts, lunched, dined, and had their snack and their supper all at the same time; and they gorged themselves with more than one cold patty which the dead gentleman's chaplains (who rarely fail to provide themselves with plenty) had brought with them on the sumpter-mule. But there was another misfortune, which Sancho considered the worst of all, namely, that they had no wine, nor even a drop of water to drink. And, moreover, they were parched with thirst.

Sancho, however, perceiving that the meadow they were in was covered with green and tender grass, said to his master: "I am sure, master, that there must be some fountain or brook near by which waters this grass and keeps it fresh, so we should move on a bit further, in the hope of running across something which will quench this terrible thirst of ours. Why, it's even more painful than hunger itself."

Don Quixote agreed, and taking Rozinante by the bridle, and Sancho his ass by the halter (after he had placed upon him the remains of the supper), they began to plod forward through the meadow, groping their way, for the night was pitch dark and they could see nothing. They had scarcely gone two hundred paces when they heard a great noise of water, as if it fell headlong from some high steep rock. The sound cheered them greatly and they stopped to listen whence it came. But suddenly they heard another loud noise which drowned straightway all their joy, especially Sancho's, who was by nature timid and faint-hearted. They heard, I say, regular thuds, mingled with the rasping of iron and chains. These sounds with the furious roar of the water would have struck terror into any heart less brave than Don Quixote's. The night, as I have said, was dark, and they happened to enter a grove of tall trees whose leaves, rustling in the gentle breeze, made a low, whispering sound so that the loneliness of the place, the darkness, the noise of the water and the rustling of the leaves all caused horror and fright, especially as they found that neither the thuds ceased, nor the wind slept, nor morning approached. In addition to all this, they had not the remotest idea where they were.

But Don Quixote, stout-hearted as ever, leapt on to Rozinante, seized his buckler, brandished his spear, and said: "Friend, I would have you know that I was born, by Heaven's grace, in this age of iron to revive in it the Golden Age. I am he for whom are reserved all great perils and valorous feats. I am he who shall revive the deeds of the Round Table, the Twelve Peers of France and the Nine Worthies. Mark well, trusty and lawful squire of mine, the darkness of this night, the strange silence, the dull, confused murmur of the trees, the dreadful noise of the water we came in search of, which seems to precipitate itself headlong down from the steep mountains of the moon; the constant thumping of the blows wounding and paining our ears. If all of those things together and each by itself are enough to strike terror, fear and amazement into the heart of Mars, how much more in one who is not accustomed to such adventures? Yet all that I describe for you serves but to rouse and awaken my courage, and causes my heart almost to burst in my bosom with longing to encounter this adventure, however great it may be. Therefore, tighten Rozinante's girths a little, and God be with you! Wait here three days for me, and no more. If I do not return in that time, you may return to our village, and from thence; for my sake, to El Toboso, where you must say to my incomparable Lady Dulcinea that her captive knight died attempting exploits that might make him worthy to be called hers."

When Sancho heard his master say these words he began to weep piteously, and said: "Master, I do not know why you wish to undertake this dangerous adventure. It is now

86

night; no one sees us here; we can easily turn aside and slip away out of the zone of peril, even though we don't drink for three days, and since no one sees us there will be no one to mark us down as cowards. Furthermore, I have many a time heard the priest of our village, with whom you, sir, are well acquainted, say in his sermons that 'he who seeks danger perishes therein': so it is not right to tempt God by undertaking such a monstrous exploit, out of which you cannot escape except by miracle. It ought to be enough for you that Heaven saved you from being blanketed as I was, and rescued you safe and sound from the hosts of enemies who escorted the dead man. And even if all this is not enough to soften your heart of stone, let you be moved by the thought that no sooner will you have left me than I shall, through the mighty fear in me, hand over my soul to whoever pleases to take it. I, sir, left my country, wife and children to come to serve you, believing that I should rise to be more, not less: but as covetousness bursts the bag, so it has torn my hopes, just when they were most lively, and I was expecting that unlucky and accursed island which you so often promised me. Instead of all that, I find that you are now ready to leave me all forlorn in this desolate spot far from a human soul. For God's sake, master, don't do me such a wrong, and if you will not give up this enterprise, put it off at least until the morning. For, according to the bit of science I learnt when I was a shepherd, the dawn is hardly three hours off, seeing that the Horn's mouth is above our head and shows midnight in the line of the left arm."[2]

"How can you, Sancho, see where this line is made, or where this mouth or top of the head may be, when the night is so dark that not a single star appears in the sky?"

"Yes, that is true," said Sancho; "but fear has many eyes, and sees things under the earth, and much more in the sky. And besides, we may now assume that dawn is not far off."

"Let it be as little off as it pleases," answered Don Quixote. "It shall not be said of me now or in days to come that tears or prayers prevented me from doing my duty as a knight. So I pray you, Sancho, keep silent, since God, Who has filled me with courage to attempt this unseen and terrible adventure, will take care to watch over my safety and console you in your sadness. What you must do now is to tighten the girths of Rozinante and remain here, for I will quickly return alive or dead."

Sancho, seeing that his master's mind was made up and

2 Ursa Minor resembles in shape a curved hunting-horn. The hour was calculated by facing the Horn and stretching the arms horizontally so as to represent a cross. The time was indicated by the relative position of the Horn to the arms.

hat his tears, entreaties and prayers were of no avail, determined to use his wits and see if he could by hook or by crook make him wait until daybreak. And so, when he was tightening the girths of the horse, he softly and without being observed, tied the halter of his ass to both Rozinante's legs, in such a way that when Don Quixote wished to depart he could not, for his horse was not able to go a step except by jumps.

Sancho Panza, seeing the success of his trick, said: "Look, sir, how Heaven has been moved by my tears and prayers and has decreed that Rozinante shall not be able to go a step. If you insist on urging, spurring and whipping him, it means angering Fortune, and, as the saying goes, 'kicking against the pricks'."

This threw Don Quixote into a state of desperation, and yet the more he spurred Rozinante on, the less would he move. At last, without noticing that the horse's legs were tied, he thought it best to remain quiet until dawn or until Rozinante would move on. Having no idea that Sancho was the cause of the trouble, he said to him: "Well, Sancho, since Rozinante is unable to move, I am content to wait here until the smile of Dawn, though I weep to think how long she will be in coming."

"No need to weep, sir," answered Sancho. "I'll tell you stories from now till daylight, unless you wish to dismount and snatch a little sleep in the green grass, after the fashion of knights-errant, so that you may be all the fresher in the morning for the unimaginable adventure."

"Who talks of dismounting and sleeping?" said Don Quixote. "Am I one of those knights who rest in times of danger? Sleep, you who were born to sleep, or do what you please, for I will do what I think becomes my profession."

"Don't be angry, good master," answered Sancho. "I didn't mean that." Then, drawing near to his master, he placed one hand on the pommel of his saddle and the other on the back of it, and he nestled up against the knight's left thigh, not daring to stir from him the breadth of a finger; so frightened was he by the thuds which still continued to sound in regular succession.

In this manner master and man passed the night, and Sancho, when he saw that morning was near, cautiously undid Rozinante. As soon as Rozinante felt himself free, though he was by no means a mettlesome steed, he revived and began to paw the ground; for (by his leave be it spoken) he was a stranger to all curveting and prancing. Don Quixote, noticing that Rozinante moved, took it for a good sign, and an omen that he should attempt the tremendous adventure.

And now the dawn had risen and the surrounding objects

appeared distinctly, and Don Quixote saw that he was among some tall chestnut trees that cast a very dark shadow. He perceived that the hammering did not cease, but could not discover what caused it, and so without delay he gave a taste of his spurs to Rozinante and turned back again to bid Sancho farewell. He ordered him to wait there for him three days at the longest, and that if he did not return by then, to take it for certain that it was God's will that he should end his days in that perilous adventure. He again repeated to him the message which he had to carry to Lady Dulcinea, and assured him that he need not be anxious about the reward for his services, since before leaving his village he had made his will. In that will Sancho would find himself gratified as regards his wages, in proportion to the time he had served; but, if God rescued his master safe and sound from the coming danger, he might reckon himself absolutely sure of obtaining the promised island.

At this point Sancho began to weep afresh at the pitiful words of his good master, and he determined not to leave him until the completion of this adventure. Don Quixote was somewhat moved by the tears of his squire, but not enough to weaken in any degree his resolve; and so, hiding his feelings as best he could, he rode forward towards the place whence both the noise of the water and of the thuds seemed to proceed. Sancho followed him on foot, leading by the halter his good Dapple, who was the constant companion of his good and evil fortune. Having gone a good distance through those shady chestnut trees, they came to a little meadow lying at the foot of some rocks, down which a might cataract of water descended. At the foot of the rocks were some huts, so roughly built that they seemed more like ruins than habitable dwellings, from whence came the din and clatter which still never ceased.

Rozinante shied at the noise of the water and the hammering, but Don Quixote quieted him and cautiously drew near to the huts, recommending himself devoutly to his lady, and beseeching her to favour him in his mighty enterprise: and by the way, he also prayed to God not to desert him. Sancho never left his master's side, but stretched out his neck and looked between Rozinante's legs to see if he could discover the cause of all his fears.

When they had gone about another hundred paces, they turned a corner and there before their eyes was the true and undoubted cause of that hideous and terrible noise that had kept them all the night in such suspense and fear. It was (do not, kind reader, take it too bitterly to heart) nothing worse than six fulling-hammers whose alternate strokes produced that terrifying sound of thuds.

When Don Quixote saw what it was, he stood mute and ashamed. Sancho looked at him and saw how he hung down his head upon his breast with all the appearance of one who is abashed. Don Quixote looked at Sancho and saw that his cheeks were swollen with laughter, with evident signs that he was in danger of bursting. Don Quixote's melancholy was not so great that he could help smiling at the sight of Sancho; and Sancho, when he saw his master beginning to laugh, burst out loud and long with such force that he had to put his hands to his sides to prevent them from splitting. Four times he ended and four times he started again. Don Quixote now began to wish him in hell, especially when he heard him say in a gibing, mimicking manner: "You must know, friend Sancho, that I was born because Heaven in this our age of iron wished to revive the age of gold: I am he for whom are reserved all dangerous, great and valorous feats." And he went on repeating the greater part of what Don Quixote had said when they first heard the dreadful sounds.

Don Quixote, seeing that Sancho was mocking him, became so enraged that he lifted up his lance and gave him two such whacks that, if he had caught him on his pate, the knight would have saved himself from paying his wages, unless it were to his heirs.

Sancho now saw that his jests were reaping a bitter harvest, and he was afraid his master might go further, so he said very humbly: "Please, good master, I swear I was only joking."

"Though you may be joking, I am not," answered Don Quixote. "Come here, Master Merryman. Do you imagine that, if those fulling-hammers had been some perilous adventure, I would not have shown the requisite courage to undertake and achieve it? Am I, being as I am a knight, to distinguish noises, and to know which are those of mills and which are of giants? Especially if (which is indeed the truth) I have never seen any fulling-mills in my life, as you have—pitiful clod-hopper that you are, who were born and bred among them. Turn those six hammers into giants and cast them at me, one by one, or all together, and if I do not turn them all with their heels up, then mock me as much as you please."

"Say no more, kind master," said Sancho. "I confess I have joked too far. Henceforth you may be sure that I will not once open my lips to jest at your doings, but only to honour you as my master and lord."

"If you do that," answered Don Quixote, "your days will be long in the land, for next to our parents we are bound to respect our masters, as if they were our fathers."

XIII. *The noble adventure and rich prize of Mambrino's helmet, and the liberation by the Knight of a number of ne'er-do-wells*

ABOUT THIS TIME IT BEGAN TO RAIN, AND SANCHO WOULD HAVE entered one of the fulling-mills for shelter, but Don Quixote had taken such a marked dislike to them, on account of the late jest, that he would not go in. Turning to the right, they struck into another road like the one which they travelled the day before. Soon after, Don Quixote espied a man on horseback, who wore on his head something that glittered like gold. Scarcely had he seen him when he turned to Sancho, saying: "I am sure, Sancho, that there is no proverb that is not true, for all proverbs are maxims drawn from experience, the mother of all knowledge; especially that one which says: 'When one door shuts another opens.' I say this because if Fortune closed the door upon us last night in our quest, by deceiving us with the fulling-mills, she now opens wide another leading to a better and more certain adventure. If I do not succeed in this, the fault will be mine, and I shall not excuse myself this time by laying the blame on my ignorance of fulling-mills, or on the darkness of the night. I say this because, if I mistake not, there comes towards us one who wears on his head the helmet of Mambrino,[1] about which I took the oath you know of."

"Take heed, sir, what you say, and more what you do," said Sancho, "for I should prefer not to meet any more fulling-mills which would hammer and mash us out of our senses."

"Devil take you," replied Don Quixote, "what has a helmet to do with fulling-mills?"

"I don't know," answered Sancho, "but if I might speak as I used, I would give you such reasons that you should see that you were mistaken in what you say."

"How can I be mistaken in what I say?" said Don Quixote. "Tell me! Do you not see that knight riding towards us on a dapple grey steed, with a helmet of gold on his head?"

"What I see and make out," replied Sancho, "is nought but a man on a grey ass like my own, carrying on his head something that shines."

[1] This enchanted helmet was originally forged for the Saracen king Mambrino. It was captured by Rinaldo. See Ariosto: *Orlando Furioso*, xviii. 151-3, l. 26.

91

"Well, that is Mambrino's helmet." said Don Quixote. "Stand aside and leave me alone with him: you shall see how, in order to save time, I will end this adventure without speaking a word, and remain master of the helmet I have so long desired."

"I'll take jolly good care to stand out of the way," replied Sancho; "but God grant, I repeat, it may turn out all spice and not fulling-mills."

"I have already told you," said Don Quixote, "not to think of mentioning the fulling-mills again: otherwise—by God—I will hammer the soul out of your body."

Sancho then held his peace, fearing lest his master should carry out the threat which he had uttered so forcibly.

Now the truth of the matter concerning the helmet, the horse, and the knight which Don Quixote saw, was as follows. In that neighbourhood there were two villages, one of which was so small that it contained neither shop nor barber, but the larger had both; so the barber of the larger village served also the smaller. It now happened that in the latter there lay a sick man needing a blood-letting, and another who wished to have his beard trimmed; for which purpose the barber came, bringing with him his brass basin. And by chance as he travelled it rained, so to save his hat, which must have been a new one, from staining, he clapped the basin on his head, and the basin, being clean scoured, glittered half a league off. He rode upon a grey ass, as Sancho said, and that was the reason why Don Quixote took him to be a knight with a helmet of gold riding on a dapple grey steed, for everything he came across he with great ease adapted to his extravagant notions of chivalry. And when he saw the unfortunate rider draw near, without halting to parley he ran at him with lance couched, putting Rozinante to a full gallop, with the intention of piercing him through and through. And when he came close to him, without checking his furious pace, he cried out: "Defend yourself, base caitiff, or hand over to me, of your own free will, what so rightly belongs to me."

The barber, so unexpectedly seeing this wild apparition dashing against him, had no other way of avoiding the thrust of the lance than to fall off his ass on to the ground. But no sooner did he touch the earth than he sprang up nimbler than a deer and scampered over the plain faster than the wind, leaving the basin on the ground behind him. With this Don Quixote was satisfied, and said that the pagan had been a wise man, for he had imitated the beaver, who, when closely pressed by the hunters, tears off with his teeth that which he knows by instinct to be the object of pursuit. He then ordered Sancho to take up the helmet, and the latter lifting it up, said: "By heaven, the basin is a good one, and is worth eight reals if it is worth a farthing." He gave it to his master, who placed it on his head, and turned it about from side to side in search of the vizor. Seeing that he could not find it, he said. "Doubtless the pagan for whom this famous helmet was first forged had a very big head, and the worst of it is that half the helmet is missing." When Sancho heard him call the basin a helmet he could not restrain his laughter, but then, suddenly remembering his master's anger, he stopped laughing at once.

"What are you laughing at, Sancho?" said Don Quixote.

"I laugh," answered the latter, "to think of the great head the pagan owner of this helmet had; it is for all the world like a barber's basin."

"If you want to know my views," replied Don Quixote. "I say this piece of the enchanted helmet must have fallen by some strange accident into some one's hands that did not know its great worth. Seeing it was of pure gold, he melted down one half and made of the other half this object, which seems, as you say, to be a barber's basin. But to me, who knows what it really is, its transformation makes no matter, for I will have it repaired at the first village where I can find a smith, in such a way that it will not be surpassed or even equalled by that which the god of smiths himself made and forged for the god of battles. Meanwhile I shall wear it as well as I can, for something is better than nothing, all the more as it will suffice to protect me against a blow from a stone."

"Yes, it will suffice," said Sancho, "if they do not shoot from a sling, as the two armies did, when they crossed your worship's grinders and broke the pot containing that blessed beverage which made me spew up my inside."

"I do not mind having lost the balsam," said Don Quixote, "for, as you know, Sancho, I have the recipe for it in my memory."

"So have I, too," answered Sancho; "but if I ever make or try it again in my life, may that be my last hour on earth. Besides, I do not intend to put myself in the way of needing it, for I intend to keep myself with all my five senses from being wounded or from wounding anyone. As to being tossed again in a blanket, I say nothing, for it is difficult to prevent such mishaps; and if they do come, there's nothing to be done but hunch your shoulders, hold your breath, close your eyes, and let yourself go whither luck and the blanket will please. But leaving all this aside, tell me, sir, what we are to do with this dapple grey steed, which looks so like a grey ass, and which that poor devil Martino, or whatever his name is, left behind ownerless when he was unsaddled by you? By the way he kicked up the dust and took to his heels he doesn't intend to return, and by my beard I tell you the dapple beast's a good one."

"I am not accustomed," said Don Quixote, "to ransack those I vanquish, nor is it the practice of knighthood to take from them their horses and leave them on foot, unless the victor lost his own in the fight. In such a case it is lawful to take that of the enemy, as won in fair fight. Therefore, Sancho, leave the horse or ass, or whatever you wish to call it, for when the owner sees that we have departed he will come back for it."

"God knows, I would like to take him," answered Sancho, "or at least swap him for mine, which, I think, is not as good. The laws of knighthood must for sure be strict if they don't even allow the swapping of one ass for another. But I'd like to know whether I might exchange a bit of the harness."

"I am not quite sure of that," said Don Quixote, "and as it is a matter of doubt, until I get information on the matter, I will allow you to exchange them, provided your need is extreme."

"So extreme," answered Sancho, "that if they were to harness my own person, I could not need them more."

So saying, he made an exchange of hoods,[2] as the saying goes, and decked out his ass with a thousand fineries and made him look vastly better. They breakfasted on the remains of the rations they had plundered from the sumpter-mule, and quenched their thirst in the mill-stream, but without turning their faces towards the hateful fulling-mills. Now that their spleen was eased and all choleric and even melancholy humors had disappeared, they mounted; without choosing any particular way, according to the fashion of knights-errant, they followed whither Rozinante was pleased to lead them; for he was a guide to his master as well as to Dapple, who always plodded along in love and good fellowship wherever he led the way. They soon, however, returned to the highway, which they followed at random without forming a plan.

As they rode onwards, Don Quixote raised his eyes and saw about a dozen men on foot, strung together on a great iron chain like beads. The chain was fastened round their necks and they were handcuffed. With them were two men on horseback and two others followed on foot. The horsemen had firelocks, and those on foot, pikes and swords.

As soon as Sancho saw them he said: "This is a chain of galley-slaves, people forced by the King to go to the galleys."

2 This is a reference to the custom at Rome when the cardinals and prelates of the Curia changed their hoods and cloaks of fur for those of silk at Whitsuntide.

"How! People forced?" answered Don Quixote. "Is it possible that the King forces anybody?"

"I don't say that," answered Sancho, "but they are people condemned for their offences to serve the King in the galleys."

"Then it is a fact," replied Don Quixote, "however you put it, that these folk are being taken to their destination by force and not by their own free will."

"That is so," said Sancho.

"Then," said his master, "here is the opportunity for me to carry out my duty, which is to redress grievances and give help to the poor and the afflicted."

"I beg you, sir," said Sancho, "to consider that justice, which is the King himself, does no violence to these folk; but only punishes those who have committed crime."

By this time the chain-gang came up, and Don Quixote in very courteous words asked those in charge to be good enough to inform him why they conducted people away in that manner. One of the guardians on horseback replied that they were slaves condemned by His Majesty to the galleys, and that there was no more to be said, nor ought Don Quixote to desire any further information.

"Nevertheless," answered Don Quixote, "I should be glad to hear from every one of them individually the cause of his disgrace."

To this the guardian on horseback answered: "Though we have here the register of the crimes of all these unlucky fellows, this is no time to produce and read them. Draw near, sir, and ask it from themselves. No doubt they'll tell you their tales, for men of their sort take delight in boasting of their rascalities."

With this leave, which Don Quixote would have taken for himself if they had not given it, he went up to the gang and asked the first man for what crimes he found himself in such straits.

The man answered that it was for being in love.

"For that and no more?" cried Don Quixote. "If folk are sent to the galleys for being in love, I should have been pulling an oar there long ago."

"My love was not of the kind your worship imagines," replied the galley-slave; "mine was that I loved too much a basket of fine linen, which I embraced so lovingly, that if the law had not taken it from me by violence, I should not of my own free will have forsaken it even to this present day. I was caught in the act so there was no need for torture. The case was a short one. They gave my shoulders a hundred lashes and in addition three years hard in the 'gurapas', and that's an end of it."

"What are 'gurapas'?" said Don Quixote.

"'Gurapas' are galleys," answered the convict, who was a young man of about twenty-four, born, as he said, at Piedrahita.

Don Quixote put the same question to the second, who returned no answer, for he seemed too downcast and melancholy to speak. But the first one spoke for him and said: "Sir, this gentleman goes for being a canary bird—I mean a musician or singer."

"Is it possible," said Don Quixote, "that musicians and singers are sent to the galleys?"

"I should say so, sir," replied the galley-slave; "there's nothing worse than to sing under torture."

"Well," said Don Quixote, "I on the contrary have heard the saying 'who sings in grief, procures relief'."

"Down here it's the exact opposite," said the slave; "for here, he who sings once, weeps the rest of his life."

"I do not understand it," said Don Quixote. One of the guards then said to him: "You know, sir, among these unsanctified folk 'to sing under torture' means to confess on the rack. They put this poor sinner to the torture, and he confessed that he was a stealer of cattle; and because he confessed he was condemned to the galleys for six years, with the addition of two hundred stripes which he carries on his shoulders. He's always sad and pensive, for the other thieves bully, abuse and despise him because he confessed and hadn't the courage to say a couple of nos. For as they say 'a nay has as many letters as a yea,' and it is good luck for a criminal when there are no witnesses and proofs, and his fate depends on his own tongue. In my opinion there's a power o' reason in that."

"I think so likewise," said Don Quixote, and he passed on to where the third slave stood, and put to him the same question as to the others.

The man replied quickly and coolly, saying: "I'm off to their ladyships the galleys because I wanted ten ducats."

"I will give you twenty with all my heart to free you from that misfortune," said Don Quixote.

"That," replied the slave, "would be like one who has money in the middle of the sea, and yet is perishing of hunger, because he can get no meat to buy with it. I say this, because if I'd had the twenty ducats your worship offers me at the right time, I would have greased the lawyer's palm with them and so sharpened my advocate's wit. If that had happened I should now have been strolling about in the market-place at Toledo instead of being trailed along here like a greyhound. But God is great; patience and mum's the word."

Don Quixote passed on to the fourth, who was a man of venerable appearance, with a white beard reaching below his chest. No sooner was he asked the reason for his being there than he began to weep and he would not answer a word; but the fifth convict lent him a tongue, and said: "This honest gentleman is off for four years to the galleys, after having appeared in the usual procession dressed in full pomp and mounted."

"That means, I suppose," said Sancho, "carried to shame in view of the whole people."

"You've said it," answered the galley-slave, "and the offence for which they gave him this punishment was for having been an ear-broker, and a body-broker too. What I mean to say is that this gentleman goes for pimping and for fancying himself as a bit of a wizard."

"If it had been merely for pimping," said Don Quixote, "he certainly did not deserve to go rowing in the galleys, but rather deserved to command them and be their captain. For the profession of pimp is no ordinary office, but one requiring wisdom and most necessary in any well-governed state. None but well-born persons should practise it. In fact it should have its overseers and inspectors, as there are of other offices, limited to a certain appointed number, like exchange-brokers. If this were done, many evils would be prevented, which now take place, because this profession is practised only by foolish and ignorant persons such as silly waiting-women, page-boys and jesters of few years' standing and less experience, who, in moments of difficulty, where the utmost skill is needed, allow the tit-bit to freeze between their fingers and their mouth and scarcely know which is their right hand. I should like to go on and give reasons why it is right to make special choice of those who have to fill such an important office in the state, but this is not the place to do it. Some day I will tell my views to those who may provide a remedy: at present I only wish to say that the sorrow I felt at seeing your grey hairs and venerable countenance in so much distress for pimping has entirely vanished when I learn that you are a wizard; though I know well that there are no sorceries in the world which can affect and force the will, as some simple people imagine. Our will is free and no herb nor charm can compel it."

"That is true, sir," said the old man; "and indeed I was not guilty of witchcraft: as for being a pimp, I couldn't deny it, but I never thought there was any harm in it, for all my intention was that the whole world should enjoy themselves and live together in peace and quiet without quarrels or troubles. But my good intentions could not save me from going to a place whence I've no hope of return,

97

laden as I am with years and so worried with bladder trouble which does not give me a moment's rest." He now began to weep as before; and Sancho was so sorry for him that he drew from his purse a four-real piece and gave it to him in charity.

Don Quixote passed on and asked another what his offence was. He answered with much more pleasantness than the former: "I am here because I played a little too much of a game with two cousins of mine and with two other sisters who were not mine. In short, I carried the game so far with them all that the result of it was the increasing of my kindred so intricately that there is no casuist who can resolve it. It was all proved against me; I hadn't a friend, and I hadn't a farthing: my neck was in the utmost danger: they gave me six years in the galleys: I consented, for it was my own fault: I am young: let my life last and time will bring everything about. If you, sir, have anything about you to relieve us poor devils, God will repay you in heaven and we will have care on earth to ask God in our daily prayers to give you as long and prosperous a life and health as your kind presence deserves."

This convict was dressed in a student's habit, and one of the guards told Don Quixote that he was a great talker and a fine Latin scholar.

Behind all these came a man about thirty years of age, of very comely looks, except that he had a squint. He was differently tied from the rest, for he wore a chain to his leg, so long that it wound around his whole body. He had besides, around his neck, two iron rings, one of which was fastened to the chain, and the other called a keep-friend or friend's-foot had two irons which came down from it to his waist, at the ends of which were fixed two manacles. These held his hands fast locked with a great padlock, so that he could neither put his hand to his mouth nor bend down his head to his hands.

Don Quixote asked why this man was loaded with more fetters than the rest. The guard answered that it was because he had committed more crimes than all the rest put together, and that he was such a desperate rascal that, though they carried him fettered in that way, they were not sure of him but feared that he might cut and run for it.

"What crimes did he commit," said Don Quixote, "that have deserved no greater penalty than being sent to the galleys?"

"He is going for ten years," said the guard, "which is the same as civil death. I need only tell you that this man is the famous Ginés de Pasamonte, *alias* Ginesillo de Parapilla."

"Master commissary," said the galley-slave, "don't go so

fast, and don't let us start defining names and surnames. Ginés is my name, not Ginesillo, and Pasamonte is my family name, not Parapilla, as you say. Let every man first look to himself and he'll do a good deal."

"Keep a civil tongue, mister out-and-out robber," answered the commissary. "Otherwise we'll shut you up, whether you like it or not."

"I know," answered the galley-slave, "that man goes as God pleases: but one day someone of you will know whether my name is Ginesillo de Parapilla or not."

"Don't they call you that, you lying trickster?"

"They do," answered Ginés; "but I'll make them stop calling me by that name or I'll shear them where I don't care to mention in company. And now, sir, if you have aught to give us, hand it out now and godspeed, for you tire us with your enquiries about other men's lives. If you want to know mine. I am Ginés de Pasamonte, whose life has been written by these very thumbs of mine."

"He speaks the truth," said the commissary: "he himself has written his own history—as good a one as you could wish, and he pawned the book in the gaol for two hundred reals."

"Aye, and I intend to redeem it," said Ginés, "even if it stood at two hundred ducats."

"Is it so good?" said Don Quixote.

"It is so good," answered Ginés, "that it means trouble for *Lazarillo de Tormes* [3] and for all that have written or shall write in that style. What I say is that it tells home truths and truths so pretty and entertaining that no fiction equals them."

"What is the title of the book," asked Don Quixote.

"The Life of Ginés de Pasamonte," answered Ginés himself.

"Is it finished?" said Don Quixote.

"How can it be finished," answered Ginés, "when my life isn't finished yet? What is written tells everything from my birth down to the last time when I was packed off to the galleys."

"Then you have been there before?" said Don Quixote.

"To serve God and the King," answered Ginés; "on the last occasion I was there for four years, and I know already the taste of hard tack and the lash. I'm not too sorry to return there, for I'll have an opportunity of finishing my book. I've still many things to say, and in the galleys of Spain there's more than enough leisure, though I don't need much for what I have to write, because I have it by heart."

"You seem to be a clever fellow," said Don Quixote.

[3] The first of the Picaresque novels. Burgos, 1554.

"Aye, and an unlucky one," replied Ginés; "for bad luck always pursues genius."

"It pursues knaves," interrupted the commissary.

"I've already told you, sir commissary," answered Pasamonte, "not to go so fast. The lords of the land didn't give you that rod to persecute us poor devils that are here, but to guide and lead us where His Majesty has ordered. If not, by the life of . . . ! I'll say no more;—perhaps one day the dirty work that was done in the inn the other day may come out in the wash. Meanwhile, mum's the word! Let every man live well and speak better. Now let us move on, for we've had too much of this diversion."

The commissary raised his rod to strike Pasamonte in answer to his threats, but Don Quixote intervened, asking him not to ill-treat the convict since it was only fair that one who had his hands so tied up should be somewhat free with his tongue. Then, turning towards the gang, he said: "I have gathered from all you have said, dearest brethren, that although they punish you for your faults, yet the pains you suffer do not please you, and that you go to them with ill will and against your inclination. I realize, moreover, that perhaps it was the lack of courage of one fellow on the rack, the want of money of another, the want of friends of a third, and finally the biased sentence of the judge, which have been the cause of your not receiving the justice to which you were entitled. Now all this prompts, nay, even compels me to perform on your behalf the task for which I was sent into the world, and for which I became a knight-errant, and to which end I vowed to succour the needy and help those who are oppressed by the powerful. But as it is prudent not to do by evil means what can be done by fair, I wish to entreat these gentlemen, your guardians and the commissary, to be kind enough to loose you and let you go in peace, since there are many others who may serve the King on better occasions, for it seems to me a harsh thing to make slaves of those whom God and nature made free. This I ask of you in a peaceable and quiet manner, and if you grant my request, I shall give you my thanks. If, on the other hand, you will not grant it willingly, then shall this lance and sword of mine, wielded by my invincible arm, force you to do my bidding."

"This is pleasant doting," answered the commissary. "You have ended your ranting with a fine joke, and no mistake. Do you want us to hand over to you those the King has imprisoned? As if we had the authority to let them go, or you to order us to do it. Go your way, good sir, and pleasant journey: settle the basin straight on your pate, and don't go looking for a cat with three legs."

"You are a cat, a rat and a knave," answered Don Quixote.

Without another word he ran at him so fiercely and without giving him time to defend himself, that he struck him to the ground badly wounded by his lance. It was lucky for the knight that this was the one who carried the firelock. The guards were astounded at this unexpected event. Then they recovered themselves, and the horsemen drew their swords, the footmen clutched their pikes, and all of them threw themselves upon Don Quixote, who quietly waited for their attack. No doubt he would have been in great danger, if the slaves, seeing a chance of liberty, had not broken the chain by which they were tied together. The hubbub was such that the guards, first of all trying to prevent the galley-slaves from getting loose, then defending themselves against Don Quixote who attacked them, did nothing to any purpose. Sancho, on his side, helped to release Ginés de Pasamonte, who was the first that leaped free and unfettered upon the plain. The latter then set upon the fallen commissary, relieved him of his sword and firelock and by dint of aiming first at one and then at another cleared the plain of guards, for they all fled no less from Pasamonte's firelock than from the volley of stones which the liberated slaves fired at them.

Don Quixote then called all the galley-slaves together, and they gathered round to hear what he commanded, and he addressed them as follows: "It is the duty of well-bred people to be grateful for benefits received, and ingratitude is one of the most hateful sins in the eyes of God. I say this, sirs, because you know what favour you have received from me, and the only return I wish and demand is that you all go from here laden with the chains from which I have just freed your necks to the city of El Toboso. There you are to present yourselves before the Lady Dulcinea del Toboso, and tell her that her Knight of the Rueful Figure sent you there to commend his service to her. You are to tell her, furthermore, point by point, the details of this famous adventure, and when you have done this, you may then go your ways."

Ginés de Pasamonte answered for all the rest, saying: "That which you, sir, demand, is impossible to perform, because we must not travel the roads together, but go alone and separate, so that we may not be found by the men of the Holy Brotherhood, who will be sure to come out to search for us. What you can and ought to do is, to change this service and duty to the Lady Dulcinea del Toboso into a certain number of *Ave Marias* and *Credos*, which we shall say for your worship's intention. And this we may do by night or by day, resting or on the run, at peace or at war: but if you think that we are now going to return to the fleshpots of Egypt—to our chains, I mean—and start off on the road to El Toboso, you might as well imagine that it's already night-time, whereas it is not yet ten o'clock in the morning. To expect this from us is like expecting pears off an elm tree."

"I vow then," said Don Quixote in a rage, "Sir whoreson Don Ginesillo de Parapilla—or whatever you call yourself, that you will go alone, with your tail between your legs and bearing the whole length of chain on your back."

Pasamonte, who was a truculent fellow (he now understood that Don Quixote was not very sane, seeing the foolish way in which he had tried to set them free), would not stand being abused in this manner, so he winked at his companions, and they, from a distance, began to rain a shower of stones on Don Quixote, whose buckler gave him scant cover; and poor Rozinante paid no more attention to the spur than if his flanks were made of bronze. Sancho took cover behind his ass, and by this means sheltered himself against the squall of stones which burst about them. Don Quixote was less able to shield himself against the countless stones, and at last they stretched him on the ground. Scarcely had he fallen when the student Ginés jumped upon him, and, taking the basin from his head, gave him three or four blows with it on the shoulders and then struck it repeatedly on the ground, almost breaking it to pieces. They then stripped him of a tunic he wore over his armour, and they would have seized his hose too, had they not been hindered by his greaves. They took Sancho's cloak, leaving him in his underclothes, and after dividing among themselves the rest of the spoils they made the best of their way off, each one on his own, with more thought of escaping the Holy Brotherhood than of dragging their chains to Lady Dulcinea at El Toboso.

The ass, Rozinante, Sancho and Don Quixote remained alone. The ass, with drooping head, stood shaking his ears every now and then as if he thought the storm of stones was not yet over. Rozinante, overthrown, lay beside his master on the ground. Sancho in his underclothes was trembling at the thought of the Holy Brotherhood; Don Quixote was most downcast to see himself so ill-treated by those to whom he had done such service.

XIV. *Don Quixote's strange adventure in the Sierra Morena*

DON QUIXOTE, FINDING HIMSELF IN A BAD WAY, SAID TO HIS squire: "Sancho, I have always heard it said that to do a kindness to rogues is like pouring water into the sea. If I had listened to your advice, I might have avoided this trouble. But now that it is over, we must be patient and take warning for another time."

"If your worship takes warning, you may call me a Turk. But, as you say, you might have escaped this mischief if you had followed my advice. Now listen to me, and you will avoid a still greater danger. For, let me tell you, it is no use blathering about chivalries to the Holy Brotherhood—they do not care two farthings for all the knights-errant there are in the world. Already I'm fancying I hear their arrows whizzing about my ears.[1]

"You, Sancho, are naturally a coward: however, to prevent your saying that I am obstinate and never followed your advice, I will take your counsel this time and hide myself from the terrors you fear so greatly. But it must be on one condition, that you never tell anyone that I withdrew from this danger through fear, but only to comply with your entreaties. If you say otherwise, you lie, and once for all I denounce you as a liar every time you say or think it."

"Master," answered Sancho, "to withdraw is not to run away, nor is it wise to stay when there is more peril than hope, and it's a wise man's duty to protect himself today for the morrow. Though I'm only a rough clod-hopper of a fellow, I've a smattering of what is called good government: so don't repent of having taken my advice, but mount Rozinante (if you're able; if not, I'll give you a hand) and follow me. I've a shrewd notion that for the present we'll need our heels more than our hands."

Don Quixote mounted Rozinante, without another word; and, Sancho leading the way on his ass, they entered the neighbouring Sierra Morena. Sancho's intention was to pass through it and get out at Viso or Almodóvar del Campo, and hide themselves for some days among those rocky wastes so as to escape the notice of the Holy Brotherhood. He was encouraged to this course by finding that the provisions carried on his ass had escaped scot-free from the skirmish with the galley-slaves—a thing which he looked upon as a miracle, considering what the slaves had taken away and how zealously they had searched for booty.

They arrived that night in the heart of the Sierra Morena, and there Sancho determined to spend that night, and, indeed, as many days as their food would last. Accordingly, they bivouacked between two rocks, among a number of cork trees. But destiny, which according to the opinion of those whose lives are not illuminated by the light of true faith, arranges and adjusts all things its own way, so ordained that Ginés de Pasamonte the celebrated trickster and robber, whom Don Quixote by his valour and folly had released from his chains,

[1] Officers of the Holy Brotherhood carried cross-bows and they were permitted to execute robbers caught in the act, and hang their bodies on trees.

103

also resolved to hide himself among the same mountains, and destiny led him to the very spot where Don Quixote and his squire were hiding. Moreover, he arrived just in time to recognize the two of them, and when he did so he let them sleep. And, as the wicked are always ungrateful, and necessity drives men to evil deeds, and present advantage obliterates all future considerations, Ginés, who was neither grateful nor good-natured, determined to steal Sancho Panza's ass. As for Rozinante he did not fancy him, for he did not consider him either pawnable or saleable. Sancho slept on blissfully, and as he lay, Ginés stole his ass, and before dawn he was so far distant as to be past finding.

The rosy dawn arose bringing joy to the earth but only grief to Sancho Panza, for he missed his Dapple. And finding himself deprived of him he began to utter the saddest and most pitiful lamentation in the world. At the sound of his cries Don Quixote awoke and heard him say: "O child of my bowels! Born in my own house, plaything of my children, comfort of my wife, envy of my neighbours, relief of my burdens, and, lastly, support of half my person, for with the twenty-six farthings which you earned daily, I paid half my expenses!"

Don Quixote, when he heard this lament and knew the cause of it, comforted Sancho as best he could, and begged him to be patient, promising to give him a bill of exchange for three out of the five asses he had left at home. Sancho was comforted by this promise, dried his tears, moderated his sobs and thanked Don Quixote for the favours he had done him.

And as they advanced farther into the mountains Don Quixote felt glad at heart, for those places seemed to him suitable for the adventures he was in search of. He reminded himself of the marvellous incidents which had happened to knights-errant in similar wild places; and his mind was so entirely wrapped up in these things that he thought of nothing else. As for Sancho, his only concern (now that he thought himself out of danger) was to cram his belly with the remains over from the spoils; so he trudged along after his master, burdened with all the things that his ass should have carried, but as he walked he took out of the wallet one piece of food after another and shovelled it into his paunch. While he was thus engaged he would not have given a farthing for any adventure in the world.

Just then he raised his eyes and saw that his master had stopped and was trying to lift with the point of his lance some object that lay upon the ground. He hastened to see whether he wanted his aid, and reached his side just as he was lifting up a saddle-cushion with a portmanteau fastened to it. They were half-rotten, in fact falling to pieces, but so heavy that Sancho had to help his master to lift them up. The latter ordered him to see what was in the portmanteau, and Sancho obeyed him as quickly as he could. Although it was shut with a chain and padlock, Sancho could see through the tears and holes what was in it, namely, four fine holland shirts and other linen garments, both unsoiled and of delicate material, besides a handkerchief containing a little heap of gold crowns. No sooner did he find the latter than he exclaimed: "Blessings on heaven, which has given us an adventure worth something!" After further searching he found a little memorandum book richly bound. Don Quixote asked him for this, but bade him keep the money for himself. For this favour Sancho kissed his hands, and taking all the linen out of the bag he rammed it into the provision-wallet. When Don Quixote saw this, he said: "I think, Sancho (it cannot be possible otherwise), that some traveller must have lost his way in the mountains and run across thieves who slew him and buried him in this desolate spot."

"That is impossible," said Sancho, "for if they had been robbers, they would not have left this money here."

"True," said Don Quixote; "I cannot imagine what can have happened. But wait a moment: let us see if there is anything written in this little memorandum book by which we may discover what we want to know." He opened it, and the first thing he found in it was a rough copy of a sonnet, but written in a most legible hand, which he read aloud to Sancho. Turning over the leaves of the pocket-book, he found other verses and letters, some of which he could read, others he could not; but they all consisted of complaints, lamentations, suspicions, likes, dislikes, favours, slights, some of them pompous, others mournful. While Don Quixote was examining the book, Sancho ransacked the portmanteau, without leaving a corner in that or in the saddle-cushion which he did not scrutinize; nor was there a seam he did not rip, nor a flock of wool he did not pick. Such was the covetousness which the golden treasure of a hundred crowns had aroused in him! And though he found no more, he considered himself over and above rewarded by his present find for the blanketings, the vomitings of the balsam, the benedictions of the pack-staves, the buffets of the carrier, the loss of the saddle-bags, the theft of his cloak; not to mention the hunger, thirst and fatigue he had endured in his good master's service.

The Knight of the Rueful Figure was eager to know who was the owner of the portmanteau, concluding from the sonnet and letters, the money in gold, and the fine linen, that it must belong to some noble lover, who had been driven to desperate straits by the disdain and ill-treatment of his mistress. But as there was no one in this rough, un-inhabitable spot to satisfy his curiosity, he ambled on aim-lessly, taking any road that Rozinante chose (he always chose those he found passable), firmly convinced that among these rocky wastes he would meet with some strange adventure.

As he rode on he saw a man on top of a neighbouring knoll, leaping from rock to rock and tuft to tuft with amazing agility. He seemed to be half-naked, with a thick, black beard, his hair long and matted, his feet unshod and his legs bare. He wore breeches of tawny-coloured velvet, but so torn to rags that his skin showed in places. His head, too, was bare, and although he ran by with all haste, as we said be-fore, yet the Knight of the Rueful Figure was able to note all these details. But although he tried he could not follow him, because Rozinante was too feeble to travel over those rough places, especially as he was by nature slow-footed and phlegmatic. Don Quixote then made up his mind that the fugi-tive was the owner of the saddle-cushion and the portmanteau, and he resolved to go in search of him, even if he should have to spend a whole year in the mountains to find him. So he ordered Sancho to make a short-cut by one side of the mountain while he went the other, in the hope that perhaps they would come across the man who had vanished so sud-denly out of their sight.

"I cannot do that," replied Sancho, "for as soon as I leave you, sir, fear seizes hold of me and fills me chock-full of a thousand different terrifying fancies. Let me say, once and for all, that in future I don't stir a finger's breadth from your presence."

"So be it," replied he of the Rueful Figure. "I am well pleased that you wish to avail yourself of my courage; it will not fail you, even though the soul in your body deserts you. Follow me, then, step by step, or as best you can, and use your eyes as lanterns: we shall go round this hill, and perhaps we may meet the man we saw, who beyond doubt is the owner of the portmanteau."

Sancho replied: "Surely it would be far better not to look for him at all: for if we find him and he turned out to be the owner of the money, there is no doubt that I'll have to give it back to him. It would be better, without taking this futile trouble, to let me keep it faithfully until the true owner turns up: perhaps by that time I shall have spent it all, and in that case the King will hold me guiltless."

"You are mistaken, Sancho," answered Don Quixote, "for now that we suspect who the owner is, we are obliged hence-forth to look for him and restore him his money."

With these words he clapped spurs to Rozinante, and Sancho followed him on foot carrying (thanks to Ginesillo de Pasamonte) his load on his back. When they had gone round part of the mountain they found in a stream a dead mule, half devoured by dogs and pecked by crows—a discovery which confirmed their belief that the man who had fled from them was the owner of the portmanteau and saddle-cushion. As they were looking at it, they heard a whistle, like that of a shepherd, and there appeared on their left a great number of goats, and, behind them, near the top of the mountain, was the goatherd—an aged man. Don Quixote shouted to him to come down to where they stood: and the goatherd shouted back, enquiring what had brought them to that lonely place, which was seldom or never trodden by any but the feet of goats, wolves or other beasts that prowled about those places. Sancho answered that they would tell him everything if only he would descend. The goatherd came down and said as he approached: "I'll bet yous were lookin' at the mule lyin' stiff in the gap yonder: faith an' skin he's lyin' in the self-same spot this sixmonth: tell me now, have either of ye caught e'er a sight of his masther?"

"We have met with nobody," replied Don Quixote, "but we discovered a saddle-cushion and a portmanteau not far from here."

"Sure, I too was after findin' that same one," said the goatherd, "but I wouldn't take it up in me hands, no, nor go near it; I was afear'd some bad luck might fall on me, an' I be held for thievin': for the divil's a sly one, to be sure; many's the time a man do hit his foot on a wee bit of a stone that do make him stumble an' fall—an' he not knowin' the why nor the wherefore."

"That's what I say," answered Sancho: "I, too, found it and I wouldn't go within a stone's throw of it: there I left it and there it stays, for I don't want a watchdog with a bell on it."

"Tell me, my good man," said Don Quixote; "do you know who is the owner of these things?"

"All I can tell ye," said the goatherd, "is that t'would be a matter o' six months ago when a fine, handsome young fella came to the sheepfold beyant—'tis a round nine mile from where we're standin'. He was ridin' that selfsame mule that's lyin' there an' with the selfsame saddle-pad an' trunk as yes found but didn't touch. He asked us which was the most hidden part of the mountain, an' we told him this was: an' we were after tellin' the truth, for if yes go three mile further yes mightn't find yer way out. Faith an' I'm wonderin' how yes found yer way in here so aisy. When the young fella heard our answer he turns his bridle an' away wid him in the direction we showed him towards them mountains beyant. Not a sight of him did we get for many a day until all of

a sudden he pops up in the way of one of our herds. Not a
word out of him—but he jumps on the herd, an' knocks
hell out of him. Then he takes all the bread an' cheese off
the herd and off he skips again into the mountains. When
we got wind of this, some of us went to fetch him an' we spent
a full two days in the lonesomest places in the mountains
lookin'; in the end sure we found him hidin' in the hollow
of an oul' cork tree. Out he comes to us meek as a lamb, wid
his clothes in ribbons an' his face burned be the sun—sure
'twas mighty hard to know him an' he in this state. He gave
us a soft answer; 'An,' sez he, 'don't wonder at what I'm after
doin'. This,' sez he, 'I have to do as a kind of penance given
me for me many sins.' We asked him who he was, but there
was no gettin' a word out of him. We begged him also to
tell us where we'd find him, an' he needin' food, for we'd gladly
bring it to him, an' we said if this didn't suit him, he was to
come an' ask for it widout liftin' it off the herds. 'I give yes
me thanks, to be sure,' sez he, 'an' I'm beggin' yer pardon for
me violence, an' I promise,' sez he, 'in future I'll ask for food
in God's name widout troublin' a soul.' He, for sure, was a
comely lad an' even the likes of us country folk could see he
was highborn. Then all of a sudden he stopped speakin'
an' held his tongue for a long while, wid his two eyes starin' out
of his head at the ground, an' we standin' there wonderin'
what would be the end of the fit that was on him. 'Twould
break your heart to see him, an' he starin' an' starin' widout
stirrin' an eyelid, bitin' his lips, frownin' somethin' awful.
'Twas easy seen the fit of madness was on him. We hadn't long
to wait, for suddenly he riz up an' made a leap at the man
next him wid such ragin' fury that he'd have bitten him, aye
an' beaten him to death if we hadn't pulled him off. All the
time he kept shoutin': 'Traitor Fernando: here you'll pay
me the injury ye did me: my hands will tear the heart out
of ye!' Then widout another word out of him he ran away
an' plunged into the thorn bushes where we couldn't follow
him. We think he has fits of madness that do return betimes to
him, an' some fella called Fernando must have done him a
power of harm to drive him to that state. An', gintlemen, I
must tell yes that yesterday meself and four young lads made
up our minds to go searchin' for him an' to take him be the
soft talk or be force to the town of Almodóvar, eight leagues
away, to see if he can be cured, or to find out if he has e'er a
relation to whom we can restore him. This, gintlemen, is all I
can tell yes, but yes may be sure that the owner of them things
yes found is the selfsame poor man yes seen, an' he dashin'
by like the wind."

Don Quixote was astonished at what he heard from the
goatherd and, as he was eager to know who the unhappy mad-

man was, he resolved to search the whole mountain, leaving no corner or cave unexplored until he should find him. But fortune favoured him more than he expected, for, even as he was speaking to the goatherd, the young man appeared in a neighbouring gorge of the Sierra descending towards them, and muttering to himself unintelligible words. His clothes were such as have been described, only differing in this, that when he drew near, Don Quixote noticed that he wore a leather jerkin, which, though torn to pieces, still retained the perfume of amber. From this he guessed that the young man was a person of quality. As the youth drew near he greeted them in a harsh voice but with great courtesy. Don Quixote returned the salute with equal politeness, and, alighting from Rozinante, with graceful demeanour went to meet him, and clasping him in his arms, embraced him as though he had known him for a long time.

The other, whom we may call the Ragged One of the Sorrowful Figure, as Don Quixote was of the Rueful Figure, after allowing himself to be embraced, drew back a little, and, laying his hands on Don Quixote's shoulders, stood gazing at him as if he wished to ascertain whether he knew him. He was, perhaps, no less amazed at the figure, demeanour and armour of Don Quixote, than the knight was at him.

The first to break the silence was the Ragged One, who addressed Don Quixote as follows: "Truly, sir whoever you may be, for I know you not, I thank you with all my heart for your courtesy towards me, and would that I could repay you as you deserve."

"My wish," cried Don Quixote, "is to serve, and I conjure you, sir, by what in this life you have loved or do love most, to tell me who you are and what has brought you to live and die like a brute beast in these solitudes—a dwelling-place so unsuitable to your rank, if I may judge from your person and attire. And I swear by the order of chivalry which I received, though an unworthy sinner, and by the profession of knight-errant, that if you gratify me in this, I will serve you with all the energy which it is my duty to exert, either in overcoming your troubles or, if that cannot be, in helping you to lament them."

The Knight of the Wood, hearing the Knight of the Rueful Figure talk in this manner, kept staring at him from head to foot; and after gazing at him again and again, he said at length: "If you have anything to eat, give it to me for God's sake, and after I have eaten I will do all that you ask in return for the kindness you show me."

Sancho straightway drew from his wallet, and the goatherd from his scrip, provisions which satisfied the Ragged One's hunger; but he ate what they gave him like a distracted person, and with such ravenous speed that he made no interval between one mouthful and the next: indeed he rather devoured than ate, and during his meal neither he nor the others spoke a word. Having ended his repast, he made signs to them to follow him, which they did, and he led them to a little green field behind a rock near by. When they arrived, he threw himself down on the grass and the rest did likewise. Not a word was spoken until the Ragged One, having composed himself, said: "If it is your pleasure, gentlemen, to hear in a few words the story of my immense misfortunes you must promise not to interrupt the thread of my sad story; for directly you do I shall stop telling it."

Don Quixote, in the name of all, promised not to interrupt him, and with this assurance the Ragged One began his story thus: "My name is Cardenio; my birthplace one of the best cities in Andalusia; my lineage noble; my parents rich and my misfortune so great that it must have been mourned by my parents and felt by my relations, though their wealth could do nought to lighten it; for riches are of little avail in the calamities imposed by destiny. In that city there dwelt a heavenly damsel, whom love had crowned with all the glory I could ever desire: such is the beauty of Luscinda, a lady as well-born and rich as myself, though more fortunate and less constant than my honourable thoughts deserved. This Luscinda I loved and adored from my earliest years, and she loved me with that innocent affection that was natural at her tender age. Our parents knew of our attachment and were not sorry to see it, for they saw that it could only end in a marriage sanctioned by our birth and wealth. Alas, how many letters have I written to her! What sweet and virtuous answers did I receive! How many songs did I compose, how many love verses, wherein I declared my love, described its passion, cherished its memories, and indulged its fancies! Then finding myself sorely troubled and being consumed with longing, I resolved to ask her of her father for my lawful wife. He answered that he thanked me for the desire I showed to honour him and to honour myself with his beloved one, but that as my father was alive it was by right his business to make that request. For if it were not done with his goodwill and pleasure, Luscinda was not the woman to be taken or given secretly.

"I thanked him for his kindness, and, feeling there was reason in what he said, I hastened to my father to tell him of my desires. When I entered his room he was standing with a letter open in his hand, and before I could speak he gave it to me, saying: 'By this letter, Cardenio, you may learn the wish the Duke Ricardo has to do you a favour.' This Duke Ricardo, as you surely know, gentlemen, is a grandee of Spain, whose dukedom is situated in the best part of Andalusia. I took the letter and read it, and it was so very kind that it seemed to me wrong if my father did not do what he asked. For he wanted me to be a companion—not a servant—to his eldest son, and offered to advance me in life in accordance with the good opinion he had of me. On reading the letter I was struck dumb with consternation, and still more especially when I heard my father say: 'Cardenio, you must be ready to leave in two days, and to do what the duke wishes. You should thank your stars that such a future lies open to you.'

"The day of my departure arrived: I spoke one night to my dear Luscinda and also to her father, and begged him to wait a few days and not to give her in marriage to anyone until I knew what Duke Ricardo's plans for me were. He promised not to bestow his daughter elsewhere, and she confirmed it with a thousand vows and swoonings. At last, I arrived at the home of Duke Ricardo, who received and treated me with great kindness, but the one who rejoiced most at my coming was his second son, Fernando, a young man who was noble, gallant and very comely. In a short time he became so intimate a friend of mine that it was the subject of general comment; and though the elder son treated me with much favour it did not compare with the affection lavished upon me by Don Fernando. Now, since friends communicate all their secrets to one another and my feelings for Fernando were deeply sincere, he told me all his thoughts and desires, and confided to me a love affair of his own which caused him much anxiety. He had fallen in love with the daughter of a farmer, who was his father's vassal. Her parents were rich, and she herself was so beautiful, modest, wise and virtuous that no one could decide which of those qualities she most excelled in. In any case, the charms of the fair farmer's daughter so inflamed the heart of Don Fernando that he resolved to promise her marriage in order to triumph over her chastity, for he knew that she could not be conquered by any other means. Prompted by my friendship, I tried by all the arguments I could think of to dissuade him from his purpose, but finding it in vain, I resolved to tell the story to his father the duke. But Don Fernando, who was clear-sighted and shrewd, suspected my intentions, for he feared that I should not, owing to my position as faithful servant, be able to keep back from my master a matter that was so prejudicial to his honour. So to put me off the scent he said that he could find no better way of banishing the remembrance of her beauty than by leaving home for a few months. Therefore his plan, he said, was for both of us to go back to my father's house, on the excuse of seeing and buying horses in my native city, which is famous for producing the best in the world.

"No sooner did he make this suggestion than, swayed by my own love, I gave my entire approval to his plan, because it gave me so good an opportunity of seeing once more my dear Luscinda. I therefore encouraged him and begged him to put it into operation as soon as possible, for absence would tell in the end in spite of the strongest inclination. I found out afterwards that when he made his proposal to me he had already, under the title of husband, enjoyed the favours of the maiden, and was only waiting for an opportunity to divulge the truth with safety to himself, for he was afraid of what the duke, his father, would do when he should hear of his escapade. Now, love in most young men is not love but lust, and as its ultimate end is pleasure, it ceases once that subject has been attained; and what appeared to be love must disappear because it cannot pass the limits assigned to it by nature, whereas true affection knows none of such limitations. I mean to say that no sooner had Don Fernando enjoyed the farmer's daughter than his desires weakened and his amorous impulses cooled. If at first he had pretended that he would absent himself in order to get rid of his passions, he now earnestly endeavoured to go away to avoid fulfilling his promises. The duke gave him leave, and ordered me to go with him.

"We arrived at my native city, and my father entertained him according to his rank. I again saw Luscinda. My love for her revived (though indeed it had never grown cold) and, to my sorrow, I told Don Fernando all about it, for I thought by the laws of friendship it was not right to hide anything from him. I described Luscinda's beauty, charm and wit in such glowing terms that my praises stirred in him a desire to see a damsel enriched with such rare virtues. To my misfortune, I gratified his wish and showed her to him one night by the light of a candle at the window where we were wont to speak together. He saw her in her light dress, and such was her beauty that he straightway forgot every fair lady he had seen hitherto. He was struck dumb, he lost his senses, he was entranced, and so deeply in love as you will see in the course of my sad story. And what inflamed his passion (which he hid from me), was that he happened to see a letter she had written asking me to beg her father again to give consent to our marriage. So sensible and full of tenderness was the letter that when he had read it he said that Luscinda possessed in her person all the beauty, grace and understanding of the rest of womankind. Yet I must confess that I took no pleasure in hearing her thus

112

praised and I began to suffer from a strange feeling of jealousy. I did not mistrust the goodness and faith of Luscinda, but at the same time I felt a vague fear for the future. So Don Fernando continued to read the letters I sent to Luscinda and those she wrote to me, on the plea that he took great pleasure in our wit; and one day it happened that Luscinda asked me to give her a book of chivalry, of which she was very fond, entitled *Amadis of Gaul . . ."*

Don Quixote had hardly heard him mention a book of chivalry when he cried: "If, my good sir, you had told me that your lady Luscinda was a reader of knightly adventures, you need not have said anything else to make me understand the high quality of her mind. So do not waste any more words describing her beauty and worth, for now I assert that owing to her devotion to such books, Lady Luscinda is the fairest and most accomplished woman in all the world. Pray pardon me for having interrupted your story, but when I hear anything said about chivalry and knights-errant, I can no more keep from speaking of them than the sunbeams can help giving warmth or the moon moisture. Therefore pardon me and continue."

While Don Quixote was speaking, Cardenio held his head down, apparently in deep thought, and although Don Quixote told him twice to continue his story, he did not raise his head nor answer a word. After a long pause he lifted his head and said: "I cannot get it out of my head, nor can anyone in the world persuade me to the contrary, indeed he who believes otherwise must be a blockhead—that Master Elisabat, that arrant rogue, was the paramour of Queen Madasima."

"That is not true, I swear," answered Don Quixote in great rage. "It is the height of malice, or rather villainy, to say so. Queen Madasima was a very noble lady, and it is not to be presumed that so high a princess would grant her favours to a bone-setter, and whoever states to the contrary, lies like a rogue, and I will make him understand it, on foot, on horseback, armed or unarmed, by night or by day, as he likes best."

Cardenio stood gazing fixedly at Don Quixote, for now the mad fit was on him, and he was in no condition to continue his story; nor would Don Quixote have listened to him, so irritated was he by what he had heard about Queen Madasima. What a strange thing it was to see him take her part as though she had been his true and natural princess! Such was the power those accursed books had over him. And Cardenio, who was now raving, when he heard himself called a liar and a rogue in addition to other opprobrious epithets, took exception to the jest, and seizing a stone that lay close to him, he threw it with such force at Don Quixote's chest that he knocked him over on his back. Sancho Panza, seeing his master so roughly handled, set upon the madman with his clenched fists, but the Ragged One with one blow laid him at his feet, after which he stood on him and kicked him to his heart's content. The goatherd, who tried to defend him, suffered the same fate. When the madman had vanquished and drubbed them all, he departed from them calmly and peaceably, and disappeared in the mountain scrub. Sancho rose in a rage to find himself so mauled and kicked without cause, and ran at the goatherd to be revenged on him, saying that he was at fault for not having warned them that this man was subject to mad fits at times; for had they known, they would have been on their guard.

The goatherd answered that he had told him, and if he had not paid attention to his warning, it was not his fault. Sancho Panza replied; the goatherd did likewise, and the dispute passed from words to blows, for they caught hold of one another's beards and punched away with such fury that if Don Quixote had not pacified them, they would have battered one another to bits. Sancho, still holding the goatherd fast, kept saying: "Let me alone, Sir Knight of the Rueful Figure, this fellow is a yokel like myself: he's not dubbed a knight, so I may safely get my satisfaction for the wrong he has done me, by fighting with him hand to hand like a man of honour."

"That is true," said Don Quixote; "but I know that he is in no way culpable for what has happened." Having pacified them with these words, he again asked the goatherd if it would be possible to find Cardenio, for he was most eager to know the end of his story. The goatherd repeated what he had said at first, namely, that he did not exactly know his haunts, but that if they wandered about these parts, they would be sure to meet him, sane or mad.

XV. The continuation of the adventure in the Sierra Morena

DON QUIXOTE TOOK LEAVE OF THE GOATHERD, AND MOUNTing once again on Rozinante, he commanded Sancho to follow him, which he did most unwillingly. They travelled at a slow pace, entering little by little into the thickest and roughest part of the mountains. Sancho Panza was dying to converse with his master, but wanted him to began talking first, so that he might not disobey his orders. At last, being unable to endure such prolonged silence, he burst out: "Please, sir, give me your blessing and permission to depart. I want to go home to my wife and children, with whom, at least, I shall be allowed to chat and gossip to my heart's content. If you, sir, want me to bear you company through these lonely places without letting me open my lips when the whim takes me, you might as well bury me alive. If fate only allowed beasts to speak as they did in the times of Aesop, it wouldn't be so bad, for I'd be able to talk to Rozinante as much as I pleased and in that way I could bear my mishaps. But 'tis tough luck, and not to be borne in patience, for a man to roam all his life in search of adventures, without meeting aught but kicks, blanketings, brickbats and punches, and all the while have to keep his mouth sewed up, not daring to say what's on his mind, just as if he was as dumb as a doorpost."

"I understand you, Sancho," answered Don Quixote: "you are dying for me to take off the embargo I have laid on your tongue. Consider it revoked and say what you please, on condition that this revocation only lasts while we are traveling through these mountains."

"So be it," said Sancho, "let me talk now, for what's to come God alone knows: so now, taking advantage of my licence, I ask what your worship meant by standing up so sturdily for that Queen Magimasa, or whatever she called herself? And what on earth did it matter whether that abbot was the boy friend or not? If you had let that pass, seeing you weren't his judge, I'm sure the madman would have continued his story, and we could have avoided the cobble-stone tattoo, the kicks and more than half a dozen back-handers."

"Truly, Sancho," said Don Quixote, "if you knew as well as I do how honourable and high-minded a lady Queen Madasima was, I am sure you would agree that I was very patient not to smash to pieces the mouth that uttered such blasphemous words; for it is grievous blasphemy to say or to think that a Queen would lie with a barber-surgeon. The true story is that Master Elisabat was very prudent and full of sound judgment, and served the Queen as her tutor and physician. But it is folly, deserving of the severest punishment, to imagine that she was his mistress, and to show you that Cardenio did not know what he was saying, you must remember that when he said it he was out of his senses."

115

"So say I," replied Sancho; "no one ought to take the words of a madman seriously."

"Every knight-errant," answered Don Quixote, "is bound to stand up for the honour of women, whoever they may be, against sane or mad, especially of sovereigns of such high degree as Queen Madasima, to whom I was particularly attracted owing to her good qualities. I therefore beg you, Sancho, do keep silent and cease meddling with what does not concern you. Let your five senses convince you that whatever I have done, do, or shall do, is very reasonable and is in accordance with the laws of chivalry, which I know better than all the knights-errant that ever professed them in the world."

"Master," replied Sancho, "is it a good rule of chivalry that we should go wandering up and down through these mountains after a madman, who perhaps, when he is found, will take it into his head to finish what he began—not his story, but the breaking of your head and my ribs?"

"Peace, I say, Sancho, once again!" said Don Quixote; "for you must know that it is not only the wish to find the madman that brings me into these wastes, but because I intend to carry out an adventure which will win me everlasting fame and renown over the whole face of the earth."

"Is it a dangerous adventure?" asked Sancho Panza.

"No," answered the Knight of the Rueful Figure, "though the dice may turn up blank instead of sixes, yet everything depends upon your diligence."

"My diligence?" said Sancho.

"Yes," said Don Quixote; "for if you return quickly from the place where I intend to send you, my penance will soon be over, and my glory will then commence. I do not want to keep you any longer in suspense, and so I shall explain the meaning of my words. You must know, Sancho, that the famous Amadis of Gaul was one of the most perfect of all the knights-errant. And as he was the morning star and sun of all valiant knights, so we who fight under the banners of love and chivalry ought to imitate him in all he did. Since this is the case, friend Sancho, the knight-errant who imitates him best will be the most certain of arriving at pre-eminence in chivalry. And one of the occasions upon which the knight especially displayed his prudence, worth, courage, patience, constancy and love, was when he changed his name to Beltenebros and retired to do penance on Peña Pobre[1] after Lady Oriana had disdained his love. And as I may more easily imitate him in this than in cleaving giants,

---

[1] *Amadis of Gaul*, ii. 1-9. It was a very high rock seven leagues out at sea. It was called "Poor Rock" because none can live there save in great poverty.

beheading serpents, killing dragons, routing armies, shattering fleets and dissolving enchantments, and because these wilds are so suitable for the purpose, I have no reason to neglect the opportunity which presents itself to me."

"What do you intend to do in this God-forsaken spot?" asked Sancho.

"Have I not told you already," replied Don Quixote, "that I mean to copy Amadis of Gaul by acting here the part of a despairing, mad and furious lover?"

"I am sure," said Sancho, "that the knights who went through these penances must have had some reason for doing so; but what cause have you, sir, for going mad? What lady turned you down? What signs have you discovered that her ladyship Dulcinea del Toboso has committed any foolishness either with Moor or Christian?"

"That is just the point of it," said Don Quixote; "and that is where I have my subtle plan. A knight-errant who goes mad for a good reason deserves no thanks or gratitude; the whole point consists in going mad without cause. Therefore, Sancho, my friend, do not waste any more time in advising me to give up so rare, so happy and so unparalleled an imitation. Mad I am and mad I shall remain until you return again with the answer to a letter which I mean to send by you to my Lady Dulcinea. If the answer is such as I deserve, my penance will end; if not, I shall go mad in good earnest. Now tell me, Sancho, have you kept safely the helmet of Mambrino?"

"Heavens above, Sir Knight of the Rueful Figure," answered Sancho, "I cannot keep my patience listening to some things you're saying, and I sometimes think all you tell me of knighthood, kingdoms, empires and islands is all windy blather and lies. For to hear you saying that a barber's basin is Mambrino's helmet, and not to find out your mistake in four days, makes me wonder if your brain isn't cracked. I'm carrying the basin right enough in my bag, all battered and dented, and I intend to take it home, repair it and soap my beard in it some day when I return to my wife and children."

"I swear by the same oath," said Don Quixote, "that you have the shallowest pate that any squire has or ever had. Is it possible that you have travelled so long with me and not found out that all the adventures of a knight-errant appear to be illusion, follies and dreams, and turn out contrariwise? Not that things are really so, but because in our midst there is a host of enchanters, for ever changing, disguising and transforming our affairs, according as they wish to favour or destroy us. So, what you call a barber's basin is to me Mambrino's helmet, and for another person it has some other shape altogether: and it was rare foresight on the part of the wise man, my ally, to make it appear to others a basin, whereas it really and truly is Mambrino's helmet; because since it is of such great value, all the world would persecute me in order to obtain it; now, since they think it is nothing but a barber's basin, they do not trouble about it."

As they were conversing, they arrived at the foot of a lofty mountain, which stood like a mighty hewn rock apart from the rest. At the foot flowed a gentle rill which watered a green and fertile meadow planted with many wild shrubs and flowers. This was the place the Knight of the Rueful Figure chose for his penance; and gazing on the scene he began to cry out in a loud voice: "Here I elect to do my penance. This is the spot where my flowing tears shall swell the waters of this crystal stream, and my unending sighs shall stir the foliage of these mountain trees. O Dulcinea del Toboso, day of my night and star of my fortunes, consider the state to which thy absence has reduced me. I beg of thee to give me what my faith deserves."

With these words he alighted from Rozinante and, taking off the saddle and the bridle, gave him a slap on his haunches, saying: "He who gives thee liberty lacks it himself: O steed, famous for thy deeds, how luckless art thou in thy destiny! Begone where thou wilt."

When Sancho heard all this, he could not help saying: "God's peace be with the fellow who saved us the trouble of unharnessing my Dapple, for he surely would have had plenty of slaps and speeches in his honour. But if the ass were here, I wouldn't allow him to be unharnessed, for there's no reason for it. He had nothing to do with love or despair any more than I, who was once his master when it pleased God. But in truth, Sir Knight of the Rueful Figure, if my departure and your madness take place in earnest it would be well to re-saddle Rozinante that he may make up for the loss of my ass, and save me time in coming and going; for if I do the journey afoot I don't know when I shall arrive or return, since, to tell you the honest truth, I am mighty poor on my legs."

"As you will," said Don Quixote; "but you must not go away for three days yet, for I want to have time to let you see what I am saying and doing for my lady's sake, that you may tell her about it."

"What more have I to see," said Sancho, "than what I have already seen?"

"How much you know about it!" said Don Quixote: "why, I have yet to tear my garments, scatter my armour about and bang my head against these rocks, and other things of the kind which will amaze you."

"For the love of God," said Sancho, "take care how you go knocking your head against the rocks, for you may run up against so nasty a one that your plan of penance will be brought to nought. If you insist on the knocks on the head, I should content myself, if I was you, seeing that this business is all sham and make-believe, with striking your head against water, or some soft thing like cotton, and put the onus on me. I'll tell my lady that I saw you banging your pate against the point of a rock that was harder than a diamond."

"I thank you, friend Sancho, for your good intentions," answered Don Quixote, "but I want you to realize that all these actions of mine are not for mockery, but are very much in earnest, for if it were otherwise, I should be breaking the rules of chivalry, which forbid me to tell a lie, on pain of being an apostate; and if I do one thing instead of another it is the same as telling a lie. And so the knocks on the head must be real hard knocks without anything imaginary about them. It will be necessary, therefore, to leave me some lint to cure them, since fortune deprived us of the balsam."

"It was worse to lose the ass," answered Sancho, "for with him we lost the lint and everything; but please, sir, don't remind me of that cursed medicine again: the very name of it turns my soul, not to mention my stomach, inside out. As for the three days which you allow me for seeing your mad frolics, I'd beg you to count them already gone by; I'll take all for granted and judged, and I'll tell wonders to my lady. Now write the letter and send me swiftly on my way, for I'm longing to come back and deliver you from this purgatory where I'm leaving you."

"Purgatory, you call it, Sancho," said Don Quixote. "Call it rather hell, or worse, if anything can be worse."

"I've heard it said," answered Sancho, "that 'from hell there is no retention'."

"I do not know," said Don Quixote, "what *retention* means." [2]

"Retention," answered Sancho, "means that he who is once in hell never does nor ever can get out again. But it'll be the reverse for you, sir, or it'll go hard with my feet, if I only have the spurs to ginger up Rozinante. Once I get safe and sound to El Toboso and into the presence of my Lady Dulcinea, I'll tell her such a tale of the mad, foolish frolics (for they're no better) which you have done, and are still doing, that I'll make her as soft as a glove, even though I find her tougher than a cork tree. And as soon as I get her sweet and honeyed answer, I'll be back as swift as a witch on a broomstick, and deliver you from your penance."

[2] He means that from hell "nulla est redemptio."

119

"How shall we manage to write the letter here?" said Don Quixote.

"And the ass-colt order," added Sancho.

"All shall be included," said Don Quixote, "and since we have no paper, we should write as the ancients did, on leaves of trees, or on tablets of wax, though it will be as hard to find wax as paper. But now that I come to think of it, there is Cardenio's pocket-book. I will write in that, and you must see that it is copied out upon paper in good round hand at the first village where you find a schoolmaster or sacristan to transcribe it for you."

"What about your signature?" said Sancho.

"The letters of Amadis were never signed," replied Don Quixote.

"That is all very well," said Sancho, "but the order for the ass-colts must be signed, for if it is copied out they'll say the signature is false, and then I'll remain without my ass-colts."

"The order for the ass-colts will be signed in the diary," said Don Quixote, "and when my niece sees it she'll make no difficulty in executing it. As for the love-letter, you must end it thus: 'yours till death, the Knight of the Rueful Figure'. It does not matter if it is written in a strange hand, for as far as I can remember, Dulcinea can neither read nor write, nor has she ever seen my handwriting. For our love for each other has always been of the platonic kind, never going beyond an occasional modest glance at each other; and even that was so rare that I can truly swear that, during the twelve years I have loved her more than the light of those eyes of mine which the earth must one day consume, I have not seen her more than four times. In fact, I even doubt if she ever noticed me gazing at her—such was the reserve and seclusion in which her father, Lorenzo Corchuelo, and her mother, Aldonza Nogales, brought her up."

"Oho!" cried Sancho, "the daughter of Lorenzo Corchuelo! Is she the Lady Dulcinea del Toboso, otherwise called Aldonza Lorenzo?"

"That is she," said Don Quixote, "and she deserves to be the mistress of the universe."

"I know her well," said Sancho; "and I assure you she can pitch the iron bar as well as the strongest lad in our village. God save us! Why, she's a lusty lass, tall and straight, with hair on her chest, and I'll bet she'll pull the chestnuts out of the fire for any knight-errant now or to come who has her for wife. God, what a woman she is! What a pair of lungs she has, and what an arm! I remember one day she climbed to the top of the church belfry to call her father's ploughmen who were working in a fallow field, and though they were more than half a league off, they heard her as plain as though close by: and the best of her is that she's not at all coy, for she's a great hand at courting, always joking with the boys and making game of everyone. Now I'm telling you, Sir Knight of the Rueful Figure, that you not only may and ought to go daft about her, but you'd be right to be desperate and hang yourself; for everyone who hears of it will say you did very well, even though the devil himself carried you away. I wish I was gone, if only to catch a glimpse of her; for it's many a day since I seen her, and I'm sure she's changed by now; for there's nothing spoils a girl's face more than to be always working in the fields, exposed to sun and weather. To be frank with your worship, I've been mistaken up to this, for I thought really and truly all this while that the Lady Dulcinea was some princess with whom you were in love, or at least some person of such great qualities as to deserve the rich presents you have sent before I became your squire. But when all's said and done, what good can it do the Lady Aldonza Lorenzo—I mean the Lady Dulcinea del Toboso—to have the vanquished whom you send, or may send, falling upon their knees before her? For perhaps at the time they arrive she may be carding flax or threshing, and they would be all mortified at the sight of her, and she would laugh or maybe poke fun at the present you'd sent her."

"I have told you, Sancho, many times before now," said Don Quixote, "that you are too great a prattler. It is enough for me to think and believe that the good Aldonza Lorenzo is beautiful and chaste; as to her lineage it matters not, for no enquiry concerning it is necessary, and as for myself—I regard her as the greatest princess in the world."

"Your worship," replied Sancho, "is always in the right and I am the ass. I don't know why I mentioned an ass —one shouldn't talk of halters in the house of the hanged. Come, give me the letter, sir, and God be with you, for I'm off."

Don Quixote took out the pocket-book and, stepping aside, began with much composure to write the letter. When he had finished, he called Sancho to him and read him the following missive:

Letter of Don Quixote to Dulcinea del Toboso.

DEAR SOVEREIGN LADY,
  The sore wounded one, O sweetest Dulcinea del Toboso, sends thee the health which he wants himself. If thy beauty disdains me, although inured to suffering, I shall ill support this care, which is not only violent but lasting. My good squire Sancho will tell thee, O ungrateful fair and most beloved enemy,

121

of the state wherein I remain for thy sake. Should it be thy pleasure to favour me, I am thine. If not, do what thou wilt, for by ending my life I shall satisfy both thy cruelty and my desires.
Thine until death,
THE KNIGHT OF THE RUEFUL FIGURE.

"By my father's life," said Sancho, "it is the finest thing that ever I heard in all my life. And now, master, will you please stick on the other side of the leaf the order for the three ass-colts and sign it very plain, that people may know your hand at first sight."

"With pleasure," said Don Quixote. Having written it, he read as follows:

DEAR NIECE,

At sight of this my first bill of ass-colts, give order that three out of the five I left at home in your keeping be delivered to Sancho Panza my squire: which three colts I order to be delivered and paid for by the like number received of him here; and this, with his acquittance, shall be your discharge. Done in the heart of the Sierra Morena the 22nd August, this present year.

"That's well done," said Sancho; "now you've only to sign it."

"It wants no signing," said Don Quixote. "I need only put my flourish, which is the same thing and is sufficient not only for three but for three hundred asses."

"And now," said Sancho, "let me saddle Rozinante and be off. For I intend to start immediately without staying to see these mad frolics which you are going to play. Now I think of it, master, how shall I be able to find my way back to this out-of-the-way spot?"

"Mark the place well," said Don Quixote, "and I will endeavour to remain near it. Moreover, I will mount to the top of one of the highest rocks so that I may see you coming. Also it would be well to cut down some boughs and strew them after you as you go, that they may serve as marks to find your way back, like the clue in Theseus's Labyrinth."

Sancho did this and asked his master's blessing; then, not without many tears on both sides, took leave of him; and mounting upon Rozinante he rode towards the plain, strewing the boughs at intervals as his master directed him. Thus he departed, although Don Quixote still insisted that he should see him perform if it were but a few of his pranks. He had hardly gone a hundred paces when he turned back and said: "Sir, what you said was true, and it would be better for my conscience if I saw at least one of your mad pranks; though to tell you the truth I've seen enough of them in seeing you stay here."

"Did I not tell you so?" said Don Quixote. "Wait but a moment, Sancho, I will do it as quickly as you can say the Creed."

Then stripping off hastily his breeches he remained in nought but skin and shirt: straightway he cut a couple of capers and did two somersaults on the ground with his head down and his legs in the air. Sancho, to avoid seeing such a display, turned the bridle and rode away, fully satisfied to swear that his master was stark, staring mad.

XVI. The penance Don Quixote performed in the Sierra Morena, and the plan of the curate and the barber

DON QUIXOTE, WHEN HE FOUND HIMSELF ALONE, CLIMBED to the top of a high mountain and spent his days imitating the deeds of Amadis, when that peerless knight did penance on Peña Pobre, weeping abundantly there until Heaven rescued him in his great tribulation. Our knight thus passed his time, walking about, and writing, and cutting on the barks of trees, or tracing in the fine sand, many verses of a plaintive character, some of them in praise of his Dulcinea. He sighed and called upon the fauns, the silvan deities of the woods, the nymphs of the streams and the mournful echo to listen and answer his laments; or else he went in search of herbs to sustain himself until Sancho should return: and if the latter had tarried three weeks instead of three days, the Knight of the Rueful Figure would have become so disfigured that the mother who bore him would not have recognized him.

Now, however, it is proper to leave him to his sighs and versifying and relate what happened to Sancho Panza on his journey as envoy. The squire, after turning into the highway, took the road which led to El Toboso, and arrived the next day at the inn where the mishap of the blanket had befallen him. He no sooner saw it than he imagined that he was once again flying through the air, so he determined not to enter the inn, although it was then dinner-time, and he had a mighty appetite for some warm food, as his diet had been confined to cold meat for many days past. This longing made him draw near to the inn, but he was still in some doubt as to whether he should enter it or not. As he stood wondering, there came out of the inn two persons, who recognized him at once, and the one said to the other: "Tell me, Master Licentiate, is that horseman over there not Sancho Panza, who went off with Don Quixote to be his squire?"

"It is," said the licentiate: "and that is our Don Quixote's nag." No wonder they knew him so well, for they were the curate and the barber of his village, who had made the search and formal process against the books of chivalry. So, wanting to hear news of Don Quixote, they went up to him and said: "Friend Sancho Panza, where have you left your master?" Sancho Panza knew them at once, and resolved to conceal the circumstances and the place of retreat of his master. So he answered that his master was detained in a certain place by affairs of great importance, which he swore by the two eyes in his head he could not disclose.

"No, no, Sancho Panza," said the barber: "that story will not do. If you do not tell us where he is, we must imagine (as we do already) that you have robbed and slain him, since you are riding his horse. So find us the horse's owner or there'll be a shindy."

"There's no reason to threaten me," answered Sancho. "I'm not the kind who robs or kills anybody. Let every man's luck kill him or the God who made him. As for my master, he's enjoying himself doing penance in the midst of yon mountains."

He then rapidly, without pausing a moment, told them in what state he had left his master, the adventures that had befallen them, and how he was carrying a letter to the Lady Dulcinea del Toboso—the daughter of Lorenzo Corchuelo, with whom the knight was up to the ears in love.

Both of them were astonished at what they heard. Although they already knew the nature of Don Quixote's madness, yet every new detail they heard caused them fresh amazement. They asked Sancho Panza to show them the letter he was carrying to Lady Dulcinea del Toboso. He said it was written in a pocket-book, and that he was ordered to get it copied out at the first village he came to. The curate then said that if he would give it to him, he would copy it out in good hand. Sancho Panza then thrust his hand into his bosom to search for the little book, but he could not find it, nor would he have found it, if he had searched till doomsday, for he had left it with Don Quixote. The knight had not given it to him, and he had forgotten to ask for it.

When Sancho failed to find the book, he turned as pale as death, and rapidly feeling all over his body he saw clearly that it was not to be found. Without more ado, he clutched hold of his beard, and with both his hands tore out half his hair, and gave himself half a dozen blows on his nose and mouth and bathed them all in blood. When the curate and barber saw this, they asked him what was the matter that he should treat himself so roughly.

"What is the matter?" answered Sancho: "why I've let

slip through my fingers in one instant three ass-colts—aye, and each of them was as sturdy as a castle."

"How is that?" replied the barber.

"I've lost the pocket-book," answered Sancho, "in which the letter to Dulcinea was written, and a bill signed by my master, in which he ordered his niece to give me three colts out of the four or five he had at home." With that he went on to tell them of the loss of Dapple.

The curate comforted him by telling him that as soon as they had found his master, they would make him renew the order upon paper according to law, for those written in a pocket-book would not be accepted as valid. This comforted Sancho and he said he did not mind having lost the letter to Dulcinea, for he could almost say it by heart, and so they might write it down when and where they pleased.

"Say it then, Sancho," said the barber, "and we will write it out." Then Sancho stood still and began to scratch his head and tried to remember the letter. He stood first on one leg and then on the other, and looked first at the ground, then at the sky. Then, after biting off half the nail of one finger and keeping his hearers for a long time in suspense, he said: "God help me, Father, may the devil take anything I remember of the letter, though I'm sure at the beginning it said: 'High and suffering lady!' "

"I am sure," said the barber, "it did not say 'suffering' but 'superhuman' or 'sovereign' lady."

"So it did," said Sancho. "Then, if I'm not mistaken it went on . . . if I'm not mistaken: 'the layman sleepless and wounded kisses your hand, ungrateful and most unknown beautiful one'; and then it said somewhat about health and sickness that he sent; and so it scampered along until it ended with 'yours till death; the Knight of the Rueful Figure'."

They were both much amused at Sancho's good memory, and they praised it much, begging him to repeat the letter twice, that they too might learn it by heart and write it down in due time. Three times Sancho repeated it and three times he added three thousand more follies. Then he told them other things about his master, but not a word did he say about being tossed in a blanket in that very inn which he now refused to enter. He told them also how his master, as soon as he had received a good despatch from his Lady Dulcinea, would set to work to become emperor, or at least king (for so it was arranged between them), and it was a very easy thing for him to become one, such was his courage and the strength of his arm. And when this came to pass, his master would arrange a marriage for him (by then he would be a widower at least) with a maid of honour of the empress, heiress to a large rich estate on the mainland, without any islands female

125

or male, for he was not interested in them any more. Sancho said all this foolishness with so much gravity, wiping his nose from time to time, that the two were still more amazed at the vehement nature of Don Quixote's madness, which had swept along in its wake the senses of that poor ignorant fellow. They did not, however, wish to weary themselves trying to convince him of his foolishness, as it didn't harm his conscience, and they thought that if they left him as he was, he would amuse them by his sallies. So they told him to pray for the health of his master.

"For my part," answered Sancho, "I'm resolved to pray Heaven to land him into places where he'll do the best for himself and reward me into the bargain."

"You talk like a wise man," said the curate, "and you will act like a good Christian. But we must now discover a way of rescuing your master from that useless penance you say he is doing. So let us go into the inn to arrange our plans, and, incidentally, to get our dinner, for it is now time." Sancho told them to go in, but said he would prefer to wait for them outside, and that he would tell them another time the reason why. He begged them, however, to bring him something nice and hot to eat, and some barley for Rozinante. They went into the inn, and after a while the barber brought him out some meat.

After much discussion between the curate and the barber on the best means of accomplishing their purpose, the curate thought of a plan exactly suited both to Don Quixote's humour, and to their purpose; which was, that the curate should dress himself up as a damsel-errant and the barber should do the best he could to equip himself as her squire. In that disguise they would go to the place where Don Quixote was undergoing penance, pretending that she was an afflicted and distressed damsel, and would beg a boon which he as a valiant knight-errant could not refuse to grant; and this should be a request that he should follow her whither she should lead him, to redress an injury inflicted on her by a wicked knight. Besides this, she was to pray him not to command her to take off her mask, nor to enquire of her condition, until he had secured her justice against that wicked knight. He was certain that Don Quixote would consent to do all he was asked, and by this stratagem they would get him away from that place and carry him home, where they would try to see if his strange madness could be cured.

The barber approved of the curate's notion, so they resolved immediately to carry it out. They borrowed a gown and a head-dress from the innkeeper's wife, leaving with her in exchange the curate's new cassock. The barber made for himself a great beard out of the tail of a pied ox into which the innkeeper used to stick his curry-comb. The land-lady asked them what they wanted these things for, and the curate told her briefly all about Don Quixote's madness, and how that disguise was necessary to bring him away from the mountain where he was at the moment. The innkeeper and his wife then realized that the madman was their former guest, the maker of the balsam and the master of the blanketed squire. So they told the barber and curate all about him, without omitting what Sancho had been so eager to conceal. Meanwhile the landlady dressed the curate up in a manner that could not be excelled. She made him put on a cloth gown with stripes of black velvet, each a span in width, all slashed, and a bodice of green velvet, trimmed with white satin, both of which might have been made in the days of King Wamba.[1] The curate would not consent to wear a woman's head-dress, but put on a little white quilted cap which he used as a nightcap. Then he tied one of his black taffeta garters around his head, and with the other made a kind of mask and fixed it on in such a way that it covered his face and beard very neatly. He then covered his pate with his hat, which was so large that it served him as a sun-shade, and, wrapping his cloak around him, he seated himself upon his mule sideways like a woman. The barber mounted also, with a beard that reached to his waist, of a colour between sorrel and white, resembling the one we mentioned before, which was made out of the tail of a pied ox.

They took leave of all, not forgetting the good Maritornes, who promised, though a sinner, to say a whole rosary that God might give them success in so arduous and Christian a business as that which they had undertaken. But no sooner had they left the inn than the curate had a sudden notion that he was not doing right in dressing up as a woman, and that it was unbecoming for a priest to go about in such a costume, even though the motive was good. So he told the barber his scruples, and asked him to change clothes with him, for he said it was more fitting that the barber should be the afflicted lady, whereas he would act the part of the squire. In this way, his priestly dignity would be safe, but if the barber did not agree, he was determined not to go on any farther, even if the devil ran away with Don Quixote.

Sancho now came up, and when he saw the two of them dressed in such a manner, he nearly burst his sides laughing. The barber let the curate have his way, who, after exchanging his clothes, began to tutor the other how to act his part and what words to use to Don Quixote, in order to persuade him to accompany them and leave the place he had chosen for his futile penance. The barber replied that without any of

[1] The last of the Gothic Kings of Spain, 672-82.

his lessons he would play his part to a nicety, but he refused to put on the gown until they came near Don Quixote's retreat. So he folded it up, and off they went under the guidance of Sancho Panza, who told them about the madman they met in the Sierra, but kept a discreet silence about the portmanteau and its contents; for though a fool, the fellow had a spice of covetousness.

The next day they arrived at the spot where Sancho had strewn the branches to mark where he had left his master. When he saw them he told them that this was the entrance to the mountain pass and it was time for them to dress up in their disguise, if that was necessary for the delivery of his master. For they had told Sancho before that their disguise was of the greatest importance in the task of rescuing his master from the wretched life he had chosen, and they solemnly warned him not to tell the knight who they were. They also said that if Don Quixote asked, as they were sure he would, whether he had delivered the letter to Dulcinea, he was to say that he had done so; but as she could not read, she had sent her answer by word of mouth, commanding her knight, on pain of her displeasure, to return to her at once on an affair of great importance. By this plan they were sure they could bring him back to a better way of life and give him the possibility of soon becoming emperor or king. Sancho listened to all this talk and stamped it clearly on his memory, and thanked them warmly for promising to advise his master to become emperor. He also suggested that it would be best for him to go on in advance to find him and deliver his lady's answer, for, perhaps, that alone would be enough to bring Don Quixote away from the mountains, and they would then be spared all their trouble. They agreed with Sancho, and resolved to wait until he came back with news of his master. Sancho then went off into the mountain gorge and left them in a pleasant spot by a tiny stream of clear water shaded by overhanging rocks and trees.

It was the month of August, when in those parts the heat is very great, and it was about three in the afternoon when Sancho left them. The curate and the barber were resting in the shade at their ease when they heard the sound of a voice, not accompanied by any instrument, singing very sweetly and melodiously. The song surprised them, for they did not think this was the place in which to find so good a singer. The song ended in a deep sigh, and they listened attentively, in the hopes of hearing more, but the music changed into sobs and heart-rending lamentations, so they went in search of the unhappy person, whose voice was no less beautiful than his complaints were mournful. They had not gone far, when, in turning the corner of a rock they saw a man of the same figure that Sancho had described when he had told them the story of Cardenio. The man did not show astonishment when he saw them, but stood still with head bent upon his breast in a pensive posture; and after glancing once in their direction, he did not raise his eyes off the ground. The curate, who was a well-spoken man (being already acquainted with his misfortune), went up to him and in a few kind words begged him to abandon that wretched kind of life, lest he should meet with the greatest of all misfortunes, which was to perish in that lonely spot.

Cardenio, who at the moment was in his right mind, and quite free from his mad fit, replied: "Whoever you may be, good sirs, I see clearly that, unworthy as I am, Heaven sends to me in this lonely heath, far from human society, kind people, who would persuade me to depart with them and dwell in some better place. But they do not know, as I do, that by running away from my present wretchedness I shall fall into still greater misery. They probably consider me a fool or a madman, and no wonder, for my consciousness of my misfortune is so overwhelming and my ruin so complete, that at times I become like a stone devoid of all knowledge and sensation. I became aware of this when people showed me the traces left by me when this terrible madness masters me, but I can only lament in vain, curse my evil destiny and excuse my outrageous deeds by telling the cause of them to all who wish to listen to me. For wise men perceiving the cause will not wonder at the effects, and though they give me no remedy, yet at least they will not condemn me; for the anger they feel at my extravagances will turn to pity for my sufferings."

The curate and the barber, who wanted nothing better than to hear the cause of his misfortune from his own lips asked him to tell his story, and promised they would do nothing by way of remedy or consolation but what was agreeable to him.

Then Cardenio began his story, and told them all that he had told Don Quixote and the goatherd some days previously, but on this occasion there was no fit of madness to interrupt the tale, so that he had leisure to continue it to the end. When he reached the point about the letter which Don Fernando found in the book of *Amalis of Gaul,* Cardenio said that he knew it well by heart and that it was as follows:

Luscinda to Cardenio.

'Each day I discover in thee qualities which drive me to hold thee dear; and therefore, if thou wouldst desire to have me discharge this debt of mine, without serving a writ on my honour, thou mayst easily do it. I have a father who knows thee, and loves me likewise dearly. He, without forcing my inclinations, will grant whatever thou mayst justly wish for, if thou really dost value me as much as thou sayst and I believe.'

129

"It was this letter," continued Cardenio, "that moved me to ask Luscinda again in marriage; it was this letter, also, which kindled Don Fernando's desire to ruin me before my happiness could be complete. I told Don Fernando how Luscinda's father expected mine to ask for her hand, and how I dared not speak to my father about it for fear he would refuse his consent, not because he was ignorant of the beauty and worth of Luscinda, but because he did not wish me to marry so soon, or at least not until he had seen what the Duke Ricardo would do for me. Finally I told him that I dared not reveal it to my father because I was full of vague apprehensions and a sad foreboding that my desires would never be accomplished.

"Don Fernando then offered to speak on my behalf to my father and persuade the latter to ask for Luscinda's hand. How could I imagine that Don Fernando, a noble gentleman and my own friend, would take such malicious pains to deprive me of my one ewe-lamb? But so it was! Don Fernando, thinking that my presence was an obstacle to his plans, resolved to send me to his elder brother on the plea of borrowing some money from him to pay for six horses which Fernando had bought. Could I forestall such treachery? Could I even suspect it? Surely not: on the contrary, I cheerfully agreed to do his errand. That night I spoke with Luscinda, and told her what had been arranged between Don Fernando and myself, and I assured her that all would turn out well. And she, no more suspecting the treachery of Don Fernando than I did myself, begged me to return speedily, since she believed that our wishes would be accomplished as soon as my father made the marriage proposal. I know not whence it was, but as she spoke, her eyes filled with tears and a lump in her throat prevented her from uttering another word.

"I set out on my journey sorrowful and pensive, for my soul was full of gloomy thoughts and fears, and yet I did not know what I imagined or feared—clear tokens of the tragic misfortune that awaited me. I reached the town to which I was sent, and delivered my letters to Don Fernando's brother, who received me well but did not allow me to return home at once. Much to my disgust he delayed me there eight days, using the money as a pretext. This was all a trick of the false Fernando, for his brother had no lack of money with which to send me home at once. In this way I remained there, much to my sorrow, and it seemed to me impossible to endure life so many days apart from Luscinda, especially as I had left her in such a state of sadness.

"But four days later, there came a man in search of me with a letter, which, by the handwriting, I knew to be Luscinda's. I opened it, not without alarm, knowing that it must be some serious matter which would make her write to me, for she did it so rarely. I asked the bearer, before I read the letter, who had given it to him, and how long he had taken to make the journey. He replied that, passing by chance at midday through a street in the city, a very beautiful lady had called to him from a window. Her eyes were full of tears and she spoke hurriedly, saying: 'Brother, if you are a good man, as you seem to be, I pray you take this letter to a person named in the address, and if you do this you will perform a Christian act. And in case you want money to do it, take what you find wrapped up in this handkerchief.' 'With those words,' the messenger went on, 'she threw out of the window a handkerchief in which was wrapped a hundred reals, this gold ring which I am wearing, and the letter which I have given you. I made signs to her that I would do what she asked, and as I know you very well, sir, I determined not to trust any other messenger, but to deliver it with my own hands. And so I have made this journey, which you know is some eighteen leagues, in sixteen hours.'

"While the good-natured messenger was speaking, I stood trembling with the letter in my hand, until at last I took courage and opened it and read the following words:

'The promise Don Fernando gave thee, that he would persuade thy father to speak to mine, he has kept more for his own gratification than thy own interest. Know then that he has asked me in marriage, and my father, carried away by his rank and position, has accepted this proposal with such alacrity that the marriage is to be solemnized two days hence, and with such privacy that, except Heaven, only a few of our own family are to witness it. Imagine my feelings! Consider if thou shouldst not return at once. Whether I love thee or not the end of this affair will prove. God grant this may reach thy hand before mine is compelled to join his that keeps his promised faith so ill.'

"Such were the words of her letter, and they caused me at once to set out on my journey without waiting for the end of Don Fernando's business, for I knew now that it was not a matter of buying horses, but the pursuit of his own pleasure, that had led Don Fernando to send me to his brother. The fury I felt towards Don Fernando, joined to the fear I had of losing the jewel I had won by so many years of patient love, lent me wings, and I arrived at my native city as quickly as though I had flown, just in time to see and speak with Luscinda.

"I entered the city secretly, and left my mule at the house of the honest messenger who had brought my letter, and fortune was just then so propitious to me that I found Luscinda at the grating of the window, the constant witness of our loves. We saw each other—but how? Who is there in the world who can boast that he fathoms and thoroughly understands the confused thoughts and variable condition of women? None, I am sure. As soon as Luscinda saw me, she said: 'Cardenio, I am attired in wedding garments, and in the hall there waits for me the traitor and my covetous father, with other witnesses, who shall see my death rather than my marriage. Be not troubled, dear friend, but try to be present at this sacrifice. If my words cannot avert it, I carry a dagger hidden about me, which will be more decisive, for it will put an end to my life and thus give thee a proof of the love I have ever borne thee.'

"I answered her in great distress, saying: 'Sweet lady, if thou dost carry a dagger, I also carry a sword to defend thy life or to kill myself, should fortune be against us.' I do not think she could have heard those words, for she was called away, and I roused myself from my grief as best I could and went into the house, for I knew well all the entrances and exits. Owing to the confusion of the whole household nobody noticed me, and I managed to place myself in the recess formed by the window of the hall, which was covered by two pieces of tapestry drawn together. From there I could see all that went on in the hall without anyone seeing me.

"The bridegroom entered the hall, wearing his ordinary dress. His groomsman was a first cousin of Luscinda, and no one else was in the room but the servants of the house. In a little while Luscinda came out of her dressing-room, accompanied by her mother and two of her maids, adorned as her quality and beauty deserved and courtly pomp could afford. My agony of mind gave me no time to note what she wore. I was only able to note the colours, which were crimson and white; and I remember the glitter with which the jewels and precious stones shone in her head-dress and on every part of her robes. They were, however, surpassed by the singular beauty of her fair golden hair, in the glory of which the brilliance of her jewels and the blaze of the four torches in the hall seemed to be lost.

"When they were all assembled, the priest entered, and having taken each by the hand, asked: "Will you, Lady Luscinda, take the Lord Don Fernando for your lawful husband, as our Holy Mother the Church commands?' I thrust my head and neck out of the tapestry to hear what Luscinda answered. The priest stood waiting for a long time before she gave it, and then, when I expected that she would take out the dagger to stab herself, or unloose her tongue to utter one word of truth for my good, I heard her say in a faint and languishing voice: 'I will.'

"Then Don Fernando said the same, and, giving her the ring, the knot was tied. But when the bridegroom approached

132

to embrace her, she put her hand to her heart and fell fainting in her mother's arms.

"It only remains to tell in what a state I was, when in that 'I will' I heard all my hopes cheated, Luscinda's words and promises false, and myself debarred from evermore receiving what I lost in that instant. I burned with rage and jealousy. The whole household was in uproar when Luscinda fainted, and her mother, unfastening her bodice to give her air, found in her bosom a paper which Fernando seized and went aside to read by the light of a torch. When he had read it, he sat down in a chair, laying his hand upon his cheek with manifest signs of melancholy discontent, without attending to any of the remedies that were being applied to his spouse to bring her back to her senses.

"As I saw that all the household was in confusion, I ventured forth, not caring whether I was seen or not, but determined, if seen, to do so desperate an act that the whole world would understand the just indignation that was seething in my breast, by chastising the false Don Fernando and the fickle, swooning traitress. But my fate, to reserve me for greater misfortunes, if there can be greater, ordained that at that instant I had the use of my reason, which has since failed me. So instead of taking vengeance on my worst enemies (it would have been easy to do so, seeing that they were so ignorant of my presence), I determined to take it on myself, and condemn myself to the penalty they so richly deserved. I left the house and came to where I had left my mule. I had it saddled, and without a word of farewell to anybody I rode out of the city like another Lot, not daring to turn back and look at it again.

"All night I travelled, and about dawn I came to one of the passes of these mountains, through which I wandered for three days more, without road or path, until I came to a valley not far from here. Then I asked some herds where the most lonely part of the Sierra was, and they directed me to this spot, where I instantly resolved to spend the rest of my days. In one of these rocky passes my mule fell dead through weariness and hunger, or, what is more probable, to be delivered of so useless a burden. My usual dwelling-place is the hollow of a cork tree, which is large enough to shelter my wretched body. The goatherds, who live in the mountains, give me food out of charity, laying it on the rocks or on the ways where they think I shall pass. They tell me, when they meet me in my sane moods, that at other times I rush out into the paths and take from the shepherds by force those provisions which they would willingly give me. Thus I spend my miserable life, waiting until Heaven may be pleased to bring it to an end, or drive out of my memory all thoughts of the

133

beauty of Luscinda or the injury done me by Don Fernando. This, gentlemen, is my melancholy tale: do not trouble yourselves, I beg, to advise or persuade me, for it will produce no more effect than a medicine prescribed by a famous doctor for a patient who rejects it. I wish to have no health without Luscinda, and I feel certain that my woes cannot even end with death."

Here Cardenio finished his long, unfortunate love story.

XVII. The quaint and delightful adventure that befell the curate and the barber in the same Sierra

AS SOON AS CARDENIO HAD FINISHED HIS STORY, THE CURATE was about to say some words of comfort when he was prevented by hearing a mournful voice near by crying out: "Please God I may find here a secret burial-ground for this wretched body of mine. Here in this rocky desert I may die in peace. Alas, how miserable I am: I am happier in the company of these crags than in the society of faithless man, for nobody on earth can advise me in my difficulties, or redress my wrongs."

The curate and all those with him heard those words, and, thinking that the person who uttered them must be close at hand, they rose and began the search. Hardly had they gone twenty paces when they saw behind a big rock a boy sitting under an ash tree. He wore a peasant's dress, but, as he was bending down to wash his feet in a stream that flowed past, his head was turned away from them. They drew near so silently that he did not hear them, for his whole attention was absorbed in the task of bathing his legs in the brook. They wondered at the whiteness and beauty of his feet, which did not seem to have been made for treading the furrows or following the ox and plough, as his dress seemed to suggest. The curate, who went in front, made a sign to the others to crouch down, or hide themselves behind a rock, whence they could watch what he did. The youth was clad in a grey-coloured cape of two folds, girded closely round his body with a white towel; his breeches, gaiters and hunting-cap were of grey cloth. His gaiters were now pulled up and exposed his bare legs which were the colour of white alabaster. After bathing his delicate feet, he wiped them with a handkerchief which he took out of his cap, and in doing so he raised his head and showed to those who were looking at him a face of such incomparable beauty that Cardenio said in a low voice to the curate: "Since this is not Luscinda it can be no human creature." The youth then took off his cap, and shook his

134

head, whereupon a mass of hair, that the sun might have envied, fell about his shoulders. They then perceived that the peasant was a woman, yea, one of the most beautiful they had ever seen. Her golden locks fell down in such profusion that they not only covered her shoulders, but concealed all her body, except her feet; and her snowy fingers served her for a comb. Her beauty made the three onlookers impatient to find out who she was, and they now resolved to show themselves. At the sound they made in approaching, the maiden raised her head and thrust aside her tresses with both hands to see what it was that had startled her. No sooner did she perceive them than she rose hastily, and, without waiting to put on her shoes or tie up her hair, seized her bundle and started to run away full of alarm; but she had run six paces when her delicate feet, unable to bear the roughness of the stones, stumbled, and she fell to the ground.

The three ran to her assistance, and the curate was the first to speak to her, saying: "Stay, madam, whoever you are: those you see here have no wish but to help you. There is no reason for you to run away from us."

To this she made no reply, being ashamed and bewildered, but the curate, taking her by the hand, continued: "Madam, your hair reveals to us what your costume would conceal, a sure proof that it can be no slight cause that has hidden your beauty in such an unworthy disguise and brought you to this lonely place where we have found you. Let us at least offer you our advice and counsel in your distress, for kind words will be of service to you, no matter how great your sorrow. Tell us your good or evil fortune that we three may help you as best we can."

While the curate spoke the disguised lady stood like one stupefied, gazing at them fixedly without opening her lips, as if she were some village rustic, when he is suddenly shown some strange new sight. But as the curate said more to the same purpose, she gave a deep sigh and said: "Since these mountains cannot conceal me, and my dishevelled hair betrays my secret, it would be foolish for me to disguise my words. Therefore I thank you all, gentlemen, for your courteous offer of advice, and I will tell you something of my misfortunes, though I would far sooner draw the veil of silence over them."

All this she said in such a sweet voice, and in so sensible a manner, that they were still more charmed by her, and they again begged her to tell her story. To this she replied by putting on her shoes and binding up her hair, and seating herself upon a rock with her three hearers around her. Then, brushing away a few tears from her eyes, she began in a calm, clear voice the story of her life.

135

"In Andalusia there is a certain town from which a great Duke takes his name, which makes him one of our grandees, as they are called in Spain. He has two sons. The elder is heir to his estates, and apparently to his good qualities, the younger, heir to I know not what, unless it be his evil qualities. To this nobleman my parents are vassals, of humble degree, but still so rich that if nature had bestowed upon them birth equal to their wealth, I should not now be in this wretched state; for their want of rank is probably the cause of all my misfortunes. They are but farmers, plain, honest people, and of the kind called old, rusty Christians, who by their wealth and handsome way of living are by degrees acquiring the name of gentlemen. But what they valued above rank or riches was their daughter, sole heiress of their fortune; and I was always treated by them with the greatest indulgence and affection. I was the light of their eyes, the staff of their old age and the sole object of all their hopes. And as I was the mistress of all their affection, so also was I mistress of all their goods. It was I who engaged and dismissed the servants; I kept the account of all that was sown and reaped; the produce of their oil-mills, their wine-presses, their cattle and sheep, their beehives—in a word, of all that a rich farmer like my father could possess. I was both steward and mistress, and I performed my duties to their entire satisfaction. The spare hours that were left from management of the farm I spent in sewing, spinning and lace making, or else, when there was time, I would read some devout book or practise upon my harp, for it was my experience that music calms the troubled spirit. Such was the life I led in my father's house. I lived so busy and retired an existence that I might have been a cloistered nun; for when I went to Mass it was early in the morning, accompanied by my mother, and so heavily veiled that my eyes saw no more ground than the space where I set my feet. Nevertheless the eyes of love, or rather of idleness, sharper than those of a lynx, discovered that I had attracted the interest of Don Fernando, the younger son of the duke whom I mentioned to you."

No sooner did she mention the name of Don Fernando than Cardenio's face changed colour, and the curate and barber noticing it, feared that he would break out into one of his mad fits. But he remained quiet, fixing his eyes attentively on the maiden, suspecting who she was; while, she, without noticing Cardenio's excitement, continued her story.

"No sooner, then, had Don Fernando seen me than he was smitten with a violent passion as his behaviour soon showed. To shorten the account of my many misfortunes, I shall pass over in silence the devices Don Fernando employed to declare his love: he bribed all my servants, he gave gifts to my relations: every day was a festival in our street, and at night no one could sleep on account of his serenades. Innumerable letters from him came, I know not how, into my hands, full of amorous declarations and protestations. All of which, nevertheless, so far from softening my resistance, rather hardened it, as if he had been my mortal enemy: not that his importunate pleadings displeased me, for I confess that I felt flattered by the attentions of a gentleman of his high rank. Besides, we women, no matter how ugly we are, always love to hear men call us beautiful. However, it was my virtue which opposed all those temptations, and the continual admonitions of my parents, who had already clearly perceived the intentions of Don Fernando, for he had not cared whether the whole world should know it. My parents told me that they relied on my virtue and prudence, and at the same time they begged me to consider the inequality between myself and Don Fernando. Thus cautioned, I maintained the utmost reserve towards him, and never encouraged him in the hope of reaching his desires. But all my modest behaviour, which he took for disdain, only inflamed his lustful passion—that is the name I wish to give to it—if he had truly loved me, you would not have heard this tale of mine.

"Don Fernando having heard that my parents intended to give me in marriage to somebody, resolved to defeat their purpose. And one night as I was in my room, with the door locked and only my maid present, he suddenly appeared before me. I was so terrified at his presence that I lost the power of speech, and as I was about to faint he caught me in his arms. Then he began to plead with sighs and tears and with such a semblance of true affection that I, a poor, simple girl, without experience, began to put some faith in him, though I was far from moved by his protestations to anything more than pure compassion. When I recovered somewhat from my fears, I said to him: 'If my life depended on the sacrifice of my honour, I would not preserve it on such terms; and though I am within your arms, you have no power over my mind. I am your vassal—not your slave. Your noble rank does not give you the right to insult me, who have an equal claim to self-respect as you have yourself. I despise your riches and distrust your words; neither am I to be won by your sighs and tears. Had you obtained the sanction of my parents, and honourably demanded my hand, I might have listened to proposals—but to no others than those of a lawful husband.'

" 'If that be all, beauteous Dorothea,' said the treacherous man, 'here I pledge you my hand; and let all-seeing Heaven and that image of Our Lady witness the agreement.' Don Fernando then took up the holy image and called upon it to witness our betrothal, and he pledged himself by the most solemn vows to become my husband, though I begged him to consider how angry his father would be when he would know that he had married the daughter of one of his own vassals. On the morning that followed that fatal night, Don Fernando before he departed drew a valuable ring from his finger and put it on mine, promising that he would always be true to me, and from that moment I felt that I was betrothed to him, and that he truly intended to make me his wife, in spite of the duke's opposition. That treacherous man visited me only once more, though access was free to him, as I had become his own, and would remain so until he felt disposed to let the world know that I was his wife. I was unable to see him for a month, either in the street or in church, though I understood that he was still in the town. Ah, how sad and bitter those days and hours were to me, when I first began to doubt and disbelieve my lover's faith. I had to keep watch on my tears, and wear a happy face for fear my parents should find out the reason of my unhappiness. All this time of doubt, however, came to an end in an instant. For at last it was announced in the town that Don Fernando had married, in a neighbouring city, a damsel of great beauty and of noble birth called Luscinda, and there were many strange tales told of their wedding."

Cardenio, hearing the name of Luscinda, did nothing but shrug his shoulders, bite his lip, bend his brows and shed tears. But Dorothea did not interrupt the thread of her story, and continued: "When the sad news reached my ears, I was inflamed with rage and fury. I devised a plan which I put into execution that very night. I borrowed this apparel of a shepherd youth in my father's service, to whom I disclosed all my misfortunes and begged him to accompany me to the city where I understood my enemy sojourned. I packed up in a linen pillow-case some dresses and some money and jewels, and at night secretly left my father's house attended only by my servant. In two days and a half I arrived at my journey's end, and the first person I asked told me the whole story of Don Fernando's wedding. He told me that at the time of the wedding, after Luscinda had uttered her consent to be Fernando's wife, she had fainted, and there fell from her bosom a letter written in her own hand, in which she said that she could not be the wife of Don Fernando because she was betrothed to Cardenio, a gentleman of that city. The letter went on to say that she intended to kill herself at the end of the ceremony, and upon her was found a dagger, which seemed to bear out what she said. Don Fernando seeing this, and thinking that Luscinda had mocked and flouted him, would have stabbed her with the dagger, if her parents had not prevented him. After this, I was told that Don Fernando fled; and I learnt that Cardenio had been present at the wedding, and, hearing her words, had vanished from the city in despair, leaving a letter behind declaring the wrongs Luscinda had done to him. The whole city were talking of nothing else, and they talked still more when it was known that Luscinda was missing from her father's house, and that her parents had almost lost their reason in their distress.

"What I heard revived my hopes and I preferred not to have found Don Fernando than to have found him married; for it seemed that the door was not yet wholly shut against my relief. But before I left the city on my search, I was told there was a proclamation made by the public crier, offering a large reward for anyone who should bring me back to my parents. As soon as I heard the proclamation I left the city with my servant, who even then began to give tokens that he faltered in the loyalty he had promised to me, and both of us together entered that same night the thick woods of the mountain, fearing lest we might be found. But as they say, one evil calls another and misfortunes never come singly; for my servant, who up to this had been faithful and reliable, no sooner saw me in this lonely place than, dismissing all regard for God or his mistress, he began to make love to me. When I answered him with severe and bitter words, he would have used force, but merciful Heaven favoured me and gave me the strength to push him down a precipice, where I left him, whether dead or alive I know not, for, in spite of my terror and weariness, I fled from the spot with utmost speed. After that I took service with a herdsman and have lived for some months in these wilds, always endeavouring to be out of doors, so as to conceal those tresses which have now so unexpectedly betrayed me. Yet all my care was fruitless, for my master at last noticed that I was no man but a woman, and the same evil thoughts sprang up in his breast that had possessed my servant. In case I might not have found the same means to free myself from his violence, I sought my safety in flight, and have endeavoured to hide myself among these rocks. This, gentlemen, is my tragic story: consider whether the sighs and tears you have witnessed have not been more than justified."

When Dorothea had finished her story she remained silent, while her flushed face showed the shame and agony of her soul. Those who heard her speak were much affected by her tale, and the curate was about to comfort her, when

139

Cardenio interrupted him and took her by the hand, saying: "You, lady, then, are the beautiful Dorothea, only daughter of rich Clenardo?" Dorothea was amazed when she heard her father's name spoken by a person of such poverty-stricken appearance as Cardenio, and answered: "Who are you, friend, that you know my father's name so well? For, unless I am mistaken, I did not mention him once in my story."

"I am," said Cardenio, "the unlucky one to whom Luscinda was betrothed; and I, too, suffer, owing to the evil deeds of that man who betrayed you: you see me now reduced to nakedness and misery—deprived even of human pity, and, what is worst of all, minus my reason except when Heaven pleases. But the story you have told gives me hopes that there may yet be happiness for both of us. Luscinda has openly declared that she is mine and so cannot marry another; and Fernando cannot marry Luscinda because he is yours. And I vow, on the faith of a gentleman and a Christian, never to forsake you until I see you in the possession of Don Fernando."

The curate then begged them to accompany him to his village, where they might take counsel on the best measures to be adopted in their troubles; an offer which they gratefully accepted. The barber, who had hitherto been silent, now added his kind words of welcome, and he briefly related the reason which had brought them to that place and the extraordinary madness of Don Quixote. They were interrupted by the voice of Sancho Panza, who, not finding them where he had left them, was shouting as loudly as he could.

They went to meet him, and asked for Don Quixote. Sancho told them that he had found him almost naked, in his shirt, lean and yellow, half dead with hunger, and sighing for Lady Dulcinea: and although he had told him that she commanded him to travel to El Toboso, yet he declared that he had made up his mind not to appear before her until he had done deeds worthy of her favour.

The curate now told Cardenio and Dorothea their plan for Don Quixote's cure, or at least for decoying him to his own home. Upon which Dorothea said she would be better able to act the part of distressed lady than the barber, especially as she had clothes with which she could perform it to the life. She told them, furthermore, to put entire trust in her talents, as she had read many books of chivalry, and was well acquainted with the style in which distressed damsels were accustomed to beg their boons from knights-errant.

"The sooner we start our work the better," said the curate: "Fortune seems to be propitious to our undertaking." Dorothea straightway took from her bundle a dress of very rich stuff, a short mantle of showy green silk, and from a little casket she extracted a necklace and other jewels. With these she adorned herself so richly that she had all the air of a great lady. Her high spirits, her wit and beauty, charmed them all, and they agreed that Don Fernando must be a man of poor taste to have slighted such beauty. But her greatest admirer was Sancho Panza, who thought (and it was true) that never in his life had he seen so fair a creature. He earnestly begged the curate to tell him who the lady was, and what she was doing in these out-of-the-way places.

"This beautiful lady, brother Sancho," answered the curate, "is, to say the least, heiress in the direct male line of the great kingdom of Micomicon, and she has come in search of your master, to ask of him a boon, namely, to redress a wrong which a wicked giant has done to her. And owing to the fame of your master, which has spread through all lands, this beautiful princess has come all the way from Guinea to seek him."

"Happy search makes happy finding," said Sancho Panza: "especially if my master has the luck to undo the wrong by wiping out the whoreson giant you mention: kill him he surely will, if he meets him, unless he turns out to be a ghost, for he has no power over that kind. Now the important point is that my master should afterwards marry this lady—by the way, I don't know her grace, so I cannot call her by her name."

"Her name," answered the curate, "is Princess Micomicona, for her kingdom is called Micomicon. As to your master's marriage, I shall do my best to arrange it."

Sancho was no less satisfied with these answers than the curate was amazed at his simplicity, and to see how firmly he had fixed in his imagination the ravings of his master.

Dorothea had now mounted the mule, and the barber had fitted on his ox-tail beard, so they told Sancho to guide them to Don Quixote; and they warned him not to say that he knew the curate or the barber, since on that depended all his fortune, for, if he did, Don Quixote would never leave the mountain and would never become emperor. Neither the curate nor Cardenio would go with them; the latter, that he might not remind Don Quixote of their quarrel; the curate because his presence was not then necessary; so they let the others go on in front, while they followed slowly on foot.

Having travelled about three-quarters of a league, they found Don Quixote clothed, though still unarmed, in a wild, rocky spot. As soon as Sancho told Dorothea that this was Don Quixote, she whipped up her palfrey, closely followed by the barber, who jumped from his mule and ran to help his lady alight. Quickly dismounting, she threw herself on her knees before Don Quixote, and, refusing his attempts to raise her, spoke as follows: "Never will I rise from this position, most valiant and invincible knight, until thou dost grant me a boon, which will not only redound to thy honour and renown, but also benefit the most injured and disconsolate damsel that ever the sun beheld. And if the valour of thy mighty arm be equal to what I have heard of thy immortal fame, thou canst indeed give assistance to a luckless woman, who, attracted by the scent of thy great ability, comes from a far-distant land to seek thy help."

"Beauteous damsel," replied Don Quixote, "I will not answer one word nor hear aught of thy affairs till thou dost rise from the ground."

"I will not rise, my lord," answered the afflicted lady, "until I have obtained from thee the boon I beg."

"I grant it, dear lady, provided it be not anything detrimental to my King, my country, or to her who keeps the key of my heart and liberty."

"No injury will be done to any of them, my good lord," replied the downcast damsel.

Then Sancho Panza went up and whispered softly in his master's ear, saying: "Your worship may well grant the request she makes, for it is a mere trifle: all that is required is to polish off a huge brute of a giant, and she that demands it is the Princess Micomicona, Queen of the great kingdom of Micomicon in Ethiopia."

"Let her be what she will," said Don Quixote, "I will do my duty towards her." Then turning to the damsel, he said: "Rise, most beautiful lady, since I grant thee any boon thou wishest to ask of me."

"What I ask of thee," said Dorothea, "is that thy grace will at once accompany me whither I guide thee, and that thou shouldst promise me not to undertake new adventures until thou hast avenged me on the traitor who, contrary to all human and divine law, has usurped my kingdom."

"I grant thy request," said Don Quixote, "and therefore, lady, thou canst dispel the melancholy that oppresses thee, for this mighty arm of mine shall restore thee to thy kingdom."

The distressed damsel struggled to kiss his hand, but Don Quixote, who was a most courteous knight, would not permit it. He made her rise, and embraced her with much gentleness and courtesy.

He now ordered Sancho to tighten Rozinante's girths and help him to arm himself. Sancho took down the armour from a tree, where it hung like a trophy; and Don Quixote, when he was armed, cried out: "In God's name let us depart to assist this great lady."

The barber was still on his knees, trying his best to hide his laughter and to prevent his beard from falling off, for, if it had, their ingenious stratagem would perhaps have miscarried. Seeing that the boon was already granted and that Don Quixote was prepared to carry out his engagement, he got up and took his lady by the hand, assisted her to mount the mule, and when both he and Don Quixote had mounted, they were ready to start. As for Sancho, who trudged along on foot, he felt again the aching grief for the loss of Dapple, but he bore it cheerfully, reflecting that his master was on the way to marry a princess, and so become at least King of Micomicon; though he was sorry to think that country was populated by negroes, and that when he became a ruler his vassals would be black. But then remembering a special remedy, he said to himself: "What care I if my subjects be blacks? What have I to do but ship them off to Spain, where I may sell them for ready money with which I may buy some title or office, on which I may live at ease all the days of my life? No! I might as well go to sleep like a blockhead if I have not the gumption to sell thirty thousand niggers in the twinkle of an eye! By God! I'll make them fly, little and big: even if they're blacker nor coal I'll turn them into white and yellow boys with the true ring out of them. Come on, all of you: I'm licking my fingers already." After these reflections, he went on in such good spirits that he forgot about the fatigue of travelling on foot.

While this was going on, Cardenio and the curate, who had been hiding in the bushes, observed all that happened and now wanted to join them. The curate, who was a cunning plotter, devised an excellent expedient; for, with a pair of scissors which he carried in a case, he quickly cut off Cardenio's beard, then put on him a grey cape and gave him his own black cloak, while he himself remained in his breeches and doublet. Cardenio's appearance was thus so changed that if he had looked in a mirror he would not have known himself. When they caught up with Don Quixote and his party, the curate, after gazing for some time earnestly at the knight, at last ran towards him with open arms, crying out: "In a good hour is this meeting with my countryman, the mirror of knighthood, Don Quixote of La Mancha, flower and cream of nobility, protector of suffering mankind, quintessence of knight-errantry." Having uttered those words, he embraced Don Quixote on his left knee.

The knight was amazed at these words, and began to gaze closely at the features of the speaker. Then he recognized him as the curate, and would immediately have dismounted, but the latter refused to allow him. "Father," said he, "you must allow me to alight: 'tis not right that I should remain on horseback and so reverend a person as you travel afoot."

"I will on no account," replied the curate, "consent to your dismounting: for 'twas on horseback your grace performed the mightiest exploits this age has witnessed. As for myself, an unworthy priest, I shall be satisfied if one of these gentlemen of your retinue will allow me to mount behind him."

"I did not think of that, reverend father," answered Don Quixote, "but I know that my lady the princess will for my sake order her squire to lend you the saddle of his mule."

"I will most certainly," said the princess, "and I know that my squire is the last man to allow a priest to go afoot when he may ride."

"That is most certain," said the barber, and got off his mule at once.

The curate now mounted, but it unfortunately happened that, as the barber was getting upon the crupper, the mule, which was a hired one, and consequently a vicious jade, lifted up her hind legs twice or thrice in the air and kicked out with such fury that if she had knocked Master Nicholas on the chest or head he would have consigned his ramble after Don Quixote to the devil. He was, however, thrown to the ground, and as he rolled over, his beard fell off and lay on the ground: and all he could do was to cover his face with both hands, and cry out that his teeth were stove in. Don Quixote, seeing that huge mass of beard torn from the jaw without blood and lying at a distance from the squire's face, said: "This, I swear, is one of the greatest miracles I ever saw in my life. The beard has been whisked as clean from his face as if it had been shaven off."

The curate, seeing the risk they ran of their plan being found out, went over to where Master Nicholas was lying moaning and with one jerk clapped the beard on again, muttering as he did so some Latin words which, he said, were a charm for fixing beards.

Don Quixote was amazed at what he saw, and begged the curate to teach him that charm; for he was sure that as it wrought a perfect cure, it must be good for even more dangerous injuries. The curate agreed to teach him the art some other day.

They now agreed that the curate should mount first and all three should ride by turns until they came to the inn, which was about two leagues distant.

XVIII. Dorothea's inventiveness and other entertaining matters

THE THREE OF THEM WERE NOW MOUNTED—THAT IS TO SAY, Don Quixote, the princess and the curate, and three were on foot, namely, Cardenio, the barber and Sancho Panza. Don

Quixote said to the damsel: "Let your highness, madam, lead the way whither it most pleases thee."

But before she could answer, the curate said: "Towards what kingdom will you guide us? Will it be towards that of Micomicon? Methinks it must be so or I know little of kingdoms." She, being well versed in everything, knew that she had to answer "yes," so she said: "Yes, sir, my way lies towards that kingdom."

"If it be so," said the curate, "you must pass through the village where I live, and from thence you must take the road to Cartagena, where you may, with good fortune, embark. If there be a favouring wind, a calm sea and no storm, you will come in the space of nine years in sight of the great lake Meona—I mean Meotis—which is little more than a hundred days' journey from your highness' property."

"You are mistaken, good sir," said she, "for it is not two years since I departed from that place, and I assure you I have never had good weather, yet in spite of that I have managed to see what I so longed for, the famous Don Quixote of La Mancha, whose glory reached my ears the moment I set foot in Spain, and impelled me to seek him to commend myself to his courtesy and entrust my just cause to his invincible arm."

"No more," cried Don Quixote. "Cease, I pray, these encomiums. I am a sworn enemy to flattery, and though I know what thou sayest is the truth, yet do such discourses offend my chaste ears. What I can say, madam, is, that whether I have courage or not, I will use it in thy service, even were I to lose my life. But, waiving all this for the moment, tell me, Sir Licentiate, what has brought you to these parts, alone, without servants, and so lightly equipped that I am filled with amazement."

"To that," replied the curate, "I shall give a brief answer. Master Nicholas, the barber, and myself travelled to Seville to collect certain sums of money which a relative of mine, who many years ago went to the Indies, had sent me. And passing yesterday through these parts, we were set upon by four highwaymen, who stripped us to our very beards, and in such a manner that the barber thought fit to put on a false one; and as for this youth who is with us (pointing to Cardenio), they made him a new man. And the best of it all is that it is rumored hereabouts that those who robbed us were certain galley-slaves, who say they were set at liberty, almost in this very spot, by a man so valiant that, in spite of the commissary and the warders, he released them all. Doubtless he must be out of his wits, or he must be as great a knave as they, or else some fellow devoid of soul and conscience, to loose the wolf among the sheep, the fox among the hens, the fly amid the honey. He has defrauded justice and rebelled

145

against his King and natural lord, since he went against his just commands: he has, I say, robbed the galleys of their limbs and stirred up the Holy Brotherhood, which has been reposing these many years, and, finally, he has done a deed which may not be a gain to his body and may bring everlasting damnation to his soul."

Sancho had told the curate and the barber of the adventure of the galley-slaves, which his master accomplished with so much glory, and therefore the curate laid stress upon it in referring to it, to see what Don Quixote would say or do. The knight, however, did not dare to say that he had been the liberator of those worthies, but his colour changed at every word the curate spoke.

"Well, these," continued the curate, "were the fellows who robbed us, and may God out of His mercy pardon the man who hindered them from receiving the punishment they so richly deserved."

The curate had scarcely ended, when Sancho burst out: "Faith and skin, your reverence, he who did that deed was my master, and that not for want of warning, for I told him beforehand that it was a sin to deliver them, since they were all going to the galleys for being the most arrant rogues."

"Blockhead!" exclaimed Don Quixote; "it is not the duty of knights-errant to examine whether the afflicted, enslaved and oppressed whom they meet by the way are in evil plight and anguish because of crimes or misfortunes. Their concern is simply to relieve them because they are needy and in distress, looking at their sorrow and not at their rogueries. I came across a rosary or string of poor unhappy wretches, and I did for them what my religion demands of me; as for the rest, come what may: and saving the presence of his reverence and his holy office, if anyone sees aught amiss in what I have done, I say that he knows little of the principles of chivalry, and, furthermore, he lies like a misbegotten son of a whore, and this I will make him know with my sword, which can give the full answer." Saying this, he set himself firmly in his stirrups, and clapped down his morion; for the barber's basin, which he called Mambrino's helmet, he carried hanging at his saddle-bow until he could repair the damage it had received from the galley-slaves.

Dorothea, who had a sprightly wit, now understood Don Quixote's crazy humour, and that they all, with the exception of Sancho Panza, made fun of him, so she resolved to play her part, and, seeing him so enraged, she said to him: "Sir Knight, be pleased to remember the boon you promised me: you are bound by it not to engage in any other adventure, be it ever so urgent: so calm your wrath, for if his reverence had known that it was by your unconquered arm the galley-slaves were

146

freed, he would have put three stitches through his lips, and even bitten his tongue thrice, rather than have spoken a word of disparagement against you."

"That I dare swear," said the curate, "and I would even have snipped off one of my whiskers." [1]

"Madam," answered Don Quixote, "I will hold my peace and stifle the just anger which has risen in my breast, and will go quietly and peacefully until I have obtained for thee the promised boon. Tell me, therefore, without delay, what is thy grievance and who, how many, and of what kind are persons on whom I have to take due, sufficient and entire revenge."

To this Dorothea replied: "Willingly will I do what you ask, if the tale of my sorrows and misfortunes be not wearisome to you."

"Not in the very least, dear lady," answered Don Quixote.

To which Dorothea replied: "Well, then, will you all favour me with your attention?"

At this Cardenio and the barber drew near to hear the witty Dorothea invent her story, and likewise did Sancho, who was as much deceived by her as his master. She, after settling herself in her saddle, with a preliminary cough and various other gestures, began with much good humour to tell her story as follows: "In the first place, I would have you know, gentlemen, that my name is——" Here she paused a moment, for she had forgotten the name the curate had given her. He, however, came to her rescue, for he understood why she hesitated, and he said: "It is no wonder that your highness should be troubled and embarrassed in telling your misfortunes. Those who suffer deeply are wont to lose their memories, so that they even forget their own names, as seems to have happened to your ladyship, who has forgotten that she is called the Princess Micomicona, heiress of the great kingdom of Micomicon. With this hint your highness may easily recall all you wish to relate."

"That is true," answered the damsel, "and from now onwards I do not think it will be necessary to give me any more hints, for I shall be able to bring my truthful story to a safe conclusion. The King, my father, was called Tinacrio the Sage, and was very learned in what they call the magic art. He discovered by his science that my mother, Queen Xaramilla, would die before him, and that soon afterwards he also should depart from this life and I be left an orphan, without father or mother. He used to say, however, that this did not trouble him so much as the knowledge that a certain mammoth giant, called Pandafilando of the Sour Face, lord of a great island near our border, when he should hear that I was an orphan would cross over with a mighty force into my kingdom and

[1] In the days of Cervantes the clergy, who are nowadays clean-shaved, all wore moustaches and chin-tufts. (Clemencin.)

take it from me, without leaving me even a tiny village in which to take refuge; but that I could spare myself all this disastrous ruin if I married him. My father warned me that when this came to pass I should not stay to defend myself, and so cause the slaughter of all my loyal subjects, but should set out at once for Spain, where I should find relief in my distress as soon as I met a knight-errant whose fame would then extend through all that kingdom. His name would be, if I remember rightly, Don Azote or Don Gigote." [2]

"Don Quixote, you mean, lady," cried Sancho Panza; "otherwise called the Knight of the Rueful Figure."

"That is true," answered Dorothea. "He said, furthermore, that he was tall of stature, with a withered face, and on his right side, under the left shoulder, or near to it, he would have a grey mole with some hairs like bristles on it."

On hearing this, Don Quixote said: "Hold my horse, son Sancho, and help me to strip, for I wish to know if I am the knight of whom the wise King prophesied."

"Why do you wish to strip?" said Dorothea.

"To see if I have that mole of which your father spoke," answered Don Quixote.

"No need to strip," said Sancho: "I know your worship has a mole of that same kind in the middle of your backbone; 'tis a sign that you're a sturdy man."

"That is enough," said Dorothea, "for among friends we should not be too particular. Whether it is on your shoulder or on your backbone is of little consequence: it is enough that there is a mole, and let it be where it please, since it is all one flesh. And, indeed, the moment I landed at Osuna I heard so many of your exploits that my heart at once told me you were the man I had come to seek."

"But, dear lady," said Don Quixote, "how didst thou land at Osuna, seeing that it is not a seaport?"

Before Dorothea could reply the curate interposed, saying: "Her highness meant to say that, after she had landed at Málaga, Osuna was the first place where she heard news of you."

"That is what I meant to say," said Dorothea.

"Now we are all set fair," said the curate: "let your majesty continue."

"Nothing remains for me to say," answered Dorothea, "save that having had the good fortune to meet the noble Don Quixote, I already consider myself Queen and Mistress of my whole kingdom, since he, out of his courtesy and generosity, has granted my request of going wherever I may please to lead

[2] "Azote" means a whip. "Gigote" (French "gigot") meant originally, according to Covarrubias, the flesh of a sheep's leg. The word is applied to "quijote"—the thigh-piece of armour.

him. And I shall straightway conduct him into the presence of Pandafilando of the Sour Face, that he may kill and restore to me all that has been so unjustly usurped. For all this must come to pass to the letter as the wise Tinacrio, my father, has foretold. And, moreover, if the knight of the prophecy, when he has cut off the giant's head, should wish to marry me, I should consent at once, without demur, to become his lawful wife, and give him possession of my kingdom together with my person."

"What do you think of this, friend Sancho?" said Don Quixote. "Did I not tell you so? See how we have a kingdom now to rule and a queen to marry."

"Faith an' I'll swear we have," said Sancho. "May a curse light on the whoreson knave who doesn't wed the moment Sir Pandahilado's weasand is slit: the Queen's a poor-looking baggage, is she? Faith an' I wish all the fleas in my bed were no worse!" And so saying he cut a couple of capers, and showed every sign of delight. Then catching the reins of Dorothea's mule and making her stop, he fell down on his knees before her and begged her to give him her hand to kiss in token that he acknowledged her as his Queen and Mistress. The rest of the party with the greatest difficulty managed to hide their laughter to see the madness of the master and the simplicity of the man. Dorothea gave him her hands and promised to make him a great lord in her kingdom when Heaven should permit her to recover and enjoy it. Sancho then uttered such words of thanks that they all increased their laughter.

"O exalted and noble lady," cried Don Quixote, "I confirm again the boon I promised thee, and I swear I shall go with thee to the end of the world until I meet that fierce enemy of thine, whose proud head I intend, with God's help and my right arm, to cut off with the blade of this—I will not say good sword, thanks to Ginés de Pasamonte, who carried off my own." These words he uttered in a low tone; then raising his voice he said: "And after I have cut it off and restored thee to thy realm in peace, how thou wilt dispose of thine own person will depend upon thy discretion, for so long as I keep my memory engrossed, my will enslaved and my mind enthralled by her—I say no more—it is impossible for me to think of facing the thought of marriage, even if it were with the Phoenix itself."

Sancho was so disgusted at his master's refusal to marry that he raised his voice and cried out angrily: "By my soul, Sir Don Quixote, I swear your worship is not in your right senses. How else is it possible for you to have any hesitation about marrying so high a princess as this one here? Do you imagine fortune is going to offer you at every corner such a piece of good luck as she holds out now? Do you by any

chance think my Lady Dulcinea is more beautiful? By no
means, not by a long chalk. Faith an' I'll hold that she don't
come up to the shoe of this lady here. Bad 'cess to it! A fair
chance I have of getting my grip on the countship if you, sir,
go fishing for mushrooms at the bottom of the sea: [3] get married—get married at once, in the devil's name, and clutch a
hold of this kingdom which is dropping into your hands free,
gratis and for nothing. Then when you are king, make me a
marquis, a governor, and to hell with 'em all!"

Don Quixote, when he heard these blasphemies against his
lady, could not bear it any longer, so, raising his lance, without speaking a word to Sancho or by your leave, he gave him
two such blows that he stretched him flat on the ground; and
if Dorothea had not called out to him not to give the fellow
any more, he would have killed his squire there and then.

"Do you imagine, foul serf," said he after a pause, "that
you are always going to be allowed to take me by the breech,
and that all the sinning is to be on your side and the pardon-
ing on mine? Then give up thinking so, you excommunicated
rogue, for I am sure that is what you are, since you have let
your tongue rip against the peerless Dulcinea. Do you not
know, rascally drudge, that if it were not for the valour she
infuses in mine arm, I would not have enough strength to kill
a flea? Tell me, mocker of the viperish tongue, who do you
think has won this kingdom, and cut off the head of this giant,
and made you marquis (for all this I consider already accomplished), if it be not the power of Dulcinea using my arm as
the instrument of her deeds? She fights in me, and conquers
in me, and I live and breathe, and have my life and being in
her. O whoreson rascal, how ungrateful you are when you see
yourself raised from the dust of the earth to be a titled lord,
and respond to such a benefit by speaking ill of her who bestowed it upon you!"

Sancho was not too much hurt to hear what his master said.
He jumped up nimbly and ran behind Dorothea's palfrey, and
from there said to his master: "Tell me, sir, if you are not
going to marry this great princess, it is clear the kingdom will
not be yours—what favours then will you be able to bestow
on me? That is what I'm complaining of. Marry once and for
all this Queen, now that we have her here—rained down as it
were from the sky—and ye may later on go back to my Lady
Dulcinea, for there must be plenty of kings in the world
who've kept mistresses. As to the matter of beauty, I've nought
to say on that score; but, if you ask me the truth, I'm of the

[3] "Pedir cotufas en el golfo" was a proverb meaning to seek for the
impossible. "Cotufas" and "chufas" were the tubers of a kind of sedge
which was a dainty in Valencia. It served to make the popular Spanish
drink called "horchata."

opinion that they're both fine, though I've never seen the Lady Dulcinea."

"How, you wicked blasphemer, you have not seen her!" cried Don Quixote. "Did you not just now bring me a message from her?"

"I mean," replied Sancho, "that I didn't see her long enough to judge of her beauty, and her good parts, piece by piece; but in the lump she looked well enough."

"Now I forgive you," said Don Quixote; "and do you forgive my wrath towards you, for first impulses cannot be curbed at will."

"I see that only too clearly," answered Sancho, "and in my case the longing to talk is the first impulse: I can't help blurting out what comes to the tip of my tongue."

"Nevertheless," said Don Quixote, "take heed, Sancho, what you say, for 'the pitcher that goes so often to the well'—I say no more."

"Well, then," answered Sancho, "God is in Heaven, who sees all our trickery; He'll judge who does most harm—I in not speaking well or you, sir, in not doing so."

"No more of this," said Dorothea. "Go, Sancho, kiss your master's hand and beg his pardon. For the future be more cautious in your praises and in your disparagements: speak no evil of that Lady Tobosa, whom I do not know except that I am her humble servant. Put your trust in Heaven and you will get an estate to live upon like a prince."

Sancho went up hanging his head and begged his master's hand, who gave it with a grave air, and, after he had kissed it, Don Quixote gave him his blessing and told him to go on a little, for he had something to enquire about and things of great importance to discuss with him. Sancho did so, and, the two going a little away from the rest, Don Quixote said: "Since your return I have had no time to question you concerning the message which you bore and the answer you brought back: now that fortune allows us time and place, do not deny me the happiness which you are able to give me by your good tidings."

"Ask me what you please, sir," answered Sancho: "I bet I'll get out as well as I got in; but I beg you, sir, not to be so full of revenge in the future."

"What do you mean, Sancho?" said Don Quixote.

"I mean," replied Sancho, "that the blows you gave me a moment ago were more on account of the quarrel the devil raised between us the other night than for what I said against my Lady Dulcinea whom I love and reverence like a relic, though to be sure she is not one, only because she belongs to you."

"No more of this, Sancho," said Don Quixote, "for it

offends me. I pardoned you then and you know the common saying—'new sin, new penance.'"

Just at this moment they saw a man coming along the road towards them, riding upon an ass, and as he came nearer he appeared to be a Gypsy; but Sancho Panza, who, when he saw an ass, followed it with eyes and heart, had no sooner caught sight of the man than he recognized Ginés de Pasamonte, and by the thread of the Gypsy he discovered the reel, his ass. This was the truth, for it was Dapple on which Pasamonte was riding, who, to avoid being recognized, and to sell the ass, had dressed himself up like a Gypsy, for he understood the language of that folk as well as many other tongues as if they were his own. Sancho saw and knew him, and no sooner had he recognized him than he called out loudly to him: "Ah, Ginesillo the robber! Give up my jewel, let go my darling, don't rob me of my comfort. Return me my ass, give up my delight! Clear off, whoreson thief, and hand over what is not your own!"

There was no need for so many words and menaces, for at the very first Ginés jumped down, and, making off at a racing speed, in a moment fled away and disappeared. Sancho ran to his Dapple, and embracing him, cried: "How have you been my darling, Dapple of my eye, my sweet companion?" Then he kissed and fondled him as if he had been a human creature. The ass held his peace and allowed himself to be kissed and caressed by Sancho without answering a word. They all came up and congratulated him on having found Dapple, especially Don Quixote, who told him that he would still give him the three ass-colts, for which Sancho thanked him.

While the knight and his squire rode on ahead, the curate said to Dorothea that she had acted very cleverly both in the conciseness of her story, and in its resemblance to the books of chivalry. She said she had often amused herself by reading them, but she did not know where lay the provinces and seaports, and therefore she had made a guess when she said that she had landed at Osuna.

"So I understood," said the curate, "and therefore I hastened to set it right. But is it not strange to see how readily this unfortunate gentleman believes all these lying fictions, merely because they resemble the style and manner of his foolish books? Another remarkable thing about it is that, notwithstanding the absurdities this worthy gentleman utters in matters touching his madness, if other topics be discussed, he discourses on them most rationally and shows himself possessed of a clear judgment and an excellent understanding."

XIX. The delightful conversation between Don Quixote and his squire Sancho Panza, and other happenings

WHILE THE REST OF THE COMPANY WERE ENGAGED IN SUCH conversation, Don Quixote addressed Sancho as follows: "Friend Sancho, let bygones be bygones: put away all angry and spiteful thoughts and tell me where, when and how you found Dulcinea? What was she doing? What did you say to her? How did you talk to her? What answer did she make? How did she look when she read my letter? Who copied it for you? Tell me all, without adding a jot or lying to give me pleasure, for I wish to know everything."

"Master," replied Sancho, "if I must speak the truth nobody copied out the letter, for I carried no letter at all."

"That is true," said Don Quixote, "for I found the pocket-book, in which it was written, two days after your departure. I was very troubled thereat, for I did not know what you would do without the letter. I believed that you would return as soon as you missed it."

"I would have done so," said Sancho, "had I not learnt it by heart when you read it to me, so that I repeated it to a parish clerk, who copied it out of my head, word for word, so exactly that he said that in all his life he had never read such a pretty letter."

"Do you still remember it by heart?" asked Don Quixote.

"No, sir," answered Sancho, "for after I gave it, seeing that it was of no further use, I let myself forget it. If I remember, it had 'Suffering'—I mean 'Sovereign Lady,' and the ending: 'Thine till death, the Knight of the Rueful Figure.' Between those two things I put in three hundred hearts and loves and mine eyes."

"All this does not displease me, so continue,'" said Don Quixote. "You arrived; now what was the Queen of Beauty doing? Surely you found her stringing pearls or embroidering some device with golden threads for this her captive knight."

"No, that I did not," answered Sancho, "she was winnowing two bushels of wheat in a back-yard of her house."

"Why, then," said Don Quixote, "you may reckon that each grain of wheat was a pearl when touched by her hands; did you note, my friend, the wheat—was it the white or brown sort?"

" 'Twas neither, but red," answered Sancho.

"Then I assure you," said Don Quixote, "that, winnowed

by her hands, it made the finest white bread. But go on; when you gave her my letter: did she kiss it? Did she put it upon her head? [1] Did she use any ceremony worthy of such a letter? Or what did she do?"

"When I went to give it to her," answered Sancho, "she was all set on her job, winnowing away with a power of wheat in her sieve, and says she to me: 'Lay down that letter on yon sack: I can't read it till I've sifted all that's here.' "

"Cunning lady!" cried Don Quixote, "she must have done that so that she might read and enjoy it at leisure; go on then, Sancho, and tell all she said about me, and what you said to her: leave not a drop in the inkhorn."

"She asked me nothing," replied Sancho, "but I told her the state you were in for her sake, doing penance for her, naked from the waist upwards, shut up among these rocks like a savage, sleeping on the ground, eating bread without a table-cloth, never combing your beard, but spending your time weeping and cursing your fortune."

"There you were wrong," said Don Quixote. "I do not curse my fortune, but rather bless it, for it has made me worthy of the love of so high a lady as Dulcinea del Toboso."

"Aye, so high is she," answered Sancho, "that she's a good hand taller than I am."

"How is that, Sancho?" said Don Quixote; "have you measured with her?"

"Aye," answered Sancho, "for when I was helping her raise a sack of wheat on to an ass, we came so close together that I couldn't help seeing that she was taller than me by a good span."

"True," answered Don Quixote, "her stature is adorned with a thousand million graces of soul. Now there is one thing you must not deny me, Sancho. When you approached her, did you not perceive a Sabaean odour, an aromatic fragrance, something sweet—I cannot find a name to describe it—a scent, an essence, as if you were in some dainty glove shop." [2]

"All I can vouch for," said Sancho, "is that I got a whiff of something rammish and manlike: this must have been because she was a-sweating and a bit on the run."

"It could not have been that," answered Don Quixote, "but you must have had a cold in your head or else smelt yourself; for I know well the scent of that rose among thorns, that lily of the fields, that liquid amber."

"That may be so," answered Sancho, "for many a time I've noticed the same smell off myself as I perceived off her lady-

---

[1] To put a letter on the head before opening it signified to do the writer the greatest possible honour.

[2] It was the custom in those days for glovers to scent the gloves.

154

ship Dulcinea; but there's no wonder in that, for one devil is the dead spit of another."

"Well, then," continued Don Quixote, "now that she has done sifting her wheat and has sent it to the mill: what did she do when she read the letter?"

"She did not read it," answered Sancho, "for she said she could neither read nor write. She tore it up into tiny pieces, saying that she did not wish to give it to anybody to read, for fear her secrets might be known all over the village. She said it was enough to hear what I had told her by word of mouth about your love for her, and all you were doing for her sake, and finally she begged me to tell you, sir, that she kissed your hands, and that she was more eager to see you than to write to you. And that she prayed and commanded you on sight of this present to leave these thorn-bushes, give up your mad moonshining and set out at once on the road to El Toboso, unless something else of greater importance turns up, for she had a mighty longing to see you. She laughed a good deal when I told her they called you the Knight of the Rueful Figure. I enquired whether that chap, the Biscayan, had been there with her. She said 'yes', and that he was a decent fellow. I asked also about the galley-slaves, but she said she had not yet seen any of them."

"So far so good," said Don Quixote, "but tell me, what jewel did she bestow upon you at your departure as a reward for the news you had brought her? For it is a well-known, ancient custom among knights-errant and their ladies to give to their squires, damsels, or dwarfs who bring good tidings, some rich jewel as a reward for their welcome news."

"That may be so," replied Sancho; "and a good custom it was, I'm thinking; but it must have been in the days gone by, for nowadays 'tis only customary to give a chunk of bread and cheese, for that was what my Lady Dulcinea gave me over the palings of the yard, when I took my leave of her; and, by the way, 'twas plain ewe's milk cheese."

"She is wonderfully generous," said Don Quixote; "and if she did not give you a gold jewel, it was doubtless because she had none there with her; but as the proverb says, 'sleeves are good even after Easter'.[3] When I see her, all will be set right. Do you know, Sancho, what amazes me? The swiftness of your return: why, it seems to me as if you went and came back through the air, for you have been away only a little more than three days, although El Toboso is more than thirty leagues from hence. Therefore I am convinced that the wise magician, who takes care of my affairs and is my friend, must have helped you in your journey without

[3] "Buenas son las mangas después de Pascua." A proverb meaning "better late than never."

your being aware of it. Remember there are wizards who snatch up a knight-errant sleeping in his bed, and without his knowing how, he awakes the next day more than a thousand leagues from the place where he fell asleep. If it were not for this, knights-errant would not be able to help one another in their perils as they do now on all occasions. For one may be fighting in the mountains of Armenia with some dragon or fierce serpent, or some other knight, where he is getting the worst of the battle, and is at the point of death. Then, just when he least expects it, he sees another knight, his friend, descend from somewhere on top of a cloud, or in a chariot of fire, who was shortly before in England; he helps him and delivers him from death. All this is done by the skill and wisdom of those wise enchanters who look after valorous knights. So I do not find it difficult to believe that you went to El Toboso and back, since, as I have said, some friendly wizard must have flown through the air with you without your being aware of it."

"That may be so," said Sancho, "for I give you my word Rozinante went as if he had been a Gypsy's ass with quicksilver in his ears."[4]

"With quicksilver you say," answered Don Quixote, "aye, and with a legion of devils besides, for they are folk who travel and make others travel without being tired, as far as they please. But putting all this aside, what do you think I ought to do about my lady's order to go and see her?"

"God save us, sir!" said Sancho, "what a pitiful state your worship's poor brain is in, to be sure! Tell me, sir, do you intend to travel to El Toboso for nothing, and to let slip so rich and rare a match as this one, where they give you a kingdom in dowry? Why, I've heard say that it's more than twenty thousand leagues round about, and stored with lashings of all that life requires—aye, and bigger it is than Portugal and Castile lumped together. Hush, for the love of God! Be ashamed of what you've said, and take my advice (pardon me) and marry her in the first village that has a parish priest. If not, let the curate here do it, and remember that I'm of age to give advice and what I'm giving you now comes pat, for better sparrow in hand than a vulture on the wing,[5] and he that has good and chooses ill, 'tis only his fault if he chooses ill."

"Look here, Sancho," answered Don Quixote, "if you advise me to marry so that I may be king when I have slain the giant and be able to bestow upon you the favours I

---

[4] To put quicksilver in an animal's ear to make him go faster, is still a Gypsy trick in Spain today.

[5] Our familiar equivalent is "a bird in the hand is worth two in the bush."

promised, you must know that I can do that without marrying, for I will impose an extra condition before going into battle, namely, that upon my coming off a conqueror, they shall give me as my fee a portion of the kingdom, even if I do not marry the princess, and this I can give anyone I please; to whom would you have me give it if not to you?"

"That is clear," answered Sancho; "but mind, sir, you select it towards the sea, so that if the life doesn't suit me, I may be able to ship away my nigger subjects and do with them what I said before. Don't worry yourself to go just now to see Lady Dulcinea, but go off and kill the giant and let us make an end of this job, for I'm sure it will bring great honour and profit."

"I tell you, Sancho," said Don Quixote, "that you are in the right: I will follow your advice by going first with the princess rather than visiting Dulcinea."

At this moment Master Nicholas the barber shouted to them to wait awhile, for they wanted to halt and drink at a small spring near by. Don Quixote stopped, to Sancho's great relief, for he was by this time tired of telling so many lies, and feared that his master would trip him so with his own words. For although he knew that Dulcinea was a peasant lass of El Toboso, yet he had never seen her in all his life. They all dismounted near the fountain and with the scanty provisions the curate had brought from the inn they satisfied, as best they could, their great hunger.

While they were thus engaged, a young lad passed by who looked very earnestly at all those who sat around the spring, and after a moment ran up to Don Quixote, and, embracing his legs, began to weep bitterly, saying: "Ah, my lord! Do you not know me? Look at me closely. I am the boy Andrew whom you loosed from the oak tree to which I was tied."

Don Quixote recognized him at once, and taking him by the hand, turned to those who were present, and said: "To show you all how important it is to have knights-errant in the world to set right the wrongs and injuries which are done by insolent and wicked men, you must know that a few days ago, as I rode through a wood, I heard some cries and very piteous lamentations as of a person afflicted and in distress. I hastened instantly to the place, and there I found tied to an oak this boy whom you see here. This rejoices my heart, for he will check me if I do not speak the truth. I say that he was tied to an oak tree, stark naked from the waist upwards, and a doltish fellow, whom I afterwards learnt to be his master, was scourging him with the reins of his mare. As soon as I saw him I asked the master the reason for his cruelty. The boor replied that he was flogging him because he was his servant, and that he had been guilty of carelessness due rather to rascality than stupidity. The lad then said: 'Sir, he beats me only because I ask him for my wages'. The master then made a number of speeches and excuses, which I heard but did not believe. I made him at once untie the boy, and forced him to swear an oath that he would take him home and pay him every real upon the nail, aye, and perfumed too. Is this not true, Andrew, my son? Did you not notice the authority with which I ordered him, and how humbly he promised to do my bidding? Answer. Do not hesitate. Tell these gentlemen what happened, that they may learn how necessary it is to have knights-errant on the road."

"All that you say is very true, sir," answered the boy, "but the end of the business was very different to what you imagine."

"How different?" asked Don Quixote. "Did the boor not pay you then?"

"He not only did not pay me," answered the boy, "but no sooner had you gone out of the wood, and we were alone again, than he tied me to the same tree and gave me afresh so many stripes that left me flayed like Saint Bartholomew. And at each stroke he cracked some joke to make a mock of you, sir, and if I hadn't felt such pain, I'd have laughed at what he said. As a matter of fact he left me in such a state that I have been in hospital ever since, getting myself cured of the injuries which that rascally boor did me. For all this you, sir, are to blame, for if you had ridden on your own way, and not meddled in other folk's affairs, perhaps my master would have been content to give me a dozen or two stripes, and then he would have let me go and paid me what he owed. But, because you abused him so unreasonably, and called him so many foul names, his anger rose, and as he could not revenge himself on you, as soon as he was alone, he let loose the storm upon me, in such a manner that I'm afraid I'll never be a man again as long as I live."

"The trouble was," said Don Quixote, "that I went away. I should not have departed until I had seen you paid, for I might well have known that no churl will keep his word if he finds it does not suit him to keep it. Nevertheless, Andrew, you do remember how I swore that if he did not pay you, I would return and seek him out and find him, even if he should hide himself in the belly of a whale."

"That is true," replied Andrew, "but it was all of no use to me."

"You will see presently whether it is of use or not," said Don Quixote. And so saying he got up hastily and commanded Sancho to bridle Rozinante, who was feeding while they ate. Dorothea asked him what it was he meant to do. He answered that he meant to go in search of the boor and punish him for his bad conduct, and make him pay Andrew to the last farthing, in spite of all the boors in the world. She answered, begging him to remember that he could not undertake any other adventure, according to his promise, until he had finished hers, and as he knew this better than anyone else, he would have to stifle his anger until he returned from her kingdom.

"That is true," answered Don Quixote; "and Andrew must have patience until I return, for once more I vow and promise afresh never to rest until he is satisfied and paid."

"I don't believe these vows," said Andrew; "I'd sooner at the present moment have enough money as would help me on my way to Seville than all the revenge in the world. Give me something to eat, and take with me, and may God be with you, sir, and with all knights-errant, and may they be as erring to themselves as they have been to me."

Sancho took out of his bag a chunk of bread and cheese, and, giving it to the lad, said: "Take it, brother Andrew, for each of us has a share in your misfortune."

"What share have you in it?" said Andrew.

"This share of bread and cheese which I give you," answered Sancho, "for God knows whether I shall have need of it again or not. For I'd like you to know, my friend, that we squires to knights-errant suffer great hunger and rough luck, aye, and other things which are rather felt than told."

Andrew grabbed his bread and cheese, and, seeing that nobody gave him anything else, bowed his head and took the road in his hands, as the saying is.

But before he went, he said to Don Quixote: "For the love of God, sir knight-errant, if you meet me again, even though you see me being cut to pieces, do not come to my aid, but leave me to my misfortunes. No matter how great they are they will not be as great as those that spring from your help, and may God lay a curse on you and all the knights-errant that ever were born in the world."

Don Quixote jumped up to chastise him, but he set off running so fast that no one attempted to follow him. Don Quixote was much ashamed at Andrew's story, and the others made great efforts not to burst out laughing, and so put him to utter confusion.

When they had finished their welcome repast they saddled at once and, without any adventure of note, they arrived next day at the inn which was Sancho Panza's dread and terror, and though he would rather not have entered it, yet he could not avoid doing so. The landlord, the hostess, her daughter, and Maritornes, seeing Don Quixote and Sancho return, went to welcome them with affection and joy. The knight received them with solemn courtesy and told them to prepare a better bed than they gave him the last time; to which the landlady replied that if he paid better than the last time she would give him one fit for princes. Don Quixote answered that he would, and they prepared a reasonably comfortable bed for him in the same cock-loft where he had lain formerly. Then he went off to bed at once, because he was tired and weary, both in body and mind. He had hardly locked himself in when the landlady rushed at the barber and, seizing him by the beard, she cried: "By the Cross, my tail will no longer be used for your beard: give me back my tail: my husband's thingummy is lying about on the floor—which is a disgrace—I mean his comb, which I used to stick in my tail."

The barber would not give it to her, though she tugged away until the curate told him to hand it over to her as they no longer needed that disguise. The barber might now appear in his own shape and tell Don Quixote that after he had been robbed by the galley-slaves he had fled for refuge to this inn. As for the princess's squire, they could say that she had sent him on in advance to give notice to those of her kingdom that she was on her way back bringing with her one who would give them all their freedom. On this the barber willingly gave up the tail to the landlady, together with the other things they had borrowed for Don Quixote's liberation.

All the people in the inn were struck with Dorothea's beauty and the handsome appearance of the shepherd-boy Cardenio. The curate made them prepare the tastiest dinner the inn could provide, and the landlord, in the hope of better payment, got ready in a short time a reasonably good meal. All this was done while Don Quixote slept, and they were of opinion that it was best not to wake him, for they thought it would do him more good to sleep than to eat.

XX. *Don Quixote and his company at the inn*

DON QUIXOTE WAS STILL SLEEPING WHEN THE DINNER WAS served, and the company, consisting of the landlord, his wife, his daughter and Maritornes as well as the travellers, talked at table of the knight's strange craze and of the condition in which they had found him. The landlady told them of what had happened between him and the muleteer, and, glancing round to see if Sancho was present, and not seeing him, she told them the tale of his tossing in the blanket to the great amusement of the whole company.

The curate then said that it was the books of chivalry which had turned Don Quixote's head.

"I don't know how that can be," said the landlord, "for in my opinion there is no finer reading in the world, and I've two or three of them here with other writings, which have truly been the breath of life to me, and to many others. When it is harvest time, the reapers often do gather during the midday heat, and there is always someone able to read who takes up one of those books. Then about thirty of us gather round him, and we sit listening to him with so much delight that it keeps off a thousand grey hairs. Speaking for myself, when I hear tell of those furious and terrible blows which the knights hand out, I'm longing to be doing the same myself, and I'd like to be listening to them day and night."

"I'm of the same opinion," said the landlady. "I never have a quiet moment in the house except when you are listening to the reading, for then you're so bemused that you forget to scold me."

"That's the honest truth," said Maritornes, "and I, too, love to hear those lovely goings on, especially when they tell how a lady is lying under an orange tree wrapped in the arms of her knight, and the duenna keeping guard for them, dying of envy herself and all of a dither. I tell you 'tis as sweet as honey."

"And what about you, young lady?" said the curate to the landlady's daughter.

"Ah, Father," said she, "I don't know. I also listen to them, and though I don't understand, I take pleasure in hearing them. But I don't like the blows which delight my father; only the lamentations which the knights make when they are away from their ladies sometimes make me weep, so much pity do I feel for them."

"Would you mend their sorrows then, young gentle-woman," said Dorothea, "if they wept for you?"

"I do not know what I would do," answered the girl. "I only know that there are some of these ladies so cruel that their knights call them tigers and lions and a thousand other foul names. But, Lord save us! What kind of people are they? Can they be so heartless and unfeeling that they prefer to let an honourable man die or go mad rather than give him a kind look. For my part I do not know why they show all this skittish coyness: if they pretend to be honest women why don't they marry them, seeing that they long for nothing else?"

"Hold your tongue, child," said the landlady. "You seem to know a great deal of these matters, and it is not right for girls to know or to talk so much."

"His reverence," answered she, "asked me and I could not help answering him."

"We need here," said the curate turning to the barber,

161

"our friend Don Quixote's housekeeper and niece. Meanwhile, my good host, beware of those books of chivalry, and may God grant you do not limp on the same foot as your guest Don Quixote."

"Not so," answered the landlord. "I shall not be such a fool as to turn knight-errant, for I see plainly that it is not the fashion today to do as they used in the times when these famous knights are said to have wandered about the world."

Sancho came in during the preceding conversation, and was so confounded and depressed to hear them say that knights-errant were no longer of any use, and that books of chivalry were full of follies and lies, that he resolved in his heart to see the end of the expedition of his master, and if it did not turn out as happily as he expected, to return home to his wife and children and to his former occupation.

At this moment the company heard a great noise coming from the garret where Don Quixote was sleeping. A few moments later Sancho Panza, who had gone to investigate, returned, rushing wildly back, shouting at the top of his voice: "Come quickly, sirs, and help my master who is up to the neck in the toughest battle my eyes have ever seen. Lord save us, he has dealt the giant, the enemy of the Lady Princess Micomicona, such a slash that he has sliced his head clean off like a turnip."

"What are you saying, friend?" said the curate. "Are you in your wits, Sancho? How the devil can it be as you say, when the giant is at least two thousand leagues from here?"

By this time the noise outside had increased, and they heard Don Quixote shouting out: "Stand back, robber, rascal, rogue! Now I have you in my power. Your scimitar will not save you!" And it seemed as if he were slashing away at the walls.

"Do not stand there listening," said Sancho, "but go in and stop the fight or help my master, although now there will be no need, for I'm sure the giant is already dead, and is giving an account to God of his wicked life. I saw his blood flooding the floor, and his head tumble off as big as a great wineskin."

"Hang me," cried the landlord on hearing this, "if Don Quixote or Don Devil has not been slashing at one of the skins of red wine standing at the head of his bed, and the wine that is spilt must be what this fellow takes for blood."[1]

Saying this, he rushed into the room, followed by the

---

[1] In Spain wine in the country inns is kept in large pig-skins. The hairy side within is covered with pitch—a custom which is mentioned by the Hispano-Romano poet Martial.

others, and they found Don Quixote in the strangest situation in the world. He was in his shirt, which was not long enough in front to cover his thighs, and behind was six inches shorter: his legs were long, lanky, hairy and none too clean. On his head he wore a little greasy red cap which belonged to the landlord. Round his left arm he had wrapped the bed-blanket to which Sancho bore a grudge (and he knew why), and in his right hand he held his drawn sword with which he was slashing about on all sides, shouting as if he were truly battling with a giant. And the strangest of all was that his eyes were closed: he was still asleep, and dreaming that he was in battle with the giant. His imagination was so intently fixed upon the forthcoming adventure that it made him dream he had arrived at the kingdom of Micomicon, and was already at war with his foe. And he had given so many slashes to the skins, thinking that he was giving them to his enemy, that the room was flooded with wine. At this sight the landlord flew into a towering rage and rushed at Don Quixote, and with clenched fists began so to belabour him that if Cardenio and the curate had not pulled him off he would have finished the war for the giant. In spite of all this, the poor knight did not wake up until the barber brought a large bucket of cold water from the well and threw it all over his body. The shock awoke Don Quixote, but not so completely as to make him realize his plight. Dorothea, seeing how short and flimsy were his garments, would not go in to watch the fight between her champion and his rival. Sancho meanwhile was searching all over the floor for the head of the giant, and as he could not find it he cried: "Now, I'm sure all in this house is enchanted, for last time in this very spot where I am now, they gave me a rare pucking and pummelling without my being any the wiser as to who gave it to me, for I couldn't see a soul. Now this head is nowhere to be seen, though I saw it cut off with my two eyes and the blood streaming from the body like from a fountain."

"What blood or what fountain are you cackling about, you enemy of God and his saints?" said the landlord. "Can't you see, you scoundrel, that they are nought else but the skins ripped open, with all their red wine swimming in this room? May I see the soul who ripped them open swimming in hell."

"All I know," answered Sancho, "is that if I'm so unlucky as not to find the head of the giant, why, my earldom will melt away like salt in water." Sancho awake was worse than his master asleep, so greatly had the latter's promises turned his brain.

The landlord was in despair at seeing the crass stupidity of the squire and the mischief done by his master, and he swore that it would not be as on the last occasion, when they went off without paying; that the privilege of knighthood would be no excuse for refusing to foot the bill for this time and the other, and he would soon make them pay for the plugs that would have to be put on the burst wineskins. The curate, meanwhile, was holding Don Quixote's hands, who, believing that he had finished the adventure and was in the presence of Princess Micomicona herself, fell on his knees before the curate and said: "Your highness, noble and beautiful lady, may live henceforth in safety, without any fear that this ill-born monster might do you harm. I, too, am liberated this day from the promise I made to you, for by the help of almighty God and through the favour of the lady by whom I live and breathe, I have so well accomplished my task."

"Didn't I say so?" cried Sancho, hearing these words of his master. "To be sure I wasn't drunk. Look now how my master has salted down the giant: the bulls are on their way.[2] My earldom is safe."

Who could refrain laughing at the follies of the two—master and servant? All of them did laugh except the landlord, who wished himself in hell. At length, however, the barber, Cardenio and the curate managed with much ado to get Don Quixote to bed again, and they left him sleeping, for he was utterly worn out. They let him sleep, and went out to comfort Sancho Panza for not having found the giant's head. As for the innkeeper, they had more difficulty in pacifying him, for he was in despair at the sudden death of his wineskins, and the landlady kept scolding and bawling out: "In an evil hour that knight-errant came into my house! I wish to God my eyes had never seen him, for he has cost me dear. Last time he went off with the price of a night's supper, bed, straw and barley for himself, his squire, his horse and his ass, saying that he was a knight-adventurer (God send him bad adventure and to all the adventurers there are in the world), and therefore wasn't bound to pay a thing, for so it was written in the rules of knight-errantry. Then on his account this other gentleman comes along and takes away my tail, and returns it with more than a halfpennyworth of damage, the hair so scraped off that it's of no further use to my husband. Then, as the climax to all, he bursts my skins and spills my wine: may I see his blood spilt! But let him not think it, for by the bones of my father and the soul of my mother, they'll pay

2 "Ciertos son los toros" is a phrase taken from the bullring and used proverbially. It expresses the feelings of relief of the spectators when they see the preparations for the bullfight nearing completion. There is no longer any room for doubts.

me every farthing on the nail or my name is not what it is and I'm not my father's daughter."

Thus the landlady went on in a great rage, and she was abetted by the worthy Maritornes. As for the daughter she held her peace, but now and then she smiled. The curate at length calmed the storm, promising to satisfy them as best he could for their loss of wine and skins, and especially for the damage to the tail of which they made so great a fuss. Dorothea comforted Sancho Panza, telling him that if it should turn out that his master had cut off the giant's head, she promised once she found herself peacefully settled in her kingdom, to give him the best earldom she had. Sancho was comforted by this, and insisted to the princess that she might depend upon it that he had seen the head of the giant, aye, and it had a beard which reached to the waist, and if it could not be found it was because everything that took place in that house happened by enchantment, as he had found the last time he had stayed there. Dorothea said she believed him, and bade him not to worry, for all would turn out to his heart's content.

XXI. *Other strange adventures at the inn*

JUST THEN THE LANDLORD, WHO WAS STANDING BY THE INN door, cried out: "Here is a fine troop of guests coming. If they stop here, we may sing 'O be joyful!' "

"Who are they?" asked Cardenio.

"Four men on horseback," answered the landlord: "they're riding Moorish fashion,[1] with lances and targets, and all of them are wearing black masks on their faces. Along with them rides a woman in white on a side-saddle, also with her face covered, and two lads on foot."

"Are they near?" asked the curate.

"So near," replied the landlord, "that they are now arriving."

Hearing this, Dorothea veiled her face, and Cardenio went into Don Quixote's room. They hardly had time to do this when the whole party, of whom the landlord had spoken, entered the inn. The four horsemen, who were of gallant bearing, having dismounted, went to help the lady in the side-saddle to alight; and one of them, taking her in his arms, placed her upon a chair that stood at the door of the room into which Cardenio had entered. All this while neither she nor they took off their masks, or said a word; but the lady, as she sank back in the chair, breathed a deep sigh and

[1] The Moorish mode of riding was "a la jineta" with very short stirrups.

165

let fall her arms as one who was sick and faint. The footmen led the horses away to the stable.

As soon as the curate saw this, he was curious to learn who they were that came to the inn in such strange attire and kept so close a silence, so he followed the footmen and asked one of them what he wanted to know. The latter answered: "Faith, yer reverence, an' I can't tell you who they be, but they seem to be folk of no mean quality, especially he who took in his arms the lady you're after seein'. This I'm sayin', because the rest keep bowin' and scrapin' to him, an' his word is law to them."

"But the lady—who is she?" asked the curate.

"I can't tell you that neither, Father," answered the footman, "for I've not caught a glimpse of her face the whole journey. I've heard her many a time sighin' an' moanin' her heart out. It's no wonder that we know no more than what we've told you: sure it's no more nor two days that myself and my comrade have been in their company, for they ran across us on the road an' persuaded us to go wid them to Andalusia, promisin' to pay us well."

"Have you heard the name of any of them?" asked the curate.

"No, Father," replied the lad: "sure they travel widout a word out of them: we hear nought but the sighin' an' sobbin' of the poor lady. It's my honest belief that wherever she's goin', she's goin' agin her wish. I'd say be her dress she is a nun or is goin' to become one, which is more likely. Who knows? Perhaps she has no leanin' towards bein' a nun and that's what has her so down in the mouth."

"That may be so," said the curate. Leaving them, he came back to Dorothea, who, hearing the veiled lady sigh so, moved by natural compassion, went up to her and said:

"What ails you, dear lady? If it is anything that women have the power and experience to relieve, let me offer you my service and goodwill."

To this the unhappy lady made no answer, and, though Dorothea again spoke kind words to her, she remained silent, until the masked gentleman—the one whom the footmen had said the rest obeyed—came up and said to Dorothea: "Lady, do not trouble yourself to offer anything to that woman, for she never shows any gratitude no matter what is done for her: and do not try to make her answer you, unless you wish to hear some falsehood."

"I have never told one," said the lady who till then had kept silence. "It is because I am so truthful and so averse to falsehood that I now find myself in this miserable state.

166

And I call you to witness this, for it is my pure truth which causes you to be so false and lying."

Cardenio heard those words very clearly and distinctly, for he was close to her who uttered them, since the door of Don Quixote's room was all that separated them from one another. No sooner had he heard them than he cried out: "Heavens above! What is this I hear? What voice is that I hear?"

The lady, startled by his exclamation, turned her head, and as she could not see who uttered them, she rose to her feet and would have entered the room, but the gentleman stopped her and would not let her move a step. In the sudden commotion her mask fell off her face and showed a countenance of incomparable beauty. But she was pale and terror-stricken and she rolled her eyes, looking here and there, like one distraught, with such an expression of suffering that Dorothea and all who beheld her were moved to deep pity, though they did not know the cause. The cavalier held her firmly by the shoulders, and as he was thus busied, he could not hold up his own mask, which fell from his face. As it did so, Dorothea, who also was upholding the lady, raised her eyes and saw that he who held her in his arms was her own husband, Don Fernando. No sooner did she recognize him than breathing out from the bottom of her heart a long and most pitiful "Oh" she fell back in a faint, and if the barber had not by good fortune been close at hand she would have fallen to the ground. The curate at once made haste to take off her veil and throw water on her face, and as soon as he uncovered it, Don Fernando—for it was he who was holding the other lady in his arms—knew her and stood like one dead at the sight of her, yet, nevertheless, he did not relax his hold of Luscinda. But she struggled to free herself from his arms, for she recognized Cardenio by his cry, and he had recognized her. Cardenio, who heard the groan which Dorothea uttered as she fell in a swoon, believing it was his Luscinda, ran out of the room in fear and trembling, and the first thing he saw was Don Fernando holding Luscinda in his arms. Don Fernando then recognized Cardenio, and all three, Luscinda, Cardenio and Dorothea, stood in dumb amazement, scarcely knowing what had befallen them. They all gazed silently at one another: then the first to break the silence was Luscinda, who addressed Don Fernando as follows: "Leave me, Don Fernando, for the sake of what is due to yourself, if for no other reason. Let me cling to the wall of which I am the ivy, to the protection of one from whom neither your threats, your promises, nor your bribes could separate me. See how heaven by mysterious and unaccountable ways has led me

167

into the presence of my true husband, and well you know by a thousand costly proofs that only death can drive him from my memory."

By this time Dorothea had come to herself, and hearing Luscinda's words she realized who she was, but seeing that Don Fernando did not yet release her from his arms, nor yield to her entreaties, she roused herself as much as she was able and cast herself at his feet, shedding a flood of tears, and thus addressed him: "Ah, dear lord, if the beauty you now hold in your arms had not dazzled your eyes, you would have seen by this time that she who is kneeling at your feet is the forlorn, miserable Dorothea. I am that humble country girl to whom you promised marriage. I am she who lived a happy innocent life until, seduced by your promises and by the apparent sincerity of your affection, she surrendered to you the keys of her freedom. How ungrateful you were for such a gift is now only too manifest! Do not, however, think that I have come hither through ways of dishonour. Sorrow and despair alone have driven me since I found myself deserted by you. Remember, dear lord, that the matchless love I have for you may compensate for the beauty and high rank of her for whom you abandon me. You cannot be the fair Luscinda's, for you are mine; nor can she be yours, for she belongs to Cardenio. You seduced my innocence and played upon my simplicity: you were not blind to my condition: you know well how I submitted to your will and so you may not plead that you were deceived. Since it is so, and since you are both a Christian and a gentleman, why do you put off making me as happy at last as you did at first? If you refuse to acknowledge me for what I am, your true and lawful wife, allow me at least to become your slave, for provided I be under your protection I shall count myself fortunate. But do not abandon me to the vile gossip of the streets to my shame: do not bring sorrow on my aged parents who have ever been your faithful vassals. And now, my lord, all I wish to say in conclusion is that, whether you will or not, I am your wife; witness your words, witness your handwriting, witness Heaven which you called upon to witness the promise you made to me. And if all this should fail, your own conscience will not fail to murmur words of self-reproach and trouble every enjoyment in your life."

These and other arguments the sorrowful Dorothea urged in so affecting a manner, that all who were present, even those who had come with Don Fernando, could not help giving her their sympathy.

As for Don Fernando, he stood gazing fixedly at Dorothea without saying a word until she had finished her speech and began to sigh and sob in such a way that all but a heart of bronze would have melted with pity. At last, overwhelmed with remorse and admiration, he opened his arms and setting Luscinda free, cried: "You have conquered, O beautiful Dorothea, you have conquered. Who could have the heart to deny so many truths together?"

Luscinda, who was still faint, would have fallen to the ground when Don Fernando released her, but Cardenio, who was standing near by her, started forward and, clasping her in his arms, said to her: "These arms shall protect you, my faithful and beloved mistress. God grant at last you will now find rest."

At these words Luscinda raised her eyes to Cardenio, and, having assured herself that it was he, regardless of all forms, cast her arms about his neck and embraced him, saying: "O Cardenio, you are my true lord and master."

What a strange sight for Don Fernando and for all the company! They were amazed at such an unforeseen incident. Dorothea thought that Don Fernando changed colour, and made a move as though to take vengeance on Cardenio: she saw his hand move in the direction of his sword. No sooner did the thought flash across her mind than swiftly she clasped him round the knees and embraced them, saying: "For God's sake and your own good name, I beg you to calm your anger and peacefully allow those two lovers to live untroubled all the days that Heaven will be pleased to grant them. If you do this, you will give proof of your noble, generous soul, and the world will recognize that reason weighs more with you than passion."

While Dorothea was saying this, Cardenio, though he held Luscinda in his arms, did not take his eyes off Don Fernando, for he was resolved, if he saw him make a hostile move, to defend himself and resist to his last gasp any who should take sides against him. But at this point Don Fernando's friends, the curate, and the barber gathered round Don Fernando and begged him to yield to Dorothea's entreaties, and to reflect that it was the will of Heaven which had brought them together in such an unexpected place. The curate told Don Fernando to bear in mind that death alone could separate Luscinda from Cardenio, and even though the edge of the sword should divide them, they would consider theirs a most happy death. He added that in cases that do not admit of remedy it was wisest for him to conquer himself and show a generous soul by freely leaving the lovers to enjoy the blessing which Heaven had granted them. Moreover, he should turn his eyes towards the lovely Dorothea who had such strong claims upon him, not only because of her great love for him, but because he had made promises to her which, as a Christian and a man of honour, he was bound to perform.

Don Fernando's manly heart at last was softened, and allowed itself to be vanquished by those truths so forcibly urged. He embraced Dorothea, saying: "Rise, my dear lady: it is not right that she who is the mistress of my soul should kneel at my feet. If I have not until now given you any proofs of what I say, surely it has been by the will of Heaven, that I might learn to value you after seeing how loyal and constant is your love for me."

So saying he kissed her again and pressed his face to hers with so much tender emotion that he could scarcely restrain his tears of love and repentance. Indeed, all the company present were so moved that they began to shed tears so copiously, some in their own happiness, and some for that of others, that one would have thought some grim calamity had befallen them. Even Sancho Panza wept, though he said afterwards that, as far as he was concerned, he cried only because he saw that Dorothea was not Queen Micomicona as he had imagined, from whom he expected so many favours. Then Don Fernando asked Dorothea to tell him how she had come to that place so far from her home. She, in a few well-chosen words, told the story she had before told to Cardenio, and the company were so interested that they wished it had lasted longer, such was the charm with which Dorothea described her sad experiences. Then Don Fernando related what he had done after finding in Luscinda's bosom the paper in which she declared that she was Cardenio's wife. He said that he wanted to kill her, and would have done so if her parents had not prevented him. He then left the house full of shame and rage, determined to avenge himself at the first opportunity. Next day he heard that Luscinda had left her parents' house and had fled no one knew whither. Within a few months he had learnt that she was in a certain convent, intending to stay there all the days of her life if she could not spend them with Cardenio. As soon as he heard this, he chose three gentlemen to help him, and went to the place where she was. One day when the convent gate was open he entered and found Luscinda in a cloister talking with a nun. Straightway he snatched her away without giving her time to resist. From there he brought her to a certain village, where they provided themselves with all they needed for carrying out the project. He said that when Luscinda found herself in his power, she lost all consciousness, and that when she came to her senses she did nothing but weep and sigh without speaking a word. And so, in silence and in tears, they had come to this inn, which to him meant Heaven, where all the misfortunes of the world have their end.

170

XXII. The story of the famous Princess Micomicona continued, and our Knight's subtle discourse concerning arms and letters

SANCHO HEARD ALL THIS CONVERSATION WITH NO SMALL GRIEF of mind, for he saw that all his hopes of an earldom were vanishing like smoke, and that the lovely Princess Micomicona was changed into Dorothea, the giant into Don Fernando, while his master was sound asleep, careless of all that happened. Dorothea could not believe that the happiness she enjoyed was not a dream. Cardenio and Luscinda were of the same mind, and Don Fernando gave thanks to Heaven for the favour shown to him, and for having extricated him from that intricate labyrinth when he was on the point of losing his honour and his soul. In a word, all in the inn were contented and happy at the fortunate way in which those desperate difficulties had been solved. The curate, who was a man of sound sense, settled every matter satisfactorily and congratulated each one upon his good fortune; but the most jubilant person of all was the landlady, because Cardenio and the curate had promised to pay for all the damage done by Don Quixote.

Only Sancho, as we said before, was downcast, sorrowful and miserable, and so he went with a melancholy face to his master, who was then just awaking, and said: "Sir Rueful Figure—you may sleep away till kingdom come without bothering to kill any giant or restore the princess to her country, for all that is done and finished with already."

"I can believe that," answered Don Quixote, "for I have had the most terrific battle with the giant that ever I had all the days of my life; but with one backstroke, swish, I tumbled his head to the ground, and his blood gushed forth, so that streams ran along the earth as if they had been of water."

"As if they had been of red wine, you might have said, sir," replied Sancho. "I want to tell your worship, if you don't know it already, that your dead giant is no other than a slashed wineskin, and the blood is a dozen gallons of red wine which were contained in its belly, and the cut-off head is the whore that bore me, may the devil roast it all."

"What are you saying, you mad fool?" answered Don Quixotte. "Are you in your senses?"

"Please get up, sir," said Sancho, "and you'll soon see what a fine day's work you've done, and what we'll have to pay: you'll see the Queen transmogrified into a private lady called

Dorothea, and a power of other things which will flabbergast you."

"I would marvel at nothing," replied Don Quixote. "If you remember rightly, on the last occasion when we were here, I told you all that happened in this place was due to enchantment. It would be no wonder if the same were true now."

"I should believe every word," answered Sancho, "if my tossing in the blanket had been of that kind. It was not so, but darned real and true; when I saw the innkeeper, who's here this day, holding the end of the blanket, and tossing me up to the sky joking all the while, with as much mirth as muscle. When it comes to knowing fellows, I'm of the opinion, though I may be a simple poor sinner, that there's precious little enchantment but a power of bruising and bad luck."

"All right," said Don Quixote, "God will remedy it: come give me my clothes; I want to see those transformations you speak of."

Sancho gave him his clothes, and, while he was dressing, the curate told Don Fernando and the rest of Don Quixote's mad pranks and of the trick they had used to get him out of the Peña Pobre, where he imagined he was exiled through his lady's disdain. The curate, furthermore, told them that since the good fortune of Lady Dorothea prevented them from continuing with their scheme, it was necessary to invent some other way of taking him home to his village. Cardenio offered to carry on what they had begun and said that Luscinda should act the part of Dorothea.

"No," cried Fernando, "it must not be so: I wish Dorothea herself to carrry out her plan, and provided the worthy knight's home is not too far from here, I shall be very pleased to help in his cure."

"It is not more than two days' journey," said the curate.

"Even if it were more," replied Don Fernando, "I should be happy to travel there to accomplish so good a work."

At this moment Don Quixote sallied forth clad in all his accoutrements, with Mambrino's helmet, which was dinted, on his head, his buckler on his arm, and leaning on his sapling or lance. Don Fernando and his companions were spellbound by the knight's extraordinary appearance: they marvelled at the contrast between his shrivelled, yellow face, half a league long, the job lot of his arms, and his grave courtly behaviour, and they kept silence to hear what he would say. The knight, gazing fixedly at the fair Dorothea, with great gravity and calmness spoke as follows: "I am informed, beautiful lady, by this my squire, that thy grandeur has been annihilated and thy condition destroyed, for instead of being a queen and a mighty princess, thou art now become a private damsel. If this has been done by command of the necromancer-king, thy father, because he was afraid I could not give thee the necessary help, I say that he has not and does not know the half of his own art, and he has never understood the histories of chivalry. If he had read and studied them with as much attention and detail as I have, he would have found at every step that many knights of less fame than myself have accomplished much more difficult exploits than this one. Truly it is not a mighty deed to slay a paltry giant, no matter how arrogant he may be; why, not so many hours ago, I came to grips with him and . . . I will be silent, lest they may tell me that I lie. But time which reveals all things, will tell all when we least expect."

"You came to grips with two wineskins, not with a giant," cried the landlord.

Don Fernando, however, told him to be silent and not to interrupt Don Quixote, who continued his speech thus: "In time, I say, noble and disinherited lady, if for the reason I have mentioned thy father has made this transformation in thee, do not trouble thyself, for there is no peril upon earth so great but my sword shall cut open a way through it, and by throwing thy enemy's head to the ground I shall set thy crown upon thine own head within a few days."

Don Quixote said no more, but waited for the princess to reply. She, knowing Don Fernando's wish that she should continue their plan of deception until Don Quixote had been led home to his village, answered gravely and pleasantly: "Whoever told you, valiant Knight of the Rueful Figure, that I had been altered and transformed did not speak truly, for I am the same today as yesterday. It is true that certain fortunate incidents have made some change in me, for they have given me my heart's desire; yet for all that I have not ceased to be what I was before, and I still am resolved to avail myself of the aid of your doughty and invincible arm. Therefore, my good lord, restore to my father his honour and consider him as wise and prudent, for by his magic he has found me so sure a remedy for all my misfortunes. For I am convinced, sir, that had it not been for you, I should never have attained the happiness I now enjoy. Most of these gentlemen here present will bear witness to the truth of my words. All that remains now is that tomorrow morning we set out on our journey, for today we shall not be able to travel far. As for the happy issue I expect, I put my trust in God and your invincible spirit."

Thus spoke the wise Dorothea, and Don Quixote having heard her, turned to Sancho in great indignation, saying: "I take mine oath, Sanchokin, that you are the veriest rapscallion in all Spain. Tell me, you thieving gadabout, did you not say just now that this princess was turned into a damsel named Dorothea? And that the head I believed I had cut off a giant was the whore who pupped you, along with other follies that threw me into the greatest confusion I have ever known in all the days of my life? I swear (he looked up to Heaven and gritted his teeth) I have a mind to wreak such havoc upon you as will put some sense into the brains of all the lying knights-errant squires there ever shall be in the world."

"I beg you, master, calm yourself," answered Sancho, "for I may well have been deceived about the changing of Princess Micomicona. But as regards the giant's head or at least the ripping of the wineskins, and the blood being red wine, I swear to almighty God I'm not deceived. Why, the skins are lying there slashed at the head of your bed, and the red wine has made a lake of the chamber. If you don't believe me, you'll see it in a jiffy when his honour the landlord asks you for damages. As for the rest, I'm mighty glad the Queen is as she was, for I'm as keen on my share as any neighbour's son would be."

"I now say, Sancho," replied Don Quixote, "you are a blockhead, but pardon me. We have had enough of this."

"Enough indeed," said Don Fernando, "and let no more be said. Since my lady the Princess says she will go away tomorrow, and as it is too late to depart today, let us spend the night in pleasant conversation. Tomorrow we will all bear company to Don Quixote, for we wish to witness the valiant and amazing exploits which he is to perform in the course of his great adventure."

Supper was now prepared, and they all seated themselves at a long table such as one finds in a refectory, for there was not a square or round one in the inn. They gave the head and principal seat to Don Quixote, though he tried to refuse it, but when he had taken it, he insisted that the Lady Micomicona should sit by his side, as he was her champion. Then Luscinda, Don Fernando, Cardenio and the others seated themselves and they enjoyed a pleasant supper. Don Quixote added to their entertainment; for he now felt the urge of the same spirit which had filled him with eloquence at the goatherds' supper in the Sierra Morena, and so, instead of eating, he addressed them as follows: "Truly, gentlemen, if we consider well, great and unheard-of-sights are witnessed by those who profess the order of knight-errantry. What man living today who should enter the gate of this castle, and behold us seated here, would judge and believe us to be what we are? Who would say that this lady by my side is the great queen we all know her to be, and that I am that Knight of the Rueful Figure so celebrated abroad by the mouth of fame? There is no doubt that this art and profession surpasses all that men have ever invented; and it is all the more deserving of esteem as it is subjected to more dangers. Away with those who say that letters win more fame than arms! Whoever they may be, I will tell them they do not know what they are saying. The reason which they generally give, and on which they rely, is that the labours of the mind exceed those of the body, and that arms are exercised by the body alone, as though it were the business of porters alone, requiring mere physical strength, and as though the profession of arms did not demand acts of courage which need high intelligence; or as though the mental powers of the warrior, who has to command an army or defend a besieged city, were not called into play as well as those of his body. Nay, let it be seen whether bodily strength will enable him to guess the designs of the enemy, his stratagems and problems, overcome difficulties and ward off the dangers which threaten. No, these are all operations of the understanding, in which the body has no share. Since, then, arms as well as letters require mind, consider which of the two minds is exerted most, the scholar's or the warrior's. This will be determined by the ultimate end and goal to which each directs his energies, for the intention most to be esteemed is that which has for object the noblest end. The aim and goal of letters (I am not now speaking of divine letters, whose sole aim is to guide and elevate the soul of man to Heaven, for with that sublime end none can be compared), I speak of human letters, whose end is to regulate distributive justice, and give to every man his due: to apply good laws and cause them to be strictly observed: an end most certainly generous and exalted, and worthy of high praise, but not so glorious as the aim of arms, which is peace, the greatest blessing man can enjoy in this life; for the first good news which the world ever received was that brought by the angels on the night that was our day when they sang in the skies: 'Glory be to God in the highest and peace on earth to men of good will'; and the salutation which the blessed Master of Heaven and earth taught his disciples when they entered any house was: 'Peace be to this house'; and many times He said to them: 'My peace I give unto you, my peace I leave you—peace be with you'—a precious legacy indeed, given and bequeathed by such a hand! A jewel without which, neither in Heaven nor on earth can there be any happiness. This peace is the true end of war, and by war and arms I mean the same thing. If we admit this truth, that the end of war is peace, and that in this it excels the end of letters, let us consider the physical toils of the scholar and of the warrior and see which are the greater."

Don Quixote uttered his discourse in such a rational manner that none who heard him could take him for a madman.

On the contrary, as most of them were gentlemen who were connected with the profession of arms, they listened to him with great pleasure as he continued, saying: "I say, then, that the hardships of the student are, first of all, poverty (not that all are poor, but I wish to put the case as strongly as possible), and when I have said that he endures poverty, no more need be said of his wretchedness, for he who is poor lacks every comfort in life. He suffers poverty in various ways; in hunger, in cold, in nakedness, and sometimes in combination of all. Nevertheless, he does get something to eat, even though it may be later than at the accustomed hour, either from the scraps off the rich man's table, or from the soup at the convent gate—that last miserable resource which the students call among themselves 'Going as a souper'. Nor do they fail to find some neighbour's brazier or ingle which, if it does not warm them, at least diminishes the extreme cold; and so they sleep tolerably well at night under cover. I will not descend to other more trivial details, such as the want of shirts, the lack of spare shoes, the scanty and threadbare clothing, the greedy guzzling they go in for when good luck sets a banquet before them. This is the hard and rugged path they tread: sometimes they stumble, then they rise only to fall again, until they reach the eminence which they covet. And after having escaped these Scyllas and Charybdises, as though wafted onwards by the wings of favourable Fortune, we have seen them rule and govern the world from an arm-chair, their hunger converted into feasting, their cold into refreshment, their nakedness into rich raiment, and their sleep on a mat to repose on fine linen and damask—the just reward for their virtuous efforts. But their hardships when compared with those of the warrior fall far short of them as I shall now show you.

"When we consider the soldier we find that there is no one poorer in poverty itself, for he depends on his wretched pay, which comes late or never, or on what he grabs with his own hands, at the imminent risk of his life and his conscience. Sometimes his nakedness is such that his slashed doublet serves him both for full-dress and shirt; and in the midst of winter, in the open country, he has nothing to warm him against the rigours of the heavens but the breath from his mouth, which, as it issues from an empty place, must needs come forth cold against the laws of Nature. But let him wait till night comes, when he hopes to restore himself from those discomforts in the bed which awaits him. It will only be his fault if that bed prove too narrow, for he may measure out on the earth as many feet as he pleases, and toss himself thereon at will without fear of rumpling the sheets. And now suppose the day and hour arrives for receiving his degree—I mean suppose the day of battle has come, when they will put upon his head the tasselled doctor's cap,[1] made of lint, to heal some wound from a bullet which perhaps has passed through his temples, or left him maimed of an arm or leg. And if this should not happen, and Heaven in its mercy keep him safe and sound, he will probably remain as poor as ever. If he is to secure any promotion at all he will need another and yet another engagement, and he must come off victorious in every one of them ere he can better himself: and such miracles are rare indeed.

"Now tell me, gentlemen, if you have ever considered how much fewer are those who have been rewarded by war than those who have perished by it? Without doubt you must answer that there is no comparison between them: the dead are countless; whereas those who survive to win the rewards may be counted in numbers less than a thousand. The opposite is true of scholars, for by their salaries (I will not mention their perquisites) they have enough to provide their needs: therefore the soldier's reward is less though his toil is greater. It may be said in reply to this, that it is easier to reward two thousand scholars than thirty thousand soldiers, for the former are rewarded by giving them employments which must of course be given to men of their profession; whereas the latter cannot be recompensed except from the property of the master whom they serve; and this impossibility adds greater weight to my argument, which is very difficult to decide. Let us take up again the question of the pre-eminence of arms over letters, which has never been settled, for the partisans of each can bring cogent arguments in support of their own side.

"It is said in favour of letters that without them arms could not subsist, for war also has its laws and is subject to them, and laws fall within the province of letters and men of letters. To this the partisans of arms reply that without them laws could not be maintained, for by arms states are defended, kingdoms are preserved, cities are protected, roads are made safe and seas cleared of pirates. Indeed, without arms, kingdoms, monarchies, cities, sea-ways and land-ways would be subject to the ruin and confusion which war brings with it as long as it lasts and has licence to use its privileges and powers. Besides, it is a well-established maxim that what costs most is, and ought to be, valued most. Now, to achieve eminence in letters costs a man time, vigils, hunger, nakedness, dizziness in the head, indigestion, and other inconveniences I have already mentioned. But to arrive by all the grades to be a good soldier costs a man all that it costs the student, only in

[1] The tassel or "borla," which was sewn on to the University cap, was the sign of a doctor's degree.

so much greater degree that there is no comparison between them, for at every step he is in danger of losing his life. What fear or poverty can threaten the student compared to that which faces a soldier who, finding himself besieged and stationed as sentry in the ravelin or cavalier of some beleaguered fortress, perceives that the enemy is mining towards the place where he stands, yet must not stir from there on any pretext nor shun the danger which so nearly threatens him? All that he can do is to give notice to his captain of what is happening, hoping that he may remedy it by some counter-mine, but he must stand quietly his ground in fear and momentary expectation of suddenly flying up to the clouds without wings and dashing down to the abyss against his will. And if this be thought a small danger, let us see if it is equalled or surpassed by the clash between two galleys prow to prow, in mid-ocean. Both of them locked and grappled together leave the soldier no more space than two feet of plank at the beak-head to stand upon; but, though he sees in front of him so many ministers of death threatening him as there are pieces of artillery pointing at him from the opposite ship, not farther than a lance's length from his body, and though he sees that the first slip of his foot will land him in Neptune's bottomless gulf, nevertheless, with undaunted heart, inspired by glory which spurs him on, he allows himself to be a mark for all their fire, and endeavours to force his way by that narrow path into the enemy's vessel.[2] And what is most to be admired is that scarcely has one fallen, never to rise again until the end of the world, when another takes his place; and if he, too, drops into the sea, which lies in wait like an enemy ready to devour him, another and yet another succeeds without any time elapsing between their deaths. In all the perils of war there is no greater courage and boldness than this. Blessed were those ages which were without the dreadful fury of those diabolical engines of artillery, whose inventor, I truly believe, is now receiving in hell the reward for his devilish invention, by means of which a base and cowardly hand may deprive the most valiant knight of life. While such a knight fights with all the bravery and ardour which fire gallant hearts, without his knowing how or whence there comes a random ball, discharged by one who perhaps ran away in terror at the flash of his own accursed machine, and cuts short and ends in an instant the life of one who deserved to live for centuries to come. When I consider this, I have a mind to say that I am grieved in my soul at having undertaken this profession of knight-errantry in so detestable an

[2] This passage describing a soldier's experiences in a sea-fight is probably taken from Cervantes' own memory of that famous day of Lepanto in 1571, when he bore himself so gallantly on the most exposed part of the deck of the Spanish galleon *La Marquesa*.

age as this wherein we live. For, although no peril can daunt me, still it troubles me to think that powder and shot may deprive me of the chance of making myself famous and renowned for the strength of my arm and the edge of my sword over all the known earth. But Heaven's will be done! I shall win all the greater fame, if I am successful in my quest, for the dangers to which I expose myself are greater than those which did beset the knights of past ages."

Don Quixote delivered this long harangue while the rest were taking their supper, and he forgot to raise a morsel to his mouth, though Sancho Panza more than once told him to eat, saying that afterwards there would be time to talk as much as he pleased. Those who had listened to him felt sorry that a man who seemed to possess so good an understanding and such powers of reason, yet should lose them so entirely when dealing with his sinister and accursed chivalry. The curate told him that he was quite right in all he had said in favour of arms, and that he himself, although a scholar and a graduate, was of the same opinion. They then ended their supper, and the hostess, her daughter and Maritornes went to prepare Don Quixote's chamber, where they had arranged that the ladies should pass the night. Sancho lay down to sleep on his ass's harness and the rest of the company settled themselves as best they could. Don Quixote, however, prepared to keep guard over the castle, lest some giant or rascally adventurer, tempted by the treasure of beauty it contained, might make an attack. He accordingly sallied out of the inn to take his post at the castle gate, and soon throughout the inn there reigned a profound silence.

XXIII. *Other unheard-of adventures at the inn*

ALL INSIDE THE INN WERE ASLEEP EXCEPT THE INNKEEPER'S daughter and her servant, Maritornes. They knew Don Quixote's weak points, and they resolved to play some trick on him, or at least spend a little time listening to his nonsense, as they saw him outside armed and mounted on guard.

Now it so happened that there was no window in the inn on that side which overlooked the fields, but only a hole in the loft, out of which the straw was thrown. At this hole the two demi-maidens took up their position, whence they could see him heaving from time to time such deep and mournful sighs that it seemed as if each one would tear his soul asunder. And they heard him say in a soft, soothing and amorous voice: "O my lady, Dulcinea del Toboso, summit of all beauty, quintessence of discretion, treasury of charm and ideal of chastity! What may thy grace be doing at this moment? Art thou, perchance, thinking of thy captive knight, who for thy sake has subjected himself to so many perils? Give me swift tidings of her, O three-faced luminary! Perhaps even now thou art gazing upon her, envious of her beauty, as she paces through some gallery of her sumptuous palace, or leans over some balcony, considering how she may, without risking her virtue or dignity, calm the pangs which my poor, aching heart endures for her; or meditating on what glory she may bestow on my sufferings, what solace she may give to my cares, and finally, what life to my death, what guerdon to my long service. And thou, O sun! who now art busy saddling thy horses to sally forth betimes to see my lady, I must beseech thee when thou seest her, to salute her in my name. But beware that thou dost not kiss her on the face, or I shall be more jealous of thee than thou wert of that swift-footed, faithless Daphne who made thee sweat and run over the plains of Thessaly, or by the banks of Peneus—I do not exactly remember where it was that thou didst run in thy jealous and amorous frenzy."

So far had Don Quixote proceeded in his mournful soliloquy, when the innkeeper's daughter softly called to him, whispering: "Dear sir, come this way, if you please."

At this signal Don Quixote turned his head, and saw by the light of the moon, which was then at its highest, that they beckoned him from the hole which he imagined to be a window, and even with gilded bars suitable to such a castle as he conceived that inn to be. At once he believed, in his strange fancy, that again, as once before, the beautiful damsel, daughter of the lord of the castle, conquered by love of him, was come to tempt him. Being in this fancy, and unwilling to show himself discourteous and ungrateful, he turned Rozinante about and came over to the hole, and when he saw the two girls, he said: "I take pity on you, beauteous lady, because you have fixed your love where it is not possible for you to meet with the response your great virtues and nobility deserve. Yet you ought not to blame this miserable knight-errant, whom love has wholly disabled from paying court to any other than to her whom, from the first moment, he made absolute mistress of his soul. Pardon me, therefore, good lady, and retire to your chamber, and do not reveal to me any further your desires, that I may not appear ungrateful to you. But if your love for me suggests to you any way wherein I may serve you other than by returning your passion, demand it straightway, for I swear to you by that sweet absent enemy of mine, to gratify you unconditionally, even if you were to demand a lock of Medusa's hair, which was all snakes, or even the beams of the sun enclosed in a phial."

"My lady needs none of that, Sir Knight," said Maritornes.

"What does she want then, wise duenna?" asked Don Quixote.

"Only one of your beautiful hands," said Maritornes; "that she may satisfy the longing that brought her to this window, putting her honour in such danger that if her lord and father came to know it, the least he would do would be to slice off her ear."

"I should like to see him do it!" answered Don Quixote. "He had best beware of what he does, unless he wishes to have the most disastrous end that ever a father had in this world, for having laid violent hands on the delicate limbs of his enamoured daughter."

Maritornes not doubting that Don Quixote would give up his hand as she had requested, and having made up her mind what to do, descended from the loft and went to the stable, whence she took the halter of Sancho Panza's ass, and hastened back with it to the hole, just as Don Quixote had stood upon Rozinante's saddle that he might more easily reach the barred window at which he thought the lovesick damsel was standing. As he stretched out his hand to her, he cried: "Take, lady, this hand, or as I should rather say, this lash of evildoers. Take this hand, I say, which no other woman has ever touched, not even she herself who holds complete possession of my whole body. I give it to you, not that you may kiss it, but that you may behold the contexture of the sinews, the knitting of the muscles, the large and swelling veins, whence you may learn how mighty is the force of that arm to which belongs such a hand."

"We'll soon see," said Maritornes. Then, making a running knot in the halter, she cast it on the wrist of his hand, and, descending from the hole, she tied the other end very tightly to the bolt of the hay-loft door.

Don Quixote, feeling the roughness of the halter about his wrist, exclaimed: "My lady, you seem rather to rasp than to clasp my hand, but yet I pray you not to handle it so roughly, since it is not to blame for what you suffer through my adverse inclinations, nor is it right that you should vent your displeasure on so small a part of me: consider that those who love well do not so ill avenge."

But there was no one now to give heed to those words of Don Quixote, for as soon as Maritornes had him tied up, she and the other one, almost bursting with laughter, ran away and left him fastened in such a manner that it was impossible for him to loose himself. He was standing, as we said before, on Rozinante's saddle, with his whole arm stuck through the hole and tied to the bolt of the door, and he was in great fear that if Rozinante budged ever so little on either side he would be left hanging by the arm.

Therefore he did not dare to make the least movement, though he might well have expected, from Rozinante's patience and mild temper, that he would stand without stirring for a whole century. Finding that he was trussed up and that the ladies had vanished, Don Quixote straightway began to imagine that all this had been done by way of enchantment, as the time before when the enchanted Moor of a muleteer had drubbed him in that same castle. Then he cursed himself for his foolishness in venturing to enter the castle a second time after his bad experience on the first occasion, for it was a maxim with knights-errant, that when they had attempted an adventure and had not come well out of it, it was a sign that it was reserved not for them but for some other, and therefore they were not bound to attempt it a second time. Yet for all this he pulled his arm to see if he might release himself, but he was so well tied that all his efforts were in vain. It is true that he pulled his arm cautiously, lest Rozinante should stir, and although he longed to get down into his seat on the saddle, yet he could do nought but stand upright or wrench off his arm. Many times did he wish for the sword of Amadis against which no enchantment had power. Then he began to curse his stars; then he spoke at length upon how his presence would be missed in the world during the time he remained there enchanted, as he believed he was; then he again remembered his beloved Dulcinea del Toboso; then he would call on his good squire Sancho Panza, who, buried in sleep, stretched out upon his pack-saddle, did not mind even the mother who bore him. At last the morning found him so full of despair and confusion, that he bellowed like a bull, for he had no hope that the day would bring him any cure for his sufferings, which would be everlasting, seeing that he was enchanted. He was all the more convinced of this inasmuch as Rozinante had not budged ever so little, and he concluded that he and his horse would remain in that state without eating, drinking or sleeping, until the evil influences of the stars had passed, or some great magician had disenchanted him.

In this he was greatly deceived, for scarcely did day begin to break when there arrived four horsemen at the inn door, well equipped, with firelocks on their saddle-bows. They knocked loudly on the inn door, which was still shut, and Don Quixote, hearing from where he stood sentinel, cried out in a loud and arrogant voice: "Knights or squires, or whoever ye may be, you have no right to knock at the gates of this castle, for it is abundantly clear that at such an hour as this either those who are within are sleeping, or else are not in the habit of opening their fortress until the sun has spread his beams over the whole land. Therefore stand back and wait

182

until it be clear day, and then we will see whether it be right or no to open our gates to you."

"What the hell castle or fortress is this," cried one of them, "that makes us observe such ceremonies? If you are the innkeeper, tell them to open the door, for we are travellers: we only want to feed our horses before moving on: we're riding post-haste."

"Do you think, gentlemen, that I look like an innkeeper?" answered Don Quixote.

"I don't know what you look like," replied the other, "but I'm sure you're talking nonsense in calling this inn a castle."

"It is a castle," said Don Quixote, "and one of the best in this province, and it has people inside who had a sceptre in their hand and a crown on their head."

"You should have said it the other way round," said the traveller, "the sceptre on their head and the crown on their hand.[1] Probably, if we get down to facts, there is a company of players within: they often wear those crowns and sceptres you're speaking of. But I don't believe people worthy of crown and sceptre would lodge in so paltry an inn, where they keep such silence as they do here."

"You know little of the world," replied Don Quixote, "for you ignore the chances that are wont to happen in knight-errantry."

The companions of the man who asked the questions, being wearied of this discourse, began again to knock furiously at the door, and this time to such effect that they not only waked the innkeeper but also all the guests. The former then got out of bed and enquired who was knocking.

In the meantime it happened that one of the horses on which the four strangers rode came sniffing round Rozinante, who stood melancholy and sad, with his ears down, bearing without budging his outstretched master. But being, after all, made of flesh, though he seemed to be of wood, he could not help feeling sympathy and turning to smell at him who made these advances. But scarcely had he moved one step, when Don Quixote's two feet, which were close together, slipped, and the knight slid from the saddle and would have fallen to the ground had he not remained hanging by the arm. This caused him so much pain that he felt as though his wrist was being cut away, for he hung so near to the ground that he touched it with the tips of his toes. This increased his misery, for, feeling how little was wanted to set his feet flat on the ground, he strained himself desperately to reach it, like those who are undergoing the torture of the strappado. They hover between touching and not touching,

[1] This is a reference to the custom in those days of branding criminals on the hand with the crown.

183

and they themselves aggravate their own sufferings owing to their eagerness to stretch themselves, under the delusion that with a little more stretching they will reach the ground.

So great was the outcry made by Don Quixote that the landlord hastily opened the inn door and ran out to see who it was that roared so loud. Maritornes, whom the cries had also awakened, guessing what it was, ran to the hay-loft and, without anyone seeing her, untied the halter which held up Don Quixote, and he fell at once to the ground in the sight of the landlord and the four travellers, who came up to him and asked him what made him roar so loud. He, without answering, slipped the halter from his wrist, and, rising to his feet, leaped on Rozinante, braced on his shield, couched his lance, and, wheeling round the field, rode back at a half-gallop, crying out: "Whoever shall dare to say that I have been justly enchanted, provided my lady, Princess Micomicona, will give me leave to do it, I say that he lies and I challenge him to single combat."

The travellers were amazed at his words, but the landlord told them not to mind him, for he was out of his wits. And so they paid no further attention to him and went into the inn. Don Quixote when he saw that none of the four took any account of him, or answered his challenge, was ready to burst with rage and fury; and if he could have found in the ordinances of his chivalry that a knight-errant might undertake another enterprise after he had pledged his word and faith not to attempt any until he had finished what he had promised first, he would have attacked them all, and made them answer against their will. By this time those in the inn were fully aroused and they gathered round the landlord to welcome the new arrivals. While they were talking to the four travellers, they heard a great hubbub outside. The cause of this was that two guests, who had lodged there the night before, seeing all the people occupied with the new guests, had tried to slip away scot-free without paying what they owed. But the landlord, who paid more attention to his own than to other men's business, laid hold of them as they were going out of the door, and demanded his money. Furthermore, he abused them for their dishonest conduct, in such terms that they answered with their fists; and with such vigour that the poor landlord was obliged to shout for help. The landlady and her daughter saw no one at hand who might have given help, except Don Quixote, so the daughter cried to him: "Help! Sir Knight, by the power which God gave you: help my poor father, whom two scoundrels are thrashing like a bundle of corn!"

Don Quixote answered deliberately and with great gravity: "Beauteous damsel, your prayer cannot at the present time be granted, for I am not permitted to engage in any new ad-

184

venture until I have finished the one I have promised to carry through. All I can do for your service is what I now say to you. Run and tell your father that he must fight on as best he can, and not allow himself to be conquered, while I ask permission from Princess Micomicona to help him in his distress. If she will give me leave, you may be sure that he will be delivered."

"As I am a sinner," cried Maritornes, who was standing near by, "before you get the leave you mention, my master will be in the next world."

"Allow me, lady, to get the leave I speak of," replied Don Quixote, "and it will matter little whether he be in the next world or no. For I will bring him back again in spite of the next world, or at least, I will so revenge myself on those who shall have sent him there that you will be well content."

Without saying more, he went in and knelt before Dorothea, praying her in knightly and courtly phrases that she would give him leave to go and help the governor of the castle, who was then in grave distress.

The princess granted him leave very willingly, and he, instantly buckling on his shield and laying hands on his sword, ran to the inn door, where the two guests were still mauling the landlord. But as he arrived he slowed up and stood still, although Maritornes and the landlady asked why he delayed in assisting their master and husband.

"I delay," said Don Quixote, "because it is not lawful for me to lay hands upon my sword against squire-like men who are not dubbed knights. But call my squire Sancho here, for his duty is to take up this defence and vengeance."

All this took place outside the inn door, where fisticuffs and buffetings were being bandied about with gusto, all to the cost of the landlord and the rage of Maritornes, the landlady and her daughter, who were in despair at having to witness the cowardice of Don Quixote and the ill-treatment their master, husband and father was suffering. However, though the laws of chivalry did not allow Don Quixote on this occasion to fight, he soon established peace between the combatants, and by his persuasiveness and fair words more than through threats he made the guests pay what the landlord demanded. All now would have been at peace in the inn, if the devil, who never sleeps, had not so ordered it that at this moment another traveller arrived there. This was none other than the barber from whom Don Quixote had taken Mambrino's helmet and Sancho Panza the harness of the ass, which he had exchanged for his own. And while this barber was leading his beast to the stable he happened to catch sight of Sancho Panza mending some part of the pack-saddle. As soon as he saw him he knew him, and at once rushed at him, crying: "Ah, mister thief, I've nabbed you. Give up my basin and my harness you stole from me!"

Sancho, finding himself attacked so suddenly, and hearing those rough words, with one hand clutched the pack-saddle and with the other gave the barber such a buffet that he bathed his jaws in blood. But for all that the barber held fast his grip of the saddle, and cried out so loud that all the people in the inn ran out, hearing the noise and scuffle.

"Help here, in the name of the King and justice," shouted the barber: "this thief and highwayman wants to kill me because I'm trying to get back my own goods."

"That's a lie," cried Sancho; "I'm no highwayman. My master Don Quixote won these spoils in fair battle."

Don Quixote was now present and very glad to see how well his squire defended himself and attacked the enemy, and from that time forth he took him to be a man of courage, and resolved in his mind to have him dubbed knight on the first opportunity that should offer, for he thought that the order of knighthood would be well bestowed on him.

"Gentlemen," cried the barber, "this pack-saddle is as surely mine as the death I owe to God, and I know it as well as if I had brought it into the world, and there is my ass in the stable who won't let me lie; if not, try it on him, and if it doesn't fit him to a hair, call me an infamous rascal. And what's more, on the very day when they took my pack-saddle they robbed me also of a new brass basin that had never been used and was worth a crown."

Here Don Quixote could no longer contain himself, and, thrusting himself between the two combatants to separate them, he deposited the pack-saddle on the ground that it might be in sight of all until the dispute should be decided, and said: "Gentlemen, see clearly and manifestly the error into which this worthy squire has fallen. See how he calls that a basin, which was, is, and always shall be, the helmet of Mambrino, which I won from him by force in fair battle, and made myself lord of it by right and lawful possession. In regard to the pack-saddle I do not interfere; but I can say that my squire Sancho asked my leave to take away the trappings from the horse of this vanquished coward, that he might adorn his own with them. I gave him leave, and he took them. As to these being turned from a horse's trappings into an ass's pack-saddle, I can give no other reason but the common one, namely, that these transformations are wont to take place in the affairs of chivalry. To confirm the truth of my words, run, friend Sancho, and bring me the helmet which this good fellow declares to be a basin."

"Faith, master," said Sancho, "if we have no better proof of our story than what you say, the helmet of Malino is as much a basin as this fellow's trappings are a pack-saddle."

"Do what I command," replied Don Quixote: "I cannot believe that all things in this castle are governed by magic."

Sancho went for the basin and brought it, and as soon as Don Quixote saw it, he took it in his hands and said: "See, gentlemen, with what face can this squire declare that this is a basin, and not the helmet that I have mentioned. I swear to you, by the order of chivalry which I profess, that this is the very same helmet which I won from him. Nothing has been added or taken away from it."

"There's no doubt about that," said Sancho, "for since my master wore it till now, he only fought one battle in it, when he freed that unlucky chain-gang. Indeed if it hadn't been for that same basin-helmet he'd not have escaped so free as he did, for there was a devil of a lot of stone-throwing."

"Now, gentlemen," cried the barber, "what do you think of those who still hold that this is not a basin but a helmet?"

"If anyone shall say the contrary," said Don Quixote, "I will make him know, if he is a knight, that he is lying, aye, and if he's a squire, that he is lying a thousand times."

Now our own barber, Master Nicholas, was present all this time. He knew Don Quixote's humour, and he had a mind to encourage his folly and carry the jest further, to make them laugh, and so he addressed the other barber as follows: "Sir Barber, or whoever you are, know that I am also of your profession, and hold a certificate more than twenty years, and I am well acquainted with all the instruments of the barber's art, every one of them. Moreover, in my youth I was a soldier, and I know what a helmet is like, and a morion, and a close-casque, and other kinds of soldier's gear. Therefore I say, always subject to better judgment, that this piece which is before us, and which this good gentleman holds in his hand, not only is not a barber's basin, but is as far from being one as black is from white and truth from falsehood. It is a helmet, though, in my opinion, not a complete one."

"No, truly," said Don Quixote: "it lacks half, namely, the beaver."

"That's true," said the curate, who perceived his friend's intention, and Cardenio, Don Fernando and his companions affirmed likewise.

"Lord save us!" cried the befooled barber: "is it possible that so many honourable gentlemen should say this is not a basin but a helmet? Sure, this is enough to strike a whole university dumb with amazement, no matter how wise it be. Enough said; if this basin is a helmet, then this pack-saddle too must be a horse's trappings."

"To me it looks like a pack-saddle," said Don Quixote, "but I have already said I do not interfere in the matter."

"Whether it be a pack-saddle or trappings," said the curate, "it is only Don Quixote who can say, for in these matters of chivalry all these gentlemen and myself bow to his knowledge."

"By heaven, gentlemen," said Don Quixote, "so many strange and unaccountable things have befallen me in this castle on the two occasions I have stayed here that I would not dare to make a positive affirmation concerning anything contained in it, for I imagine that all here works by enchantment. On the first occasion, a Moorish magician in the castle troubled me greatly, and Sancho suffered at the hands of certain of his followers, and last night I remained hanging by this arm for close on two hours, without knowing how or why I fell into that mischance. Therefore, it would be rash on my part to interfere in so perplexing a business. For those who say this is a basin and not a helmet I have given my answer, but I will leave it to others to decide whether this be a pack-saddle or the trappings of a horse."

All this was the subject of great laughter to those who knew Don Quixote's humour, but to those who were ignorant of it, it seemed the greatest nonsense in all the world, especially to the four travellers who had arrived at the inn early in the morning, and to three others who had just arrived and who had the appearance of officers of the Holy Brotherhood, as in fact they were.

But he who despaired most of all was the barber whose basin had been transformed before his very eyes into the helmet of Mambrino, and whose pack-saddle would doubtless turn into the rich trappings of a horse. All of them laughed to see how Don Fernando took their votes, whispering in their ear so that they might declare in secret if that precious object they had quarrelled so much about were a pack-saddle or horse-trappings.

After he had taken the votes of those who knew Don Quixote, he said in a loud voice: "The truth is, my good man, that I am tired of asking so many opinions, for no sooner do I ask what I want to know than they answer me that it is absurd to say that this is an ass's pack-saddle and not the trappings of a horse—aye, and of a well-bred horse at that. So you must have patience: in spite of you and your ass, this is not a pack-saddle but horse-trappings, and you have made your case very badly."

"May I never have a share in Heaven," cried the barber, "if all you gentlemen be not deceived! So may my soul appear before God as this pack-saddle appears to me a pack-saddle and not horse-trappings. But laws go as kings will, I'll say no more, and in truth I'm not drunk, nor have I broken my fast, sinner though I be."

The barber's simplicity made them laugh as merrily as did the vagaries of Don Quixote, who now said: "There is nothing more to be done here except for everyone to take his own, and let Saint Peter bless what the Lord has given."

One of the travellers now spoke, saying: "If this be not a planned joke, I can't for the life of me understand why men of sense, as all those here seem to be, can have the face to say that this is not a basin, nor that a pack-saddle. I'll swear by (here he hurled a round oath) that all the people on earth will not convince me that this is no basin and this no jackass's pack-saddle."

"Perhaps it might be a she-ass's," said the curate.

"It is all the same," said the traveller. "The only point is whether it is or is not a pack-saddle, as you say."

Then one of the three troopers of the Holy Brotherhood, who had heard the dispute and the question, exclaimed indignantly: "It is as much a pack-saddle as my father is my father, and he who says, or shall say, to the contrary, must be sodden with drink."

"You lie like a base-born knave!" answered Don Quixote. Then raising his lance, which he had never let out of his hand, he aimed such a blow at the trooper's head that had he not jumped aside it would have laid him flat on the ground. The lance was broken into splinters against the ground, and the other troopers, seeing their companion so roughly handled, raised the hue and cry, shouting for help in the name of the Holy Brotherhood. The landlord, who was one of that body, ran at once for his staff of office and his sword and took his place beside his companions. The barber seeing the house was turned topsy-turvy, laid hold again of his pack-saddle, and Sancho did the same. Don Quixote set hand to his sword and attacked the troopers, and Cardenio and Don Fernando took his side. The curate kept shouting, the landlady screaming, her daughter weeping, Maritornes howling, while Dorothea stood frightened and Luscinda fainted away. The barber drubbed Sancho; Sancho mauled the barber; Don Fernando knocked one of the troopers down and trampled him underfoot to his heart's content. The landlord bawled at the top of his voice again for help to the Holy Brotherhood. Thus the whole inn was nought but wails, shouts, screams, dismay, confusion, alarms, disasters, slashes, cudgellings, kicks and spilling of blood.

In the midst of all this chaos, tumult and hurly-burly, Don Quixote suddenly took it into his mind that he was launched hell-for-leather into the discord of Agramante's camp,[2] and so he cried aloud in a voice that thundered through the inn:

[2] Proverbial for a fierce battle. From *Orlando Furioso*, cxxvii.

"Hold back, all of you! Sheath all your swords! Keep the peace and let all hearken to me, if ye wish to live!"

At the sound of his mighty voice they all stopped fighting, and he continued, saying: "Did I not tell you, gentlemen, that this castle was enchanted, and that some legion of demons must live here? As proof of what I say, note with your own eyes how the discord of Agramante's camp has been transplanted among us. There they fight for the sword, here for the horse, yonder again for the eagle, there for the helmet, and we are all of us fighting, and not one of us understands the other. Come, therefore, your reverence, and make peace between us, for by almighty God it is great wickedness that so many gentlemen of quality here should kill one another for such trivial matters."

The troopers, who did not understand the language of Don Quixote, and found themselves ill-used by Don Fernando, Cardenio and comrades, would not be pacified, but the barber gave in, for both his beard and his pack-saddle had been pulled to bits in the fight; Sancho, as a good servant, was attentive to the slightest hint of his master. The landlord alone insisted that they had to punish the insolent behaviour of that madman who was continually creating a hubbub in his inn. At last the row died down for the moment; the pack-saddle remained a horse-caparison until the day of judgment, the basin a helmet, and the inn a castle, in the imagination of Don Quixote. But the devil, who is the enemy of concord and the adversary of peace, finding himself despised and mocked and with nought but a scanty profit from the chaos in which he had involved them all, resolved to try his hand once more and stir up fresh quarrels.

Now it happened that the troopers, when they heard the quality of their adversaries in the brawl, retired from the fray, believing that, no matter what happened, they would get the worst of it. But one of them, who had been drubbed and kicked, suddenly remembered that among some warrants in his possession he had one against Don Quixote, whom the Holy Brotherhood had ordered to be taken into custody for liberating the galley-slaves; thus confirming Sancho's just fears. No sooner did this thought come into his mind than he tried at once to ascertain whether the description of Don Quixote on the warrant tallied with the man who stood before him. He took from his bosom a parchment scroll and began to read it slowly, for he was not good at reading, and at every word he came to he fixed his eyes on Don Quixote, comparing the details in his warrant with those of the knight's face. He found that this, beyond all manner of doubt, was the very man described in the warrant. As soon as he felt sure of this, he folded his parchment, held the warrant in his left hand, while with the right he seized Don Quixote by the collar with so tight a grip that he could hardly breathe, at the same time crying aloud: "Help for the Holy Brotherhood! To show you that I'm asking for it in earnest let your reverence read this warrant, where it states that this highway robber is to be arrested."

The curate took the warrant and saw that all the trooper said was true, and that the description therein applied to Don Quixote. The knight, on his side, however, finding himself ill-used by that base-born knave, felt his choler rising to such a fever height that all the bones in his body began to crackle: he caught the trooper by the throat with both hands so that if he had not been rescued by his companions he would have given up the ghost there and then before the knight slackened his grip. The landlord, who was under the obligation of helping those of his office, rushed to take his part. The landlady, seeing her husband engaged again in battle, raised a fresh outcry, which was caught up by Maritornes and her daughter, who invoked the help of Heaven and all the company.

Sancho, when he saw what was afoot, cried out: "God almighty! It's true what my master says of the enchantments of this castle: it's not possible for a man to live an hour here in peace and quiet."

Don Fernando parted the trooper and Don Quixote, and, to the relief of both of them, unlocked their grip on one another. Nevertheless, the troopers still kept on demanding their prisoner and calling on the company to help them to tie up and hand over the highway robber to them, in accordance with the laws of the King and the Holy Brotherhood.

Don Quixote laughed when he heard them say these words, and exclaimed: "Come hither, filthy, base-born crew! Do you call me a highway robber because I liberated those in chains, freed those who were bound, aided those who were wretched, raised the fallen and succoured the needy? O infamous brood! Your understanding is too mean and base for you to deserve that Heaven should communicate to you the power which lies in knight-errantry: you are even unworthy to be shown the sin and ignorance in which you wallow, when you refuse to revere the shadow, much more the actual presence, of a knight-errant! Come hither, ye that are not troopers but thieves in a troop, highway robbers with licence from the Holy Brotherhood! Tell me, who was the idiot who signed a warrant for the arrest of such a knight as I am? Who was he who did not know that knights-errant are free from all jurisdiction? That their law is their sword, their charters their courage, their statutes their own will? Who is the blockhead, I say again, who is not aware that there exists no patent of nobility with so many privileges and exemptions as that which a knight-errant acquires the day he is dubbed a knight and devotes himself to the stern exercise of chivalry? What knight-errant ever paid poll tax, customs, queen's patten money, king's tribute, toll or impost? What tailor ever took money from him for a suit of clothes? What constable ever lodged him in his castle and made him pay his scot? What king did not seat him at his own table? What maiden did not fall in love with him and surrender herself to his will and pleasure? And, lastly, what knight-errant was there, is, or shall be in the world, who has not the courage, single-handed, to give four hundred drubbings to four hundred troopers if they stand in his way?"

While Don Quixote was uttering this oration, the curate was trying to persuade the troopers that the knight was out of his wits, as they could perceive by his words and his actions, and that even if they did arrest him, they would have to release him afterwards as a madman. To this the trooper who had the warrant answered that he was not there to pass judgment on Don Quixote's madness: he had just to carry out the orders of his superior officer.

"Nevertheless," said the curate, "this time you must not take him away; nor do I believe that he will let himself be taken." The curate brought forward so many arguments and Don Quixote himself did so many eccentric things that the troopers would have had to be as mad as he was not to discover the knight's infirmity. At last they were convinced, and they even agreed to act as arbiters and make peace between the barber and Sancho Panza, who still nursed their quarrel with great bitterness. As for Mambrino's helmet, the curate, secretly and unperceived by Don Quixote, gave eight reals for the basin, and the barber wrote out a receipt in token of the settlement. The landlord, however, had not turned a blind eye on the compensation which the curate had paid to the barber: he now demanded Don Quixote's reckoning as well as payment for the damage to his skins and the loss of his wine, and he swore that neither Rozinante nor Dapple should budge from the inn until he was paid to the last farthing. The curate settled all, Don Fernando paid the bill, and everybody now rested in peace and tranquillity, so that the inn no longer resembled the discord of Agramante's camp, as Don Quixote had said, but the peace and quiet of the Augustan age.

XXIV. The amazing method of our Knight's enchantment and how he returned to his village

DON QUIXOTE, NOW THAT HE FOUND HIMSELF FREE FROM all quarrels, both his own and his squire's, thought it was high time for him to continue the journey he had begun, and bring to an end the great adventure for which he had been called and chosen. Therefore with firm resolution he went and cast himself upon his knees before Dorothea, but she would not allow him to utter a word until he rose, and so to obey her he stood up and said: "It is a well-known proverb, beauteous lady, that 'diligence is the mother of good luck'; and in nothing is this truth more clearly shown than in the affairs of war, in which rapidity of action forestalls the designs of the enemy, and snatches the victory before the adversary has time to be on the defensive. All this I say, high and worthy lady, because it seems to me that our further stay in this castle is without profit, and may turn out to our disadvantage, as we many find out some day. For who knows but thy enemy the giant may have already learned by spies how I intend to destroy him, and our delay may give him the opportunity of fortifying himself in some impregnable castle, against which even the might of my untiring arm will be of little avail? Therefore, dear lady, let us by our diligence hinder his plans, and let us depart quickly with good fortune on our side."

Don Quixote said no more and awaited calmly for the answer of the beautiful princess. She, with a lordly air and in a style adapted to Don Quixote's, replied as follows: "I thank you, Sir Knight, for the desire you show to assist me in my great need, like a knight whose function is to protect the orphans and the distressed. Heaven grant that your desires and mine may succeed, that you may see there are grateful women on earth. As for my departure, let it be at once, for I have no other will than that which is yours. Therefore dispose of me as you will, for she who has once given you the defence of her person, and has committed into your hands the recovery of her estates, ought not to seek to do otherwise than as your wisdom shall suggest."

"By the hand of God," cried Don Quixote, "since a lady thus humbles herself to me, I will not lose the opportunity of raising her up and setting her upon the throne she has inherited from her sires. Let us depart immediately, for my wishes are spurring me on to the journey, and there is a saying that in delay there is danger. Since Heaven has never created nor hell ever seen one to frighten or intimidate me, go saddle me Rozinante, Sancho, and get ready your ass and the queen's palfrey, and let us take leave of the castellan and these gentlemen and depart instantly."

Sancho, who was present during all this, said, wagging his head from side to side: "O master, master! There's a deal more mischief done in the village than is noised abroad: with all due deference to the good bodies, I'm saying it."

"What can be noised abroad in any village or in any of the cities of the world to my discredit, you bumpkin?"

"If you get into a rage, master," answered Sancho, "I'll

hold my tongue and omit to say what I'm bound as a good squire and an honest servant to tell you."

"Say what you will," replied Don Quixote, "provided your words are not intended to rouse fears in me. You, when you fear, behave like yourself; whereas I behave like myself when I fear not."

"As I'm a sinner," answered Sancho, "that's not it. But I'm certain and positive that this lady who calls herself queen of the great kingdom of Micomicon is no more a queen than my own mother. If she were what she says, she wouldn't at every head's turn and behind every door be nuzzling with somebody of the present company."

Dorothea blushed at Sancho's words, for it was true that her husband, Don Fernando, had every now and then, on the sly, gathered with his lips part of the prize his love had earned. Sancho had noticed this and he thought such wanton behaviour rather became a courtezan than the queen of a great kingdom. Dorothea was neither able nor willing to answer him, but let him continue, which he did as follows: "I'm telling you this, master, because if after we have travelled highways and byways and endured bad nights and worse days, he that is disporting himself in this inn is to snaffle the fruit of our labours, there's no need to fash myself saddling Rozinante, harnessing Dapple, or getting ready the palfrey. In fact we'd be wiser to stay still, and let every drab stick to her spinning and let us be off to our dinner."

Heavens above! What a mighty rage surged in Don Quixote's bosom when he heard his squire utter those unmannerly words! It was so great that, with faltering voice and stammering tongue, with fire blazing from his eyes, he said: "O base-born scoundrel! Ill-mannered, vulgar, ignorant, ill-spoken, foul-tongued, insolent and audacious back-biter! Do you dare to utter such words in my presence and in the presence of these distinguished ladies? How dare you conceive such rude and insolent thoughts in your muddled imagination? Leave my presence, monster of nature, treasury of lies, storehouse of deceits, depository of rascalities, inventor of mischiefs, publisher of follies, enemy of the respect due to royalty! Begone! Never appear before me, on pain of my wrath."

Saying this, he arched his brows, puffed out his cheeks, glared about him on every side, and stamped his right foot on the ground, thus showing his pent-up rage.

At these words and furious gestures Sancho fell into such a fit of cowering and cringing that he would have been glad if the earth had opened that instant beneath his feet and engulfed him. He was at a loss what to say or do, so he turned his back to hasten out of the presence of his angry master.

But the tactful Dorothea, who understood perfectly the humours of Don Quixote, said, to pacify him, the following words: "Do not be offended, Sir Knight of the Rueful Figure, at the idle words your good squire has spoken. Perhaps he said them not without some cause; for, considering his good sense and Christian understanding, we could not suspect him of wishing to slander or accuse anyone falsely. We must, therefore, believe that doubtless, as you have yourself said, Sir Knight, in this castle all things are subject to enchantment, and Sancho must have seen, through that diabolical illusion, what he believes he saw, so much to the prejudice of my honour."

"I swear by almighty God," said Don Quixote, "that your highness has hit the mark, and some evil spectre must have appeared to this sinner Sancho, which made him see what he could not have seen except by magic, for I know too well the goodness and the innocence of this poor unhappy wretch, and that he is incapable of bearing false witness against a living soul."

"So it is, and so it shall be," said Don Fernando: "therefore, Señor Don Quixote, you must pardon him, and restore him to your bosom, *sicut in principio,* before these apparitions drive him out of his senses."

Don Quixote said he pardoned him, and the curate went for Sancho, who came in very crestfallen, and, after falling down on his knees, humbly begged his master's hand. The latter gave him his hand, and, after letting him kiss it, gave him his blessing, saying: "Now, Sancho, my son, you will be thoroughly convinced of the truth of what I have told you many times, namely, that all things in this castle come about by means of enchantment."

"I do believe so," said Sancho, "except that business in the blanket, which really happened in the ordinary way."

"Do not believe it," answered Don Quixote: "if it had been so, I would have avenged you then and I am ready to do so now. But neither then nor now could I see anyone on whom I could take vengeance for that injury."

In spite of this, Sancho's folly never reached to such a pitch that he could believe it was not the absolute truth without any shadow of doubt, that he had been tossed in a blanket by persons of flesh and bone, and not by visionary phantoms, as his master believed.

The illustrious company had now been two days in the inn, and thinking it was time to depart, they considered how without giving Dorothea and Don Fernando the trouble of accompanying Don Quixote back to his village, on the pretext of restoring the Princess Micomicona, the curate and the barber might take him with them and get him cured at home. This was the plan they decided upon. They made a bargain with a waggoner, who happened to pass by with his team of oxen, to carry our knight in the following manner. They made a kind of cage of trellised poles, large enough to hold Don Quixote in it comfortably, and then Don Fernando and his companions together with the troopers and the landlord, by the direction of the curate, covered their faces and disguised themselves so that they might appear to Don Quixote to be different persons to any he had seen in the castle. This being done, they entered the room silently where he lay sleeping peacefully, little recking of such an accident, and, seizing him forcibly, they tied up his hands and feet very firmly so that when he started out of his sleep he could not move nor do anything but stare and wonder at the strange faces he saw before him. And straightway his disordered imagination suggested to him that these were the phantoms of that enchanted castle, and that without any doubt he was enchanted, for he could neither move nor defend himself. All this turned out exactly as the curate, the inventor of the scheme, had anticipated. Sancho alone, of all who were present, was in his right mind as well as in his own clothes; for though he was wellnigh infected with his master's infirmity, yet he could not help knowing who all these counterfeit phantoms were, but he did not dare to unseal his lips until he should see what would be the result of this assault and seizure of his master. The latter, likewise, did not say a word, but submissively awaited the outcome of his misfortunes.

The outcome was that they brought in the cage and shut him in, nailing the bars so well that they could not easily be burst open. They then hoisted him on to their shoulders, and, as he was carried out of his chamber, a voice was heard—as dreadful a voice as the barber could muster (not the pack-saddle barber, by the way), which said: "O Knight of the Rueful Figure, be not downcast at thy imprisonment, for so it must be that the adventure to which thy bravery has committed thee may be more speedily accomplished. That shall be accomplished when the furious Manchegan lion shall mate with the white dove of El Toboso after they have humbled their stately necks beneath the soft yoke of matrimony. From this unheard-of union there shall come forth to the light of day doughty whelps, who shall rival the ramping talons of their valiant sire. And this shall come to pass ere the god who pursues the fleeting nymph shall twice have visited in his swift and natural course the bright constellations. And thou, O most noble and obedient squire that ever had sword in belt, beard on chin, smell in nose, be not dismayed nor discontented to see the very flower of knight-errantry carried away before thine eyes, for in a short time, if it pleases the great artificer of the world, thou shalt see thyself so exalted and sublimated that thou shalt not know thyself, and neither shalt thou be cheated of the promises which thy good lord has made to thee. I assure thee, on behalf of the sage Mentironiana, that thy wages shall punctually be paid to thee, as thou shalt see in due course. Follow, therefore, the steps of the brave, enchanted knight, for it is right that ye should go where you will both remain. I am not allowed to say any more, so farewell. I now return whither I alone know."

As he finished the prophecy the barber raised his voice in pitch, and then modulated it in such a soft pathetic tone that even those who were in the plot well-nigh believed that what they heard was real. Don Quixote was comforted by this prophecy, for he at once understood its whole meaning, and saw that it promised him the fortune of being wedded to his beloved Dulcinea del Toboso, from whose womb should spring the whelps, his sons, to the eternal glory of La Mancha. Being convinced of the sincerity of the prediction, he lifted up his voice and sighing deeply he said: "O thou, whoever thou art, who hast foretold this great happiness for me, I beg thee to entreat the wise magician who directs my fortunes, not to allow me to perish in this prison wherein they have now put me, until I see accomplished the incomparable promises they have made me. If this come to pass, I shall glory in the chains which bind me, and this pallet on which I lie will be no hard field of battle, but a soft bridal bed of down. And as concerns my squire Sancho Panza, I trust in his goodness of heart and conduct, that he will not abandon me in good or evil fortune. For though it should happen through his or my hard lot that I shall not be able to bestow on him the island which I have promised him, yet at least he shall not lose his wages, for in my will, which is already made, I have set down what he is to have."

Sancho Panza bowed respectfully, and kissed his master's two hands, which were tied together. Then the phantoms hoisted the cage on to their shoulders, and placed it on the ox-waggon.

When Don Quixote found himself cooped up in that manner in the cart, he said: "Many learned histories have I read of knights-errant, but never have I read, nor seen, nor heard, that they carried enchanted knights in this manner, and as slowly as these lazy animals seem to go. They are always carried through the air with amazing rapidity, enveloped in some thick, dark cloud, or in a chariot of fire, or mounted upon a hippogriff or some such animal. To be carried off in an ox-cart! By the living God, it fills me with shame! Perhaps, however, the chivalries and enchantments of our day follow a different road from that followed by the ancients. As I am a new knight and the first to revive the forgotten exercise of knight-errantry, perchance new ways of enchantment and new methods of carrying the enchanted have come into fashion. What do you think, Sancho, my son?"

"I don't know what to think," answered Sancho, "for I'm not so well up in the scriptures-errant. But still an' all I'd swear that the ghosts we've seen are not too Catholic."

"Catholic?" answered Don Quixote: "My sainted father! How can they be Catholic when they are all devils who have put on weird shapes to accomplish their purpose, and put me into this state? If you wish to convince yourself, touch them and feel them, and you will find they have no bodies and are made of air; they only exist to our eyes."

"Faith, sir," replied Sancho, "an' I've touched 'em already, and this devil here who's so busy is as plump as a partridge, and has another characteristic very different from what you'd find in devils: for I've heard tell that devils smell of sulphur and other foulness; but this one smells of amber half a league off." Sancho said this of Don Fernando, who, being a fine gentleman, must have smelt as Sancho said.

"Do not wonder at this, friend Sancho," answered Don Quixote. "I tell you, the devils are very cunning, and though they carry smells about them, they do not smell, for they are spirits. And if they do smell, it is not of good things, but of such as are foul and fetid. The reason is that wherever they are, they take hell with them, and there is no relief for them from its torments. Wherefore if you think that this devil you speak of smells of amber, either you are deceiving yourself or he is deceiving you by making you believe he is not a devil."

All this conversation took place between master and servant. Now Don Fernando and Cardenio feared that Sancho would discover their stratagem, for he had already suspected that something was afoot, so they resolved to hasten their departure. They called the landlord aside and ordered him to saddle Rozinante and put the pack-saddle on Sancho's ass. This was done without delay. Cardenio hung on one side of Rozinante's saddle-bow the buckler and on the other side the basin, and he made signs to Sancho to get up on his ass and take Rozinante by the bridle. But before the cart began to move, the landlady, her daughter and Maritornes came out to say farewell to Don Quixote, and they pretended to shed sorrowful tears at his misfortunes. The knight addressed them as follows: "Do not weep, good ladies: all these misfortunes are the lot of those who profess what I profess. If these disasters did not befall me, I would not consider myself a famous knight-errant, for such mishaps do not happen to knights of small repute. Forgive me, fair ladies, if unwittingly I have given you any cause for annoyance, and pray to God that I may be delivered from these fetters which some evil-minded magician has cast about me. If ever I am freed from them, never shall I forget to requite the favours ye have bestowed upon me in this castle."

While this was taking place between the ladies of the castle and Don Quixote, the curate and the barber took leave of Don Fernando, Cardenio and their companions, and especially of Dorothea and Luscinda. The order of the cavalcade was as follows: first went the cart, guided by its owner: on either side marched the troopers with their cross-bows: then came Sancho Panza on his ass, leading Rozinante by the bridle: in the rear of all rode the curate and barber upon their sturdy mules (both wore their masks that they might not at once be recognized by Don Quixote): the whole procession moved on with great solemnity, travelling no faster than the slow pace of the oxen permitted. Don Quixote sat in his cage, with his hands tied and his legs stretched out, leaning against the bars, as silently and patiently as if he had not been a man of flesh but a statue of stone. And thus silently and slowly they journeyed for about two leagues, when they came to a valley which the waggoner thought a suitable place for resting and feeding his oxen. Here in this green and pleasant spot the company determined to unpack the provisions and banquet in the shade of the trees. While these preparations were being made, Sancho, seeing that the curate and the barber, whom he regarded as suspicious persons, were not at his elbow, went up to his master's cage, and said: "Master, I must unburden my conscience and tell you what's happening about this enchantment of yours: it is this—that yon two who are riding along with us here with their faces masked, are the priest and the barber of our village. I'm thinking that they've played this trick of carrying you in this manner, out of pure envy of you, sir, because you outdid them in famous deeds. Now, if I'm right in this, it follows that you're not enchanted but bamboozled and befooled. To prove this, I'd like to ask you one question: if you answer me as I think you will, you'll lay your finger on this trick and you'll find that you're not enchanted but gone daft in the head."

"Ask what you will, Sancho, my son," replied Don Quixote. "I will answer all your questions. But when you say that those who accompany us are our townsmen the curate and the barber, I tell you that you are mistaken: those persons who accompany us are no more the curate and the barber than I am a Turk. As to your queries, make them, for I will answer you, even if you continue questioning me until tomorrow morning."

"Blessed Virgin!" cried Sancho in a loud voice. "Is it possible, master, that you're so thick-skulled and brain-sick? It's the honest truth I'm telling you, and there's more roguery than magic in this trouble of yours, as I'll clearly prove. Now what I want is for you, sir, to tell me the whole truth, without adding or subtracting aught from it, as all should speak and do speak who exercise the profession of arms, as you do, under the title of knights-errant."

"I tell you I will lie in nothing," answered Don Quixote; "make an end of your questions, for in truth I am weary, Sancho, of your supplications and preambles."

"I'm asking, master," replied Sancho, "with all respect, whether since you have been cooped up, or as you call it enchanted, in this cage, you have had any longing to do the greater or lesser business, as the saying goes?"

"I do not understand," answered Don Quixote, "what you mean by doing the business: explain your meaning."

"Is it possible, sir," said Sancho, "that you do not know what the greater or the lesser business is? Why, children at school are suckled on it. It means whether you feel inclined to do what nobody else can do for you."

"Ah! Now I understand you, Sancho. Yes, I have often had the inclination, and I have it at the present moment. Help me now—all is not clean with me."

"Ah!" cried Sancho, "now I've caught you: this is what I longed to know with all my heart and soul. Come now, sir, can you deny what everyone says in these parts when a person is in the dumps? It is always said, 'I don't know what's the matter with so-and-so; he doesn't eat, nor drink, nor sleep, nor answer pat when you ask him a question: surely he must be enchanted'. So it's as plain as a pikestaff that they who don't eat, nor drink, nor sleep, nor do the natural doings I speak of, are enchanted. But they who have the longing you have, and eat and drink when they can get it, are not enchanted."

"You are right, Sancho," replied Don Quixote, "but I have told you that there are many kinds of enchantment and perhaps they change with the times from one kind to another. I know and I am convinced that I am enchanted, and that is enough for the peace of my conscience. If I were not enchanted, I should be greatly perturbed to think that I had let myself be cooped up in this cage like a lazy coward when there are so many distressed in the world who need my protection."

"For all that, master, you should try and get out of this prison, and I'll guarantee to help you and release you from it so that you may mount again your good Rozinante: he's so crestfallen that he must be enchanted too. But once we've done this, let us try our luck once more and go off in search of adventures, and if all doesn't turn out well, there'll be time enough to return to the cage."

Sancho Panza then went up to the curate and begged him to allow his master to leave the cage for a short while, otherwise that prison could not remain so clean as the decency of such a knight as his master required. The curate understood and said he would be very willing to grant his request, but for the fear lest Don Quixote, finding himself free, would play one of his pranks, and go off where no one would ever find him. Sancho, however, replied that he would go bail for his not running away, and Don Quixote pledged his word as a knight not to leave without the consent of his captors.

The curate then uncaged him, and he, finding himself outside his gaol, was overjoyed. The first thing he did was to stretch himself, and then he went up to Rozinante and gave him a few slaps on the haunches, saying: "I still put my faith in God and in His blessed Mother, O flower and mirror of steeds! I trust that soon we two shall find our wish fulfilled; you, with your master on your back, and I on top of you, exercising the function for which God sent me into the world." Saying this, Don Quixote went apart with Sancho to a remote spot, whence he returned much relieved, and with a still greater wish to carry out the designs of his squire.

Shortly afterwards, while Don Quixote and Sancho were seated conversing with the curate and the barber and the rest of the company, they heard the sound of a trumpet, so mournful that it made them turn towards the place whence it seemed to come. Don Quixote was the most excited of them all when he heard the sound, and he cried straightway: "Methinks the sad notes of yon trumpet do summon me to some new adventure."

He rose to his feet and strove to discover where the sound came from. All of a sudden he saw descending a hill a number of men, clad in the white habits of penitents. Now the clouds that year had denied the earth their moisture, so through all the valleys of that region, processions, public prayers and penances were ordered to beseech Heaven to open the flood-gates of its mercy and send them rain. It was for this purpose, therefore, that the people of a neighbouring village were coming in procession to a holy shrine which stood on a hill at the edge of the valley. Don Quixote, as soon as he saw the strange attire of the penitents, did not pause to recall the many occasions on which he had seen a similar sight before, but immediately he imagined that it was some kind of adventure which was reserved for him alone as knight-errant. He was all the more confirmed in his opinion on seeing an image clothed in black which they bore, and which, he was sure, must be some great lady carried away by ruffians and unmannerly churls. No sooner did this thought flash through his mind than he rushed over to Rozinante, who was grazing near by, and, taking off the bridle and buckler which hung from the pommel of the saddle, he bridled him in an instant. Then, asking Sancho for his sword, he mounted Rozinante and, bracing his buckler, he cried in a loud voice to all present: "Now, valiant company, ye shall see how necessary it is that there should be in the world knights who profess the order of knight-errantry: now, I say, shall ye see, in the restoration of that captive lady to liberty, whether knights-errant ought to be valued!"

So saying, he clapped his heels to Rozinante (for spurs he had none), and at a half-gallop (for we nowhere read, in all this truthful history, that Rozinante ever went at full speed), he advanced to encounter the penitents, though the curate and the barber tried to stop him. But it was in vain, for not even the voice of Sancho detained him, as he shouted: "Master, where are you going? What devils in your heart are driving you on to attack our Catholic faith? Mind, sir, bad 'cess to me, yon is a procession of penitents, and that lady they're carrying on the stretcher is the most blessed image of the Immaculate Virgin. Take heed, sir, what you're doing: this time you're in for what you've not bargained for."

Sancho wearied himself in vain, for his master was so set upon encountering the penitents in their sheets, and upon freeing the lady in black, that he heard not a word, and, even if he had, he would not have turned back though the King himself had commanded him. When he reached the procession he stopped Rozinante, who already wanted to rest a little, and in a hoarse, angry voice he cried out: "You there, who cover up your faces probably because you are evil, halt and pay heed to my words!"

The first to halt were those who were carrying the image. Then one of the four priests who chanted the litanies, noticing the strange appearance of Don Quixote, the leanness of Rozinante, and other ludicrous details, answered him, saying: "Brother, if you have anything to say, say it quickly, for these brethren of ours are scourging their flesh, and we cannot, nor is it right that we should, stop to listen to anything that may not be said in two words."

"I will say it in one," replied Don Quixote. "You must instantly free that beauteous lady whose tears and sad appearance show clearly that you are bearing her away against her will, and have done her some grievous wrong. But I, who came into the world to redress such injuries, will not allow you to move one single step forward till you have restored to her the liberty she desires and deserves."

From these words all who heard them concluded that Don Quixote must be some madman, and they began to laugh heartily. But their laughter only served to add gunpowder to the knight's fury, for without another word he drew his sword and attacked the litter. One of those who carried it, leaving the burden to his comrades, stepped forward to encounter Don Quixote, brandishing a forked pole, on which he supported the litter while resting, and with it he parried the heavy stroke which the knight aimed at him. The force of the stroke snapped the pole in two, but with the stump that was left in his hand he dealt the knight such a smack on the shoulder of his sword-arm that his buckler was unable to shield him against the rustic onslaught, and down came poor Don Quixote to the ground in a bad way. Sancho, who came panting after him, seeing him fall, called out to his assailant not to strike him, for he was a poor enchanted knight who had done nobody any harm all his life. The peasant stopped, not, however, on account of Sancho's appeal, but because he saw that Don Quixote stirred neither hand nor foot. And, believing he had killed him, he hastily tucked up his habit to his girdle, and set off, running like a deer across the country.

By this time all Don Quixote's company had come up to where he lay, but those in the procession, seeing them running in their direction, among them troopers of the Holy Brotherhood with their cross-bows, feared some trouble. So they clustered in a circle about the image; the penitents lifted their hoods, grasping their lashes; the priests brandished their tapers, and all waited for the attack, with the firm resolve to defend themselves, and if they could, to take the offensive against their aggressors. But fortune arranged matters better than they expected, for Sancho did nothing but cast himself upon the body of his master, making over him the most sorrowful and at the same time the most laughable lament in the world, for he truly believed Don Quixote was dead. The squire with tears in his eyes cried: "O flower of chivalry, who by one single blow of a cudgel hast finished the course of thy well-spent years! O thou credit to thy race, honour and glory of all La Mancha, aye, of the whole world, which through loss of thee will be overrun with evil-doers, who will no longer fear punishment for their iniquities! O thou, liberal above all the Alexanders, since for a mere eight months' service thou hast given me the best island which the sea surrounds! O thou, who wast humble with the haughty and arrogant with the humble! Resister of perils, sufferer of affronts, lover without cause, imitator of the good, scourge of the wicked, enemy of the base! In a word, knight-errant, which is the highest thing anyone could say!"

At the cries and groans of Sancho, Don Quixote revived, and said: "He who lives absent from thee, sweet Dulcinea, endures far greater sufferings than these. Help, friend Sancho, to lift me into the enchanted car, for I am no longer in a condition to press the saddle of Rozinante, for this shoulder of mine is broken to pieces."

"That I'll do with all my heart, dear master," replied

Sancho, "and let us go back to our village in company with these gentlemen, and there we will make schemes for another sally, that may be more profitable to us."

"You speak well, Sancho," answered the knight, "it is prudent for us to wait until the evil influence of the stars, which now reigns, passes away."

The curate and the barber approved this resolution, and they placed Don Quixote in the waggon as before. The procession resumed its former order and continued on its way. The troopers refused to go on any farther, so the curate paid what was owing and discharged them. The party now consisted only of the curate, the barber, Don Quixote, Sancho, and good Rozinante, who bore all the ups and downs as patiently as his master. The waggoner yoked his oxen, and, having laid Don Quixote on a bundle of hay, plodded his way at his usual calm, deliberate pace, following the directions of the curate, and at the end of six days reached Don Quixote's village. They made their entrance at noon, and as it happened to be Sunday all the people were in the market-place when the waggon passed through. Everyone rushed to see who was in it, and when they recognized their townsman they were amazed. A boy ran off at full speed to give the news to his housekeeper and niece that their master was coming home, lean and yellow, stretched full length on a bundle of hay in an ox-cart. It was a pathetic thing to hear the cries of the two ladies, the blows they gave themselves, the curses they uttered afresh against the books of chivalry, especially when they saw Don Quixote enter the door of his house.

As soon as she received news of Don Quixote's arrival Sancho Panza's wife ran thither, and, as soon as she saw Sancho, her first enquiry was whether the ass had come home in good condition. Sancho replied that he was in better health than his master.

"Thanks be to God," said she, "for this great favour. Now tell me, husband, what good have you got from your squireships? What petticoat have you brought for me? What dainty shoes for your children?"

"I've brought you nought of that kind, dear wife," said Sancho; "but I've other things of more consequence."

"I'm glad to hear so," answered the wife; "show me those things of more consequence. I'm dying to see them, to gladden my heart, for I've been mournful and down in the mouth all those ages you've been away."

"I'll show them to you at home, wife," said Sancho. "For the present, hold your soul in patience. Please God we may sally out another time in search of adventures and you'll soon see me Count or Governor of an island—not one of those round here, but the finest that can be found."

"May the Lord be pleased to grant it, husband, for we're in sore need of it. Tell me now: what's all this about islands? —I don't catch your meaning."

"Honey is not for an ass's mouth," answered Sancho. "You'll see in good time, wife; aye, and you'll be struck of a heap at hearing yourself called 'Ladyship' by all your vassals."

"What are you prating about ladyship, islands and vassals?" cried Juana Panza, for that was the name of Sancho's wife.

"Don't fash yourself, Juana, and be in too much of a hurry: it's enough for you to know that I'm telling the truth, so mum's the word. But I can tell you one thing by the way, namely, that there's nought in this world so pleasant as for an honest, decent man to be squire to a knight-errant on the prowl for adventures. 'Tis true, I must say, that most we knocked up against were not so comfortable as a body would wish, for out of a hundred that we met, the ninety-nine usually fell out cross and crooked. I know by experience, but when all's said and done, it's a fine thing to be gadding about spying for chances, crossing mountains, exploring woods, climbing rocks, visiting castles, lodging in inns at our own sweet will, with the devil a farthing to pay."

While this conversation was passing between Sancho Panza and Juana Panza his wife, Don Quixote's housekeeper and niece received the knight, undressed him and put him into his old bed. He looked at them with eyes askance, for he could not make out where he was. The curate told the niece to have great care of her uncle, and to be on the constant look-out lest he might escape again. The two women were sore worried lest they should again lose their master and uncle, the moment he should find himself a little better.

Indeed, the sequel to this history proved that their fears were not groundless.

PART TWO

1. *Diverting interviews between Don Quixote, Sancho Panza, the bachelor Samson Carrasco and others*

THE CURATE AND THE BARBER REMAINED NEARLY A MONTH without visiting Don Quixote, lest they should revive his recollection of what had taken place. They did not, however, refrain from visiting his niece and housekeeper, and they urged them to be careful to treat him well and give him comforting things to eat and such as were good for heart and brain, for it was manifest that all his troubles came from that quarter. The two women replied that they did so and would continue to do so with all possible care and kindness, for they noticed that their master now and then began to show signs of being in his right senses. This piece of news gave great satisfaction to the curate and the barber, for it served to prove that they had acted rightly in bringing him back enchanted in the ox-cart, as has been described in this great and accurate history. So they determined to pay him a visit and test the progress of his cure, though they thought that was scarcely possible; but they agreed not to utter a word connected with knight-errantry so as not to run the risk of ripping open wounds which were still so tender.

They found him sitting up in bed clad in a green baize waistcoat and a red Toledo cap, so dried up and shrivelled that he looked as if he had turned into a mummy. He welcomed them cordially, and to their questions about his health he replied intelligently in very well-chosen words. In the course of their conversation they discoursed on so-called reasons of state and systems of government, correcting this abuse and condemning that, reforming one practice and abolishing another, in fact each of the three set himself up as a new law-giver, a modern Lycurgus, or a brand-new Solon; and so completely did they remodel the state that they might as well have cast it into a furnace and drawn out something quite different from what they had put in; and on all the subjects they touched, Don Quixote spoke with such good sense that the two examiners believed without a shadow of doubt that he was quite recovered and in his full senses.

The niece and the housekeeper were present at the conversation and could not find adequate words to thank God for seeing their master so clear in his mind. The curate, however, then changed his original plan, which was not to touch upon matters of chivalry, and resolved to test Don Quixote's recovery thoroughly to see whether it was genuine or not; so, ranging from one subject to another, he came at last to talk of the news that had come from the capital. Among other things he said that they had it for certain that the Turk was descending with a powerful fleet, but no one knew what his purpose was, or where the mighty storm would burst. And owing to this fear, which almost every year rouses men to arms, all Christendom was on the *qui vive*, and His Majesty had made provision for the defence of the coasts of Naples and Sicily and the island of Malta.[1]

To this Don Quixote answered: "His Majesty has acted

[1] This is a pointed reference to the naval power of the Turks which was a continual threat to Spain and Italy during the 16th and 17th centuries, in spite of the great victory of Lepanto in 1571.

like a most prudent warrior in providing for the safety of his realms in time, so that the enemy may not find him unprepared; but if he would follow my advice, I would counsel him to adopt a measure which I fancy His Majesty little thinks of at the present moment."

No sooner did the curate hear these words than he said to himself: "God protect you, poor Don Quixote! It looks as if you are tumbling from the pinnacle of your madness into the depths of your simplicity."

But the barber, who had the same suspicions as the curate, asked Don Quixote what kind of measures did he think they should adopt; perhaps, indeed, they might be added to the long list of impertinent suggestions that are usually offered to princes.

"My suggestions, Mr. Scrape-beard, will not be impertinent but highly pertinent," said Don Quixote.

"No harm meant," said the barber, "but experience has shown that most of the suggestions offered to His Majesty are either impossible, absurd, or damaging to King and country."

"But my suggestion," answered Don Quixote, "is neither impossible nor absurd, but the easiest, the justest, readiest and simplest which could suggest itself to the mind of man."

"You are slow in telling us about it, Señor Don Quixote," said the curate.

"I don't want to tell it here now," said Don Quixote, "for fear it might reach the ears of the Lords of the Council tomorrow, and some other person carry off the thanks and reward for my pains."

"As for me," said the barber, "I give my word here and before God that I'll not tell what you say to a soul."

"I am sure," said Don Quixote, "that your word is good, for I know that you are an honest man."

"Even if he were not," said the curate, "I'll go bail for him, and vouch that in this matter he'll be as mum as a dumb man, under pain of any penalty imposed by the court."

"But who will go bail for your reverence?" said Don Quixote.

"My profession," replied the curate, "which is to keep secrets."

"By my troth!" exclaimed Don Quixote at this, "what else has His Majesty to do but to order by public proclamation all the knights-errant who are roving about Spain to gather in the capital on a certain day, and even if no more than half a dozen come, there may be one among them who alone would be strong enough to annihilate the total might of the Turk? Pay attention, both of you, and follow me. Is it, mark you, an unheard-of exploit for a single knight-errant to cut to bits an army of two hundred thousand men as if all together had but one throat or were made of almond-paste?

Nay, tell me, how many histories are filled with these wonders? Supposing the famous Don Belianis were alive at this moment ('twere an evil hour for me, I don't speak for anyone else), or any one of the innumerable offspring of Amadis of Gaul! If any one of them were alive today, and were to face the Turk, 'pon my faith I would not be in the latter's shoes. But God will look to His own people, and will provide someone who, if not so resolute as the knights-errant of old, will at least not be inferior to them in courage. A knight-errant I intend to die; let the Turk descend or ascend whenever he pleases and muster as great forces as he can. God knows my meaning, so I'll say no more."

At this point they heard the housekeeper and the niece, who had withdrawn from the conversation, crying out loudly in the courtyard, so they all ran out to see what was wrong.

They found them remonstrating indignantly with Sancho Panza and holding the door against him, while he was trying to push his way in to see Don Quixote. "What does the feckless lout want in this house?" cried they. "Off with you to your own haunts, brother, for it is you and no one else who deludes my master, and leads him roving over hill and dale."

To which Sancho replied: "Housekeeper of Satan! It's myself am deluded and led rambling over hill and dale, and not your master. He it is who led me on a jaunt all over the world, and you are wide of the mark. He it was tricked me away from home with his colloguing, promising me an island, which I'm still waiting for."

"May foul islands choke you, accursed Sancho," said the niece. "What are those islands of yours? Is it something tô eat, you glutton and gormandizer?"

"It's nought to eat," replied Sancho, "but something to govern and rule, and better than four cities or four judgeships at court."

"For all that," said the housekeeper, "you don't come in this door, you bag of mischief and sack of knavery. Go off and govern your own house, till your own allotment, and rid your empty pate of islands and islets."

The curate and the barber were greatly amused by the words of the trio, but Don Quixote was afraid lest Sancho might blab and blurt out a whole heap of mischievous follies, and touch upon points which might not redound entirely to his credit. So he called to him and made the two women hold their tongues and let him come in. Sancho entered, and the curate and the barber took their leave of Don Quixote. They now despaired of his cure, seeing how fixed he was in his crazy fancies and how much absorbed in his accursed nonsensical chivalry. Said the curate to the barber: "You will see, my friend, how, when we least expect it, our gentleman will spread his wings for another flight."

"I'm sure of it," replied the barber, "but the madness of the knight does not astonish me as much as the simplicity of the squire, who believes so firmly in that island that all the disappointments imaginable will not drive it out of his noddle."

"May God help them both," said the curate. "Let us be on the watch that we may see what comes of this crazy alliance of master and man. Both of them seem to have been cast in the same mould, and the eccentricities of one would not be worth a doit without the simplicity of the other."

"That is true," said the barber. "I should like very much to know what both are talking about at this moment."

"I am sure," answered the curate, "that the niece or the housekeeper will tell us later, for they'll not refrain from listening."

Meanwhile Don Quixote shut himself up in his room with Sancho, and when they were alone he said: "I am deeply grieved, Sancho, that you still say that it was I who took you from your cottage, when you know that I myself did not stay at home. We set out together, together we wandered. We have had the same fortune and the same luck. If they tossed you in a blanket once, they drubbed me a hundred times, and this is the one advantage I have over you."

"That was only right," replied Sancho, "for, according to what your worship says, misfortunes belong rather to knights-errant than to their squires."

"You are wrong, Sancho," said Don Quixote, "according to the saying *quando caput dolet,* etc."

"My own is the only language I understand," said Sancho.

"I mean to say," said Don Quixote, "that when the head aches all the other members suffer; and so, being your lord and master, I am your head, and you are a part of me since you are my servant; and thus the evil that touches or shall touch me should hurt you, and what touches you should give pain to me."

"So it should be," said Sancho, "but when I as a member was tossed in the blanket my head stood on the other side of the wall, looking on while I was flying through the air, and did not feel any pain at all; now if the members are forced to feel the head's pain, so it should be forced to feel their pain."

"Do you mean to say now, Sancho," said Don Quixote, "that I did not suffer when they were tossing you in the blanket? You must not say so or think so, for I felt more pain then in my spirit than you in your body. But put that aside for the present; there will be plenty of time later to consider and settle that point. Tell me, Sancho, my friend, what do they say about me in the village? What do the common people think of me? What do the nobles and the gentry say? What of my valour; what of my achievements; what of my courtesy? How do they say about the enterprise I have undertaken to revive and restore to the world the now forgotten order of chivalry? In short, Sancho, I want you to tell me what has come to your ears; you must tell me without exaggerating praise or mitigating blame; for loyal vassals must speak the truth to their lords, without exaggerating it through flattery or lessening it through vain deference. I wish to impress upon you, Sancho, that if the naked truth reached the ears of princes, without the trappings of flattery, times would be different and other ages would more fitly be reputed iron than ours, which I hold to be of gold. Follow this advice, Sancho, and report clearly and loyally all you know."

"That I will do most willingly, master," replied Sancho, "on condition that you will not be vexed at what I say."

"Speak freely, Sancho, and without any circumlocution."

"Then the first thing I have to say is that the common people consider you a mighty great madman and me no less a simpleton. The gentry say that you have not kept within the bounds of your quality as gentleman and have made yourself into a Don[2] and snatched at a knighthood, though you've but four vine-stocks and two acres of land, with a tatter behind and another in front. The knights say they don't want to have the hidalgos in opposition to them, especially those squireling-gentry who black their own shoes and darn their black stockings with green silk."

"That," said Don Quixote, "has nought to do with me, for I am always well dressed and never patched; ragged I may be, but ragged more from the wear and tear of my weapons than from time."

"As to your worship's valour, courtesy and exploits," continued Sancho, "there are different opinions. Some call you mad but droll: others, valiant but unfortunate; others, courteous but impertinent. Then they go sticking their noses into so many things that they don't leave a whole bone either in your worship or in myself."

"Remember, Sancho," said Don Quixote, "that whenever virtue is found in an eminent degree it is persecuted. Few or none of the famous men that have lived escaped being slandered by malicious tongues. Julius Caesar, the most high-spirited, wise and valiant of captains, had the reputation of being ambitious, and not over clean in his garments or in his morals. Alexander, whose deeds of prowess earned him the name of Great, was held to be somewhat of a drunkard. Of Hercules, the hero of many labours, it is said that he was lascivious and soft. Of Don Galaor, the brother of Amadis

[2] Today the title of Don is given by courtesy to everyone. In the days of Cervantes it was much more restricted.

of Gaul, it was rumoured that he was more than excessively lustful, and of his brother that he was tearful. Therefore, Sancho, when such good men's reputations are blasted, the calumnies at my expense may well pass, if they are not more serious than what you have mentioned."

"Ah, but there is the rub, body of my father!" replied Sancho.

"Is there more, then?" asked Don Quixote.

"Faith, an' we still have to skin the tail," said Sancho. "All up to this is just tarts and fancy bread; but if your worship wants to know all about the calumnies they fling at you, I'll bring someone anon who'll tell you the lot of them without missing an atom, for last night the son of Bartholomew Carrasco, who has been a student at Salamanca, came home—made a bachelor, and when I went to shake him by the hand, he told me that your worship's history is already told in a book by the name of *The Imaginative Gentleman, Don Quixote of La Mancha;* and, says he, they mention me in it by my own very name of Sancho Panza, and the Lady Dulcinea del Toboso too, and many a thing which happened to us when we were alone, which made me cross myself for amazement to think how the history-writer could have got wind of what he wrote."

"I assure you, Sancho," said Don Quixote, "that the author of our history must be some wise magician, for from such spirits nothing is hidden."

"Your worship may be right," answered Sancho, "but if you wish me to bring the bachelor here, I'll go off for him in a trice."

"You will do me a great favour, my friend," said Don Quixote, "for your tidings hold me in suspense, and I shall not eat a mouthful until I have heard the whole story."

"Then I'll be off for him," said Sancho. And leaving his master he went away to look for the bachelor, with whom he returned after a little while, and all three had a most diverting colloquy.

Now the bachelor, though his name was Samson, was no giant in stature, but was a very great wag. He was of sallow complexion, very sharp-witted, about four-and-twenty years of age, with a round face, a flat nose, and a large mouth —all signs of a mischievous disposition, and of one fond of joking and making fun, as he showed straightway, for no sooner did he see Don Quixote than he dropped on his knees before him, saying: "Let your mightiness give me your hands to kiss, Sir Don Quixote of La Mancha! For by the habit of St. Peter which I wear, though I hold no more than the first four orders, your worship is one of the most famous knights-errant that have ever been, or will ever be in all the round surface of the earth. Blessings on the Cide Hamete

Benengeli, who has written the history of your doughty deeds, and double blessings on the connoisseur who took the pains to have it translated from Arabic into our Castilian vulgar tongue for the universal entertainment of the people."

Don Quixote made him rise, and said: "So it is true that there is a history of me, and that it was a Moor and a wise man who wrote it?"

"So true is it, señor," said Samson, "that I believe there are today in print more than twelve thousand volumes of the said history. For proof you have only to ask Portugal, Barcelona and Valencia, where they have been printed, and it is rumoured that it is being printed at Antwerp, and I am convinced that there is not a country or language in the world in which it will not be translated.[3] And, mark you, it does not need a commentary to explain it, for it is so clear that there is nought in it to puzzle anyone. Children turn its leaves, young people read it, grown-ups understand it, and old folks commend it. In a word, it is so well thumbed and read and learnt by heart by people of all sorts that no sooner do they see any lean hack than they cry out: 'There goes Rozinante'. And those who are most given to reading it are the pages, for no lord's antechamber is without its copy of *Don Quixote*. When one lays it down, another takes it up; one pounces upon it, and another begs for it. In short, the said history is the most pleasing and least harmful entertainment that ever was known, for there is not in the whole of it even the semblance of an immodest word, or a thought that is other than Catholic."

"Does the author promise a second part?" said Don Quixote.

"He does," said Carrasco, "but he says he has not found it, nor does he know who has it; and we are in doubt whether it will come out or not. And therefore on this account, and because some hold that second parts are never any good, and others that enough has been written about Don Quixote, it is thought that there will be no second part; though some who are rather of a jovial than of a saturnine temperament say: 'Let us have more Quixoteries; let Don Quixote charge and Sancho talk, and come what may, we'll be content'."

"What is the author's intention, then?" said Don Quixote.

"Why," replied Samson, "as soon as he has found the history, which he is now searching for with extraordinary pains, he will straightway give it to the press, influenced rather by the profit he will draw from doing so than by any praise."

At this point, Sancho observed: "Does the author look for money and profit, does he? It'll be a wonder if he hits

---

[3] When Cervantes was writing Part II of *Don Quixote*, Shelton's translation of Part I had already appeared in England.

the nail on the head; for there'll be nought but hurry, hurry like a tailor on Easter Eve, and works done in a hurry are never finished as tidily as they should be. Let this Mister Moor, or whatever he is, keep his eye on what he is doing, for myself and my master will give him such a power of rubble and mortar in the matter of adventures and accidents that he could contrive not only a second part but a hundred. The good man evidently thinks we are lying asleep here in the straw, but let him hold our feet for the shoeing and he'll soon find which foot we limp on. What I mean to say is that if my master would take my advice we would be at this very moment in the field, undoing wrongs and righting injuries, as is the usage and custom of knights-errant."

Sancho had hardly uttered these words when the neighing of Rozinante reached their ears, which neighing Don Quixote recognized as a happy omen, and he determined to make another sally in three or four days from that time. Announcing his intention to the bachelor, he asked advice as to where he should start his expedition. The bachelor replied that in his opinion he ought to go to the kingdom of Aragón, and the city of Saragossa, where in a few days from that date certain solemn joustings would be held at the festival of St. George, at which he might win fame over all the knights of Aragón, which would be to win it over all the knights in the world. He promised Don Quixote's most honourable and valiant resolution, but warned him to be more cautious in affronting perils, seeing that his life did not belong to him, but to all those who needed him to protect them in their misfortunes.

"This is just what I object to, Mister Samson," said Sancho at this point. "My master here sets upon a hundred armed men as a greedy boy would upon half a dozen water-melons. Body of the world, Mister Bachelor, there are surely times for attacking and times for retreating, and we don't want it always to be 'Saint James and close Spain!'[4] Besides, I've heard tell (I think 'twas my master himself if I remember right) that the mean of valour lies between the extremes of cowardice and rashness. If this is so, I don't want him to take to his heels without good reason, or to make an attack when the odds require the opposite. But, above all, I warn my master that if he takes me with him it must be on condition that he is to do all the fighting, and that I am not to be obliged to do anything but look after his person in what concerns cleanliness and comfort. In this I am ready to dance attendance upon him; but to think that I have to lay hands on the sword, even against rascally churls of the baser kind with their hatchets, is a foolish thought.

[4] This was the battle-cry of the Spaniards in the Middle Ages.

I, Mister Samson, don't expect to win the fame of a fighting man, but only that of the best and most loyal squire that ever served knight-errant; and if my master Don Quixote, in return for my many faithful services, should be pleased to give me some island of the many he says he's bound to meet with in these parts, I'll be profoundly grateful. And if he should not give it to me, I'm just as I came into the world, and a man must not live on the favours of anyone but God. Moreover, my bread will taste as well, aye, and still better, without a government than with one. For how do I know that in these governorships the Devil may not have laid a trap for me, to make me stumble, fall and break my grinders? Sancho I was born and Sancho I mean to die. Nevertheless, if Heaven fairly and squarely, without trouble or risk, were to hand me an island or something like it, I am not such a fool as to fling it away, for there is also a saying that 'where they give thee a heifer, run with the halter', and 'when good luck comes thy way, take it home with thee'."

"Brother Sancho," said Carrasco, "you have spoken like a professor, but put your trust in God and in your master, Don Quixote, for he will give you not an island but a kingdom."

"It is all the same, be it the greater or the lesser," answered Sancho, "though I can tell Mister Carrasco that the kingdom my master gives me will not be flung into a sack all full of holes, for I've felt my pulse and I find myself sound enough to rule kingdoms and govern islands, and I've told my master as much long before now."

"Take care, Sancho," said Samson, "for office changes manners, and, perhaps, when you find yourself governor, you will not recognize the mother who bore you."

"That may be true," replied Sancho, "of those who are born in a ditch among the mallows, but not of those who have four fingers' depth of honest old Christian fat on their souls, as I have.[5] Nay, just take a look at my disposition: do you think that is likely to show ingratitude to anyone?"

"God grant it may not," said Don Quixote. "We shall see this when the governorship comes along: I seem to see it already."

After much discussion it was decided that the departure should take place within eight days from that date. Don Quixote charged the bachelor to keep it a secret, especially from the curate and Master Nicholas the barber, and from his niece and his housekeeper, lest they should prevent him from carrying out his laudable and valiant purpose. All this Carrasco promised, and then departed, charging Don Quixote to keep him informed, whenever possible, of his good or evil

[5] Sancho was very proud of being an Old Christian ("Cristiano viejo rancio"), that is to say, without any mixture of Jewish or Moorish blood.

fortunes. Thus they said farewell to each other, and Sancho went away to make the necessary preparations for their expedition.

11. What passed between Sancho Panza and his wife on one side and Don Quixote, his niece and housekeeper on the other

SANCHO WENT HOME IN SUCH HIGH SPIRITS THAT HIS WIFE noticed his glee a bowshot away, so much so that she asked him: "What ails you, Sancho friend, that you are so merry?"

To which he replied: "Wife, if God were willing, I'd be right glad to be less merry than I am this instant."

"I don't get your meaning, husband," said she, "and I don't know what you are at, when you say that you would be glad, if God were willing, not to be happy, for though I'm a fool, I don't know how a body can be happy for not being so."

"Listen, Teresa," replied Sancho; "I'm merry because I've a mind to go back to serve my master, Don Quixote, who means to be going out a third time to look for adventures, and I'm going with him again, for my needs will have it so, and also the hope that cheers me with the thought of finding another hundred crowns like those we have spent. Mind you, I'm sad at having to leave you and the children, and if God would be pleased to give me my daily bread dry-shod and at home, without dragging me over byways and crossroads—and He could do it for a mere song by merely willing it—no doubt my happiness would be stronger and more enduring, for now 'tis mixed with sorrow at our parting. So I was right in saying I would be glad, God being willing, not to be so happy."

"Look here, Sancho," answered Teresa, "since you're become a limb to a knight-errant you talk so round-about there's no understanding you."

"'Tis enough if God understands me, wife," replied Sancho, "for He is the Understander of all things, that's all I need say. But mind, sister, you must look after Dapple for the next three days, so that he may be fit to bear arms. Double his feed; and have an eye to the pack-saddle and the rest of his harness, for it's no wedding we are going to, but round the world to engage in the game of give-and-take with giants and dragons and monsters, and to hear hissings and roarings, bellowings and howlings. Aye, and all this would be mere lavender, if we hadn't to deal with Yanguesans and enchanted Moors."

"I'm quite ready to believe, husband," answered Teresa, "that squires-errant don't eat their bread for nothing, so I'll be always praying to our Lord to deliver you quickly from all those hard knocks."

"I tell you, wife," answered Sancho, "that if I did not feel convinced I'd see myself governor of an island before very long, I would drop dead on the spot."

"Not at all, husband," said Teresa. "Let the hen live though it be with the pip: live, and let the Devil take all governments in the world. Without one you came out of your mother's belly; without one you've lived till now, and without one you'll go or be carried to your grave, when God is willing. How many are there in the world who live without a government, yet continue to exist all the same, and are counted in the number of the people? The best sauce in the world is hunger, and as the poor are never without that, they always eat with gusto. But take heed, Sancho, if you're lucky and find yourself with some government on your hands, don't forget me and your children. Remember that your son Sanchico is now turned fifteen, and it's reasonable he should go to school, if his uncle the abbot intends to put him into the Church. Remember, too, that your daughter Marí-Sancha will not die if we get her wed, for I have a shrewd suspicion that she's every bit as keen to get a husband as you are to see yourself governor, and, when all's said and done, a daughter looks better badly married than well kept."

"By my faith," answered Sancho, "if God brings me any kind of government, my dear wife, I'll marry Marí-Sancha so high that they'll not reach her without calling her 'my lady'."

"Not on your life, Sancho," replied Teresa: "marry her to her equal, that's the safest plan, for if you take her out of clogs and put her into high-heeled shoes, and change her grey flannel petticoat into hoops and silk gowns, and out of plain Marcia and 'thou' you transmogrify her into 'Doña So-and-so' and 'my lady', the poor girl won't know whether she's on her head or her heels and at every turn she'll fall into a thousand blunders, showing the thread of her coarse homespun."

"Whisht, you foolish woman," said Sancho: "all she has to do is to practise it for two or three years, and then the ladylike airs and dignity will come naturally to her; and suppose they don't, what odds? Provided she becomes 'my lady', come what may."

"Measure yourself by your equals, Sancho," answered Teresa: "don't try to raise yourself higher, and remember the proverb that says: 'wipe your neighbour's son's nose and take him into your house.' Surely 'twould be a fine business to marry our María to some toff of a count or grand gentleman, who, when he felt inclined, would treat her like dirt, calling her country joan, clod-hopper's bairn and spinning sister. Not on my life, husband: not for that have I had my daughter all these years, I tell you. You, Sancho, fetch the money, and leave the marriage business to me. Why, there's Lope Tocho, Juan Tocho's son, a lusty, live lad that we know; I've seen him making eyes at the girl, and I know she'll be well matched to him, since he's our equal, and we'll have her always under our eyes, so that we'll all be one family, parents and children, grandchildren and sons-in-law; why, the blessing of God will be with the lot of us. So I won't have you marrying her in those courts and gaudy palaces, where they won't know what to make of her, nor will she know what to make of herself."

"Come here, blockhead and wife for Barabbas," cried Sancho; "what do you mean by trying, without why or wherefore, to hinder me from marrying my daughter to one who'll give me grandchildren that'll be called 'Your ladyship'? Look here, Teresa, I've always heard my elders say that he who doesn't know how to enjoy good luck when it's nigh shouldn't grumble when it passes him by; and now that it's knocking at our door, we shouldn't shut it out. Let us spread our sails before the favouring breeze. Can't you see, you dolt," continued Sancho, "that it will be best for me to clap myself into some profitable governorship, which will lift our feet out of the mud, and marry Marí-Sancha to whom I please? Then you'll see how they'll call you Doña Teresa Panza, and seat you in church on rugs, cushions and finery right in the face of the high-born ladies of the town. No, stay as you are, neither growing nor waning, like a tapestry figure. Well, mum's the word for the present. Sanchica will be a countess, whether you will or no."

"Do you know what you are saying, husband?" replied Teresa. "I for one am afraid that this countess business will be the ruin of my daughter. However, do as you please, make her a duchess or a princess: I tell you it will not be with my will and consent. I've always been a lover of equality, brother, and I can't stand people giving themselves airs when they should not. They christened me Teresa— a plain, simple name, without any of those additions or tags or ornaments of Dons or Doñas. Cascajo was my father's name, and as I'm your wife they call me Teresa Panza, though strictly they ought to call me Teresa Cascajo, but 'Kings go as the laws will'; and I'm satisfied with this name without sticking a 'Don' on the top of it to make it so heavy that I cannot carry it, and I don't want to make people gossip about me when they see me all dolled out as countess or governor's wife. Look at the airs Lady Slut gives herself! 'Twas only yesterday she was not above stretching a hank of flax, and went to Mass with the tail of her skirt over her head instead of a cloak; and today she struts in a farthingale, with her brooches and swagger, as if we didn't know her! If God preserves me in my seven senses, or five, or as many of them as I have, I've no intention of letting them see me make such a show. You, brother, be off, and become a government or an island, and swagger to your heart's content; by the years of my mother, neither my daughter nor myself will stir a foot from our village, for the honest woman is the one with the broken leg who bides at home, and to be doing her bit is as good as a feast for the decent girl. Be gone, I tell you, with Don Quixote to your adventures, and leave us to our misadventures, for God will mend them provided we be good, and I'm sure I don't know who put the Don on him, for neither his father nor his grandfather had it."

"I declare," cried Sancho, "you must have some devil in that body of yours. God bless us, woman, what a power of things you've strung together, one after the other, without head nor tail. What have Cascajo, the brooches, the proverbs, and the airs to do with what I'm saying? Listen, dolt and nincompoop (I'm right to call you this, seeing that you don't grip my meaning and you go tearing away from good fortune); if I said that my daughter had to throw herself down from a tower, or go gallivanting all over the world as Doña Urraca[1] wished to do, there would have been some reason for not submitting to my will; but supposing in an instant, and in less than the twinkling of an eye, I clamp the 'Don' and 'my lady' to her back, and fetch her out of the stubble and place her under a canopy, on a pedestal, and on a couch with more velvet cushions on it than there are Moors in the clan of the Almohades.[2] Why won't you agree, and fall in with what I wish?"

"Do you know why, husband?" answered Teresa; "because of the proverb which says: 'who covers thee, discovers thee'. All skip by the poor man after giving him a hasty glance, but they keep their eyes glued on the rich man, and if the said rich man was once upon a time poor, 'tis then you would hear the sneering and the gossiping and the continued spite of the backbiters, and in the streets here you'd find them swarming as thick as bees."

[1] Dona Urraca, the daughter of King Ferdinand I of Castile, when she heard that her father had divided his realms among his four sons, and had left her nothing, declared that she would roam like a loose woman through the world, and would give her body to the Moors for money and give it gratis to the Christian warriors. Moved by such a threat the King gave her Zamora, which in consequence became the scene of many a bloody battle. The incident is described in one of the ancient ballads with which Sancho, as a true Manchegan peasant, was familiar.

[2] Sancho makes a play upon the word "almohadas" (cushions) and Almohades—a Moorish Dynasty who succeeded the Almoravides in South Spain in 1145.

"Look here, Teresa," said Sancho, "and pay heed to what I'm going to tell you, for maybe you've never heard it all your life: and remember that I'm not airing my own opinions, but those of the reverend father who preached in this village last Lent, and who said, if I remember right, that if a person, whom fortune has raised from his lowly state to the height of his present prosperity, be well-bred, liberal, courteous to all, and does not seek to vie with those who were noble from ancient times, rest assured, Teresa, that no one will remember what he was, and all will respect him for what he is—that is to say, all except the envious, from whom no prosperous fortune is safe."

"I can't make head nor tail of you, husband," answered Teresa: "do what you will, and don't break my head with your orating and speechifying. And if you have revolved to do what you say . . ."

"Resolved, you should say, woman," said Sancho, "not revolved."

"Don't start argufying with me, husband," said Teresa. "I speak as God pleases, and am content to call a spade a spade, and I say that if you're set on having a government, take your son Sancho with you, and teach him from this day how to hold one, for sons should inherit and learn the trades of their parents."

"As soon as I get it," said Sancho, "I will send for him by post, and I will send you money, of which I'll have lashings, for you'll always find people ready to lend it to governors when they have none. And mind you dress him so as to hide what he is and make him look what he has to be."

"You send the money," said Teresa, "and I'll dress him up as gaudy as a branch on Palm Sunday."

"Then we both agree that our daughter is to be a countess," said Sancho.

"The day I see her a countess," replied Teresa, "I'll feel that I'm burying her; but once again I say, do as you please, for such is the burden we women receive at birth, to be obedient to our husbands no matter how doltish they may be."

And with this she began to weep in real earnest, as though she already saw Sanchica dead and buried. Sancho consoled her by saying that though he would have to make her a countess, he would postpone doing it as long as he could. So ended their conversation, and Sancho went back to see Don Quixote and make arrangements for their departure.

Now, while Sancho Panza and his wife held their irrelevant conversation, the niece and the housekeeper of Don Quixote were not idle, for by a thousand signs they began to perceive that their uncle and master intended to break away the third time, and return to his, for them, ill-errant chivalry. They tried every method of diverting him from his unlucky notion, but they might as well have preached in the desert or hammered on cold iron. Among many other arguments they used, the housekeeper said to him: "Truly, master, if you do not stay still and quiet at home, and cease rambling over hill, over dale, like a restless spirit, looking for what they call adventures, but which I call misfortunes, I shall have to call upon God and the King to send some remedy."

To which Don Quixote replied: "I know not what answer God will give to your complaints, housekeeper, nor what His Majesty will answer either. I do, however, know that if I were king I would refuse to answer the innumerable petitions which are presented to him every day, for one of the greatest of the many troubles kings have is being obliged to listen to all and to answer all, and therefore I would not wish that my affairs should worry him."

Whereupon the housekeeper said: "Tell us, master, are there no knights at His Majesty's court?"

"There are plenty of them," answered Don Quixote, "and it is right there should be, for the adornment of the princely dignity and the exaltation of the monarchy."

"Then why should your worship not be one of those who serve their king and lord in his court, without moving a step?" said she.

"Look here, dear lady," said Don Quixote, "all knights cannot be courtiers nor can all courtiers be knights-errant, nor ought they to be. There must be all sorts in the world, and even though we may all be knights, there is a vast difference between one and another, for the courtiers, without leaving their chambers or the threshold of the court, roam all over the world by looking at the map, without spending a farthing, and without suffering heat or cold, hunger or thirst. But we, the true knights-errant, in sun, in cold, in the open, exposed to the wrath of the heavens by night and by day, on foot and on horseback, we meander over the whole earth on our own feet. Nor is it only enemies in pictures that we know, but in their own real bodies, and on every occasion, no matter how great the risk, we attack them, without minding childish details or the laws of the duel; whether one carries or does not carry a shorter sword or lance; whether one bears on his person relics or any hidden subterfuge; whether the sun has to be divided and shared between the combatants or not; and other ceremonious rites of the sort that are observed in single combats of man to man, which you know nothing about, but I do.³ And I would

³ These remarks of Don Quixote are an echo of ancient chivalry which established a rigid code of knightly behaviour. It was a cardinal rule that the combatants should be equally mounted, that their lances and swords should be of the same length, and that in duels the sun should be equally divided between them—that is to say, that the rays

have you know, also, that the true knight-errant, though he should see ten giants, who not only touch the clouds with their heads but pass through them, and walk each of them on two huge towers instead of legs, and whose arms are like the masts of mighty vessels, and each eye like a great mill-wheel, burning fiercer than a glass-furnace, he must on no account be frightened by them. Rather, with gallant courage and fearless heart he must attack them, and, if possible, vanquish and lay them low in one instant, even if they be armed with the shells of a certain fish, which, they say, are harder than diamonds, and instead of swords wield trenchant blades of Damascus steel, or clubs studded with spikes of the same metal, such as I myself have seen more than twice. All this I have said, housekeeper, that you may see the difference that exists between one kind of knight and another; and it would be well if every prince gave more value to this second, or, more properly speaking, first kind of knights-errant, for, as their histories tell us, some among them have been the salvation, not merely of one kingdom, but of many."

"Ah, master," cried the niece, "remember that all you say about knights-errant are fables and lies. Their histories, if they were not burnt, certainly deserved each of them to be wrapt in a sambenito⁴ or to bear some mark by which they might be known as infamous and corrupters of good manners."

"Now, by almighty God the life-giver," cried Don Quixote, "if you were not my own sister's daughter I would chastise you so for the blasphemous words you have uttered, that the whole world would resound with it. What! Is it possible that a young hussy who can scarcely manage a dozen of bobbins of lace should have the impudence to wag her tongue and make disparaging remarks about the histories of knights-errant? What would Sir Amadis say if he heard such a thing? He, no doubt, would forgive you, for he was the most meek and courteous knight of his time, and, moreover, a great protector of damsels. But others might have heard you who would not have let you escape so easily, for all are not courteous and well-mannered, some are vain, swaggering rascals: nor are all who call themselves gentlemen⁵ to be taken at their own valuation; for some are gold, others are of base alloy, and all look like gentlemen, but not

should face sideways between them, so that neither should have the sun at his back. A chivalrous knight would have scorned taking an unfair advantage over his adversary in those days—in the days before Satan invented high explosives and totalitarian war.

⁴ The sambenito, short for "saco benedicto," was the garment worn by penitents under sentence by the Inquisition. It was a short yellow shirt with a red cross in front.

⁵ The word "caballero" means "gentleman" as well as "knight." Cervantes used the word in its former sense in the passage.

all are able to stand the touchstone of truth. There are low fellows who blow themselves up to bursting-point to appear gentlemen, and others of exalted rank who would seem to be dying to pass for men of the vulgar herd. The former rise through ambition or virtue; the latter sink through indolence or vice. And it is necessary to have knowledge and discernment in order to distinguish these two kinds of gentlemen, so alike in name and so different in actions."

"God save us!" cried the niece; "to think that you should be so knowing: why, if need be, you could mount a pulpit or go preaching through the streets; and yet here you are, so blind and deluded as to make yourself out valiant when you are old, strong when you are sick, a straightener of crooked ways when you yourself are bent crooked with age, and, above all, a knight when you are not one, for though hidalgos[6] may be so, the poor cannot."

"There is much reason in what you say, niece," answered Don Quixote, "and I could tell you things about birth that would astonish you, but for fear of mingling sacred with profane subjects, I refrain. I want to impress upon you, my dear simpletons, that there is great confusion among lineages and that only those appear great and illustrious which show themselves so by the virtue, wealth and generosity of their owners. I spoke of virtue, wealth and liberality, because a great man who is vicious will only be a great doer of evil, and a rich man who is not liberal will be only a miserly beggar; for the possessor of wealth is not made happy by possessing it, but by spending it—and not by spending as he pleases, but by knowing how to spend it well. To the poor gentleman there is no other way of showing that he is a gentleman than by virtue, by being affable, well-bred, courteous, gentle-mannered and helpful; not haughty, arrogant or censorious, but above all by being charitable, for by two maravedis given with a cheerful heart to the poor, he will show himself as liberal as he who distributes alms to the sound of a bell; and no one who sees him adorned with the virtues I have mentioned, will fail to recognize and judge him, though he know him not, to be of good stock. Indeed it would be a marvel if this was not so, for praise has always been virtue's guerdon, and those who are virtuous cannot fail to be praised. There are two roads, my daughters, by which men can travel and reach wealth and honours; one is that of letters, the other that of arms. As for myself, I have more of arms than of letters, and I was born, to judge by my inclination to arms, under the influence of the planet Mars. I am, therefore, almost forced to follow that road, and by it I have to travel in spite of the whole world, and

[6] An hidalgo is a noble by birth. A caballero in addition to noble birth had to possess wealth.

it will be useless for you to weary yourselves in persuading me that I should resist what Heaven wills, fortune ordains, reason demands, and, above all, my own inclination dictates. Knowing as I do the innumerable toils that are the accompaniments of knight-errantry, I know, too, the infinite benefits which are its guerdon. I know that the path of virtue is very narrow, and the road of vice broad and spacious: I know their ends and goals are different, for that of vice though wide and spacious, ends in death, and that of virtue, narrow and full of toil as it is, in life, not life that has an ending but in that which has no end. I know, as our great Castilian poet says:

> By these rough paths we mount, upon our way
> Towards the heights of immortality,
> which none can reach who . . ."

"Ah, woe is me!" cried the niece, "so my uncle is a poet, too! He knows everything, and there's nought he cannot do; why, I'll bet if he had a mind to turn mason, he could build a house as easily as a cage."

"I promise you, niece," answered Don Quixote, "if these knightly thoughts did not monopolize all my faculties, there would be nothing I could not do, nor any handicraft I could not acquire, even so far as making bird-cages and tooth-picks."

Just then a knocking at the door was heard, and when they enquired who was there, Sancho Panza answered that it was he. No sooner did the housekeeper hear who it was than she ran away to hide herself so as not to see him, so bitterly did she hate him. The niece then opened the door and his master welcomed him with open arms, and the two shut themselves up in his room, where another conversation ensued.

When the housekeeper saw that Sancho Panza was closeted with her master she guessed what was afoot, and feeling certain that the result of their conference would be a third sally, she snatched her cloak, all full of trouble and anxiety, and set off in search of the bachelor Samson Carrasco, thinking that as he was a well-spoken person and a new acquaintance of her master, he might be able to convince him to abandon his mad enterprise. She found the bachelor walking to and fro in the courtyard of his house, and straightway, perspiring and all of a flutter, she threw herself at his feet. Carrasco, seeing how distressed she was, said to her: "What is this, Mistress Housekeeper? What has happened? You look as if you were heart-broken."

"Nothing, Señor Samson," said she, "only that my master is breaking out, breaking out for sure."

"Whereabouts is he breaking out, Señora?" asked Samson: "has he broken any part of his body?"

"He is not breaking out," she replied, "unless it be

223

through the door of his madness. I mean, dear Mister Bachelor, that he is about to break out again (this will be the third time) to hunt all over the world for what he calls ventures, though I can't make out why he calls them thus. The first time he was brought back to us slung across the back of an ass, and drubbed all over; the second time he came home in an ox-cart, shut up in a cage, in which he convinced himself he was enchanted, and the poor fellow was in such a state that the mother who bore him would not have known him, so lean and yellow was he, with his eyes deep sunk in the recesses of his skull. To bring him back to a shadow of his former self cost me more than six hundred eggs, as God knows, and all the world, and my hens, that won't let me tell a lie."

"I can believe you," replied the bachelor, "for they are so good, and so fat, and so well-fed, that they would not say one thing for another even if they burst for it. In short then, Mistress Housekeeper, is there nothing else, or is there any further trouble in addition to what we are afraid Don Quixote may do?"

"No, Señor," said she.

"Well, then," answered the bachelor, "don't worry, and go home in peace, and get something hot ready for my breakfast, and while you are walking along, say the prayer of St. Apollonia,[7] that is, if you know it. I'll follow presently and you'll see marvels."

"Poor me!" answered the housekeeper, "do you want me to say the prayer of St. Apollonia? That would be grand if 'twas a toothache my master had, but it's in his brains only that he has it,"

"I know what I'm saying, Mistress Housekeeper: be off and don't start arguing with me: you know I am a bachelor of Salamanca, and no one can 'bachelor' more than that," replied Samson. With this the housekeeper departed, and the bachelor went immediately to look for the curate, to make certain arrangements which we shall relate in due time.

Now let us turn to Don Quixote and Sancho who were closeted together. Said Don Quixote: "Sancho, my friend, come to the point: what does Teresa say?"

"Teresa says," replied Sancho, "that with your worship it should be 'fast bind, fast find'; and that now's the time for more writing and less talking; for he who settles doesn't tangle; since 'a bird in hand is better than two in the bush'. And I say that a woman's counsel is bad, but he who won't take it is mad."

"And so say I," answered Don Quixote. "Speak, friend

---

[7] A joke of the bachelor. St. Apollonia was the patron of those who suffered from toothache. The Manchegans today still recite spells to her to relieve their aching molars.

Sancho, go on; today pearls are dropping from your lips."

"The fact is," answered Sancho, "that as your worship knows, we are all of us mortal—here today and gone tomorrow, and Death eats the lamb as soon as the sheep, and nobody can promise himself more hours of life in this world than God wishes to give him, for Death is deaf, and when he comes to knock at our life's door he is always in a hurry, and neither prayers, nor force, nor sceptres, nor mitres can delay him, as the common saying goes, and as they tell us from the pulpits."

"That is quite true," said Don Quixote, "but I don't know what you are getting at."

"What I'm getting at," said Sancho, "is that you should settle some fixed salary, which you would pay me monthly while I'm in your service, out of your estate, for I don't want to trust to rewards which arrive late or never; God help me with what is my own. In short, I want to know what I'm earning, whether it is much or little, for upon one egg set the hen, and 'many a mickle makes a muckle', and provided one gains something there is nothing lost. To be sure, if it should happen (which I neither believe nor expect) that your worship would give me the island you promised me, I'm not the one to be ungrateful or grasping, and I would be willing to have the said island valued and stopped out of my wages."

"I understand you," answered Don Quixote, "and I have penetrated to the depths of your thoughts and I know the mark you are shooting at with the countless arrows of your proverbs. Listen, Sancho: I would willingly fix your wages if I could discover an instance in any of the histories of knights-errant which would give even the faintest hint of what their squires used to get by the month or the year. But I cannot remember reading of a knight-errant having given fixed wages to his squire. I only know they served for a reward, and that when they least expected it, if their masters were lucky, they found themselves rewarded with an island, or something equivalent, or at least they were given a title and a lordship. And so, if such hopes and inducements, Sancho, persuade you to return to my service, you are welcome, but it is ridiculous to imagine that I am going to turn topsy-turvy the ancient usage of knight-errantry. Go back to your home, Sancho, and expose my intentions to your Teresa, and if she is willing and you are willing to be on reward with me, *bene quidem;* if not, we remain friends as before, for if the dovecote does not lack food, it will not lack pigeons; and remember, my son, that a good hope is better than a poor holding, and a good complaint than bad pay. I speak in this way, Sancho, to show you that I too can pour out as thick a shower of proverbs as you can, and, in short, I mean to say that if you don't want to come on reward with me, and run the same chance as I run, God be with you and make a saint of you. I shall find plenty of squires more obedient and willing and not so thick-headed and talkative as you."

When Sancho heard his master's firm and resolute words, the sky became clouded for him and the wings of his heart drooped, for he had believed that his master would never go without him for all the wealth in the world. While he stood there moody and dejected, Samson Carrasco arrived, with the housekeeper and the niece, who were eager to hear what arguments he would employ to dissuade their master from setting out in quest of adventure. Samson, a consummate wag, went up and embraced him as before, saying in a loud voice: "O flower of knight-errantry! O shining light of arms! O honour and mirror of the Spanish nation! May it please Almighty God in His infinite power to grant that the person or persons who hinder or disturb your third sally may lose their way in the labyrinth of their schemes and never accomplish what they most desire." Then turning to the housekeeper, he said: "Mistress Housekeeper, you may well give up saying the prayer of St. Apollonia, for I know that the spheres have positively determined that Señor Don Quixote should put into operation his new and lofty enterprises, and I should lay a heavy weight upon my conscience did I not urge this knight not to curb his strong arm, for as long as he remains inactive he is defrauding those who have been injured, of the means of having their wrongs redressed. Forward, then, my lord Don Quixote, and let your worship and highness set out today rather than tomorrow. If anything is needed in order to pursue your design, here am I to supply it with my person and estate; and if it were necessary that I should attend upon your magnificence as squire, I should consider it the height of good fortune."

At these words Don Quixote turned to Sancho and said: "Did I not tell you, Sancho, that there would be squires in plenty? Take note that he who offers his services is no other than the renowned bachelor Samson Carrasco, the perpetual joker and diverter of the Salamantine schools. But let this new Samson remain in his own country, and, in honouring it, bring honour to his venerable parents, for I will be content with any squire, now that Sancho does not deign to come with me."

"But I do deign," said Sancho, with his eyes full of tears, "never will they say of me, master, 'the bread partaken, the company forsaken'. Sure, I don't spring from any ungrateful stock, for all the world knows, and especially my village, who the Panzas were from whom I descend. Besides, I have learnt through word and deed of your worship's desire to do me favour, and if I have been a bit of a bargainer on the score of my wages, it was only to please my wife, who, when she takes it into her head to press a point, no hammer drives the hoops of a cask as she drives a man to do what she wants. But, after all, a man must be a man, and a woman a woman, and as I'm a man anywhere in the world, which I can't deny, I'll be one in my own house, in spite of anybody. So there's nought for us to do but take to the road at once."

Don Quixote and Sancho now embraced and became friends, and, with the approval of the great Carrasco, who became henceforth their oracle, it was settled that in three days they should depart. As for the housekeeper and the niece, they tore their hair, they clawed their faces, and they made a lament over the approaching departure of their master as if it was his death. During the three days, Don Quixote and Sancho provided themselves with what they thought necessary. Then, Sancho having placated his wife and Don Quixote his niece and housekeeper, they sallied forth at nightfall without being seen by a soul save the bachelor, who insisted on keeping them company half a league from the village. They took the road to El Toboso. Don Quixote was mounted on his good Rozinante and Sancho on his old Dapple, his wallets stored with eatables and his purse full of money, which his master gave him in case of need. Samson, after embracing the knight, returned to the village, and the pair went on their way to the great city of El Toboso.

III. The fortunes of Don Quixote on the way to his lady-love, the trick devised by Sancho for her enchantment, and the strange adventure of the cart of Death

Don Quixote and Sancho had hardly said farewell to Samson when Rozinante began to neigh and Dapple to sigh, which both knight and squire took as a good sign and a most lucky omen, though to tell the truth the sighs and brays of Dapple were louder than the neighings of the horse, whence Sancho concluded that his good fortune was to exceed and overtop that of his master, basing his arguments upon some kind of fortune-telling which he had learnt, goodness only knows where, for history does not relate. Only he was heard to say, when he stumbled or fell, that he wished he had not left his home, for by stumbling or falling he could get nothing but a torn shoe or a broken rib, and I must say that though he may have been a fool, he was not wide of the mark on this point. Said Don Quixote: "Sancho, my friend, night is coming on and we shall be unable to reach El Toboso by daylight, for there I am determined to go before I undertake any other adventure; and there I shall receive the blessing and kind permission of the peerless Dulcinea. When she gives it to me I feel sure that I shall bring to a fortunate conclusion every perilous enterprise, for nothing in this life makes knights-errant more valiant than finding themselves favoured by their ladies."

"So I believe," replied Sancho, "but I think it will be difficult for your worship to speak with her or see her, at least, so as to receive her blessing, unless she flings it over the wall of the yard where I saw her the first time, when I took her the letter telling of the mad follies your worship was doing in the Sierra Morena."

"Did you really think those were yard walls, Sancho," said Don Quixote, "where you saw that never-sufficiently-celebrated grace and beauty? They must have been the galleries, corridors, or porticoes, or whatever they call them, of some rich and royal palace."

"That may be so," answered Sancho, "but to my eyes they look like mud walls, unless, of course, my memory cheats me."

"In any case, let us go there, Sancho," answered Don Quixote. "Provided I see her, it is the same to me whether it be over a wall, at a window, or through the chinks and gaps in a garden fence, for any beam from the sun of her beauty that reaches my eyes will light up my understanding and strengthen my heart, so that I shall be supreme and un-equalled in wisdom and valour."

"To tell you the truth, master," said Sancho, "when I saw that sun of the Lady Dulcinea del Toboso, it was not bright enough to throw out beams; this must have been because her worship was winnowing that wheat I spoke to you about, and the heap of dust she raised clouded her face and darkened it."

"What! Do you still insist," cried Don Quixote, "on believing and maintaining that my Lady Dulcinea was winnowing wheat—a task and occupation utterly at variance with what is done by ladies of rank, who are reserved for other pursuits that will display, a bow-shot away, their refinement and quality? You fail to remember, O Sancho, the lines of our poet wherein he paints for us the labours of the fair nymphs in their crystal dwellings, who rose from their beloved Tagus and seated themselves upon the verdant meadow to embroider those rich stuffs which the ingenious poet describes as woven and interwoven with gold, silk and pearls.[1] In like manner must my lady have been busied when you saw her, only that the envy which some wicked enchanter bears against me transforms all things that give me pleasure into shapes different from their own. For this reason, if the

[1] Garcilaso de la Vega in the third eclogue.

history of my deeds, which they say is now in print, was written by some wise man who was an enemy of mine, I am afraid he may have mingled a thousand lies with one truth and turned aside to relate idle tales that have nought to do with the course of truthful history. O envy, root of countless evils and cankerworm of the virtues! All the vices, Sancho, bring certain pleasures with them, but envy brings nought but discord, rancour and rage."

"That is what I say, too," answered Sancho, "and I suspect that in that legend or history which the bachelor told us he had seen about us, my reputation goes all topsy-turvy, jolting up and down here and there helter-skelter, sweeping the streets, as the saying is. Nevertheless, on the faith of an honest man, I never said a bitter word of any enchanter, nor am I well enough off to be envied. To tell you the truth, I am a bit roguish and I've a streak of cuteness in me, but it's all covered by the broad cloak of my simplicity, which is always natural and never put on. Why, if I'd nought else to my credit but my believing, as I do believe firmly and truly, in God and the Holy Catholic and Roman Church, and being a mortal enemy of the Jews, as I am, the historians ought to have mercy on me and treat me well in their writings. Well, let them have their say: naked I was born, naked I am, I neither lose nor win; and if I do find myself put into books and bandied about all over the world, I don't care a fig. Let them say what they like about me."

In these, and similar discussions they spent that night and the following day, without encountering anything worth noting, much to Don Quixote's mortification; but at last, the next day, at nightfall, they came in view of the great city of El Toboso, at the sight of which Don Quixote's spirits rose and Sancho's sank, for he did not know Dulcinea's house, nor in all his life had he ever seen her, any more than his master. Thus they were both anxious—one to see her, and the other because he had not seen her; and Sancho could not imagine what he would do when his master sent him into El Toboso. At last Don Quixote made up his mind to enter the city when night had fallen, and they halted until the time came, among some oak trees near the city.

'Twas on the stroke of midnight, a little more or less when the knight and his squire quitted the wood and entered El Toboso. The town lay in deep silence, for all the inhabitants were asleep, resting at full length, as the saying goes. The night was fairly clear, though Sancho wished it had been quite dark, so that he might find in the darkness an excuse for his folly. Not a sound was heard all over the town but the barking of dogs, which deafened Don Quixote's ears and disturbed the heart of Sancho. Now and then an ass brayed, pigs grunted, cats miaoued, and the various noises grew in intensity in the stillness of the night. All this the enamoured knight regarded as an evil omen. Nevertheless, he said to Sancho: 'Sancho, my son, lead on to the palace of Dulcinea, perchance we may find her awake."

"Body of the sun, what palace am I to lead on to," answered Sancho, "when the one I saw her highness in was only a tiny house?"

"She must have retired, then," said Don Quixote, "to some little apartment of her palace to enjoy herself with her damsels, as is customary among great ladies and princesses."

"Señor," said Sancho, "if your worship insists, in spite of me, that the Lady Dulcinea's house is a castle, is this an hour, think you, to find the door open; and is it fitting for us to be knocking till they hear us and open the door, thus putting the whole household in uproar and confusion? Do you think we are visiting the houses of our wenches like rakes who come and knock and enter at any hour, no matter how late it is?"

"Let us first make sure of finding the palace," answered Don Quixote, "and then I will tell you what it is right for us to do. But look, Sancho: either my eyesight is bad, or that great dark mass yonder should be Dulcinea's palace."

"Let your worship lead the way," said Sancho, "perhaps it may be so; though I see it with my eyes and touch it with my hands, I'd believe it as much as I believe it's now daylight."

Don Quixote led the way and after advancing about two hundred paces he came upon the mass that caused the shadow, and found that it was a great tower. He then knew that the building was no castle, but the principal church of the village. So he said: " 'Tis the church we have come upon, Sancho."

"So I see," replied Sancho. "God grant we may not come upon our graves, for it's no good sign to find oneself gadding about in a graveyard at this time of the night; and this happens after my telling your worship, if I remember right, that this lady's house is in a blind alley."

"May God curse you for an arrant blockhead," cried Don Quixote; "where have you ever found castles and royal palaces built in blind alleys?"

"Señor," answered Sancho, "every land has its customs: perhaps it is usual here in El Toboso to build palaces and grand houses in blind alleys. I beg you, therefore, to let me have a look about these streets and alleys here: perhaps in some corner or other I may butt into this palace, and I hope I may see the dogs devouring it, for dragging us into this goose chase!"

"Speak respectfully, Sancho, of the affairs of my lady," said Don Quixote; "let us keep our feast in peace, and not throw the rope into the well after the bucket."

"I'll keep my peace," answered Sancho, "but how can I have the patience to listen to your worship telling me that you want me, after only one glimpse of my lady's house, to know it always and find it in the middle of the night, when you yourself can't find it, though you must have seen it thousands of times?"

"You will drive me desperate, Sancho," said Don Quixote. "Come here, you heretic: have I not told you a thousand times that never once in my life have I seen the peerless Dulcinea, nor have I ever crossed the threshold of her palace? I am enamoured only by hearsay, and owing to the great reputation she possesses for beauty and wit."

"I agree now," answered Sancho, "and I'll add that if you have never seen her, neither have I."

"That is not true," replied Don Quixote, "for you yourself told me that you saw her winnowing wheat when you brought back an answer to the letter which I sent by you."

"Don't trouble about that, master," said Sancho. "I must tell you that my glimpse of her and the answer I brought you back were by hearsay too. I can no more tell who the Lady Dulcinea is than I can punch the sky above."

"Sancho, Sancho," said Don Quixote, "there are times for joking and times when jokes are out of place. If I say that I have neither seen nor spoken to the lady of my soul there is no reason why you should say that you have not spoken to her or seen her, when you know that the opposite is true."

While the two were thus conversing they saw a man with a pair of mules approaching, and from the noise the plough made as it was dragged along they judged him to be a labourer who had risen before dawn to go to his work. Such was the case. The labourer came along singing the ballad which begins:

" 'Twas an evil day befell the men of France
    In the chase of Roncesvalles."

"May I be slain, Sancho," cried Don Quixote, when he heard the words, "if any good will come to us this night. Do you hear what he is singing?"

"Aye, I do," said Sancho, "but what has the chase of Roncesvalles to do with what we have to do?"

When the labourer came up, Don Quixote said: "Can you tell me, good friend, and may God speed you, where is the palace of the peerless princess Doña Dulcinea del Toboso?"

"Señor," replied the fellow. "I'm a stranger here myself and I've been only a few days in the village doing a bit of farm work for a rich farmer. In that house opposite the curate and the sacristan live, and both or either of them will give your worship an account of this princess, for they have a list of all the folk of El Toboso. All the same, I don't believe there's a single princess in the length and breadth of the village. There are many ladies, sure enough, aye and of quality too, and each one of them may well be a princess in her own house."

"Then, my friend, the lady I am seeking must be one of those," said Don Quixote.

"That may be," answered the labourer. "God be with you, for here comes the daylight." Without waiting to hear any more questions, he whipped up his mules and moved on. Sancho, seeing that his master was perplexed and somewhat dissatisfied, said to him: "Master, the day will be soon upon us, and 'twill not be wise for the sun to find us in the street. It will be better for us to leave the city, and for your worship to hide in some neighbouring wood, and I'll return by day and search in every corner for the house, castle or palace of my lady. I'll be mighty unlucky if I don't find it, and as soon as I have found it I'll speak to her ladyship and tell her where your worship is waiting for her directions how you may visit her without any damage to her honour and reputation."

"Sancho," replied Don Quixote, "I willingly accept the advice you have given me. Come on, son, let us look for a place where I may hide, while you return to seek my lady."

Sancho was in a fever to get his master out of the village, lest the latter might discover the lie about the answer which he had brought to him in the Sierra Morena on Dulcinea's behalf, so he hastened their departure, and two miles from the village they found a grove in which Don Quixote hid himself. Sancho then turned about, whipped up Dapple and set off, leaving Don Quixote behind, seated on his horse, resting in his stirrups and leaning on his lance, filled with sad and troubled fancies. There we shall leave him while we follow Sancho Panza, who took leave of his master in no less anxious and meditative frame of mind, so much so indeed that as soon as he had left the grove he looked round, and seeing that Don Quixote was out of sight, he dismounted from the ass and, seating himself at the foot of a tree, began to converse with himself, saying: "Now, tell us, brother Sancho, where your worship is going. Are you in search of some ass you've lost? Not at all. Then what are you looking for? I'm looking for a mere nothing—a princess and, in her, for the sun of beauty and the whole sky together. And where do you expect to find what you mention, Sancho? Where? In the great city of El Toboso. Well, and on whose behalf are you going to look for her? For the famous knight, Don Quixote of La Mancha, who rights wrongs, gives food to them that are thirsty and drink to them that are hungry. That's all very well, but do you know her house, Sancho? My

232

master says it must be some royal palaces or proud castles. And have you ever caught a stray glimpse of her? Neither I nor my master ever saw her. And do you think it would be fair and proper if the people of El Toboso, once they found out that you were here with the intention of snaffling their princesses and meddling with their ladies, were to come and batter your ribs with cudgels and leave not a whole bone in your body? Indeed they would be perfectly in their rights if they refused to admit that I am under orders, and that in the words of the ballad:

> A messenger, my friend, thou be,
> No penalty may fall on thee.

Don't you put your trust in that, Sancho, for the Manchegan folk are as hot-tempered as they are honest, and they won't let a soul touch them on the raw. By God, if they smell your purpose you're in for a bad time, I tell you. To hell with it, you whoreson rogue: let the bolt fall on someone else! Not at all: I am not going looking for three feet in a cat to please another; for, when all's said and done, tracking Dulcinea up and down El Toboso will be as bad as looking for a needle in a bundle of hay or a scholar in Salamanca. 'Tis the devil incarnate has landed me into this kettle of fish and no one else!"

Such was the conversation Sancho held with himself, and the only result of it was that he continued the conversation as follows: "Well, there's a cure for everything except death, under whose yoke we all have to pass, whether we like it or not, when our time is up. I've seen by a thousand signs that this master of mine is a madman and fit to be tied, and as for myself I'm not far behind him; if there's a word of truth in the proverb that says: 'tell me the company you keep and I'll tell you what you are', and the other: 'not with whom you are bred, but with whom you are fed'. Now if he's mad, as he truly is, and of a madness that appeared when he said the windmills were giants, the friars' mules dromedaries, and the flocks of sheep armies of enemies, and many other things to the same tune, 'twill not be very hard to make him believe that the first peasant wench I come across here is the Lady Dulcinea, and if he doesn't believe it, I'll swear on oath (and if he swears I'll swear again. If he persists, I'll persist the more, and in this way, no matter what happens, my word will always top the mark. Perhaps if I hold out in this way I shall put an end to his sending me on messages of this kind another time. On the other hand, perhaps he will think, as I imagine he will, that one of the wicked enchanters, who, he says, have a grudge against him, has changed her form to do him an injury."

With these thoughts Sancho lulled his conscience, and con-

233

sidered his business as good as settled. He stayed there until the afternoon so as to make Don Quixote think that enough time had elapsed for him to have gone to El Toboso and back. And all turned out so luckily for him that when he rose to mount Dapple, he saw three peasant-girls coming from El Toboso towards him, mounted on three ass-colts or fillies. As soon as Sancho saw them, he galloped back to his master, Don Quixote, and found him sighing and uttering a thousand amorous lamentations. When Don Quixote saw him, he said: "What news, friend Sancho? Am I to mark this day with a white stone or a black?"

"Your worship," replied Sancho, "had better mark it with red ochre as they do the lists of the professors' chairs [2] that the lookers-on may read their names clearly."

"So you bring good news, then," said Don Quixote.

"So good," answered Sancho, "that your worship has nought to do but clap spurs to Rozinante and ride out into the open country. There you'll see the Lady Dulcinea, who with two of her damsels, is coming to visit your worship."

"Holy God! what are you saying, Sancho, my friend?" said Don Quixote. "Mind you do not deceive me, and try to beguile my real sadness with false joys."

"What advantage would I get by deceiving your worship," answered Sancho, "especially when my truth is about to unfold itself? Spur on, master, and you'll see the princess our mistress coming robed and adorned, in fact, like herself. Her ladies and she are all one shimmer of gold, all clusters of pearls, all diamonds, all rubies, all brocade of more than ten folds; their hair flowing down their shoulders like so many sunbeams playing with the wind; and, above all, they're coming along mounted on three piebald nackneys, the finest you'd see anywhere."

"Hackneys, you mean to say, Sancho," said Don Quixote.

"Well," said Sancho, "hackneys and nackneys are much the same. But let them come as they will; there they are, the finest ladies you could wish for, especially my lady the Princess Dulcinea, who dazzles one's senses."

"Let us go, Sancho, my son," replied Don Quixote, "and as a reward for bringing me these tidings, which are as welcome as unexpected, you may have the best of the spoils of my next adventure. If this is not enough, I'll bequeath you the fillies I shall get from my three mares, which, as you know, are in foal on our town common."

"I'll stick to the foals," replied Sancho, "for I'm not so sure that the spoils of the first adventure will be good ones."

By this time they had come out of the wood, and saw the three village lasses close at hand. Don Quixote gazed along the

[2] This is a reference to those who had received the degree of Doctor, in Spanish Universities. Their names were painted on the walls in red.

road towards El Toboso, and, seeing nobody but the three peasant girls, he was all disturbed, and asked Sancho whether he had left them outside the city.

"Outside the city?" answered Sancho. "Are your worship's eyes in the back of your head that you can't see them coming along towards us, and there she is shining like the sun itself at noon?"

"I see nothing, Sancho," said Don Quixote, "but three peasant girls on three asses."

"Now God save me from the Devil," replied Sancho: "is it possible that your worship mistakes three hackneys, or whatever they're called, which are as white as driven snow, for asses? By the Lord, I'd pluck my beard out by the roots if that were the case."

"Well, I must say, Sancho, my friend," said Don Quixote, "that they are as truly jackasses or jenny-asses as I am Don Quixote and you Sancho Panza: at least, that is how they appear to me."

"Whisht, master!" exclaimed Sancho, "don't say that, but skin your eyes, and come and do homage to the lady of your thoughts, who is now close at hand." With these words he rode on to welcome the three village lasses, and dismounting from Dapple, caught hold of one of the asses of the girls by the halter, and sinking on both knees to the ground, he said: "Queen and princess and duchess of beauty, may it please your arrogance and greatness to receive into your favour and good disposition this captive knight of yours who is standing there turned into marble stone, all worried and unnerved at finding himself in the presence of your magnificence. I am Sancho Panza, his squire, and he is the much-wandered knight, Don Quixote of La Mancha, otherwise called the Knight of the Rueful Figure."

Don Quixote had now sunk on his knees beside Sancho, and with eyes starting out of his head he kept staring at her whom Sancho called queen and lady. As he saw in her nothing but a village lass, not even good-looking at that, for she was moon-faced and snub-nosed, he was perplexed and confounded, without even daring to open his lips. The girls, too, were thunderstruck at seeing those two men, so different in appearance, on their knees, trying to prevent their companion from passing on. She, however, who had been stopped, broke silence, and exclaimed in a coarse, angry voice: "Get out of the way, bad 'cess to you, and let us pass: we're in a hurry." To which Sancho replied: "O princess and universal lady of El Toboso: how comes it that your magnanimous heart is not softened by the sight of the pillar and support of knight-errantry on his knees before your sublimated presence?"

One of the others, when she heard these words, cried: "Whoa there, you! I'll curry-comb you like my father-in-law's she-ass! Look how the bits of gentlemen try to make fun of us village girls, as if we weren't as good a hand at cracking jokes as themselves. Be off on your way and let us be off on ours: you'd better, I'm telling you."

"Get up, Sancho," said Don Quixote at this, "for I see that Fortune, 'unsated with the evil she hath done me',[3] has seized possession of all the ways by which any comfort could reach the wretched soul imprisoned in my fleshly body. And thou, O loftiest perfection of all virtue that can be desired! extremity of human courtesy! sole relief of this afflicted heart which adores thee, now that a wicked enchanter persecutes me, bringing clouds and cataracts into my eyes, transforming thy unequalled loveliness and changing thy features into those of a poor labouring girl—who knows, too, if he has not at the same time turned mine into those of some monster to make them abominable in thy sight?—do not refuse to look upon me with loving tenderness, and consider that, by kneeling thus to thy deformed beauty, I am giving the surest token of my soul's humble adoration of thee."

"Come, come, tell it to my grandfather!" cried the girl. "It's little I care for your saucy love-palaver! Get out of the way and let us go. We'll say thank-ye."

Sancho drew aside to let her go, delighted at having so successfully extricated himself from his intrigue. No sooner did the girl who had acted Dulcinea find herself free than she pricked her "nackney" with a spike she had at the end of a stick, and started to gallop across the field. The ass, however, feeling the point of the spike more acutely than usual, began to curvet and caper in such a way that it flung the Lady Dulcinea to the ground. Don Quixote, seeing this, rushed over to raise her up, while Sancho tightened up the pack saddle, which had slipped under the ass's belly. When the saddle was fixed, Don Quixote wished to lift his enchanted lady in his arms and set her upon the ass, but drawing back a little, she took a short run, and, placing both hands on the ass's crupper, sprang into the saddle lighter than a falcon and landed astride like a man.

"By St. Roch," cried Sancho, "our lady is swifter than a falcon, and can teach the cleverest Cordoban or Mexican how to mount in Moorish fashion.[4] In one leap she sprang over the crupper of the saddle, and without spurs she is making the hack race like a zebra. Why, the rest of her damsels are all flying like the wind."

This was the truth, for as soon as they saw Dulcinea in the

---

[3] A quotation from the third eclogue of Cervantes' favourite poet, Garcilaso de la Vega.

[4] That is to say, with short stirrups ("a la jineta"), as opposed to "a la brida," with long stirrups.

saddle they all pricked on after her and dashed away at full speed, without looking behind them for more than half a league. Don Quixote gazed after them, and when they had disappeared he turned to Sancho and said: "Sancho, what do you think now? How enchanters must loathe me! See how far their spite and hatred go when they try to deprive me of the happiness of seeing my lady in her own proper form. Truly was I born to be an example of misfortune, and a target at which the arrows of adversity are aimed. Notice, too, Sancho, that those traitors were not satisfied merely to change and transform my Dulcinea, but they changed and transformed her into a shape as low and ugly as that of the village girl yonder, and not content with that, they deprived her of something that is the property of ladies of quality, to wit, the fragrant perfume which always emanates from those who spend their lives amidst sweet amber and flowers. For I must confess, Sancho, that when I approached to lift Dulcinea upon her hackney (as you say it was, though I thought it was a she-ass), she gave me such a whiff of raw garlic that my very soul reeked of the pestiferous odour."

"O vile, spiteful enchanters!" cried Sancho at this; "bad 'cess to you: would that I could see the lot of you strung by the gills like pilchards on a twig! A power of evil you can do, and do! It should have been enough for you, ye rogues, to have changed the pearls of my lady's eyes into cork galls, her hair of purest gold into the bristles of a red ox's tail, and, in short, all her features from good to bad, without interfering with her smell, for even by that alone we might have guessed what was hidden under that ugly skin; though to tell the honest truth, I never noticed her ugliness but only her beauty, which was enhanced in value by a mole which she had on her right lip, like a moustache, with seven or eight red hairs like threads of gold, and more than a span in length."

"Now," said Don Quixote, "since the moles of the face always correspond to those of the body, Dulcinea must have another mole on the broad of her thigh corresponding to the side on which she has one on her face. All the same, hairs of such a length as you have mentioned are very long for moles."

"I surely can tell you, master, that they were there as plain as the day for the eye to see."

"I believe it, friend," answered Don Quixote, "for nature bestowed on Dulcinea nothing that was not perfect and well-finished. Wherefore, if she had a hundred moles similar to the one you have described, they would not be moles but moons and glittering stars. But tell me, Sancho, about that pack-saddle—for so it seemed to me when you were fixing it: was it a flat-saddle or a side-saddle?"

"Neither one nor t'other," replied Sancho; "it was a jennet-saddle,[5] with a field-covering of such value that it was worth half a kingdom."

"Again I say," cried Don Quixote, "and I shall say it a thousand times, that I am the most unfortunate man in the world not to have seen all this!"

The roguish Sancho had more than enough to do to hide his mirth at hearing the crazy ravings of his master, whom he had so nicely deceived. At last, after much further talk, they remounted their beasts, and pursued their journey. Don Quixote was mightily dejected, for he kept meditating on the cruel trick the enchanters had played upon him in changing his Lady Dulcinea into the mean shape of a village girl, nor could he imagine any method by which he might restore her to her original form. So absorbed was he in those reflections that without being aware of it he loosened his hold on Rozinante's reins, who, noticing the liberty granted to him, stopped at every step to crop the fresh grass which abounded in that plain. Sancho Panza roused him from his reverie, saying: "Master, sadness was made for men and not for beasts, but if men let themselves give way too much to it, they turn into beasts. Let your worship pull yourself together, and be your old self again. Come, grip hold of Rozinante's reins, rouse yourself and show that spirit which knights-errant ought to have. What the devil is all this? Are we here or in France? Let the Devil run away with all the Dulcineas in the world: the health of a single knight-errant is worth more than all the enchantments and transmogrifications on earth."

Don Quixote was about to answer Sancho Panza, but he was prevented by a cart which passed across the road, laden with the strangest figures that could be imagined. He who drove the mules and acted as carter was a hideous demon: the cart was open to the sky, without wicker tilt or awning. The first figure that presented itself to Don Quixote's eyes was that of Death himself with a human face: next to him was an angel with large painted wings. At one side was an emperor with a crown, to all appearance of gold, on his head. At the feet of Death was the god called Cupid, without his bandage over the eyes but with his bow, quiver and arrows. There was also a knight armed cap-à-pie, except that he wore no morion or helmet but only a hat adorned with plumes of varied colours. With these there were others of different faces and costumes. At this unexpected encounter Don Quixote became somewhat disturbed, and Sancho was struck with terror. But on second thoughts Don Quixote rejoiced, for he

[5] The "silla a la jineta" was a saddle adapted for ladies riding with high pommel and cantle and short stirrups. In La Mancha today it is still the custom for women to ride astride.

believed that some new perilous adventure was at hand; so, under this impression, and with the firm intention of facing any danger, he halted in front of the cart and cried out in a loud, threatening voice: "Carter, coachman or devil, be quick to tell me who you are, whither bound, and who are the people you are carrying in your coach, which resembles rather the boat of Charon than an ordinary cart."

To which the Devil, stopping the cart, answered courteously: "Señor, we are players of Angulo El Malo's [6] company: we have been acting the play of the 'Parliament of Death' this morning in a village behind yonder hill, seeing that 'tis the octave of Corpus Christi; [7] and we have to act it this evening in that village which you can see from here; and because it is so near at hand, and to save ourselves the trouble of undressing and dressing again, we go in the costumes in which we play. That lad there goes as Death, the other as an angel; that woman, who is the manager's wife, is the Queen; another one is a soldier; that one is the Emperor, and I am the Devil, and I'm taking one of the leading parts. If there's aught else you wish to know about us, ask me, and I'll know how to answer to the point, for since I'm the Devil, I'm up to everything."

"By the faith of a knight-errant," answered Don Quixote, "when I saw the cart I imagined that some great adventure was at hand, but I declare that one must touch with the hand what appears to the eye, if one would be undeceived. God speed you, good people, and carry on your festival. Remember, if there is anything wherein I may be useful to you, I will do it willingly, for from childhood I have always been fond of the masquerade, and in my youth I had a craving for the play."

While they were talking, chance willed it that one of the company, clad in motley, with a great number of bells, and bearing on the end of a stick three ox-bladders fully-blown, came up to them. This clown, then, sidling up to Don Quixote, began twirling his stick and banging the ground with his bladders and capering with shrill jingling of bells. At the sight of this weird apparition Rozinante began to shy so violently that Don Quixote was unable to hold him in, and, taking the bit between his teeth, he set off at a canter across the plain with greater speed than the bones of his anatomy

[6] Angulo El Malo was a well-known manager of a theatrical company in the days of Cervantes.

[7] Ever since the Middle Ages it was customary in Spain to perform on the feast of Corpus Christi short religious dramas called "Autos Sacramentales." They were performed in the open streets on carts drawn by oxen. The most famous writer of these plays was Calderón, to whom Shelley bore tribute by his reference to the "starry autos of Calderón." The actors in Spain travelled from town to town in open carts as here described. The Church abolished "Autos Sacramentales" in 1765.

ever gave promise of. Sancho, thinking his master was in eminent danger of being thrown, jumped off Dapple and ran in haste to help him, but by the time he reached him he was already stretched on the ground, and Rozinante was lying beside him, for he had fallen with his master—the usual end of his frisky exploits. And no sooner had Sancho left his beast to go to the help of Don Quixote than the dancing devil with the bladders leapt upon Dapple and buffeting him with them, by the fear he caused and the clatter more than by the smart of the blows, made him fly across the country towards the village where they were going to hold their festival. Sancho saw the flight of Dapple and the fall of his master, and did not know which of the two disasters he should attend to first; but, in the end, like a good squire and good servant, he let his love for his master prevail over his affection for his ass, though every time he saw the bladders rise in the air and fall upon the hindquarters of Dapple he felt the gripings and terrors of death, and he would rather have had those blows fall upon the apples of his own eyes than upon the least hair of his ass's tail. In such turmoil and perplexity he came to where Don Quixote lay in a sadder plight than he would have wished. After helping him to mount Rozinante, he said: "Señor, the Devil has carried off Dapple."

"What devil?" asked Don Quixote.

"The fellow with the bladders," answered Sancho.

"Then I will get him back," said Don Quixote, "even if he were shut up with him in the deepest and darkest dungeons of hell. Follow me, Sancho, for the cart goes slowly, and I will take the mules as payment for the loss of Dapple."

"There's no need to worry, master," said Sancho; "let you keep your anger in check, for I see now that the Devil has already let Dapple go, and he's coming back to his lair." And so indeed it turned out, for the Devil, after falling with Dapple in imitation of Don Quixote and Rozinante, set off on foot to the village, and the ass returned to his master.

"Nevertheless," said Don Quixote, "it will be well to make one of those in the cart pay for the Devil's discourtesies, even if it were the Emperor himself."

"Drive such a thought out of your mind, master," replied Sancho. "Follow my advice, and never meddle with actors, for they're favoured folk. I myself have seen an actor taken up for two murders, and yet get off scot-free. Remember that, as they're rollicking folk of pleasure, everyone favours and protects them, and helps and treats them with consideration, especially when they are members of the royal companies and with a charter, and almost every one of them dresses and makes up as a prince."

"In spite of all that," said Don Quixote, "the player devil is not going to go away boasting, even if the whole human race favours him."

Saying this, he turned towards the cart, which was now near the village, and shouted loudly as he rode: "Stay! halt! ye merry, festive band! I want to teach you how to treat asses and animals that serve the squires of knights-errant!" So loud were the shouts of Don Quixote that the folk in the cart heard and understood the purpose of him who had uttered them. Death in a trice leap from the cart, and after him the emperor, the devil carter and the angel, nor did the queen and the god Cupid lag behind. Then all armed themselves with stones and drew themselves up in a line, ready to receive Don Quixote on the points of their pebbles. Don Quixote, when he saw them drawn up in such a gallant squadron with their arms raised ready to let fly a massive discharge of stones, reined in Rozinante, and began to consider in what manner he could assail them with the least danger to his person. As he halted, Sancho came up and, seeing that he was about to attack such a well-drawn-up squadron, said to him: "It would be stark, staring madness to engage upon such an enterprise. Remember, dear master, that against 'gutter ammunition',[8] aye, and lashings of it, too, there is no defensive armour in the world unless you shut yourself up in a bronze bell, and, besides, you should remember that it is rash rather than brave for a single man to attack an army where Death takes part, and emperors fight in person, with good and wicked angels to lend a hand. And if this reflection will not make you keep quiet, perhaps you will do so when you know for certain that among all those folk yonder, though they look like kings, princes and emperors, there's not one single knight-errant."

"Now indeed," said Don Quixote, "you have hit the point which can and should turn me from my resolve. I cannot and should not draw my sword, as I have many a time told you, against one who is not dubbed a knight. It is for you, Sancho, if you care, to take vengeance for the injury which has been done to the ass, and I from here will help you by shouting out salutary advice."

"There is no reason to take vengeance on anybody," answered Sancho, "for a good Christian never takes it for wrongs, and besides, I'll make my ass submit his wrong to my good will, and that means to live at peace as long as Heaven grants me life."

"Since that is your resolve," replied Don Quixote, "good Sancho, wise Sancho, Christian Sancho, honest Sancho, let us leave these phantoms alone and go off in search of worthier adventures, for I see that this country will not fail to provide us with many marvellous enterprises."

He then wheeled about; Sancho went to catch his Dapple;

8 Slang phrase for pebbles.

Death and all his flying squadron returned to their cart and continued their journey. Thus the terrifying adventure of the cart of Death ended happily, thanks to the wise advice which Sancho Panza gave his master.

IV. The strange adventure that befell the gallant Don Quixote with the brave Knight of the Mir-

DON QUIXOTE AND HIS SQUIRE SPENT THE FOLLOWING NIGHT beneath some tall and shady trees, and the former, at Sancho's persuasion, partook of the food from the store carried by Dapple. While they were at supper, Sancho said to his master: "Señor, what a fool I should have been if I had chosen for my reward the spoils of the first adventure accomplished by your worship, instead of the foals of the three mares! Well, well, a sparrow in the hand is better than a vulture on the wing."

"Nevertheless, Sancho," replied Don Quixote, "if you had let me attack as I wished, the empress's gold crown and Cupid's painted wings would have fallen to you as spoils, for I would have seized them by force and put them into your hands."

"The sceptres and crowns of stage emperors," answered Sancho Panza, "are never made of real gold, but only of brass-foil or tin."

"That is true," said Don Quixote, "the ornaments of the drama should not be real, but only make-believe and fiction like the drama itself: indeed, Sancho, I want you to turn a kindly eye upon the play and in consequence upon those who represent and compose it, for they are all productive of much good to the state, placing as they do before us at every step a mirror in which we may see vividly portrayed the actions of human life; nothing indeed more truly portrays us as we are and as we would be than the play and the players.[1] Now tell me, have you never seen a play acted in which kings, emperors, pontiffs, knights, ladies and divers other characters are introduced? One plays the bully, another the rogue; this one the merchant, that the soldier; one the wise fool, another the foolish lover. When the play is over and they have divested themselves of the dresses they wore in it the actors are all again upon a level."

"Yes, I've seen it," answered Sancho.

[1] Compare Hamlet's speech to the players in Act 3, Sc. 2. "The purpose of playing, whose end, both at the first and now, was and is, to hold, as 'twere, the mirror up to nature; to show virtue her own feature, scorn her own image, and the very age and body of the time his form and pressure."

"Well, then," said Don Quixote, "the same happens in the comedy and life of this world, where some play emperors, others popes, and, in short, all the parts that can be brought into a play; but when it is over, that is to say, when life ends, death strips them all of the robes that distinguished them one from the other, and all are equal in the grave."

"A brave comparison!" said Sancho, "though not so new, for I've heard it many a time, as well as that one about the game of chess, how, so long as the game lasts, each piece has its special office, and when the game is finished they are all mixed, shuffled and jumbled together, and stored away in the bag, which is much like ending life in the grave."

"Sancho," said Don Quixote, "you are becoming daily less doltish and more wise."

"Yes, master, for some of your wisdom must stick to me," said Sancho, "just as land that is, of itself, barren and dry, will eventually, by dint of dunging and tilling, come to yield a goodly crop. What I mean to say is that your worship's talk has been the dung which has fallen upon the barren soil of my poor wit, and the time during which I have served you and enjoyed your company has been the tillage. With the help of this I hope to yield fruit like any blessing, in such plenty that it will not slide away from the paths of good breeding that you have made in my shallow understanding."

Don Quixote laughed at Sancho's affected style of speech, and perceived that what he said about his improvement was true, for from time to time he spoke in a way that astonished him, though on most occasions when Sancho tried to talk in argument, and in a lofty style, his speech would end by toppling down from the peak of his simplicity into the abyss of his ignorance. And where he showed his culture and his memory best was in his use of proverbs, no matter whether they came pat to the subject or not, as must have been seen already and noted in the course of this history.

In such conversation they spent a great part of the night, but Sancho felt a wish to let down the hatches of his eyes, as he used to say when he wanted to sleep. So, having unharnessed Dapple, he left him free to crop the abundant pasture. He did not take the saddle off Rozinante, as his master's express orders were that so long as they were in the field or not sleeping under a roof, Rozinante was not to be unsaddled; it was, by the way, an ancient custom, established and observed by knights-errant, to take off the bridle and hang it on the saddle-bow; but to remove the saddle from the horse—never on your life! Sancho observed this rule, and gave him the same liberty he had given Dapple, whose friendship for Rozinante was so unequalled and so close that a tradition handed down from father to son says that the author of this true history wrote some chapters on the subject which, in order to preserve the

243

propriety and decorum due to so heroic a history, he did not include. At times, however, he forgets this resolve and describes how as soon as the two beasts were together, they would scratch one another, and how, when they were tired or satisfied, Rozinante would lay his neck across Dapple's more than half a yard beyond, and the pair would stand in that position, gazing thoughtfully on the ground, for three days, or at least so long as they were left alone, or hunger did not compel them to look for food.

Sancho at last fell asleep at the foot of a cork tree, and Don Quixote dozed under a robust oak. But a short time only had elapsed when a noise he heard behind him awoke the latter, and, standing up, he gazed in the direction the noise came from, and spied two men on horseback, one of whom, letting himself slip from the saddle, said to the other: "Dismount, friend, and take the bridles off the horses, for, methinks, this spot abounds in grass for them and in silence and solitude for my love-sick thoughts." Saying this, he stretched himself upon the ground, and as he flung himself down the armour he wore clattered—a manifest proof by which Don Quixote knew him to be a knight-errant, and, going over to Sancho, who was fast asleep, he pulled him by the arm, and, after rousing him with no small difficulty, he said to him in a low voice:

"Brother Sancho, we have an adventure."

"God send us a good one," said Sancho, "and where, master, may mistress adventure be?"

"Where, Sancho?" answered Don Quixote. "Turn your eyes, and you will see stretched yonder a knight-errant, who, methinks, is not too happy, for I saw him fling himself off his horse and throw himself on the ground with signs of dejection, and as he fell his armour clattered."

"But how does your worship make out this to be an adventure?" said Sancho.

"I do not insist," answered Don Quixote, "that this is a full adventure, but it is the beginning of one, for this is the way adventures begin. But listen, for he seems to be tuning a viol or lute, and by the way he is spitting and clearing his throat he must be preparing to sing something."

Sancho would have replied, but the Knight of the Wood's voice, which was neither very good nor very bad, stopped him, and both listened attentively to the plaintive song. At the end the knight uttered "Woe's me!" in such a piteous tone that it seemed to be wrung from the inmost depths of his heart.

"I' faith," said Sancho, "yon knight seems the kind who'll go on weeping and moaning a month without ceasing."

This was not so, however, for the Knight of the Wood, hearing voices near him, ceased his lamentation, stood up and called out in a loud but courteous voice: "Who goes there?

Who are you? Are you, perchance, of the band of the happy or of the afflicted?"

"Of the afflicted," answered Don Quixote.

"Then come to me," said he of the Wood, "and you will come to the very fountain-head of sorrow and affliction."

Don Quixote, when he heard such gentle and courteous words, went over to him, and so did Sancho.

The melancholy knight took Don Quixote by the arm, saying: "Sit down here, Sir Knight. Now that I have found you in this place, where solitude and night, the natural couch and proper dwelling of knights-errant, keep you company, I need no further proof that you belong to their number."

To this Don Quixote answered: "I am a knight-errant as you say, and though in my soul sorrows, disasters and misfortunes have taken up their abode, yet they have not driven out my pity for the miseries of others."

While this conversation was proceeding, they were seated side by side upon the hard sward, in peace and good company, not in the manner of men who at break of day would have to break one another's heads.

"Are you, Sir Knight, perchance, in love?" enquired the Knight of the Wood.

"To my woe, I am," answered Don Quixote, "though the sorrows arising from well-placed affections should be accounted blessings rather than calamities."

"That is true," replied he of the Wood, "provided disdain do not unbalance our reason and understanding, for if exaggerated it resembles vengeance."

"I was never disdained by my lady," said Don Quixote.

"No, surely not," said Sancho, who stood close by, "my lady is as meek as a lamb, and softer than butter."

"Is this your squire?" asked he of the Wood.

"Yes, he is," said Don Quixote.

"This is the first time I have ever seen a squire," said he of the Wood, "who dared to speak while his master was speaking. Anyhow, there is mine over there, who is as tall as his father, and it cannot be proved that he has ever opened his lips when I was speaking."

"I' faith," said Sancho, "I have spoken and am fit to speak before one as great, and even . . . and perhaps . . . but let it be . . . it'll be worse to stir it about."

The Squire of the Wood then took Sancho by the arm, saying, "Let us two go where we can talk squire-like together, and leave these gentlemen, our masters, to butt at each other, telling the story of their lives. I wager the day will find them at it without having settled anything."

"With all my heart," said Sancho, "and I'll tell your worship who I am, that you may judge whether I deserve to be counted among the number of most talkative squires."

The two squires then withdrew to one side, and a dialogue passed between them as droll as that of their masters was serious.

The Squire of the Wood said to Sancho: "We squires to knights-errant do indeed lead a hard life of toil and 'tis true to say that we eat our bread by the sweat of our brows, which is one of the curses God laid upon our first parents."

"It may also be said," observed Sancho, "that we eat it in the chill of our bodies, for who suffers more heat and more cold than the wretched squires of knights-errantry? Indeed it would not be so bad if we had something to eat, for sorrows are lighter when there's bread to eat; but there are times when we go a day or two without breaking our fast, unless it be on the wind that blows."

"All that can be put up with," said he of the Wood, "when we have hopes of a reward, for unless he serves an especially unlucky knight-errant, a squire is sure after a little time to find himself at least rewarded with a handsome government of some island or a tidy countship."

"I've told my master already," said Sancho, "that I'll be content with the government of some island, and he's so noble and generous that he has promised it to me many a time."

"As for me," said he of the Wood, "I'll be content with a canonry for my services, and my master has already assigned me one."

"Your master," said Sancho, "must then be a knight in the ecclesiastical line, and can grant such favours to his good squire, but mine is only a layman, though I do remember some wise, but, in my opinion, intriguing folks, who tried to persuade him to have himself made archbishop. He, however, would be nothing but an emperor, and I was trembling all the time lest he should become bitten with the fancy of going into the Church, for I didn't consider myself suitable to hold offices in it. In fact I may as well tell you that, though I look like a man, I'm just a beast as far as the Church is concerned."

"Ah! That's where you are wrong," said he of the Wood, "'those insular governorships are not all plain sailing; some are twisted, some poor, some dreary, and, in short, the loftiest and best regulated brings with it a heavy load of worry and trouble, which the unlucky wight to whose lot it has fallen bears upon his shoulders. Far better would it be for us who profess this plague-stricken service to return to our homes and there spend our days in more pleasant occupations, such as hunting and fishing: for where in the world would you find a squire so poor as not to have a hack, a couple of greyhounds and a fishing-rod with which to while away the time in his own village?"

"I'm not in need of any of these things," said Sancho. " 'Tis true I've no hack, but I've an ass that is worth twice as much as my master's horse. God send me a bad Easter, and that the next one, if I would swap him, even if I got four bushels of barley to boot. You'll laugh at the value I'm putting on my Dapple—for dapple is the colour of my ass. As for greyhounds, I'm in no want, for there are lashings of them in my home town, and surely the finest sport of all is where it's at other people's expense."

"Truly and earnestly, Sir Squire," said he of the Wood, "I've made up my mind to give up the drunken frolics of these knights of ours, and go back to my village and bring up my children, for I've three like three Oriental pearls."

"I've two," said Sancho, "fit to be presented to the Pope in person, especially a girl whom I'm rearing to be a countess, please God, though in the teeth of her mother."

"And how old is this lady who is being brought up to be a countess?" enquired he of the Wood.

"Fifteen years, more or less," replied Sancho, "but she's as tall as a lance, and as fresh as an April morning, and as strong as a porter."

"Those qualities," said he of the Wood, "fit her to be not only a countess but a nymph of the greenwood. Ah, the frisky whore! What spunk the jade must have!"

To this Sancho replied somewhat sulkily: "She's no whore, nor was her mother, nor will either of them be, please God, so long as I'm alive; and do you keep a civiller tongue on you. Considering that you've been reared among knights-errant, who are the last word in courtesy, I don't think your language is becoming."

"O how little you understand the language of compliments, Sir Squire," answered he of the Wood. "Do you mean to tell me that you don't know that when any horseman lands a good lance-thrust at a bull in the square, or when anyone does anything very well, the people are accustomed to say: 'how well the whoreson rogue has done it!' and that which seems to be insulting in the phrase is high praise? Come, señor, let you disown the sons or daughters whose actions don't earn their parents such compliments."

"Yes, I do disown them," answered Sancho, "and in the same way you may heap a whole bawdyship straightway on me, my wife and my children, for all they do and say is over and above deserving of like praise. And that I may see them again, I pray God deliver me from mortal sin, which is the same as delivering me from this dangerous squire business into which I've fallen for the second time, baited and bribed by a purse with a hundred ducats in it that I found one day in the heart of the Sierra Morena. And I tell you the Devil is always putting before my eyes, here, there and everywhere, a bag full of doublooms, which I'm for ever turning over with my hand, and hugging it, and carrying it home with me, to make investments and settle rents, and live like a prince. So long as I think of this, I don't care a fig for all the toils I endure with this fool of a master of mine, whom I know to be more of a madman than a knight."

"Hence the common saying that 'covetousness burst the bag'," said he of the Wood; "but if you mean to talk of such men, let me tell you that there is no greater in the world than my master, for he is one of those of whom it is said: 'care for his neighbour kills the ass', for he makes a madman of himself in order that another knight may recover the wits he has lost, and he goes about looking for what, were he to find it, may, for all I know, hit him in the snout."

"Is he by any chance in love?" asked Sancho.

"He is," said he of the Wood, "with a certain Casildea of Vandalia, the rawest and most hard-boiled lady in the world, but 'tis not on the score of rawness that he limps, for he has other greater plans rumbling in his belly; you'll hear him speak of them before long."

"No matter how smooth the road, there's sure to be some rut or hollow in it," said Sancho. "In other houses they cook beans but in mine 'tis by the potful; madness has always more followers and hangers-on than wisdom; but if the common saying is true, that to have a friend in grief gives some relief, I may draw consolation from you, for your master is as crazy as mine."

"Crazy but valiant," answered he of the Wood, "and more roguish than crazy or valiant."

"Mine is not like that," replied Sancho: "I mean he has nought of the rogue in him. On the contrary, he has a soul as simple as a pitcher: he could not do harm to anyone, but good to all, nor has he any malice in him; why, a child would convince him 'tis night at noon-day, and 'tis on account of this simplicity that I love him as I love the cockles of my heart, and I can't invent a way of leaving him, no matter what piece of foolishness he does."

"Nevertheless, brother and señor," said he of the Wood, "if the blind lead the blind, both are in danger of falling into the ditch. It is better for us to retire quickly, and get back to our dens, for those who seek adventures don't always find good ones."

Sancho kept on spitting from time to time, and as the charitable Squire of the Wood noticed that his spittle was gluey and somewhat dry, he said, "It seems to me that all this talk of ours has made our tongues stick to our palates, but I have a loosener, hanging from the saddle-bow of my horse, which is quite good", and getting up, he came back a moment later with a large skin of wine and a pasty half a yard long—which is no exaggeration, for it was composed of a domestic rabbit so big that Sancho, as he held it, took it to be a goat, not to say a kid, and gazing at it he said: "Is this what you carry along with you, señor?"

"What were you thinking then?" said the other. "Am I perchance some mean homespun, water-drinking squire? I carry a better commissariat on my horse's crupper than a general does when he is on the march."

Sancho fell to, without any need of pressing: in the dark he gobbled lumps as large as the knots on a tether, observing as he ate: "You are indeed a trusty and a loyal squire, round and sound, grand and gorgeous, as is proved by this feast, which, if it has not come here by magic, seems like it at least; and not like me, poor devil, who am only carrying in my saddle-bags a scrap of cheese so hard that you could brain a giant with it, and, to keep it company, a few dozen carob beans and as many filberts and walnuts. Thanks to the poverty of my master and the idea he has and the rule he follows, that knights-errant must not feed on anything except dried fruits and the herbs of the field."

"By my faith," replied he of the Wood, "my stomach is not made for thistles or wild pears from the woods. Let our masters keep to their opinions and laws of chivalry, and eat what is prescribed. As for me, I carry my meat baskets and this wineskin slung from my saddle-bow, whether by their will or no, and I'm so devoted to her, aye, and so arrantly fond of her, that hardly a minute passes without my giving her a thousand kisses and hugs."

Saying this, he put the skin into Sancho's hands, who raising it up pressed it to his mouth and remained gazing at the stars for a quarter of an hour. When he had finished his drink he let his head fall on one side, and, heaving a deep sigh, he exclaimed: "O whoreson rogue, what a Catholic liquor it is!"

"There you are," said he of the Wood when he heard Sancho's exclamation. "See how you have praised my wine by calling it 'whoreson'."

"Well," said Sancho, "I confess that I'm aware 'tis no dishonour to call a body whoreson when we mean to praise him. Now tell me, señor, by the life you love best, is this Ciudad Real wine?"

"'O peerless wine-taster!" said he of the Wood. "From there and from nowhere else has it come, and it is a few years old too."

"Trust me for that," said Sancho. "I knew I'd make a successful guess as to where it came from. Would you believe me, señor, when I tell you that I've such a great natural instinct in testing wines that no sooner do I smell one of them than I can tell its country, its kind, its flavour and age, the changes it will undergo, and every detail concerning the said wine. But you needn't wonder, for I've had in my family on my father's side the two finest wine-tasters La Mancha has known for many a long year, and to prove what I'm saying I'll tell you what happened to them. They were both given wine from a cask to try, and they were asked their opinion about its condition, quality, goodness or badness. One of them tested it with the tip of his tongue, the other did no more than hold it to his nose. The first said that the wine tasted of iron; the second that it had a flavour of Córdoban leather. The owner declared that the cask was clear, and the wine had no blending which could have imparted a taste of iron or leather. Notwithstanding this the two famous wine-tasters stuck to their point. Time went by; the wine was sold, and when the cask was cleansed, a small key was found in it hanging to a leather thong. Consider now whether one who comes of such a stock is able to give an opinion in such matters."

"Since that is so," said he of the Wood, "let us give up going in search of adventures, and since we have loaves, don't let us go looking for tarts, but return to our cots, for there God will find us if it be His will."

"I'll serve my master till he gets to Saragossa," said Sancho, "then, maybe, we'll come to an understanding."

In the end the two worthy squires talked so much and drank so much that they had need of sleep to tie up their tongues and allay their thirst, for to quench it was impossible. And so the pair of them, clinging to the now nearly empty wineskin and with half-chewed morsels in their mouths, fell fast asleep: and there we will leave them for the present to relate what took place between the Knight of the Wood and him of the Rueful Figure.

The Knight of the Wood said to Don Quixote, "I wish you to know, Sir Knight, that my destiny, or rather my choice, led me to become enamoured of a certain lady, the peerless Casildea de Vandalia. I call her peerless, because she has no peer, either in bodily stature, station or beauty. This Lady Casildea repaid my honourable desires by forcing me, as his stepmother did Hercules, to engage in many perilous exploits, promising me, at the end of each, that, with the end of the next, I should attain the object of all my hopes. But my labours have gone on increasing link by link until they are past counting, nor do I know which is to be the one which will finally announce the accomplishment of my honourable passion. On one occasion she ordered me to go and challenge that famous gaintess of Seville known as the Giralda,[2] who is as valiant and strong as if made of brass, and though never stirring from one spot, is the most changeable and volatile woman in the world. I came, I saw, I conquered, and I made her keep still and on one point (for none but north winds

[2] This is the brass statue of Faith, fourteen feet in height, which is perched on the top of the great tower of the Cathedral of Seville, and serves as a weathercock. The tower was erected by the Moors in the 13th century, and afterwards was transformed into a belfry.

blew for more than a week). On another occasion she made me go and weigh the mighty Bulls of Guisando,[3] an enterprise that should have been recommended to porters rather than to knights. Another time she commanded me to fling myself into the pit of Cabra[4]—an unheard-of peril—and bring her back a detailed account of what is hidden in its abyss. I stopped the motion of the Giralda; I weighed the Bulls of Guisando; I descended into the pit and drew to the light of day the secrets of its abyss, and yet my hopes are as dead as dead can be, and her orders and disdains as much alive as ever. And now her last command is for me to go through all the provinces of Spain and compel all the knights-errant wandering there to confess that she is the most beautiful woman alive today, and that I am the most valiant and the most enamoured knight on earth. In accordance with her demand I have already travelled over the greater part of Spain, and have vanquished many knights who have had the presumption to gainsay me, but my greatest pride and boast is that I have conquered in single combat that so famous knight Don Quixote of La Mancha, and made him confess that my Casildea is more beautiful than his Dulcinea. By this victory alone I consider that I have conquered all the knights in the world, for the said Don Quixote has vanquished them all, and since I have vanquished him, his glory, his fame and his honour are forthwith transferred to my person, and his innumerable exploits are now set down to my account and have become mine."

Don Quixote was astounded to hear such words from the Knight of the Wood, and he was a thousand times on the point of telling him he lied, and had the word "liar" on the tip of his tongue, but he restrained himself as best he could in order to make him confess the lie out of his own mouth. So he said to him calmly, "I say nothing about your worship, Sir Knight, having vanquished most of the knights of Spain, and even of the world, but I am doubtful whether you have conquered Don Quixote of La Mancha. Perhaps it may have been some other knight who resembled him, though indeed there are few like him."

"How! Not vanquishd him?" said he of the Wood. "By heaven above us, I fought Don Quixote and vanquished him, and overcame him. He is a man of tall stature, gaunt features, lanky shrivelled limbs; his hair is turning grey, his nose is aquiline and a little hooked, and his moustaches are long, black and drooping. He goes into battle under the name of 'The Knight of the Rueful Figure', and he has for squire a

[3] The Bulls of Guisando are four rough granite figures of animals in the district of Avila.
[4] The pit of Cabra in the district of Cordoba is traditionally supposed to be the shaft of an ancient mine.

peasant called Sancho Panza. He presses the back and curbs the reins of a famous horse called Rozinante, and, finally, he has for mistress of his will a certain Dulcinea del Toboso, once upon a time known as Aldonza Lorenzo, just as mine, whose name is Casildea, and who comes from Andalusia, I call Casildea de Vandalia. If all these tokens do not suffice to vindicate the truth of my words, here is my sword which will compel incredulity itself to give credence to it."

"Softly, Sir Knight," said Don Quixote, "and listen to what I am about to say. You must know that this Don Quixote you speak about is the greatest friend I have in the world, in fact I may say that I regard him as I would my very self, and by the precise tokens you have given of him I am sure that he must be the same whom you vanquished. On the other hand, I see with my eyes and feel with my hands that it is impossible for him to be the same, unless, perhaps, that particular enemy of his, who is an enchanter, may have taken his shape in order to allow himself to be vanquished so as to cheat him of the fame that his noble exploits as a knight have won him throughout the world. To confirm this I must tell you that only a short while since, these said enchanters, his enemies, changed the shape and person of the fair Dulcinea del Toboso into a vulgar and mean village lass, and in the same manner they must have transformed Don Quixote. If all this does not suffice to convince you of the truth of my words, here stands Don Quixote himself: he will maintain it by arms, on foot or on horseback, or in any way you wish."

With these words he stood up and gripped his sword, waiting for the decision of the Knight of the Wood, who in a voice equally calm replied: "A good payer needs no sureties. He who managed to vanquish you once when transformed, Señor Don Quixote, may well hope to conquer you in your proper person. But since it is not right for knights to perform their deeds in the dark like highwaymen and bullies, let us wait till daylight, that the sun may look down on our achievements. And it must be a condition of our battle that the vanquished shall remain entirely at the mercy of the conqueror, provided that what is imposed shall be becoming a knight."

"I am more than satisfied with these conditions," answered Don Quixote. And so saying, they went to seek their squires, whom they found snoring, and they were in the same posture as when sleep first waylaid them. They roused them and ordered them to prepare the steeds, for at sunrise the two knights would engage in bloody single combat. When Sancho heard the news he was thunderstruck and all of a dither with fear for the safety of his master, because of the tales which he had heard the Squire of the Wood tell of his knight's powers. Without saying a word, however, the two knights went off in search of their beasts, for the three horses and Dapple had smelt each other and were by this time all together. On the way, he of the Wood said to Sancho: "You must know, brother, that fighting men from Andalusia are accustomed, when they are seconds in any combat, not to stand idle with their hands folded while their champions are engaged. I'm saying this to remind you that while our masters are fighting, we, too, must have a fight, and knock one another to splinters."

"That custom, Sir Squire," replied Sancho, "may be current among the bullies and fighting men you mention, but never in any circumstances among the squires of knights-errant. At least I have never heard my master speak of such a custom, and he knows all the rules of knight-errantry by heart. But even if it is an express rule that squires should fight while their masters are fighting, I don't intend to follow it, but to pay the penalty that might be imposed on peacefully-minded squires like myself, for I'm sure it will not be more than a couple of pounds of wax.[5] I would prefer to pay that, for I know it will cost me less than the plasters I'll have to pay for in healing my head, which I already reckon to be smashed in two pieces. Furthermore, I cannot fight, for I've no sword and never in my life carried one."

"I know a good remedy for that," said he of the Wood. "I've here two linen bags of the same size: you take one, and I'll take the other, and we'll have a bout of bag-blows on equal terms."

"If that's the way it goes," answered Sancho, "I'm game, but I'm thinking such a fight will beat the dust out of us rather than hurt us."

"That mustn't happen," replied the other, "for we'll put into the bags, to keep the wind from blowing them away, half a dozen fine smooth stones, all of the same weight. In this way we'll be able to pound one another without doing much damage."

"Body of my father," said Sancho, "what a nice kind of sable skins and pads of cotton wool he's putting into the bags to save breaking our heads and mashing our bones to powder! But even if they were filled with pads of raw silk, I tell ye, my dear sir, there's to be no fighting for me. Let our masters fight and take their medicine, but let us eat, drink and be merry, for Time is anxious enough to snatch away our lives from us without our going out in search of appetizers to finish them off before they reach their season and drop off the tree for very ripeness."

"Still," said he of the Wood, "we must fight, if only for half an hour."

5 Religious Confraternities imposed such a fine upon their members for trifling offenses.

"Not on your life," replied Sancho: "I'm not going to be so churlish or ungrateful as to pick any quarrel, no matter how trifling, with one whom I have eaten and drunk with; besides, who the devil could manage to fight in cold blood, without anger or annoyance?"

"I'll provide a remedy for that," said he of the Wood. "Before we start fighting I'll walk nicely and gently up to your worship and give you three or four buffets which will land you at my feet. By this means I'll rouse your choler though it be sleeping sounder than a dormouse."

"Faith and I've a trick against yours that's just as good," replied Sancho. "I'll take up a stout cudgel, and before your worship gets near enough to raise my choler I'll send yours to sleep with such sound whacks that it will not awake until in the next world, where all know that I'm not the kind of man to let my face be messed about by anyone. Let each man watch out for his own arrow—though, mind you, the better way would be for everyone to let his choler sleep in peace, for no one knows the heart of his neighbour, and many a man comes for wool and goes back shorn: and God always blessed the peacemakers and cursed the peace-breakers; for if a baited cat, who's shut in, turns into a lion, God knows what I, who am a man, shall turn into. So from now onwards, I warn you, Mister Squire, that I'll put down to your account all the harm and damage that may come of our quarrel."

"I agree," said he of the Wood; "God will send the dawn and all will be as right as rain."

And now a thousand kinds of little painted birds began to warble in the trees, and with their blithe and jocund notes seemed to welcome and salute the fresh dawn, who already was showing her beautiful countenance through the gates and balconies of the East, shaking from her tresses countless liquid pearls, and the plants bathing in that fragrant moisture seemed likewise to shed a spray of tiny white gems; the willow trees distilled sweet manna, the fountains laughed, the brooks murmured, and the meadows clad themselves in all their glory at her coming. But hardly had the light of day allowed him to see and distinguish things, when the first object that Sancho Panza caught sight of was the Squire of the Wood's nose, which was so big that it almost overshadowed his whole body. It is said, indeed, that it was of huge size, hooked in the middle, all covered with warts, and of a mulberry colour like an egg-plant, and it hung down two fingers' length below his mouth. Now the size, the colour, the warts and the hook of the aforesaid nose made its owner's face so hideous that Sancho, as he gazed at it, began to shudder hand and foot, like a child in a fit of epilepsy, and he resolved in his mind to let himself be given two hundred buffets rather than allow his choler to provoke him into attacking that monster. Don Quixote looked at his adversary, and found that he had already his helmet on, with the vizor down, so that he could not see his face, but he noticed that he was a muscular man, though not very tall in stature. Over his armour he wore a surcoat or cassock of some stuff, which seemed to be the finest cloth of gold, all bedizened with a quantity of little moons of glittering looking-glass, which gave him a most gallant and showy appearance. Above his helmet fluttered a great cluster of green, yellow and white plumes, and his lance, which was leaning against a tree, was very long and thick, and had a steel point more than a palm in length.

Don Quixote noted all, and from what he saw he inferred that the said knight must be very powerful; but for all that he did not fear as Sancho did, but with a noble courage he addressed the Knight of the Mirrors, saying: "If, Sir Knight, your great longing to fight has not exhausted your courtesy, I would beg you earnestly to raise your vizor a little that I may see if the gallantry of your countenance corresponds with that of your accoutrement."

"Whether, Sir Knight, you are vanquished or victor in this enterprise," answered he of the Mirrors, "you will have more then enough time and opportunity to see me. If I do not now satisfy your request, it is because, in my opinion, I should wrong the beauteous Casildea de Vandalia by wasting time in raising my vizor before forcing you to confess what you know I demand."

"Well," said Don Quixote, "while we are mounting our steeds you can surely tell me if I am the Don Quixote whom you said you vanquished."

"To that we answer," said he of the Mirrors, "that you are as like the knight whom I vanquished as one egg is like another, but as you say that enchanters persecute you, I dare not say whether you are the aforesaid or not."

"That is enough," said Don Quixote, "to convince me of your deception; however, to relieve you of your misapprehensions, let our horses be brought, and in less time than you would take in raising your vizor, if God, my lady, and my arm prevail, I shall see your face, and you shall see that I am not the vanquished Don Quixote you consider me to be."

Therefore, cutting short further words, they mounted on horseback, and Don Quixote turned Rozinante's reins in order to take up the requisite ground for charging back upon his rival, while he of the Mirrors did the same; but Don Quixote had hardly gone twenty paces when he heard himself called by the Knight of the Mirrors, who said, when each had returned half-way: "Remember, Sir Knight, that the condition of our battle is that the vanquished, as I said before, shall be at the disposal of the victor."

"I know it already," answered Don Quixote, "but there is a proviso that what is commanded and imposed upon the vanquished must not transgress the bounds of chivalry."

"That is understood," replied he of the Mirrors.

Just at this moment the amazing nose of the squire presented itself to Don Quixote's view, and he was no less astonished to see it than Sancho had been, so much so that he took him for some monster or else for a human being of some new species which is rarely seen on the face of the earth. Sancho, seeing his master go off to take up his ground, did not want to remain alone with the nosy individual, for he was afraid lest one flick of that nose on his own should end the battle as far as he was concerned, and leave him stretched on the ground either with the blow or with the fright; so he ran after his master, holding on to one of Rozinante's stirrup-leathers, and when he thought it was time to turn about, he said: "I beg your worship, master, before you turn to charge, to help me climb up on yonder cork tree, where I may witness your gallant encounter with this knight at better ease and comfort than from the earth."

"I am rather of the opinion, Sancho," said Don Quixote, "that you would even mount a scaffold to see the bulls without danger."

"To tell you the truth," replied Sancho, "the fearsome nose of that squire has me all of a dither and full of terror, so that I dare not stay near him."

"It is, indeed, such a one," said Don Quixote, "that were I not what I am, it would strike fear in me too. So come, I will help you to climb up where you will."

While Don Quixote stopped to let Sancho climb into the cork tree, he of the Mirrors took as much ground as he considered necessary, and, thinking that Don Quixote had done likewise, without waiting for any sound of trumpet or other signal to direct them, he wheeled his horse, which was no swifter or better-looking than Rozinante, and at his top speed, which was no more than an easy trot, advanced to meet his foe, but noticing that he was busy hoisting Sancho up into the tree, he drew rein and halted mid-way, for which his steed was profoundly grateful, for it was unable to move. Don Quixote, imagining that his rival was careering down on top of him, drove his spurs vigorously into the lean flanks of Rozinante and made him dash along in such style that, as history relates, this was the one occasion when he was seen to make an attempt to gallop, for on all others he did no more than plain easy trotting; and with this unheard-of fury he charged at him of the Mirrors, who stood digging the spurs into his horse up to the buttons, without being able to make him stir an inch from the spot where he had halted in his career. At this lucky critical moment did Don Quixote bear down upon his adversary, who was in difficulties with his horse and embarrassed with his lance, for he could neither manage it nor was there time to put it into the rest. Don Quixote, however, paid scant heed to such embarrassments, but in perfect safety and without taking any risks crashed into him of the Mirrors with such force that, in spite of himself, he threw him to the ground over the horse's crupper; and so great was the fall that he lay apparently dead, not stirring hand or foot. No sooner did Sancho see him fall than he slid down the cork tree, and ran at top speed to where his master was, who, after dismounting from Rozinante, stood over the Knight of the Mirrors. Unlacing his helmet to see if he was dead and to give him air if haply he were alive, he saw— who can say what he saw without arousing the wonder, as- tonishment and awe of all who hear it? He saw, history says, the very face, the very figure, the very aspect, the very phys- iognomy, the very effigy, the very image of the bachelor Samson Carrasco. As soon as he saw it, he cried out in a loud voice: "Come, Sancho, and behold what you have to see but not to believe: make haste, my son, and learn what wizards and enchanters are able to accomplish."

Sancho came up, and when he saw the face of the bachelor Carrasco, he began to cross himself a thousand times and bless himself as many more. All this time the prostrate knight showed no signs of life, and Sancho said to Don Quixote: "In my opinion, master, you should stick your sword into the mouth of this one who looks like the bachelor Carrasco, and perhaps in him you will kill one of your enemies, the enchanters."

"That is good advice," said Don Quixote, "for of enemies the fewer the better." Then drawing his sword he was about to put into operation Sancho's advice, when the Squire of the Mirrors came up, now minus the nose which had made him so hideous, and cried out in a loud voice: "Mind what you are doing, Señor Don Quixote, that man lying at your feet is your friend the bachelor Samson Carrasco, and I am his squire."

"And what about the nose?" said Sancho, seeing him with- out his former hideous appendage.

"I have it here in my pocket," said the latter, and sticking his hand into his right pocket he drew out a clownish nose of varnished pasteboard of the kind we have already described. Sancho then, after peering at him more and more closely, exclaimed in a loud voice of amazement: "Holy Mary pro- tect us! Isn't it Tom Cecial, my neighbour and gossip?"

"Who else would I be?" replied the unnosed squire. "Tom

Cecial I am, gossip and friend, Sancho Panza, and I'll tell you presently of the means, the vagaries, the schemings that brought me here; but in the meantime, beg and beseech your master not to touch, maltreat, wound or kill the Knight of the Mirrors whom he has lying at his feet, for without any manner of doubt 'tis the bold and ill-advised bachelor Samson Carrasco, our fellow-townsman."

At this moment he of the Mirrors came to his senses, and Don Quixote no sooner saw it than he held the naked point of his sword to his face, saying: "You are a dead man, Knight, unless you confess that the peerless Dulcinea del Toboso surpasses your Casildea de Vandalia in beauty; and as well as this, you have to promise that if you survive this combat and fall, you will go to the city of El Toboso and present yourself before her on my behalf, leaving her to do with you what she pleases. And if she leaves you to your own devices, you must return and seek for me (the trail of my deeds will guide you in my direction) and tell me all that has taken place between her and you. These are conditions that do not depart from the terms of knight-errantry."

"I confess," said the fallen knight, "that the torn and dirty shoe of the Lady Dulcinea del Toboso is better than the ill-combed though clean beard of Casildea, and I promise to go and return from her presence to yours, and give you a complete and detailed account of what you ask me."

"You have also to confess and believe," added Don Quixote, "that the knight you vanquished was not, nor could be, Don Quixote of La Mancha, but somebody else who resembled him, just as I confess and believe that you, though you appear to be the bachelor Samson Carrasco, are not he, but another like him, and that my enemies have conjured you up before me in his shape that I may restrain and moderate my impetuous wrath and make humane use of my glorious victory."

"I confess, judge, and consider everything to be as you confess, judge and consider it," answered the crippled knight. "Let me rise, I pray you, if the shock of my fall will allow it, for I am indeed in a very bad way."

Don Quixote helped him to rise, with his squire Tom Cecial, from whom Sancho never for an instant took his eyes, and whom he questioned incessantly, proving thereby to his own satisfaction that the latter was truly the Tom Cecial he said he was. But Sancho was so impressed by what his master had said about the enchanters having changed the figure of the Knight of the Mirrors into that of the bachelor Samson Carrasco, that he was unable to believe the truth of what he saw with his own eyes. In fine, both master and man remained under their delusion, and so he of the Mirrors and his squire, feeling down in the dumps and out of tune with

the world, took their departure from Don Quixote and
Sancho, intending to look for some place where the knight's
ribs might be plastered and strapped. Don Quixote and Sancho once more proceeded on their journey towards Saragossa.
The former rode onwards in great spirits; he was extremely
pleased, elated, not to say vainglorious, at having won a victory over such a valiant knight as he imagined him of the
Mirrors to be, and from his knightly word he expected to
learn whether his lady still continued to be enchanted, for the
said vanquished knight was bound, on pain of ceasing to be
one, to return and give him a report of what took place between himself and her.

But if Don Quixote was thinking of one thing, he of the
Mirrors was certainly thinking of another. In fact the latter at
that moment had no other thought than to find some place
where he might get poulticed, as we have said before. The
history then says that when the bachelor Samson Carrasco
counselled Don Quixote to resume his knight-errantry which
he had laid aside, he did so in consequence of a conference he
had previously held with the curate and the barber upon the
measures to be taken to induce Don Quixote to stay at home
in peace and quiet without exciting himself over his accursed
adventures. At that conclave it was decided by the unanimous
vote of all, and at the special instance of Carrasco, that Don
Quixote should be allowed to set out, as it was impossible to
restrain him, and that Samson should sally forth as a knight-
errant, and join battle with him, for which a pretext could
readily be found, and vanquish him—an easy matter, they
thought—and that it should be agreed and regulated that the
one conquered should remain at the mercy of his conqueror.
And once Don Quixote was vanquished, he should be ordered to go back to his village and home, and not leave it for
two years or until some other command was imposed upon
him, all of which conditions Don Quixote would carry out
without fail rather than break the laws of chivalry. During the
period of his seclusion, he might possibly forget his foolish
notions, or else an opportunity might be found of discovering
a sure remedy for his madness.

Carrasco undertook the task, and Tom Cecial, Sancho's
gossip and neighbour, a merry, scatter-brained fellow, offered
his services as squire. Samson armed himself as has been
described, and Tom Cecial, to avoid being recognized by his
gossip when they met, fitted on over his own natural nose
the false one already mentioned. And so they followed the
same road as Don Quixote, and very nearly reached him in
time to be present at the adventure of the cart of Death, and
at last they met in the wood, where all that the wise reader
has read took place. And if it had not been for the extraordinary fancies of Don Quixote, who took it into his head that

the bachelor was not the bachelor, Sir Bachelor would be for ever incapacitated from taking his degree as licentiate, all through not finding nests where he expected to find birds.

Tom Cecial, seeing how badly their plans had turned out, and what a wretched end their expedition had come to, said to the bachelor: "For sure, Master Samson Carrasco, we've met with our deserts. 'Tis easy to plan and start an enterprise, but most times 'tis hard to get out of it safe and sound. Don Quixote is mad, and we are sane, but he comes off safe and sound, with the laugh into the bargain, while you, master, are left drubbed and downcast. Tell us now, who is the greater madman, he that is so because he can't help it, or he who is so of his own free will?"

To which Samson replied: "The difference between these two madmen is, that he who is so perforce will be one for ever, but he who is so of his own accord can leave off being one whenever he likes."

"That being so," said Tom Cecial, "I was mad of my own accord when I agreed to become your squire, and, of my own accord, I wish to leave off being one and go back home."

"You may please yourself," replied Samson, "but to imagine that I am going home until I have given Don Quixote a beating is an absurdity, and it is not my wish to make him recover his wits that will drive me to hunt him now, but a lust for revenge, for the aching of my ribs will not let me form a more charitable resolve."

The two conversed in such a manner until they reached a town where by good fortune they found a bone-setter who cured the hapless Samson. Tom Cecial went home, leaving him behind nursing his revenge, and the history will return to him at the proper time, but now it must frolic along with Don Quixote.

V. The happily terminated adventure of the lions, and the story of Camacho's wedding feast

DON QUIXOTE CONTINUED HIS JOURNEY FULL OF THE JOY, satisfaction and high spirits we have described, fancying himself the most valiant knight-errant in the world owing to his late victory. All the adventures that might happen to him from that day onwards he reckoned as already successfully accomplished; he despised enchanters and enchantments, and he gave no thought to the innumerable beatings he had received in the course of his knight-errantry, nor to the stoning which had knocked out half his teeth, nor to the ingratitude of the galley-slaves, nor to the bold insolence of the Yanguesans who had belaboured him with their staves. Finally he said to himself that if he could only discover a method of disenchanting his Lady Dulcinea, he would not envy the highest good fortune which the most fortunate knight-errant of past ages ever achieved or could achieve. He was riding along entirely absorbed in these fancies, when Sancho said to him: "Isn't it strange, master, that I've still before my eyes that monstrous and hugeous nose of my gossip Tom Cecial?"

"Can it be, Sancho, that you really believe that the Knight of the Mirrors was the bachelor Samson Carrasco, and his squire Tom Cecial, your gossip?"

"I don't know what I'm to say to that," answered Sancho. "I only know that the details he gave me about my house, my wife and my children, no one but himself could have given me; and as for his face, once he had removed the nose, 'twas the very face of Tom Cecial, for I've often seen him in my village, and there was but a wall between my house and his; and the tone of his voice was just the same."

"Let us be reasonable, Sancho," replied Don Quixote. "Now tell me how it can be argued that the bachelor Samson Carrasco would come as a knight-errant armed with arms offensive and defensive to do battle with me? Have I, perchance, ever been his enemy? Have I ever given him cause to have a grudge against me? Am I his rival, or does he make profession of arms that he should envy the fame I have earned in them?"

"Yes, but what shall we say then," replied Sancho, "about that knight, whosoe'er he was, being the very image of the bachelor Carrasco, and his squire the dead spit of my gossip, Tom Cecial? And if that is enchantment, as your worship says, was there no other form in the world for them to take the likeness of?"

"It is all," said Don Quixote, "an artifice and trick of the malignant magicians who persecute me, and who, guessing that I was to be victorious in the conflict, settled that the vanquished knight should display the face of my friend the bachelor in order that my affection for him might intervene to halt my sharp blade and restrain my mighty arm and moderate the righteous indignation of my heart, so that he who sought to rob me of my life by trickery should save his own. And in proof, you know already, Sancho, through experience, which cannot lie or deceive, how easy it is for enchanters to change some countenances into others, making the beautiful ugly and the ugly beautiful, for not two days ago you saw with your own eyes the beauty and elegance of the peerless Dulcinea in all its perfection and natural grace, while I saw her in the ugly and mean form of a coarse country wench, with cataracts in her eyes and a stinking breath from her mouth. Seeing that the perverse enchanter

261

caused such a wicked transformation, it is no wonder that he effected that of Samson Carrasco and of your gossip, in order to snatch away my victory. Nevertheless, I console myself, because, when all is said and done, I have been victorious over my enemy, no matter what shape he took."

"God knows the truth of all," answered Sancho. Knowing as he did that the transformation of Dulcinea had been a device and trick of his own, he was not at all pleased by his master's wild fancies; but he did not like to reply, for fear of saying anything that would reveal his trickery.

As the discourse was not much to his taste, he turned aside from the road to beg a little milk from some shepherds who were milking their ewes near by.

Just then Don Quixote, happening to raise his head, perceived a waggon covered with royal flags coming along the road they were travelling, and, convinced that this must be some new adventure, he shouted to Sancho to bring him his helmet. At that moment Sancho was buying some curds from the shepherds, and, being flustered by his master's hurried call, he did not know what to do with them or how to carry them, so, not to lose them, for he had already paid for them, he thought it best to pour them into his master's helmet, and, using this clever shift, he turned back to see what his master needed. Don Quixote cried out to him: "Give me that helmet, my friend, for either I know precious little of adventures, or what I see yonder is one which should require me to arm myself."

The squire, as he had no time to take out the curds, had to give it him just as it was. Don Quixote took it, and, without noticing what was in it, clapped it on his head hastily, and as the curds were pressed and squeezed, the whey began to pour down over Don Quixote's face and beard, which gave him such a start that he exclaimed to Sancho: "What's this, Sancho? I think my head is softening, or my brains are melting, or else I am sweating from head to foot. And if I am sweating 'tis certainly not from fear. Now I am truly sure that the adventure is a terrible one which I must face. Give me something to wipe myself with, for this copious sweat is blinding my eyes." Sancho held his tongue and handed him a cloth, thanking God that his master had not found out the truth.

Don Quixote wiped himself and took off the helmet to see what it was that made his head feel cool, and seeing the white mess inside the helmet he put it up to his nose, and sniffing he said: "By my Lady Dulcinea del Toboso, these are curds you have put here, you treacherous, impudent, ill-favoured squire."

To which with calm composure Sancho replied: "If they are curds, master, give them to me, and I'll eat them; but let the Devil eat them, for it must be he who put them there. But how could you ever imagine that I would have the impudence to soil your worship's helmet? Indeed you must already know the culprit. In faith, master, from the understanding which God has given me, I am convinced that I too must have enchanters who persecute me as a creature and limb of your worship, and they must have put that nasty mess there in order to drive your patience into anger and make you drub my ribs as you are wont to do; but this time they have missed their mark, for I put my trust in my master's good sense; he must have considered that I have no curds or milk, or anything of the kind, and if I had, 'tis in my belly I would put it and not in the helmet."

"That may be," said Don Quixote. When he had wiped clean his head, face, beard and helmet, he put it on, and sitting himself firmly in his stirrups, feeling for his sword and grasping his lance, he cried: "Now come what may: here I stand ready to face Satan himself in battle."

The waggon with the flags now approached. In it was nobody, but the carter rode one of the mules and a man was seated in front. Don Quixote stood in front of it, and said: "Whither are you going, brothers? What cart is this? What have you got in it? What flags are those?"

To this the carter replied: "The cart is mine, but in it is a fine pair of caged lions which the Governor of Oran is sending as a present to His Majesty, and the flags are of the King, our master, and signify that what is inside the cart is his property."

"Are the lions large?" asked Don Quixote.

"So large," said the man at the door of the waggon, "that none larger, or even as large, have ever crossed from Africa into Spain. I am the keeper and I've carried many, but never a pair like these. They are male and female; the male is in the front cage, and the female in the one behind. They are now very hungry, for they've eaten nought today, so 'twere best for your worship to stand aside, for we must make haste to reach the place where we may give them their feed."

To this Don Quixote answered, smiling slightly: "Lion-whelps to me? To me lion-whelps? At such a time too? Then, by God, those gentlemen who send them here will soon see whether I am the man to be frightened by lions. Dismount, my good man, and since you are the keeper, open the cages and drive out those beasts. In the midst of this open field I will let them know who Don Quixote of La Mancha is, in spite of the enchanters who have sent them to me."

The carter tried to remonstrate with Don Quixote, but the latter then said sharply: "I swear, Sir Rogue, that if you don't open the cages at once I'll stitch you to the cart with this lance."

The carter then, seeing the grim determination of the armed phantom, said to him: "Please, sir, for charity's sake, let me unyoke the mules and place myself in safety along with them before the lions are unleashed, for if they kill them on me I'm ruined for life, seeing that all I possess is this cart and the mules."

"O man of little faith," replied Don Quixote, "get down and unyoke, and do what you will: soon you will see that your toils were in vain, and you might have spared yourself the trouble."

The carter got down and in haste unyoked, and the keeper called out in a loud voice: "Bear witness all who are here, how against my will and under compulsion I open the cages and let loose the lions. And I protest to this gentleman that all the harm and mischief these beasts shall do will be put to his account, together with my wages and dues as well. You, sir, take cover before I open: as for myself, I am sure they will do me no harm."

Hearing this, Sancho besought his master with tears in his eyes to give up such an enterprise, compared with which that of the windmills, and the fearsome one of the fulling-mills, and, in fact, all the deeds his master had attempted in the whole course of his life, were nought but cakes and fancy bread. "Look, sir," quoth he, "here there is no enchantment nor anything of the kind, for between the bars of the cage I have seen the paw of a real lion, and I infer that a lion with such a paw must be bigger than a mountain."

"Fear, at any rate," answered Don Quixote, "will make it seem bigger to you than half the earth. Retire, Sancho, and leave me. If I die here, you know our old compact. You will go straight to Dulcinea; I say no more."

Sancho now began to weep over his master's death, for this time he firmly believed that it would come for him from the claws of the lions. He cursed his fate and called it an unlucky hour when he took it into his head to take service with him again. Nevertheless, despite all his tears and groans he took good care to flog up Dapple so as to drive him a good distance away from the cart.

While the keeper was engaged in opening the first cage, Don Quixote was wondering whether it would not be best to do battle on foot, instead of on horseback, and in the end he decided to fight on foot, for he was afraid lest Rozinante might take fright at the lions. He therefore sprang off his horse, flung his lance aside, braced his buckler on his arm, drew his sword and advanced at leisurely speed to take up his position in front of the cart, commending himself to God and then to his Lady Dulcinea.

The keeper, seeing that Don Quixote had taken up his position, and that it was impossible for him to avoid letting loose the male lion without falling under the rage of the wrathful and undaunted knight, opened wide the doors of the first cage, containing, as we have said, the male lion. The beast was now seen to be of extraordinary size and of grim and awful aspect. The first thing he did was to turn round in the cage in which he lay, and extend his claws and stretch himself out at his full length. Then he opened his mouth and yawned very leisurely, and with about two palms-length of tongue, which he put out, he licked the dust from his eyes and washed his face. When this was done, he put his head out of the cage and gazed all around with eyes like blazing coals, a sight that would have struck terror into rash bravery itself. Don Quixote alone stood looking at him intently, longing for him to leap out of the cart and come to close grips with him, when he hoped to hack him to pieces.

Up to this point did his unheard-of madness raise him. The noble lion, however, more courteous than arrogant, took scant notice of such childish bravado, but after looking around about him, as we have said, turned his back and showed Don Quixote his hinder parts, after which coolly and calmly he flung himself down in the cage. Seeing this, Don Quixote ordered the keeper to prod him and tease him to make him come out.

"I will not so," replied the keeper, "for if I excite him, the first he will tear to pieces will be myself. Be content, sir, with what you've done, which leaves no more to be said on the score of courage, and don't try to tempt fortune a second time. The lion has the door open; he's free to come out or not; since he hasn't come out up to this, he won't come out all day. Your worship's sturdy heart has been already shown to the world; no gallant champion, to my way of thinking, is bound to do more nor challenge his enemy and wait for him on the field. If his rival don't come, to him sticks the disgrace, and the man who waits his ground carries off the crown of victory."

"That is true," said Don Quixote; "close the door, my friend, and now give me, in the best form you are able, a voucher to prove what you have seen me do; to wit, how you did open for the lion, that I waited for him, that he did not come, that still I waited for him, that still he did not come out, but lay down again. I am not bound to do more. Away with enchantments, and God protect right, truth and true chivalry! Close the door, as I have said, while I make signs to the fugitives to return and hear this exploit from your lips."

The keeper did so, and Don Quixote, sticking on the point of his lance the cloth with which he had wiped the shower of curds off his face, began to signal to those who were still continuing to flee, though looking round at every step.

Sancho, happening to notice the signal of the white cloth, exclaimed: "May I be blowed, if my master has not conquered the wild beasts, for he's calling us!"

They stopped, and saw that it was Don Quixote who was making signals, and, losing some of their fear, they approached little by little, until they clearly heard the voice of Don Quixote calling to them. At length they reached the cart, and as they came up Don Quixote said to the carter: "Yoke your mules once more, my friend, and continue your journey, and you, Sancho, give him two gold crowns for himself and for the keeper, as a compensation for the delay they have had through me."

"I'll give them with a heart and a half," said Sancho, "but what has happened to the lions? Are they alive or dead?"

Then the keeper gave a detailed account of the encounter, praising to the skies the power and valour of Don Quixote, at whose sight the cowed lion dared not to come out of his cage, though he had held the door open a good while, and that it was only because he had told the knight that it was tempting Providence to excite the lion and force him to come out, as he wanted him to do, that the knight had, against his will, allowed him to close the door.

"What do you think of this, Sancho," said Don Quixote: "are any enchantments able to prevail against true valour? The enchanters may be able to rob me of fortune, but of courage they cannot."

Sancho gave the gold crowns, the carter yoked up, the keeper kissed Don Quixote's hands for the guerdon received and promised to give an account of the brave exploit to the King himself as soon as he saw him at court.

"Then," said Don Quixote, "if His Majesty should happen to ask who performed it, you must say the Knight of the Lions, for it is my wish that from this day onwards there may be changed, altered and transformed the name which till now I have borne of the Knight of the Rueful Figure. In this I follow the ancient custom of knights-errant, who changed their names when they pleased or when it suited them."

The cart of the lions then went on its way and Don Quixote and Sancho went theirs. They had not travelled far when they met a couple of either priests or students and a couple of peasants, mounted on four asses. One of the students carried, wrapped up in a piece of green buckram, what seemed like a small piece of scarlet cloth and two pairs of stockings of rough homespun; the other carried nothing but two new fencing foils with their buttons. The peasants were laden with other things which showed that they came from some large town where they had bought them, and were taking them home to their village. The peasants as well as the students were struck with the same amazement that all felt who saw Don Quixote for the first time, and were dying to know who this strange individual, so unlike other men, could be. Don Quixote greeted them, and after finding out that their road was the same as his, offered them his company, and begged them to slacken their pace, as their ass-fillies travelled faster than his horse. Then to oblige them he told them in a few words who he was and the office and profession he followed, which was that of a knight-errant seeking adventures all over the earth, saying that his name was Don Quixote of La Mancha, and that his appellative was the Knight of the Lions.

All this was Greek or gibberish to the peasants, but not so to the students, who at once noticed what was wrong with the brain of Don Quixote. Nevertheless, they regarded him with admiration and respect; and one of them said to him: "If your worship, Sir Knight, has no fixed road, following as you do the example of those who seek adventure, come with us and you will see one of the finest and richest weddings that up to this day have ever been celebrated in La Mancha, or for many leagues round."

Don Quixote then asked if it was some prince's, to deserve such ceremonies.

"It is not," replied the student, "but of a farmer and a farmer's daughter, but he is the richest in all this country, and she is the fairest beauty men have ever seen. The celebration will be rare and extraordinary, for the bridal ceremonies will be held in a meadow adjoining the village of the bride, whom they call Quiteria the Fair, and the bridegroom is called Camacho the Rich. She is eighteen years of age and he is twenty-two, and they are a well-matched pair, though those who know by heart all the pedigrees in the world would say that the family of the beautiful Quiteria is better than Camacho's. Nevertheless, no one gives a thought to that nowadays, for riches can solder many a crack. In any case, Camacho is free with his money, and he has taken the fancy of screening the whole meadow with boughs and covering it overhead, so that the sun will find it difficult to get in to reach the grass that covers the soil. He has organized dances also, both of swords and of little bells, for there are in the village folk who can jingle and clatter the bells to perfection. I won't mention clog-dancers, for he has engaged a host of them. But none of those, nor the many things I have omitted to mention, will make this wedding more memorable than those which I suspect the unfortunate Basilio will do there.

"This Basilio is a youth from the same village as Quiteria and he dwelt in the house next door to that of her parents, a circumstance that gave Cupid the opportunity of reviving in the world the long-forgotten loves of Pyramus and Thisbe; for Basilio loved Quiteria from his tender years, and she responded to his passion with countless innocent demonstrations of affection. And so, the loves of the two children, Basilio and Quiteria, were the talk of the whole village. As they grew up, the father of Quiteria resolved to deny to Basilio his accustomed entrance to his house, and to avoid all worrying doubts and suspicions, he arranged to marry his daughter to Camacho the Rich, as he did not approve of marrying her to Basilio, who had not such a plentiful share of Fortune's as of Nature's gifts: for, speaking truthfully without envy, he is the most athletic youth we know, a great thrower of the bar, a first-rate wrestler, and a fine ball player; he runs like a deer, leaps like a goat, bowls over the nine-pins as if by magic, sings like a lark, plays the guitar so that he makes it speak, and, above all, wields a sword like the best of them."

"For that one accomplishment alone," said Don Quixote at this, "the youth deserves to marry, not only the fair Quiteria, but Guinevere herself, were she alive today, in spite of Launcelot and of all who should try to prevent it."

"Say that to my wife," said Sancho Panza, who up to this had listened in silence. "She won't allow any to marry save with his equal, for she sticks to the proverb 'every ewe with its mate'. Now what I would like is that this worthy Basilio (I'm taking a fancy to him already) should marry the Lady Quiteria, and eternal life and rest—I meant to say the opposite—to those who try to prevent those who love one another from marrying."

To this the student bachelor replied: "From the moment Basilio heard that the fair Quiteria was to be married to Camacho the Rich he has never been seen to smile, or heard to speak a rational word; but he always goes about full of sadness, talking to himself and giving clear tokens that he has lost his wits. He eats nought but fruit, and when he sleeps 'tis in the fields on the hard earth like a brute beast. From time to time he gazes at the sky, and at other times he fixes his eyes on the ground in such a distracted way that he resembles a clothed statue with its drapery billowing in the wind. Indeed, he shows such signs of a heart overwhelmed by passion that we who know him are convinced that when tomorrow the fair Quiteria says 'Yes', 'twill be his death sentence."

"God will find a better way," exclaimed Sancho, "for God who gives the sore gives the plaster. Nobody knows what's in store. There are many hours between now and tomorrow, and in one, aye, in a minute, the house topples down; and I've seen the rain falling and the sun shining at the same time. Many's the time a fellow goes to bed hale and hearty, and can't budge an inch the next day. And tell me now: is there anyone who can boast that he has put a spoke in the wheel of Fortune? Not on your life; and between a woman's 'yea' and 'nay' I'd not risk putting a pin's point, for there wouldn't be room for it. If you tell me Quiteria loves Basilio heart and soul, then I'll give him a bag full of good luck, for I've always heard that love looks through spectacles that make copper seem gold, poverty riches, and tear-drops pearls."

"When are you going to stop, Sancho, a plague on you?" said Don Quixote. "When you begin to string together your proverbs and tales, only Judas himself would understand you—may he seize you! Tell me, blockhead, what do you know about spokes or wheels, or anything else?"

"Don't be cross with me, master," replied Sancho, "for you know that I was not reared at court or trained at Salamanca."

"That is true," said the student, "for those who have been brought up in the tanneries and the Zocodover[1] cannot talk like those who stroll about all day in the cathedral cloisters, and yet they are all Toledans. Now I, gentlemen, for my sins have been a student of canon law at Salamanca, and I pride myself on expressing my thoughts in clear and significant language."

"Aye," said the other student, "if you hadn't taken more pride in your skill with those foils you carry than in your skilful use of language, you would have come out at the top in your degree examination instead of at the bottom."

"Look here, bachelor," replied the first student, "you have the most mistaken opinion in the world about skill with the sword if you think it useless."

"It is not my opinion," retorted Corchuelo, for that was the name of the second student, "but a well-known fact, and if you wish me to prove it to you here and now, you have the swords there, and now we have an opportunity. I have a steady wrist and a strong arm, which with my courage will make you confess that I am not wrong. Dismount and try out your measured steps, circles, angles, and science, for I hope to make you see stars at noon with my rough-and-ready art, in which next to God I put my trust. There is no one alive who will make me turn back, and not a living man whom I will not force to give ground."

"As regards turning your back or not," answered the former, "I don't concern myself, though who knows but the very spot where you first plant your feet may be the

[1] The square at Toledo which was the meeting-place of picaroons and peasants.

opening of your grave—I mean that you might lie dead there as a result of the swordsmanship you despise."

"We shall see presently," replied Corchuelo, and, alighting briskly from his ass, he snatched one of the foils which his companion carried on his.

"This is not the way to settle the affair," said Don Quixote at this point: "I want to be the umpire of this fencing bout, and judge of the oft undecided question." Then dismounting from Rozinante and grasping his lance, he planted himself in the middle of the road at the moment when the student who was expert at fencing advanced against his adversary with easy and graceful step, while the latter on his side rushed on, darting fire from his eyes, as the saying goes. The two peasants of the company, without alighting from their asses, served as spectators of the mortal tragedy; the slashes, lunges, down strokes, back strokes, and wrist strokes which Corchuelo dealt were innumerable, and came thicker than hailstones. He attacked like a raging lion, but then he met a blow on the mouth from the button of his adversary's foil that stopped him in his mad onrush, and he was made to kiss it as though it were a relic, though not with as much devotion as relics are wont to be kissed.

The licentiate finally counted off with lunges every one of the buttons of the short cassock which Corchuelo wore, tearing the skirts into strips, like the tentacles of a cuttle-fish. Twice he knocked off his hat, and so bedevilled and bamboozled him that out of sheer rage and vexation he took his foil by the hilt and hurled it away with such force that one of the peasants that were there, who happened to be a scrivener and who went to fetch it, testified later that it went about three-quarters of a league away from him, a testimony which has served and still serves to prove incontestably how brute force is conquered by skill.

Corchuelo sat down worn out, and Sancho went up to him, saying: "By my faith, Sir Bachelor, if you'll take my advice you'll never challenge anyone to fence again, but only to wrestle and throw the bar, for you've the youth and sinews for that; but as for those so-called fencers, I have heard tell as how they can put the point of a sword through the eye of a needle."

"I'm satisfied with having tumbled off my ass,"[2] Corchuelo replied, "and with having learnt through experience a truth of which I was so ignorant." With these words he got up and embraced the licentiate, and they became better friends than ever, and without waiting for the scrivener who had gone for the sword, as they thought he would be a long time, they determined to push on so as to arrive at Quiteria's village, to which they all belonged.

[2] A proverb meaning to be undeceived.

It was nightfall, but before they reached the village it seemed to them all as if in front of it there was a sky filled with countless glittering stars. At the same time they heard sweet, confused sounds of various instruments, such as flutes, tambourines, psalteries, pipes, tabors and timbrels, and when they drew near they saw that the trees of a bower, which had been erected at the entrance of the village, were all filled with illuminations, which were undisturbed by the wind, for it blew so softly that it had not even the strength to rustle the leaves of the trees. The musicians were the funmakers at the wedding, for they roamed through that gay pleasure-ground in bands, some dancing, others singing, and others playing the various instruments we have already mentioned. Indeed, it seemed as though mirth and gladness were frisking and gambolling all over the meadow. Some others were briskly erecting platforms, from which people might more comfortably see the plays and dances that were to be performed the next day on the spot dedicated to the celebration of the marriage of Camacho the Rich and the obsequies of Basilio. Don Quixote refused to enter the village, though the peasant and bachelor urged him to do so, giving as an excuse that it was the custom of knights-errant to sleep in the fields and woods in preference to populated places, even though it might be under gilded roofs, and so he turned aside from the road, much against Sancho's will, and bivouacked in the open.

Scarcely had fair Aurora given shining Phoebus time to dry up the liquid pearls on her golden hair with the heat of his rays when Don Quixote, shaking off sloth from his limbs, sprang to his feet and hailed his squire, Sancho, who still lay snoring. Before awaking him, Don Quixote addressed him, saying: "O fortunate one above all who inhabit the face of the earth, since without envying or being envied you sleep with mind at rest. Ambition does not make you anxious, nor does this world's empty pomp worry you, since your wishes extend no farther than to provide for your ass. The servant sleeps, and his master watches, thinking how he is to feed him, to better his lot and grant him favours."

To all this Sancho made no answer, because he was asleep, nor would he have wakened up so soon as he did, had not Don Quixote roused him to his senses with the butt-end of his lance. He awoke at last, drowsy and lazy, and, looking round on all sides, he exclaimed: "Unless I'm mistaken there comes from yon bower a steam and a scent reeking a great deal more of fried rashers than of thyme and rushes. A wedding that begins with such smells, by my sainted soul, must have lashings and plenty in store."

"Stop, you glutton," said Don Quixote: "come, let us

watch these nuptials, and see what forlorn Basilio will do."

"Let him do what he pleases," replied Sancho. "Fancy wanting to marry in the clouds and being without a farthing to his name. By my faith, master, I'm thinking that the poor man should be content with what he can get, and he shouldn't be ferreting for dainties at the bottom of the sea."

"Hold your tongue, Sancho," said Don Quixote, "and come along with me, for the instruments we heard last night are already beginning to gladden the valleys again, and no doubt the nuptials will be celebrated in the cool of the morning and not in the heat of the afternoon."

Sancho obeyed his master, and after putting the saddle on Rozinante and the pack-saddle on Dapple, the two mounted and rode leisurely towards the bower of trees. The first object that caught Sancho's eye was a whole ox spitted on a whole elm tree, and in the fire over which it was roasting there was burning a good-size mountain of faggots; and six earthenware pots, which stood round the blaze, had not been made in the common mould, for they were six half wine-jars, and each could hold a whole slaughter-house of meat. Whole sheep were swallowed up and hidden in them as if they had been mere pigeons. Innumerable were the hares already skinned and chickens plucked, which hung on the trees ready for burial in the pots; innumerable too were the birds and game of divers kind hanging from the branches that the air might cool them. Sancho counted more than sixty wineskins of more than eight gallons each, and all filled, as it afterwards turned out, with generous wines. There were also rows of loaves of the whitest bread, like heaps of wheat piled up on the threshing-floors, the cheeses arranged like open brick-work formed a wall, and two cauldrons full of oil, bigger than dyers' vats, served to fry the pastry, which when fried was drawn out with two mammoth shovels and plunged into another cauldron of prepared honey that stood near by. There were more than fifty cooks and cook maids, all of them clean, busy and buxom. In the swollen belly of the ox were twelve tender little sucking-pigs, which, sewed up within, gave a delicious flavour to its meat. As to the spices of different kinds, they seemed to have been bought not by the pound but by the quarter-hundredweight, and all lay open to view in a big chest. Indeed, the preparations for the wedding, though in rustic style, were plentiful enough to feed an army.

Sancho noticed all, inspected all, and fell in love with all. The first that caught his fancy were the flesh-pots, from which he would most willingly have extracted a fair helping of stew. Then the wineskins monopolized his attentions; and lastly the fritters in the pan, if indeed one could call those swollen cauldrons pans. And so, unable to resist his impulses any longer, he went up to one of the cooks and in civil though hungry words begged leave to soak a crust of bread in one of the pots. To which the cook answered: "Brother, this is not a day over which hunger holds sway, thanks to Camacho the Rich. Dismount and look if there is a ladle handy, and skim off a hen or two; and much good may they do you."

"I don't see one," said Sancho.

"Wait," cried the cook; "well, blast me for a sinner, but you're a dainty and bashful customer and no mistake!" and so saying he seized a pot, and dipping it into one of the huge half jars, drew out in it three hens and a couple of geese, saying to Sancho: "Tuck into this, my friend, and break your fast on these mere skimmings until dinner-time comes."

"I've nothing to put it into," said Sancho.

"Then take pot and all," said the cook, "the wealth and joy of Camacho supply all demands."

While Sancho was thus busily engaged, Don Quixote was watching the entrance through one part of the bower of about twelve peasants mounted on twelve beautiful mares richly caparisoned, with a number of little bells jingling on their breast-plates. The peasants, who were all clothed in festive garments, gathered together in a marshalled troop, and ran many races over the meadow, shouting jubilantly as they ran: "Long live Camacho and Quiteria! He is as rich as she is fair, and she is the fairest in the world!"

Hearing this, Don Quixote said to himself: "It is clear that these folks have never seen my Dulcinea del Toboso. If they had, they would moderate their praise of the Quiteria."

Soon afterwards various companies of dancers began to enter at different points the leafy enclosure. Among them was one of sword-dancers, about twenty-four youths, of gallant bearing, all dressed up in the whitest linen, with headdresses of different colours embroidered in fine silk. One of the peasants on the mares asked the leader, an athletic youth, if any of the dancers had hurt himself.

"Up to the present, thank God," said he, "none of us are hurt: we are safe and sound," and he began at once to wheel and twist with the rest of his troop in such skilful fashion that, although Don Quixote was accustomed to see similar dances, he thought he had never seen any as good as this. He also admired another of twelve beautiful maidens, none of whom seemed to be less than fourteen or more than eighteen years of age. They were clad in green stuff, their locks were partly plaited and partly flowing loose, but all so golden that they rivalled with sunbeams, and over them they wore garlands of jasmine, roses, amaranth and honeysuckle.

273

They were led by a venerable old man and an ancient matron, who, nevertheless, were more active and athletic than one would have expected from their years. A Zamoran bagpipe gave them music, and so they with modesty in their glances and nimbleness in their feet thus proved themselves the best dancers in the world.

Behind them there came a masque of the kind they call "speaking dances". It was made up of eight nymphs grouped in two rows; of one row "Love" was leader; and of the other "Interest". The former was adorned with wings, bow, quivers and arrows; the latter clad in a rich dress of gold and coloured silks. In front of all the nymphs then came a castle of wood drawn by four savages, clad in ivy and hemp dyed green, and so lifelike that they well-nigh frightened Sancho. On the front of the castle and on each of the four sides it bore the inscription "Castle of Modesty". Four skilful tambourine and flute players made sweet music, and when the dance had opened, "Love", after executing two figures, lifted his eyes and aimed an arrow against a solitary maiden who stood between the turrets of the castle. After discharging his arrow at the top of the castle he retired to his place in the dance. Then all the characters of the two dancing bands advanced and retired after executing its figures. All mingled together, forming chains and dissolving again with spontaneous, joyous rhythm, and whenever "Love" passed in front of the castle he shot up his arrows at it, while "Interest" broke gilded balls against it. At length, after they had danced a good while, "Interest" drew out a large purse, made from a brindled catskin, which seemed to be full of coin, and flung it at the castle; such was the force of the blow that the planks fell asunder and left the damsel exposed and defenceless. "Interest" then advanced accompanied by his band, and throwing a big golden chain over her neck, made a show of leading her away a prisoner. No sooner was this seen by "Love" and his followers than they all tried to rescue her, and their actions they mimicked in the form of a dance, accompanying them with the tambourine. The savages made peace between them, and after skilfully readjusting the planks of the castle, the damsel once again shut herself up in it. and the dance ended amid the great applause of the bystanders.

Don Quixote asked one of the nymphs who had composed and arranged the dance. She replied that it was a curate of that village, who had a great talent for such masques.

"I will wager," said Don Quixote, "that the said curate or bachelor is a greater friend of Camacho than of Basilio, and that he is better at writing satire than at Vespers: he has fitted most cleverly the talents of Basilio and the riches of Camacho into the dance."

Sancho, who was listening to all that was said, exclaimed: "The king is my cock: [3] I'll stick by Camacho."

"It is indeed easy to see," said Don Quixote, "that you are a boor, and one of those who always cheer for the winner."

"I don't know what kind I am," replied Sancho, "but I know full well that I'll never get such elegant skimmings off Basilio's pots as these I've got off Camacho's," and showing him the pot full of geese and pullets, he snatched up one and began to eat with great gusto, saying: "A fig for the talents of Basilio! what you have is what you're worth. As my grandmother used to say, there are only two families in the world, the *Haves* and the *Haven'ts*; and she always stuck to the *Haves*, and to this day, master, people prefer to feel the pulse of *Have* than of *Know*. An ass covered wtih gold looks better than a horse with a pack-saddle. So once more I say I stick by Camacho, from whose pots come the plenteous skimmings of geese and hens, hares and rabbits. But from Basilio's, if any come to hand or to feet, they'll only be dish-rinsings."

"Have you finished your harangue, Sancho?" said Don Quixote.

"I'll soon have finished it," replied Sancho, "for I see you receive it with annoyance; if 'twere not for that, there would have been enough work cut out for three days."

"Please God, Sancho," said Don Quixote, "I may see you dumb before I die."

"At the speed we're going," replied Sancho, "before you die, master, I shall be chewing clay, and then, perhaps, I'll be so dumb that I'll say ne'er a word until the end of the world, or, at least, until the day of judgment."

"Even if that should happen, Sancho," said Don Quixote, "your silence will never make up for all you have talked, are talking and will talk all your life. Besides, it is only natural that my death will come before yours, so I never expect to see you dumb, not even when you are drinking or sleeping, and what more can I say?"

"In good faith, master," replied Sancho, "it is no use trusting the fleshless one, I mean Death, who devours the lamb as soon as the sheep, and, as I've heard our curate say, tramples with equal feet upon the lofty towers of kings and the lowly huts of the poor. This lady is more powerful than dainty, she is not at all squeamish; she devours all and does for all; and she packs her saddle-bags with people of all kinds, ages and ranks. She is not a reaper who sleeps her siestas, for she reaps at all hours, and she cuts down the dry grass as well as the green. She does not appear to chew, but bolts and gobbles all that is put before her, for she has a dog's hunger which is never satisfied. And though she has no belly, she seems to have the

[3] Metaphor from cock-fighting. The victorious cock was called "the king."

275

dropsy, and is thirsty to drink all the lives of those that live, as one drinks a jug of cold water."

"Say no more, Sancho," said Don Quixote, "don't spoil it and risk a fall, for truly what you have spoken about in your rustic speech is what a good preacher might have said. I tell you, Sancho, that if your wisdom was equal to your mother wit, you could take a pulpit in hand and go preaching your fine sermons through the world."

"He preaches well who lives well," replied Sancho, "and I know no other theologies than that."

"You don't need them," said Don Quixote, "but I cannot make out how it is that the fear of God being the beginning of wisdom, you, who are more afraid of a lizard than of Him, should know so much."

"Let you, master, judge your chivalries and stop meddling with the fears and boasts of others, for I'm as proper a God-fearing man as any neighbour's son. Now leave me to mop up these skimmings, for all the rest is nought but idle talk for which we'll have to give an account in the next life." With these words, he began a fresh attack upon his pot with such hearty gusto that he even aroused the appetite of Don Quixote.

While master and squire were conversing, they heard loud shouts and a great noise, which came from the men on the mares as they galloped shouting to receive the bride and bride-groom, who were approaching surrounded by countless musical instruments and festive pageantry, and accompanied by the priest, the relatives of both, and the notabilities from the neighbouring villages, all dressed up in their finery. When Sancho saw the bride, he cried: "By my faith she's not dressed like a farmer's daughter but like a fine court lady! Lord bless us, as far as I can make out, the necklace she's wearing is of rich coral, and her green Cuenca stuff is thirty-pile velvet; and mark the trimming of white linen, I swear it's satin! Now have a look at her hands—are they not adorned with jet rings?— may I be struck dumb if they're not rings of gold, genuine gold, and set with pearls as white as curdled milk, every one of them worth an eye out of one's head! Whoreson wench, what tresses she has! If they're not false, I've never seen longer or more golden all the days of my life. Now see how gallantly she carries herself, and mark her figure! Wouldn't you compare her to a palm tree moving along laden with bunches of dates? That's what the baubles look like which she's wearing, dangling from her hair and her throat. 'Pon my soul, I swear she's a bonny lass, she'll sail on an even keel through the shoals of Flanders."

Don Quixote laughed at Sancho's naïve and rustic words of praise, but he thought that, with the exception of his Lady Dulcinea del Toboso, he had never seen a more beautiful woman. The fair Quiteria looked a little pale, probably on

276

account of the bad night which brides always spend preparing themselves for their wedding on the following day.

The procession advanced towards a theatre that stood on one side of the meadow, adorned with carpets and boughs, where they were to plight their troth and from which they were to witness the dances and masques. Just as they arrived at the spot, they heard a loud outcry behind them, and a voice crying: "Tarry a moment, thoughtless and hasty people!"

At these cries they all turned their heads, and saw the man who had uttered them. He was dressed in a black garment slashed with crimson patches like flames. He was crowned (as they saw presently) with a garland of mournful cypress, and carried in his hand a long staff. As soon as he drew near they all recognized him as the gallant Basilio; and they all anxiously waited to see what the end of his words would be, for they feared that some catastrophe might take place owing to his appearance at such a moment. He approached at last, wearied and breathless, and planting himself in front of the bridal pair, he dug his staff, which had an iron spike at the end, into the ground; then, turning pale, and gazing fixedly at Quiteria, he addressed her in a hoarse, trembling voice as follows: "Well dost thou know, faithless Quiteria, that according to the holy law which binds us, thou canst take no husband so long as I am alive; nor art thou ignorant either that while I waited for time and my industry to improve my fortunes, I never failed to observe the respect due to thy honour; but thou, after casting behind thee all thy obligations to my love, art resolved to surrender what is mine to another whose wealth gives him not only good fortune but also happiness. Long live the rich Camacho! May he live many happy years with the ungrateful Quiteria, and let poor Basilio die, Basilio whose poverty clipped the wings of his happiness and brought him to the tomb."

With these words he seized hold of the staff which he had stuck in the earth, and leaving half of it in the ground, he showed that it served as a scabbard to a fair-sized rapier which was enclosed within. Then, planting what might be called the hilt in the ground, with an agile spring and with calm, deliberate purpose he threw himself upon it. In an instant the blood-stained point and half the blade appeared at his back, and the hapless man lay stretched on the ground, bathed in blood, pierced by his own weapon.

His friends at once ran up to his assistance, filled with sorrow at his pathetic fate, and Don Quixote, leaving Rozinante, hastened also to help, and taking him up in his arms, found that he had not yet expired. They wanted to draw out the rapier, but the priest who was present was of opinion that they should not extract it until he had confessed him, for if they drew it out he would die at once. Basilio, however, reviving slightly, said in a faint, sorrowful voice: "If thou, cruel Quiteria, wouldst only consent in this last fatal moment to give me thy hand as my bride, I might still imagine that my rashness could be pardoned, since by its means I reached the bliss of being thine."

The priest, when he heard this, said that he should attend to the salvation of his soul rather than to the lust of the body, and that he should beg God's pardon for his sins and for his act of desperation. To this Basilio replied that he was resolved not to confess unless Quiteria first gave him her hand in marriage, for that happiness would strengthen his will and give him breath for confession.

Don Quixote, hearing the wounded man's petition, cried out in a loud voice that Basilio's request was just, reasonable and easy to comply with, and that Señor Camacho would be no less honoured in receiving the Lady Quiteria as the widow of the valiant Basilio than if he received her from her father. "All that is needed in this case," said he, "is a mere 'yes', and no other consequence can come from pronouncing it, for the nuptial couch of this marriage must be the grave."

Camacho listened to all this in perplexity and bewilderment, and he knew not what to do or say, but the pleas of Basilio's friends were so urgent, as they besought him to allow Quiteria to give her hand to Basilio, lest the latter's soul be lost, leaving this life so wickedly, that they compelled him to say that provided Quiteria wás willing, he would agree, since it was to delay only for a moment the fulfilment of their desires. Then all ran up to Quiteria, and some with entreaties and others with tears, and others again with cogent arguments, begged her to give her hand to poor Basilio. But she, without answering a word, sad and distracted in appearance, advanced to where Basilio lay with eyes upturned and breathing painfully, muttering between his teeth the name of Quiteria, and, as it seemed, about to die like a heathen and not a Christian. Kneeling by him, she asked for his hand more by signs than by vords. Basilio, opening his eyes and gazing fixedly at her, said: "O Quiteria, thou fatal star of mine! I now entreat of thee that the hand thou demandest of me and wouldst give me, be not given out of complaisance nor to deceive me again. I beseech thee to confess and say that without forcing thy will thou art giving me thy hand as thy lawful husband, for it is not right that thou shouldst deceive me in a state like this, nor play tricks upon one who has always been so loyal to thee."

With these words he began to swoon away, and the by-standers thought that every moment would be his last. Quiteria, full of modesty and bashfulness, taking hold of Basilio's right hand with her own, said: "No force could bend my will, and therefore of my own free will I give thee the hand of a lawful wife, and take thine if thou dost give it freely, being untroubled by the calamity thy hasty act has brought upon thee."

"Yes, I give it," said Basilio, "with the clear understanding that Heaven has been pleased to grant me, and thus I give myself to be thy husband."

"And I," replied Quiteria, "give myself to be thy wife, whether thou livest many years or they carry thee from my arms to the grave."

"I'm thinking," said Sancho at this point, "that for one so badly wounded this young gentleman has a lot of talk out of him. They should make him ease off his billing and cooing and attend to his soul: to my way of thinking, he has more of it on the tip of his tongue than between his teeth."

When Basilio and Quiteria had joined hands, the priest with tears in his eyes pronounced his blessing upon them, and prayed Heaven to grant good repose to the soul of the newly wedded man. But he, no sooner had he received the blessing than he sprang swiftly to his feet and with surprising agility drew out the rapier which had been sheathed in his body. All the bystanders were astounded, and some, more simple than enquiring, began to shout: "A miracle, a miracle!" But Basilio replied: "No miracle, no miracle; but a strategem, a strategem!"

The priest, perplexed and amazed, hastened to examine the wound with both hands, and found that the knife had passed not through Basilo's flesh and ribs, but through a hollow iron tube fitted to that place, full of blood so prepared (as was afterwards ascertained) as not to congeal. In short, the priest and Camacho and all the bystanders realized that they had been fooled and deceived. The bride showed no trace of displeasure at the trick, but, on the contrary, when she heard people saying that the marriage, being fraudulent, would not be valid, declared that she confirmed it afresh; wherefore they all inferred that the two had planned the whole affair secretly together. As a result Camacho and his supporters became so enraged that they turned to vengeance, and unsheathing many swords they attacked Basilio, but in a moment an equal number were drawn in his defence, while Don Quixote leading off on horseback, with his lance couched and his shield as cover, made them all give way. Sancho, who never derived any pleasure from such deeds, straightway took refuge among the flesh-pots from which he had drawn his delicious skimmings, for he was sure that such a place would be respected as a sacred place. Don Quixote in a loud voice kept crying: "Hold, gentlemen, hold! We have no right to exact vengeance for the wrongs that love does to us. Remember that love and war are the same thing, and since it is permissible in war to make use of stratagems to overcome the enemy, so in the contests of love the tricks and wiles employed to achieve the end desired are allowable, provided they do not bring injury or dishonour on the beloved one. Quiteria belonged to Basilio and Basilio to Quiteria according to the just and benevolent dispensation of Heaven above. Camacho is rich and can purchase his pleasure when, where and how he pleases. Basilio has nought but this one ewe lamb, and no one, however powerful he may be, shall take her from him. Those two whom God hath joined together man cannot put asunder, and he who attempts it must first pass the point of this lance." Saying this, he brandished the lance so fiercely that he struck terror into all who did not know him.

So deep an impression did Quiteria's disdain produce upon Camacho that it caused him to banish her straightway from his thoughts. The persuasive words of the priest, who was a man of wisdom and good sense, prevailed upon him, and in this way he and his followers were pacified. And the rich Camacho, to show that he felt no resentment at the trick which had been played upon him, insisted that the festivities should continue as if he were really getting married.

Neither Basilio, however, nor his wife, nor their followers would take any part in them, and they departed to Basilio's village: for even the poor, if they are virtuous and wise, have those who will follow, honour and uphold them, just as the rich have their minions and flatterers. They took Don Quixote away with them, for they considered him a man of courage and mettle. Sancho alone was downcast at not being able to take part in the magnificent feast and festival of Camacho, which lasted until nightfall. Dejected and despondent he followed his master, who joined Basilio's party, and behind him he left the flesh-pots of Egypt, though in his heart he carried them along with him; and the skimmings in the pot, which by now were almost consumed, evoked in his mind the glory and abundance of good cheer he was losing. And so, sulkily and pensively, though not hungrily, he followed on Dapple in the wake of Rozinante.

VI. *The great adventure of the Cave of Montesinos, in the heart of La Mancha, to which our gallant Don Quixote gave a happy termination*

THE NEWLY-WEDDED COUPLE LAVISHED MANY FAVOURS UPON Don Quixote, for they felt themselves under an obligation to him for the zeal he had shown in defending their cause, and they lauded his wisdom no less than his valour, considering him a Cid in arms and a Cicero in eloquence. Worthy

Sancho enjoyed three days' hospitality at the expense of the pair, from whom he learnt that the sham wound was not a stratagem arranged with the fair Quiteria, but one planned by Basilio, who foresaw the result they had witnessed. It is true to add, nevertheless, that he had informed his friends of his designs, that they might, at the right moment, back up his plan and ensure the success of his trick.

"Trick it should not be called," said Don Quixote, "seeing that it aimed at virtuous ends. The marriage of lovers is a most excellent end, for the greatest enemy of love is hunger and continuous want. Love is all gaiety, enjoyment and happiness, especially when the lover possesses the beloved object, and poverty and want are their declared foes." All this he said in order to persuade Basilio to give up practising the talents he was skilled in, for though they brought him fame, they earned him no money, and to set himself to acquiring a livelihood by lawful and industrious means, which are always within the possibilities of prudent and painstaking men. The poor man who is a man of honour (if indeed a poor man can be a man of honour) when he possesses a beautiful wife has a jewel, and if she is taken from him, his honour is taken and slain. The beautiful and honourable wife, whose husband is poor, deserves to be crowned with the laurels and the crowns of victory and triumph. Beauty by itself attracts the desires of all those who recognize it, and the royal eagles and birds that soar on high swoop down upon it as upon a tasty lure; but if to this beauty be joined want and penury, then the crows, the kites and other birds of prey attack it, and she who stands firm against such trials deserves indeed to be called the crown of her husband.

"Remember, O wise Basilio," added Don Quixote, "that a certain sage, I know not who, held that there was not more than one good woman in all the world, and he advised everyone to think and believe that this one good woman was his own wife, and so he would live happily. I myself am not married, nor, so far, has it even come into my mind to be so; nevertheless, I would dare to give advice to anyone who might ask it, as to the mode in which he should seek a wife to marry. The first thing I would advise him is to pay more attention to reputation than to fortune, for the good woman does not win a good name solely by being good, but by appearing so: for looseness and public frivolity do greater injury to a woman's honour than secret misdeeds. If you bring a good woman home to your house it will be an easy matter to keep her good, and even improve her in that goodness. But if you bring home a bad one, you will find it a hard task to mend her ways, for it is not easy to pass from one extreme to another. I do not say it is impossible, but I consider it difficult."

Sancho, who had been listening to all this, said to himself: "Whenever I say a word that has a bit of marrow and substance about it, this master of mine straightway says that I ought to take a pulpit in my hand and roam the world preaching fine sermons; but I say of him that when he starts stringing sentences and giving counsels, not only might he take a pulpit in his hand, but two on each finger, and go into the market-places with the cry, 'Who'll buy my wares?' on his lips. Devil take you for a knight-errant, what a number of things you know! I used to think to myself that the only things he knew had to do with chivalry, but there's not a thing he doesn't peck at nor dip his spoon into."

Sancho kept mumbling to himself so loud that his master overheard him, and asked: "What are you muttering about, Sancho?"

"I'm not saying or murmuring anything," said Sancho, "only saying to myself that I wish I had heard what your worship has just said before I got married. Perhaps I'd say now: 'The ox that's loose licks himself well'."

"Is Teresa so bad then, Sancho?" said Don Quixote.

"She's not too bad," replied Sancho, "but she's not very good, at least she's not so good as I would like her to be."

"You do wrong, Sancho," said Don Quixote, "to speak ill of your wife, for she is the mother of your children."

"We're both all square," answered Sancho; "she speaks ill of men when she's got the whim, especially when she's jealous—then Satan himself couldn't stomach her."

They remained three days with the newly-married couple, by whom they were treated right royally. Don Quixote asked the fencer-licentiate to get them a guide to conduct them to the Cave of Montesinos of which so many wonderful things were related in those parts, for he had a great wish to explore it and to see with his own eyes if the wonders reported were true. The licentiate replied that he would get him a cousin of his own, a famous scholar, one much given to reading books of chivalry, who would be very glad to guide him to the mouth of the cave, and would show him the lakes of Ruidera, which were also famous all over La Mancha, and even all over Spain. The cousin arrived later on, with a she-ass in foal, whose pack-saddle was covered with a many-coloured piece of sackcloth. Sancho saddled Rozinante, harnessed Dapple, and stocked his saddle-bags, to which we should add those of the cousin, which likewise were well supplied. And so, commending themselves to God and taking leave of all, they set out on the road leading to the famous Cave of Montesinos.

On the way Don Quixote and his companions spent their time in pleasant conversation, and that night they lodged at a little village, which, the cousin said, was only two leagues distant from the Cave of Montesinos. He added that if Don Quixote was determined to enter it, he would need to provide himself with ropes, so that he might be tied up and lowered into its depths. Don Quixote said that even if it reached to the abyss he was determined to see where it ended. So they bought about a hundred fathoms of rope, and next day at two o'clock in the afternoon they arrived at the cave. Its mouth is wide and spacious, but full of thorn and wild fig bushes and brambles and briars, so thick and intertwined that they completely close it up.[1]

When they caught sight of it, the cousin, Sancho and Don Quixote dismounted, and the first two straightway tied up the latter very firmly with the ropes, and, while they were binding him and winding them round him, Sancho said: "Mind what you're doing, master: don't bury yourself alive, or put yourself where you'll be like a flask lowered down into a well to cool. Surely 'tis no affair of yours to be exploring this place, which must be worse nor an underground dungeon."

"Tie me up and hold your peace," replied Don Quixote. "Such an enterprise as this has been reserved for me."

The guide then said: "I pray you, Sir Don Quixote, to note and examine with a hundred eyes all that is inside the cave. Perhaps there may be things which I may include in one of my books."

"The drum is in hands which will know well how to beat it," said Sancho.

When Don Quixote's binding was over, he said: "It was remiss of us not to have provided ourselves with a little bell to be tied on the rope close to me. By the sound you would know that I was still descending and was alive. However, since that is impossible, let God's hand guide me." So saying, he fell upon his knees and in a low voice he offered up a prayer to Heaven, beseeching God to help him and give him success in his new perilous adventure. Then in a loud voice he cried: "O mistress of my actions and movements, most illustrious and peerless Dulcinea del Toboso, if it is possible for the prayers and the supplications of thy venturesome lover to reach thy ears, by thy incomparable beauty I beseech thee to listen to them, for they do but beg thee not to refuse me thy favour and protection at this moment when I need them so urgently. I am about to plunge myself—to engulf and sink myself in the abyss which yawns at my feet, only to make the world recognize that if thou dost favour me there is no impossible feat which I may not accomplish."

[1] The route to this cave passes through the plain of Montiel by the lake of Ruidera. The cave is deep and according to the local Manchegans it continues for several kilometres and ends in the feudal castle of Rochefrias.

With these words, he approached the cavern, and, finding that it was not possible to let himself down or make an entrance unless by force of arm or by cutting a passage, he drew his sword and began to cut away the brambles at the mouth of the cave. At the noise he made, a great number of crows and jackdaws fluttered out so thickly and with such a rush that they knocked Don Quixote down, and if he had been as superstitious as he was a good Catholic, he would have taken it for an evil omen, and would have refused to bury himself in such a place. At last he rose to his feet, and seeing that no more crows came out, or night birds such as bats which had flown out at the same time as the crows, he let the cousin and Sancho give him rope, and he began to lower himself into the depths of the dread cave. As he entered it Sancho gave him his blessing, and made a thousand signs of the Cross over him, saying: "May God and the Rock of France and the Trinity of Gaeta guide you, O flower, cream and skimming of knights-errant! There you go, you bully of the world, heart of steel, and arm of bronze. Once more, may God guide you and bring you back safe and sound to the light of this world of ours you are leaving to bury yourself in darkness."

The cousin likewise offered up similar prayers and supplications.

Don Quixote, as he descended, called out for more and more rope, and they gave it to him little by little. When his shouts, which sounded from the cave as through a funnel, could not be heard, they had already uncoiled the hundred fathoms of rope. They were of opinion that they should pull up Don Quixote again as they had no more rope to give him. They waited, however, for about half an hour, and then began to gather in the rope with great ease and without any weight, a sign which made them believe that Don Quixote had remained inside. Sancho, when he realized this, wept bitterly and pulled away in great haste in order to learn the worst. But when they came to about eighty fathoms they felt a weight, which cheered them up considerably. At last, at ten fathoms, they saw Don Quixote clearly, and Sancho shouted to him, saying: "Welcome back, master, we fancied you were staying down there to found a family."

Don Quixote answered not a word, and when they had pulled him up they saw that his eyes were shut and he appeared fast asleep.

They laid him on the ground and untied him, but still he did not awake. Then they turned him over this way and that, and so shook him and rolled him about that at last he came to himself, and stretched himself as if he had just awakened from a deep sleep. Looking round him from one side to another, like one who had great fear on him, he cried: "God forgive you, friends: you have snatched me from the most delightful vision that any human being has ever beheld. Now indeed I know that all the pleasant things of this life pass away like a shadow and a dream, or wither like the flowers of the field. O hapless Montesinos! O sore wounded Durandarte! O unlucky Belerma! O tearful Guadiana, and ye luckless daughters of Ruidera, who show by your waters the tears your eyes did shed!"

The cousin and Sancho listened with great attention to the words of Don Quixote, who uttered them as though they were torn from his very bowels. They besought him to explain what he meant, and tell them what he had seen in the hell below.

"Hell do you call it?" said Don Quixote: "do not call it thus, for it does not deserve such a name, as you will see presently."

He then begged them to give him something to eat, as he was very hungry. They spread the cousin's saddle-cloth on the grass, and visited their saddle-bags; and seated together in good brotherly fellowship they lunched and supped at the same time.

Then when the saddle-cloth was removed, Don Quixote said: "Now, my sons, hearken to my words, both of you." It was then about four o'clock in the afternoon, when the sun veiled itself behind clouds and shone with subdued light, so that Don Quixote was enabled to relate without heat and discomfort what he had seen in the Cave of Montesinos. He began as follows: "About twelve or fourteen fathoms down in the depth of this dungeon, on the right hand, there is a recess big enough to contain a large cart with its mules. A tiny ray of light enters through some chinks or crevices which are open to the earth's surface. This recess I saw when I was weary and downcast at finding myself dangling in the air by the rope and travelling down through that dark region below, without any clear idea of where I was going, so I determined to enter it and rest myself for a moment. I shouted to you not to let out more rope until I should ask for it, but you must not have heard me. I then gathered in the rope you were letting down, and after making a coil of it I sat down upon it, meditating all the while on what I ought to do in order to lower myself to the bottom of the cavern, seeing that I had no one to hold me up. While I was thus perplexed, suddenly and without warning a deep sleep fell upon me, and without the why or the wherefore I awoke, and found myself in the midst of the most delightful meadow that Nature could create or the most vivid imagination visualize. I opened my eyes, I rubbed them, and found that I was not asleep but wide awake. Nevertheless, I felt my head and my heart to make sure that I myself was there

285

and not some vain spectre, but the touch, the feeling, the discourse I held with myself, proved to me that I was the same then as I am here at this moment. Then I saw before me a sumptuous royal palace or castle, with walls that seemed to be made of clear, transparent crystal, and through two great doors that opened I saw a venerable old man approach towards me, clad in a long cloak of purple-coloured serge that trailed on the ground. He wore over his shoulders and breast a scholar's green satin hood, and his head was covered with a black Milanese cap, and his snow-white beard fell below his waist. He carried no arms at all, only a rosary of beads that were bigger than fair-sized walnuts—indeed each tenth bead was like a moderate-sized ostrich egg. His bearing, his gait, his gravity and his imposing presence held me spellbound with admiration. He came up to me, and the first thing he did was to embrace me closely. Then he said: 'For many an age, valiant knight Don Quixote of La Mancha, we who inhabit these enchanted solitudes have waited to see you, that you may announce to the world what lies buried in the deep cavern which you have entered, called the Cave of Montesinos, an exploit reserved for your invincible heart and spirit. Come with me, illustrious sir, for I wish to show you the wonders which this transparent palace contains, whereof I am the governor and perpetual chief warden, for I am Montesinos himself, after whom the cave is named.'

"No sooner had he said that he was Montesinos than I asked him if the story told in the world above was true, namely, that he had cut the heart of his great friend Durandarte out of his breast with a little dagger, and carried it to the Lady Belerma, in accordance with Durandarte's instructions at the point of death. He replied that the story was correct in all particulars save in the matter of the dagger, for it was not a dagger, nor little, but a burnished poniard sharper than an awl."

"That same poniard," said Sancho, "must be one of those made by Ramón de Hoces the Sevillian."

"I do not know," said Don Quixote, "but it could not have been made by that poniard-maker, for Ramón de Hoces lived yesterday, whereas the affair of Roncesvalles, where this misfortune took place, was many years ago. But this matter is not of importance, it does not disturb or alter the truth of the story."

"You are right," said the cousin. "Pray proceed, Señor Don Quixote, for I am listening to you with the greatest pleasure in the world."

"And I am no less pleased to tell the story," said Don Quixote. "Well, to continue, the venerable Montesinos led me into the palace of crystal, where, in a lower hall all made of alabaster and extremely cool, there stood an elaborately carved marble tomb, on top of which I saw a knight stretched at full length, not of bronze or marble, but of actual flesh and bone He had his right hand (which to my eyes appeared somewhat hairy and sinewy, a sign that its owner was of great muscular strength) placed over his heart, but before I could question Montesinos, he, on seeing me gaze in amazement at the tomb, said: 'This is my friend, Durandarte, flower and mirror of the true lovers and valiant knights of his time. He is kept enchanted here, as I am myself, and many other men and women, by that Gallic enchanter Merlin, who, they say, was the Devil's son, but, in my opinion, he is no Devil's son, for he knows, as the saying goes, a point more than the Devil. How or why he enchanted us, no one knows, but time will reveal the reason at no distant date. What amazes me is that I should know as surely as that it is now day, that Durandarte ended his life in my arms, and that after his death I extracted his heart with my own hands, and, indeed, it must have weighed a couple of pounds, for, according to scientists, he who has a large heart is endowed with greater valour than he who has a small one. Now since the knight did really die, how comes it that he moans and complains from time to time as if he were alive?'

"As he said these words the wretched Durandarte cried aloud:

'O my cousin Montesinos!
Heed, I pray, my last request:
When thou seest me lying dead
And my soul from my corpse has fled,
With thy poniard or thy dagger
Pluck the heart from out my breast,
And hie thee with it to Belerma.'

"On hearing these words the venerable Montesinos sank upon his knees before the hapless knight and, with tears in his eyes, exclaimed: 'Long since, Sir Durandarte, my dearest cousin, have I done what you bade me on the rueful day when I lost you. I took out your heart as best I could, without leaving the slightest piece of it in your breast: I wiped it with a lace handkerchief; I went off with it by the road to France, after having first laid you in the bosom of the earth with tears so plentiful that they sufficed to wash and cleanse my hands of the blood which stained them when I groped in thy bowels. Then, O cousin of my soul, more by token, at the first place I reached after leaving Roncesvalles, I sprinkled a few pinches of salt on your heart that it might not smell badly, and so I might bring it, if not fresh, at least pickled, into the presence of Lady Belerma, whom with you and me, and Guadiana your squire, the duenna Ruidera and her seven daughters and two nieces, and other friends, Merlin the Wizard keeps here enchanted these many years. And though five hundred years have passed, not one of us has died. Ruidera and her daughters and nieces alone are missing, for Merlin, pitying them for the tears they had shed, changed them into so many lagoons, which now in the world of the living and in the province of La Mancha the people call the Lagoons of Ruidera.[2] The seven daughters belong to the kings of Spain and the two nieces to the knights of a very holy order, called the Order of St. John. Guadiana, your squire, who also was bewailing your fate, was changed into a river of his own name, but when he reached the surface of the earth and saw the sun of another heaven, so great was his sorrow at finding that he was leaving you, that he plunged into the bowels of the earth. Nevertheless, as he cannot avoid following his natural course, from time to time he comes forth and shows himself to the sun and the world. The lagoons I have mentioned supply him with their waters, and with their help and the help of many others he enters Portugal in all his pomp and glory. But wherever he goes he shows his sadness and melancholy, and takes no pride in breeding choice and tasty fish, but only coarse and tasteless kinds, very different from those of the golden Tagus. All this, my cousin, I have told you many times before, but since you make me no answer, I am afraid you do not believe me, or do not hear me, which greatly distresses me, as God knows. Now I have news to give you, which, while it may not alleviate your sorrows, will by no means increase them. Learn that you have here before you (open your eyes and you will see) that great knight about whom the magician Merlin has prophesied so many things: that Don Quixote of La Mancha, I say, who anew, and to better purpose than in the past, has revived in the present the already forgotten order of knight-errantry. By his aid and favour we may be disenchanted, for great deeds are reserved for great men.'

" 'And if this does not take place,' replied the hapless Durandarte in a swooning voice: 'if this may not be, then, O cousin, I say: patience and shuffle the cards.' And turning over on his side he relapsed into his former silence without speaking another word.

"And now a great outcry and lamentation arose, accompanied by deep groans and pitiful sobbings. I turned round and saw through the walls of crystal in another hall a procession of two lines of fair damsels all clad in mourning, with white turbans of Turkish fashion on their heads. Behind, in the rear of the procession, walked a lady, for so her dignity

[2] La Ruidera or Roydera was in reality a Moslem castle in the neighbourhood of the lakes to which it gave its name. It was captured from the Moors in 1215.

proclaimed her to be, also clothed in black, with a white veil so long and ample that it kissed the ground. Her turban was twice as large as the largest of any of the others; she had eyebrows that met together, her nose was rather flat, her mouth was large but her lips red; her teeth, which at times she showed, were few and not well set, though as white as peeled almonds. She carried in her hands a fine handkerchief, and in it, as well as I could make out, a mummified heart, for it was all dried up and pickled. Montesinos said that all those in the procession were servants of Durandarte and Belerma, who were enchanted there with their master and mistress, and that the last one, she who bore the heart wrapped up in the handkerchief, was the Lady Belerma, who, with her damsels, four days a week walked in that procession, and sang, or rather wept, her sorrowful dirges over the body and wretched heart of his cousin. He added that if she appeared to me somewhat ugly, or at least not so beautiful as fame reported, it was because of the bad nights and the worse days she spent in that enchantment, as I could see by the dark circles round her eyes and her sickly complexion. 'And,' said he, 'her sallowness and the rings round her eyes do not come from the periodical ailment common to women, for it is many months and even years since it has happened at her gates, but from the grief her own heart suffers for that object which continually she holds in her hands; it brings back to her memory the misfortune of her luckless lover. If it were not for this, scarcely would the great Dulcinea del Toboso, so renowned in all these parts, aye, and even in all the world, equal her in beauty, charm and wit.'

" 'Go slow, Señor Don Montesinos,' quoth I. 'Tell your story rightly, for you are aware that all comparisons are odious, and there is no reason to compare one person with another. The peerless Dulcinea del Toboso is what she is, and Doña Belerma is what she is and has been, and there let the matter rest.'

"To which he answered: 'Forgive me, Señor Don Quixote, for I confess that I was wrong in saying that the Lady Dulcinea could scarcely equal the Lady Belerma, for it was enough for me to learn, I know not by what indications, that you are her knight to make me bite my tongue before I compared her to aught but heaven itself.' After this satisfaction which the great Montesinos gave me, my heart recovered from the shock it had received at hearing my lady compared to Belerma."

"And yet I'm amazed," cried Sancho, "that your worship did not jump upon the old fellow and kick every bone in his body, and tear out his beard, without leaving a hair in it."

"Nay, Sancho, my friend," said Don Quixote, "it would

not have been right for me to do so, for we are all bound to show respect to the aged, even though they be not knights, but especially to those who are, and who become enchanted. I am certain that I owed him nothing in the matter of the many other questions and answers which passed between us."

At this point the cousin remarked: "I cannot understand, Señor Don Quixote, how in so short a space of time as you were down below you were able to see so many things and to say and answer so much."

"How long is it since I went down?" asked Don Quixote.

"A little more than an hour," replied Sancho.

"That cannot be," answered Don Quixote, "for night came when I was down there, and then morning, and again a night and a morning three times, so that, by my reckoning, I have been three days in these remote regions hidden from the upper world."

"My master must be right," said Sancho, "for since everything that has happened to him is by enchantment, perhaps what seems an hour to us would seem three days and nights down there."

"That must be so," said Don Quixote.

"Did you, dear sir, eat anything all that time?" asked the cousin.

"I have not broken my fast," answered Don Quixote, "nor did I feel hunger even in imagination."

"Do the enchanted eat?" enquired the cousin.

"They do not eat," answered Don Quixote, "nor do they void excrement, but it is thought that their nails, hair and beard grow."

"And do the enchanted ones sleep, master?" asked Sancho.

"Certainly not," replied Don Quixote, "at any rate during the three days I spent with them no one closed an eye, neither did I."

"This is a point," said Sancho, "where the proverb comes pat: 'Tell me the company you keep and I'll tell you what you are.' You, master, kept company with enchanted fellows who were fasting and watching—what wonder, then, that you neither ate nor slept while you were with them? But forgive me, master, if I tell you that of all you've said up to the present, God seize me—I was just going to say the Devil—if I believe a single word."

"What!" cried the cousin, "could Don Quixote tell a lie? Why, even if he wished to do so, this was no time for him to invent such a load of lies."

"I don't believe my master tells lies," answered Sancho.

"If not, what do you believe?" asked Don Quixote.

"I believe," said Sancho, "that this fellow Merlin, or these enchanters who bewitched the whole crew your worship says you saw and talked to down below, has piled your imagination with all that hotch-potch you have been unloading on us, and all that still remains to tell."

"That might be, Sancho," replied Don Quixote, "but as a matter of fact it is not so, for all that I have told you I saw with my own eyes and touched with my own hands. Now, what will you say when I tell you now that among the countless marvellous things Montesinos showed me, he pointed out three peasant girls who were capering and frisking like she-goats over those delightful fields, and no sooner had I caught sight of them than I recognized one as the peerless Dulcinea del Toboso, and the other two as the same country wenches that were with her and to whom we spoke on the road from El Toboso? I asked Montesinos if he knew them. He answered that he did not, but thought they must be some enchanted ladies of quality, for it was but a few days since they had made their appearance in those meadows. He added that I should not be surprised at that, because many ladies of past and present times were enchanted there in various strange shapes, and among them he recognized Queen Guinevere and her duenna Quintañona, who poured out the wine for Launcelot.

"When from Brittany ne came."[3]

As soon as Sancho Panza heard his master say this, he thought he would lose his wits, or else die with laughter, for since he knew the truth about the pretended enchanting of Dulcinea and had been himself her enchanter and the concocter of all the evidence, he made up his mind beyond all shadow of a doubt that his master was out of his wits and mad as a March hare. So he said to him: "It was a bitter day, dear master, when you went below to the other world, and 'twas an unlucky moment when you met Señor Montesinos, who has so transmogrified you for us. Up here, master, you were as right as rain and in your full senses, such as God has given you, uttering your maxims and giving counsels at every turn, and not as you are now, blabbing the greatest balderdash that ever was known."

"I know you, Sancho," replied Don Quixote, "so I pay no heed to your words."

"No more do I to yours," said Sancho, "even though you beat me or kill me for those I've spoken or mean to speak, if you don't correct and mend your own. But tell me, now that we're at peace, what made you recognize the lady our mistress? If you did speak to her, what did you say, and what did she say in reply?"

"I recognized her," said Don Quixote, "because she wore the same clothes as when you showed her to me. I spoke to her, but she did not answer a word, but only turned her

[3] From the ballad on Launcelot which Don Quixote quoted in the first adventure in the inn (Part I, ch. ii).

back on me and fled, and she ran at such a pace that an arrow would not have overtaken her. I wanted to follow her, and would have done so if Montesinos had not advised me not to weary myself in doing so, for it would be in vain, especially as the hour was approaching when it would be necessary for me to leave the cavern. He told me, moreover, that in time he would tell me how he, Belerma and Durandarte, and all who were there, were to be disenchanted. What pained me, most of all was that while Montesinos was speaking to me, one of the two attendants of the hapless Dulcinea came up to me without my having seen her coming, and, with tears in her eyes, said to me in a low, agitated voice: 'My Lady Dulcinea del Toboso kisses your worship's hands, and beseeches you to let her know how you are, and since she is in great need, she also entreats your worship as earnestly as she can to be so good as to lend her, upon this new dimity petticoat I have here, half a dozen reals, or as many as you have, which she promises to repay in a very short time.' Such a message amazed me, so turning to Montesinos I said: 'Is it possible, Señor Montesinos, that persons of quality, who are enchanted, can suffer need?' He replied: 'Believe me, Señor Don Quixote, that which is called need is the fashion all over the world: it reaches to all, and even extends to the enchanted. And since the Lady Dulcinea del Toboso sends to borrow the six reals, and the security is apparently good, there is nothing for it but to give them to her, for she must no doubt be in sore straits.'

" 'I will not take a pledge for her,' I replied, 'nor can I yet give her what she asks, for all I have is four reals', which I gave her (they were those which you, Sancho, gave me the other day to hand as alms to the poor I met on the road), and I said: 'Tell your mistress, my dear friend, that I am sore distressed to hear of her troubles and I wish I were a Fúcar[4] to relieve them, and I wish her to know that I cannot be, and ought not to be, in health, seeing that I lack her pleasant company and witty conversation. So I beseech her as earnestly as I can to allow herself to be seen and greeted by this her captive and foot-weary cavalier. You must tell her also that when she least expects it she will hear that I have made a vow, like that which the Marquis of Mantua made to avenge his nephew Baldwin, when he found him dying on the mountain-side, which was, not to eat bread off a tablecloth, with some other trifles he added, until he had avenged him. And I will do the same: not to rest, and to wander over the seven regions of the earth more

---

[4] Fúcar is the Spanish form of Fugger, the name of famous bankers at Augsburg who became the Rothschilds of the sixteenth century. They helped Charles V in his wars and rose to great eminence in Spain. "Ser un Fúcar" (to be a Fúcar) was a proverbial saying, meaning to be a Croesus.

diligently than the Infante Don Pedro of Portugal, until I have freed her from enchantment.' 'All that and more your worship should do for my lady,' said the damsel in answer, and taking the four reals, instead of making me a curtsey she cut a caper which lifted her two yards into the air."

"Holy God!" shouted Sancho at this point, "is it possible that such things can happen in the world, and that enchanters and enchantments can have the power to change the good sense of my master into such crazy folly? O master, master, for God's sake, mind yourself, consider your honour, and give no credit to this empty balderdash which has destroyed your senses."

"You talk this way, Sancho, because you love me," said Don Quixote, "and because you are inexperienced in the affairs of the world everything which presents points of difficulty appears to you impossible. But after time has passed I shall tell you about some of the things I saw below, which will make you believe what I have related. Its truth admits of no reply or question."

VII. The charming episode of Master Peter's puppet show

As Don Quixote, Sancho Panza and the cousin rode on, they came across a youth who was plodding along in front of them at a slow rate, and they quickly caught up on him. He carried a sword over his shoulder, and slung on it a bundle or parcel of his clothes, as it seemed, probably his breeches, a cloak and a shirt, for he had on just a short velvet jacket, which was frayed and glossy like satin in spots, and as he was minus his breeches his shirt was sticking out: his stockings were of silk, and his shoes were square-toed like those worn at court. He was about eighteen or nineteen years of age—a blithe and merry-faced lad, and to all appearance, of an active disposition. He went along singing "seguidillas" to enliven the boredom of his journey. And as they reached him he was just finishing one, which the cousin learnt by heart, and which ran thus:

> I'm off to the wars for the want of pence.
> If I had any money I'd show more sense.

The first to speak to him was Don Quixote, who said: "You travel very lightly, gallant sir. Whither are you bound, may we ask, if it please you to tell us?"

The youth answered: "The heat and my poverty are the reasons for my travelling so lightly, and it's to the wars I'm going."

"How poverty?" asked Don Quixote. "The heat I can understand."

"Sir," replied the youth, "in this bundle here I carry a pair of velvet breeches to match the jacket I'm wearing. If I wear them out on the road I shall not be able to cut an honourable figure in the city, and I've not a penny with which to buy others. And so I travel along in this fashion to keep cool, until I overtake some companies of infantry that are not twelve leagues away, with whom I shall enlist, and after that there will be plenty of baggage waggons in which to travel to the port of embarkation, which they say is Cartagena. I would rather have the King as lord and master, and serve him in the war, than some seedy pauper at court."

"Do you get a bounty,[1] by any chance?" asked the cousin.

"If I had served some Spanish grandee or some distinguished personage," replied the lad, "I wager I would get one, for that is what happens to those who serve good masters, and from the servants' hall they rise to be ensigns and captains, or to get a good pension allowance. But I have served job-hunting fellows—the kind whose keep and wages were so paltry and wretched that they would spend half on starching their ruffs; indeed, it would be a miracle if a fortune-hunting page[2] could ever come by any good fortune whatever."

"Now tell me, for goodness' sake," said Don Quixote, "is it possible that all the time you served you never were able to get a livery?"

"They gave me two," replied the page, "but as the man who leaves a religious order before being professed is stripped of his habit and receives his own clothes in return, so my masters gave me back my own, for once their business at court was over they returned to their homes and took back the liveries they had given simply for show."

"What stinginess!" said Don Quixote. "Nevertheless, you are lucky to have left the court with so worthy an object in view, for there is nothing on earth more honourable or more profitable than first of all to serve God, and then your King and natural lord, especially in the profession of arms, by which is won, if not more wealth, at least more honour than by letters, as I have said many a time. And mark my words, my son: it is better for a soldier to smell of gun-powder than of civet, and when old age descends upon you in this honourable profession, even though you may be full of wounds and crippled and lame, at least it will not come upon you without honour, and that honour no poverty will be able to lessen, especially as they are now making an order that old and crip-

[1] This was an extra sum above the ordinary pay. As the common soldier's pay was very small it was usual for youths of good family who enlisted to receive an extra gratuity from their commander. Cervantes himself was rewarded in this way by Don John of Austria, on account of his valiant conduct at Lepanto.

[2] Cervantes speaks of his own early experience as page-adventurer and soldier through the medium of this dashing young soldier of fortune.

pled soldiers should be supported and relieved.[3] It is not well to treat such men after the fashion of those who emancipate their negro slaves when they are old and unable to work, and, after casting them out of their houses with the name of freemen, make them slaves to hunger, from which they cannot hope to be emancipated except by death. For the present I will say no more; but get up behind me on my horse till we come to the inn, and there you shall dine with me and tomorrow continue your journey, and may God reward you as your intentions deserve."

The page did not accept the invitation to mount, but he did that to dine at the inn, and at this point they relate that Sancho muttered to himself: "God save you for a master! Is it possible that a man who can say so many good things as he has said just now, should say that he saw the impossible tomfooleries which he relates about the Cave of Montesinos? Well, well, time will tell."

It was about nightfall when they arrived at the inn, and Sancho was pleased to note that his master took it for a real inn, and not for a castle as he usually did. Sancho and the cousin straightway went off to the stable to see to their beasts, and to Rozinante they gave the best manger and the best stall in the stable.

Just then there came in at the door of the inn a man entirely clad in chamois leather, hose, breeches and doublet, who cried out in a loud voice: "Mr. Landlord, have you room? Here's the fortune-telling monkey, and the puppet show of *The Releasing of Melisendra*."

"Faith and skin!" cried the landlord, "here's Master Peter! That means there's a grand night in store for us."

(I forgot to say that the said Master Peter had his left eye and nearly half his cheek covered with a patch of green taffeta, a sign that there was something wrong with all that side of his face.)

"You're welcome, Master Peter," said the landlord, "but where are the ape and the show? I don't see them."

"They're not far off," replied he of the chamois leather, "but I came on in advance to find out if there was any room."

"I'd put the Duke of Alba[4] himself out to make room for

3 These words were used by Cervantes, the wounded ex-serviceman, in an ironical sense. During the reign of Philip II, after the glorious battle of Lepanto, Spain was thronged with poor discharged soldiers who roamed through the country living by their wits like the heroes of Alemán and Quevedo. It was only 150 years after the death of Cervantes that a pension for ex-servicemen was introduced.

4 This refers to the Grand Duke of Alba, the conqueror of Portugal, and hero of the poet Garcilaso de la Vega, whose name was on the lips of every Spaniard in the days of Cervantes. It was one of the Duke's family—a Prior of the Order of St. John—who had founded Don Quixote's so-called birthplace, Argamasilla de Alba. The Grand Duke had died in 1583.

Master Peter," said the landlord. "Bring in the ape and the show. There are folk in the inn this night who'll pay to see them and the tricks of the monkey."

"May luck come of it," answered he of the patch, "and I'll lower the price, and be well satisfied if I only pay my expenses. So I'll go back and speed up the cart with the ape and the puppet theatre." With that he went out of the inn. Don Quixote then asked the landlord who Master Peter was, and what show and what ape he had with him. The landlord answered: "This is a famous puppet-showman, who for a good while has been roaming about this Mancha de Aragón,[5] exhibiting the show of Melisendra liberated by the famous Don Gaiferos, one of the best and best-acted stories that have been seen in this part of the kingdom for many a year. He also has with him an ape with the most amazing gift ever seen among apes or imagined among men. For if you ask him anything, he listens attentively to the question, and then jumps upon his master's shoulder, and drawing close to his ear tells him the answer, and Master Peter immediately proclaims it. He says far more about past events than about things to come, and though he does not give the correct answer in all cases, he generally makes no mistake, so that he makes us believe that he has the Devil in his inside. He charges two reals for every question if the monkey answers; I mean if his master answers for him, after he has whispered into his ear. And so it is believed that this same Master Peter is very rich. He is a 'gallant man' as they say in Italy, and a boon-companion, and leads the finest life in the world; he talks more than six, drinks more than a dozen—all at the cost of his tongue, his ape and his show."

At this point Master Peter returned, and in a cart followed the show and the ape—a big animal, without a tail, with buttocks like felt, but not a bad face. As soon as Don Quixote saw him, he questioned him, saying: "Tell me, sir fortune-teller, what fish do we catch, and what is to become of us? See, here are my two reals." He then ordered Sancho to give them to Master Peter, and the latter answered for the ape: "Sir, this animal does not answer or give information about things that are to come. Of things that are past, he knows something, of the present a little."

"By God," said Sancho, "I wouldn't give a farthing to learn what's over and done with me, for who knows that better than I do myself? And 'twould be mighty foolish for me to pay for what I know. Nevertheless, seeing that he knows things present, here are my two reals, and tell me, most monkeyish sir, what my wife Teresa Panza is doing now, and how is she enjoying herself?"

[5] The eastern part of La Mancha. It derived its name from a village there called Monte de Aragón.

Master Peter refused to take the money, saying: "I'll not take payment in advance or until the service has been given." And after he had given with his right hand a couple of slaps on his left shoulder, the ape with one leap perched himself upon it, and putting his mouth to his master's ear began to chatter his teeth rapidly, and after keeping this up for the space of a credo, with another leap he skipped to the ground. At the same instant Master Peter ran over and sank on his knees before Don Quixote, embracing his legs as he exclaimed: "These legs I embrace as I would the two Pillars of Hercules! O illustrious reviver of the now-forgotten knight-errantry! O never sufficiently celebrated knight, Don Quixote of La Mancha, courage of the swooning, buttress of those about to fall, arm of the fallen, staff and consolation of the unfortunate!"

Don Quixote was astounded, Sancho agape, the cousin speechless, the page astonished, the landlord puzzled, and, in short, everyone amazed at the words of the puppet-master, who continued: "And you, good Sancho Panza, the best squire to the best knight in the world, be of good cheer, for your good wife Teresa is well, and she is at this present moment carding a pound of flax, and more by token she has at her left hand a jug with a broken spout that holds a tidy what-for of wine, with which she cheers herself at her work."

"That I can well believe," said Sancho. "She's a lucky one, and if she weren't jealous, I wouldn't exchange her for the giantess Andandona,[6] who, according to my master, was a very clever and decent woman. My Teresa is one of those who won't let themselves want for aught, even though their heirs should have to foot the bill."

"Now I say," cried Don Quixote, "that he who reads much and travels much, sees and knows a great deal. I say this because who could persuade me that there are apes in the world that can divine, as I have now seen with my own eyes? For I am that very Don Quixote of La Mancha this worthy animal has spoken of, though he has exaggerated somewhat my virtues. But whatever I may be, I give thanks to Heaven, which has endowed me with a soft and compassionate heart, always inclined to do good to all and harm to no one."

"If I had money," said the page, "I would ask Mr. Monkey what will happen to me in the peregrination I am making."

To this Master Peter, who had risen from Don Quixote's feet, replied: "I have already said that this little beast does not answer questions about the future, but if he did, not having money would not matter, for to oblige Señor Don Quixote here present I would renounce all the profits in the world. And now, since I am indebted to him, and to please him,

[6] The giantess of *Amadis of Gaul*.

297

I will set up my puppet show and entertain all who are in the inn, without any charge whatever."

As soon as he heard this news the landlord was delighted beyond measure, and pointed out a place where the show might be erected, which was done at once.

Now Don Quixote was not too well pleased with the ape's divinations, as he did not think it right that an ape should divine things past or future. And so, while Master Peter was preparing his show, he retired with Sancho into a corner of the stable, where, without being heard by anyone, he said to him: "Listen, Sancho, I have considered carefully the extraordinary talent of this ape, and I am convinced personally that without doubt this Master Peter must have made a pact, tacit or express, with the Devil."

"If the packet is express from the Devil," said Sancho, "it must be a very dirty one, but what good is it to Master Peter to have such packets?"

"You do not understand me, Sancho," said Don Quixote. "I only mean to say that he must have made some bargain with the Devil, to impart this power to the ape, so that he may earn his living, and after he has grown rich he will hand over to him his soul, for this is the aim of the universal enemy of mankind. What makes me believe this is that I observe that the ape only answers about things past or present, and the Devil's knowledge extends no further, for the future he knows only by conjecture, and that not always, for God alone knows the times and the seasons, and for Him there is neither past nor future: all is present. Since this is so, it is clear that the ape speaks in the style of the Devil, and I am astonished that they have not denounced him to the Holy Office and questioned him, and extracted from him by whose virtue he divines. For surely this ape is no astrologer, nor his master either, nor do they know how to cast a horoscope, such as is so much the fashion in Spain that there is not a wench, or page, or old cobbler who does not claim to set up a figure as easily as pick up a knave of cards from the ground, bringing to nought, with their lies and their ignorance, the wonderful truth of science. One lady I know asked one of those astrologers whether her little lap-dog would be in pup and would bring forth, and how many and of what colour the pups would be. The astrologer, after casting his horoscope, responded that the bitch would be in pup and would bring forth three pups, one green, another scarlet, and the third mottled, provided that the said bitch should be covered between eleven and twelve o'clock, by day or night, and that it should be on a Monday or a Saturday. What actually happened was that two days later the bitch died of indigestion, and Sir Astrologer won the reputation in that town of being a famous planet-ruler."

"Nevertheless," said Sancho, "I wish, master, you would tell Master Peter to ask his ape if what happened to you in the Cave of Montesinos is true. As for me, with all respect to your worship, I hold that it was all moonshine and lies, or at least dreams."

"That may be," replied Don Quixote, "but I shall follow your advice, though I have some scruples about doing so."

At this point Master Peter came to look for Don Quixote and tell him that the puppet-show was now in order, and that his worship should come to see it, for it was well worth seeing. Don Quixote told him what was in his mind, and asked him to enquire from the ape whether the things that had taken place in the Cave of Montesinos were imaginary or real, for in his opinion they seemed to partake of both. Master Peter, without answering, went to fetch the ape, and placing him before Don Quixote and Sancho, said: "Listen, Mr. Ape, this gentleman wishes to know whether certain things which happened to him in the cave called the Cave of Montesinos were false or true."

Making the usual sign, the ape jumped on to his left shoulder, and appeared to whisper in his ear. Then Master Peter said: "The ape says that the things your worship saw or that happened to you in that cave were part false and part true. That is all he knows on this question, but if your worship wishes to know more, he will answer on Friday next all that you ask him, for his power is now exhausted and will not return until Friday, as he has said."

"Did I not say, master," said Sancho, "that I could not believe the truth of all the stories you told me, no, nor even half of them?"

"The future will tell, Sancho," answered Don Quixote. "Time, the discoverer of all things, leaves nothing that it does not drag into the light of the sun, even though it be buried in the bosom of the earth. But enough of that, let us go and see Master Peter's show, for I am sure it must contain some novelty."

"Some, do you say?" said Master Peter. "This show of mine has sixty thousand novelties in it. Let me tell you, Señor Don Quixote, this is one of the things most worth seeing in the whole world, but *operibus credite et non verbis*, and let us set to work, for it's growing late, and we have a lot to do and to say and to show."

Don Quixote and Sancho obeyed him, and went to where the show was set up and uncovered, plentifully supplied on all sides with lighted wax tapers, which gave it a gay and festive air. Master Peter took his place inside it, for it was he who had to work the puppets, and a boy, a servant of his, stood outside to act as interpreter and explain the mysteries of the show. He held a wand in his hand to point out the figures as they emerged upon the stage. All those who were guests in the inn were already settled in front of the show, and some were standing, but Don Quixote, Sancho, the page and the cousin were given the best places.

Now all were silent, and everyone was hanging on the lips of the interpreter of the wonders of the show, when drums and trumpets were heard within and the sound of cannon. When the noise ceased, the boy lifted up his voice and said: "This true story which is here represented before your worships is taken word for word from the French chronicles and from the Spanish ballads which are in the mouths of the folk and in the mouths of the boys who roam the streets. It tells of the release by Señor Don Gaiferos of his wife Melisendra, who was a captive in Spain in the power of the Moors in the city of Sansueña, for so they called the city which is now named Saragossa. Let your worships see there how Don Gaiferos is a-playing at backgammon, according to what they are singing:

> Gaiferos is at tables[7] playing,
> For Melisendra, alas, is forgotten.

And that character who appears over there with a crown on his head and a sceptre in his hand is the Emperor Charlemagne, the supposed father of Melisendra, who being angered at his son-in-law's idleness and negligence comes forth to chide him. Note, good folks, with what stern vehemence he scolds him; why, you would fancy he was going to give him half a dozen raps with his sceptre. Aye, indeed, there are authors who say that he did give them, and they were well laid on too; and after saying many a thing about endangering his honour through not trying to release his wife, he said, so they say: 'I've said enough, look to it!'

"Take notice, gentlemen, how the Emperor turns his back and leaves Don Gaiferos fuming and frothing: see now how in a blaze of choler he flings the board and the pieces from him, and calls in haste for his armour, and begs his cousin Don Roland for the loan of his sword Durindana. And Don Roland refuses to lend it, and offers him his company in the difficult enterprise which he is undertaking. But the valiant, choleric hero will have none of it, saying that he alone suffices to rescue his wife, even though she were gaoled in the deepest centre of the earth. Thereupon he goes in to arm himself to start at once upon his journey. Turn your eyes, gentlemen, to yon tower over there, which you must imagine to be one of the towers of the Alcázar of Saragossa, now called the Aljafería. That lady who appears on the balcony, dressed in Moorish fashion, is the peerless Melisendra, who many a time

[7] The game of "tablas" or tables was a very ancient game resembling our backgammon. It was played with dice.

used to look out from thence upon the road to France, and console herself in her captivity by turning her imagination towards Paris and her consort. Note, too, a new incident which now takes place, one such as, perhaps, was never seen before. Can ye not see yon Sir Moor, who stealthily on tiptoe, with his finger to his mouth, creeps up at the back of Melisendra? See how he gives her a kiss right in the centre of her lips, and how she hastens to spit it out and wipe them with the white sleeve of her smock. Look how she weeps and tears her lovely hair, as though it were to blame for the trespass. See, too, that stately Moor who stands in the corridors over there: he is King Marsilio of Sansueña, who, having seen the other Moor's insolence, at once orders him to be arrested (though he was a relative, and a great favourite) and to be given two hundred lashes, and to be led through the most crowded streets of the city, with criers going before and the officers of the law behind. And there you see them come out to execute the sentence, though the crime has hardly been committed, for among the Moors there are no indictments nor remands, as amongst us."

At this point Don Quixote cried out in a loud voice: "Boy, boy, on straight with your story, and don't go off into curves and crossways, for proof after proof is needed if we would establish a truth."

"Boy, do as the gentleman bids you, and don't go in for variations," cried Master Peter from within, "and you'll always be right. Stick to your plain song, and don't trouble about counterpoints, for they are liable to break down from being too subtle."

"I'll do so," replied the boy, and continued: "This figure you see here on horseback, clad in a Gascon cloak, is Don Gaiferos himself. His wife (now that she has been avenged of the insolent behaviour of the amorous Moor), standing on the battlements of the tower with calmer and more tranquil mien, converses with him, thinking him to be some stranger, and addresses him in the words recorded in the ballad which says:

> Sir Knight, if you to France are bound,
> Pray ask for my spouse, Don Gaiferos.

The rest I'll not repeat, because prolixity begets weariness. It is enough to see how Don Gaiferos makes himself known to her, and Melisendra by her joyful gestures makes it plain to us that she has recognized him, and, furthermore, we see her let herself down from the balcony and place herself on the crupper of her good husband's horse. But, alas, hapless lady, the lace of her under-petticoat has caught on one of the iron bars of the balcony and there she is, dangling in the air without being able to reach the ground. But watch how mer-

301

ciful heaven sends aid in our sorest need. Don Gaiferos approaches, and without minding to see whether her rich petticoat is torn or not, he seizes her and by force pulls her to the ground. Then with one leap he sets her on the crupper of his horse, astride like a man, and bids her hold on tight and clasp her arms round his neck so as to cross them on his breast to avoid falling off, for the Lady Melisendra was not accustomed to such a way of riding. See also how the neighing of the horse shows his joy at the gallant and beautiful burden he carries in his lord and lady! See how they wheel round and leave the city and merrily gallop along the road to Paris! Go in peace, O peerless pair of true lovers! May you reach in safety your longed-for fatherland, and may fortune place no hindrance to your lucky journey: may the eyes of your friends and kinsmen see you enjoying in peace and tranquillity the remaining days of your life, and may they be as many as those of Nestor!"

Here Master Peter once more cried out: "Keep it plain and simple, boy, don't go in for high flights: all affectation is bad."

The interpreter made no answer, but went on: "There was no lack of idle eyes that look out for everything, to see Melisendra descend and mount the horse. Straightway they ran with the news to King Marsilio. He at once ordered them to sound the alarm. See how quickly it is done, and how the whole city shakes with the booming and pealing of the bells from the towers of all the mosques."

"Not so," said Don Quixote at this point. "In this point of the bells Master Peter is altogether wrong, for bells are not used among the Moors, but drums and a kind of shawm like our clarion. It is surely a great absurdity to ring bells in Sansueña."

On hearing this, Master Peter stopped ringing, and said: "Don't single out trifles, Señor Don Quixote, and don't expect perfection which is impossible to find. Do they not play in these parts almost every day a thousand comedies full of a thousand absurdities, and, in spite of that, they run their course successfully and are listened to, not only with applause, but admiration and all the rest? Go on, boy, and let them have their say. Provided I fill my money-bags, let them show more absurdities than there are motes in the sun."

"That is the truth," replied Don Quixote.

The boy continued: "See what a numerous and shining cavalcade rides out from the city in pursuit of the two Catholic lovers! What a number of trumpets are blaring! What a number of clarions ringing! Listen to the drums and timbrels beating! I'm afraid they'll overtake them, and we'll see them brought back tied to the tail of their own horse, which would be a horrifying spectacle."

Don Quixote, seeing such an array of Moors and hearing

such a strident din, thought it was his duty to help the fugitives, so springing to his feet he cried in a loud voice: "Never, as long as I live, will I allow an outrage to be committed in my presence to so famous a knight and so gallant a lover as Don Gaiferos. Halt! base-born rabble! Follow him not, nor pursue him, or with me ye do battle!"

And suiting the action to the word, he drew his sword and with one bound he planted himself by the show. Then with extraordinary speed and violence he began to shower blows upon the puppet Moors, knocking over some, beheading others, maiming this one and demolishing that. And among many more, he delivered one down-stroke, which, if Master Peter had not ducked, huddled, and side-stepped, would have sliced off his head as easily as if it had been made of almond-paste. Master Peter kept shouting, "Stop, Señor Don Quixote! Look and you'll see that those you're knocking over and killing are not real Moors, but only little paste-board figures! See, sinner that I am, how you're wrecking and ruining my whole livelihood."

Don Quixote, however, did not stop raining slashes, down-strokes, slashes and back-strokes, and at last, in less than the time required for saying two credos he knocked the whole show to the ground, with all its fittings cut to pieces, King Marsilio severely wounded, the Emperor Charlemagne with his crown and head slit in two. The whole assembly of listeners was thrown into confusion; the ape fled to the roof of the inn; the cousin was afraid, the page was crouching with fear, even Sancho Panza himself was in a state of great alarm, for, as he swore after the squall had passed, he had never seen his master in such a mad passion.

Now that the complete destruction of the show had been accomplished, Don Quixote became somewhat calmer, and said: "I wish I had here before me at the present moment all those who do not or will not believe how useful knights-errant are in the world. Consider, if I had not been here present, what would have become of the valiant Don Gaiferos and the fair Melisendra? I wager that by this time those curs would have overtaken them and done them some terrible wrong. Wherefore, long live knight-errantry above everything that lives on earth this day!"

"Let it live, and welcome," said Master Peter in a faint voice, "and let me die, for I'm so unlucky that I may say with King Rodrigo:

'Yesterday I was the lord of Spain;
Today there's not a battlemented town
That I may call my own.'

Hardly half an hour, nay, barely a moment ago I saw myself lord of kings and emperors, with my stables, my chests and

303

bags full of countless horses and gay dresses without number, but now I see myself forlorn and desolate, poor and a beggar, and above all, without my ape, for I swear my teeth will have to sweat before I'm able to catch him again. And all this has happened because of the rash fury of this knight here, who, they say, protects orphans and redresses wrongs and does other charitable deeds. In my case alone his noble intentions have failed, blessed be the loftiest thrones of heaven! Indeed, Knight of the Rueful Figure he must be, for he has disfigured mine."

Sancho Panza was moved by Master Peter's words, and said to him: "Don't cry and complain, Master Peter: you're breaking my heart. I want you to know that my master, Don Quixote, is so Catholic and scrupulous a Christian that if he once realizes that he has done you any wrong he will pay up and make it up to you, aye, and with something over and above besides."

"If only Señor Don Quixote pays me for some part of the damage he has done me, I'll be well satisfied, and his worship will salve his conscience, for he will not be saved who keeps what belongs to another against the will of the owner, and makes no restitution."

"That is true," said Don Quixote, "but up to the present I am not conscious of having anything that belongs to you, Master Peter."

"What!" cried Master Peter. ' And these relics strewn about the hard, sterile ground—what scattered and annihilated them but the invincible force of that mighty arm of yours? Whose are those corpses but mine? With whom did I earn my livelihood if not with them?"

"Now I am fully convinced," said Don Quixote, "of what I have often believed, that these enchanters who persecute me are for ever conjuring up before my eyes figures like these, and then they turn and transform them into what they please. Truly I declare to you gentlemen, who hear me, that all that has taken place here seemed to me to happen really: that Melisendra was Melisendra, Don Gaiferos—Don Gaiferos, Marsilio—Marsilio, and Charlemagne—Charlemagne. It was for this reason that my anger rose within me, and in order to be loyal to my vow of knight-errant I wished to give aid and protection to those who were fleeing, and with this virtuous intention I did what you have seen. If the result has been the opposite, it is not my fault, but that of the wicked beings who persecute me. Nevertheless, I am willing to condemn myself in costs for my error, though it did not proceed from malice. Let Master Peter see what he wants for the damaged figures, for I offer to pay him for them in good and current money of Castile."

Master Peter bowed to him, saying: "I expected no less from the unique Christian spirit of the valiant Don Quixote of La Mancha, the true helper and protector of all needy and distressed vagabonds. Mr. Innkeeper here and the great Sancho Panza shall be the arbiters and assessors between your worship and me of what these damaged figures are worth or might be worth."

The landlord and Sancho agreed to act, and then Master Peter lifted from the ground King Marsilio of Saragossa, minus the head, and said: "You can see how impossible it is to restore this King to his former state, therefore I think, subject to your better judgment, that I should receive for his decease, end and demise the sum of four and a half reals."

"Go on," said Don Quixote.

"Well, for this split from top to bottom," continued Master Peter, taking up in his hands the cleft Emperor Charlemagne, "it would not be too much to ask five reals and a quarter."

"That's no small sum," said Sancho.

"Not too much, all the same," replied the landlord. "Let us settle the difference and give him five reals."

"Give him the five a quarter reals," said Don Quixote. "In such a great misfortune as this, a quarter more or less makes precious little difference; but conclude the business quickly, Master Peter, for the supper hour approaches and I am somewhat hungry."

"Now, for this puppet," said Master Peter, "which is the fair Melisendra, and is minus its nose and eye, I want—mind you I'm being fair to you—two reals and twelve maravedis."

"It must be the work of the Devil," cried Don Quixote, "if Melisendra and her husband are not at least at the French frontier, for the horse they rode seemed to me to fly rather than gallop, so there is no reason to sell me a cat for a hare [8] by showing me a noseless Melisendra, when she is now, if all goes well, enjoying herself to her heart's content in France with her husband. May God give everyone his deserts, Master Peter, and let us play fair and square. Proceed."

Master Peter, perceiving that Don Quixote was swerving from the path of reason and returning to his old craze, was determined not to let him escape, so he said: "This must not be Melisendra but one of her handmaidens. So just give me sixty maravedis and I'll be content and count myself well paid."

In this manner he continued to put a price on the many shattered puppets, which afterwards the two arbitrators reduced to the satisfaction of both sides. The total reached the sum of forty reals and three quarters, and in addition to this sum, which Sancho straightway paid, Master Peter asked two reals for his trouble in catching the ape.

"Give them to him, Sancho," said Don Quixote, "not to

[8] A proverbial expression meaning to cheat somebody.

305

catch the monkey but to get monkey drunk,[9] and I would willingly give two hundred this instant as reward for good news to anyone who could tell me for certain that Lady Melisendra and Señor Don Gaiferos are now in France among their own folk."

"No one can tell us that better than my ape," said Master Peter, "but there's no devil can catch him now. However, I expect affection and hunger will make him search for me tonight. Anyhow, God's dawn will soon be here and we shall see."

And so the puppet-show squall passed, and all took supper in peace and good fellowship at Don Quixote's expense, for he was of a most liberal disposition. Shortly after daybreak the cousin and the page took leave of Don Quixote. The former set off for home, and the latter continued his journey, towards which Don Quixote contributed a dozen reals. Master Peter did not want to enter into any more arguments with Don Quixote, whom he knew exceedingly well,[10] so he rose before the sun, and, collecting together the remains of his show and his ape, he, too, went off in search of his adventures. The landlord, who did not know Don Quixote, was no less amazed by the knight's generosity than by his madness. Finally, after Sancho, by his master's orders, had paid him very well, the two said farewell to him and left the inn at about eight o'clock in the morning for the open road.

VIII. The Knight's adventure with a fair huntress

THAT DAY, AT SUNSET, AS THEY CAME OUT OF A WOOD, DON Quixote gazed over a green meadow and at the other end he noticed some people, and when he drew near he saw that they were a hawking party. He came closer and perceived among them an elegant lady on a palfrey or milk-white nag caparisoned with green trappings and a silver side-saddle. The lady herself was clad in green of so rich and gorgeous texture that comeliness seemed to be personified in her. On her left she bore a hawk, a token by which Don Quixote knew that she must be some great lady and the mistress of all those hunters, which was true; so he said to Sancho: "Run, Sancho, my son, and say to that lady of the palfrey with the hawk that I, the Knight of the Lions, kiss the hands of her noble beauty, and if her excellency grants me leave I will go myself to kiss them, and serve her to the best of my power and as her highness shall

[9] Mona (she-monkey) is a slang expression for a drunken orgy.
[10] Because he is no other than our rascal galley-slave Ginés de Pasamonte (called Ginesillo de Parapilla by Don Quixote) whom the knight liberated in the Sierra Morena (Part I, ch. xiii). Ginés showed his lack of gratitude by stealing Sancho's ass while he was asleep. For fear of being recognized by the officers of justice he covered his left eye with a patch and set himself up as puppet-master.

command. Mind, Sancho, how you speak, and be careful not to intrude any of your proverbs into your message."

"I' faith," said Sancho, "you've got a fine intruder here! Leave that to me! Sure, this is not the first time in my life that I've carried messages to high and full-blown ladies."

"Except for the message you carried to the Lady Dulcinea," said Don Quixote, "I am not aware that you ever carried any other, at least in my service."

"That's true," replied Sancho, "but a good payer needs no sureties, and when there's plenty in the house the supper's soon ready—I mean there's no need to warn or tip me the wink about aught, for I'm a match for all, and I know a wee bit about everything."

"I am sure of that, Sancho," said Don Quixote. "Good luck to your journey, and God guide you."

Sancho went off at top speed, spurring Dapple out of his usual pace, and came to where the fair huntress was, and dismounting, knelt before her, saying: "Fair lady, that knight over there, called the Knight of the Lions, is my master, and I'm his squire, and at home they call me Sancho Panza. This same Knight of the Lions, who was called a short while ago the Knight of the Rueful Figure, sends by me to say may your greatness be pleased to give him leave that, with your good pleasure and consent, he may come and carry out his wishes, which are, as he says and I do believe, nought else than to serve your lofty nobility and beauty, and if you give it, your ladyship will do something that will redound to your honour, and he will receive a most marked favour and contentment."

"Truly, good squire," answered the lady, "you have delivered your message with all the details and formalities which such embassies require. Rise up from the ground, for it is not meet that the squire of so great a knight as He of the Rueful Figure, of whom we have heard a great deal, should remain on his knees. Rise, my friend, and tell your master that I welcome him to the services of myself and my husband the duke, in a country house we have here."

Sancho got up, delighted as much by the beauty of the good lady as by her high breeding and courtesy, and, above all, by what she had said about having heard of his master, the Knight of the Rueful Figure, and if she did not call him Knight of the Lions it must have been because he had only recently taken the title. "Tell me, brother squire," asked the duchess (her title is unknown),[1] "about this master of yours: is he not

---

[1] According to the commentator Pellicer, Cervantes drew the duke and duchess from real life. The originals were Don Carlos de Borja and María Luisa de Aragón, Duke and Duchess of Villahermosa, and the castle where all the adventures took place was theirs in the neighbourhood of Pedrola. In 1905 the Duchess of Villahermosa, their descendant, gave festivities in Pedrola in celebration of the third centenary of the publication of Part I of the immortal work.

one of whom a history is in print called *The Ingenious Gentleman, Don Quixote of La Mancha,* who has for the mistress of his heart a certain Dulcinea del Toboso?"

"He's the very same, my lady," answered Sancho, "and that squire of his who figures, or ought to figure, in the said history, and whom they call Sancho Panza, is myself, if they haven't changed me in the cradle—I mean, in the press."

"I'm delighted to hear all this," said the duchess. "Go, brother Panza, and tell your master that he is welcome to my estates, and that nothing could happen which could give me more pleasure."

Sancho returned to his master in high spirits with this agreeable answer, and told him all the great lady had said to him, praising to the skies, in his rustic speech, her great beauty and her courtesy. Don Quixote preened himself in his saddle, set his feet taut in the stirrups, fixed his visor, dug his spurs into Rozinante, and with easy bearing advanced to kiss the hands of the duchess. She had sent for her husband and told him, while Don Quixote was approaching, all about the message. Now, the duke and the duchess had read the First Part of this history, and were, therefore, well aware of Don Quixote's crazy humour, so they awaited his coming with the greatest eagerness, for they intended to follow his humour and treat him as a knight-errant as long as he stayed with them, with all the accustomed ceremonies which they had read about in the books of chivalry, of which they were very fond.

Don Quixote approached with vizor raised, and as he made signs of wishing to dismount, Sancho hastened to hold his stirrup, but in getting down off Dapple he was unlucky enough to catch his foot in one of the ropes of the pack-saddle in such a way that he could not free it but remained hanging by it with his face and chest to the ground. Don Quixote, who was unused to dismount without having the stirrup held for him, imagining that Sancho had by this time caught hold of it, shot his body off with a lurch and brought with him Rozinante's saddle, which no doubt was badly girthed, with the result that both saddle and he came to earth, not without discomfiture to him, and plenty of curses which he mumbled against the luckless Sancho, who still lay prone with his foot tangled in the halter. The duke ordered his huntsmen to go to the aid of the knight and squire, and they raised Don Quixote, who, though badly shaken by his fall, limped along as best he could and knelt before their graces. But the duke would not permit it; on the contrary, he dismounted from his horse and went over to embrace Don Quixote, saying: "I am sorry, Sir Knight of the Rueful Figure, that your entry into my estate should have been so unfortunate; but the carelessness of squires is often the cause of worse accidents."

"That which has befallen me in meeting you, valiant

308

Prince," replied Don Quixote, "cannot be unfortunate, even if my fall had dragged me down into the bottomless abyss, for the glory of having seen you would have raised and rescued me from it. My squire, God's curse upon him, is more skilled at loosening his tongue to utter impertinences than in tightening the girths of a saddle to keep it steady. But wherever I may be, fallen or risen, on foot or on horseback, I shall always be at your service and at that of my lady the duchess, your worthy consort, worthy mistress of beauty and universal princess of courtesy."

"Gently, my lord Don Quixote of La Mancha," said the duke. "Where my lady Doña Dulcinea del Toboso is, it is not right that other beauties should be praised."

Sancho who was now released from his noose, was standing close by and put in his word before his master could answer, saying: "There's no denying, in fact we must assent emphatically, that the Lady Dulcinea del Toboso is very beautiful, but the hare jumps up where one least expects it, and I've heard tell that what we call Nature is like a potter who makes vessels of clay, and he who makes one fine vase can just as well make two, or three, or a hundred. I say this, because, 'pon my word, my lady the duchess is no whit behind my mistress the Lady Dulcinea del Toboso."

Don Quixote turned to the duchess, saying: "Your highness may consider that no knight-errant in the world ever had a more droll or talkative squire than I have. And he will prove the truth of my words if your loftiness is pleased to accept my services for a few days."

To this the duchess made answer: "I value the worthy Sancho highly for being droll, because it is a sign that he is shrewd, for drollery and humour, as you, Señor Don Quixote, are well aware, are not housed in dullards. And since good Sancho is droll and humorous, henceforth I set him down as shrewd."

"And talkative," added Don Quixote.

"So much the better," said the duke; "one cannot utter many witty things in few words: so not to waste time in mere talk, come, great Knight of the Rueful Figure . . ."

"Of the Lions, your highness should say," said Sancho, "for now there is no Rueful Figure."

"He of the Lions let it be," continued the duke. "Now let the Knight of the Lions come to a castle of mine which is near by, where he shall be welcomed as befits his exalted state."

By now Sancho had girthed Rozinante's saddle, and Don Quixote having mounted, the duke sprang on to his own fine horse, and with the duchess between them, they set out for the castle. The duchess insisted that Sancho should ride by her side, for she took infinite pleasure in hearing his shrewd comments. Sancho needed no pressing, but shoved himself among the three and made a fourth in the conversation, to the great amusement of the duchess and the duke, who considered themselves fortunate indeed to welcome to their castle so noble a knight-errant and so aberrant a squire.

Before the company reached the castle, the duke rode on in advance and gave orders to his servants how they were to treat Don Quixote, and so when Don Quixote came up to the castle gates with the duchess, two lacqueys or grooms, clad from head to foot in what are called morning-gowns of fine crimson satin, ran out and caught Don Quixote in their arms almost before he could see or hear them, saying: "Let your highness go and help my lady the duchess to dismount from her horse."

Don Quixote did as he was bid, and great compliments passed between the two over the business, but in the end the duchess's determination prevailed, and she would not dismount from her palfrey save in the arms of the duke, saying that she was not worthy of imposing so great a burden upon so great a knight. At length the duke came out to take her down, and as they entered a great courtyard two fair maidens approached and threw over Don Quixote's shoulders a long mantle of the finest scarlet cloth,[2] and in a moment all the galleries of the court were thronged with the men and women servants of the duke and duchess, crying: "Welcome, flower and cream of knights-errant." Then all poured little phials of perfumed water over Don Quixote and the duke and duchess. All this astonished Don Quixote, and for the first time he felt thoroughly convinced that he was a knight-errant in fact and not in imagination, for he saw himself treated in the same way as he had read that such knights were treated in past ages.

Sancho, forsaking Dapple, attached himself to the duchess and entered the castle, but his conscience pricked him at having left his ass forlorn, so he went up to a grave duenna who had sallied out with the rest to receive the duchess, and in a low voice said to her: "Mistress González,[3] or whatever your worship's name may be . . ."

"My name is Doña Rodríguez de Grijalba," answered the duenna. "What is your will, brother?"

To which Sancho made reply: "I wish your worship would do me the favour to go out to the castle gate, where you'll find a dappled ass of mine: please give orders for them to put him in the stable, or put him there yourself, for the poor fellow is easy scared, and can't stand being left on his lonesome."

"If the master is as wise as the servant," said the duenna,

[2] A scarlet mantle lined with ermine was the customary garment worn by knights when they had put off their armour.
[3] González was a very common name among duennas, and Rodríguez among pages.

"we're in a nice fix. Off with you, brother, and bad luck to you and him who brought you here! Go mind your own ass: we duennas are not used to jobs of that kind."

"Faith, and I've heard my master tell," quoth Sancho, "and, mind you, he's a wizard for stories—of how Launcelot when he came from Britain, said that ladies waited on him, and duennas on his nag; and, when it comes to my ass, I wouldn't swap him for Sir Launcelot's horse."

"If you are a jester, brother," said the duenna, "keep your jokes for the right occasion where they'll be paid for, from me you'll get naught but a 'fig'."[4]

"In that case," quoth Sancho, " 'tis sure to be a ripe one, and if years count, you certainly won't lose the trick by too few points."

"Whoreson knave," said the duenna, blazing with anger, "if I'm old or no, that is God's business, not yours, you garlic-stuffed rascal!" She said all this in such a loud voice that the duchess heard it, and turning round and seeing the duenna so heated and her eyes so flaming, asked her with whom she was bickering.

"With this fine fellow here," said the duenna, "who respectfully requests me to go and put an ass of his that is at the castle gate into the stable. And he brings it up as an example that they did the same I don't know where, when some ladies waited on a certain Launcelot and duennas on his nag, and, what is more serious, he ends up by calling me an old woman."

"That I would consider," replied the duchess, "the greatest insult that anyone could inflict upon me." Then to Sancho she said: "Remember, Sancho, my friend, that Doña Rodríguez is quite a young lady, and that head-dress she wears more by authority and custom than because of years."

"May the rest of mine be unlucky," replied Sancho, "if I said it with that intention. I only said it because I've so great a fondness for my ass; and I thought I couldn't recommend him to a more kind-hearted soul than the lady Doña Rodríguez."

Don Quixote, who was listening, then said to him: "Is this suitable conversation, Sancho, for such a place?"

"Master," replied Sancho, "everyone must speak out his needs, wherever he may be: here I remembered Dapple, and here I spoke of him. Had I thought of him in the stable I would have spoken of him there."

The duke then remarked: "Sancho is quite right, and there is no reason why he should be blamed. Dapple will receive fodder in plenty. Sancho may set his mind at rest; the ass shall be treated like himself."

While this conversation, amusing to all except Don Quixote,

4 An insulting gesture.

was going on, they went upstairs and led the knight into a hall hung with rich cloth of gold and brocade. Six maidens relieved him of his armour and waited on him as pages, all of them trained by the duke and duchess as to what they had to do, and how they were to treat Don Quixote so that he might believe that he was being tended as a knight-errant. After his armour had been removed he stood there in his tight-fitting breeches and chamois-skin doublet, a long, lean, lanky figure, with cheeks that kissed each other on the inside; a figure that would have excited the handmaidens to outbursts of merriment had they not taken care to hide their laughter (which was one of the strict orders they had received from their master and mistress). They asked him to let himself be stripped that they might put a shirt on him, but he would not allow it, for he said that modesty was as becoming to knights-errant as valour.[5] However, he told them to give the shirt to Sancho, and after shutting himself up with him in a room where there was a luxurious couch, he undressed and put on the shirt, and then, finding himself alone with Sancho, he said to him: "Tell me now, you clown of today and noodle of yesterday—do you think it was right of you to offend and insult a duenna so worthy of reverence and respect as that one? Was that the time to think of your Dapple, or are those lordly gentlemen the kind who would let the beasts go hungry when they treat their owners in such elegant style? For God's sake, Sancho, keep an eye to yourself, and do not show the yarn, for fear they may see what coarse, brutish stuff you are spun of. Remember, you sinner, that well-bred and honourable servants cause their master to be respected, and that one of the greatest advantages which princes possess over other men is that they have servants as good as themselves to wait on them. Do you not see, you unlucky bane of mine, that if they find out you are a coarse clod-hopper or a clownish loony, they will think that I am some roaming quack or a knight of straw?[6] No, no, Sancho, my friend, shun such pitfalls, for he who trips into being a droll chatterbox, at the first stumble drops into a despised clown. Bridle your tongue, reflect and chew the cud before you let your words escape from your mouth, and remember that we have arrived at a point whence, by the help of God and the strength of my arm, we shall come forth greatly advanced both in fame and fortune."

[5] In the romances of chivalry it was customary for damsels to undress the knights who visited the castle and clothe them in fresh garments.

[6] These diatribes of Don Quixote suggest that the knight was slightly nettled at the praise lavished on Sancho by the duke and duchess for his sallies. Perhaps the knight may have felt a touch of jealousy at the prominence accorded to Sancho by his hosts, who had already read and enjoyed the First Part of the great book.

Sancho promised his master faithfully that he would sew up his mouth and bite off his tongue rather than utter a word that was not fitting and well-considered, and he told him not to be anxious about the point in question, for no one would ever discover through him who they were.

Don Quixote then dressed himself, put on his baldric with his sword, threw the scarlet mantle over his shoulders, placed on his head a hunting-cap of green satin which the maidens had given him, and thus arrayed sallied out into the great hall, where he found the damsels drawn up in two rows, half on one side and half on the other, all of them with vessels for washing the hands, which they presented with many courtesies and ceremonies. Then came twelve pages, with the seneschal, to conduct him to dinner, as his host and hostess were already awaiting him. Placing him between them, they led him with much pomp and circumstance into another hall, where there was a sumptuous table laid with but four covers. The duchess and the duke came out to the door of the dining-hall to receive him, and one of those graver ecclesiastics that rule noblemen's houses; one of those that, not being born princes themselves, never know how to teach those who are how to behave as such; that would measure the greatness of great folk by their own narrowness of mind; that, trying to teach their pupils to practise economy, end by making them miserly. One of this kind, I say, was the grave prelate who came out with the duke and duchess to receive Don Quixote.[7]

Many courtly compliments were exchanged, and at last, placing Don Quixote between them, they took their places at the table. The duke invited Don Quixote to sit at the head of the table, and though he refused, the host was so pressing in his request that the knight had to take it. The ecclesiastic sat opposite to him, and the duke and duchess at the sides. All this time Sancho stood by, gaping with amazement at the honour paid to his master by these princes; and observing all the ceremonies and formalities that passed between the duke and his master to persuade the latter to take his place at the head of the table, he said: "If your worships would give me leave, I'll tell you a tale of what happened in my village about this matter of seats."

No sooner had Sancho said this than Don Quixote trembled, for he was sure that his squire was about to deliver

---

[7] Some commentators say that the portrait of this ecclesiastic is drawn from the confessor to the Duke of Bejar, who nearly succeeded in persuading the duke to refuse the dedication of the First Part of *Don Quixote*. Others say it refers to Bartolomé Leonardo de Argensola the poet. He and his brother Lupercio prevented the Conde de Lemos from dispensing patronage to other writers. There are, however, frequent references in Spanish literature of the sixteenth and seventeenth centuries to the despotic behaviour of confessors in noblemen's houses.

himself of some piece of tomfoolery. Sancho looked at him, and straightway understood, so he said: "Don't be afraid, master, that I'll go astray or say anything that won't hit the nail on the head. I haven't forgotten the advice your worship gave me a while ago about talking much or little, well or ill."

"I remember nought of it, Sancho," answered Don Quixote; "say what you want, but say it quickly."

"Well, what I'm going to say," quoth Sancho, "is as true as my master Don Quixote here will not let me lie."

"As far as I am concerned, Sancho, you may lie to your heart's content, I will not put an obstacle in your way, but take heed what you are going to say."

"I've so heeded and re-heeded it," said Sancho, "that I'm safe and sound as the bell-ringer in the watch-tower, as you'll see from the sequel."

"I should advise your highnesses to give orders for the removal of this idiot," exclaimed Don Quixote, "for he will utter a deal of absurdities."

"By the life of the duke," said the duchess, "let no one attempt to take Sancho from me. I am very fond of him, for I know he is very wise."

"Wise may the days of your holiness be,"[8] said Sancho, "for the good opinion you have of me, though I don't deserve it. This is my story. A gentleman of my village sent an invitation . . . a wealthy man he was, and of quality too, for he was one of the Alamos of Medina del Campo, and married Doña Mencía de Quiñones, the daughter of Don Alonso de Marañón, Knight of the Order of Santiago, that was drowned in the Herradura . . . about whom there was that quarrel, years ago, in our village, in which, as far as I can understand, my master Don Quixote was mixed up, and out of which little Thomas the scapegrace received a wound, the son of Balbastro the blacksmith he was. . . . Isn't all this true, my dear master? By your life say so . . . otherwise these lords here may take me for a lying chatterbox."

"So far," said the ecclesiastic, "I take you more for a chatterbox than a liar, but later on I do not know what I shall take you for."

"You quote so many witnesses and proofs, Sancho," said Don Quixote, "that I have to admit that you must be telling the truth; go on and shorten the story, for at the rate you are going it will take you two days to finish it."

"He must not shorten it," said the duchess. "On the contrary, to please me, he should tell it in his own way, even though it takes him six days to finish it. They would, indeed, be the best I ever spent in my life."

"Well, then, I say, gentlemen," continued Sancho, "that

---

[8] Sancho in his attempt to appear well-bred to the duke and duchess uses absurdly incongruous forms of address.

this said gentleman, whom I know as well as I do my own hands, for 'tis but a bow-shot from my house to his, invited a poor but decent labourer . . ."

"Get on, brother," cried the ecclesiastic, "at the rate you are going you will not stop your story till the next world."

"I'll stop less than half-way, please God," said Sancho. "And so I say that this labourer arriving at the house of the aforesaid gentleman who had invited him . . . God rest his soul, for he's now dead; and more by token, they say, he had an angel's death . . . I wasn't there, for just at that time I had gone off to reap at Tembleque . . ."

"By your life, my son," cried the ecclesiastic, "come back quickly from Tembleque and finish your story, without burying the gentleman, unless you want to have more funerals."

"Well, it so happened," said Sancho, "that as the two of them were, as I said, about to sit down to table . . . sure, I fancy I can see them clearer than ever . . ."

The duke and duchess were highly amused at the irritation displayed by the worthy ecclesiastic at Sancho's pauses and long-winded manner of telling his story. As for Don Quixote, he was chafing with wrath and vexation.

"Well, as I was saying," continued Sancho, "as the two were about to sit down to table, as I said, the labourer insisted that the gentleman should take the head of the table, and the gentleman insisted upon the labourer's taking it, for in his own house the other should do as he was bid, but the labourer, who prided himself on his politeness and good-breeding, would not allow it, so the gentleman out of sheer exasperation, put both his hands on his guest's shoulders and forced him to sit down, saying: 'Sit down, you clodhopper, for where I sit that is the head of the table!' So there's the story, and 'pon my word, I think it comes pat here."

Don Quixote turned a thousand colours, and his tanned face looked like jasper. The duke and duchess suppressed their merriment for fear lest Don Quixote might get in a temper, once he saw through Sancho's mischievous meaning. So to change the conversation, and to keep Sancho from uttering further absurdities, the duchess asked Don Quixote what news he had of the Lady Dulcinea, and if he had sent her lately any presents of giants or evil-doers, for he must have conquered many.

To which Don Quixote replied: "Señora, my misfortunes, though they had a beginning, will never have an end. I have conquered giants, and I have sent her miscreants and evil-doers, but where could they find her if she is enchanted and transformed into the ugliest peasant wench that can be imagined?"

"I don't know," said Sancho, "to me she seems the most beautiful creature in the world,—at any rate in agility and in leaping she's the equal of any tumbler. I' faith, Señora duchess, she leaps from the ground on to an ass like a cat."

"Have you seen her enchanted, Sancho?" asked the duke.

"Have I seen her!" answered Sancho. "Who the devil was it but myself that first thought of the enchantment business? She's as much enchanted as my father."

The ecclesiastic, when he heard them speaking of giants and evil-doers and enchantments, suspected that this must be Don Quixote of La Mancha, whose history the duke was continually reading; and he himself had often taken him to task, telling him how foolish it was to read such fooleries, and convincing himself of the truth of his suspicion, he addressed the duke very angrily, saying: "Your Excellency, sir, will have to give an account to God for what this good man is doing. This Don Quixote, or Don Idiot, or whatever you call him, is not, to my mind, so big a blockhead as your Excellency would make out, when you encourage him to continue his extravagant absurdities." Then turning to Don Quixote he said: "And you, crack-skull, who put it into your pate that you are a knight-errant, and that you conquer giants and capture miscreants? Go on your way, with good luck to you as my parting words. Go back to your home and rear your children if you have any, and look after your estate, and give up roaming through the world, with mouth agape, swallowing wind, and making those who know you, and those who do not, laugh at you. Where in heaven's name have you found that there are or ever were knights-errant? Where are there giants in Spain, or marauders in La Mancha, or enchanted Dulcineas, or all the medley of daft deeds that they tell about you?"

Don Quixote listened attentively to the words of that reverend gentleman, and no sooner did he perceive that the latter had done talking than, regardless of the presence of the duke and duchess, he sprang to his feet, trembling from head to foot like a man dosed with mercury, and said in an excited, stammering voice: "The place where I am, those in whose presence I find myself, and the respect I have and have always had for the profession to which your reverence belongs, bind the hands of my just indignation. For this reason and because I know, as all know, that the weapon of gownsmen is the same as that of women, namely, the tongue, so with mine I will enter into equal combat with your reverence, from whom we might have expected good counsels rather than infamous abuse. Pious and well-intentioned blame requires different behaviour and other methods. In any case, by rebuking me publicly and in such bitter terms you have exceeded the bounds of just rebuke, for that should consist of gentleness rather than of rudeness. And it is not right, without knowing aught of the sin which is reproved, to call the sinner blockhead and idiot. Now tell me, your reverence, for which of the follies you have noticed in me do you condemn and abuse me, and bid me go home and look after my house and wife and children, without knowing whether I have any? Is nought else needed than to slip into other men's houses by hook or by crook and rule over the masters, and, after having been reared in the straitened circumstances of some seminary, and without having ever seen more of the world than is contained within twenty or thirty leagues around, to proceed to lay down the law for chivalry, and pass judgment on knights-errant? Is it, perchance, a vain business, or is the time ill-spent, which is spent in roaming the world, not seeking its pleasures but its hard toils by which good men ascend to the abode of immortality? If knight, if grandees, if nobles and men of high birth considered me an idiot, I should consider it as an irreparable affront; but I do not care a farthing if clerks who have never entered or trod the paths of chivalry should mark me down as an idiot. Knight I am and knight I will die, if it pleases Almighty God. Some choose the broad road of proud ambition; some that of mean and servile flattery; some that of deceitful hypocrisy, and a small number that of true religion; but I, influenced by my star, follow the narrow path of knight-errantry, and in practising that calling I despise wealth but not honour. I have redeemed injuries, righted wrongs, chastised insolence, conquered giants and trampled on monsters. I am in love, for no other reason than that it is an obligation for knights-errant to be so; but though I am, I am no lustful lover, but one of the chaste, platonic kind. My intentions are always directed towards virtuous ends, to do good to all and evil to none. If he who so intends, so acts, and so lives deserves to be called an idiot, it is for your highnesses to say, most excellent duke and duchess."

"By God, that's great," cried Sancho. "Say no more, dear lord and master, in your defence, for there's no more in the world to be said, thought or persevered in, and, besides, when this gentleman denies, as he has done, that there are or ever have been knights-errant in the world, can we wonder that he knows nought of what he has been talking about?"

"Are you by any chance, brother," said the ecclesiastic, "the Sancho Panza they talk about, to whom your master has promised an island?"

"Aye, so I am," replied Sancho, "and I'm the one who deserves it as well as anyone else. I'm one of your 'Stick to the good and you'll be one of them', and I'm of the 'Not with whom you're bred, but with whom you've fed' tribe, and of your 'He who leans on a good tree, good shelter has he'. I've leant on my master, and many a month I've been going in his company, and, please God, I'll turn out just such another as he; long life to him and long life to myself, for he'll have no lack of empires to command, nor I of islands to govern."

317

"No, Sancho, my friend, certainly not," said the duke, "for I, in the name of Don Quixote, confer upon you the governorship of an odd one of mine, which is of no mean quality."

"Kneel down, Sancho," said Don Quixote, "and kiss his excellency's feet for the boon he has conferred upon you."

Sancho did as he was told, but on seeing this the ecclesiastic rose from the table in a rage, exclaiming: "By the habit I wear, I must say that your Excellency is as fooled as those two sinners. Is it a wonder that they are mad, when we see sane people sanctioning their madness? Let your Excellency stop with them, but as long as they remain in this house I shall stay in mine, and save myself the trouble of rebuking what I cannot remedy." And without saying another word or eating another morsel, he went off, in spite of all the entreaties of the duke and duchess. It must be admitted, however, that the duke did not say much, owing to his amusement at the other's uncalled-for rage.

When he had finished laughing, he said to Don Quixote: "You have answered for yourself so nobly, Sir Knight of the Lions, that there is no need to demand further satisfaction, for this, though it appears an offence, is not one at all: for, as women can give no offence, no more can ecclesiastics, as you yourself know better than I."

"That is true," said Don Quixote, "and the reason is, that he who cannot be offended cannot give offence to anyone. And, although a little while ago I said that I might have received offence, I now say certainly not; for which reasons I ought not to feel, nor do I feel, aggrieved at what that worthy man has said to me. I only wish that he had stayed a little longer that I might have convinced him of his error in thinking and saying that there are not and never have been knights-errant in the world. If Amadis or any of his countless descendants had heard his words, I am sure I know it would not have gone well with his reverence."

"I'll swear it wouldn't," said Sancho. "Why, they would have given him a slash that would have slit him from top to bottom like a pomegranate or an over-ripe melon. They were not the fellows to stand such jokes! I'm sure if Rinaldo of Montalvan had heard the words of the little man, he would have landed him such a clout on the mouth that he wouldn't have spoken for the next three years: let him have a scrap with them and he'll see how he'll get out of their hands!"

The duchess, as she listened to Sancho, was ready to die with laughter, and in her mind she considered him a funnier fool and a greater madman than his master, and there were many there who were of the same opinion.

Don Quixote at length became appeased, and the dinner came to an end. When the cloth was removed, four maidens came in, one holding a silver basin, another a jug also of silver, a third with two fine white towels on her shoulder, and the fourth with her arms bared to the elbow, and in her white hands (they certainly were white) a round ball of Naples soap. The girl with the basin approached, and with grace and arch impudence shoved it under Don Quixote's beard. Though he was mystified by such a ceremony, he said not a word, for he supposed it was a custom of that country to wash beards instead of hands, and so he stretched out his own as far as he could; and at the same instant the jug began to pour water upon it, and the maiden with the soap rubbed his beard rapidly, raising snow-flakes, for the lather was no less white, not only over the beard, but all over the face and eyes of the submissive knight, who was obliged to keep them tightly shut. The duke and the duchess, who had not been informed of this ceremony, waited to see how this strange washing would end. The barber-maiden, when she had covered him with a handful of lather, pretended that there was no more water, and told the girl with the jug to go for some more, while Señor Don Quixote would wait. She did so, and Don Quixote remained there, the strangest and most laughable figure imaginable. All present, and there were many, stood watching him, and when they saw him there with half a yard of neck, and that exceedingly brown, his eyes shut and his beard full of lather, it was a marvel of discretion that they were able to stifle their laughter. The damsels who were in the joke kept their eyes lowered, not daring to look at their master and mistress; the latter felt anger and laughter surging within them, and they knew not what to do, whether to punish the girls for their impudence, or to reward them for the amusement they derived from seeing Don Quixote in such a plight.

At last the maiden with the jug returned and they finished washing Don Quixote, and then the girl with the towels wiped him and dried him thoroughly; and all four together, after dropping him a deep curtsey, were about to depart, when the duke, who was afraid Don Quixote might see through the joke, called the maiden with the jug, saying: "Come and wash me, and mind there is enough water." The girl, who was quick-witted and active, came and placed the basin for the duke as she had done for Don Quixote, and in a trice they had him well soaped and washed, and after wiping and drying him, they made their curtsey and departed. It was known later that the duke had sworn that if they had not washed him as they had washed Don Quixote he would have punished them for their saucy impudence, which they had cleverly atoned for by soaping him as well.

Sancho observed the ceremony of the washing with deep attention, and he said to himself: "God bless us! If it were only the custom in this country to wash the beards of squires as well as of knights! For, by God and my soul, I've sore need of it, and I'd take it as a kinder favour if they were to give us a bit of a scrape with the razor."

"What are you muttering to yourself, Sancho?" asked the duchess.

"I was saying, my lady," he replied, "that in the courts of other princes I've always heard tell that when the cloth is removed they give water for the hands but not suds for the beards. And so 'tis good to live much to see much, though, to be sure, they say too that he who lives a long life must face much strife. Still, to face one of these same washings must be rather pleasure than pain."

"Do not worry, friend Sancho," said the duchess; "I will make my maids wash you, and even put you in the bath if necessary."

"I'll be content with the beard," said Sancho, "at any rate for the present. As for the future, 'tis God's will what'll happen."

"Carry out the worthy Sancho's request, seneschal," said the duchess, "and do exactly what he wishes."

The seneschal replied that Señor Sancho should be served in everything, and with that he went off to dinner, taking Sancho with him, while the duke and duchess and Don Quixote remained at table talking of many and various things, but all touching on the profession of arms and knight-errantry.

The duchess begged Don Quixote to describe the beauty and features of the Lady Dulcinea del Toboso, for by her reputation abroad, she must be the fairest creature in the world, even in La Mancha. Don Quixote sighed when he heard the duchess's request, and said: "If I could tear out my heart, and lay it on a plate on the table before your highness's eyes, I would spare my tongue the trouble of saying what can hardly be thought of, for your excellency would see her portrayed in full. But why should I now attempt to describe feature by feature the beauty of the peerless Dulcinea? That is a burden worthy of other shoulders than mine."

"Nevertheless," said the duke, "Señor Don Quixote would give us great pleasure if he would depict her for us; I am sure that even in a rough sketch she will be the envy of the fairest."

"I would do it, certainly," said Don Quixote, "had the mishap which befell her lately not blurred her in my mind's eye, a mishap that makes me ready to weep for her rather than describe her. For your highnesses must know that a few days ago when I went back to kiss her hands and receive her blessing and permission for this third sally, I found her enchanted and transformed from a princess into a peasant girl, from fair to foul, from angel to devil, from fragrant to pestiferous, from well-spoken to boorish, from gentle to tomboyish, from light to darkness . . . in short, from Dulcinea del Toboso into a coarse Sayagan wench."[9]

"There is," said the duchess, "one doubt which persists in my mind, and I cannot help feeling somewhat of a grudge against Sancho Panza. My doubt arises from the fact that in the First Part of the aforesaid history it is related that Sancho Panza, when he carried on your worship's behalf a letter to the said Lady Dulcinea, found her winnowing a sack of wheat, and, by token, the story says it was red wheat; a thing which makes me doubt the greatness of her lineage."

To this Don Quixote replied: "My lady, your highness must know that everything or almost everything that happens to me exceeds the ordinary limits of what happens to other knights-errant, whether it is ruled by the inscrutable will of destiny, or by the malice of some envious enchanter. Now, since it is an established fact that most famous knights-errant have some special gifts, I infer that I may perhaps have some gift of this kind. It is certainly not that of being invulnerable, for on many occasions experience has proved to me that I am of tender flesh and not at all impenetrable. Neither is it the gift of being proof against enchantment, for I have already seen myself cast into a cage into which the whole world would not have been powerful enough to put me save by force of enchantment. But since I managed to free myself from that, I am inclined to believe that there is no other power that can harm me. Now these enchanters, seeing that they cannot use their vile magic upon my person, revenge themselves on what I love most, and try to rob me of life by ill-treating that of Dulcinea by whom I live. And so I am convinced that when my squire carried my message to her, they changed her into a peasant girl, engaged in so mean an occupation as winnowing wheat; though I have already said that this wheat was neither red wheat nor wheat at all but grains of Orient pearl. As a proof of all this, I must tell your highnesses that, when I went to El Toboso a little while ago, I could not find the palace of Dulcinea, and the next day, though Sancho, my squire, saw her in her proper shape, which is the most beautiful in the world, to me she appeared as a coarse, ugly peasant wench, and by no means well spoken, she who is refinement itself. All this I have said for fear any should mind what Sancho said about Dulcinea's winnowing, for as they changed her to me, it is no wonder if they changed her to him. Besides, I want your highnesses to understand that Sancho Panza is one of the drollest squires that ever served a knight-errant. Sometimes of so acute a simplicity that it is no small enjoyment to guess whether he is simple or cunning, he has roguish tricks which condemn him as a knave, and

[9] Sayago, in the province of Zamora, was where Castilian was worst spoken, and the people there were considered very uncouth and rustic.

321

blundering ways which confirm him a fool. He doubts everything and yet believes everything; when I imagine he is crashing head-foremost into folly, he bobs up with some shrewd or witty thing which sends him shooting up to the skies. After all, I would not exchange him for another squire, even if they were to give me a city to boot, and for this reason I am in doubt whether it will be well to send him to the government your highness has conferred upon him, though I perceive that he possesses a certain talent for this business of governing. With a little trimming of his understanding he should manage his governorship as successfully as the King does his taxes, especially as we know by long experience that to be a governor does not require much cleverness or book learning, for there are a hundred about here who can hardly read, and yet govern as ruthlessly as gerfalcons."

The conversation between the duke, the duchess and Don Quixote had reached this point, when they heard many voices and a great din in the palace. All of a sudden Sancho burst abruptly into the hall, quivering with excitement, with a straining-cloth for a bib, and followed by a number of lads, or rather kitchen scullions and other underlings, one of whom carried a small pail full of water, which from its colour and dirt was evidently dish-water. The lad with the pail pursued him and chased him hither and thither, trying hard to shove it under his beard, and another one of the scullions made an attempt to wash it.

"What does this mean, brothers?" asked the duchess. "What do you want to do to this good man? What! Do you not know that he is governor-elect?"

To which the barber-scullion replied: "The gentleman won't let himself be washed, as the custom is, and as the duke my master was washed and the gentleman his master."

"Yes, I will," answered Sancho, in a blaze of wrath, "but I'd like it to be done with cleaner towels, with cleaner lye and hands not so dirty, for there's not so much difference between me and my master that he should be washed with angel's water[10] and me with devil's lye. The customs of the countries and the palaces of princes are only good when they do not cause annoyance, but the custom of the washing which they follow here is worse than that of the flogging of penitents[11] I'm clean in the beard and I don't need such refreshings. And whoever tries to wash me or touch a hair of my head—I mean of my beard—speaking with all due respect, I'll give him such a puck that my fist will be rammed in his

10 Water scented with rose, thyme and orange.
11 In Holy Week it was customary for penitents ("disciplinantes") to flog themselves as they walked in procession through the streets. To cleanse oneself thus from sin was called by the folk "jabonadura" or "soaping."

skull, for such *cirimonies* and soapings look more like horse-play than entertainment."

The duchess was ready to die with laughter when she saw the rage of Sancho and heard his words, but Don Quixote was not pleased to see his squire so vilely adorned with the spotted towel and surrounded by the kitchen underlings, so after making a low bow to the duke and duchess, as though he begged for permission to speak, he addressed the rabble in a dignified tone: "Ho there, gentlemen! Leave this lad alone, and go back to where you came from, or wherever else you will: my squire is as clean as any other person, and these little pails are as irritating to him as a narrow-mouthed drinking-cup would be. Take my advice and leave him alone, for neither he nor I understand this joking business."

Sancho caught the word from his master, and continued, saying: "Just let them come and play their jokes on the loutish clodhopper: I'll stand up to the lot of them, as sure as it's now night-time! Let them bring me a comb here, or whatever they please, and curry this beard of mine, and if they get anything out of it that offends against cleanliness, let them clip me crosswise."[12]

At this the duchess, laughing all the while, said: "Sancho Panza is right in all he has said, and will be right in all he shall say. He is clean, and, as he says himself, he does not need to be washed, and if our ways do not suit him, his soul is his own. Besides, you ministers of cleanliness have been exceedingly remiss and thoughtless, I do not know whether I should not say audacious, to bring pails and wooden utensils and kitchen dish-clouts, instead of basins and jugs of pure gold and towels of holland, to such a person and such a beard. Indeed, after all, you are a low ill-bred crew, and since you are rascals, you cannot help showing the grudge you bear against the squires of knights-errant."

The roguish scullions, and even the seneschal who was with them, believed that the duchess was speaking in earnest, so they took the straining-cloth off Sancho's chest, and all full of confusion they fled from the hall.

Sancho, when he found himself released from what, in his opinion, was a great peril, threw himself on his knees before the duchess, and said: "From great ladies we expect great favours. I cannot repay what your ladyship has done for me this day but by longing to see myself dubbed a knight-errant so that I might spend all the days of my life serving so high a lady. I'm a labouring man, my name is Sancho Panza, I'm married, I've children, and I'm serving as a squire. If in any of those ways I can serve your highness, I'll be no longer in obeying than your ladyship in commanding."

[12] This was the punishment meted out to blasphemers and usurers in ancient times.

"It is easy to see, Sancho," said the duchess, "that you have learnt to be courteous in the very school of courtesy. It is easy to see, I mean, that you have been reared in the bosom of Señor Don Quixote, who is, of course, the cream of compliments and the flower of ceremonies, or *cirimonies,* as you say. May such a master and such a servant be fortunate! One is the cynosure of knight-errantry and the other is the star of squirely loyalty. Rise, friend Sancho: I will repay your courtesy by making the duke, my lord, grant you as soon as he can the favour of governorship which was promised."

And so the conversation ended. Don Quixote went away to take his siesta, but the duchess begged Sancho, if he was not eager to sleep, to come and spend the afternoon with her and her damsels in a very cool chamber. Sancho replied that, true enough, he usually slept four or five hours in the heat of the summer days, but to serve her excellency he would try his hardest not to snooze even a single hour that day, and would come in obedience to her command.

IX. *The amusing discourse that passed between the duchess and Sancho, and the disenchantment of Dulcinea*

WHEN SANCHO, IN ACCORDANCE WITH HIS PROMISE, VISITED the duchess in her apartments that afternoon, she was so delighted to listen to his talk that she made him sit down beside her on a low seat, though Sancho out of pure good-breeding wanted not to sit down. The duchess, however, told him he was to sit down as governor and talk as squire, for in both respects he deserved even the throne of the Cid Ruy Diaz the Campeador. Sancho shrugged his shoulders, obeyed and sat down, and all the damsels and duennas of the duchess crowded round him, listening in deep silence to what he would say. But it was the duchess who was the first to speak.

"Now that we are alone," said she, "and there is no one here to hear us, I wish Sir Governor would resolve some doubts I have, rising out of the history of the great Don Quixote that is now in print. One of these doubts is that since the good Sancho never saw Dulcinea, I mean the Lady Dulcinea del Toboso, nor took Don Quixote's letter to her, for it was left in the memorandum book in the Sierra Morena, how did he dare to invent the answer and all that about finding her winnowing wheat, seeing that the whole story was a joke and a lie, and so much to the prejudice of the peerless

Dulcinea's reputation, and so injurious to the quality and loyalty of a good squire?"

When he heard these words, Sancho, without answering, got up from his chair, and with noiseless steps, with his body hunched up and a finger placed to his lips, went all round the room lifting the hangings, after which he returned to his seat, and said: "Now, my lady, that I've seen there is not a soul listening to us on the sly, only the bystanders, I'll answer what you've asked me without fear or dread. And the first thing I'll say is that I consider my master Don Quixote to be stark staring mad, though at times he says things that to my mind, and indeed to everybody's, are so wise, and run in such a straight furrow, that Satan himself could not have said them better. Nevertheless, truly and without question I'm convinced he's daft. Now, since I've got this fixed in my pate I can risk making him believe things that have no head nor tail, like that business about the answer to the letter, and the other of six or eight days ago, which is not yet written out in history, namely, the enchantment of my Lady Dulcinea, for I made him believe she's enchanted, though there's no more truth in it than over the hills of Ubeda."[1]

The duchess then said: "Owing to what worthy Sancho has told me, a doubt keeps springing up in my mind, and a kind of whisper reaches my ears which says: 'If Don Quixote is mad, crazy and cracked, and Sancho Panza, his squire, knows it, and yet serves and follows him, and relies on his vain promises, there is no doubt that he is more of a madman and a fool than his master. Since that is so, it will be bad for you, my lady duchess, if you give the said Sancho an island to govern, for how can he who does not know how to govern himself be able to govern others?' "

"By God, my lady," said Sancho, "that doubt of yours had a timely birth. But your ladyship should speak out plain and clear. I know what you say is the honest truth, and if I had a head on my shoulders I'd have left my master this long time. But this is my fate and my bad luck: I can't help it. I must follow him; we're from the same village; I've eaten his bread; I love him well; I'm grateful to him; he gave me his ass-colts, and above all I'm faithful, and so it's quite impossible for anything to separate us except the man with the pickaxe and shovel.[2] And if your highness does not want to give me the government you promised, God made me without it, and perhaps if you don't give it to me 'twill be all the better

---

[1] To go over the hills of Ubeda ("ir por los cerros de Ubeda") means, according to Covarrubias, to say anything without foundation. There are no hills round Ubeda. The words, it would seem, are the beginning of an old forgotten ballad and are used proverbially like our English phrase "the flowers that bloom in the spring . . ."

[2] A synonym for the grave-digger.

325

for my conscience, for though I'm a fool I know the proverb 'to her hurt the ant grew wings',[3] and maybe Sancho the squire will get to heaven sooner than Sancho the governor: 'they bake as good bread here as in France'; and 'by night all cats are grey'; and "tis hard luck on the man who hasn't broken fast by two in the afternoon'; and 'there's no stomach a hand's breadth bigger than another', and it can be filled 'with straw or hay', as the saying goes; and 'the little birds of the field have God for their purveyor and feeder'; and 'four yards of Cuenca cloth keep a man warmer than four of Segovia broadcloth';[4] and 'on leaving this world and going under, the prince travels as narrow a path as the journeyman'; and 'the Pope's body fills no more feet of soil than the sacristan's'; and no matter if the one is higher than the other, for when we go into the pit we all have to shrink, and make ourselves small, or they make us shrink in spite of us, and then . . . good-night to us. And I say again that if your ladyship does not want to give me the island because I'm a fool, I'll know how to care nought about it like a wise man. I've heard it said that 'behind the Cross stands the Devil', and that 'all that glitters is not gold', and that from among the oxen, the ploughs and the yokes, Wamba the husbandman was made King of Spain, and from among the brocades, and jollities, and riches, Roderick was taken to be devoured by snakes, if the verses of the old ballads don't lie."

"To be sure they don't lie," cried Doña Rodríguez, the duenna, who was one of the listeners. "There's a ballad that says they put King Roderick alive into a tomb full of toads, snakes and lizards, and that, two days after, the king cried out from within the tomb in a low, plaintive voice:

'They nibble me now, they nibble me now,
    In the part where I most did sin.'

According to that, the gentleman here is quite right in wishing to be a labouring man rather than a king, if he is to be eaten by vermin."

The duchess could not restrain her laughter at her duenna's simplicity, nor from marvelling at the language and proverbs of Sancho, to whom she said: "Worthy Sancho knows that what a knight ever promises he tries to fulfil, even at the cost of his own life. The duke, my lord and husband, though he is not a knight-errant, is none the less a knight, and so will keep his word about the promised island, in spite of the envy and malice of the world. Be of good heart, Sancho; when you least expect it you will find yourself seated on the throne of

[3] Because when she flew the birds gobbled her up. The proverb warns those who rise through luck to a position above their deserts. They meet with the ruin they would have avoided had they remained in obscurity.

[4] Cuenca coarse cloth was the cheapest and Segovia material was the finest and most expensive.

326

your island, and you will grasp firm hold of your governorship, and you may even expect to exchange it for another of three-bordered brocade.[5] But I charge you to mind how you govern your vassals, for I warn you they are all loyal and well-born."

"About that business of governing them well," said Sancho, "there's no need to charge me to do it, for I'm naturally charitable, and full of pity for the poor; and 'don't go stealing the loaf from him who kneads and bakes'; and by the Sign of the Cross they're not going to load the dice against me. I'm an old dog, so I know all about their whistle; I can keep my eyes skinned if need be, and I don't let black spots flicker before my eyes, for I know where the shoe pinches. I'm saying this, because I'll be always ready to give the good a helping hand, but I won't let the bad put a foot near me. Besides, my view is that in this business of governing the beginning is what counts, and maybe after being governor for a fortnight I'll lick my fingers for such a tasty job, and know more about it than about ploughing and reaping for which I was reared."

"You are right, Sancho," said the duchess, "for no one is born educated, and bishops are made out of men and not out of stones. But let us return to the subject we were discussing a short while ago, namely, the enchantment of the Lady Dulcinea. I am convinced that your idea of deceiving your master by making him believe that the peasant girl was Dulcinea, and that if he did not recognize her it must have been because she was enchanted, was all a contrivance of one of the enchanters who persecute Don Quixote. For I know from a good source that the coarse country wench who leaped on the ass was and is Dulcinea del Toboso, and that you, my good Sancho, though you fancy yourself the deceiver, are the one who is deceived. And remember that we, too, have enchanters here who wish us well and tell us clearly and unmistakably what happens in the world; so believe me, Sancho, that leaping country lass was and is Dulcinea del Toboso, who is as much enchanted as the mother that bore her. When we least expect it, we shall see her in her own proper figure, and then Sancho will come out of the delusion in which he lives."

"That may well be," said Sancho Panza, "and now I'm willing to believe what my master says about what he saw in the Cave of Montesinos, when he says he saw the Lady Dulcinea del Toboso in the dress that I said I had seen her in when I enchanted her all at my own sweet will. Now, it must have been all the reverse, as your ladyship says, for it cannot be supposed that I could with my weak and feeble wits con-

[5] This phrase means that Sancho will exchange his governorship at a later date for one that is more profitable. In La Mancha it is a common saying when a child appears in a new suit of clothes, for his relations to greet him and wish him luck in the words: "May you reject it for another of finer stuff" ("que le deseche con otro de tela superior").

trive so clever a trick in a moment, nor do I think my master is so mad as to believe that I could do so. But, my lady, your excellency must not think me ill-natured, for a blockhead like me is not bound to understand the wicked plots of those wicked enchanters. I contrived all that to avoid a scolding from my master, Don Quixote, but not with any intention of injuring him. If the whole business has gone awry, there is a God in heaven who judges our hearts."

"That is true," said the duchess, "but tell me, Sancho, what do you think about the Cave of Montesinos, for I should be glad to know."

Sancho then told her, word for word, what we have already related about that adventure, and when she heard it the duchess said: "From this incident we may infer that, since the great Don Quixote says he saw there the same peasant wench whom Sancho saw on the way from El Toboso, it is, no doubt, Dulcinea, and that there are very active and interfering enchanters about here."

"That's what I say," said Sancho, "and if my Lady Dulcinea is enchanted, that will be so much the worse for her. It's not my job to engage in a brawl with my master's enemies, who must be many and in great numbers. The honest truth is that the one I saw was a peasant wench, and I took her for a peasant wench. And if that was Dulcinea, do not blame me and raise a fuss about it. Nevertheless, there they are, blathering at me every instant, saying: 'Sancho said it, Sancho did it, Sancho come, Sancho go!' As if Sancho was a nobody, and not that same Sancho who's now roaming all over the world in books, according to Samson Carrasco, and he for sure is one bachelored by Salamanca, and fellows of that kind surely don't tell lies, except when the whim bites them or it's well worth their while. So there's no reason why anybody should barge into me. Besides, I've a good reputation, and as I've heard my master say: 'a good name's worth more nor great riches'. If they only shove me into this government they'll see wonders, for he who has been a good squire will be a good governor."

"Now, Sancho," said the duchess, "'twere best for you to go and take your rest, and we shall talk at greater length by and by, and give orders how you may soon go and shove yourself, as you say, into the government."

Sancho again kissed the duchess's hand, and besought her to grant him the favour of seeing that good care was taken of his Dapple, for he was the light of his eyes.

"What is Dapple?" said the duchess.

"My ass," replied Sancho. "Instead of giving him that name, I'm used to call him Dapple. I asked this lady duenna here to take care of him when I entered the castle, but she flew into a temper as if I had called her old or ugly, though it should be more natural for duennas to feed asses than to give orders in halls. God bless us and save us! What an edge a gentleman of my village had against those ladies!"

"He must have been some gross fellow," said Doña Rodríguez, the duenna. "If he had been a gentleman he would have set them above the horns of the moon."

"Now let us have no more of this," said the duchess: "hush, Doña Rodríguez, and you, Señor Panza, calm yourself, and leave Dapple to my charge. As he is Sancho's treasure, I'll put him on the apple of my eye."

"Provided he's in the stable I'm satisfied," replied Sancho, "for neither he nor myself is worthy to remain one instant on the apple of your eye, and I'd prefer to stick daggers into myself than agree to it."

"Take him to your governorship, Sancho," said the duchess, "and there you'll be able to entertain him as you like, and even pension him off."

"Don't think, my lady, that you've exaggerated," said Sancho; "I've seen more than two asses go to governorships so there's nothing strange in my taking mine with me."

Sancho's words made the duchess laugh, and after sending him to bed, she went away to report to the duke the conversation that had passed between herself and the squire.

With the duke she plotted and arranged to play a joke upon Don Quixote which would be unusual and in accordance with knight-errantry style, and she took as her starting-point the story Don Quixote had told them about the Cave of Montesinos. What astonished the duchess more than anything else was the credulity of Sancho, who actually believed that Dulcinea had been enchanted, whereas it was he himself who had been the enchanter and the play-boy in all that affair. She and the duke, therefore, gave orders to their servants as to how they should behave, and six days later they took Don Quixote to a hunt with as great a retinue of huntsmen and beasts as any crowned king could muster.

They gave Don Quixote a hunting suit and Sancho one of the finest green cloth; but Don Quixote refused to put his on, saying that he would soon have to return to the hard exercise of arms, and could not carry wardrobes and stores with him. As for Sancho, he took what they gave him, intending to sell it as soon as he had an opportunity.

The appointed day arrived. Don Quixote put on his armour and Sancho dressed himself, mounted Dapple (for he would not give him up though they offered him a horse) and joined the band of huntsmen. The duchess came out richly attired, and Don Quixote, courteous and gallant as always, held the rein of her palfrey,[6] though the duke did not wish to allow it.

6 This was the highest token of respect that a knight could give to a lady.

At last they reached a wood between two high mountains, where, after arranging hiding-places and snares, and scattering the people to their various beats, the hunt began with great noise, shouting and tally-ho, so that with the barking of the hounds and the blaring of the horns they could not hear one another speak. The duchess dismounted, and with a sharp hunting spear in her hand, took up her station in a place where she knew the wild boars were accustomed to pass.[7] The duke and Don Quixote likewise dismounted and posted themselves by her side. Sancho took up a position behind all of them, without dismounting from Dapple, whom he did not dare to leave lest some mishap might befall him.

Scarcely had they taken their places on foot in the line of their retainers, when they saw a gigantic boar, pressed by the hounds and followed by the huntsmen, careering towards them, gnashing his teeth and tusks, and dashing the foam from his mouth. As soon as he saw him Don Quixote braced his shield on his arm, drew his sword, and advanced to meet him: the duke with his hunting spear did likewise, but the duchess would have gone in front of all of them had the duke not prevented her. Sancho alone, when he saw the beast at bay, jumped off Dapple, took to his heels as hard as he could, and in sheer desperation tried in vain to scramble up a tall oak tree. But half-way up, while he clung to a branch, as bad luck would have it, the branch snapped, and in his fall he was caught by a stump of the tree and remained suspended in the air unable to reach the ground. Finding himself in this position and feeling his suit was beginning to rip, and thinking that the ferocious beast would reach him if he came that way, he began to bellow so lustily for help that all who heard and did not see him believed that some wild animal had its teeth in him. In the end the tusked boar fell pierced by the many spears that pressed upon him, and Don Quixote, turning round at the shouts of Sancho, saw him hanging from the oak head downwards, and Dapple, who did not forsake him in his calamity, standing close beside him. He went over and unhooked Sancho, who, when he found himself free and on the ground, examined the rent in his hunting-suit and was deeply grieved, for he thought that suit was worth an inheritance to him.

They laid the mighty boar upon a sumpter-mule, and having covered it with sprigs of rosemary and branches of myrtle, they bore it away as the spoils of victory to some large field-tents which had been pitched in the middle of the wood, where they found the tables laid and dinner served in such sumptuous style that it was easy to see the greatness and magnifi-

---

[7] By a law of 1611 firearms were prohibited in hunting. Two years after the publication of Part II of *Don Quixote*, in 1617, firearms were permitted.

cence of the host and hostess. Sancho, as he showed the rents in his torn suit to the duchess, remarked: "If it had only been hunting hares or little birds, my suit wouldn't be in such a pickle; I'm blest if I can see what pleasure there is in lying in wait for an animal that may murder you with his tusk if he gets a go at you. I remember once hearing an old ballad that says:

> 'By bears be you devoured
> Like Favila of old'."

"That was a Gothic king," said Don Quixote, "who, when following the chase, was eaten by a bear."

"That's just what I'm saying," answered Sancho, "and I'd sooner kings and princes didn't expose themselves to such dangers for the sake of a pleasure which, in my opinion, should not be one at all, for it consists in killing an animal that has done no harm to anyone."

"You are mistaken, Sancho," replied the duke, "for hunting is the most suitable and necessary exercise of all for kings and princes. The chase is the image of war: it has its stratagems, wiles, ambushes by which one can overcome the enemy in safety; in it we have to bear extreme cold and intolerable heat; indolence and sleep are scorned; bodily strength is invigorated; the limbs of one who takes part in it are made supple, and indeed it is an exercise which can be taken without harming anyone and with benefit to many. And the best point about it is that it is not for everybody, as other kinds of sport are, except hawking, which also is only for kings and great lords. So, Sancho, change your opinion, and when you are governor, go in for hunting, and you will soon find that one loaf will do you as much good as a hundred."[8]

"By no means," replied Sancho: "a good governor should have a broken leg and keep at home. Wouldn't it be a fine thing if people came to see him on business, foot-weary, and he's away in the woods enjoying himself? Sure, that way the government would go to hell altogether! By my faith, sir, hunting and amusements are more for lazybones than governors. Now my bit of amusement will be a game of trumps[9] at Easter, and bowls on Sundays and holidays. Them huntings and such-like don't suit my temper or my conscience."

"God grant it may be so," said the duke, "but there's many a slip 'twixt cup and lip."

"Come what may," answered Sancho, " 'a good payer needs no sureties', and God's help is better than rising at dawn —and . . . ' 'tis the belly carries the feet, not the feet the

8 This is an old slang phrase meaning "you will be a hundred times the better for it."

9 An old game called "Triunfo envidado," the ancient English country card game of Brag.

belly': I mean that if God helps me and I do what I ought honestly, there's no doubt I'll govern better than a robber chief.[10] Just let them stick a finger in my mouth and see if I bite or no."

"May the curse of God and His saints light upon you, Sancho," cried Don Quixote. "When will the day come, as I have often told you, when I shall hear you speak a single connected sentence without proverbs? I beseech you, my lord and lady, pay no heed to this idiot: he will grind your souls, not between two but between two thousand proverbs, which he drags in as much in season and as much to the purpose as . . . May God grant as much health to him as to me if I wish to hear them!"

"Sancho Panza's proverbs," said the duchess, "give me more pleasure than others that are more to the purpose and more reasonably introduced."

As they conversed in this pleasant manner they sallied forth from the tent into the wood, and they spent the day visiting the hunters' posts and ambushes. Then night fell, which was not so clear or calm as might have been expected at such a season (for it was then midsummer), but bringing with it a strange dim light which greatly helped the scheme of the duke and duchess. And so when it began to be dusk, a little after twilight, suddenly the whole wood seemed to be on fire, and from far and near countless trumpets and other military instruments sounded and resounded, as if many squadrons of cavalry were passing through the wood. The blaze of the fire and the noise of the martial clarions almost blinded the eyes and deafened the ears of all those that were in the wood. Soon all heard innumerable "lelilies", or cries such as the Moors utter when they ride into battle: trumpets and clarions blared, drums rattled, fifes skirled, so unceasingly and so fast that he could not have had any senses who did not lose them at the confused din of so many instruments. The duke was dumbfounded, the duchess astonished, Don Quixote wondered, Sancho trembled; in fact, even those who were in the know were frightened. Through fear, they kept silence when a postillion, disguised as a devil, passed in front of them, blowing, instead of a bugle, a huge hollow horn, which bellowed a harsh, terrifying sound.

"Ho there! brother courier," said the duke: "who are you? Where are you going? What warriors are those who seem to be passing through the wood?"

To which the courier answered in a deep, horrifying voice: "I am the Devil; I am searching for Don Quixote of La Mancha; those who come yonder are six troops of enchanters who are bringing on a triumphal car the peerless Dulcinea del

---

[10] To govern like a gerfalcon ("mejor que un gerifalte") was a slang phrase meaning "like a thief."

Toboso. She is enchanted and comes, together with the gallant Frenchman Montesinos, to give instructions to Don Quixote as to how she is to be disenchanted."

"If you were the Devil, as you say, and as your appearance shows," said the duke, "you would have recognized the said knight, Don Quixote of La Mancha, for he stands before you."

"By God and my conscience," replied the Devil, "I did not notice him, for my mind is so busy with many things that I forgot the main reason for my presence here."

"This surely must be an honest kind of Devil," said Sancho, "and a good Christian into the bargain, for if he wasn't, he wouldn't swear by God and his conscience. I'm certain that even in hell itself there must be some good folks."

The Devil then, without dismounting, turned to Don Quixote, saying: "To thee, the Knight of the Lions (may I see thee in their claws), the unlucky but valiant knight Montesinos sends me, bidding thee to tell thee to wait for him at the very spot where I may find thee, as he is bringing with him the lady called Dulcinea del Toboso, to show thee how thou may'st disenchant her. Now, since there is no further reason for my coming, I shall stay no more. May devils of my kind remain with thee, and good angels with these noble lords and ladies."

After these words he blew his monstrous horn, turned his back, and went away without waiting for an answer from anyone.

They all felt fresh wonder, especially Sancho and Don Quixote; Sancho because, in spite of the truth, they insisted that Dulcinea was enchanted; Don Quixote, because he was unable to convince himself whether all that had taken place in the Cave of Montesinos were true or not. While he was pondering deeply over these problems, the duke said to him: "Do you mean to wait, Señor Don Quixote?"

"Why not?" replied the knight. "Here will I wait, fearless and steadfast, though all hell should assail me."

"Well, if I see another devil and hear another horn like the last one, I'll wait here as much as in Flanders," said Sancho.

By now night had closed in more completely, and many lights began to flit through the wood, just as the dry exhalations from the earth, that look like shooting-stars to our eyes, flicker in the heavens. At the same instant a frightful noise was heard, like that made by the massive wheels of ox-waggons, which, it is said, put to flight even wolves and bears, so harsh and continuous is their creaking. In addition to this din, there was a further tumult which made the company feel as if in the four corners of the wood four separate battles were going on at the same time: in one quarter resounded the heavy thunder of artillery; in another countless muskets were crackling; close at hand could be heard the shouts of men fighting hand to hand; while in the distance they could hear the echoing Moorish war-cries. In a word, the bugles, horns, clarions, trumpets, drums, cannon, musketry, and, above all, the hideous creaking of the waggons, made up so confused and terrifying a din that Don Quixote had to harden his heart to face it. Sancho, however, gave way, and fell down in a faint on the hem of the duchess's skirts; but she sheltered him, and ordered her servants to throw water on his face. This was done, and he came to his senses just as one of the cars with the screeching wheels reached the spot where he lay. It was drawn by four plodding oxen, all covered with black trappings; on each horn they had fixed a large blazing torch of wax. On the top of the waggon a raised seat had been constructed, on which was seated a venerable old man with a beard whiter than the very snow, and so long that it fell below his waist. He was clad in a long robe of black buckram: for, as the cart was furnished with a host of candles, it was easy to make out everything that was in it. Guiding it were two ugly devils, also clad in buckram, with faces so hideous that Sancho, having caught one glimpse of them, shut his eyes tight so as not to see them again. When the waggon had come up to them, the venerable old man rose from his lofty seat, and, standing up, cried out in a loud voice: "I am the sage Lirgandeo", whereupon the cart passed on without another word. Behind it came another waggon of the same form, with another old man enthroned, who, when the cart stopped, said in no less solemn a tone: "I am the sage Alquife, the great friend of Urganda the Unknown". Whereupon the waggon passed on. Then a third cart appeared of the same sort, but the man seated on the throne was not old like the rest, but robust and of forbidding aspect. When he stood up like the others, he cried out in a voice that was hoarser and more devilish: "I am Arcalaus the Enchanter, the mortal enemy of Amadis of Gaul and all his kin", and passed on. The three waggons, after moving on a short distance, halted, and the jarring screech of their wheels ceased. Then they heard nothing but the sound of sweet concerted music, which gladdened the heart of Sancho, for he took it to be a good omen, and he said to the duchess, from whom he did not stir a step: "My lady, where there's music there can't be mischief".

"Neither where there are lights and brightness," replied the duchess.

To which Sancho answered: "Fire gives light, and bonfires give brightness, as we see by those that surround us, and, perhaps, they may burn us; but music is always the sign of feasting and merriment."

"Time will tell," said Don Quixote, who was listening.

Keeping time to the pleasing music, they saw advancing towards them what is called a triumphal car, drawn by six grey mules, caparisoned with white linen, on each of which was mounted a "torch-bearing penitent",[11] also clad in white, with a large lighted wax taper in his hand. The car was twice and even three times as large as the former ones, and in front of it and on the sides stood twelve more penitents, white as snow, all with their lighted tapers, a sight which aroused fear as well as wonder; and on a raised throne was seated a nymph clad in a thousand veils of silver-tissue, with countless leaves of gilded tinsel, which made her appear, if not richly, as least showily apparelled. She had her face covered with a fine, transparent veil, in such a way that its folds did not prevent the beautiful features of the maiden from being distinguished, while the multitude of lights enabled all to judge her beauty and her years, which seemed not to have reached twenty nor to be under seventeen. Beside her was a figure in a so-called robe of state [12] reaching to the ground, and with his head enveloped in a black veil. As soon as the car arrived in front of the duke, the duchess and Don Quixote, the music of the clarions stopped and then that of the harps and guitars on the car, and the figure in the robe stood up and, throwing it apart and removing the veil from his face, disclosed plainly before all the figure of Death itself, fleshless and hideous; at which sight Don Quixote felt uneasy, Sancho frightened, and the duke and duchess made a show of nervousness. This living Death, standing up, spoke in a sluggish, sleepy voice as follows:

"Merlin I am, miscalled the Devil's son
In lying annals authorized by time,
Of magic prince; of Zoroastric art
Monarch and archive, with a rival eye
I view the efforts of the age to hide
The doughty deeds of errant cavaliers
Who are, and ever have been, dear to me.
Enchanters, and magicians, and their folk
Are harsh, austere, malevolent,
But not so mine,—soft, tender, amorous
My nature, and its joy doing good to all.
In the dim caverns of the gloomy Dis,
Where now my soul abides amid my spells,

"My mystic squares and characters, there came
Unto my pitying ears the plaintive voice
Of peerless Dulcinea, the Tobosan maid.

11 In ancient days in Spain there were two classes of penitents at Seville: (1) torch-bearing penitents ("disciplinantes de luz") who carried lighted tapers in the processions; (2) blood penitents ("penitentes de sangre") who flagellated themselves in the procession so that their blood spurted over their white habits.
12 Robes of state worn by persons of distinction were called "trailers" ("rozagantes") because they reached the ground.

I learnt of her enchantment and sad fate,
How she from noble dame became transformed
To peasant wench; and touched with tender pity,
I searched the volumes of my devilish craft,
Closing my soul in this grim skeleton,
And hither have I come to give relief
To woes so great, and break the cursed spell.
O lady! Thou the glory and the pride of all
Who case their limbs in coats of steel and adamant!
Light, lantern, pilot, star and cynosure
Of those who scorn the sloth of feather beds,
And seek the hardy toils of blood-stained arms!

"To thee, I speak, great hero! ever praised,
Spain's boasted pride, La Mancha's peerless knight,
Don Quixote wise and brave, to thee I say,
For peerless Dulcinea del Toboso
Her pristine form and beauty to regain,
'Tis needful that yon Sancho Panza squire
Three thousand and three hundred stripes should lay
On both his brawny buttocks bar'd to heaven,
Such as may sting and tease and hurt him well:
The authors of her woes have thus decreed,
On such an errand, lords and ladies, have I come."

"Faith and skin!" cried Sancho at this, "three thousand lashes indeed! I'd as soon give myself three stabs in the belly with a dagger as these stripes: devil take this method of disenchanting! I don't see what my arse has to do with enchantings! By God, if Master Merlin hasn't found another way for disenchanting the Lady Dulcinea del Toboso, she may go enchanted to her burial."

"I will take you, Don Clown, gorged with garlic," cried Don Quixote, "and tie you to a tree naked as when your mother bore you, and not three thousand three hundred, but six thousand six hundred lashes will I give you, aye, and so well laid on that three thousand three hundred hard tugs shall not tug them off. And answer me not a word, else will I tear out your heart!"

Hearing this, Merlin said: "This must not be so, for the stripes which the good Sancho has to receive must be of his own free will and not by force, and at whatever time he pleases, for no term is fixed. And, furthermore, he is allowed, if he wishes, to commute by half the infliction of this whipping; he may let it be done by another's hand, even though it be somewhat weighty."

"Neither another hand nor my own, nor one weighty or for weighing, shall touch my bum! Did I by any chance bring Mistress Dulcinea del Toboso into the world, that my bottom should pay for the sins her eyes have committed. My master, yes,—he's a part of her, for isn't he always calling her 'my life' and 'my soul' and his stay and prop:—he may and ought to whip himself for her, and bear all the pains needed

336

for her disenchanting. But imagine me whipping myself! Not on your life, I pronounce."[13]

Hardly had Sancho ceased speaking when the silvery nymph, who was beside the ghost of Merlin, stood up, and, removing the thin veil off her face, disclosed one that was extraordinarily beautiful; and with masculine assurance and in no very ladylike voice addressed Sancho Panza in the following words: "O wretched squire, with the soul of an empty pail, the heart of a cork tree, and bowels of flint and pebbles: if they had ordered you, brazen-faced sheep-stealer, to throw yourself headlong from some tall tower; if, enemy of mankind, they had asked you to swallow a dozen toads, two dozen lizards, and three dozen adders; if they had requested you to butcher your wife and children with some sharp murderous scimitar, 'twere no marvel had you shown yourself squeamish and pig-headed. But to make such a song about three thousand three hundred lashes, what every poor snivelling charity-boy gets every month, it is enough to amaze, confound and stupefy the compassionate bowels of all who hear it, nay, even of all who will hear it in the course of time. Turn, wretched, hard-hearted animal, turn, I say, your startled owl's eyes upon these pupils of my eyes that have been compared to glittering stars, and you will see them weeping tears, drop by drop, trickle by trickle, making furrows, tracks and paths over the fair meadows of my cheeks. Let it move you, sly, ill-conditioned monster, to see my blooming youth—still in its teens, for I am nineteen and have not reached twenty,—withering and wasting beneath the coarse shell of a rude peasant wench; and if I now do not look like one, it is because of a special favour granted to me by the Lord Merlin, here present, solely that my beauty may soften you: for the tears of beauty in affliction turn rocks into cotton-wool and tigers into sheep. Lay on, lay on those fleshy globes of yours, you loutish untamed beast, revive from sloth your lusty vigour which only urges you to eat and eat, and restore me the silken softness of my skin, the gentleness of my disposition, and the beauty of my face. And if for me you will not relent, or come to reason, do so for the sake of that poor knight who is beside you, your master, I mean, whose soul I see even at this instant sticking crosswise in his throat, not ten inches from his lips, waiting only for your harsh or gentle answer, either to fly out of his mouth or go back again into his stomach."

Don Quixote, when he heard this, felt his throat, and turned to the duke, saying: "By God, my lord, Dulcinea speaks truly, for I have my soul stuck crosswise in my throat, like the nut of a cross-bow."

"What do you say to this, Sancho?" asked the duchess.

[13] "Abrenuncio" was the liturgical word used in refuting the Devil.

"I say, my lady," replied Sancho, "what I said before, that as for the lashes, I pronounce them."

" 'Renounce' you should say, Sancho, and not as you say it," said the duke.

"Leave me alone, your highness," answered Sancho: "I'm in no mood at present to go quibbling and hair-splitting about niceties or a letter more or less, for these lashes they have to give me, or I have to give myself, have put me in such a dither that I don't know what I'm saying or doing. But I'd like to know from the lady here, my Lady Dulcinea del Toboso, where she learnt this way of begging that she has. She comes to ask me to lay open my flesh with lashes, and she calls me 'soul of an empty pail' and 'loutish untamed beast' and a whole string of bad names, which the Devil is welcome to. Is my flesh made of brass? Do I care a hang whether she's enchanted or no? What hamper of white linen, shirts, kerchiefs, or socks—not that I wear them—does she bring with her to coax me? No, nothing but one piece of abuse after another, though she must remember the old saying that 'an ass with a load of gold goes lightly up a mountain'; and that 'gifts break rocks'; and 'praying devoutly but hammering stoutly'; and 'a bird in hand is worth two in the bush'. Then, there's my master, who, instead of stroking my neck and petting me to make me turn to wool and carded cotton, says if he catches me, he'll tie me naked to a tree and double the ration of lashes. These tender-hearted gentlemen should have been aware of what they were doing: 'tis not a mere squire but a governor they're ordering to whip himself, just as if it was a case of 'drink with cherries'.[14] Let them learn—curses upon them!—let them learn how to beg and how to ask, and how to behave themselves, for there's a time for all things, and people are not always in a good humour. At the present instant I'm bursting with grief at seeing my green suit all torn, and here they are coming to ask me to whip myself of my own free will, when I've as little stomach for it as I would for becoming an Indian chieftain."

"Well, the truth is, Sancho my friend," said the duke, "if you don't become softer than a ripe fig, you shall not get the government. A nice thing it would be for me to send my islanders a cruel governor with flinty bowels, who won't hearken to the tears of afflicted damsels, nor to the prayers of wise, imperious, and antique enchanters and sages. In short, Sancho, either you must whip yourself or they must whip you, or you shan't be governor."

[14] "To drink with cherries" ("beber con guindas") is a proverbial phrase used ironically in the sense of putting one good thing upon another. Clemencin compares it to the phrase "honey upon a jam tart." We might compare it with our phrase "to paint the lily."

"My lord," replied Sancho, "won't you give me two days' time to examine what's best for me?"

"No, certainly not," said Merlin. "Here, at once, in this place the matter must be settled. Either Dulcinea will return to the Cave of Montesinos and to her former state of peasant wench, or else in her present form she will be carried off to the Elysian Fields, where she will wait until the number of lashes is completed."

"Come, dear Sancho," said the duchess, "pluck up good courage and show some return for your master Don Quixote's bread you have eaten. We are all bound to serve him and please him for his kind nature and noble chivalry. Say 'yes', my son, to this whipping: leave the Devil to his own devices: faint heart ne'er won fair lady: you know very well that a stout heart breaks bad luck."

To this Sancho replied with irrelevant words, which he addressed to Merlin: "Well, your worship, Lord Merlin, tell me this; when that devil courier came here with a message from Señor Montesinos, he ordered my master to wait here for him, as he was coming to arrange how the Lady Dulcinea del Toboso was to be disenchanted, yet up to the present we have not seen Montesinos, nor anyone like him."

To which Merlin replied: "The Devil, friend Sancho, is a blockhead and a great rascal. I sent him in search of your master, but with no message from Montesinos but from me, for Montesinos is in his cave expecting, or rather waiting for, his own disenchantment, for in his case the tail has yet to be played.[15] If he owes you anything, or you have any business to transact with him, I will bring him to you, and put him where you please. But, for the present, make up your mind to agree to this whipping penance, and, believe me, it will be of much profit both to your soul and your body, to your soul because of the charity with which you perform it, to your body, because I know that you are of a sanguine complexion, and it will do you no harm to draw a little blood."

"There are many doctors in the world—even the enchanters are doctors," replied Sancho, "but since they all tell me so, though I personally don't see it, I say I am willing to give myself three thousand three hundred lashes, provided I may give them whenever I please, without any fixing of days or times; and I'll try to wipe off the debt as soon as possible, that the world may enjoy the beauty of the Lady Dulcinea del Toboso, for it now appears, contrary to what I believed, that she is truly beautiful. I insist too, on a further condition, namely, that I am not to be bound to draw blood from

15 Meaning that the most difficult part of the business has yet to be done.

myself with the whipping, and that if any of the lashes happen to be fly-swatters they are to count. *Item,* that if I make a mistake in the reckoning, Lord Merlin, as he knows all, shall make it his business to keep count, and let me know how many fall short or are over the number."

"There will be no need to let you know about those that are over," said Merlin, "for the moment you reach the exact number the Lady Dulcinea will at once become disenchanted, and will come full of gratitude to give thanks to the good Sancho, and even rewards for his good work. So you need not be particular about too many or too few lashes. Heaven forbid that I should cheat anyone, even in a hair of his head."

"Well, then, in God's hands let it be," said Sancho, "I abide by my hard fortune. I say that I accept the penance, with the conditions we have agreed."

Hardly had Sancho uttered these last words when the music of the clarions struck up once more, and again a host of muskets were discharged, and Don Quixote hung on Sancho's neck, giving him a thousand kisses on the forehead and on the cheeks. The duke and duchess and all the by-standers expressed the greatest satisfaction, and the car began to move on. As it passed, the fair Dulcinea bowed to the duke and duchess and made a low curtsey to Sancho.

And now the joyous smiling dawn came on apace; the tiny flowers of the field revived, raised their heads, and the crystal waters of the brooks, murmuring over the white and grey pebbles, flowed along to pay their tribute to the expectant rivers; the glad earth, clear sky, pellucid air, calm light, each and all together gave manifest tokens that the day which came treading on the skirts of the dawn would be fine and unclouded. The duke and duchess, pleased with their hunt and with having carried out their plans so successfully, returned to the castle, resolving to continue their joke, which gave them more amusement than anything in the world.

X. Don Quixote's advice to Sancho Panza, and the latter's departure to his island

NEXT DAY THE DUCHESS ASKED SANCHO WHETHER HE HAD made a beginning with his penance for disenchanting Dulcinea. He replied, 'yes', and said that he had given himself five stripes that night. The duchess then asked him what he had given them with, and he replied, with his hand.

"That," said the duchess, "is more like giving oneself slaps than stripes: I am sure that the sage Merlin will not be satisfied with such softness. Worthy Sancho, you must make a scourge of thorns, or a knotted cat-o'-nine-tails, which will make you smart, for 'tis with blood that the letter enters,[1] and the freeing of so great a lady as Dulcinea will not be granted so cheaply; and take heed, Sancho, that works of charity which are performed half-heartedly are without merit and of no avail." [2]

To this Sancho made answer: "If your ladyship will give me a scourge or proper rope's end, I'll lam myself with it, provided it does not hurt too much, for I must tell you that though I'm a rustic, there's more cotton-wool than tough hemp in my flesh, and it won't do for me to play hell with myself for the good of anybody else."

"By all means," replied the duchess. "Tomorrow I will give you a scourge that will be just the thing for you, and will adapt itself to the tenderness of your fleshy parts, as if they were both sisters."

"Then," said Sancho, "I must tell your highness, dear lady of my soul, that I've written a letter to my wife, Teresa Panza, giving her an account of all that has happened to me since I left her. I have it here in my bosom, and all it needs is the address. I'd be grateful if your discretion would read it, for I think it runs along in the governor style, I mean in the way governors ought to write."

"But who dictated it?" asked the duchess.

"Who indeed but myself, sinner that I am?" replied Sancho.

"And did you write it yourself?" said the duchess.

"Not I," answered Sancho, "for I can neither write nor read, though I can make my mark."

"Let us see it," said the duchess, "for I'll dare wager you show in it the quality and quantity of your wit."

Sancho took out an open letter from his bosom, and handing it to the duchess, she saw that it ran as follows:

Sancho Panza's Letter to his Wife, Teresa Panza.

Well-whipped maybe I was, but 'tis a fine mount I have. If a good governorship I have. a good hiding it cost me. This thou wilt not understand now, my Teresa, but by-and-by 'twill become clear to thee. I want to tell thee, Teresa, that I mean thee to ride in a coach, for that is only right, seeing that every other way of going is like cats on all-fours. Thou art a governor's wife: see if anybody is back-biting thee. I send thee here a green hunting-suit that my lady the duchess gave me; alter it so as to make a petticoat and bodice for our daughter. Don Quixote, my master, I hear tell in these parts, is a sensible madman and a droll

[1] This was an ancient proverb adopted as a motto by the flagellants and those who mortified the flesh. It corresponded to our phrase: "there is no argument like the stick."

[2] The last clause ("Y advierta, Sancho, que las obras de caridad que se hacen tibia y flojamente, no tienen mérito ni valen nada") which appears in the first edition of 1615 was ordered to be expurgated by the Holy Inquisition in 1619, though no objections were made to all the rest of the work.

blockhead, and I am by no means behind him. We have been in the Cave of Montesinos, and the sage Merlin has laid hands on me to help him for disenchanting Dulcinea del Tobosa, her that is called Aldonza Lorenzo over yonder. With three thousand three hundred stripes, less five, that I'm to give myself, she will be left as disenchanted as the mother that bore her. Say not a word of this to a soul; for mention your business to folks, and some will say 'tis white, others 'tis black. I'll be starting hence in a few days for my governorship, and I'm going there with a hugeous wish to make money, for they do tell me all new governors start out with the same wish. I'll feel the pulse of it and will let thee know if thou art to come and be with me or no. Dapple is well and sends his humble wishes. I'm not leaving him behind though they carry me off to be Grand Turk. My lady the duchess kisses thy hands a thousand times; mind thou send her back by return two thousand, for nought costs less nor is cheaper than civilities, as my master says. God has not been good enough to give me another bag with another hundred crowns, like the one the other day; but don't let that vex thee, Teresa dear, for he who sounds the bell is safe, and 'twill all come out in the wash; only it worries me greatly what they tell me,—that once I get the taste of it, I'll eat my hands off after it, and if that's so 'twill not turn out cheap for me; though to be sure, maimed and crippled alms-folk pick up a pretty benefice of their own in the alms they beg. So by one way or an other thou wilt be rich and in luck. God give it thee as He can and keep me to serve thee.

From this castle, the 20th of July, 1614.

Thy husband, the governor,
SANCHO PANZA.

When she had finished reading the letter, the duchess said: "On two points the worthy governor goes a little astray: one is in saying or letting it be understood that this governorship has been bestowed upon him for the lashes that he has to give himself, when he knows (and he cannot deny it) that when my lord the duke promised to him, no one dreamt that there were lashes in the world. The other is that he shows himself here to be very covetous, and I don't want him to turn out the opposite to what I expected, for 'greediness bursts the bag', and the covetous governor misgoverns justice."

"That's not my meaning, lady," said Sancho, "and if you think the letter doesn't run as it should, there's nought to do but tear it up and make a new one, and maybe it will be a worse one if 'tis left to my gumption."

"No, no," replied the duchess, "this one is all right: I'll show it to the duke."

They then went out into a garden where they were to dine, and the duchess showed Sancho's letter to the duke, who was highly delighted with it. He then bade Sancho prepare himself and be in readiness to take possession of his governorship, for his islanders were already longing for his arrival as for rain in May. "Friend Sancho," he continued, "the island I am presenting you with all my heart is ready made, round and sound, right fertile and plentiful, where if you know aught of management you may with the riches of the earth purchase an inheritance in heaven."

"Well, then," replied Sancho, "let me have the island, and I'll do my best to be such a governor that, in spite of knaves, I'll fly up to heaven. And, mind you, it's no covetousness neither that makes me forsake my cottage and set myself up as a somebody, but the longing I have to taste what it's like being a governor."

"Once you taste it," said the duke, "you will eat your hands off after it; so sweet is it to command and be obeyed. And I am certain that, when your master becomes an emperor (this is bound to happen as his affairs proceed so well), it would be impossible to tear his power from him, and his only regret will be that he was not made one sooner."

"Faith, sir," answered Sancho, "I imagine it must be pleasant to govern, though 'twere no more nor a flock of sheep."

"May I be buried with you, Sancho," replied the duke, "if you don't know something about everything, and I hope you will be as good a governor as your wisdom leads me to believe. But enough of this for the present: tomorrow you will surely depart to your island, and this evening you shall be provided with suitable apparel and with all things necessary for your journey."

"Clothe me as you will," said Sancho, "I'll still be Sancho Panza."

"That is true," said the duke, "but clothes should always be suitable to the office and rank which is held: it would not be well for a lawyer to dress like a soldier, or a soldier like a priest. You, Sancho, are to be dressed partly like a lawyer and partly like a captain, for in the government I am giving you, arms are as necessary as letters, and a man of letters as needful as a swordsman."

"As for letters," replied Sancho, "I've precious few, for I scarce know my A B C, but still if I can but remember my Christ-cross [3] 'tis enough to make me a good governor; and as for my arms, I'll handle those they give me till I fall, and God be my support."

"With such intentions," said the duke, "Sancho cannot go astray."

Don Quixote then arrived, and after hearing the news and that Sancho was immediately to depart to his government, with the duke's leave he took him aside to give him some good advice concerning his conduct in the discharge of his office. And when he entered his chamber, he shut the door,

[3] The cross which is put at the beginning of the alphabet.

and almost forced Sancho to sit beside him. Then in a quiet, deliberate voice he said: "I give Heaven infinite thanks, Sancho, my friend, that even before I have met with response to my fondest hopes, good fortune has gone out to welcome you. I who had trusted in my own success for the reward of your good services, find myself at the beginning of my advancement, while you before your time, and beyond all reasonable expectation, have crowned your wishes. Some bribe, importune, solicit, rise early, pray, insist, and yet at the end do not obtain what they desire, while another comes and without knowing why nor wherefore finds himself spirited into a position of rank and authority which many others had sought in vain. There is indeed much truth in the saying that 'merit does much, but fortune more'. You, who in my eyes are the veriest blockhead, without burning the midnight oil or rising betimes, without any toil or trouble, by simply breathing the air of knight-errantry, find yourself the governor of an island in a trice, as if it were a mere trifle, All this I say, Sancho, to let you know that you should not attribute the favour you have received to your own merits, but give thanks, first to Heaven, which disposes things so kindly; and, in the next place, to the essential greatness of the profession of knight-errantry. When you are convinced of what I have already told you, pay heed, my son, to me, your Cato,[4] who will be your guide, and counsellor, and North Star, to steer you safely into port out of that stormy sea on which you are about to embark; for, mark you, Sancho, a post of influence and deep responsibilities is often no better than a bottomless gulf of confusion.

"First of all, O my son, fear God, for to fear Him is wisdom, and if you are wise you cannot err.

"Secondly, consider what you are, and try to know yourself, which is the most difficult study in the world. From knowing yourself you will learn not to puff yourself up like the frog that wished to rival the ox; and when you remember having been a swineherd in your own country, that thought will be in the flushed exaltation of your pride like the peacock's ugly feet."

"Aye, it is true," said Sancho, "that I once was a hogdriver, but it was when I was but a slip of a lad. When I grew up to be a bit more of a man I drove geese, not hogs. But all this doesn't seem to me to fit the case, for all governors don't come of royal stock."

"That is true," replied Don Quixote, "wherefore those who are not of noble descent must grace the dignity of the office they bear with mildness and civility, which when accompanied with prudence will enable them to escape the

[4] He refers to the famous *Disticha Catonis,* a book of aphorisms which served as text in all the schools and was called *The Cato.*

malicious mischief-makers, from which no estate is exempt. Show pride, Sancho, in your humble origins, and do not scorn to say that you spring from labouring men, for, when men see that you are not ashamed, none will try to make you so; and consider it more deserving to be humble and virtuous than proud and sinful. Countless are those who, though born of low extraction, have risen to the highest posts of Church and State.

"Remember, Sancho, if you make virtue your rule in life, and pride yourself on acting always in accordance with such a precept, you will have no cause to envy princes and lords, for blood is inherited, but virtue is acquired, and virtue in itself is worth more than noble birth. Seeing that this is so, if, by chance, one of your poor relations comes to visit you in your island, do not reject or affront him, but, on the contrary, welcome and entertain him; for this way you will please God, who insists that none of the beings created by Him should be scorned. If you send for your wife to be with you (for it is not right that those appointed to governments should be long separated from their spouse), teach, instruct and refine her native coarseness, for all that a wise governor can accomplish is often thrown away and brought to nought by an ill-bred, foolish woman.

"If you should become a widower (as may well happen), and your position entitles you to a better match, do not choose one who will serve you as a hook and fishing-rod, or as one who cries—'I will not take it, but throw the coin in my hood', for, believe me, whatever the judge's wife receives, the husband must account for at the Final Judgment, and he shall be made to pay fourfold for all that he has not accounted for during his life.

"Never let arbitrary law rule your judgments: it is the vice of the ignorant, who make a vain boast of their cleverness.

"Let the tears of the poor find more compassion, but not more justice, from you than the pleadings of the wealthy.

"Be equally anxious to sift out the truth from among the offers and bribes of the rich and the sobs and entreaties of the poor.

"Whenever equity is possible and is called for, let not the whole rigour of the law press upon the guilty party; for a rigorous judge has not a better repute than one who is compassionate.

"If by any chance your scales of justice incline to one side, let pity weigh more with you than gold.

"If you should have to give judgment in the case of an enemy of yours, forget your injuries and concentrate upon the true facts of the case.

"Don't let passion blind you in another man's case, for

345

the mistakes you will commit are often without remedy, and will cost you both reputation and fortune.

"When a beautiful woman appears before you to demand justice, blind your eyes to her tears and deafen your ears to her lamentations and give deep thought to her claim, otherwise you may risk losing your judgment in the one and your integrity in the other.

"When you have to punish a man, do not revile him, for the penalty the unhappy man has to suffer is sufficient without the addition of abusive language.

"When a criminal is brought before you, treat him as a man subject to the frailties and depravities of human nature, and as far as you can, without injuring the opposite party, show pity and clemency, for though one attribute of God is as glorious as another, His mercy shines more brightly in our eyes than His justice.

"If you follow these precepts, Sancho, your days will be long and your renown eternal, your rewards will be without number, and your happiness unimaginable. You shall marry your children to your heart's content, and they and your grandchildren shall receive titles. You will live peaceful days cherished by all men, and when, after a gentle, ripe old age, Death steals upon you, your grandchildren's children with their tender and pious hands shall close your eyes."

Sancho listened most attentively to his master's instructions, and tried his best to commit them to memory, that he might hereby be enabled to support the burden of government and acquit himself honourably. Don Quixote continued as follows: "Now let us consider the regulation of your own person and your domestic concerns. In the first place, Sancho, I want you to be clean in your person. Keep your finger-nails pared, and do not allow them to grow as some do, who in their ignorance imagine that long nails embellish their hands, whereas such long finger-nails are rather the claws of a lizard-hunting kestrel. Do not wear your clothes baggy and unbuttoned, Sancho, for a slovenly dress is proof of a careless mind; unless as in the case of Julius Caesar, it may be attributed to cunning.

"Investigate carefully the income of your office, and if you can afford to give liveries to your servants, supply them with garments that are decent and durable rather than garish and gaudy; and give what you save in this way to the poor. That is to say, if you have six pages to clothe, clothe three and give what remains to three poor youths. Thus you will have attendants both in heaven and earth. This original way of giving liveries has never been followed by the vainglorious great ones of this world.

"Do not eat either garlic or ónions, lest the stench of your breath betray your humble birth.

"Walk slowly and gravely; speak with deliberation, but not so as to give the impression that you are listening to yourself, for all affectation is hateful.

"Eat little at dinner, and still less at supper, for the health of the whole body is forged in the stomach.

"Drink with moderation, for drunkenness neither keeps a secret nor observes a promise.

"Be careful, Sancho, not to chew on both sides of your mouth at once, and do not on any account eruct in company."

"Eruct," quoth Sancho, "I don't know what you mean by that."

"To eruct," said Don Quixote, "means to belch, but since this is one of the most beastly words in the Castilian language, though a most significant one, polite people, instead of saying 'belch', make use of the word 'eruct' which comes from Latin, and instead of 'belchings' they say 'eructations'. And though some do not understand these terms, it does not much matter, for in time use and custom will make their meanings familiar to all, and it is by such means that languages are enriched."

" 'Pon my word, master," said Sancho, "I shall make a special point of remembering your advice about not belching, for, to tell you the honest truth, I'm mighty given to it."

"Eructing, Sancho, not belching," said Don Quixote.

"From now on," replied Sancho, "I'll say eructing, and please God I'll never forget it."

"Furthermore, Sancho, you must not overload your conversation with such a glut of proverbs, for though proverbs are concise and pithy sentences, you so often drag them in by the hair, that they seem to be maxims of folly rather than of wisdom."

"God alone can remedy that," answered Sancho, "for I know more proverbs than would fill a book, and when I talk, they crowd so thick and fast into my mouth that they struggle which shall get out first. And the tongue starts firing off the first that comes, haphazard, no matter if it's to the point or no. However, in future I'll take good care not to let any fly save 'tis beneficial to the dignity of my place, for 'where there's plenty the guests can't be empty'; and 'he that cuts doesn't deal'; and 'he's safe as a house who rings the bells'; and 'he's no fool who can spend and spare'."

"There, there you are, Sancho!" said Don Quixote, "on you go, threading, tacking and stitching together proverb after proverb til nobody can make head or tail of you! With you 'tis a case of 'my mother whips me yet I spin the top!' Here am I warning you not to make such an extravagant use of proverbs, and you then foist upon me a whole litany of old saws that have as much to do with our present business as 'over the hills of Ubeda'. Mind, Sancho, I do not condemn a proverb when it is seasonably applied, but to be for ever stringing proverbs together without rhyme or reason makes your conversation tasteless and vulgar.

"When you ride on horseback, do not throw your body back over the crupper, nor keep your legs stiff and straddling from the horse's belly; nor yet so loose, as if you were still riding Dapple. Remember that the air of sitting a horse distinguishes a gentleman from a groom.

"Be moderate in your sleep; for he who rises not with the sun enjoys not the day; and remember, Sancho, that diligence is the mother of good fortune, and sloth, her adversary, never accomplished a good wish.

"There is one final piece of advice which I wish to give you; though it has nought to do with the adornment of your body, I would have you remember it carefully. It is this . . . Never allow yourself to discuss lineage, or the pre-eminence of families, for if you compare them, one is sure to be better than the other, and he whose claim you have rejected will hate you, and he who is preferred will not reward you.

"Now with regard to your dress, you should wear breeches and hose, a long coat, and a cloak somewhat longer; as for wide-kneed breeches or trunk-hose, do not think of them: they are not becoming either to gentlemen or governors.

"This is all the advice I can think of giving you for the present. As time goes on, if you let me know the state of your affairs, I shall give you further instructions as the occasions warrant."

"Master," said Sancho, "I know that all you have told me is mighty wholesome and profitable, but what good can they be to me when devil a one of them can I keep in my head? I grant you, I'll not forget that about paring my nails, and marrying again, but as for all the rest of that tangled hotch-potch you've given, blest if I can remember a single quirk; it has already swept by like the clouds of yester-year. So you must give it to me in black and white. It's true I cannot write nor read, but I'll give it to my father confessor for him to hammer them into my noddle so as I'll remember them at the right moment."

"As I am a sinner," said Don Quixote, " 'tis a scandal for a governor not to be able to read or write! For I must tell you, Sancho, that when a man has not been taught to read, or is left-handed, it means one of two things: either that he comes of very humble parents, or that he was of so way-ward a nature that his teachers could get no good of him. This is, indeed, a grave defect in you, and therefore I want you to learn to write at least your name."

"I can sign my name well enough," quoth Sancho, "for when I was steward of the Brotherhood in my village, I learnt how to scrawl a kind of letters, like what they mark on bales of cloth, which, they told me, spelt my name. Besides, I can always let on that my right hand is lame, and so another can sign for me, for there's a remedy for all things but death. And now that I've the staff of office in my hand I'll do as I please, for as the saying goes, 'he whose father is mayor' [5]—and am I not governor, which is more than mayor, I'm thinking? So let them backbite and be-devil my name, they'll come for wool and I'll send them home shorn, for 'his home tastes good whom God loves'; . . . besides, 'the rich man's follies pass current for wise deeds', so I being rich, you see, and governor, and free-handed too into the bargain, as I intend to be, there'll be no fault to find in me. It is always so: 'plaster yourself with honey and you'll have flies in plenty', as my grandma used to say; 'tell me what you have and I'll tell you what you're worth'; and 'there's no taking vengeance on a man well-rooted'."

"A curse upon you, Sancho," cried Don Quixote, "may sixty thousand devils take you and your proverbs! For the past hour you have been stringing and streeling them and choking me with them. Take my word for it, those proverbs will one day bring you to the gallows; they will drive your people in sheer desperation into open rebellion. Tell me in God's name, where in the world do you rake them up? Who taught you to apply them? As for me, I sweat as if I were digging and delving before I utter one, and apply it properly."

"Before God, master," replied Sancho, " 'tis a trifling matter puts you into such a wax. Why in the Devil's name should you mind if I make use of my own goods and chattels? I've no other stock; proverbs and still more proverbs, that's all there is to my name; and just now I've four on the tip of my tongue, all pat and purty like pears in a pannier—but mum's the word: I'm dumb, for silence is my name." [6]

"That's not your name, then," quoth Don Quixote, "for you are all tittle-tattle and stubbornness. Still, I would fain know these four famous proverbs that come so pat to the purpose, for though I keep rummaging my memory, which is a pretty good one, I am thankful to say I cannot for the life of me call one to mind."

"Where would you find any better than these?" said Sancho: " 'Between two grinders never clap your thumbs'; and 'When a man says "Get out of my house, what would you have with my wife?" there's no more to be said'; and 'Whether the pitcher hits the stone, or the stone hits the pitcher, 'tis the worse for the pitcher'. All those, master, fit to a hair. Let no one meddle with his governor or his deputy,

[5] The complete proverb is: "He whose father is mayor goes safe to his trial" ("El que tiene el padre alcalde, seguro va a juicio").

[6] Sancho makes a pun on his name. The proverb is "to keep silence is called holy" ("santo"). Sancho changes "santo" to Sancho.

349

or he'll rue it, like him who claps a finger between two grinders, and though they're not grinders 'tis enough provided they be teeth. Next, 'tis no good giving any backchat to a governor, any more than arguing with a man who says, 'get out of my house, what business have you with my wife?' And as for the stone and the pitcher, even a blind man may see that. So he who sees a mote in another man's eye should first look to the beam in his own, that people may not say of him, 'The dead woman was afraid of the one with her throat cut'; besides, master, you know that 'a fool knows more in his own house than a wise body in another man's'."

"That is not so, Sancho," replied Don Quixote, "for the fool knows nothing, either in his own or in any other house, for no substantial knowledge can be erected upon so bad a foundation as folly. But let the matter rest, Sancho, for if you govern badly, though the fault will be your own, the shame will be mine. However, I am comforted by the thought that I have done my duty in giving you the best counsel in my power. Thus I am relieved of my obligation and promise. So God speed you, Sancho, and direct you in your government, and deliver me from the anxiety I feel lest you will turn that hapless island topsy-turvy, which, indeed, I might prevent by letting the duke know what you are, and telling him that your gorbellied, paunch-gutted little carcase is nought else but a bag full of proverbs and sauciness!"

"Listen, master," answered Sancho, "if you think I'm not fit for this government, I'll renounce it from now on, for I'm fonder of a black nail-paring of my soul than of my whole body, and as plain Sancho I can continue to live as well upon bread and onions as Governor Sancho upon capon and partridge. Besides, when we're asleep we're all alike, great and small, rich and poor. And if you, master, would call to mind who first put this whim of government into my noddle; who was it but yourself? For, as for me, I know no more about governing islands than a vulture; and if you think the Devil will collar me when I become governor—remember that I'd rather go up to heaven as plain Sancho than down to hell as governor."

"By heaven, Sancho," said Don Quixote, "these last words of yours are enough to prove you worthy to govern a thousand islands. You have a good disposition, without which knowledge is valueless. Recommend yourself to God and try never to go wrong in your intention; I mean, strive with determination to do right in whatever business occurs, for heaven always favors good desires. And now let us go to dinner, for I believe their highnesses are waiting for us."

After dinner, Don Quixote gave Sancho, in writing, the copy of his verbal instructions, telling him to get somebody to read them to him. But the squire had no sooner got them than he dropped the paper, which fell into the duke's hands, who communicated them to the duchess, and they both were amazed at the madness and good sense of Don Quixote. And so continuing their merry humour, they sent Sancho that afternoon with a numerous retinue to the place that was for him to be an island.

Sancho departed with his train. He was dressed like a scholar, and wore over the long robe a loose, slashed coat of clouded camlet, and a cap of the same stuff. He was mounted upon a mule, which he rode with short stirrups in the Moorish fashion, and behind him, by the duke's order, was led Dapple, caparisoned with gaudy trappings of silk, which so delighted Sancho that every now and then he turned his head to gaze upon him, and thought himself so lucky that now he would not have changed fortunes with the Emperor of Germany. He kissed the duke and duchess's hands at parting, and when it was time to receive his master's blessing, the Don wept and the squire blubbered outright.

Now, beloved reader, let the worthy Sancho depart in peace, and in a happy hour. When we come to describe his conduct in office you may well expect over two bushels' weight of laughter, but for the moment let us hearken to what befell his master that night. And if this does not make you hold your sides laughing, at least you will grin like a monkey, for the noble knight's adventures are always bound to create either surprise or merriment.

As soon as Sancho had departed, Don Quixote felt an acute sense of loneliness, and had it been in his power to cancel the commission and deprive Sancho of his government, he would have done it there and then. The duchess, perceiving his melancholy, enquired the cause of it, adding that if it was because of Sancho's absence, she had plenty of squires, duennas and damsels, all ready to serve him to his heart's content.

"It is true, my lady," answered Don Quixote, "I miss Sancho, but that is not the principal cause of my apparent sadness, and I must decline your grace's kind offers, all save the goodwill with which they are tendered. Furthermore, I entreat your excellency to allow me to wait upon myself in my own apartment."

"In truth, Señor Don Quixote," said the duchess, "I cannot allow that. You shall be served by four of my maidens, all as blooming as roses."

"To me," replied Don Quixote, "they will not be roses, but thorns pricking my very soul. They will no more enter my chamber than fly. If your grace wishes to confer further favours upon me, unworthy as I am, I beseech you to suffer me to be alone, and leave me without attendants in my chamber, that I may keep a wall between my passions and my modesty. I will not abandon this rule of mine for all your grace's liberality to me. Indeed, I would rather sleep in my clothes than allow anyone to undress me."

"Enough, enough, Señor Don Quixote," answered the duchess, "I will give orders that not so much as a fly shall enter your chamber, much less a damsel. I am not so inconsiderate as to urge anything that would cripple the exquisite sense of decency of Señor Don Quixote, for I am well aware that the most conspicuous of all his virtues is modesty. You shall undress and dress by yourself, your own way, how and when you please. No one shall molest you, and in case some natural necessity might oblige you to open your door during the night, care shall be taken to supply your room with the needful vessels. And may the great Dulcinea del Toboso live a thousand centuries, and may her name be extended all over the earth's circumference, since she has merited the love of so valiant, so chaste and honourable a knight, and may the kindly heavens inspire the heart of our Governor Sancho Panza to finish his flogging penance speedily, that the world may again enjoy the beauty of so noble a lady."

Don Quixote returned thanks to the duchess, and after supper retired to his chamber, not allowing anybody to attend him, lest he should feel inclined to transgress the bounds of chaste decorum which he always observed towards his Lady Dulcinea. He therefore closed the door of his chamber after him, and undressed himself by the light of two wax candles. But, alas, as he was striving to pull off his hose, about four-and-twenty stitches in one of his stockings gave way, which made it look like a lattice window. The good knight was extremely afflicted, and would have given there and then an ounce of silver for a drachm of green silk—I say green, because his stockings were of that colour.

At this point the author of our history could not forbear exclaiming: "O fatal poverty, why do you insist on persecuting gentlemen and well-born souls more than other people? Why do you oblige them to smoke their shoes for lack of wax, and wear on the same threadbare garment odd buttons of silk hair, and even glass? Why must their ruffs be, for the most part, pleated and not starched? Wretched is the poor gentleman who, to ginger up his honour, starves his body, and fasts unseen with his door locked; then putting on a brave face, sallies forth into the street, picking his teeth,[7] though that is an honourable hypocrisy, seeing that he has eaten nothing and thus has nought to pick! Wretched is he whose honour is extremely shy, and who thinks that at a league's distance people can see the patch on his shoe, the

[7] The dandies of the day used to wear their tooth-picks on their hats.

352

sweat stains on his hat, the threadbareness of his clothes, and even the cravings of his famished belly."

Such were the melancholy reflections that Don Quixote recalled as he gazed on the rent in his stocking. However, he consoled himself when he found that Sancho had left him a pair of travelling-boots, which he resolved to put on the next day. At last he went to bed, pensive and heavy-hearted, being no less depressed at the absence of Sancho than at the misfortune of his stocking, which he would have darned, even with silk of another colour—one of the most significant tokens of gentlemanly poverty.

He then put out the lights, but it was a sultry night, and he could not settle down to rest; so he got up, and opened slightly a casement that looked into a beautiful garden. No sooner had he done this than he heard voices below. He listened and could hear their words:

"Do not press me to sing, dear Emerencia: you know, ever since this stranger came to our castle, and my eyes beheld him, I cannot sing, I can only weep. Besides, my lady does not sleep sound, and I would not for worlds let her find us here."

"Pray, my dear Altisidora," said the other, "do not be uneasy, for surely the duchess is fast asleep. But as for the lord of your desires, he is certainly awake, for I heard him just now open his window. Sing, my love-sick friend, in a soft, sweet voice, to the sound of your harp."

"Alas, my dear Emerencia," replied Altisidora, "I fear lest my song should betray my heart, and that those who know not the mighty power of love may take me for a wanton damsel. But come what may, I will venture, for better a blush on the face than a stain on the heart." So saying she began to prelude on the harp so sweetly that Don Quixote was ravished, and straightway there crowded into his imagination a host of adventures he had read about in his vain books of chivalry—such as casements, gardens, serenades, courtships, swoonings with which his memory was well stored—and he felt convinced that some damsel of the duchess had become enamoured of him and was struggling with her modesty to conceal her passion. Although he was somewhat afraid of yielding to temptation, he resolved to resist all allurements; so, commending himself fervently to his Lady Dulcinea, he decided to listen to the music, but to let the damsel know that he was awake he gave a feigned sneeze, which pleased the two ladies in the garden below, for they wished above all things that he should hear them. After the love-sick Altisidora had finished her serenade, the courted knight sighed deeply and said to himself: "Why am I so unhappy a knight that no damsel can gaze at me without falling in love? Why is the peerless Dulcinea so unlucky that she may not be permitted to enjoy alone my incomparable constancy? Queens, what do ye want from her? Empresses, why do ye persecute her? Maidens of fifteen, why do ye plague her? Take notice, ye enamoured band, that to Dulcinea alone I am paste and sweetmeats, and to all others flint; to her I am honey, and to you I am gall. Let Altisidora weep or sing, let the lady despair on whose account I was drubbed in the castle of the enchanted Moor.[8] Boiled or roasted, Dulcinea's I must be, in spite of all the wizards on earth."

With this he hastily closed the casement and threw himself upon his bed, feeling gloomy and out of sorts as if some misfortune had befallen him. There we will leave him for the present, to follow the fortunes of the great Sancho Panza, who wishes to begin his famous government.

XI. How Sancho Panza governed his island

SANCHO AND HIS SUITE CAME TO A TOWN THAT HAD ABOUT A thousand inhabitants, and was one of the best the duke possessed. They gave him to understand that it was called the island of Barataria, either because Barataria was really the name, or because he had obtained it at so cheap a rate.[1] When he arrived at the gates of the town (for it was walled) the chief officers of the town-council came out to welcome him, the bells were rung, and with popular demonstrations of joy and with pomp and circumstance the people conducted the new governor to the church to give thanks to heaven. After some ludicrous ceremonies they gave him the keys of the town, and consecrated him as perpetual governor of the island of Barataria. The garb, the beard, the plumpness and squatness of the new governor surprised all who were not in the secret, and even those (and there were many) who knew about it were inclined to wonder.

At last, after leaving the church they carried him to the Court of Justice and placed him on the throne, and the duke's steward said to him: "My Lord Governor, it is an ancient custom in this island that he who takes possession must answer some difficult and intricate questions that are put to him, and by his answers the people feel the pulse of his understanding, and thus judge whether they ought to rejoice or to be sorry for his coming."

While the steward was saying this to Sancho, the latter was gazing at an inscription in large letters on the wall opposite his seat, and as he could not read, he asked what was the meaning of that which was painted on the wall.

[8] Part I, ch. ix.
[1] "Barato" means "cheap."

"Sir," said they, "it is there written on what day your excellency took posssession of this island, and the inscription says: 'This day, such a day of this month, in such a year, the Lord Don Sancho Panza took possession of this island, may he long enjoy it'."

"Now tell me: who is this man they call Don Sancho Panza?"

"Your lordship," answered the steward, "for we know of no other Panza in this island but the one seated on this throne."

"Well, take note, brother," said Sancho, "that the 'Don' does not belong to me, nor ever did to any of my family. I'm called plain honest Sancho and all of us have been Panzas, without any Dons or Doñas added to our names. I'll bet there are more Dons than stones in this island. But I'll say no more, God understands me, and, perhaps, if my government lasts only a short while I'll weed out those swarms of Dons that for sure must be as plaguesome as mosquitoes. Come on with your questions, Mr. Steward, I'll answer as best I can, whether the town be sorry or not sorry."

Just then two men came into the court, one dressed as a country fellow, the other like a tailor, with a pair of shears in his hand. "My Lord Governor," said the tailor, "I and this farmer here are appearing before your worship. Yesterday this honest man came to my shop (saving your presence, I'm a tailor, and free of my company, thanks be to God),[2] and putting a piece of cloth in my hands, he says to me: 'Sir, is there enough of this to make me a cap?' So I measures the stuff and answers him yes. Now, as I see it, he must have fancied that I was out to snaffle some of his cloth, for he was a bad-natured cuss, and us tailors have a bad repute. 'Tell me kindly,' says he, 'might there be not sufficient for two caps?' I smells out what he's driving at, so I tells him there was. Then he, sticking to his knavish intentions, goes on increasing the number of caps, and I saying yes, all the time till we reach five caps. Just now he has come for them, and I gives them to him. But what does he do then? He refuses to pay me for the making, and says I must either give him back his cloth or pay for it."

"Is all this true, brother?" asked Sancho.

"Yes, sir," answered the man, "but let your worship make him show you the five caps he made for me."

"With pleasure," replied the tailor, and then, bringing his hand from under his cloak, he showed the five caps on the ends of his fingers, saying: "Here are the five caps this good man ordered me to make, and by God and my conscience,

[2] Tailors had a very bad reputation in those days, so the tailor begs for the indulgence of those present.

none of the cloth is left, and I'm ready to submit the work to the judgment of the trade inspectors."

All present laughed at the number of the little caps and the strangeness of the claim. Sancho reflected for a moment, and then said: "I am of opinion there's no need of long delay in this suit, and it may be decided without ado on an equitable basis, and so I give judgment that the tailor lose the making and the countryman the stuff, and that the caps be given to the prisoners in goal, so that there's an end of that."

If this sentence aroused the laughter of the bystanders, the next one certainly awakened their admiration. For after the governor's order was executed, two old men appeared before him, one with a cane in his hand which he used as a staff; the other, who had no stick, said to Sancho: "My lord, some time ago I lent this man ten crowns of gold to oblige and serve him, on condition that he should return them on demand. I did not ask him to pay them back for a good while, lest he should be put to greater straits to pay me than he was in when I had lent them. At length, thinking that he neglected to pay me, I asked for them back not once but many times, but not only does he not repay me; he denies the debt and says that I never lent him such a sum, or if I did that he has already paid me. I have no witnesses to the loan, nor has he of the pretended payment, and for that reason I would beseech your worship to put him on his oath. Yet if he will swear before your worship that he has returned the money, I will this instant forgive him before God and man."

"What do you say to this, old gentleman with the staff?" said Sancho.

"I confess, my lord," replied the old man, "that he did lend me the money, and if your worship will be pleased to lower your rod of justice, since he leaves it to my oath, I'll swear I have really and truly returned it to him."

The governor then lowered his rod, and the old man gave his staff to his creditor to hold, as though it hindered him while he was swearing; then taking hold of the cross of the rod, he swore it was true that the other had lent him the ten crowns, but that he had restored them to him into his own hand, and now having, as he supposed, forgotten this, he was continually dunning him for them. As soon as the great governor heard this, he asked the creditor what he had to say in reply to the statement just heard. The latter replied that he submitted, and could not doubt that his debtor had spoken the truth, for he believed him to be an honest man and a good Christian, and that as his memory had played him false, he would ask for his money no more. The debtor

356

then took his staff again, and, after making a low bow to the governor, he left the court.

Now Sancho had observed the defendant take his staff and walk away, and he had noticed also the resignation of the plaintiff. He bent his head over his chest, laid the forefingers of his right hand upon his forehead, and continued for a short time apparently in deep meditation. Then raising his head, he ordered the old man with the staff to be called back, and when he had returned, the governor said: "Honest friend, hand me that staff of yours; I'll be needing it."

"Certainly," answered the old man, and delivered it into his hands.

Sancho took it, and passed it over to the other old man, saying: "There, take that, and go in God's name; you are now paid."

"How, sir?" answered the old man; "is this cane worth ten golden crowns?"

"Yes," said the governor, "if not, I'm the greatest blockhead in the world, and all will now see whether or no I've the head to govern a whole kingdom."

He then ordered the cane to be split in court. As soon as this was done, ten crowns of gold were found within it. All the spectators were amazed, and considered their new governor to be a second Solomon. They asked him how he had discovered that the ten crowns were in the cane. He replied that, having noticed how the defendant gave the cane to the plaintiff to hold while he took the oath, and then swore he had returned him the money into his own hands, he afterwards took back his cane again from the plaintiff. He then took it into his head that the money in question must be inside the cane. From this, he added, they might learn that though sometimes those who govern are blockheads, yet it often pleases God to direct them in their judgment.

The trial was no sooner over than a woman entered the court, hauling after her a man dressed like a rich grazier.

"Justice, My Lord Governor, justice!" cried she in a loud voice: "and if I can't get it on earth, I'll sure get it from heaven! Lord Governor of my soul, this wicked scoundrel caught hold of me in the middle of a field and had his will of me, aye, and handled me like a dish-clout. Woe's me! He has robbed me of that which I've kept intact these three-and-twenty years, saving it from Moors and Christians, natives and foreigners. Tough as a cork I was, and preserved myself as entire as a salamander in fire or as wool in a thorn bush, and yet here is this fine fellow who comes with his clean hands to maul and mangle me to my ruin!"

"We have still to decide," said Sancho, "whether this swain's hands are clean or not." Then turning to the grazier, he said, "What do you say in answer to this woman's complaint?"

The grazier, full of confusion, replied: "Gentlemen, I'm a poor drover and pig-dealer, and this morning I left the town after selling, saving your worship's presence, four of my pigs, and what with the dues and tricky ways o' they government inspectors I had to hand over little less than the beasts were worth. Now as I was walking along the road home, quiet and peaceful like, whom did I pick up with but this woman here; and the Devil, who sticks his finger in every pie in the hope of doing us a power of mischief, tempted us and made the two of us yoke together. Then, your worship, I gave her money—'twas enough, I tell ye, to have quietened any sensible woman; but she starts cursing and argufying, and with that, she grabs hold o' me and won't let go till she lands in this court before your worship. She says I did force her, but by the sacred oath I'm taking, or hope to take, I swear she's lying. An' this, your worship, is the honest truth I'm tellin' ye— every scrap of it."

Then the governor asked him if he had any silver money about him.

"Yes, your worship," replied the grazier, "I've a matter o' twenty ducats here in my leather purse."

"Give the purse, money and all, to the plaintiff," quoth Sancho.

The grazier did as he was told, trembling; the woman took the purse, and dropped a thousand curtsies to the assembly, invoking many blessings of God upon the good governor, who took such special care of poor fatherless and motherless children and wronged virgins. Then out of the court she nimbly tripped, holding the purse tight with both hands, though first she peeped into it to see if the money in it was really silver.

No sooner had she left the room than Sancho said to the grazier, who was already in tears, for his eyes and his heart, too, were off on the trail of his purse: "Honest man, run after that woman, and take the purse from her, whether she will or not, and bring it back here."

The grazier, who was neither deaf nor a dullard, did not need to be told twice. Instantly he was away like a streak of lightning to do what he was bidden. All present were in a state of mighty expectancy, for they longed to know the issue of this suit.

In a few minutes the man and the woman came back, clinging and clutching at one another even more desperately than on the first occasion: she with her petticoat tucked up, and the purse lapped up in it, and he striving and struggling to take it from her, but in vain, so stoutly did she defend it. "Justice from God and the world!" she bawled at the top of her lungs. "See, My Lord Governor, the shameless impudence of this ruffian, who in the open street tries to rob me of the purse your worship commanded to be given to me."

358

"Has he got it from you?" asked the governor.

"Got it!" cried the woman—"I'd sooner let him take my life than my purse. A nice baby I'd be indeed! 'twould need other cats to claw my beard, and not this measly, mangy cur: pincers and hammers, crows and chisels won't wrench it from my clutches, no, not even the claws of a lion. Sooner would I let them strip my soul from my body."

"Faith, and she's saying the honest truth," said the man: "I agree she has me beaten: I confess I haven't the strength to lift it off her." So saying, he let go his hold.

Sancho then addressed the woman. "Hand me up that purse, chaste and valiant woman," said he.

The woman gave it to him, and he returned it to the man. Then he said to the violent but not violated woman: "My dear sister, if you had shown the same or even half as much courage and resolution to defend your body as you have done to defend your purse, the strength of Hercules could not have violated you. Go in God's name, and plague upon you, and don't let me find you in this island, nor within six leagues of it, on pain of two hundred lashes: away with you this instant, I say, you trickstering, brazen-faced hedge-whore!"

The woman was in a terrible fright, and slunk away, bending her head in shame and disappointment.

"Now, my good man," said the governor, "in God's name go back to your home with your money, and in future, if you don't want to ruin yourself, don't yoke with such heifers."

The countryman stammered out his thanks in rough and ready fashion, and went his way, leaving the whole court in astonishment at their new governor's judgments and decrees. An account of the entire proceedings was noted down by the appointed chronicler and immediately forwarded to the duke and duchess, who waited for it with the utmost impatience.

From the Court of Justice, Sancho Panza was conducted to a sumptuous palace, where in a great hall a magnificent banquet was prepared. As soon as he entered, he was greeted by the sound of many instruments, and four pages waited on him with water to wash his hands, which he did with great gravity. The music then ceased, and Sancho sat down to dinner at the head of the table, for there was but one seat, and the cloth was only laid for one. A certain personage, who, as it afterwards appeared, was a physician, stood by his side with a rod of whalebone in his hand. They then took off the beautiful white cloth, which covered dishes of fruit and a great variety of viands. One, who looked like a student, said grace; a page put a lace-edged bib under Sancho's chin; and another, who performed the service of butler, set a plate of fruit before him. But scarcely had he tasted it when the man with the rod touched the plate, and it was instantly snatched away by a page, and the butler put in its place another containing meat.

Yet, no sooner did Sancho try to taste it than the physician with the rod touched it, and a page whisked it away as speedily as the plate of fruit.

Sancho was astonished at this proceeding, and, looking around him, asked if this dinner was to be a conjuring game. He with the rod replied: "My Lord Governor, your meals here will follow the same usage and fashion as in other islands where there are governors. I am a physician, and I am paid a salary in this island to look after the governor of it, and so I am more careful of his health than my own. I study night and day, examining his constitution, that I may know how to cure him when he falls ill. Now the principal thing I do is always to attend him at his meals, to see that he eats what is good for his system, and avoids whatever I fancy may be prejudicial to his health and injurious to his stomach. That is why I ordered the plate of fruit to be removed, because it is too watery, and the other dish because it is too hot, and over-flavoured with spices which increase a man's thirst; for he who drinks much, destroys and consumes the radical moisture, which is the fuel of life."

"In that case," said Sancho, "this dish of roasted partridges, which seems to me well-flavoured, will do me no manner of harm."

"Stop," replied the physician, "as long as I am alive, my Lord Governor shall not eat them."

"Why so?" said Sancho.

"Because," answered the doctor, "our great master Hippocrates, the north star and luminary of medicine, says in one of his aphorisms: 'Omnis saturatio mala, perdicis autem pessima', which means, 'all repletion is bad, but that from partridges is worst of all.'"

"If that is so," said Sancho, "please, doctor, give an eye to the dishes here on the table, and see which of them will do me the most good or the least harm, and leave me my bellyful of that, without whisking it away, hey presto, with that conjuring wand of yours, for by the life God grants me as governor, I'm perishing with the hunger, and to deny me belly-fodder—say what you will, Mr. Doctor,—is the way to shorten, not to lengthen, my life."

"Your worship is right," replied the doctor, "and so I am of the opinion that you should not eat these stewed rabbits, for that is a furry kind of diet; and I wouldn't touch a morsel of that veal if I were you: had it not been roasted or pickled you might, perhaps, have had a taste, but as it is, certainly not."

"Well, then," said Sancho, "what about that hugeous dish yonder, smoking hot? I think it's an 'olla podrida';[3] seeing that it is a hodge-podge of many meats, surely I'm bound to light upon somewhat that'll be wholesome and toothsome."

[3] Boiled meat and vegetables, stew.

"By no means," quoth the doctor, "far from us be such a thought. 'Olla podrida' indeed! There is no dish in the world more injurious. Leave 'olla podrida' to canons, college rectors, or lusty gluttons at country weddings: but never let them be seen on the tables of governors, where delicacy and daintiness should be the order of the day. The reason is that simple medicines are usually more highly valued than compounds, for with simple medicines you cannot go wrong, whereas with compounds you err by altering the amount of the ingredients. Therefore, what I would at present advise my Lord Governor to eat in order to preserve his health, is a hundred or so rolled-up wafers, with a few thin slices of quince, which will sit light on the stomach and help the digestion."

When Sancho heard this, he leant back in his chair and stared at the doctor from top to toe. Then in a solemn tone he asked him what his name was, and where he had studied. The latter said in reply: "My Lord Governor, my name is Doctor Pedro Recio de Agüero; I am a native of a place called Tirteafuera, which lies between Caracuel and Almodóvar del Campo, on the right hand, and I have taken my doctor's degree in the University of Osuna."

"Then listen to me," cried Sancho in a rage, "Doctor Pedro Recio [4] of Evil Augury, native of Tirteafuera, lying between Caracuel and Almodóvar del Campo, on the right hand, graduate of the University of Osuna, and so on, take yourself out of this at once! If not, I swear by the sun above I'll take a cudgel, and, starting with yourself, I'll so rib-roast and belabour all the physic-mongers in the island that not one of them will be left—I mean of those like yourself whom I know to be ignorant quacks, for those who are wise and prudent I'll set on high and honour like so many angels. Once more, clear out of here, Pedro Recio: if not, I'll take the chair I'm sitting on and I'll crack it on your skull; let them call me over the coals for it when I give up my office, and they'll discharge me when I tell them I did God's service by killing off a bad physician who's a public executioner. Now give me something to eat: if not, let them take back their government, for an office that doesn't feed its master isn't worth a couple of beans."

The doctor quaked with fear when he saw the governor in such a rage, and he would have acted up to his name and taken himself away, but just then the sound of the post-horn was heard outside, in the street. "It's an express courier from my lord the duke," said the butler, after he had looked out the window. "It must be some important dispatch."

The courier entered, sweating with hast, and in great agitation. Pulling a packet out of his bosom, he handed it to the

[4] "Recio de agüero" means "positive of omen." "Tirteafuera" means "take thyself away."

governor, who gave it to the steward, telling him to read the superscription, which was as follows: "To Don Sancho Panza, Governor of the island of Barataria. To be delivered to him or to his secretary."

"Who is my secretary?" said Sancho.

"It is I, my lord," answered one who was present, "for I can read and write, and am, besides, a Biscayan."[5]

"With that last qualification," said Sancho, "you may well be secretary to the Emperor himself. Open the letter, and see what it says."

The new secretary did so, and, after having perused the dispatch, he said it was a business that could be told only in private.

Sancho then ordered all the company to leave the room except the steward and the butler. When the hall was cleared, the secretary read the following letter:

MY LORD DON SANCHO PANZA,

It has come to my notice that some of our enemies intend to deliver a fierce attack upon your island one of these nights. You ought, therefore, to be watchful and stand upon your guard, that you may not be caught unawares. I have also learnt through reliable spies that four men have got into the town in disguise to murder you, because your great talents make you feared. Keep a strict watch; watch carefully before you admit strangers to audience; eat nothing that is set before you. I will take care to send you assistance if you are in want of it. I rely upon your judgment.

Your friend,

THE DUKE.

From this castle, the 16th day of August, at four in the morning.

Sancho was dumbfounded at the news, and the rest appeared to be no less so. Then turning to the steward he said: "The first thing we have got to do, and do quick, is to shove that same Doctor Recio into gaol, for if anybody intends to kill me, it must be he, and that by a lingering death, the worst of all—starvation."

"Nevertheless," said the butler, "I think your worship should not eat any of the food here upon the table, for it was sent in by some nuns, and, as the saying goes, 'behind the Cross stands the Devil'."

"I don't deny it," replied Sancho, "so for the present give me a chunk of bread and about four pounds of grapes; they won't poison me. For, when all's said and done, I can't go on without eating, and if we've got to be ready for the battles that threaten us, we need to be well fed. Remember, 'tis the belly keeps the heart up, and not the heart the belly. Meanwhile, secretary, do you send My Lord Duke an

---

[5] The office of secretary was frequently entrusted to Basques on account of their reputation for loyalty.

answer, and tell him his commands shall be carried out on the nail. Remember me kindly to My Lady Duchess, and beg her not to forget to send a special messenger with my letter and bundle, to my wife Teresa Panza. Tell her I'll take this as a special favour, and that I'll serve her to the best of my power. And, by the way, you might as well include a salutation to my master Don Quixote de la Mancha, that he may see I'm always grateful to the hand that fed me. The rest I'll leave to you as a good secretary and a sturdy Biscayan. Now clear away the cloth, and bring me something to eat. Then you'll see how I'm able to deal with all the spies, cut-throats and wizards that dare to put their nose near me and my island."

At that moment a page came into the room and said to the governor: "My Lord, there is a countryman outside who wishes to have a word with your lordship about some very important business."

"It's mighty strange," cried Sancho, "how these men of business keep plaguing us! How is it that they're such blockheads as not to understand that this is not the time for business? Do they imagine that we governors and judges are made of iron and marble, and have no need of rest and refreshment like other folks of flesh and bone? By God and my conscience, if my government lasts (I've a shrewd suspicion 'twon't do so), I'll give some of those men of business a leathering."

When the lord governor at last managed to dismiss his vexatious visitor, he was much out of humour, and he continued his tirade against men of business for the benefit of the company, among whom was Dr. Pedro Recio, who had crept into the room again, after the consultation about the duke's letter was over. "Now," said Sancho, "it is clear as daylight to me that judges and governors ought to be made of brass to be able to last out against those business men, who take heed of none but themselves, and insist on being listened to at all hours and at all times, and if the wretched judge don't think fit to give an ear to their business, then they start backbiting and gossiping against him, and they'll gnaw the very flesh off his bones and rake up a power of muck about his forebears. Now, Mr. Business Man: you're a fool, and a blockhead! Don't be in such a hurry! Just keep your patience and wait for a fit moment to make your application: don't come at dinner-time, or when a man is dropping off to sleep, for, by your leave, I'd have you know that we judges are made of flesh and bone like yourselves, and we must allow nature what nature requires—unless it be myself, for I'm forbidden to eat—thanks to Doctor Pedro Recio Agüero de Tirteafuera, here present, who wants me to die of hunger, and yet swears on oath that this kind of dying is life. God grant such a life to him, and to all his crew—I mean the quacks, for the good physicians deserve palms and laurels."

All who knew Sancho Panza were amazed at the elegance of Sancho's speech, which they could not account for, unless it be that offices and responsible positions sharpen some men's minds, and stupefy others.

At length Doctor Recio Agüero de Tirteafuera gave way, and he promised the governor he should sup that night, though he transgressed all the aphorisms of Hippocrates. With this promise the governor was satisfied, and he waited with great impatience for the hour of supper, and though time, as he thought, stood still, yet the longed-for moment came at last, when they served him with cold beef hashed with onions, and some calves-feet somewhat stale. He tucked into this fare with more gusto than if they had given him Milan godwits, Roman pheasants, Sorrento veal, Moron partridges, or Lavajos geese. In the midst of his supper he turned to the doctor and said: "Listen, Mr. Doctor, from now on don't fash yourself giving me dainties and titbits, for that'll make my belly go all contrary, seeing that it's used to nought but good, honest beef, bacon, pork, goat's meat, turnips and onions; and if you give it palace fare 'twill turn queasy and sicken at them. Now what the butler might do is serve me one of them so-called 'ollas podridas' or jumble stews, and the stronger they are the better they taste, in my opinion. Mind you stuff them puddings with anything you will, provided it be eatable, and I'll take it kindly and pay you back some day. So let nobody play tricks on me, for either we are or we aren't, and let us all live and break a crust together in peace and good fellowship, for when God sends the morn 'tis morn for all. I'll govern this island fair and square without any greasing of palms, so let everyone keep his eye skinned and mind his own business, for the Devil's in the offing say I, and if they give me half a chance I'll show them wonders. No, make yourselves honey and the flies will eat you."

"Indeed, My Lord Governor," said the butler, "your worship is quite right in all that you've said, and I can assure you in the name of all the islanders that they will serve your worship with loyalty, love and goodwill, for the gentle way of governing you have shown from the outset gives them no cause to think or do anything to the disadvantage of your worship."

"I'm sure of it," replied Sancho, "and arrant fools they'd be if they did or thought otherwise, so I repeat once more, see that you take good care of my food, and Dapple's also, for that is the main point in all this business. When 'tis the right time for it we'll go our rounds, for I'm dead set on clearing this island of all kinds of rubbishy wasters, tramps and sharpers, for I want you to know, friends, that your lazy loungers in a state are like drones in a hive of bees; they eat up the honey the worker bees gather. Now I'm intending to encourage the labouring men, preserve the privileges of the gentry, reward the good, and, above all things, reverence religion and honour holy men. What do you think of my plan, good friends? Am I talking sense or simply cracking my brains to no purpose?"

"My Lord Governor, your worship speaks so well," answered the steward, "that I stand in admiration to hear a man devoid of letters as you are (for I believe you cannot read), utter so many weighty sayings, so far beyond what we expected from you when we came hither—but there you are, every day sees a fresh marvel in the world, jests turn out to be in earnest, and the biters are bit."

That night, when the governor had supped with Doctor Recio's sanction, they prepared for going the rounds. He set out accompanied by the steward, the secretary, the butler, the chronicler who was to record his deeds, a few constables and notaries, altogether making up a middle-sized battalion. It was indeed a goodly sight to see our governor marching in the midst of them, armed with his rod of office. They had hardly passed through a couple of streets when they heard the clashing of swords, and, hastening to the place whence the noise came, they found two men fighting, who stopped when they saw the officers of the law approaching. One of them said: "Help, in the name of God and the King! Are people to be attacked and robbed in the open street?"

"Hold, my good man," cried Sancho, "and tell me what's the reason for this brawl, for I'm the governor."

"My Lord Governor," interrupted his antagonist, "let me tell shortly what occurred. Your worship should know that this gentleman has just come from the gaming-house yonder, where he has won over a thousand reals, God knows how, except that I happened to be present, and against my conscience, gave judgment for him in more than one doubtful throw; and now I expected he would give me at least a mere crown in gratuity,[6] as is the custom among gentlemen of quality like myself, who are always ready in an emergency to back unreasonable claims and to prevent quarrels, but instead, up he got, after pocketing his money, and left the gaming-house. Being vexed at such conduct, I followed him and requested him civilly to give me at least eight reals, as he knew that I was a man of honour, without employment

6 It was customary for winning gamesters to give a gratuity ("dar barato") by way of courtesy, or for some other reason, to a bystander. This custom became an abuse in Spain, and many picaroons who lived upon it regarded it as their right.

or pension, seeing that my parents had brought me up to no profession. But the knave, who is as great a thief as Cacus himself, refused to give me more than four reals. Think, My Lord Governor, how shameless a fellow he must be! I swear, if your worship had not come on the scene, I would have made him spew out his winnings and taught him how to balance his accounts."

"What's your answer to this?" said Sancho to the other. He admitted that what his antagonist had said was true; he meant to give him more than four reals, for he was tipping him continually, and he held that 'tis civility wins the gratuity, and those who expect them should take graciously what is given them and not look a gift-horse in the mouth unless they know for certain that the winners are common cheats and have won unfairly. And the proof that he was a man of honour and no sharper was that he had refused the other's request, for, said he, cheats are always in the fee of the bystanders who are their accomplices.

"That is very true," said the steward. "It is for you to say, My Lord Governor, what is to be done with these two men."

"This is what must be done," replied Sancho. "You, sir, the winner, whether by fair or foul play, give immediately a hundred reals to your bully-brack here, and shell out an extra thirty for the poor prisoners. And as for you, sir, who have neither office nor pension and are a drag on this island, take your hundred reals, and some time tomorrow, at the latest, be sure to clear out of this island, nor set foot in it for ten years, unless you would finish your banishment in the next world, for if you disobey my order I'll have you swinging from a gibbet, or at least, the hangman will do the job for me. And if anyone gives any backchat he'll feel the weight of my hand."

Thereupon the one disbursed, and the other received; the first went home, and the last went out of the island. As for the governor, he commented as follows: "It won't be my fault if I don't get rid of those gaming-houses, for I've a shrewd suspicion that they're highly injurious to the state."

"As regards the house yonder," said one of the notaries, "I'm sure your worship will not be able to do away with it, for it is owned by a person of great influence, who loses a great deal more year in year out at cards than he gains. Your worship may show your authority against other gaming-houses of less note, that do more harm and shelter more abuses than those frequented by the gentry, for in them the notorious card-sharpers don't dare to play their tricks. Furthermore, since the vice of gaming has become a common practise, it is better to play in the houses of people of quality than in those of the lower classes, where from midnight

366

onwards poor fools are gulled and fleeced of everything they have in the world."

"Well, master notary," said Sancho, "I know there's a great deal to be said on the subject."

Just then two constables came up, dragging a person along with them. "My Lord Governor," said they, "we have brought to you one in disguise, who seems to be a man, but is, in fact, a woman, and no ugly one neither." They then held two or three lanterns up to her face, by the light of which they discovered the face of a girl about sixteen years of age. She was as fair as a thousand pearls, with her hair put up in a snood of gold and green silk. They noted that her stockings were of flesh-coloured silk, her garters of white taffeta, fringed with gold and seed pearls; her breeches were of green and cloth of gold, her close-fitting jacket of the same, under which she wore a fine doublet of white and gold stuff, and her shoes were white and like those worn by men. She had no sword, but a very richly wrought dagger, and her fingers were covered with a quantity of valuable rings. Everyone was struck by the maiden's beauty, but nobody knew her, and those who were in the secret of the jests to be played on Sancho were as puzzled as the rest by this unexpected incident.

The governor was thrilled by the young lady's beauty, and asked her who she was, where she was going, and why she had dressed up in those clothes.

With downcast eyes she modestly answered: "I cannot, my lord, answer so publicly what I wish so much to be kept a secret. You may, however, rest assured that I am no thief or criminal, but an unhappy maiden, whom the spur of jealousy has driven to violate the laws of decorum."

The steward, hearing this, said: "Be pleased, My Lord Governor, to order your retinue to retire, that this young lady may speak out her mind more freely." The governor did so, and they all departed, except the steward, the butler and the secretary.

The young lady then continued: "The truth is, gentlemen, that since the death of my mother ten years ago, my father has kept me in close confinement. We have a small but richly ornamented chapel in the house where we hear Mass. Now in all these years I have seen nothing but the sun in the heavens by day and the moon and the stars by night. I know nothing about the streets, squares or churches, nor about men, except my father and my brother. For many days and months I have felt deeply depressed owing to this confinement, and I have constantly longed to see the world, or at least the town where I was born, and I convinced myself that my longing was not unbecoming or unseemly in a high-born lady. When I heard people talking of bull-fights, tourneys and theatrical shows, I asked my brother, who is a year younger than I am, to tell

367

me about them, and about many other things I had never seen. He described them as best he could, but it only made me more curious to see them. At last, to shorten the story of my downfall, I prayed and besought my brother—would that I had never prayed nor besought him . . ." at this point she broke down and wept bitterly.

"Pray, my lady, continue your story," said the steward. "Your words and tears keep us all in anxious suspense."

The young lady, sobbing as she spoke, proceeded, saying: "To my misfortune I entreated my brother to lend me some of his clothes, and take me out one night to see all the town while our father was asleep. Finally he consented, and having lent me his clothes, he put on mine, which fit him exactly, for he has no trace of beard on his face, and makes a mighty pretty lady. So we slipped out of the house and took a ramble all over the town, but as we were going home we perceived a crowd of people coming our way, which my brother said was the governor's round. He then said we should have to run as fast as we could, for if we should be recognized it would be worse for us. With that he started to race away as fast as if he had wings on his feet. I hastened after him, but in my fright I fell down and was caught by the constable, who dragged me before you and your company, who must surely consider me a shameless hussy."

The truth of the girl's story was confirmed by the arrival of two other constables, who had seized the brother as he sped away. The female dress of the youth was only a rich petticoat and a cloak of blue damask edged with embroidery of gold; on his head he wore no ornament but his own hair, which looked like ringlets of gold.

The governor then addressed them as follows: "Now, my young folks, this seems to me to be nought but a childish frolic, and there was no need of all these tears and tantrums: there's no harm done. Come along with me, and we'll see you home to your father's, and perhaps he won't be any the wiser. But remember to be more careful in future and don't be so childish and eager to go gadding abroad, for 'the modest maid stays at home, as if she'd a leg broken': ' 'tis roaming ruins the hen and the maid': and 'she that longs to see, longs also to be seen'. I'll say no more."

The youth thanked the governor for his kindness, and so they both went home under an escort. When they came to the house, the young man threw a pebble up at a grated window, and presently a maid-servant, who had been watching out for them, came down and opened the door to let them in.

The governor and his retinue continued his rounds, talking all the time of the noble bearing and beauty of the brother and sister, and the great longing these poor children had to see the world by night. Sancho had a mind to arrange a match between the young man and his daughter Sanchica, and he resolved to bring it about as soon as possible, for he thought no man's son would refuse to wed a governor's daughter. And so his round ended for that night.

XII. The terrifying cat-and-bell scare experienced by Don Quixote, and the fortunes of the page that carried the letters to Teresa, wife of Sancho Panza

NOW LET US LEAVE HONEST SANCHO FOR A MOMENT AND turn to the great Don Quixote, whom we last saw in his solitary chamber, meditating on the serenade which the love-sick Altisidora had given him. He went to bed, but the harassing cares and anxieties which he brought thither with him, like so many fleas, allowed him no rest, and the disaster to his stocking added to his affliction and banished soothing sleep. When morning came, he forsook his downy bed, put on his chamois suit, and drew on his top-boots to conceal the rent in his hose. Next he flung his scarlet mantle over his shoulders, and clapped on his head his green velvet cap trimmed with silver lace. His sharp and doughty sword he slung over his shoulder by its belt, and then picking up a large rosary, which he always carried with him, he strutted along with great pomp and solemnity towards the antechamber, where the duke and duchess expected him. As he passed through a gallery he encountered Altisidora and her companion, who had purposely awaited his coming. No sooner did Altisidora see him approaching than she feigned a swooning fit, and straightway sank into the arms of her friend, who hastily began to unfasten her bodice. When Don Quixote saw this he turned to the damsel, saying: "I know the meaning of this swooning."

"You know more than I do," replied the damsel: "Altisidora is the most healthy lady in all the house, and I have never heard her utter a single sigh since I have known her. A curse upon all knights-errant who are so ungrateful. Pray, my lord Don Quixote, depart, for this poor young girl will not revive as long as you are nigh."

"Madam," replied the knight, "I beseech you to order a lute to be left in my chamber this night, and I will console as best I can this love-sick lady's grief."

And so that night, when it was eleven o'clock, Don Quixote retired to his apartment, and found the lute there as he had desired. After tuning it, he opened his casement, and hearing the sound of footsteps below he preluded on the instrument, coughed and cleared his throat, and began to sing in a somewhat hoarse though not unmusical voice a song which he had composed that day. As he sang his voice was heard by the duke and duchess, Altisidora and all the inmates of the castle. But before the knight had proceeded very far with his song, suddenly, from a corridor above his window, a rope was let down, to which over a hundred tiny tinkling bells were fastened. Immediately after that a huge sackful of cats was emptied into the window, and all had smaller bells tied to their tails. The jingling of the bells and the miaowing of the cats made such a deafening din that the duke and duchess, though the inventors of the jest, were scared, and Don Quixote himself was panic-struck. Unluckily two or three cats leaped in through the bars of his window, and darted up and down the room for all the world as if a whole legion of devils had been flying to and fro. In a moment they put out the candle lights in their frantic efforts to escape from the chamber. Meanwhile the rope with the bigger bells kept ceaselessly bobbing up and down, and scared the majority of those who were not in the secret of the plot.

Don Quixote jumped up and, seizing his sword, began to fence about him and make thrusts at the window, shouting: "Avaunt, ye malicious enchanters! Avaunt, ye wizard scum! I am Don Quixote of La Mancha, against whom your vile intentions are of no avail." Then turning his attention to the cats that were scampering up and down the room, he laid about him furiously as they made desperate attempts to get out of the window. At last they made their escape, all but one of them, which, finding itself hard pressed by Don Quixote, sprang at his face, and burying its claws and teeth in his nose, caused him such agonizing pain that he roared at the top of his lungs. When the duke and duchess heard the outcry, they guessed the cause and rushed at once to his assistance, and, having opened the door of his chamber with a master-key, they found the poor gentleman writhing in his efforts to disentangle the cat from his face. By the lights they carried they saw the unequal combat: the duke hastened to intervene and remove the beast, but Don Quixote shouted: "Let nobody take him: let me fight hand to hand with this devil, this wizard, this necromancer! I'll make him understand what it means to deal with Don Quixote of La Mancha." The cat, however, paid no heed to these blood-curdling threats, and hung on like grim death until at last the duke unhooked its claws and flung it out of the window.

Don Quixote's face was all criss-crossed with scratches, and as for his nose it was in no healthy condition; nevertheless, he was extremely indignant because they had not allowed him to bring to a victorious end his battle with the rascally enchanter. Immediately orders were given for oil of Hypericum to be brought, and Altisidora herself with her lily-white hands bound up his wounds, and while she was dressing him she whispered in his ear: "Hard-hearted knight, these misadventures have fallen you as a just punishment for your wilful obstinacy and disdain. Please God your squire Sancho may forget to whip himself, that your beloved Dulcinea may never be delivered from her enchantment, nor you ever be blessed with her embraces in the bridal bed—at least so long as I who love you shall be alive."

Don Quixote made no answer to this tirade, but he sighed deeply and then stretched himself out on his bed after he had thanked the duke and duchess, not because he was afraid of that caterwauling, bell-jingling crew of enchanters, but because he was grateful for their kindness in coming to his assistance.

The duke and duchess then left him to rest, and departed, full of regrets at the miscarriage of their jest, for they never imagined it would turn out so disastrous to the worthy knight as to oblige him, as it did, to keep to his chamber for five days. Don Quixote, indeed, as a result of his wounds, remained sullen and crestfallen, with his face swathed in bandages and scarred, not by the hand of God, but by the claws of a cat: such are the mishaps that befall knights-errant!

The duke and duchess, when they saw that the invalid's wounds would soon heal, resolved to continue their jests and make the most of the opportunities for merriment afforded by the extravagances of Don Quixote. So the page (who had acted the part of Dulcinea when it was proposed to disenchant her) was sent away to Teresa Panza with the letter from her husband, with another from the duchess herself, to which she added a costly string of coral as a present.

Now the page was a bright, intelligent lad, and being eager to please his lord and lady, set off in high spirits for Sancho's village. When he came near his destination, he saw a group of women washing in a stream, and asked them whether they could inform him whether there lived in that village a woman whose name was Teresa Panza, wife to one Sancho Panza, squire to a knight called Don Quixote of La Mancha. No sooner had he asked the question than a young wench, who was washing among the rest, answered, saying: "That Teresa Panza is my mother; that Sancho is my own father, and the same knight our master."

"In that case, damsel," said the page, "lead me straight to your mother: I've a letter and present here for her from your father."

"That I will with a heart and a half, sir," said the girl, who looked about fourteen years of age, and, leaving the clothes she was washing to one of her companions, without pausing to tidy her hair or put on her shoes, away she raced ahead of the page's horse, bare-legged and all dishevelled.

"Come on, sir, an't please you," quoth she, "for our house

is hard by the entrance to the village, and my mother is at home; but she's in a queer way, poor old soul, not hearing for many's the day what happened to my father."

"Well," said the page, "I bring tidings that will make her give thanks to God, I warrant."

At last, after leaping, running and jumping, the girl reached the house, and, before entering, she shouted at the top of her voice: "Come out, mother, come out, come out! Here's a gentleman's after bringing letters and presents from father."

At these words out came her mother, Teresa Panza, spinning a hank of flax: she was clad in a russet petticoat, so short that it seemed as if it had been cut off at the placket: with a jacket of the same colour, and her shift beneath it. She was not old, but looked as though she had turned forty, and with that, sturdy, stocky, hale, hearty and buxom.

"What's up with you, daughter?" quoth she, seeing the girl with the page. "Who's the gentleman?"

"A servant of your ladyship's," answered the page. As he spoke he dismounted and knelt humbly before the Lady Teresa, saying: "Give me leave to kiss your ladyship's hand, seeing that you are the only legitimate spouse of my lord Don Sancho Panza, lawful governor of the island of Barataria."

"Come, come, sir, no more o' this, I pray," replied Teresa: "I'm no court dame but a plain unvarnished country-woman, daughter of a humble clod-beater, and wife of a squire-errant, but not a governor."

"Your ladyship," answered the page, "is the most worthy wife of a thrice worthy governor, and as a proof of what I am saying, pray receive this letter and this present." So saying, he took out of his pocket a string of coral beads set in gold, and fastened it around her neck, saying: "This letter is from His Excellency the Governor, and another which I have for you, together with these beads, comes from Her Grace the Lady Duchess, who sends me to your ladyship."

Teresa was dumbfounded, and her daughter likewise. The girl then said: "I'll be hanged if our master, Don Quixote, hasn't something to do with this: sure, it's he must have given the government or earldom he so often promised him."

"That is so," replied the page, "and it is out of respect for Señor Don Quixote that my lord Sancho is now governor of the island of Barataria, as you may see by the letter."

"Good gentleman," said Teresa, "read it out to me, though I can spin I can't read a scrap."

"No more can I," chipped in Sanchica, "but wait here a moment an' I'll run and fetch one as can, either the bachelor Samson Carrasco, or the priest himself, who'll be leaping to hear news of father."

"You may save yourself the trouble," said the page. "I can

read, though I cannot spin, and will read it to you." Which he accordingly did, but as its contents have already been given, it is not repeated here.[1] He then produced the letter from the duchess, and read as follows:

FRIEND TERESA,

The good qualities of your husband Sancho, his honesty and good sense obliged me to persuade my husband the duke to make him governor of one of the many islands in his possession. I am informed that he is as sharp as a hawk in his government, for which I am very glad, and my lord duke likewise, and I give thanks to heaven that I have not been deceived in my choice of him for that office. For I must tell you, Madam Teresa, that it is mighty difficult to run across a good governor in this world of ours, and may heaven make me as good as Sancho shows himself in his government.

I herewith send you, my dear friend, a string of coral beads set in gold: I wish they were oriental pearls, but, as the saying goes, whoever gives you a bone won't wish you dead. The day will come when we shall get to know each other, and then God knows what may come to pass. Remember me to your daughter Sanchica, and tell her from me to get herself ready, for I mean to make a big match for her when least she expects it. They tell me that you have fine large acorns in your village; pray send me a couple of dozen of them, for I shall value them all the more as coming from your hands. And, please write me a nice long letter to let me know about the state of your health and your welfare, and if you want anything, you have only to gape and I shall guess your meaning. So heaven protect you.

Your affectionate friend,

THE DUCHESS.

From this castle.

"Lord bless us!" quoth Teresa, when she heard the letter, "what a good, plain and humble lady she is, to be sure! Let them bury me with such ladies as this, I say, and not with them haughty madams we have in our village, who, because they are gentlefolks, think the wind mustn't blow upon them, and go flaunting in style to church as stately as if they were very queens! They turn up their noses in scorn to look on a poor peasant woman, and yet, here is a good lady, who, though a duchess, calls me her friend, and treats me as if I were as high as herself, and, please God, I'll see her some day as high as the highest steeple in La Mancha. As for the acorns, sir, I'll send her ladyship a peck of them, and of such hugeous size that people will come from far and near to see and wonder. And now, Sanchica, give a hearty welcome to the gentleman: take care of his horse, and fetch some new-laid eggs from the stable, and slice some rashers of bacon, and let us feed him like a prince, for his good news and the bonny face on him deserve no less. Meanwhile I'm off to tell the glad news to the neighbours, especially to our good priest and Master Nicholas the barber, for they are and have been all along fast friends of thy father."

"I'll do as you say," replied Sanchica, "but listen, mother: you must give me half the beads, for I'm sure her ladyship was not so foolish as to send them all to you."

"They're all for thee, daughter," replied Teresa, "but let me wear them a few days round my neck, for truly they cheer my very heart."

"You will be still more cheered," said the page, "when you see what I have got in my portmanteau: a fine suit of green cloth which the governor only wore one day at a hunt, and he has sent it all to my lady Sanchica."

"May he live a thousand years!" cried Sanchica, "and the fine gentleman who brought it likewise, aye, and two thousand, if need be!"

Teresa now went out of the house with the letters in her hand, and the beads around her neck, and as she went along her fingers played on the papers as if they had been a tambourine. Meeting by chance the curate and the bachelor Carrasco, she began dancing and capering before them. "Faith and skin!" cried she, "we're no poor relations now, we've got a bit of a government! Now let the proudest painted ladyship among them turn up her nose at me, I'll give her what-for."

"What is up, Teresa Panza?" said the curate. "What madness is this? and what papers have you there?"

"No madness at all," replied Teresa, "but these are letters from duchesses and governors, and them beads I'm wearing are fine coral, and the *Ave Marias* and the *Paternosters* are of beaten gold, and I'm a governor's lady—there you are."

"Heaven be our witness," they exclaimed, "there's no understanding you, Teresa, we don't know what you mean."

"These will tell you," replied Teresa, handing them the letters.

The curate read them aloud to Samson Carrasco, and then both stared at one another in amazement. The bachelor asked who had brought the letters. Teresa said if they would come home with her they should see the messenger—a fine, handsome young man, and that he had brought her another present worth twice as much. The curate took the string of corals from her neck, and examined it again and again, and being convinced that they were genuine, he wondered still more, and he said: "By the cloth I wear, I don't know what to say or think of these letters and presents! On the one hand I see and feel the fineness of these corals, on the other I read that a duchess sends to ask for a dozen or two acorns."

"Make all this fit if you can," said the bachelor, "but let

us go and see the messenger: perhaps he may explain the difficulties which puzzle us."

They then returned with Teresa, and found the page sifting a little barley for his horse, and Sanchica cutting rashers to fry with eggs,[2] for the page's dinner. The appearance and behaviour of the youth made an excellent impression upon the curate and Samson, and after the usual exchange of civilities, the bachelor asked him to give them some news of Don Quixote and Sancho Panza, for, though they had read a letter from the latter to his wife, and another from the duchess, they were completely puzzled, and they could not for the life of them imagine what was meant by Sancho's government, especially government of an island, for they were well aware that all or most of the islands in the Mediterranean belonged to the King.

"Gentlemen," replied the page, "there is no doubt about Señor Sancho Panza being governor, but I am not going to say whether it is an island or not, I only know it is a place that has above a thousand inhabitants. As to that business about the acorns, I tell you she's so plain and so humble that there's no wonder in her sending to a peasant woman for a few, why, I've known her send to borrow a comb from one of her neighbours. For I must tell you, gentlemen, that the ladies of Aragón, though as high in rank, are not so punctilious and ceremonious as the ladies of Castile—they treat their people with greater familiarity."

Sanchica now came in with her lap full of eggs. "Tell me, sir," said she to the page, "now that my father is a governor, does he wear trunk-hose?"[3]

"I never noticed," replied the page, "but I suppose he does."

"God save us!" answered Sanchica, "what a sight father must be in tights! Isn't it funny that ever since I was born I've longed to see my father in trunk-breeches."

"You'll certainly have that pleasure, my lady, if you live. By heavens, if his government only lasts two months you'll see him travelling the roads with a winter-mask against the cold."[4]

2 Bacon and eggs were the staple diet of La Mancha in those days. Sancho in Avellaneda's continuation of *Don Quixote* calls an omelet of eggs and rashers "the Grace of God" ("gracia de Dios"). According to the ancient commentator Covarrubias, in La Mancha, eggs and rashers fried in honey were called "merced de Dios." The reason why bacon and eggs received such flattering epithets was because they were the cheapest and easiest food to prepare for such an unexpected guest as the page of the duchess. Nowadays rashers and fried eggs are called "chocolate de La Mancha."

3 Trunk-hose ("calzas atacadas") were only worn by old-fashioned gentlemen in the second half of the sixteenth century.

4 Persons of quality, especially those who were of delicate constitution, used to wear cloth masks or hoods against the cold.

The curate and the bachelor saw clearly that the page was speaking ironically, but the fineness of the corals and the hunting-suit sent by Sancho (which Teresa had already shown them), perplexed them again. Meanwhile they could not help smiling at Sanchica's fancies, and still more when her mother said: "Your reverence, do keep a sharp look-out and see if there's any of our neighbours going to Madrid or Toledo. I want them to buy me a farthingale, a round, well-made one of the newest fashion, and the best that is to be had, for as true as I'm telling you, I'm meaning to be a credit to my husband's government as far as I can, and if I get vexed, I'll go myself to that court and flaunt a coach too, as well as the best of them; for she who has a governor for husband may well have a coach, and afford it too, I'm thinking."

"Aye, you're right, mother!" said Sanchica. "I wish to heaven 'twould be today rather than tomorrow, though folks who saw me perched in our coach up beside my lady mother would jeer, saying: 'Take a look at yon trollop, the garlic-guzzler's daughter. Look how she's lolling and airing herself in the coach like she was a she-pope.' But sure let them jeer away and tread along in the muck, so long as I'm riding in my coach with my feet well above the ground. Bad 'cess year in year out to all the back-biting bitches in the world! While I go warm, let them laugh till they burst. Am I not right, dear Mamma?"

"Of course thou art, child," replied Teresa, "and indeed my good man Sancho foretold me all this, aye, and still greater luck, and thou shalt see, daughter, 'twon't stop till it has made me a countess. In luck 'tis the beginning that matters, and as I've many a time heard your dear father say (who as he's yours, so he's the father of proverbs), 'when they give you a heifer make haste with the halter': when they give you a government, grab it, and when they whistle for you with a fine fat gift, gobble it up; if not, go snoring a-bed, and when good luck raps at the door give it the go-by."

"Aye," quoth Sanchica, "what do I care if they say, when they see me preening myself and stepping it stately: 'When the mongrel in breeches was seen',[5] and all the rest of it."

"I'm forced to believe," said the curate, "that the whole race of Panzas were born with their bellies bunged up with proverbs, for I never knew one of them that didn't spurt them out at all hours, no matter what the conversation was about."

"I agree," quoth the page, "even his honour the governor utters them at every turn, and though many are wide of the

[5] The full proverb is: "When the mongrel in breeches was seen, he wouldn't recognize his friend" ("Vióse el perro en bragas de cerro, y no conoció a su compañero". It corresponds to our phrase "beggars on horseback."

mark, they give great joy to the lady duchess and my lord duke."

"Do you still mean to assure us," said the bachelor, "that this tale of Sancho's government is true, and there is a duchess who sends these letters and presents? For though we touch the presents and have read the letters, we don't believe it and we think that this is one of the adventures of our countryman Don Quixote, and so a matter of enchantment. Indeed, I've a mind to touch you and feel you to find if you are a man of flesh and bone, and not a magic messenger."

"As for myself," replied the page, "I can only say that I am really a messenger, and that his honour Sancho Panza is actually a governor; and that my lord duke and the duchess can give and have given him the said government, which, I'm told, he administers in admirable fashion. Whether this is the result of enchantment or not I leave to you to argue out, but I swear by the lives of my parents, who are living and whom I love dearly, I know nothing else about the matter."

"It may be so," replied the bachelor, "but Saint Augustine doubts."

"Doubt away to your heart's content," said the page. "I've told you the truth, and truth will always prevail over falsehood and rise to the top as oil does over water, but if you will not believe me, believe deeds, not words: come with me, one of you, and you'll see with your eyes what you will not believe by the help of your ears."

"That's the jaunt for me," quoth Sanchica: "come on, sir, take me up behind you on your nag, for I've a great longing to see my father."

"The daughters of governors," said the page, "should not travel unattended, but in coaches and litters, and with a great train of servants."

"Glory be to God!" quoth Sanchica, "I could just as well go a journey on an ass as in a coach, I'm a nice one to be namby-pamby and particular."

"Hold thy whisht, girl," said Teresa, "thou know'st not what th'art saying; the gentleman is in the right, for 'according to reason, each thing in its season.' When 'twas plain Sancho, 'twas plain Sancha, but now he's governor thou art 'my lady.' Aren't I in the right?"

"My lady Teresa says more than she thinks," said the page, "but now give me a bite of dinner, and let me go as soon as possible, for I mean to return home this night."

"Well, then, sir," said the curate, "do come with me and share a humble meal in my house, for Madam Teresa has more goodwill than good cheer to entertain so worthy a guest."

The page made a gesture of refusal, but at length felt that

it would be best to comply, and the curate was very pleased to have his company, for thus he would be able to question him at leisure about Don Quixote and his exploits.

The bachelor offered Teresa to write the answers to her letters, but she would on no account let him meddle in her affairs, for she considered him a bit of a playboy, and so she gave a roll and a couple of eggs to a young novice from the chapel who could write, and he wrote two letters for her, one to her husband and the other to the duchess, both dictated by herself, and perhaps not the worst in this great history, as we shall see by and by.

The duke and duchess were delighted to see the page on his return, for they were eager to know how he had succeeded in his embassy. They accordingly questioned him, but he replied that he could not give his report in public, nor in a few words, and so he begged their graces to give him a private audience. He then handed over the two letters to the duchess. One was addressed to "My Lady Duchess of I know not where"; the other to "My Husband Sancho Panza, Governor of the Island of Barataria, whom God prosper more years than me."

The duchess's cake, as the saying goes, would not bake until she had read her letter. So she eagerly opened it, and after hastily running her eye over it, finding nothing secret in it, she read it out aloud to the company. It was as follows:

Teresa Panza's Letter to the Duchess.

MY LADY,
    The letter your grace wrote me, made me right glad, for, i' faith, I mightily longed for it. The string of corals is very fine, and the hunting-suit of my husband doesn't fall short of it. All our village is very pleased that your honour has made my husband a governor, though not a soul will believe it, especially the curate and Master Nicholas the barber, and Samson Carrasco the bachelor. But I don't care, for so long as the thing is so as it is, let each one say what he wills; though, to tell the truth, if I had not seen the corals and the suit I would not have believed it, for the folks in this village take my husband for a dolt, and they can't for the life of them imagine what kind of government he's fit for, unless 'tis over a herd of goats. Well, God help him and guide him in the way He thinks best for His children. As for me, dear lady, I am resolved, with your kind permission, to make hay while the sun shines, and go to Court, taking my ease in a coach, and making my friends as are envious enough already, stare their eyes out when they see me riding by. And, therefore, I pray Your Excellency to bid my husband send me a tidy sum of money—and let it be sufficient, for I'm sure living at Court is expensive; bread there costs a real, and a pound of meat thirty maravedis, which is as bad as the Day of Judgment. If he doesn't want me to go, let him warn me in time, for my feet are itching to be on the tramp; and, besides, my friends and neighbours do keep

378

telling me that if I and my daughter strut about the Court stately and stylish, my husband will be better known by me than I by him; for men would be bound to ask: "What ladies are those in that coach?" And my footman will reply that 'tis the wife and daughter of Sancho Panza, governor of the island of Barataria. Thus will my husband be known, and I made much of, for "all's to be found at Rome."

I am as sorry as sorry can be, that around here there has been no gathering of acorns this year, however, I'm sending your highness about half a peck which I picked one by one with my own hands, and they were the biggest I could find—I wish they were as big as ostrich eggs.

Pray let your pomposity not forget to write to me, and I'll be sure to send you an answer, and let you know how I am in my health, and give you the news of our village, where I'm waiting and praying the Lord to preserve Your Excellency, and not forget me. My daughter Sanchica and my son kiss your ladyship's hands.

She that wishes rather to see you than to write to you,

Your servant,

TERESA PANZA.

This letter amused all the company, especially the duke and duchess, and the latter then asked Don Quixote whether it would be right to open the governor's letter, for she was sure it must be a very good one. The knight told her that he would open it to satisfy her curiosity. Accordingly he did so, and found that it was as follows:

Teresa Panza's Letter to her Husband Sancho Panza.

DEAREST HUSBAND,

I received thy letter, and vow and swear to thee, as I am a Catholic Christian, I was within two fingers' breadth of going stark staring mad for joy. Look here, my darling, when I heard thou wert made a governor, I thought I'd fall down dead with the gladness, for thou knowest how they say sudden joy will kill as soon as great sorrow. As for thy daughter Sanchica she wet herself unbeknown to herself for sheer pleasure. There before my eyes was the suit thou didst send me, and the corals my lady duchess sent was round my neck, and the letters in my hands, and the young fellow as brought them standing by my side. Yet, for all that, I thought what I was seeing and feeling was only a dream, for who could have thought that a goatherd would come to be a governor of islands? My mother used to say that "he who would see much must live long." I say this because, if I live longer, I hope to see more: faith and I'll never rest content till I see thee a tax-gatherer, or collector of customs, for though they be offices that send those as use them badly to the devil, there's lashings of money to be touched and turned. My lady duchess will tell thee the longing I have to go to Court. Think it over, and let me know thy mind, for I want to bring credit on thee by riding in a coach.

Neither the curate, the barber, the bachelor, nor even the sacristan will believe thou art a governor, and they say it's all humbug, or enchantment like all the affairs of thy master Don Quixote; and Samson says he will go and find thee out, and drive this government out of thy noddle, and Don Quixote's madness out of his brain-pan. But I only laugh at them, and look at my string of coral beads, and puzzle how to make thy suit of green into a gown for thy daughter. I sent my lady the duchess some acorns, but I wish they were of gold. Do send me some strings of pearls, if they are worn in thy island.

The news from our village is that Berrueca has married her daughter to a poor kind of a painter that came here, offering to paint anything that was going. The Corporation set him to paint the King's Arms over the town-hall; he asked them two ducats for the job, which they paid in advance; so he fell to work, and spent eight days daubing away, but at the end of that time he made nothing of it, and he said he couldn't paint such trumpery, and handed back the money. Yet, in spite of all this, he married with the name of a good workman. The truth is, he has left his paint-brushes and taken up the spade, and goes to the field like a gentleman. Pedro de Lobo's son has taken orders, and shaved his crown, meaning to be a priest. Minguilla, Mingo Silvato's grand-daughter, heard of it, and is suing him for breach of promise of marriage. Bad tongues try to hint that he has put her in the family way, but he swears by all that's holy he had nought to do with it. We have no olives this year, and there's not a drop of vinegar to be got in the village for love or money. A company of soldiers passed through here, and carried along with them three wenches out of the village: I don't tell you their names, for perhaps they'll come back, and there are sure to be fellows who will marry them, for better or for worse. Sanchica is making bone-lace, and gets eight maravedis a day clear, which she drops into a money-box to help her buy household stuff, but now that she's a governor's daughter you must give her a dowry so that she need not work. The fountain in the market-place is dried up; a thunderbolt fell upon the gibbet, and there may the lot of them end. I expect an answer to this, and thy decision as to whether I'm to go to Court or no. God grant thee more years than myself, or as many, for I wouldn't like to leave thee behind me.

Thy Wife,

TERESA PANZA.

The letters caused much applause, merriment and admiration, and, as a finishing touch, the courier now returned bringing Sancho's answer to Don Quixote. This was publicly read, and made all who had thought the governor a fool reconsider their opinion.

The duchess retired to hear from the page the account of his journey to Sancho's village, which he gave her in detail, without omitting a single circumstance. He also brought her the acorns, and a cheese which Teresa had given him. Now let us leave the duchess and the page to record the end of the government of the great Sancho Panza, the flower and mirror of all island governors.

XIII. *The violent end of Sancho's governorship, and his adventures leading to his meeting with Don Quixote*

To THINK THAT THE AFFAIRS OF THIS LIFE WILL ALWAYS remain in the same state is a vain presumption; indeed they all seem to be perpetually changing and moving in a circular course. Spring is followed by summer, summer by autumn, and autumn by winter, which is again followed by spring, and so time continues its everlasting round. But the life of man is ever racing to its end, swifter than time itself, without hope of renewal, unless in the next that is limitless and infinite. For many by natural instinct, without the light of faith, have understood the swiftness and instability of this present life, and the duration of the eternity to come. In this context, however, we allude only to the instability of Sancho's fortune, and the brief duration of his government, which so suddenly dissolved and vanished like smoke into the air.

It was now the seventh night of our governor's administration, and he was in bed, sated not with bread and wine, but worn out after judging cases, giving opinions, making statutes and proclamations. Just at the moment when sleep, in spite of the pangs of hunger, was beginning to close his eyes, all of a sudden he heard such a din of bells and shouting that he really thought the island was sinking. He started and sat up in bed, listening intently to try and find out, if possible, the cause of such an uproar. But far from discovering it, a great number of drums and trumpets added their rattling and blaring to the former noise, and such a dreadful alarm ensued that he began to quake with fear. Up he leaped from his bed and put on his slippers, on account of the damp floor, and without a stitch on him but his shirt he ran and opened the door of his chamber, and saw about twenty men come running along the galleries with lighted torches in their hands and their swords drawn, all shouting: "Arm, My Lord Governor, arm! A host of enemies has got into the island, and we are lost unless your courage can save us." Bawling at the tops of their voices and brandishing their swords, they rushed up to where Sancho stood scared and stupefied by what he saw and heard.

"Arm this instant, my lord," cried one of them, "otherwise you'll be destroyed and the whole island with you."

381

"What's the good of my arming?" replied Sancho. "Do I know a thing about arms or relief tactics? Why don't you send for Don Quixote, my master, and he'll deal with them in the twinkling of an eye and retrieve our fortunes? Alas! as I'm a sinner, I know nothing about these sudden attacks."

"How so, My Lord Governor," said another, "what's the meaning of this faint-heartedness? See, here we bring you defensive and offensive arms: arm yourself, and come with us to the market-place, and be our leader and our captain: that is your duty since you are our governor."

"Well, then, arm me and wish me good luck," quoth Sancho, and instantly they brought him two big shields, which they had provided for the occasion. Without letting him put on his other clothes they clapped the shields over his shirt; one they tied on front, the other behind. They pushed his arms through holes they had made in the shields, and fastened them so tightly together with cords that the poor governor remained cased and walled up as stiff and straight as a spindle, without being able to bend his knees or stir a single step. Next they put a lance into his hands, with which he propped himself up as best he could, and they urged him to march and lead them on and put spirit into the whole people, for, they added, there would be no doubt of victory since he was their pole-star, their lantern and their morning star.

"How can I march—bad 'cess to it!" said the governor, "when I can't stir my knee-joints with these planks digging so hellishly deep into my flesh? What you should do is to carry me in your arms, and lay me slantwise, or prop me up at some gate, which I'll defend with this spear or with my body."

"Come, come, Lord Governor," said another, " 'tis fear rather than shields that hinders your marching. Hurry and get a move on, it is high time, the enemy grows stronger and danger threatens."

The poor governor, urged and upbraided, tried to totter forwards, but down he fell full length with such a bump that he thought he had broken every bone in his body. There he lay like a huge tortoise in his shell, or like a flitch of bacon sandwiched between two boards, or like a boat keel upwards on the shore. But those jesting fellows, though they saw him lying prone, did not show him the least compassion; on the contrary, having put out their torches, they renewed their shouting and alarms, and clattered their arms unceasingly, and trampled upon the unfortunate Sancho, and slashed away at the shields so continuously that if he had not ducked his head between the bucklers it would have gone hard with him. Indeed, the poor governor, huddled up in his narrow shell, sweated with terror, and prayed with all his heart and soul to God for deliverance from such a horrible danger. Some butted into him, others fell on top of him, and one among them leaped upon his body and stood there for a long time, as on a watch-tower, giving orders to the troops. "This way, my men," he bawled in a stentorian voice, "this way the enemy is charging thickest: guard that gate over there; close yon gate; knock down those scaling ladders; bring grenades, burning pitch, resin, and kettles of boiling oil; barricade the streets with mattresses!" In short, he called for all the instruments of death, and all the gear used in the defence of a city besieged.

Sancho, bruised and battered, listened to all that was taking place, and kept saying to himself: "If only the blessed Lord would be pleased to allow this island to be captured, and if I could only see myself either dead or delivered from this hell-kitchen!"

Heaven at last heard his prayers, and, when he least expected it, he heard the shouts: "Victory, victory! The enemy is vanquished. Rise, Lord Governor, and make ready to enjoy the conquest, and divide the spoils your invincible army has snatched from the enemy."

"Lift me up," quoth Sancho in a plaintive tone, and when they had set him on his legs he said: "As to all the enemies I may have killed, let them be nailed to my forehead: I want no dividing of spoils, but I beg and entreat some friend, if I have any, to give me a sup of wine, for I'm choking with the drought, and to help me dry up the sweat that's pouring off me, for I'm turning to water."

They wiped him, gave him wine and untied the shields. Then when he sat down on the bed, what with his fright, his agony and his sufferings, he fainted away, and those responsible for the scene began to repent they had carried the joke so far. However, their anxiety passed away when they saw Sancho recover after a short time. He asked them what time it was, and they told him it was daybreak. He said no more, but began to put on his clothes in silence, while the rest looked on, wondering why he was in such haste to dress.

At length, having put on his clothes and creeping along a step at a time, because he was too much bruised to hurry, he wended his way to the stable, followed by all the company. Then going up to Dapple, he embraced him and gave him a kiss of peace on his forehead. "Come hither," said he with tears in his eyes, "my friend and partner of my toils and troubles: when you and I consorted together and had no other care in the world but mending your harness and feeding that little carcase of yours, happy were my hours, my days and my years; but since I forsook you and mounted the towers of ambition and pride, a thousand woes, a thousand torments and four thousand tribulations have entered my soul."

While he was speaking he set about saddling the ass, without anyone interrupting him. When this was done, he mounted with great difficulty, and then addressing the steward, the secretary, the butler, and Dr. Pedro Recio, and many other bystanders, he said: "Make way, gentlemen, and let me return to my former liberty. Let me go in search of the life I left, and rise again from this present death. I was not born to be a governor, nor to defend islands nor cities from enemies who wish to attack them. I know more about ploughing, digging, pruning, and planting vines, than about making laws or defending cities and kingdoms. St. Peter is all right at Rome—I mean to say that 'a man does best the job for which he was born.' In my hand a sickle is better than a governor's sceptre; and I'd rather stuff my belly with Andalusian broth,[1] the poor man's diet, than submit to a rascally physic-monger who starves me to death. I'd rather rest under a shady oak in the summer, and wrap myself up in a rough sheepskin in winter, at my own sweet will, than lie down, with the slavery of a government, in holland sheets, and dress myself up in richest sables. God be with you, gentlemen, and tell my lord the duke that naked was I born, and naked I am now; I neither lose nor win, for without a penny I came to this government, and without a penny I leave it, quite the opposite to what governors of other islands are wont to do when they leave them. Let me go, gentlemen: I must plaster myself, for I don't believe I have a single rib unbroken, thanks to the enemies who have trodden on me all night long."

"This must not be so, My Lord Governor," said Dr. Recio, "I'll give your worship a potion against falls and bruises, which will give you back your former vigour. As to your diet, I promise your honour to turn over a new leaf, and let you eat whatever you please."

"You've chirped too late, Mr. Doctor," replied Sancho, "I'd as soon turn Turk as not go. No, no! 'Once bitten twice shy' as far as this is concerned. By God, you might as soon make me fly up to heaven without wings as get me to take this or any other government, even though it were served up in a covered dish. I'm of the stock of the Panzas, and every man of us is stubborn as a mule. When once we cry 'Odd,' odd it's got to be, against the whole world, even though it be even. No, let every sheep to her mate; ne'er

[1] 'Gazpacho,' made of biscuit, oil, onions, vinegar and garlic.

stretch your feet beyond the sheet; so let me be on my way, for 'tis getting late."

"My Lord Governor," said the steward, "we would not presume to hinder your departure, although we are sorry to lose you because of your wise and Christian conduct, but your worship knows that every governor, before he leaves his government, is required to render an account of his administration."

"No man can require that of me," replied Sancho, "save My Lord Duke. To him I go, and to him I'll give a fair and square account, and since I depart as bare as I do, there's no further token needed to show that I've governed like an angel."

And so they all agreed to let him go, and they offered to supply him with whatever he might need on his journey. Sancho told them that all he required was a little barley for Dapple; half a cheese and half a loaf for himself; in such a short journey nothing more would be necessary. Then they all embraced him, and he with tears in his eyes embraced them, and departed leaving them in admiration both of his good sense and unshakable determination.

Our friend Sancho, whose feelings were a mixture of gladness and sadness, rode along on Dapple in the direction of his master, whose company pleased him more than being governor of all the islands in the world. He had not gone far from his island, city or town (for he had never troubled himself to find out what it was), when he saw six pilgrims plodding along the road with their staves, foreigners as they turned out to be, of the class that beg for alms in song. As they approached they lined up and began their song in the language of their country, but all that Sancho could understand was one word which clearly signified alms, whence he guessed that begging was the burden of their chant. Being extremely charitable, he took out of his saddle-bags the half loaf and half cheese, and gave it to them, making signs that he had nought else to give. They received his gift eagerly, saying: "Guelte, guelte."[2]

"I don't understand you," replied Sancho. "What do you want, good folks?"

One of them then pulled out of his bosom a purse, and showing it to Sancho, making him understand that it was money they wanted. Sancho, putting his thumb to his throat and shaking his hand with his four fingers upwards, made a sign that he had not a penny in the world. Then clapping heels to Dapple, he broke through them, but, as he passed, one of them, who had been gazing at him most earnestly, caught hold of him, and, throwing his arms around his waist,

[2] German for money.

cried out loud in excellent Spanish: "God save us! What do I see? Is it possible that I'm holding in my very arms my dear friend and worthy neighbour Sancho Panza? I'm sure it is, for I'm neither drunk nor dreaming."

Sancho, who was astonished to hear his name called and to be embraced by the pilgrim stranger, stared at him without speaking, but stare as he would he could not remember him.

"Is it possible, brother Sancho Panza, that you don't recall your neighbour, Ricote, the Morisco shopkeeper of your village."

Then Sancho, after giving him another close look, began to call him to mind, and at last he remembered him perfectly, and, without dismounting, he hugged him around the neck, saying: "Ricote, who the devil could recognize you in your merry-andrew's costume? Tell me now, who has frenchified you in this way? How it is you dare to come back to Spain? Why, if they find you out, you'll be in for a bad time."

"If you don't give me away, Sancho," replied the pilgrim, "I'm safe enough, for not a soul would know me in this get-up. Now let us retire to the wood yonder, where my companions mean to dine and have a nap, and you'll dine with us. They are decent, peaceable folks, I assure you, and I'll have an opportunity to tell you how I spent my time since I was forced to leave our town in obedience to the king's edict, which, as you know, so severely threatens the people of my unfortunate nation."[3]

Sancho accepted the invitation and, after Ricote had spoken to the rest of the pilgrims, they all turned into the popular wood, which was a good distance from the main road. Then they threw aside their staves and took off their pilgrims' habits, and remained in doublet and hose. They were all youths, with the exception of Ricote who was well on in years: all of them good-looking fellows, and each had his wallet, which, as it soon appeared, was well furnished, at least with peppery and spicy victuals such as would raise a raging thirst two leagues away. They stretched themselves on the ground, and using the green grass as their table-cloth they spread out on it bread, salt, knives, nuts, cheese, and some ham bones, which, though they had precious little to pick on them, could at least be sucked with relish. They brought out also a kind of black eatable called caviare, made of the roes of a fish; still better to tempt a man to pluck the leather. Even olives were not missing, and though a bit dry and unseasoned, they were most tasty. But the champion of the

[3] Between 1609 and 1613 proclamation was made ordering the expulsion from Spain of the Moriscos, *i.e.* the Moors, who, though outwardly converted, secretly practised their religion.

whole feast was six bottles of wine, for each pilgrim possessed one as his share, even honest Ricote, who from a Morisco became for the nonce a German or a Hollander, and grabbed his bottle, which in size was a match for the other five. They now began their banquet in high good-humour, and at a leisurely pace, for they dwelt upon each morsel with the utmost relish, spiking but a snippet of each dainty at a time on the end of their knife in order to make the most of it. Then, after a pause, with one accord they raised their arms and wineskins aloft into the air, and joining their mouths to the mouths of the bottles, and with their eyes fixed upwards as if taking aim at the heavens, they remained in this posture a good while, letting the heart's blood of the vessels gurgle into their bellies as they wagged their heads from side to side in token of their rapturous ecstasy. Sancho beheld all this, and not a complaint did he utter; on the contrary, wishing to comply with the good old proverb, "when in Rome, do as the Romans do," he asked Ricote for his bottle, and, taking his as the rest had done, he showed no less satisfaction. Four times the wineskins were tilted upwards with good effect, but the fifth was to no purpose, for the skins by then were flabby and as dry as a rush; a circumstance which somewhat damped their rollicking spirits. From time to time one of the pilgrims would take Sancho by the right hand, saying: "Spanish and German here all one: goot companion." Sancho would echo in response: "Goot companion, I swear to God," then he would burst into a fit of laughter lasting well-nigh an hour. And from that moment all memories of his past misfortunes faded away, for anxieties have little power over men during the time that is spent in eating and drinking. In short, no sooner was the wine finished than a deep sleep seized upon them and they lay snoring beside the remains of their feast, all except Sancho and Ricote, who had indeed eaten more but drunk less. So the two friends, leaving the pilgrims buried in their sweet sleep, went a short distance away and sat down in the shade of a beech tree, and Ricote, without once stumbling into his Morisco jargon, spoke in pure Castilian as follows:

"You are well aware, Sancho Panza, my friend, how terrified all of our race were when the edict of His Majesty was proclaimed. It certainly produced such a dread effect upon me that I almost imagined the law had already been executed upon me and my children before even the time-limit for our departure had expired. Accordingly I left our village by myself and went to seek some place beforehand, where I might conveniently convey my family without the hurry and confusion which prevailed when the rest set out;

for I knew, and so too did the elders of my race, that the edicts of His Majesty were no mere threats, as some said, but genuine laws that would be put into force within a determined time. I was all the more inclined to believe this, being aware that our people were continually plotting against the State, and I could not but think that His Majesty was inspired by Heaven to take so gallant a resolution. It is true we were not all guilty; some of us were sturdy and steadfast Christians, but we were so few in number that we were no match for those who were otherwise, and it was not safe for Spain to nurse the serpent in its bosom. And so the expulsion was just and necessary; a punishment which some might consider a mild and pleasant fate, but to us it seems the most disastrous calamity that could befall us. Wherever in the world we are we weep for Spain, for, after all, there we were born, and it is our fatherland. Nowhere can we find the compassion which our misfortunes crave; for in Barbary and other parts of Africa, where we expected to be welcomed and cherished, it is there that they treat us with the grossest inhumanity. We did not know our happiness until we had lost it, and the longing which most of us have to return to Spain is such that the majority of those who speak the language as I do, who are many, come back hither, and abandon our wives and children over there in penury; so strong is their love for their native land. Now I know by experience the truth of the saying, 'sweet is the love of one's own fatherland.'

"When I left our village I went to France, and, though I was well treated there, yet I wished to roam the world. From France, therefore, I passed into Italy, and thence into Germany, where I thought one might live in greater freedom, for the inhabitants are not over particular, and, as there is liberty of conscience, everyone lives his own way. There I took a house in a village near Augsberg, and joined these pilgrims who are accustomed to come to Spain in great numbers every year to visit its sanctuaries, which they regard as their Indies and their surest and most profitable source of income. They roam over the whole country, and there is not a village where they are not certain to get food and drink in plenty, and at least a real in money. As a rule, they manage by the end of their journey to make more than a hundred crowns clear gain, which they change into gold and hide either in the hollow of their staves or between the patches of their cloaks, or in some secret way, and thus they carry them off safely to their country, in spite of the numerous inspectors and other officers who search them before they leave.

"Now, Sancho, my friend, my real object in coming here is not to collect alms but to carry off the treasure that I left buried when I went away. As it lies in a place outside the village, I'll be able to fetch it without danger to myself. As soon as that is done, I intend to write or cross myself from Valencia to my wife and daughter, who are, I know, in Algiers, and find some means or other to get them over to a port in France, and thence carry them into Germany, where we will wait and see what God has in store for us. Francisca, my wife, I know is a good Catholic Christian, and my daughter Ricota also. Though I myself am not so far on as they are, yet I am more of a Christian than a Mohammedan, and I pray constantly to Almighty God to open the eyes of my understanding and make me know how I can best serve Him. I am, however, surprised that my wife and daughter should have preferred to go to Barbary rather than to France, where they might have lived as Christians."

"Listen, Ricote," said Sancho, "that must not have been their choice, for Juan Tiopieyo, your wife's brother, it was, who carried them off, and as he's a cunning Moor, he went where there was most money to be got. And I'll add one thing more, namely, that you may be wasting your time looking for your hidden treasure, as I heard it said that many pearls and gold coins had been seized from your brother-in-law and your wife by the inspectors."

"That may be," replied Ricote, "but I know, Sancho, they didn't touch my hidden nest-egg, for I never told them where I hid it, for fear of some accident. Now if you'll come along with me and help me to rescue this money I'll give you two hundred crowns to help you meet your obligations, for I know you've got many."

"I'd do it," answered Sancho, "but I'm not at all covetous. If I had been so, would I have left this morning an employment which might have given me enough to build the walls of my house with beaten gold, and before six months were over you'd find me eating off silver plates? For this reason, and because, to my way of thinking, it would be a piece of treason to the King if I were to help his enemies, I won't go with you, even if you were to offer me twice as much cash down."

"Now tell me," quoth Ricote, "what kind of job have you left?"

"I've left off being governor of an island, aye, such an island as I swear you wouldn't find if you were to search the world."

"Where is it?" asked Ricote.

"Two leagues from here," replied Sancho, "and it's called the island of Barataria."

"Hush, Sancho," said Ricote, "islands lie out in the sea; there are none of them on the mainland."

"Why not?" quoth Sancho. "I tell you, Ricote, my friend, I came from there this morning, and yesterday there I was governing it at my own sweet will, proud and haughty as a highwayman on his last ride. Yet for all that I turned it down, because, in my opinion, a governor's job is a mighty ticklish one."

"What did you get from your governorship?" asked Ricote.

"I got," answered Sancho, "experience enough to know that I'm no hand at governing aught else but a herd of cattle, and that the wealth a fellow earns by such governorships has got to be paid in hard labour, loss of sleep, and in hunger too, for governors of islands must eat next to nothing, especially if they have physicians to look after their health."

"I can make neither head nor tail of this," said Ricote, "in fact, it all seems flapdoodle to me, for who in heaven's name would give you islands to govern? Were they so badly off for brainy men that they had to choose you? Hold your whisht, Sancho, and come back to earth, and consider whether you'll come with me and help me carry off my hidden treasure. Indeed, I may well call it treasure, seeing there's so much of it, and I'll give you a tidy sum to live on, as I said before."

"I told you, Ricote," replied Sancho, "that I'm not willing. But set your mind at rest, I'll not give you away. Now go your way, and good luck to you, and let me go mine; for I know only too well that 'well-got wealth may meet disaster, but ill-got wealth destroys its master'."

"Sancho, my friend, I won't press you any longer," said Ricote, "but tell me now: were you by chance in our village when my wife, my daughter and my brother-in-law went off?"

"Yes, I was there," replied Sancho, "and by the same token that daughter of yours looked so handsome that the whole village turned out to see her, and all said she was the fairest creature on God's earth. She kept crying all the way, and embracing all her friends and acquaintances; and she begged all who came to see her off to pray to Our Lady for her, and that in so piteous a manner that she even made me cry, and I'm no blubberer. Faith and skin, there were many had a good mind to kidnap her on the road and hide her away, but the fear of the King's order had them cowed. He who carried on most passionately was Don Pedro Gregorio, that rich young heir you know. They say he was daft about her, and since she left he hasn't shown himself in our village. We all thought he had gone after her, to kidnap her, but we've heard nothing up to the present."

"All along I suspected that this young fellow was courting my daughter, but I always put my trust in my Ricota's virtue, so it didn't worry me to know that he loved her, for you must have heard say, Sancho, that Moorish women seldom or ever married Old Christians for love, so I'm sure that my daughter, who, I believe, minded her Christian religion more than love, would pay scant heed to the courting of this young heir."

"God grant it," replied Sancho, "otherwise 'twould be the worse for both of them. Now, friend Ricote, 'tis time to say farewell, for I want to reach my master, Don Quixote, this night."

"God be with you, brother Sancho," said Ricote: "I see my companions are stirring and 'tis time for us to continue our journey."

The two then embraced, Sancho mounted Dapple, Ricote picked up his pilgrim staff, and thus they parted.

Sancho had spent so much time conversing with Ricote that night fell when he was half a league from the duke's castle. It grew very dark, but as it was summer-time, he felt no uneasiness, and turned off the highway, intending to bivouac until morning. But, as ill-luck would have it, in searching for a place to shelter, he and Dapple all of a sudden fell into a deep hole which yawned amidst some old ruins. As he was falling he recommended his soul to God, not expecting to stop till he came to the bottom of the pit, but this did not happen, for when he had fallen a little more than eighteen feet Dapple struck the ground, and he found himself still on his back, unbruised and unscathed. Sancho felt himself all over and held his breath, wondering whether he was still safe and sound, without a bone broken; and when he found himself whole and in Catholic health he could never give adequate thanks to Heaven for his miraculous preservation. He then groped about the walls of the pit, to try if it were possible to climb out without help, but he found them all smooth, and without any footing. This grieved him exceedingly, and to increase his depression, Dapple began to groan piteously and dolefully, nor did the poor beast lament without good cause, for in truth he was in a woeful plight. "Alas," cried Sancho, "what unexpected mishaps occur at every step to those who live in this mierable world! Who would have thought that he who but yesterday saw himself seated on the throne as island governor, with servants and vassals at beck and call, should today find himself buried in a pit without a soul to come to his relief?"

Then Sancho moaned over his misfortunes, and his ass listened to what he said, but not a word did he answer, so great was the anguish and distress of the poor beast. At length, after a whole night of miserable lamentations, daylight came, and Sancho realized that there was no possibility of getting out of that place without help, so he began to shout as loud as he could, in hope that somebody would hear him, but his was a

391

"voice crying in the wilderness," as not a living soul was within hearing. He then gave himself up for dead. Seeing that Dapple was lying on the ground, he set to work to get him up on his legs, and with great difficulty he did so, though the poor animal could hardly stand. Then he took out of his saddle-bags a piece of bread and gave it to the ass, who relished it. "Better a fat sorrow than a lean one," said he to the ass, as if the latter understood him. After a time he noticed at one side of the cavern a crevice large enough for a man to squeeze through if he stooped. Having crawled through on all-fours, he found that it led into a vault which, by a ray of sunlight that came through the roof, he saw was large and spacious, and he noted that it led into another vault of equal size. After this discovery he went back to Dapple and, picking up a stone, he began digging away to remove the earth from the hole, and in a short time he made it large enough for Dapple to pass. Then, leading the ass by the halter, he went along through the various vaults to see if he could find a way out on the other side. Sometimes he was in the dusky gloom, sometimes in pitch darkness, but always in fear and trembling. "Almighty God protect me!" said he to himself, "this is all misfortune for me, but my master, Don Quixote, would take it as a rare adventure. He'd look upon these caves and dungeons as lovely gardens and gorgeous palaces of Galiana,[4] and he'd feel sure they would end in some flowering meadow or other. But here am I, a poor, feckless, chicken-hearted loon, who am for ever fancying that the earth is going to open all of a sudden under my feet and swallow me up. Welcome bad luck when it comes alone." Such were Sancho's despairing laments as he cautiously groped his way through the vaults, until at last, after going somewhat more than half a league, he saw a glimmering light, like that of day, shining through an aperture above, but which he looked upon as an entrance to another world.

There we shall leave him for an instant while we return to Don Quixote.

The knight happened that morning to be out in the country exercising his steed, and Rozinante, in one of his curvetings, pitched his feet so near the brink of a deep cave that had not Don Quixote pulled in his reins sharply he would inevitably have tumbled into it. Having managed to check his horse in time, he wheeled him round and rode up to the edge, and gazed earnestly down into the yawning chasm. All at once he heard a noise down in the depths, and, listening intently, he was able to distinguish the following words: "Hello! Above there! Is there any Christian to hear me? Is there no

[4] In Spanish tradition, a Moorish princess whose father, King Haxen of Toledo, built her a magnificent palace on the Tagus.

charitable gentleman to take pity on a sinner buried alive—a poor governor without a government?"

Don Quixote fancied it was Sancho's voice he heard, and this amazed him, so he shouted as loudly as he could: "Who are you below there? Who is it that cries for help?"

"Who should be here shouting for help but miserable Sancho Panza, governor, for his sins, and for his accursed misfortune, of the island of Barataria, formerly squire to the famous knight Don Quixote of La Mancha?"

At these words Don Quixote's wonder and alarm increased, for he then imagined that Sancho was dead, and that his soul was there doing penance. With this fancy uppermost in his mind, he said: "I conjure you as a Catholic Christian to tell me who you are: and if you are a soul in Purgatory, let me know what you want me to do for you. Since my profession is to assist and succour all that are afflicted in this world, I shall also be ready to relieve and aid the distressed in the world below, who cannot help themselves."

"In that case," said he from below, "you who are speaking to me must be my master, Don Quixote: by the tone of your voice I know 'tis none else."

"My name is Don Quixote," replied the knight, "and I think it is my duty to assist the dead as well as the living. Tell me, then, who you are, for I am astounded at what I hear. If you are my squire Sancho Panza, and are dead, and if the Devil has not carried you off, and through God's mercy you are in Purgatory, Our Holy Mother, the Roman Catholic Church, has enough suffrages to redeem you from the pains you suffer, and I will solicit her in your behalf, as far as my estate will allow. So proceed, and tell me who you are."

"Well, then," replied the voice, "I swear by whatever you will that I'm Sancho Panza, your squire, and that I never yet died in all the days of my life, but having left my government for reasons which I'll need more time to tell you, I fell into this cave, where I'm standing now, and Dapple with me, that won't let me lie—as a further proof here he is by me."

Then as if the ass had understood what his master said and wanted to back up his evidence, he began to bray so loudly that the whole cavern echoed and re-echoed.

"That is a prime witness," said Don Quixote. "I know his bray as well as if I was his parent, and I know your voice, too, dear Sancho. Wait for me; I'll hasten off to the duke's castle, which is hard by, and get people to pull you out of the pit where your sins, doubtless, have cast you."

"Make haste, I pray you, sir," quoth Sancho, "and for God's sake come back quick, for I can't bear being buried alive, and I'm dying of fear."

Don Quixote left him and hastened to the castle to tell the

duke and duchess about Sancho's mishap. They were very astonished, though they knew that he might easily have fallen down into the pit, which had been there from time immemorial. They could not, however, understand how he came to give up his government without their having been notified of his coming. They straightway sent their servants with ropes and cables to draw him out, and at the cost of many hands and much toil they pulled up Dapple and his master from the dark realms to the light of the sun. A certain student, who was one of the bystanders, when he saw it, exclaimed: "That's how all bad governors should come out of their governments, just as this sinner comes out of this deep abyss, pale, famished, and as far as I know, penniless."

Sancho heard his remark and replied: "Listen here to me, back-biter: 'tis only eight or ten days since I started to govern the island that was given to me, and in all that time I never once had my bellyful, except once; physicians have persecuted me, enemies trodden on me and battered my bones, and I've not had a moment to take bribes nor to receive what was owing to me. When all this is taken into account I didn't deserve by a long way to end up this way. But man proposes and God disposes, and He knows what's best and right for every one of us; and we should take time as it comes, and our lot as it falls; don't let anyone say, 'I'll drink no more of this water'; for where one thinks to find a flitch there's ne'er a stake to hang it on; God knows my mind and that's enough, mum's the word."

"Be not angry, Sancho, nor troubled at what is said," quoth Don Quixote, "otherwise you will never have a moment's peace. Provided your conscience is clear, let the world say what it will, for you might as well put up gates in the open country as tie up the tongues of slanderers. If a governor returns rich from his government, they say he has been a robber; if poor, then they say he was a worthless fool."

"In that case," replied Sancho, "I'm sure they'll all take me for a fool rather than a robber."

Such was their discourse as they walked along towards the castle, surrounded by a crowd of boys and others. When they arrived they found the duke and duchess waiting for them in the gallery. Sancho refused to go up to see the duke until he had stabled Dapple and given him his feed, for, said he, the poor beast had had a poor night's lodging. When that was done, he went up to the duke and duchess, and knelt down before them, saying: "My lord and lady, not through any merit of mine but because your grandeurs wished it, I went off to govern your island of Barataria. I entered it naked and naked I came away. I neither won nor lost. Whether I governed well or badly, there were witnesses who'll say what they please. I've settled problems, decided law-suits, always perishing with the hunger, for that was the wish of Dr. Pedro Recio of Tirteafuera, physician-in-ordinary to insular governors. Enemies made a set against us in the night, and after landing us into great danger, the people of the island say they were saved and won the victory by the strength of my arm. May God help them in so far as they speak the truth. Now in that time I bore all the burdens this business of governing brings with it, and I found them, by my account, too heavy for my shoulders or my ribs to bear—they are, in fact, not the arrows for my quiver. And so, before the government could knock me all of a heap I resolved to knock it all of a heap; accordingly, yesterday morning I left the island as I found it, with the same streets, the same houses, the same roofs as it had when I entered it. I've neither asked for a loan nor set myself to make a pile. Though I intended to issue some wholesome laws, I made none of them, for I was afeared they would not keep them, and that's the same as making none at all. I left the island, I repeat, without any company but my Dapple: I fell into a pit, and groped my way through it, till this morning by the light of the sun I saw the way out, but 'twas no easy matter, for if Heaven hadn't sent my master Don Quixote to rescue me, I'd have stayed there till doomsday. So now, my lord duke and my lady duchess, here's your governor Sancho Panza again, who in a mere ten days' government has learnt that he wouldn't give a fig to be a governor, not only of an island, but even of the whole wide world. Admitting this, and kissing your excellency's feet, and copying boys at play when they cry, 'you leap and I'll follow,' I give a leap out of the government, back into my old master's service again; for, after all, though with him I often eat my daily bread in fear and trembling, at least I eat my bellyfull; and, as far as I'm concerned, if only that's well stuffed, it's all the same whether it be carrots or partridges."

Here Sancho ended his long speech, and Don Quixote, who was always anxious lest his squire should utter a thousand absurdities, gave thanks to Heaven when he saw that he had ended with so few. The duke embraced Sancho, and told him he was grieved that he had left his government so soon, but that he would give him some other less troublesome and more profitable post. The duchess too embraced him, and gave orders that he should be taken care of, for he seemed to be badly bruised and in a bad way.

Don Quixote now thought it high time to leave the idle life he led in the castle, for he felt he was much to blame for allowing himself thus to be shut up, and for living indolently amidst the tempting dainties and delights provided for him, as a knight-errant, by the duke and duchess. He believed, too, that he would have to give a strict account to Heaven for leading a life so opposed to the active ideals of his profession. Accordingly he besought their graces to grant him permission to depart: they yielded to his request, though they showed him plainly that they deeply regretted his going. The duchess gave Sancho Panza his wife's letters, which he wept over. "Who would have thought," cried he, "that all the mighty hopes with which my wife puffed herself up at the news of my government should come to this at last, and that it should be my fate to return to the rambling adventures of my master, Don Quixote de La Mancha! However, I'm thankful that my Teresa was like herself, in sending the acorns to the duchess; if she hadn't sent them, and had showed herself an ungrateful woman, 'pon my word I'd be mighty sad; and 'tis a comfort that no man can say the gift was to oil a palm, for I had my government before she sent it, and isn't it right that those who receive a benefit should show themselves thankful, even though it be only a gaudy gewgaw? Naked I went into the government, and naked I came out, and so I can say with a clear conscience—and that's no small matter—naked I came from my mother's womb, and naked I am this moment: I neither win nor lose." Such were Sancho's sentiments on the day of his departure.

As for Don Quixote, he had taken leave of the duke and duchess the night before, and early next morning he sallied forth from his apartment in full armour, and descended into the courtyard. The surrounding galleries were thronged with the inmates of the castle, and the duke and duchess were there to see him set out on his adventures. Sancho was mounted upon Dapple, with his saddle-bags, his wallet and his provisions, he was as pleased as Punch because the steward had given him, unbeknown to Don Quixote, a purse containing two hundred gold crowns to defray the expenses of the journey. And now, while everyone was gazing at Don Quixote, all of a sudden the pert and witty Altisidora raised her voice from amidst the crowd of duennas and damsels of the duchess, and addressed the knight in doggerel rhymes which expressed her resentment at his departure. Don Quixote stood looking at her attentively while she chanted her doleful song, but he would not answer a word, and kept his silence. After he had made a low obeisance to the duke, the dutchess and all the company, he wheeled round Rozinante, and sallied out of the castle gate, followed by Sancho upon Dapple, and took the road leading to Saragossa.

XIV. Of what befell Don Quixote and his squire on their way to Barcelona, and an adventure which caused greater sorrow to the former than any yet

AS SOON AS DON QUIXOTE FOUND HIMSELF IN OPEN COUNTRY, safe and sound and free from Altisidora's endearments, he fancied himself in his own element, and felt all his old chivalric impulses revive. Turning to Sancho, he said: "Liberty, Sancho, my friend, is one of the most precious gifts that Heaven has bestowed on mankind; not all the treasures the earth contains within its bosom, or the ocean within its depths, can be compared with it. For liberty as well as honour man ought to risk even his life, and he should reckon captivity the greatest evil that life can bring. I say this, Sancho, because you were a witness of the luxury and plenty which we enjoyed in the castle we have just left; yet, in the midst of those seasoned banquets, and snow-cooled liquors, I suffered, or so it seemed to me, the extremities of hunger, because I did not enjoy them with the same freedom as if they had been my own, for the obligations that spring from benefits and kindnesses received, are ties that prevent a noble mind from ranging freely. Happy the man to whom Heaven has given a morsel of bread for which he is obliged to thank Heaven alone."[1]

"Nevertheless," quoth Sancho, "we should feel grateful for two hundred gold crowns which the duke's steward gave me in a little purse, which I carry next my heart as a restorative and comfort in case of need, for we'll not always run across hospitable castles; instead, we'll be more likely to meet inns where we'll be drubbed."

Late that day Don Quixote discovered among some trees a bubbling spring which revived their spirits after their wearisome journey. After taking the bridle and halter off Rozinante and Dapple, and letting them go free, the two forlorn adventurers sat down by the edge of the fountain. Sancho straightway turned to the store of his saddle-bags, and drew out what he called his belly-timber. He rinsed his mouth, and Don Quixote washed his face, by which they were refreshed in some degree; but the knight, who was out of sorts, refused to eat, and Sancho out of pure good manners re-

[1] This sentiment has a twofold meaning here, for it applies both to Don Quixote and to his creator Cervantes, whose heroic struggle and self-denial in the cause of freedom were the source of all his troubles.

frained from touching the food in front of him, waiting for his master to handsel the feast. At length, seeing that his master was so wrapped up in his fancies as to forget to lift a morsel to his mouth, he said not a word, but, casting all thoughts of good-breeding to the winds, began to stuff his belly with all the bread and cheese he could find within reach.

"Eat, friend Sancho," cried Don Quixote, "repair the decay of nature and support your life, which you have more reason to cherish than I, for I was born, Sancho, to live dying, and you to die eating."

"In that case," said Sancho (still chewing rapidly as he spoke), "you, master, won't approve of the saying, 'let Marta die, so she die well-fed.' As for myself, I've no intention of killing myself; no, I'll do like the cobbler who stretches the leather with his teeth to make it fit; I'll stretch the span of my life by eating as far as Heaven will let it run. I' faith, master, there's no greater folly in the world than for a man to despair. Take my advice, and after you've eaten, throw yourself down and have a bit of a snooze on the grass here, which is as soft as a green feather-mattress; when you awake I'll guarantee you find yourself another man."

Don Quixote followed Sancho's advice, for he was convinced the squire spoke more like a philosopher than a fool; but before doing so he said to him: "Ah, Sancho! if you would only do for me what I am now going to propose, my sorrows would be lessened and my relief more certain. All that I want you to do is this. Whilst I follow your advice and try to sleep, do you go a short distance away, and expose your bare skin to the open air. Then take the reins of Rozinante, and give yourself three or four hundred lashes as payment on account of the three thousand and odd which you are bound to give yourself in order to disenchant Dulcinea; for truly it is no small shame that the poor lady should remain enchanted owing to your carelessness and neglect."

"There's a great deal to be said on that," said Sancho, "but for the present let us both sleep, and then, 'God knows what may happen.' Remember, sir, that this lashing oneself in cold blood is a tough business, all the more when the stripes fall on a body so thinly covered and worse lined as mine is. Let my Lady Dulcinea be patient, and one day, when she least expects it, she'll see my pelt turned into a regular sieve with the belting. While there's life there's hope; which is just as good as to say, 'a promise is always a promise.'"

Don Quixote thanked him, and ate sparingly; but Sancho gorged himself. They both then lay down to sleep, leaving Rozinante and Dapple, those inseparable companions and friends, to crop at their own discretion the rich grass abounding in that meadow.

They awoke rather late in the day, mounted again and continued their journey more rapidly towards an inn which seemed to be about a league away. I say it was an inn, because Don Quixote himself called it so, contrary to his usual procedure, which was to take inns for castles. When they arrived, they asked the landlord if he had any lodgings. "Yes," he replied, "and as good accommodation as you'd find in Saragossa itself." They dismounted, and Sancho put his baggage in a room, of which the host gave him the key. Then he put Rozinante and Dapple in the stable, fed them, and returned to receive Don Quixote's orders, whom he found seated on a stone bench.

As supper-time was near, Sancho asked the host what there was to eat. "Whatever you will," he replied, "you may make your choice: soaring birds of the air, earth-bound birds,[2] fishes from the open sea: there's nothing this inn can't provide."

"We don't need all that," said Sancho, "a couple of chickens roasted will do us well, for my master is delicate and has a small appetite, and I myself am no gluttonous trencherman."

"We've no chickens," replied the innkeeper, "for the kites have eaten them."

"Well, then," quoth Sancho, "roast us a pullet, but mind 'tis a tender one."

"Lord bless us! A pullet!" replied the innkeeper. "As true as I'm telling you, I sent over fifty yesterday to be sold in town. But, setting aside pullets, you may ask for anything else."

"In that case there's sure to be a fine joint of veal or kid in the larder."

"Veal or kid, you say?" quoth the host; "I'm afraid there's none just now; 'tis all finished. Next week there'll be enough and to spare."

"Much help that'll be to us," answered Sancho. "I'll lay a bet that you can make up all these deficiencies with lashings of eggs and bacon."

"Hold on!" cried the host. "My guest must be a sly one and no mistake! I've told him I have neither pullets nor hens, and yet he expects me to have eggs! Mention some other delicacies, but don't ask for hens."

"Body of me!" quoth Sancho. "Let us come to something: tell me what you have, Mr. Landlord, and don't make me rack my brains any longer."

"Now what I really and truly have," said the host, "is a pair of cow-heels that look like calves' feet, or a pair of

2 The ironical innkeeper means hens, ducks, geese as opposed to the high-flying wild birds.

399

calves' feet that look like cow-heels, dressed with onions, peas and bacon. They are just ready, and crying out, 'come eat me, come eat me'."

"Mark them down as mine at once," said Sancho, "and let no one touch them. I'll give more for them than anybody else. In my opinion, there's nothing better in the world; give me cow's heel and you can keep your calves' feet."

"Nobody shall touch them," said the host, "for my other guests are so genteel that they bring their cook, their butler, and their larder along with them."

"If you're talking about genteel folks," quoth Sancho, "I'll say there's no genteeler person than my master, but his profession doesn't allow for any larders and butteries: we just squat down in the middle of a field and fill our bellies with acorns or medlars."

As supper was now ready and Don Quixote was still in his chamber, the innkeeper brought it to him there and he sat down comfortably to his meal. Now the room next to that occupied by Don Quixote was separated from it only by a thin partition, and he could hear distinctly the voices of the persons inside. "Don Jerónimo," said one of them, "I beseech you, till supper is brought in, let us read another chapter of the Second Part of *Don Quixote*." No sooner did the knight hear his name mentioned than he sprang to his feet, and listening with attentive ears, he heard the said Don Jerónimo answer: "Why, Señor Don Juan, do you want to read such absurdities? Whoever has read the First Part of the history of *Don Quixote* cannot possibly enjoy the Second Part." [3]

"Nevertheless," said Don Juan, " 'twere better to read it, for no book is so bad as not to have something good in it. What displeases me most about this Second Part is that the author describes Don Quixote as no longer in love with Dulcinea."

As soon as he heard these words, Don Quixote, full of rage and indignation, raised his voice and said: "Whoever shall say that Don Quixote of La Mancha has forgotten, or ever can forget, Dulcinea del Toboso, I will make him know, with equal arms, that his words stray far from the truth. Neither can the peerless Dulcinea be forgotten, nor Don

[3] It appears that Cervantes had reached the present chapter when the book by Avellaneda fell into his hands. From this point to the end he never ceased having sly, satirical digs at the anonymous coxcomb who tricked himself out in another man's plumes. Clemencín, the learned and pedantic commentator, considers this a further proof that Cervantes never revised what he had written, for if he had, he would have flayed Avellaneda in earlier chapters when the bachelor Samson Carrasco talks to the knight of his world fame. But modern commentators have shown that he parodies Avellaneda from the beginning.

Quixote ever forget her. His motto is constancy, and his profession to preserve it staunchly and without constraint."

"Who is that speaking to us?" replied one of the persons in the next room.

"Who should it be, indeed?" quoth Sancho, "but Don Quixote of La Mancha himself, who'll make good all he has said, and all he has to say, for 'a good payer needs no sureties.'"

At these words two gentlemen rushed into the room, and one of them, throwing his arms about Don Quixote's neck, said: "Your presence does not belie your name, nor can your name fail to give credit to your presence. You are indeed the true Don Quixote of La Mancha, pole-star and morning star of knight-errantry, in spite of him who has attempted to usurp your name and annihilate your exploits, as the author of this book, which I deliever to you, has tried to do in vain."

Don Quixote, without making a reply, took up the book, and after turning over some of the pages, laid it down, saying: "In glancing at this volume I have noticed three things for which the author deserves to be rebuked. First, I object to certain words in his prologue: in the second place, his language is Aragonese, for he sometimes omits the article; the third and most damaging objection is that he strays from the truth in an essential point of the history; for he says that the wife of my squire, Sancho Panza, is called Marí Gutiérrez, whereas her name is Teresa Panza,[4] and he who errs in so important a circumstance may well be suspected of errors all through the book."

At this point Sancho butted in, saying: "He's a fine history-maker, and no mistake! A fat lot he knows of the concerns when he calls my wife, Teresa Panza, Marí Gutiérrez! Turn over a few more pages, master, and see whether I'm there, and if they've changed my name too."

"By your words, friend," said Don Jerónimo, "I infer that you are Sancho Panza, squire to Señor Don Quixote."

"I am so," replied Sancho, "and I'm proud of it."

"In that case," said the gentleman, "this new author does not treat you as civilly as he ought. He makes you out a glutton and a fool, without a tittle of humour, and very different to the Sancho described in the First Part of your master's history."

"God forgive him," said Sancho, "he might have left me in my corner, for 'he who knows the fiddle should play on it'; and 'St. Peter is well at Rome.'"

The two gentlemen begged Don Quixote to go to their chamber and sup with them, as they well knew that the inn

[4] In Part I, ch. vi, Cervantes himself calls her Marí Gutiérrez.

had nothing fit for his entertainment. Don Quixote, who was always courteous, accepted their invitation, and Sancho remained with full powers over the hot-pot, and sat down at the head of the table with the innkeeper for company; for he was no less a devotee of cow's heel than the squire.

The two gentlemen asked Don Quixote which way he was travelling. He told them he was going to Saragossa, to be present at the tournament held in that city every year for the prize of a suit of armour.[5] Don Juan told him that the spurious Second Part of his history described how Don Quixote, whoever he was, had been at Saragossa at a public running at the ring, of which the author gives a measly account, defective in contrivance, mean in style, wretchedly poor in devices, and rich only in absurdities. "For that reason," said Don Quixote, "I will not set foot in Saragossa, and so the forgery of this new historian shall be exposed to the eyes of the world, and mankind will be convinced that I am not the Don Quixote of whom he speaks."

"You are wise to act thus," said Don Jerónimo, "besides, there is another tournament in Barcelona, where you may display your valour."

"So I intend," replied Don Quixote, "and now, gentlemen, I crave permission to leave you, for it is time to retire to rest; pray rank me among the number of your best friends and most loyal servants."

"Include me too," quoth Sancho, who had finished his supper and rejoined his master, "who knows, I may be good for something."

Don Quixote and Sancho then retired to their chamber leaving the two gentlemen surprised at the medley of good sense and madness they had observed in the knight, but fully convinced that these two persons were the genuine Don Quixote and Sancho Panza. Don Quixote rose early next morning, and Sancho paid the innkeeper right royally, and advised him either to boast less of the provisions of his inn or to keep it better supplied.

Before he left the inn Don Quixote enquired which was the most direct road to Barcelona. He was resolved not to pass by Saragossa, that thus he might prove the falsity of the new history, which, he understood, had so misrepresented him. For six days the knight and squire travelled on without meeting with any adventure worth recording, but on the sev-

5 As a result of his enemy's work on Don Quixote, Cervantes determines to alter his hero's course. His original intention had been to bring Don Quixote and the bachelor Samson Carrasco together at the tournament in Saragossa, for the latter knew that the knight planned to go there. From now on Cervantes draws humorous toll from his rival's libel.

enth, having lost their way, night overtook them in a thick forest of oaks or cork trees. Master and squire dismounted, and lay down at the foot of the trees. Sancho, who had already eaten his supper, in an instant let himself be wafted through the gates of sleep, but Don Quixote, being a prey to his fancies rather than to hunger, could not close his eyes. His thoughts flashed here and there and everywhere; at one moment he thought himself in the Cave of Montesinos; at another he saw his Dulcinea, who had been transformed into a peasant wench, leap upon her ass; the next moment he thought he heard the sage Merlin proclaiming the conditions required for disenchanting her. He was in despair when he remembered Sancho's uncharitable negligence, who, he believed, had given himself only five lashes—a small number indeed when compared with the great number that still remained. This reflection drove him into such a state of exasperation that he reasoned with himself as follows: "If Alexander the Great cut the Gordian knot, saying: 'to cut is just the same as to untie,' and became in that way the ruler of all Asia, why should I not try the same method now in the disenchantment of Dulcinea, and decide to whip Sancho myself, whether he will or no? For if the condition of this remedy consists in Sancho's receiving the three thousand and odd lashes, what does it matter to me whether he gives himself those stripes or another gives them to him, since the essential point is that he should receive them, from whatever hand they may come?"

With this idea uppermost in his mind he came up to the sleeping Sancho, after having first taken the reins of Rozinante and adjusted them in such a way that he might use them as a cat-o'-nine-tails. He then started to undo the tapes that upheld Sancho's breeches, though it is said that the squire had only the one in front to hold them up. Hardly had he begun his operations when Sancho awoke and was instantly on the alert. He cried out: "What's the matter? Who is trying to undo my breeches?"

"It is I," replied Don Quixote, "who am come to atone for your negligence, and to find a remedy for my torments; I have come to whip you, Sancho, and discharge, at least in part, the debt which you did engage yourself to pay. Dulcinea is perishing; you live on without caring what becomes of her; I am dying with longing; so, let down your breeches of your own free will, for I am determined in this lonely place to give you at least two thousand lashes."

"No, master, not on your life; hands off, or, by God, the deaf will hear us. The lashes I am bound to give myself must be given of my own free will and not under compulsion; and at present I'm not in the humour for flogging. Let you be content that I promise to flog and flay myself when I'm so inclined."

"It is useless to leave it to your courtesy, Sancho," said Don Quixote, "for you are hard-hearted, and though a peasant, your flesh is tender." So saying, he strove with all his might to undo the squire's breeches, but Sancho then jumped to his feet, and making for his master, gripped him, tripped him, and laid him flat on his back, whereupon, setting his right knee upon his chest, he held his hands fast, so that he could scarcely stir or draw his breath.[6] Don Quixote kept crying out: "How, traitor! Do you dare to raise a hand against your master and against the hand that feeds you?"

"I neither raise up king nor pull him down," replied Sancho, "I only defend myself, who am my lord.[7] If you promise me, master, that you'll let me alone and not try to whip me, I'll set you free; if not, 'twill be a case of

'Here and now thou diest, traitor.
Enemy of Doña Sancha'."

Don Quixote gave him his word, and swore by the life of his thoughts never to touch even a hair on Sancho's coat, but leave the whipping entirely to his discretion.

Sancho now got up and moved off to another place, a good distance away; but as he was going to lie down under another tree he felt something touch his head. Lifting up his hands, he found it to be a man's feet, with shoes and stockings on, which were dangling to and fro. Quaking with fear, he moved on to another tree, but there he found a similar pair of dangling feet. He then shouted out to his master for help. Don Quixote came up and Sancho told him that all the trees were full of men's legs and feet. Don Quixote felt them, and immediately guessing what it meant, said to his squire: "Be not afraid, Sancho, these must be the legs of robbers and bandits who have been strung up for their crimes; here it is customary for officers of the law to hang them in bands of twenties and thirties when they can catch them. From this circumstance I gather that we are not far from Barcelona." As it happened, Don Quixote was right, for when

[6] In the days of Cervantes, the men of La Mancha had the reputation of being excellent wrestlers, even when the sport had declined in Spain.

[7] A very old proverb dating from the fourteenth century. It refers to the meeting between King Pedro the Cruel and his bastard brother Enrique de Trastamara in the tent of the French knight Du Guesclin. Pedro and Enrique struggled together, and when Enrique was getting the worst of the fight Du Guesclin, according to tradition, helped him, saying: "I neither raise up king nor pull him down, I only defend my lord."

day began to break they raised their eyes and saw the bodies of bandits hanging from the trees.

If the knight and his squire were unnerved by these dead bandits, how much more did they quake when they suddenly found themselves surrounded by more than forty living bandits, who ordered them in the Catalan tongue to halt and not to move till their captain arrived. Don Quixote happened to be on foot, his horse unbridled, his lance leaning against a tree some distance away; in short, being defenceless, he thought it best to cross his hands, bow his head and reserve himself for a better opportunity. The bandits made haste to rifle Dapple, and in a trice they seized everything they could find in the saddle-bags or in the wallet. It was lucky for Sancho that he had hidden in his belly-band the duke's gold pieces and those he had brought from home; but, for all that, these worthy fellows would certainly have prodded and pried and peered all over him, sparing not even what lurked between his flesh and skin, had they not been interrupted by the arrival of their captain. He seemed to be about thirty-four years of age, of sturdy physique, his stature tall, his face austere and his complexion swarthy. He rode a strong horse, wore a coat of mail and carried two pistols on each side. Noticing that his squires (for so men of that profession are called in those parts) were about to strip Sancho, he commanded them to stop, and was instantly obeyed, and thus the belly-band escaped scot-free. He was surprised to see a lance leaning against a tree, a shield on the ground, and Don Quixote in armour and pensive, with the saddest and most melancholy face that sadness itself could devise.

Walking up to him, he said: "Do not be downhearted, my good man, for you have not fallen into the hands of some cruel Osiris, but into those of Roque Guinárt, whose nature is more compassionate than cruel."

"My sadness," replied Don Quixote, "does not arise from having fallen into your hands, O valiant Roque, whose fame reaches the ends of the earth,[8] but from my negligence in allowing your followers to surprise me with my horse unbridled: for, according to the tenets of the order of knight-errantry which I profess, it was my bounden duty to be continually on the alert, and at all hours be my own sentinel; for I would have you know, great Roque, that had they found me on horseback with my lance and my shield, they would

[8] Roque Guinart was a celebrated historical bandit, whose exploits made him the terror of Catalonia in the early years of the seventeenth century. His real name was Perot Roca Guinarda, and he came from near Vich. During the years 1607-11, he became a kind of Robin Hood figure in the popular imagination. He fought for the partisans known as the Niarros against the Cadells. In 1611 he was pardoned and was appointed captain of a "tercio" of regular troops in Naples.

have found it no easy task to vanquish me, for I am Don Quixote of La Mancha, he whose exploits echo throughout the world."

Roque Guinart straightway realized that Don Quixote's infirmity had more of madness than of valour in it, and though he had from time to time heard men speak of him, he had never believed that what was said of him was true, nor did he imagine that such a humour could exist in any man. He was, in consequence, delighted to meet him, as he now had an opportunity to investigate for himself. "Valiant knight," said he, "do not vex yourself nor exclaim against your destiny, for who knows whether by thus stumbling you may not rectify your twisted fortunes. Indeed, Heaven, by strange and unaccountable ways beyond man's comprehension, is wont to raise the fallen and enrich the poor."

Just at this time one of the scouts arrived with news that, not far off, a large company of travellers were to be seen making their way to Barcelona.

"Have you noticed," said Roque, "whether they are such as look for us, or such as we look for?"

"Such as we look for," answered the scout.

"Away, then," said Roque, "and bring them here—see that none escape."

The order was immediately obeyed and the bandits went off, leaving Don Quixote and Sancho with the chief. Meanwhile Roque addressed Don Quixote as follows: "I am sure, Señor Don Quixote," said he, "that this life of ours must appear strange to you, with its constant sequence of adventures and accidents, all of them perilous. I don't wonder it seems so to you, for I must confess that no manner of life compares with ours for hazards and anxieties. I was driven into it by a lust for vengeance, which is strong enough to sway even those whose natures are calm and peace-loving. By temperament I am gentle and humane, but, as I have said before, no sooner do I feel the wish to avenge a wrong which has been done to me, than all my good intentions fall to the ground. And once I have given way to my evil nature I feel I must go on, even in spite of my better designs; and as one fall is followed by another fall, and sin is added to another sin, my resentments and acts of vengeance have linked themselves together in such an uninterrupted chain that I find myself bearing the burden of other men's crimes as well as my own. Nevertheless, with the help of God, I hope to extricate myself from this entangled maze and bring a peaceful end to my misfortunes."

Don Quixote was surprised to hear Roque utter such sound and sensible words, for he did not expect such qualities from one whose occupation was robbing and killing. "Señor Roque," said he, "once a man recognizes his infirmity and consents to take the medicines prescribed by his physician, he has taken the first great step towards health. You are sick; you know your infirmity, and God, our Physician, will apply medicines that, provided you give them time, will certainly heal you. For sinners who are men of understanding more easily mend their ways than fools, and as your superior sense is manifest, be of good heart and trust in your recovery. If you wish to take the shortest way towards your salvation, come with me, and I will teach you to be a knight-errant: it is a profession full of toils and troubles, no doubt, but if you look upon them as penances for your misdeeds, you will save your soul in the twinkling of an eye."

Roque smiled at Don Quixote's naïve counsel and changed the subject.

By this time Roque's company of bandits had returned with their captives, who consisted of two gentlemen on horseback, two pilgrims on foot, and a coach full of women, attended by half a dozen servants, some on foot and some on horseback, and also two muleteers that belonged to the two gentlemen. They were surrounded by the victorious squires, who, as well as the vanquished travellers, stood in profound silence awaiting the sentence of the great Roque. First of all he asked the gentlemen who they were, whither they were going, and what money they carried. One of them answered: "We are captains of the Spanish infantry, sir, and are going to join our companies which are at Naples, and thus we intend to embark at Barcelona, where four galleys are about to sail for Sicily. We carry about two or three hundred crowns, which we thought a tidy sum for men of our profession, who seldom carry well-lined purses."

The same question was put to the pilgrims, who said that they intended to embark for Rome, and had between them about three score reals.

Roque then questioned the travellers in the coach, and one of the horsemen answered that the persons within were the lady Doña Guiomar de Quiñones, wife of the Regent of the Vicarship of Naples, her little daughter, a maidservant, and an old duenna, together with six servants, and their total sum of money amounted to six hundred crowns.

"So then," said Roque Guinart, "we have here nine hundred crowns sixty reals, and I think I have about sixty soldiers here. See how much falls to each, for I'm a bad accountant."

Hearing this, the highwaymen shouted: "Long live Roque Guinart and damn the dogs who seek his ruin!"

The officers looked crestfallen, the Lady Regent very
407

dejected, the pilgrims in no way pleased, at seeing their goods confiscated. Rogue held them for a while in suspense, but he did not wish to prolong their melancholy, which was visible at a bow-shot's distance, so turning to the captains, he said: "Do me the favour, gentlemen, to lend me sixty crowns, and you, Lady Regent, oblige me with eighty, as a small gratification for these worthy gentlemen of my squadron, for 'the abbot that sings for his meat must eat'. You may then depart and continue your journey without hindrance, for I'll give you a pass in case you run across any other squadrons of mine which are scattered about this region. It is not a practise of mine to interfere with soldiers, and I have no intention of failing in my respects towards the fair sex, especially, madam, when they are ladies of quality."

The captains gave cordial thanks to Roque for his courtesy and generosity, for they considered it a generous gesture of him to allow them keep their money. The lady wanted to throw herself out of the coach at his feet, but Roque would not permit it, and even begged her pardon for the injury he was forced to do in compliance with the duties of his office. The lady then ordered one of her lacqueys to pay the eighty crowns, and the captains settled their share of the debt; and as for the pilgrims, they were about to offer their "widow's mite", but Roque told them to wait a little. Then, turning to his men, he said: "Each man will get two crowns as his share of the pool, which means that there are twenty over: let ten be given to these pilgrims, and the remaining ten be given to this honest squire, so that he may say a good word about us hereafter."

Then, taking pen, ink and paper, he wrote out a passport directed to the chiefs of his various squadrons; and wishing them good luck he let them go their way, and they departed fully convinced that such a gallant, generous chief was an Alexander the Great rather than a notorious robber.

When the travellers had gone, one of the bandits mumbled in his Catalan language: "This captain of ours would do better as friar than as bandit. In future if he must be open-handed let him be it with his own."

The poor wretch spoke low, but Roque heard him, and, drawing his sword, he almost cleft his skull in twain, saying: "That's how I chastise mutiny." The rest were dumbfounded and said not a word, so great was their obedience to his authority. Roque then withdrew, and wrote a letter to a friend at Barcelona, to let him know that the famous Don Quixote of La Mancha was with him, and that as the knight was on his way to Barcelona, he would be sure to see him there on Midsummer's Day parading the strand, in full panoply, on his steed Rozinante, and followed by his squire, Sancho

Panza, upon an ass. He added, too, that he had found the knight the most entertaining and sagacious man in the world. This letter he dispatched by one of his band, who, after changing into a peasant costume, entered the city and delivered it as directed.

Don Quixote spent three days and three nights with the great Roque, and had he tarried with him three hundred years he might have still found plenty to observe and admire in that kind of life. They bivouacked at dawn on this side of the country, only to take their evening meal at the opposite side. Sometimes they fled from they knew not whom, at other times they lay in wait for they knew not whom, often forced to snatch a nap standing, and at every moment liable to be disturbed in haste by the approach of danger. They were always on the watch, sending out spies, questioning sentries, blowing the matches of their fire-locks, though they had but few, for they were chiefly armed with flint-locks. Roque passed his nights apart from his men, letting nobody know where his hiding-place was to be found; secrecy was vitally necessary owing to the continual proclamations issued against him by the Viceroy of Barcelona, and, as a consequence, he feared to trust even his own men, for fear one of them might betray him to the authorities for the price of his head. His was, indeed, a nerve-racking and unhappy life.

At last, after pursuing a hazardous journey by unfrequented roads, short-cuts and secret by-paths, Roque, Don Quixote and Sancho, attended by six squires, reached their destination. It was Midsummer-eve, at night, when they arrived at the strand of Barcelona. Roque said farewell to Don Quixote, and gave Sancho the ten crowns he had promised him. Thus they departed after many cordial greetings on both sides, and Don Quixote remained there on horseback waiting for daybreak.

It was not long before the pale face of Aurora began to peep through the balconies of the east, rejoicing the flowers and plants in the fields, while, at the same time, the ears of men were cheered by a gay rousing sound of pipes, kettle-drums and jingling bells, mingled with the tramp, tramp of horses, and the shouts of their riders sallying forth from the city. Aurora now withdrew, and the majestic sun, broad as a buckler, gradually began to rise above the verge of the horizon. Don Quixote and Sancho gazed about them and descried the sea, which they had never seen before. To them it seemed a right spacious expanse, far greater than the lakes of Ruidera which they saw in La Mancha. They saw the galleys bobbing at anchor off the shore, which, when their awnings were removed, appeared covered with flags and pennants that flickered in the wind and sometimes kissed and swept the surface of the water. From within them they heard the sound of trumpets, hautboys and clarions filling the air with martial music. Soon afterwards the galleys began to glide over the calm sea and engage in a kind of naval skirmish; and at the same time a numerous band of cavaliers, in rich uniforms and gallantly mounted, rode out from the city and completed the warlike tourney by their movements on the shore. The marines discharged repeated volleys from the galleys, which were answered by those on the ramparts and forts of the cities, and thus the air was rent by the thunder of this mimic battle, which echoed and re-echoed far and wide. The sea sparkled, the land was gay, the sky serene in every quarter save where wisps of smoke clouded it for an instant; indeed it seemed as if everything in the smiling scene contributed to gladden the heart of man.

Sancho, though, was greatly exercised in his mind to discover how those hulks that moved on the sea could have so many feet; and as for Don Quixote, he stood gazing in silent amazement upon the scene. Presently the band of cavaliers in bright uniform came galloping up to him whooping and shouting in the Moorish manner, and one of them—the person to whom Roque had written—cried in a resounding voice to the knight: "Welcome to our city, O mirror and beacon and north-star of knight-errantry! Welcome, I repeat, O valiant Don Quixote of La Mancha, not the false, spurious, and apocryphal one sent amongst us in lying histories, but the true, the legitimate, the loyal one described by the flower of all historians!"

Don Quixote made no answer, nor did the cavaliers wait for any, but wheeled about, and pranced around the knight and his squire. Then the gentleman who had spoken before addressed Don Quixote, saying:

"Be pleased, Sir Knight, to come with us, for we are all devoted friends of Roque Guinart," and Don Quixote replied: "If courtesy begets courtesy, then yours, kind sir, is akin to that of the great Roque; lead me whither you wish, for my will is yours."

The gentlemen then enclosed him in the midst of them, and proceeded towards the city accompanied by the martial music of trumpet and hautboy. But at the entrance, the father of mischief himself, or boys, who are the very devil, so ordained it that two of their number, bolder than the rest, managed to wriggle their way amid the crowd of horsemen until they reached Don Quixote and his squire. One then lifted up Dapple's tail, and the other that of Rozinante, and shoved a handful of briars under each of them. The poor animals, feeling such unusual spurs, clapped their tails only the closer, which so increased their pain that they began to curvet and plunge and kick so violently that their riders were thrown to the ground. Don Quixote, abashed and nettled at the affront, made haste to remove the sting from the tail of his long-suffering steed, and Sancho performed the same office for Dapple. The escort would have chastised the offenders, but the young scapegraces darted away with lightning rapidity and disappeared in the crowd that followed the procession. The knight and the squire then mounted again, and, amidst the blare of music and loud acclamations, proceeded on their way until they came to the stately mansion belonging to the gentleman who was to entertain Don Quixote during his stay in Barcelona.

This host, who was called Don Antonio Moreno, was a wealthy gentleman of cheerful disposition, always ready to enjoy a good-humoured jest. He resolved to extract as much amusement as he could from his guest's whimsical infirmity without offence to his person, for jests that cause pain are no jests, and pastimes that inflict an injury upon one's neighbour are unworthy of the name.

Having persuaded the knight to take off his armour, he led him to a balcony that looked out into one of the principal streets of the city, and there, in his tight-fitting chamois doublet, he exposed him to the populace, who gathered below and stood gaping at him as if he had been some strange baboon. The cavaliers in uniform again paraded in front of him, as if the ceremony were held in compliment to him alone, and not in honour of that day's solemnity.

That night the wife of Don Antonio, a most accomplished and beautiful lady, invited friends to a ball, to honour her guest and to join in the diversion created by his eccentric humour. After a sumptuous banquet, the dancing began at about ten o'clock at night. Among the ladies there were two of an arch, roguish disposition, who, though they were modest, were not unwilling to engage in a little innocent flirtation to amuse the company. They both paid court to Don Quixote, and they plied him so constantly with dancing one after another, that they wore him out in body and soul. He was, indeed, a sight to see, with his long, lean, lanky figure, his yellow complexion, and his close-fitting doublet and hose: an awkward figure too, and by no means light-footed at a saraband. The roguish ladies fussed and flattered him, and more than once they gave him private hints of their inclinations towards him, but he as often repelled them, and told them no less secretly that he was indifferent to their charms. At last their teasing so exasperated him that he cried aloud: *"Fugite, partes adversae!* Leave me in peace, unwelcome thoughts! Avaunt, ladies! Play your amorous pranks with somebody else; for peerless Dulcinea del Toboso is the

411

sole queen of my soul." With these words he sat himself down on the ground in the midst of the hall to rest, for he was utterly worn out by so much dancing. Don Antonio then gave orders that he was to be carried up to bed, and the first who came to lend a helping hand was Sancho, and, as he helped him up, he said: "Heavens above, master, you've certainly shaken your heels, and no mistake! Do you think that all brave men must be cutting capers, or all knights-errant castanet-dancers? If you do, you're in the wrong; there's men would sooner slit a giant's weasand than cut a caper. Had you been on for the clog-dance I'd have been your man, for I can slap and tap away like any gerfalcon, but as for any of your fine dancing, I can't work a stitch of it." Sancho's comments gave great amusement to the company. He led away his master and put him to bed, leaving him well muffled up, to sweat away the effects of his dance.

Some days later when Don Quixote was taking his usual morning airing on the strand, in full armour, for, as he often said, arms were his ornament and fighting his recreation, he spied a knight riding towards him, armed like himself from head to foot, with a shield on which was painted a resplendent moon, who, when he came within hearing, called out to him: "Illustrious knight and never-enough-renowned Don Quixote of La Mancha, I am the Knight of the White Moon, whose unheard-of exploits perchance may have reached your ears. Lo, I have come to enter into combat with you, and to compel you by sword to own and confess that my mistress, whoever she may be, is incomparably more beautiful than your Dulcinea del Toboso. If you will fairly confess this truth, you will spare your own life, and me the trouble of taking it. If you are resolved to fight and victory be mine, my terms require that you relinquish arms and the quest of adventures, and retire to your home for the space of one year, where you shall engage to live quietly and peaceably without laying hand to your sword, for thus you will improve your temporal and spiritual welfare. But should you vanquish me, my head shall be at your mercy, my arms and my steed shall be yours, and yours also the fame of my deeds. Consider what is best for you, and give your answer without delay, for this day must decide the issue of this affair."

Don Quixote was surprised, not to say dumbfounded, as much by the arrogance of the Knight of the White Moon's challenge, as at the subject of it, so with solemn gravity and composure he replied: "Knight of the White Moon, whose exploits have not yet come to my ears, I will swear you have never set eyes upon the illustrious Dulcinea, for if you had done so, I am confident you would never have made this claim, since the sight of her perfections must have convinced

you that there never was, nor ever can be, beauty comparable
to hers: and so, without giving you the lie, I only declare that
you are mistaken, and accept your challenge upon the spot,
this very day. Furthermore, I accept all your conditions with
the exception of the transfer of your exploits, for they are
unknown to me. I must remain contented with my own,
such as they are. Choose, therefore, your ground, and I shall
do the same, and may St. Peter bless him whom God
favours."

Meanwhile the Viceroy, who had been informed of the
arrival of the Knight of the White Moon, and that he was
holding parley with Don Quixote, hastened to the scene of
action accompanied by Don Antonio and others, firmly convinced that this must be some new jest invented by Don
Antonio Moreno or by some other knight of the city. He arrived with his retinue just as Don Quixote was wheeling
Rozinante about to take his ground, and, perceiving that
they were on the point of attacking one another, he intervened and asked what was the reason for such a sudden
encounter. The Knight of the White Moon replied that it
was a question of pre-eminence in beauty, and then briefly
told what he had said to Don Quixote concerning the conditions of the duel. The Viceroy then went up to Don Antonio
and asked him in a whisper if he knew who the Knight of
the White Moon was, or whether it was some jest they wished
to play upon Don Quixote. Don Antonio answered that he did
not know who he was, nor whether the challenge was in
earnest or not. The Viceroy was troubled by that answer, and
wondered whether he ought or ought not to let the battle
continue. At length by dint of persuading himself that it was
some jest, he withdrew, saying: "Gentlemen, if there be
no other remedy than confession or death, and if Señor Don
Quixote is stubborn in his resolve, and you, Sir Knight of the
White Moon, are obstinate likewise, then in God's name go
to it!"

The Knight of the White Moon in well-chosen words
thanked the Viceroy for what he had done, and Don Quixote
did likewise, and after recommending himself to Heaven and
his Dulcinea, he retired to take a larger compass of ground,
for he saw his opponent do the like; and then without any
flourish of triumpets or any other martial instrument to give
the signal for the onset, they both turned their horses round at
the same instant. But he of the White Moon, who was mounted
on the fleeter steed, met Don Quixote two-thirds down the
course, and hurtled into him with such fierce onslaught that,
without touching him with his lance, which he seemed
purposely to hold aloft, he brought both horse and rider to
the ground. He then sprang upon him, and said as he clapped

his lance to his opponent's vizor: "Knight, you are vanquished and a dead man if you don't confess in accordance with the conditions of our challenge."

Don Quixote, who was bruised and stunned, without lifting his vizor, and as though speaking from the tomb, said in a faint low voice: "Dulcinea del Toboso is the most beautiful woman in the world, and I am the most unfortunate knight on earth, nor is it just that my weakness should discredit this truth. Go on, knight, press on with your lance, and take away my life, since you have robbed me of my honour."

"That will I never do," said he of the White Moon; "long may the fame of the Lady Dulcinea del Toboso's beauty live and flourish! All I demand is that the great Don Quixote should retire to his village for one year, or for a period to be fixed by me, in accordance with the agreement drawn up before this battle."

The Vicery, Don Antonio and many others witnessed all that passed, and they now heard Don Quixote promise that he would fulfill all the terms of their engagement, provided nothing was required to the prejudice of his Lady Dulcinea. When this declaration was made, he of the White Moon turned about his horse, and, after bowing to the Viceroy, rode at a half gallop into the city.

The Viceroy ordered Don Antonio to follow him, and use all means to ascertain who he was.

They now raised Don Quixote from the ground, and, on taking off his helmet, they found him pale and bathed in sweat. Rozinante was in such a plight that he was unable to stir. As for Sancho, he was so sorrowful and cast down that he knew not what to say or do; sometimes he fancied that all had taken place in dreams; at others, that all was the result of witchcraft and enchantment. He found his master overthrown, and bound to lay aside his arms for a whole year. Now, he thought, his master's glory had been finally eclipsed, and his hopes of greatness vanished like smoke in the wind. He was afraid that Rozinante as well as his master would remain crippled, and it would be fortunate if no worse results ensued.

At last the knight was put into a chair, which had been ordered by the Viceroy, who was most curious to know who this Knight of the White Moon was that had left Don Quixote in such plight.

Don Antonio Moreno rode into the city after the Knight of the White Moon, who was also followed by a crowd of boys as far as his inn. As soon as the knight entered the inn, a squire came forward to take off his armour, and Don Antonio followed both of them into a small room, resolutely determined not to leave until he had discovered the identity of the stranger. When the knight found that the gentleman would not depart, he said: "As it happens, there is no reason for me to conceal myself, so while my squire disarms me, you shall hear the whole truth of my story.

"You must know, sir, that I am called the bachelor Samson Carrasco: I come from the same town as Don Quixote of La Mancha, whose madness and folly have been the cause of deep sorrow to his friends and neighbours. I myself felt particular sympathy for his sad case, and, as I believed his recovery to depend upon his remaining quietly at home, I earnestly endeavoured to accomplish that end. And so, about three months ago I sallied forth myself as a knight-errant, calling myself the Knight of the Mirrors, intending to fight and vanquish him without doing him harm, and to impose as the condtion of our combat that the vanquished should be at the mercy of the conqueror. Feeling certain of my success, I expected to send him home for twelve months, and hoped that during that time he might be restored to health. But fortune willed it otherwise, for it was he who vanquished me; he un-horsed me, and so my scheme was of no avail. He continued his journey, and I returned home vanquished, ashamed and injured by my fall. Nevertheless, I did not abandon my scheme, as you have seen this day, and, as he is so punctilious and so particular in observing the laws of knight-errantry, he is sure to perform his promise. This, sir, is my whole story, and I beseech you not to reveal me to Don Quixote, in order that my good intentions may produce their fruit and that the worthy gentleman may recover his sense, for when he is freed from the follies of chivalry he is a man of excellent under-standing."

"O sir!" replied Don Antonio, "may God forgive you for the wrong you have done in robbing the world of the most diverting madman who was ever seen. Is it not plain, sir, that his cure can never benefit mankind half as much as the pleasure he affords by his eccentricities? But I feel sure, sir bachelor, that all your art will not cure such deep-rooted madness, and were it not uncharitable, I would express the hope that he may never recover, for by his cure we should lose not only the knight's good company, but also the drollery of his squire Sancho Panza, which is enough to transform melancholy itself into mirth."

"In spite of what you say," replied the bachelor, "the stratagem has prospered, and I am confident the outcome will be favourable."

That same day the bachelor, after having his armour tied upon the back of a mule, mounted his charger and left the city for home, meeting no adventure on the way worthy of mention in this faithful history.

For six days Don Quixote was confined to his bed, dejected, melancholy, thoughtful and out of humour, and full of bleak reflections on his luckless overthrow. Sancho strove hard to comfort him, saying: "Raise your head, master, cheer up and thank your stars you've come off without even a broken rib. Remember, sir, that 'they that give must take'; and 'every stake has not its flitch'; come now, sir,—a fig for the doctor! You've no need of him. Let us be off home, and give up this gallivanting up and down, seeking adventures the Lord knows where."

And so, two days afterwards, Don Quixote, who had somewhat recovered from his bruises, set out on his journey home, followed by Sancho trudging along on foot, because Dapple was now laden with his master's armour.

XV. How Don Quixote and Sancho returned to their village

DON QUIXOTE, AS HE RODE OUT OF BARCELONA, CAST HIS EYES on the spot where he had been overthrown. "Here stood Troy! here my unhappy fate, and not my cowardice, despoiled me of the glories I had won; here Fortune made me feel her fickle changes. Here my deeds of derring-do were eclipsed; and, lastly, here fell my happiness, never to rise again!"

Then Sancho said to him: "Great hearts, dear master, should be as patient in adversity as they are joyful in prosperity; that's surely my own experience, for when I was made a governor I was as blithe and merry as a lark, and now that I'm only a poor foot-slogging squire, devil a bit am I sad: for I've heard say that she they call Fortune is a drunken, freakish drab, and blind into the bargain, so that she doesn't see what she's doing, nor does she know whom she raises nor whom she pulls down."

"You are much of a philosopher, Sancho," said Don Quixote, "and I wonder how you come to talk so sensibly, but I must tell you that there is no such thing as fortune in the world. Nothing that happens here below, whether of good or evil, comes by chance, but by the special disposition of Providence, and that is why we have the proverb that 'every man is the maker of his own fortune'. I, for my part, have been the maker of mine, but because I did not act with all the prudence necessary, my presumptions have brought me to my shame. I should have remembered that my poor, feeble Rozinante could never withstand the strong-built horse of the Knight of the White Moon. However, I risked all for adventure: I did my best, and was overthrown, and though it cost me my honour, I have not lost my integrity, and I can still perform my promise. When I was a knight-errant, bold and valiant, my actions gave lustre to my exploits, and now that I am no more than a dismounted squire I can still prove the validity of my word. Trudge on, then, friend Sancho, and let us hie us home to pass our year's novitiate. In our retirement we shall gather fresh strength to return to the profession of arms which I can never forget."

"This foot-slogging ain't so pleasant as to tempt me to go tramping to the edge of beyond, master," replied Sancho. "Let us hang up these arms of yours upon some tree in the place of one o' them gallows-birds that dangle from the branches in these parts, and when I'm sitting on Dapple's back with my feet up, we'll make whatever journeys your worship pleases. But there's little sense in thinking I can traipse along on my two feet mile after mile."

"You are right, Sancho," answered Don Quixote. "Hang my armour up as a trophy, and underneath them or about them we shall carve on the bark of the trees the inscription which was written under Roland's arms:

> Let no one dare these arms displace
> Who would not valiant Roland face."

"That's the very thing for me," quoth Sancho, "and were it not that we'll be needing Rozinante on the road, 'twould be a good idea to hang him up too."

"On second thoughts," said Don Quixote, "neither the armour nor the horse shall be treated thus. I do not want men to say 'for good service bad guerdon'."

"Them's good words," quoth Sancho, "for I've heard wise men say that the ass's fault must not be laid on the pack-saddle."

Day after day master and squire plodded their way homewards, and the nights they spent in the fields under the roof of the open sky. One night when they were conversing peaceably under the trees they heard a harsh grunting sound through the adjacent valleys. Don Quixote straightway sprang to his feet, grasping his sword: as for Sancho, he crouched down under Dapple's belly, pushing the bundle of armour on one side and fortifying the other with the ass's pack-saddle, where he lay shivering, as full of fears as his master of surprise. Meanwhile the noise grew louder and louder as the cause of it approached. Now what had happened was as follows: Some farmers were driving a herd of over six hundred swine to a certain fair, and such was the din that the beasts made with their grunting and squealing that Don Quixote and Sancho were almost deafened by it, and could not understand whence it came. But at length the huge grunting herd approached *en masse*, and, paying scant heed to Don Quixote or Sancho, rode rough-shod over them, knocking down Sancho's entrenchments and upsetting both the knight and Rozinante; and after treading and trampling knight, squire, horse, pack-saddle, armour and all, the filthy beasts rushed on leaving chaos in their wake.

Sancho was the first to realize what had occurred, so he rose to his feet as best he could, and called to his master to lend him his sword, saying that he was resolved to slay at least half a dozen of those gentlemen porkers immediately.

"Let them go, my friend," said Don Quixote; "this disgrace is the punishment which Heaven inflicts upon my guilty head, for it is just that jackals should devour, wasps sting and hogs trample on a vanquished knight-errant."

"And I'm thinking," quoth Sancho, "that Heaven also sends the gnats to sting, the lice to bite and hunger to famish us squires for attending on vanquished knights-errant. If we squires were the sons of the knights we serve, or at least related to them, why, then it would not be unreasonable to expect that we should share in their punishment even up to the fourth generation. But what have the Panzas to do with the Quixotes? Well, let us get a little sleep out of what is left of the night. Tomorrow is a new day."

Don Quixote lay down to rest under a tree, but thoughts came crowding into his mind like flies into a pot of honey: sometimes he reflected on the life he was to lead in his retirement; at others on the means needed for freeing Dulcinea from enchantment. After a long spell of silent meditation he woke up Sancho and spoke to him in a dreamy voice, as if he were raising a ghost from the dead, saying: "Alas for my poor Dulcinea to whom you, Sancho, do such grievous injury by being so remiss about your penance which would save the hapless lady from her wretched plight. Since you delay flogging that flesh of yours, may I see it mangled by wolves rather than kept in store for worms to eat."

"Master," quoth Sancho, "to tell you the honest truth, I can't for the life of me see how whaling my backside has aught to do with disenchanting the enchanted; why, sir, 'tis as though we should say: 'if thy head aches smear thy shins'. Why, I'd dare swear that in all the stories you've read dealing with knight-errantry there's no case of anyone being unbewitched by flogging. However, when I can find myself in the mood I'll chastise myself, that you may be sure."

"God grant you the grace to understand that it is your duty to relieve your mistress, for since she is mine, she must in consequence be yours, seeing that you belong to me. For my own part I wish to inform you that if you had demanded payment from me for disenchanting Dulcinea I would already have given it willingly, but I am not sure whether payment will go well into the cure, and I should not wish the reward to hinder the medicine. However, there is no harm in putting the matter to the test. Come, Sancho, name your price, and down with your breeches. Flog yourself first and then pay yourself money down, for you have all my money in your keeping."

Sancho opened wide his eyes and ears at such a tempting offer, and said to his master: "Aye, aye, sir, now you are talking: with a wife and children on my hands I'm all agog for the scheme. Tell me now, how much will you give me for each lash?"

"If I had to pay you," replied Don Quixote, "in proportion to the greatness of the case, not all the wealth of Venice, nor the silver mines of Potosí, would suffice to pay you. But pull out whatever money of mine you have in your purse and name a price for each stripe."

"There are," quoth Sancho, "three thousand three hundred and odd lashes, of which I have given myself five. Let the five count for the odd ones, and let us come to the three thousand three hundred. At three halfpence apiece (I wouldn't for the world take a farthing less) they will amount to three thousand three hundred three-halfpences. Three thousand three-halfpences make fifteen hundred threepences, which amounts to seven hundred and fifty reals, or sixpences. Now the remaining three hundred three-halfpences make a hundred and fifty threepences, and seventy-five sixpences. Add that togther and it comes to just eight hundred and twenty-five reals. This sum I'll subtract from the cash of yours that I have on me, and then I'll go home all gaudy and glad-hearted, though well whipped, for, as they say, 'he who goes a-fishing shouldn't fear a wetting'. I'll say no more."

"My blessings on you, my dearest Sancho," cried Don Quixote. "As long as Heaven is pleased to grant us life Dulcinea and I will feel compelled to serve you. If she returns to her former self, as now she must, her misfortune will turn to good fortune, and my defeat shall turn to triumph. Come, Sancho, tell me, when will you begin your flogging? I will add a hundred reals if you hasten the task."

"I'll start this very night as is," replied Sancho, "and you'll see how I lay on my naked flesh."

He then made himself a pliant whip out of Dapple's halter and withdrew behind some beech trees about twenty paces from his master. Don Quixote seeing him depart with such firm resolution, called out to him: "Sancho, my friend, do not cut yourself to pieces, and see that you do not start off at too furious a pace lest your breath fail you half-way: I mean, do not lay on so fiercely that you would kill yourself before reaching the required number. As for myself, I will stand at a distance and count the lashes on my rosary beads so that the reckoning may be fair on both sides. May Heaven prosper your pious undertaking."

"A good payer needs no sureties," answered Sancho. "I'm resolved on giving myself a decent whipping, for I suppose I needn't kill myself to work the miracle." With that he stripped himself to the waist, and seizing the whip he laid on the lashes, and Don Quixote began to count the strokes. But by the time that Sancho had applied six or eight lashes to his bare back he felt that the joke had gone too far, and he began to regret the bargain he had made. So he paused for a while and called out to his master, saying that the bargain was off, for such stripes as he was giving himself were worth at least threepence a-piece of his money.

"Go on, Sancho, my friend," answered Don Quixote, "keep your courage up. I will double the stakes."

"In that case," quoth Sancho, "God's will be done; let's have the whipping good and proper." But the cunning rogue left off flogging his own back and began to lash the trees, uttering such dismal groans every now and then that one would have thought that he was at death's door. Don Quixote, who was by nature tender-hearted, and feared lest Sancho might make an end of himself before finishing his penance and thus cheat his master of his desires, cried out: "Sancho, my friend, let this affair lie in abeyance for the moment. This physic seems mighty severe, and 'twould be wiser to give time, for Rome was not built in a day. If I have not counted wrongly, you have given yourself about a thousand stripes: that is enough for the present, for, to use a homely expression, the ass will carry his load, but not a double load."

"No, no, master," quoth Sancho, "never let it be said of me that when the wages are paid the work is stayed. Therefore, stand aside, I pray you, and let me lay on a further thousand, for I'll settle the job in two rounds and have plenty to spare."

"As you are in the humour," replied Don Quixote, "I shall retire, and may Heaven assist you."

With that Sancho returned to his task, and flayed the trees so furiously that he ripped their barks off without mercy, and raising his voice as he dealt a smashing blow at a beech tree, he cried: "Die, Samson, and all your kith and kin!" This direful cry, followed by the whistle of the lash, made Don Quixote run to the help of his squire, and seizing the halter which Sancho had twisted and wielded like a bull's pizzle, he cried: "May Fate forbid that I should be the cause of your death and the ruin of your wife and children. Let Dulcinea wait until a more auspicious occasion presents itself, and I shall live in hopes that when you have regained new strength the business may be brought to a finish to the satisfaction of all parties."

"Well, if that be your worship's will and pleasure," quoth Sancho, "then let it be; but kindly throw your cloak over my shoulders; for I'm all of a sweat and I've no wish to catch cold: we novices are in danger of that when we're first at the flogging game."

Don Quixote then took off his cloak and wrapped it around Sancho, remaining himself in shirt-sleeves; and the squire immediately fell fast asleep and never stirred until the sun awoke him.

In the morning they continued their journey and after three hours' riding they reached an inn, for Don Quixote recognized it as one, and not a castle, with moat, towers, portcullises and drawbridge as he generally fancied; for now that he had been defeated he was sane in his judgments as we shall see presently. They lodged him in a basement which was hung with old painted fabrics, such as one often sees in villages, instead of with leather hangings. One of them had the story of Helen of Troy when Paris stole her away from her husband, Menelaus, but it was very crudely painted. Another had the story of Dido and Aeneas: she was on the top of a tower, waving a sheet to her runaway guest, who was in a ship at sea, fleeing as fast as he could from her. Don Quixote noticed that Helen was not by any means unhappy at going away, for she had a roguish smile on her face, whereas Dido really did show her grief, for the tears she shed were painted as big as walnuts.

"How unfortunate," said Don Quixote, "were those two ladies that they did not live in this age of ours, and how much more unlucky am I for not having lived in theirs! I would have faced these gentlemen and saved Troy from being burnt and Carthage from being destroyed; why, by killing Paris alone all these disasters could have been prevented."

"I'll lay you a wager," quoth Sancho, "that before long there will not be an inn, tavern or barber's shop in the whole country that has not painted our lives and deeds along the walls. All the same, I'd prefer a better painter than the blockhead who has done these daubs."

"You are right, Sancho," replied Don Quixote. "That painter puts me in mind of Orbaneja, a painter from Ubeda, who, when he was asked what he was painting, would answer: 'Whatever comes out', and if he happened to draw a cock he would write underneath: 'This is a cock', lest people might think it was a fox. But now let us turn to our own affairs. Tell me truly, Sancho, are you in the mood for another round of flogging tonight? Would you like to do it indoors or in the open air?"

"Well, master," quoth Sancho, "a flogging is a flogging whether 'tis indoors or outdoors, but I prefer it among trees, for I feel that they bear me company and help me to endure my sufferings."

And so Don Quixote and Sancho spent the whole of that day in the inn, expecting the return of the night, the one to have an opportunity of ending his penitential flogging in the open air, the other to see the penance performed, since this would lead to the accomplishment of his desires.

Just then a gentleman came riding up to the inn with three or four servants, and one of them addressed him who appeared to be the master by the name of Don Alvaro Tarfe, saying: "Your worship should spend the heat of the day here. The inn seems cool and clean." Don Quixote, remembering the name Tarfe, turned to his squire, saying: "Mark my words, Sancho, I think I met this same Alvaro Tarfe before when I turned over the pages of that so-called Second Part of my history."[1]

"That's quite possible," quoth Sancho, "but just let him dismount, and then we'll question him."

The gentleman alighted and was given by the landlady a ground-floor room facing Don Quixote's apartment. When the stranger had changed into light summer garments he came out to the porch of the house, which was large and airy, and found Don Quixote walking up and down.

"Pray, sir, which way are you travelling?" said he to our knight.

"To a country town not far away where I was born," answered Don Quixote, "and pray, sir, which way are you bound?"

"To Granada, sir," replied the gentleman, "the land where I was born."

"And a fine country it is," said Don Quixote. "But do tell me, sir, I beg you, your name; for it is more important for me to know it than I can conveniently tell you."

"My name is Alvaro Tarfe," answered the gentleman.

"Then surely," said Don Quixote, "you are the same Don Alvaro Tarfe whose name occurs in the Second Part of Don Quixote of La Mancha's history that was lately published by a modern author."

"I am the very man," answered the gentleman, "and that very Don Quixote, who is the principal subject of that book, was my closest friend; it was I who drew him away from his home, or, at least, I persauded him to travel in my company to Saragossa to see the tournament; and, as it turned out, I behaved as a true friend, for had it not been for my intervention his arrogant impudence would have exposed him to a flogging at the hands of the public hangman."

"But pray tell me, sir," said Don Quixote: "am I in any way like that Don Quixote of yours?"

"Not in the least," answered the stranger.

"And had Don Quixote," said our knight, "a squire, one Sancho Panza?"

[1] Don Alvaro Tarfe is one of the characters of Avellaneda's *Don Quixote*.

"Yes," said Don Alvaro, "but though he was reported to be a comical fellow, I never heard him say a witty thing."

"To be sure," quoth Sancho, "for 'tis not every Tom, Dick and Harry that can crack a joke or say witty things; and that Sancho you mention must be some paltry pilferer or gallows-bird. For it's myself is the true and genuine Sancho Panza: I'm brimful o' God's wit! Just you try me for one year only and you'll find that scarce a minute goes by without my pouring forth such a flood of quips and cracks; why, half the time I'm unaware of my own waggery, and yet all who hear me say my jokes will be the death of them. And, as for the true Don Quixote, there you have him before you: he is the celebrated, the staunch, the wise, the loving Don Quixote of La Mancha, the righter of wrongs, the protector of orphans, the mainstay of widows, the killer of maidens; he whose one and only sweetheart is the peerless Dulcinea del Toboso: here he stands and here am I, his squire. All other Don Quixotes and all other Sancho Panzas are but delusion and dust in the eyes."

"'Pon my word, I believe what you have said," cried Don Alvaro, "for the few words you have just uttered have more humour than all that I ever heard the other Sancho Panza say; he was too much of a fool to be entertaining, and he carried his brains in his belly. For my part, I believe the enchanters that persecute the good Don Quixote sent the bad one to persecute me too. Indeed I do not know what to make of the whole matter; for though I can swear on my oath that I left one Don Quixote under surgeons' hands at the Nuncia's house in Toledo, yet here pops up another Don Quixote entirely different from mine."

"For my part," said Don Quixote, "I do not claim to be the good, but I may venture to say that I am not the bad one; and as a proof of it, sir, I can assure you that I have never in the course of my life been in Saragossa; indeed, so far from it, that hearing this spurious usurper of my name had appeared there at the tournament, I refused to go near it, being determined to expose to the world his imposture. And so I bent my course directly to Barcelona, the home of courtesy, the sanctuary of strangers, the refuge of the poor, the fatherland of patriots, the avenger of the wronged, residence of true friendship, and unique in the world for beauty and situation. And though some accidents that befell me there are unpleasant to recall and mortify me deeply, yet I find relief from my misfortune in my memories of that city. In conclusion, Don Alvaro Tarfe, I am Don Quixote of La Mancha whom fame has celebrated, and not the paltry wretch who has usurped my name and tried to arrogate to himself my honourable ambitions. I beg you, sir, as a gentleman, to be so good as to depose before the mayor of this village, that you never saw me in all your life till this day, and that I am not the Don Quixote mentioned in that Second Part, nor was this Sancho Panza, my squire, the person you knew formerly."

"With all my heart," said Don Alvaro; "but I must confess I am extremely puzzled to find at the same time two Don Quixotes, and two Sancho Panzas, so alike in name and so different in behaviour. Indeed, I must repeat that all my experience in this matter makes me believe that some witchcraft must be at the bottom of it."

"Quite so," quoth Sancho. "Your worship must have been bewitched the same as my Lady Dulcinea del Toboso; and if 'twere feasible to disenchant your worship as well as her by giving myself three thousand and odd lashes on my behind, I'd do so with a heart and a half; and what is more, they would not cost you a farthing."

"I do not understand what you mean by those lashes," said Don Alvaro.

"Thereby hangs a tale," quoth Sancho, "but 'tis too long in the telling. But if we're travelling the same way I'll tell it to you."

As it was now dinner-time, Don Quixote and Don Alvaro dined together, and the mayor happened to come into the inn with a public notary, so Don Quixote requested him to take the deposition which Don Alvaro Tarfe there present was ready to give, stating that the said deponent had not any knowledge of Don Quixote there present, and that the said Don Quixote was not the same person mentioned in a certain printed book entitled "The Second Part of Don Quixote of La Mancha", written by a certain Avellaneda, native of Tordesillas. In short, the mayor drew up an affidavit, and the declaration was completed in due form, much to the satisfaction of Don Quixote and Sancho, for they gave undue importance to the document, not realizing that their words and actions were more than enough to make the distinction apparent between the two Don Quixotes and the two Sanchos.

They started on their journey towards the evening, and about half a league from the village the road divided into two, one way leading to Don Quixote's village, and the other to Don Alvaro's destination. Don Quixote in that short interval let him know the misfortune of his defeat, with Dulcinea's enchantment, and the remedy prescribed by Merlin, at which Don Alvaro's wonder increased. After embracing the knight and his squire he left them on their way and followed his own.

Don Quixote spent that night among the trees, to give Sancho an opportunity to end his penance, but the crafty knave adopted the same methods as the night before. The barks of the beech trees paid for all, and Sancho took such good care of his back that a fly would not have been flicked off if it had chanced to alight there. But all the while Don

Quixote kept counting up the strokes and he did not miss one of them. He reckoned that with those of the preceding night they amounted to the sum of three thousand and twenty-nine. The sun, which apparently rose with more than ordinary haste to see the sacrifice, gave them the light to continue their journey. They spent that day on the road, and that night Sancho completed his task, to the great joy of his master, who waited impatiently for the moment when he might meet his Lady Dulcinea in the disenchanted state; and as he went along he scrutinized every woman he met, to see whether she was Dulcinea del Toboso, such implicit faith had he in Merlin's promises, which to him were infallible.

With these hopes and fancies in his mind they reached the top of a hill, from which they could see their village in the distance. Sancho had no sooner caught a glimpse of it than he fell on his knees and said: "Open your eyes, beloved home of mine, and here behold your son Sancho Panza come back again, if not very full of money yet very full of whipping. Open your arms and welcome your son Don Quixote too, who, though he was conquered by another, nevertheless conquered himself; that is the best kind of victory a man can wish for, and I have his own word for it. However, though I've had my fill of flogging, I've filled my pockets too."

"A truce to your foolish prattle," said Don Quixote, "and let us make a dignified entry into our native village where we may give our imaginations play and lay down the plans for our intended pastoral life." With these words they came down the hill, and went directly to their village. When they were entering Don Quixote noticed two little boys pummelling one another on the threshing-floor of the village, and he heard one say to the other: "Don't fash yourself, Pete, devil a bit of her you'll see till doomsday." Don Quixote, overhearing this, said to Sancho: "Did you catch what the boy said—'devil a bit of her you'll see till doomsday'?"

"Well, what odds?" said Sancho.

"Don't you realize that such words where applied to my affairs clearly mean that I shall never see my Dulcinea?"

Sancho was about to answer again, but was hindered from so doing by a great hue and cry of hounds and huntsmen in full pursuit of a hare, which was so hard pressed that she came and squatted for shelter just between Dapple's feet. Immediately Sancho laid hold of her and presented her to Don Quixote, but the knight kept muttering to himself: "*Malum signum! Malum signum*, . . . a hare runs away, hounds pursue her, and Dulcinea does not appear."

"You are indeed a strange man, sir," quoth Sancho. "Why not let us suppose that poor bunny here is Mistress Dulcinea, the greyhounds that followed her are those dogs the en-chanters who transmogrified her into a country lass? She races away, I catch her by the scut and hand her safe and sound to your worship. Blowed I am if I can see any harm or bad luck in this." By this time the two boys that had been fighting came up to see the hare, and when Sancho enquired why they had been fighting he was answered by the boy who had uttered the ominous words, that he had snatched from his play-fellow a cage full of crickets, which he would not give up to him again. Whereupon Sancho pulled a threepenny piece out of his pocket and gave it to the boy for his cage; and, giving it to Don Quixote, he said: "There you are, sir; all the tokens of bad luck have been brought to nought, and though I am a blockhead I'm convinced all these things have no more to do with our affairs than the clouds of yesteryear. And if I remember right, I've heard the priest of our village say that no decent self-respecting Christian should give ear to such foolishness; and I've heard you yourself, master, say not many days ago that all such Christians as troubled their heads with fortune-telling rubbish were no better than nincompoops. So without more ado let us make straight for our homes." By now the huntsmen had come up and were asking for their hare, which Don Quixote delivered up to them.

They passed on, and just as they were entering the town they perceived the priest and the bachelor Samson Carrasco at their devotions in a small field. The latter no sooner caught sight of Dapple laden with the knight's armour than they recognized their old friends, and came running to greet them with open arms. And while Don Quixote alighted and returned their embraces, the boys, who are sharp-eyed as lynxes and miss no detal, came flocking about them, saying: "Have a look, boys! Here is Sancho's ass gaudier than Mingo,[2] and Don Quixote's hack leaner than ever." Surrounded by the boys of the town and attended by the priest and the bachelor, they moved towards the house of Don Quixote, where they found the housekeeper and his niece waiting for them on the doorstep. News also had reached Teresa, the wife of Sancho Panza, and she came running half-naked with her hair all towsled, leading by the hand her daughter Sanchica. But when she found that her husband was not quite dressed up to her notions of governor's fashion, she said: "What's all this, husband? You look as if you'd plodded all the way on Shank's mare! There's not much of the governor about you, I'm thinking."

"Whisht, Teresa!" quoth Sancho, "we must take the rough with the smooth. First of all let us go home, and then I'll tell you wonders. I've money, and that after all is what counts, and I made it by my own labours without harming a soul."

"Bring home the money, my dear," said Teresa, "no matter

[2] A proverb derived from the fifteenth-century *Coplas de Mingo Revulgo.* Mingo was a synonym for an over-dressed dandy.

426

how you've earned it or where you've earned it: after all, there's nothing new in that."

Sanchica then hugged her father and asked what he had brought her home, for she longed for his return as the flowers do for the dew in May. So she caught hold of her father's waistband with one hand and pulled Dapple after her by the halter with the other, and her mother took Sancho by the arm on the other side, and away they all went to his cottage, leaving Don Quixote in his own house under the care of his niece and housekeeper, with the priest and bachelor to keep him company. Don Quixote forthwith drew the last two aside, and, without beating about the bush, gave them a short account of his defeat, and the obligation he lay under of remaining in his village for a year, which, like a true knight-errant, he was determined to observe most faithfully: and he added that he intended to become a shepherd and spend that year in the solitude of the fields and woods, giving rein to his armorous thoughts and practising the virtues of the pastoral life. Futhermore, he begged them, if more important duties were not a hindrance, to become his companions, and he assured them he would furnish them with sufficient sheep and cattle to enable them to belong to such a profession. They were struck with amazement at this new strain of madness, but considering this might be a means of preventing him from wandering from home, and hoping at the same time that within the year he might be cured of his mad knight-errantry, they approved his pastoral folly and offered their friendly co-operation in the scheme.

As luck would have it, the housekeeper and niece heard the conversation between the three on the subject of the pastoral life, so no sooner had the priest and the bachelor gone than they both burst into Don Quixote's room, and the niece cried:

"Mercy on us, uncle! What does this mean? We thought you had come to stay at home, and live there like a quiet, honest gentleman, and here you are longing to dash away into the wilderness, wool-gathering after sheep, bleating pastorals forsooth. By my troth, uncle, the straw is too old to make pipes of."

"Heaven help us, sir," quoth the housekeeper, "how will your worship be able to stand the summer's heat and the winter's frost in the open country, and the howling of the wolves? Pray, sir, you mustn't think of it: 'tis a business for those who are born and bred to it, and great strapping fellows into the bargain. Even if the worst came to the worst, 'tis better to be a knight-errant than a shepherd. Mark my words, master, and heed my counsel; I'm neither full of food nor drink, but fasting, and I'm no chicken, but fifty years of age, and I say to you: stay at home, look after your property, go

427

to confession often, do good to the poor, and let me be to blame if you go wrong."

"My dear girls, do cease your prating," Don Quixote answered. "I know best what I have to do, only help me to my bed, for I do not feel very well. Remember that whether I be a knight-errant or an errant shepherd, you will always find me ready to provide for you, you may rely on my good faith."

The niece and the housekeeper who, without doubt, were good-natured souls, undressed him, put him to bed, brought him something to eat, and made him as comfortable as possible.

XVI. *How Don Quixote fell sick, made his last will and died*

As all human things, especially the lives of men, are not eternal, and even their beginnings are but steps to their end, and as Don Quixote was under no special dispensation of Heaven, he was snatched away by death when he least expected it. Whether his sickness was caused by his melancholy reflections on his defeat, or whether it was so pre-ordained by Providence, he was stricken down by a violent fever which confined him to his bed for six days. All that time his good friends, the priest, the bachelor and the barber, often visited him, and his trusty squire Sancho Panza never left his bedside. They were convinced that his sickness was due to his sorrow at having been defeated, and his disappointment in the matter of Dulcinea's disenchantment, and so they tried in every way to cheer him: the bachelor begged him to pluck up his spirits and get up from his bed that they might begin their pastoral life, adding that he had already written an eclogue not inferior to those of Sannazaro, and that he had bought with his own money from a shepherd of Quintanar two pedigree dogs to watch their flock, one called Rufus and the other Trap. But this had no effect, for Don Quixote continued to mope as before. A physician was then sent for, who, after feeling his pulse, took a rather gloomy view of the case, and told him that he should provide for his soul's health, as that of his body was in a dangerous condition. Don Quixote received the news calmly and serenely, but his niece, his housekeeper and his squire began to weep as bitterly as if he had been laid out already. The physician was of the opinion that melancholy and mortification had brought him to death's door. Don Quixote then asked them to leave him for a little while as he wished to sleep. They retired, and he had a long, uninterrupted sleep of more than six hours, and the housekeeper and the niece were afraid he might not waken from it. At length he did awake and cried out in a loud voice: "Blessed be the Almighty for this great benefit He has granted me! Infinite are His mercies, and undiminished even by the sins of men."

The niece, who was listening very attentively to these words of her uncle, found more sense in them than there was in his usual talk, at least since he had fallen ill, and questioned him, saying: "What do you mean, uncle? Has anything strange taken place? What mercies and what sins of men are you talking about?' '

"Mercies," answered Don Quixote, "that God has just this moment granted to me in spite of all my sins. My judgment is now clear and unfettered, and that dark cloud of ignorance has disappeared, which the continual reading of those detestable books of knight-errantry had cast over my understanding. Now I see their folly and fraud, and my sole regret is that the discovery comes too late to allow me to amend my ways by reading others that would enlighten my soul. I find, dear niece, that my end approaches, but I would have it remembered that though in my life I was reputed a madman, yet in my death this opinion was not confirmed. Therefore, my dear child, call my good friends, the priest, the bachelor Samson Carrasco and Master Nicholas the barber, for I wish to make my confession and my will." There was no need for the niece to send, for presently all three arrived at the house, and Don Quixote no sooner saw them than he said: "My dear friends, welcome the happy news! I am no longer Don Quixote of La Mancha, but Alonso Quixano, the man whom the world formerly called the Good owing to his virtuous life. I am now the sworn enemy of Amadis of Gaul, and his innumerable brood; I now abhor all profane stories of knight-errantry, for I know only too well through Heaven's mercy and through my own personal experience the great danger of reading them."

When his three friends heard him talk thus, they concluded that he was stricken with some new madness, Samson then said to him: "What does all this mean, Señor Don Quixote? Now that we have just received news that Lady Dulcinea is disenchanted, and we are just about to become shepherds and spend our days singing and living like princes, you talk about turning yourself into a hermit. No more foolish tales, I beg you, and come back to your senses."

"Those foolish tales," replied Don Quixote, "which up to now have been my bane may with Heaven's help turn to my advantage at my death. Dear friends, I feel that I am rapidly sinking; therefore let us put aside all jesting. I want a priest to receive my confession, and a notary to draw up my will. Therefore pray send for the notary while the priest hears my confession."

Don Quixote's words amazed his hearers, but though they were at first sceptical about the return of his sanity, they were forced to take him at his word. One of the symptoms that made them fear he was near the point of death was the suddenness with which he had recovered his intellect, and after that he conversed with such good sense and displayed such true Christian resignation that they believed his wits had been restored at last. The priest therefore told the company to leave the room, and he confessed Don Quixote. In the meantime the bachelor hastened to fetch the notary, and presently returned with him and with Sancho Panza. The latter, hearing the news of his master's plight and finding the niece and the housekeeper in tears, began in his turn to make wry faces and finally burst out crying. After the priest had heard the sick man's confession he came out, saying: "There is no doubt he is at the point of death and Alonso Quixano the Good is in his entire right mind, so we should go in and enable him to make his will." These sad tidings burst open the floodgates of the housekeeper's, the niece's and the good squire's swollen eyes; and their tears flowed fast and furious, and a thousand sighs rose from their breasts, for, indeed, as it has been noted, the sick gentleman, whether as Alonso Quixano the Good or as Don Quixote of La Mancha, had always been so good-natured and so agreeable that he was not only beloved by his family, but by all who knew him.

The notary, with the rest of the company, then went into the sick man's chamber, and Don Quixote stated the preamble to the will, recommending his soul to Heaven and including the customary Christian declarations. When he came to the legacies he said:

"Item, I give and bequeath to Sancho Panza, whom in my madness I made my squire, whatever money he has of mine in his possesson; and whereas there are accounts and reckonings to be settled between us for what he has received and disbursed, my will and pleasure is that he should not be required to furnish any account of such sums, and whatever may remain due to me, which must be but little, be enjoyed by him as my free gift, and may he prosper with it. And as, when I was mad, he was through my means made governor of an island, I would now, in my right senses, give him the government of a kingdom, were it in my power, for his honesty and his faithfulness deserve it.

"And now, my friend," said he, turning to Sancho, "forgive me for making you appear as mad as I was myself, and for drawing you into my errors, and persuading you that there have been and still are knights-errant in the world."

"Woe's me," cried Sancho all in tears. "Don't die on me; but take my advice and live on for many a year; sure 'tis the maddest trick a man can play in his life, to yield up the ghost without more ado, and without being knocked on the head or stabbed through the belly to mope away and die of the doldrums. Shame on you, master, don't let the grass grow under your feet. Up with you this instant out of your bed, and let us put on our shepherds' clothing and off with us to the fields as we had resolved a while back. Who knows but we may find Lady Dulcinea behind a hedge and disenchanted and as fresh as a daisy. If 'tis your defeat that is tearing your heart, lay the blame on me, and say 'twas my fault in not tightening Rozinante's girths enough, and that was why you were unhorsed. You must remember, too, sir, from your books on knight-errantry how common it was for knights to jostle one another out of the saddle, and he who's lying low today may be crowning his victory tomorrow."

"Just so," said Samson; "there is good sense in what honest Sancho says."

"Go softly, I pray you, gentlemen," replied Don Quixote; "one should never look for birds of this year in the nests of yesteryear: I was mad, but I am now in my senses; I was once Don Quixote of La Mancha, but am now, as I said before, Alonso Quixano the Good, and I hope that my repentance and my sincere words may restore me to the same esteem as you had for me before. So now proceed, Mr. Notary.

"Item, I declare and appoint Antonia Quixano, my niece, here present, sole heiress of all my estate both real and personal after all my just debts and legacies have been paid and deducted out of my goods and chattels; and the first charges on the estate shall be the salaries due to my housekeeper, together with twenty ducats over and above her salary wages, which I leave and bequeath her to buy her mourning.

"Item, I appoint his reverence the priest and Señor Samson Carrasco, the bachelor, here present, to be the executors of this my last will and testament.

"Item, it is my will, that if my niece Antonia Quixano should wish to marry, it will be with none but a person who, upon strict investigation, shall be found never to have read a book of knight-errantry in his life; but if it should be ascertained that he is acquainted with such books, and that she still insists on marrying him, she is then to lose all rights to my bequest, which my executors may then distribute in charity as they think fit.

"Item, I entreat the said executors, that if at any time they happen to meet with the author of a certain book

431

entitled *The Second Part of the Achievements of Don Quixote of La Mancha,* they will in my name most heartily beg his pardon for my having been unwittingly the cause of his writing such an amount of folly and triviality as he has done. Indeed, as I depart from this life my conscience troubles me that ever I was the cause of his publishing such a book."

After finishing the will, he swooned away and stretched his body to its full length in the bed. The company were alarmed and ran to his assistance; but these fainting attacks were repeated with great frequency during the three days after he had made his will. The household was in grief and confusion, and yet, after all, the niece continued to eat her meals, the housekeeper drowned her sorrows in wine, and Sancho Panza puffed himself up with satisfaction, for the thought of a legacy possesses a magic power to remove or at least to soothe the pangs that heirs would otherwise feel for the death of their friends.

At length Don Quixote's last day came, after he had received all the sacraments, and expressed his abhorrence of books of knight-errantry. The notary, who was present, said that he had never read of any knight who ever died in his bed so peacefully and like a good Christian as Don Quixote. And so, amidst the tears and lamentations of his friends who knelt by his bedside, he gave up the ghost, that is to say, he died. And when the priest saw that he had passed away, he bade the notary give him a certificate stating that Alonso Quixano the Good, commonly known as Don Quixote of La Mancha, had died a natural death. This he desired lest any other author should take the opportunity of raising him from the dead, and presume to write endless histories of his pretended adventures. Such was the death of that imaginative gentleman Don Quixote of La Mancha, whose native place the author has not thought fit directly to mention, with the intention that all the towns and villages in La Mancha should vie with one another for the honour of giving him birth as the seven cities of Greece did for Homer. We shall omit the lamentations of Sancho, and those of the niece and the housekeeper, as also the epitaphs that were composed for his tomb, and we will only quote the following which the bachelor Samson Carrasco inscribed on it:

Don Quixote's epitaph

Here lies the noble fearless knight,
Whose valour rose to such a height;
When Death at last had struck him down,
His was the victory and renown.
He reck'd the world of little prize,
And was a bugbear in men's eyes;
But had the fortune in his age
To live a fool and die a sage.